Dakota

OR WHAT'S A HEAVEN FOR

Dakota

OR WHAT'S A HEAVEN FOR

By

Brenda K. Marshall

Institute for Regional Studies
NDSU

A version of Chapter XLI, 'In Which a Coffin
is a Bed, but an Ox is Not a Coffin,' first appeared
in *Michigan Quarterly Review*.

North Dakota Institute for Regional Studies
North Dakota State University

Printed in Canada.

International Standard Book Number (ISBN): 978-0-911042-72-6
Library of Congress Control Number: 2010929868

For Valerie
Always

Acknowledgements

This is a work of fiction. Although several of the characters in this novel, such as Moses K. Armstrong, J. B. Power, and Alexander McKenzie, are based on historical figures, I have provided them with motivations, speeches, thoughts, and chronologies from my imagination. At the same time, in an attempt to infuse the novel with a sense of verisimilitude, I have often used the letters and language of these historical figures. Although the larger story that I have told here—about the role of the Northern Pacific Railroad, the political shenanigans of the day, the settling of the territory by immigrants, and the phenomenon of the bonanza farm—is as "true" as I know how to make it, I have changed historical dates, altered events, and invented conversations and personal histories when it suited my narrative purpose. The *Far West*, for example, steamed past Bismarck with its cargo of wounded soldiers on July 5, 1876, and not on Independence Day, as I so conveniently would have it in this novel. In other words, I have relied heavily upon historical fact, but more heavily upon my imagination.

Among the several dozens of texts (including diaries, novels, histories, journals, and newspapers) consulted while writing this novel, a few were exceptionally valuable. Hiram Drache's *Day of the Bonanza* and Howard Lamar's *Dakota Territory: 1861-1889* were indispensable. Also important were *The Early Empire Builders of the Great West* by Moses K. Armstrong, *History of the Northern Pacific Railroad* by Eugene V. Smalley, *Plains Folk*, edited by William C. Sherman and Playford V. Thorson, and *History of North Dakota* by Elwyn B. Robinson. I have culled newspapers and magazines from the 1870s and 80s, especially the Dakota *Herald* and the Fargo *Argus*, for commentary upon the events of the day. Percy's essays and columns are taken from the Fargo *Argus*, *Harper's New Monthly Magazine*, and N.P. immigration brochures.

Over the years I have received a great deal of help from librarians and archivists. I would like to thank John Bye, John Hallberg and Michael Robinson for their help during several visits to the archives of the North Dakota Institute for Regional Studies (NDIRS), and for their prompt and friendly e-mail responses. The website www.fargo-history. com (created by John Caron and now managed by NDIRS) has given me as much pleasure as information. Minnesota Historical Society (MHS) Curator Linda McShannock generously spent a couple of hours with me in the vaults of the MHS showing me clothes from the period. I would like to thank the reference librarians at the Minnesota Historical Society and at the State Archives & Historical Research Library Division of the North Dakota Historical Society in Bismarck, especially Susan Dingle.

For help with the occasional phrases in Norwegian, I thank Anna Siri Sovde, Helen Muirhead, and Marian Vigan. Anita Norich provided welcome help with Yiddish-inflected English.

The University of Michigan's Rackham Graduate School generously provided funds for a research assistant. Thank you to Catherine Borden for tirelessly tracking down train schedules, diphtheria records, business records, and a host of details from Dakota Territory newspapers. I am indebted to the University of Michigan's Center for Research on Teaching and Learning for two Lecturers' Professional Development Grants (2002, 2010) in support of the research and marketing of this novel. A generous grant from the Institute for Research on Women and Gender at the University of Michigan has helped me to reach readers through my website (www.brendamarshallauthor.com) and through travel.

What a privilege it has been to work with scratchboard artist, Scott McKowen! Many thanks to Scott for the gorgeous cover art, and for his meticulous dedication to capturing the sensibility of the novel.

Megan Eckman provided delightful pen and ink illustrations (typical of nineteenth-century popular novels) that highlight moments in *Dakota* for my website. Deborah Gibson, who designed the website, was a pleasure to work with.

Tom Fricke, Peggy McCracken, Chris Stier, Keith Taylor, and Valerie Traub were early readers to whom I am grateful. More support, enthusiastic and/or technical, came from Doug Anderson, Carol Boyd, Kerry Larson, and Richard Miller.

Thanks, too, to my literary agent, Jean Naggar, for unwavering support, and to Maureen Baron for editorial assistance.

Finally, I want to thank Tom Riley, Director of the Institute for Regional Studies at North Dakota State University, for his enthusiasm and confidence in this novel, Ross Collins for his work as editor, and Deb Tanner for graphic design.

CONTENTS

BOOK ONE: PRIVATE LIFE 1

   PRE-AMBLE 2

     CHAPTER I *In Which Frances Waits* 6

     CHAPTER II *In Which We See Cracks in a Diamond* 15

     CHAPTER III *In Which We Meet J. B. Power* 18

     CHAPTER IV *In Which We Must All Go Farming* 21

     CHAPTER V *In Which an Ill Wind Blows Some Good* 29

     CHAPTER VI *In Which John and Percy Bingham Head for
                      the End of the Earth* 37

     CHAPTER VII *In Which Frances Goes Too Far* 43

BOOK TWO: THIS MASTERPIECE FOR COMMON FOLK 51

     CHAPTER VIII *In Which We Meet a Homesteading Mule* 52

     CHAPTER IX *In Which We Meet Kirsten Knudson* 70

     CHAPTER X *In which Frances is Forced to Behave Badly* 78

     CHAPTER XI *In Which the Fruit Rolls Far from the Tree* 84

     CHAPTER XII *In Which Two Dutchmen Come to Appreciate Iowa* 89

     CHAPTER XIII *In Which Little Norwegian Girls Are Like Grass* 95

     CHAPTER XIV *In Which the Bingham Family Entertains
                     a 'Fool on the Loose'* 100

     CHAPTER XV *In Which We All Need Stories* 108

     CHAPTER XVI *Scooped* 126

     CHAPTER XVII *In Which the Women Go West* 131

     CHAPTER XVIII *In Which the Impossible is Seen and Done* 139

BOOK THREE: THE FIRST LOW WASH 153

     CHAPTER XIX *In Which J. B. Power Harvests Gold* 154

     CHAPTER XX *In Which Kirsten Begins to Learn About Love* 157

     CHAPTER XXI *In Which We Consider Perspective* 164

     CHAPTER XXII *In Which We Study the Intricate Geometry of Frost* . . . 178

     CHAPTER XXIII *In Which To Go is To Be Gone* 183

     CHAPTER XXIV *In Which There is No Shame in Profit* 204

     CHAPTER XXV *In Which Peter is Robbed and Paul is Paid* 216

CHAPTER XXVI   *In Which Frances Finds a Match* 222

CHAPTER XXVII   *In Which Frances Gets to Work.* 237

CHAPTER XXVIII *Two Rocks, a Prairie Fire, and an Inquest* 247

CHAPTER XXIX   *In Which Far er Død* 256

CHAPTER XXX   *In Which Frances Gains a Little* 262

CHAPTER XXXI   *...And Loses More* 269

BOOK FOUR: A STRUGGLE WITH DIRT 277

CHAPTER XXXII   *In Which Alexander McKenzie and Governor
                Nehemiah Ordway Meet, Dance, Embrace* 278

CHAPTER XXXIII *In Which We Hear about Scallawags and Scoundrels* . . 288

CHAPTER XXXIV   *Dakota Dirt* 294

CHAPTER XXXV   *Exeunt Power* 302

CHAPTER XXXVI   *In Which What Goes Up Prefers Not to Come Down.* . 304

Chapter XXXVII *In Which A Flood Both Washes Away and Reveals* 311

CHAPTER XXXVIII *In Which the Relationship between Dirt
                and Insanity is Clarified* 320

CHAPTER XXXIX   *In Which What Recedes and Returns Fatigues.* 331

CHAPTER XL   *In Which Kirsten Is Taken for a Ride* 337

CHAPTER XLI   *In Which a Coffin is a Bed but an Ox is Not a Coffin.* . 345

CHAPTER XLII   *In Which Always is Always (Maybe)* 359

CHAPTER XLIII   *In Which a Monster is Revealed and a Friend
                is Lost: I* 369

CHAPTER XLIV   *In Which a Monster is Revealed and a Friend
                is Lost: II* 379

BOOK FIVE: A REACH AND A GRASP 387

CHAPTER XLV   *In Which She Has a Farm of Her Own* 388

CHAPTER XLVI   *In Which Percy Learns to Dance with the Ugly Ones* . . 397

CHAPTER XLVII   *In Which Percy is Hanged for a Lamb.* 405

CHAPTER XLVIII *Percy's Last Poem* 417

CHAPTER XLIX   *In Which Percy's Past Improves Whereas
                Frances' Future is Less Certain* 424

CHAPTER L   *In Which Pretty Much Everybody Misses the Train.* . . . 430

CHAPTER LI   *In Which the Bidding Begins.* 434

CHAPTER LII   *In Which Frances Learns What's What and
                Who's Who (and She's Not)* 447

CHAPTER LIII   *Our Hero.* 464

BOOK ONE: PRIVATE LIFE

*There is no private life which has not been
determined by a wider public life.*

(George Eliot, *Felix Holt*)

PRE-AMBLE

You will say that I am making this up, as if it were a small matter to invent truth. Accuse me, rather, of excess, for what can invention add to fact in a land where trains leave their rails to sail through the air, men are born of frozen beasts, and locusts feast on human flesh.

I have proof. Here is General Alfred Sully's report to the Secretary of War in August of 1864 regarding the carnivorous bugs:

A soldier on his way here lay down to sleep on the prairie in the middle of the day—the troop had been marching all night. His comrades noticed him covered with grasshoppers and awakened him. His throat and wrists were bleeding from the bites of the insects.

Or perhaps General Sully, seeking to fill the unearthly void of this strange land with words, had been provoked into exaggeration, for it was he who referred to my home as "hell with the fires out." So, I invent. I embellish. I exaggerate. It is my heritage.

In fact, it was a singularly brilliant advertising campaign by a railroad on the verge of bankruptcy that transformed Sully's "hell" into the Nile of the North. Listen, and tell me if you can name this place: "It is a land fair enough to tempt the angels in their flight to wonder whether a new and better Eden has not been formed and roofed with sapphire skies."

Yes, that's right: Dakota Territory.

The angels, as is generally the case, resisted the temptation to tarry, but Norwegians, Swedes, Danes, Finns, Icelanders, Germans, and Russians came in droves. There were Moravians and Mennonites and Methodists and Lutherans and the occasional Jew and even some Catholics. Slum dwellers pried themselves loose from the muck and stink of Eastern cities; Jews left villages in Russia to sink cement mikvahs into the prairie; newly freed black men set up tonsorial palaces in prairie towns and learned to speak Norwegian to their customers; farmers, some of them real Americans, pulled up stakes in Michigan and Nebraska and Iowa to try their luck behind a plow in the new Northwest. "Wrong side up," the Indians said, shaking their heads at the white men intent upon turning under perfectly good prairie grass.

I could begin this story of an unlikely place, composed in equal parts of excess and lack, those opposites so fully integrated into the regional psyche as to be indistinguishable, anywhere, and too much would be left out. I sort of like the part about how glaciers once covered the northern plains, but a glacial pace, Reader, would surely tax your patience. As for the millennia when Native Americans and their ancestors spent a few months of each year hunting here, that is not my story to tell. I will skip, too, the pre-territory trading and trapping days, and the stories of forts and soldiers, of treaties made and broken, and of small pox and Indian agents and graft and despair and fury, and get right to the real excitement: farming.

Once upon a time a railroad was given a land grant by the U.S. Congress to build from Duluth, Minnesota, to Puget Sound, but was given no federal money to accomplish such a thing. A Philadelphia banker named Jay Cooke said to the directors of this Northern Pacific Railroad Company, "I'll give you the money, lads. I can finance a war, surely I can finance a railroad." Then he went bankrupt, leaving the railroad with millions of acres of land and no money, and shareholders with worthless bonds. But a Northern Pacific employee had an idea: offer a land-for-shares trade, on the condition that the land be farmed, and not held for speculation. Most of the land was in eastern Minnesota and Dakota Territory, and the shareholders were in the east. Yankees. A couple of the directors of the railroad took control of gigantic parcels of land, miles and miles and miles. Other shareholders joined in to do the same. Preferring to remain with their families in New York and Philadelphia and Boston, they sent business managers to oversee operations and to farm in a brand-new way, with the newest implements and an army of seasonal laborers per field, and one crop: wheat. The newspapers, even those not on the payroll of the Northern Pacific Railroad, told stories of the magnificent "bonanza farms," and of the new land's glory, of soil so fertile that seeds cast upon the ground leapt into the sunlight in sheaves of gold. Apples grew to the size of pineapples. The climate was so salubrious that the infirm would spring from their sickbeds to grasp a plow. Best of all, a fellow could be his own boss, required to doff his hat to no man. Reports of the new Nile spread across the globe. And the people came.

Some bought land from the Northern Pacific Railroad. Some filed homestead claims. Some prospered, some failed, most just hung on. The advertisements had told the truth about the fertile land of the Red River valley of Dakota Territory, and about the miracles of sunsets that set the prairies ablaze with color, the blue skies that clapped the land with clarity, the peace of space. But they hadn't mentioned the wind, or the dust, or the hail, or the tornadoes, or the locusts. A "sea of grass" did not translate in the emigration leaflets into "no trees," and few could imagine the cramped isolation of a ten-by-twelve-foot shanty on the Dakota prairie. Inside, no privacy. Outside, no neighbors. The settlers discovered soon enough that there was no market for their wheat nearby, and, unlike the bonanza farmers, they did not get special transport rates from the railroad, or special storage rates from the elevators that were owned by the railroad. They did not receive rebates from the milling companies. They paid retail prices for their machinery. Their interest rates from the banks in the east were high; twenty percent was not uncommon.

So they told themselves the story: they were special because they could live in this place of wind and dust and hail and tornadoes and locusts, despite the railroad, the milling companies, the implement dealers, and the bankers. The story gave them back their independence.

That narrative of independence remains as powerful, as false, as necessary as ever in the Dakotas. It has become our fetish, replacing the lost object of desire, the impossible place that never was. You have been told that there is nothing there. I tell you there is too much. Even where there is nothing, there is too much of it.

And who am I?

I am an old politician, pretty close to honest, and I know the stories of this territory from before there was such a thing.

I am the Land Commissioner for the Northern Pacific Railroad, in charge of the Land and Immigration Department. Sometimes in my dreams I wear a robe and flowing beard, and behind me the multitudes flow toward this land of milk and honey.

I am a Scot from Ontario and I have come to this land to chew it up and make myself fat. Someday I will be called the "Boss of North Dakota."

I am just a girl from Norway.

I am Frances Louise Houghton Bingham, daughter-in-law of John

Bingham, wife of his son, Percy, friend of Percy's sister, Anna, and I mean for this to be my story. It, too, is a story of what a woman's patience can endure, as well as of what a woman's resolution can achieve. As to whether that refers in this case to one woman or two, you will have to make up your own mind.

And so, Reader, to Frances, alone in the bedroom she shares with her husband in his father's home in St. Paul, Minnesota. It is January of 1874. There is a photograph in her hand.

Chapter I

In Which Frances Waits

Frances caressed the intricate gilt frame that protected the photograph from her daily handling. They had been sixteen then, in number, and little more than that in years. Like several of the other girls from Miss Ardwell's Female Institute, Class of '70, Frances stood rigid in her finest white shirtwaist, its high collar clasped with the horseshoe brooch she believed she could remember at her mother's throat. Lifting her eyes to the mirror to compare her reflection there with the woman four years her junior in the photograph, Frances watched her hand rise to touch the same brooch, dusted with tiny diamonds. In the photograph Frances' hand rested lightly upon Anna's right shoulder.

Anna was, as usual, all containment, her seated posture erect, her hat, laden with waxed orange blossoms, refused the slightest slant. Frances knew the price Anna paid for that posture, the ache of disguising her spine's curve, of forcing the appearance of height from the set of her shoulders and stretch of her neck. The ugly cane hanging from the back of her chair was not part of the picture. At least it was long gone, replaced by the staff of polished ivory with its head of a swan, so like Anna, Frances had thought when she lifted it from the hands of the clerk at Cuthbertson's, elegant and of unexpected strength.

In the picture a few of Anna's curls refused to remain tucked, pinned, twisted beneath her hat. With a fingernail Frances traced their tumble onto Anna's neck. She liked to imagine that her friend had intended this hint of abandon that Frances alone could recognize. A black velvet ribbon from Anna's hat slid over her left shoulder and rested upon the shirtfront of white lace sewn into a blouse of heavy silk that Frances remembered to be of lavender stripes. The many-buttoned sleeves tightened around Anna's fine wrists as if to display the long, strong fingers in prayer upon her lap. In an act of quiet resistance, Anna had chosen to wear her cross pendant, despite Miss Ardwell's repeated disapproval of the holy symbol "cheapened," as if it were a common ornament. "We are none of us, here, Romanists," she would add, and Anna would obediently, or disobediently, perhaps, lift the cross and drop it inside her blouse, leaving Frances to imagine the metal's cool slide against warm flesh. It was Anna's single act of rebellion.

Frances had come, over the past four years, to resent the other girls in the photograph and looked forward to the day when she would have forgotten all of their names. No luck, so far, with the square-faced girl at the end of Frances' row, the one with the mournful stare. Serena Haugbeck. Frances had stumbled upon her once during a ("strictly prohibited") late night stroll about the grounds of Miss Ardwell's, not long before graduation. With a small cry Serena had clutched Frances about the neck, dampening her lace with tears. "Please, do not forget me," Serena had pled, to Frances' surprise, for they had had very little previous intercourse beyond Serena's occasional and inchoate gazes of longing, which Frances had steadfastly ignored. Frances had been disgusted by the embrace, by the leanness of the girl's desire, belied by the heavy body tucked and pressed into her corset. Frances was not unfamiliar with that leanness that allowed itself to be satisfied with so little, necessary, she supposed, for women whose role it would be to secure a husband precisely to produce his heirs, for women who would be happiest the less they knew of happiness. It was a meagerness that she could not abide.

She supposed it was possible that others had imagined her to be unfeeling. As a child there had been no tears in her eyes as she waited for her train, a satchel in her lap, a grown brother on either side of her on the bench, neither mother nor father in sight. But then, what little girl of eight is thinking "never again" with a train whistle sounding in the distance? As a young adult Frances was quite capable of looking upon infants without needing to poke, tickle, or otherwise torment the simple, drooling things. Nor did she reach out to caress the grief of others, an awful disrespect. Miss Ardwell's assistant, Miss Prior, had complained that her manner was too direct to convey grace, and had done her best to encourage Frances to "flow" with the other girls as they wove and leapt their way about the room during the morning calisthenics hour. It was all Frances could do not to rap the diminutive Miss Prior over the head with her wand each time she, gracelessly, passed the piano. But Frances did not feel the least bit severe, finding, in fact, much sport in the contemplation of her fellow man. Certainly Percy had not found her to be unfeeling.

Frances had discovered much to appreciate in Anna's older brother when they first met upon his return to St. Paul from New Haven, without the certificate of law for which he had studied, and for which, his father liked to remind Percy, he had paid. John Bingham seemed to Frances to have much in common with the fathers of several of the young men in her circle, craving that which they never had and stuffing their sons to sate themselves. Then, with each privilege bestowed—education, travel, leisure, money—they found more to condemn. Percy, predictably, had grown contemptuous of his provider. Frances claimed no great insight into the souls of humankind, but one need be neither clergy nor spiritualist, she suspected, to divine the insecurity that lay within Percy's contempt. Only in Anna's presence did Percy relax; insecurity unnecessary, contempt impossible.

Anna had spoken much, and fondly, of her brother during their years at Miss Ardwell's, so when Frances learned that he, newly returned from Yale, was to be a part of the excursion party to White Bear Lake to which Anna had invited Frances that long-past July, she was doubly eager to accept. Although Percy was his sister's senior by five years, there was still much of the boy evident in the man. He carried with him a copy of Mr. Tennyson's poems and a tidy, leather-bound diary that closed like a wallet, into which he was to later tuck a lock of Frances' hair. These diaries, Frances had since discovered—one for each year, going back into his teens—did not record daily events, social visits, changes in the weather as one would expect, but were filled, rather, with quotations from famous men, lines and verses of poems he had copied, and even the occasional poem of his own composition. Frances could not speak to his accomplishments there. She cared little for poetry herself, although she had often enough at Miss Ardwell's taken pleasure in Anna's attempts to hold back the tears Miss Alice Cary meant to wring from her readers with her catalogue of carnage from the War of the Rebellion. A far greater evil than war lay in the smoke and iron of progress, represented in Percy's poetry by the—what was it now?—"serpent in the garden of America," the railroad. His unease on the excursion train from St. Paul to White Bear Lake, however, had had little to do with the railway's "scars upon the virgin breast of the land," but rather with the realization that he was to be the only gentleman in the party, made up almost completely of merchants' wives and children. Anna had helped him to find his place in precisely the manner she would not tolerate from anyone else. She allowed herself to be the invalid in need of his constant attention.

The week that followed at the South Shore House had given Frances and Anna the opportunity to observe the manners of the many wealthy ladies visiting from eastern cities, ladies who were disappointing only in that they had chosen to enjoy their summer leisure in remote Minnesota by dressing in plain calico and brown linen. Following their leads, several of the women of the St. Paul party took to rowing their own boats, baiting their own hooks, and catching their own fish. Percy was at first as unsure of his duties in a boat as he was on the train. He proved to be just competent, at best, with an oar, and somewhat reluctant to handle worms, but it was he who was able to convince Anna to attempt the transition from land to lake, and with his greater strength helped her to her seat with little clumsiness. That is when Frances began to study Percy's conduct around Anna far more closely than she did the etiquette of the eastern ladies. From him she learned when to offer her arm, when to check the impulse, and when to look away, unnoticing, from a stumble or grimace.

On their third or fourth day on holiday Percy had offered to row an acquaintance of three hours across the lake to the depot where he was to catch the eastbound St. Paul and Duluth. This gentleman — Frances could remember only that his first name was Moses, and that he was from the wilds of Dakota — had caught Percy's attention when he mentioned that he was by profession a journalist, but having "come down with the politicking bug" was currently the representative to the United States Congress from Dakota Territory, a tonic that he proclaimed would "cure him if it didn't kill him." Frances and Anna had required very little encouraging to join them in the rowboat. Anna had come to love the ease and swiftness of travel on water, and Frances, more so, the flush that rose to Anna's cheeks. The gentleman and Percy shared the oars on the row to the depot, although it was clear that the Dakota man was more accustomed to strenuous labor, for his strokes overmastered Percy's to the point that he refrained from putting his oar to the water on each third stroke in the attempt to keep the boat on course. By the time the party arrived at the north shore, deposited the Dakota man, and turned the boat back to the hotel, Percy was himself flushed, as much with embarrassment as exertion.

Anna had leaned forward to smooth Percy's dark curls that had been lifted by the breeze. "Your talkative friend appeared to prefer resting to rowing," she had said with a smile. "It was good of you not to mention it."

Frances had forgotten Percy's response, but the image of brother and sister with their foreheads almost touching remained clear. They could have been twins. Later, as Percy helped Frances from the boat she seemed to lose her balance for just a moment, and her breast pressed against Percy's arm as he steadied her. That was the day she decided that he was a man whose touch she could tolerate. That, Frances knew, had been her good fortune, for she would have married a brute to remain with Anna.

The wedding took place less than a year later. Frances remembered turning from her new husband to accept Anna's embrace. Like Percy she needed to bend to Frances, although with Anna it was more tilt than bend, her weight transferred from the ivory staff before she allowed herself to rest for just an instant against her new sister-in-law's breast. Frances' instinct then had been to both embrace and lift, as if in her arms Anna could be released from the unsteadying tug of the earth. Anna had brushed Frances' cheek with her lips, held her for that moment, and murmured, "sister." But Frances had gently refused the title, for she could not bear to lose the pleasure of hearing her name in Anna's voice.

For the past three years, since that wedding day, Frances and Percy had lived in the John Bingham home, and there they would stay, it was understood, until Percy could "find his feet." Each evening, after Frances and Anna carried the supper dishes into the kitchen and left them to Mrs. Cook (whose economy of name Frances quite enjoyed), they would join Percy and his father, if he were home, and mother in the parlor. Rhoda Bingham sat next to the window letting in the day's last light, a light she had not seen for years, but which she insisted she could feel through clouds, through fog, through rain, through that window. Blind but certain, she would knit the blankets or mufflers that made up her work, the intricate embroidery of the past no longer possible. Occasionally she would match her voice to Anna's when Anna turned to the Bible, signaling that the evening's family time had come to an end. Frances could hear the faintest echo of Anna's voice in her mother's, made fragile less by years than by illness. Frances found the resemblance disarming, although she had learned to take care with her own voice in her mother-in-law's presence. For Rhoda Bingham alone was attuned to that which those who rely on sight for perceptions can not hear. Once, when Frances had said Anna's name, Rhoda Bingham, sitting nearby, had slowed her needles, and Frances could sense her mother-in-law suddenly listening harder. Little wonder, Frances knew, for Anna's name in her mouth sounded like nothing else that she had heard spoken in this house. Of course, Mother Bingham could not know what it was that she had heard. Dear woman, how could she suspect the impossible?

Still, Frances found it daily more difficult to keep her feelings mute. Three years ago, Frances had believed that she had brought her dreams to fruition by arranging a life with Anna by her side. But her desire, to her surprise, refused to remain static in the constant presence of her friend, so that what had once seemed to her an obvious solution had become a torment. Of late, Frances had come to think of her marriage as less a solution, than a small first step toward … what? She could not parse out the conundrum she had placed herself within, in which her husband—without whom she could not have remained with Anna— was both ally and adversary, essential, and yet the greatest obstruction to her happiness. With the exception, that is, of Anna herself, and that ever-present cross weighted upon her neck. As for Frances' father-in-law, John Bingham was very often absent from his family. On his rare evenings home, he would favor Frances with a distant smile as she poured his last cup of coffee of the day, and then, oblivious to the evening's reading, return to the notebook upon his lap, filled with numbers. Once, Frances had silently dropped a finger to his notebook to draw his attention to an error relating to the percentage of a particular sum. When her father-in-law had looked up in surprise, Frances had dared a smile of complicity.

She had returned the coffee pot to its tray and taken her seat next to Percy less than an hour ago when Percy suggested—as Anna closed the Bible upon her reading from the twelfth chapter of Second Corinthians, yet again, to Frances' dismay—that perhaps Anna would soon invite another figure into their "happy domestic sphere." He was certain he had spied a blush upon her cheek this past Sunday as she was speaking to the young minister who had stepped into the pulpit while their regular pastor recovered from his fall from the church's roof he had been helping to repair.

"I am to glory in my infirmities, rather," Anna answered, favoring Percy with a wan smile. Frances had cause to be grateful for those infirmities, for they had thus far served to make Anna invisible to potential suitors. Still, the response was chilling, and Frances must have shuddered, for Percy had placed his hand upon hers for a moment.

It was John who spoke next, embarrassing both son and daughter. "You would do well to mind your tongue, sir," he said, as if Percy were a child in need of schooling, and Anna a cripple to be protected.

Frances had watched the tension between father and son increase steadily over the past year. This could well have been due to Percy's lack of gratitude for his "opportunity" to read law, arranged for him by John Bingham with a crony who worked with the St. Paul and Pacific Railroad, but Frances believed that John Bingham was bothered by something greater than his son's reluctance to secure his own certificate of law. Although her father-in-law spoke of the "crisis" as if last September's financial panic was an event that affected all but him, Frances had begun to wonder if the comfortable home she had attained was itself less than secure. Still, she knew John Bingham to be an ambitious man, and Frances had faith in ambition. Percy, on the other hand, for all his talents, was precisely the man that his mother's influence of frailty and his father's purchased privilege had formed him to be: educated, bored, and quite lacking in initiative.

"Father, it is quite –" Anna had begun to insist when Percy broke in, pleased to enter the tug-of-war.

"I do not understand you, sir. I'm sure that Anna—"

"Please—" Anna spoke again.

"There is a great deal you do not understand," John said, overriding his daughter's plea, "not the least of which is the value of a hard day's work."

Frances had felt Percy stiffen next to her, although he kept his voice low. "You will have little trouble finding me at work amidst the clamor and racket on Fourth Street during all hours of the work week, sir, poring over contracts, deeds, and maps with the rest of the ink-stained drudges."

"And I expect that I would find you the first out of the door at the end of the day, as well."

"That is your criticism, father? That I leave the office at the end of the day? That I find it a pleasurable duty to return to my family in the evening? I see, yes, of course, I can see how—"

"Anna." Rhoda Bingham's frail voice silenced the men. She lifted her unseeing eyes to the center of the room as if she meant to conjure a presence from the atmosphere to settle the dispute. And then, anticipating the men, she spoke again. "No, it is Anna whom I need."

Frances had had to hide her smile, for Mother Bingham could make a point, leaning on Anna as Anna, in turn, leaned upon her ivory staff, mother and daughter, blind and halt, tilting toward the door, driven out by the unpleasant manners of the men. Frances had stood as well to lift the coffee tray. Although she bid the family good-night, she lingered on the other side of the parlor door, taking care to arrange some of the cups so that they would not spill, and thus caught the fragments of the argument that had begun anew. From John Bingham she heard "fortunate to find such a promising position" and "by God, you need to strike while the iron's—." Percy's responses had included, "asked no favors" and "perfectly capable" and, unfortunately, "newspaper man." That was when John Bingham's voice rose with "occupation for scoundrels and windbags," and Frances continued on to the kitchen, for father and son had begun to harmonize upon an old tune.

No, her husband was not a brute, Frances thought, setting the photograph back on the dressing table, but he was a man, and it was a Wednesday evening and her menses were not upon her. The argument below would be short. Within days of their wedding Percy had produced a much-thumbed advice tract called *The Book of Nature* ("Containing Information for Young People Who Think of Getting Married"), which he had hesitantly opened to the author's advice regarding the interval of two to three days between conjugal relations as the most healthful for men. Women, Frances read, could experience more frequent relations without suffering particular injury, although such frequency, the author warned, could prove to be "hard on their nerves."

"Indeed," Frances had responded quietly, but had not looked up from the page as she waited for Percy to speak again. When he did it was to suggest that perhaps Frances would not think it improper for him to press his "attentions" upon her twice a week, excepting those days when… and at this point Percy had begun blushing so profusely that Frances feared he would Spontaneously Combust as did that poor fellow in Mr. Dickens' *Bleak House*. "What you wish, Percy," Frances had replied, thinking to herself, the next words he speaks will be "Wednesday" and "Saturday." They were, and that (it being a Saturday) had been the end of their discussion. The next morning, however, Percy had suggested that Frances read the rest of Mr. Ashton's tract at her leisure, for there were things there she "might find of interest," given their hopes to be settled in a house of their own before they began a family. This, Frances readily did, although she discovered little information that she had not already acquired through a thorough study of the infamous Madame Beach's little book, purloined by a classmate from her mother's chest of drawers and surreptitiously passed from girl to girl at Miss Ardwell's.

At first Frances and Percy had been strangers and their intimacies brief. Percy was kind and Frances was grateful for his kindness as well as his brevity. Still, she preferred the other evenings, when her husband came to her as a friend. He had found in Frances an avid listener, for in his desire to speak of the life he had been meant to lead he had become the most willing of teachers. Through his descriptions Frances had traveled from England to Greece, through his reminiscences of his years at school she had been brought into the company of Byron and Keats, and of course, Percy's favorite, Mr. Tennyson, whom she found terribly dull. Frances preferred the Dante that Percy read aloud, less for the verse than for the exquisitely horrible etchings in the volume beautifully bound in Moroccan leather. Although Frances took greater pleasure in listening to Anna's voice, she had grown weary of Anna's choice of ever good, ever patient, ever suffering heroines, her Dorcas, Daughter of Faustina, or lately, Mrs. Gaskell's increasingly pathetic Ruth. Sometimes, as Percy read, Frances liked to compare the features brother and sister shared: hands that were strong, yet fine; fingers that squared and did not taper. Percy's emotions, too, could be read in the blueness of his eyes. He, too, signaled a question with his shoulders and head tilted forward.

Frances dropped her gaze once more to the photograph upon hearing her husband's steps. In reality, Percy and Anna were nothing alike. He was a man, and she a fantasy more real in a picture than in the room down the hall.

CHAPTER II

In Which We See Cracks in a Diamond

The knock on the door was less a request than a polite announcement, and Frances looked up at the mirror to see Percy, his color high, entering the room behind her.

"Vanquished or vanquisher?" Frances asked from her dressing table as she picked up her hairbrush, slid her thumb against the coolness of its silver handle, and passed an invitation through the mirror.

"We should be living in our own home. Oh, you need not bother," Percy assured Frances as he caught the change in her expression. "I know the arguments well. We can little afford such a luxury, and it would be a hardship on Anna to be without us now that mother requires such constant care." Percy accentuated each point with the thud of a boot dropped to the floor. He herded the boots to the heavy black oak wardrobe against the wall with his stocking feet, hung his jacket, and shrugged his suspenders from his shoulders. "But as long as I am under his roof, I must needs be the vanquished." He turned to see that Frances continued to hold the brush up for him. The unreadable half-smile that she offered as well, mediated by the mirror, was familiar. Stepping toward Frances, Percy lifted the brush from her hand, and began to brush the long tresses he gathered across his arm as if her hair were some separate darkly silken and fragile creature, and Frances was reminded of the one poem containing an inventory of her virtues that she had come upon in Percy's diaries. The poem spoke of the "unexpected" beauty of her tumbled hair, and of her eyes, "shivered with streaks of black like cracks in a diamond." Gray, Frances thought, looking into the mirror again. Gray would have been easier to rhyme.

"Is it not he who leaves the field who is the vanquished?" Frances said. "Your father has been away so much of late that I believe he must feel like a stranger in his own home. His aggression toward you, who have become the man of the house, is quite natural."

"I see you are philosophical tonight. Perhaps I have underestimated the intellectual rigor of Miss Ardwell's curriculum."

"Will you spar with me as well, Percy? Here?"

Frances' expression was no longer enigmatic, and Percy understood that he had given offense, although he could not have said how. Often his wife asked questions that only he, with his greater learning, could answer. But should he refer directly to the inferiority of her intellect or her education, the former sufficient for a woman, and the latter proper, her response was to bristle. It was in this very inconsistency that she confirmed those limitations she would deny. No matter, Percy thought, there was equal charm in the attempt and the failure.

"I did not mean to offend you with my teasing, dear. It is just that he so thoroughly irritates me that I lose all perspective, and—"

"—manners?"

"And manners. There, am I forgiven?" Percy halted his strokes for a moment and waited for Frances to reply.

"Of course, but your father does seem to be unusually preoccupied this winter, does he not?"

"Oh, he's on the run all right. Positively scrambling."

The increased vigor with which Percy reapplied the hairbrush suggested that whatever had John Bingham "scrambling" was cause for some excitement, if not pleasure. The set of Percy's mouth, however, told Frances that there would be no further disclosure on his part. He could be so tiresome at times, she thought. Clearly it was all about money, a subject her husband considered inappropriate in mixed company, even between husband and wife. Beyond the understanding of how a household must run upon a set allowance, a woman, Percy had explained, had no need to be sullied by financial matters. Exceptions— and with Percy, there were always exceptions—had to do with his periodic complaints about his own "indentured servitude" and the occasional opportunity he took to display scorn for his father's pursuit of wealth. It occurred to Frances (not for the first time) that her husband's sensibilities were not only out of step with the time, but were perhaps a bit more delicate than his family's history warranted.

Fortunately, she was not without her own resources. That John Bingham's fortunes had taken a turn for the worse with those of the Northern Pacific Railroad seemed clear. The first indication that something unusual had happened, this past September, came with the slamming of the front door as Percy, flushed with excitement, burst into the Bingham home. Passing directly through the parlor, without a word for the women sitting there, he strode into his father's study. Frances and Anna had exchanged a startled look. Rhoda Bingham continued to stare straight before her, but stopped her knitting, blinked her eyes rapidly, as if she could clear them of blindness, and asked, "Was that Percy? Has something happened?" Soon thereafter John Bingham rushed from the house, leaving Percy to assure the women that some business news had come over the wire, but it was nothing to concern them.

Almost twenty-four hours had passed before Frances could lay her hands upon a newspaper. Although the headline exclaimed, "PANIC," Frances' attention was first drawn to a fascinating report of the Yellow Fever in Louisiana that a local physician had described as taking victims as quickly as "sheep dying with the rot." The lead story was a dry thing in comparison. The great financial house of Jay Cooke and Company had failed. Other banks and businesses, it was feared, would soon topple under the weight of that catastrophe, just as the galleries of the Stock Exchange had threatened to collapse under the weight of the masses that had rushed there in alarm. Jay Cooke stood accused of misrepresenting the Northern Pacific Railroad project by vastly overrating the value of the land upon which the bonds he sold were based, although here the St. Paul Press took issue with the eastern newspapers that proclaimed "Jay Cooke's banana belt" to be, in reality, a "wild scheme to build a railroad from Nowhere, through No-Man's-Land to No Place." The Northern Pacific came in for its own share of the blame for mismanagement and for profligate spending that not even the great house of Cooke and Company could withstand.

Thirty financial houses in New York and Philadelphia failed that Friday. The following Monday eleven more closed their doors. The New York Stock Exchange closed for ten days. The Gold Exchange followed suit. The panic, Frances read, was spreading across the country, and she imagined the din of doors slamming from east to west.

Sitting at her dressing table with her husband all but forgotten behind her, Frances shuffled the clues. It was still September when John Bingham announced that Mother Bingham's poor health would make the Binghams' yearly shopping trip to New York impossible. An order to Berkey & Sloan's for a new carriage, to have been delivered in the coming spring, had been cancelled. "The Panic of '73," as it was already being called, had evidently slammed the door on the second floor bath room as well, for there had been no talk for some time of new plumbing and a zinc bath tub. The question remaining for Frances was what was she to do with her new understanding? If she were to be of use in this crisis, it would be to John, for the fate of the family was clearly in his hands. She would have liked to move to her secretary to study once again her list of small changes that could be made in the daily management of the household, but Percy's pull upon her hair reminded her that she had other duties to attend to first.

"Perhaps we could banish your father, and his affairs, from this room," Frances said as she reached behind her to take the hairbrush from Percy's hand, all the while holding his gaze in the mirror. She watched his Adam's apple rise and dip as he swallowed and bent toward her, his hands now in her hair. To her surprise Percy's grasp on her hair, gathered in his fists about each ear, tightened beyond a caress. The slight force was curiously pleasant, and Frances practiced a sudden intake of breath as she set the hairbrush next to the photograph.

CHAPTER III

In Which We Meet J. B. Power

James Buel Power set the letter he had been reading back on his desk, tapped it twice, and reached for the watch tucked into his waistcoat. By the dim light of the kerosene desk lamp he had grudgingly lit moments earlier, Power saw that he had another half hour before the 6:30 p.m. eastbound left the station for Duluth. It would be this time tomorrow evening before he reached St. Paul, and then he'd be getting onto another train for New York the next morning. It didn't make for much of a visit with Helen and the children, but that could not be helped. Thirty minutes. Plenty of time to finish the day's correspondence, this last to ... Power looked again at the letter before him ... the Jewish Agricultural and Industrial Society of St. Paul. He'd lived in St. Paul for ten years before moving his office and small staff to Brainerd and yet he'd never heard of such a thing. Moravians and Mennonites were one thing, Jews quite another, he thought, taking up his pen, and pausing for a moment to compose a beginning line.

His words would be professional and assured. And optimistic. The assumption of success, Power knew, was no small component of the same, although, and here he allowed himself a private sigh, optimism had been easier before. From the day he'd begun his professional life as a ticket and freight clerk for the New York and Erie Railroad, a lanky boy of sixteen his friends called Jimmy P, he'd believed that fortune would be available to him to precisely the degree that he was willing to hustle. Throughout the next twenty years, as Jim Power, he'd been what he called a "rustler of a living," working as a civil engineer, a surveyor, draftsman, and auditor. He was James Power when he began his work with the Northern Pacific Railroad just three years ago in 1871 as chief clerk of the Minnesota and Dakota Division of the Land Department. Expectations were high, money was plentiful, and the bulk of his work lay in keeping up with arrangements for visits and sales along the Minnesota portion of the road as it was built. The property, with open acres of fertile land, edged with forested hills and interspersed with lakes packed with fish, practically sold itself. Within a year he had been promoted to General Agent of the Division. He spent less time in the field and more time in correspondence with the N.P. Bureau of Immigration's European agents in London, Liverpool, throughout Scandinavia, and Germany. Although this correspondence, which filled several letterpress books, was signed by James B. Power, his associates had begun to call him J.B.

He had personally seen to the settlement of several colonies of Swedes, Germans, Norwegians, and Finns, the latter of which didn't so much settle as burrow in like a warren of rabbits. Just this month he'd managed to get 230 Swedes out of the N.P. reception house in western Minnesota where they'd been since December. He'd been pressed to get them out earlier, but, as he'd written to the chairman of the N.P. Land Department, Frederick Billings, "even a Swede ought not be turned out in winter." More important, of course, were the Yankees who migrated to the new Northwest. Several colonies had gathered together in New England to make their way west. The most impressive, the Red River Colony, had picked out thirty-six townships—not sections, but townships. Even the arrival of the Red River Colony, however, could not make up for the lost Russian Mennonites who had petitioned President Grant for an exemption from military service for the next fifty years, and from service as jurymen, and for the right to keep and administer their own schools as a condition for settlement. The petition had been denied. Power shook his head at the memory. A few non-binding assurances could have brought as many as forty thousand families—moral, sober, frugal and industrious—to the new Northwest. Power remained in contact with another small colony of thirty Mennonite families, but the larger opportunity had been lost.

News of the petition's denial had arrived on Power's desk in his St. Paul office in early September of the past year, and the news that followed had grown steadily worse. The daily bludgeoning that the Northern Pacific had taken in the press following September's "panic" had colony after colony of prospective settlers writing to say that they had decided to "take another look" at Kansas. Then, on September 30, 1873, not quite two weeks after the crash, came the telegram from the Northern Pacific general office in New York that changed everything.

Expect no further help from this end, take care of yourself as best you can.

Anticipating something of the sort, Power had been ready to act when the telegram arrived. He had called in and released all the land examining parties. His own staff he reduced to three clerks. Hard as relaying those decisions had been, they'd been nothing compared to informing his wife that she was to remain in St. Paul with their four children while he moved his office and those three clerks to the Company's office in Brainerd, a mid-Minnesota town that consisted of little more than the railroad shops, a depot, a livery, a general store, and a couple of saloons along the N.P. line from Duluth to Fargo. And yet, it was the right thing to do. Within thirty days he'd managed to sell some of the N.P.'s town lots in Fargo—a town in the sense that the tents along the two-year-old tracks were lined up in neat rows—as well as some pine land in Minnesota, raising enough money to pay his department's bills and leave a small surplus with which to work.

Still, six months after the crash, the situation for the Northern Pacific was dire. Track laying had come to a halt in Bismarck and there was no telling if it would ever begin again. The N.P.'s Bureau of Immigration had been closed, and the European agents brought home. Power was not privy to the decisions being made in the general offices in New York, but surely bankruptcy was near. Power thought again of the telegram's words, let a small smile draw up the edges of his hound dog face, and murmured, "Good." Take care of yourself? He would do better than that. This was the opportunity he'd been waiting for.

If it works, Power reminded himself, noticing that the window panes that looked out onto the tracks were almost dark. If it works, this will rival any advertising scheme Jay Cooke himself could have devised. Once again pulling his watch from his vest pocket, Power saw to his surprise that he had spent a full ten minutes in rare reverie. Returning to work, he quickly completed a paragraph of encouragement, and added the letter to the pile in the box on the corner of his desk. One of his clerks would see that the letters made it into the mail bag. Then J. B. Power stood and crossed the small room to retrieve his hat, coat, and satchel. For a moment he studied the engineer's map of the line from Brainerd to Bismarck tacked to the wall next to the coat rack. It looked like an elongated checkerboard spread from east to west, the government sections available for homesteads crosshatched and marked with even numbers, the alternating N.P. railroad land grant sections in white with odd numbers. With his index finger Power tapped his way west and south of Fargo a few miles to a couple of sections of slough land between the Red and the Sheyenne Rivers. "Mennonites, Moravians, and Jews," he muttered under his breath as he stepped out the door and into the March slant of ashy precipitation, a combination of falling snow and blowing dirt.

CHAPTER IV

In Which We Must All Go Farming

To J. B. Power's right the diminutive Septimus Slade alternated bites of his steak with puffs from his cigar. Power resisted the impulse to wave the smoke away. Clean-shaven and pink, with a head that seemed oddly oversized, Slade looked like an aging cherub dressed in a rumpled suit, and Power imagined the little man's feet swinging well short of the floor under the table. He owned a half dozen railroads and express companies and sat on the boards of a half dozen more. Known for a Midas touch, his approval of Power's plan would be essential if the rest of the Northern Pacific's board of directors were to be convinced at tomorrow's meeting. Slade had thus far said little beyond his original greetings to Power and the other two men sitting at their table at Delmonico's. Across from Power sat the hirsute and dour Frederick Billings, chairman of the N.P.'s Land Department. The fourth man at the table, General George Cass, was the current president of the road. Like all N.P. shareholders, the officers and directors of the road had suffered significant financial loss through the depreciation of their stocks and bonds, currently worth about ten percent of their original value.

The road's progress had, in fact, never been smooth. A transportation route through the northern tier of the country had been under consideration since the first decade of the century when Lewis and Clark completed their explorations for Thomas Jefferson. But plans for a transcontinental railroad along that course had barely begun to gain popularity when the discovery of gold in California made the Bay of San Francisco a far more attractive destination than the Puget Sound. The hopes inspired by President Lincoln's decision to charter the Northern Pacific Railroad quickly dissipated as the War of the Rebellion turned governmental interest to the country's midsection. In 1866, a handful of the nation's wealthiest men dug into their own pockets, hoping to persuade Congress that here was a business endeavor so certain of success that proven capitalists had thrown the weight of their own personal fortunes behind it. After three years of unsuccessful lobbying for financial support for the road, they gave up on Congress and turned to the deepest pocket of all, Jay Cooke & Company. Cooke agreed to issue bonds to the amount of $100,000,000 to build the railroad. An oft-reproduced map of the country showing isothermal lines bending to the north and bringing a temperate climate to Minnesota and Dakota Territory reassured investors.

Construction work on the line began that summer of '69. Track soon reached the Mississippi River where the town of Brainerd was laid out. Early in '72 the N.P. crossed the Red River that separated Minnesota and Dakota Territory. The settlement of Centralia became Fargo, the newly platted town sites along the railroad acting as a roll call of the N.P.'s board of directors. By the time the road reached Edwinton (soon to be renamed Bismarck after the Iron Chancellor) on the Missouri River deep in Dakota Territory, the speed of the road building had taken its financial toll and the Northern Pacific and Jay Cooke & Company were in financial distress.

These were the details that the country had been reading in the newspapers for over six months, along with the tales of widespread ruination brought about by Cooke's collapse and the Panic of '73. But in all the newspapers there was one part of the Northern Pacific contract that was not mentioned: the creation of a Land Department. Perhaps it did not seem pertinent, but Power believed that it held the key to saving what existed of the railroad. As chairman of the Land Department, Frederick Billings was responsible for plotting, platting, and managing town sites along the road. Next in line was the Land Commissioner, a chronically ill W. A. Howard to whom Power, as the General Agent of the Minnesota and Dakota Division, reported, but who had been unable to join the current gathering at Delmonico's. The Land Commissioner bore the responsibility for settling a "civilized" population along the one thousand miles of the planned road.

Although General Cass had arranged for the four men to meet in order to discuss Power's proposition (which would need Billings' and Slade's support if the board were to agree), the discussion thus far around the table had centered on the road's impending bankruptcy. So it was with some relief that Power heard General Cass, whose one military command had been of a steamer on Lake St. Clair, turn his nautical metaphors toward the business at hand.

"Our creditors have been lenient thus far," Cass was saying, "but we may be forced to declare insolvency within the month. If you have ideas for restructuring, as you say, Billings, I'd like to hear them. In the meantime, we need not be idle. We are now in shoal water and all hands must take hold and lift over the bar until we get into deep water below. It won't do to tie up to the shore and wait for a rise to carry us over. Perhaps we have not all been in agreement with decisions made thus far," Cass hesitated as if expecting a response from Septimus Slade, who continued to chew and puff without looking up, "but there isn't a Northern Pacific man who does not believe that the future of this country resides in the new Northwest. There will be a day when Brainerd, Fargo, and Bismarck will rival the finest cities of the eastern seaboard. If, that is, we find the means to rescue the Northern Pacific Railroad. Mr. Power, I believe, has spotted an opportunity from the crow's nest and now cries, 'Land Ho!'"

"Doctor Power, we'll have to call him, if he can save this bleeding amputee, hemorrhaging our good money."

Slade's was an inauspicious entry into the conversation, but Power saw his way immediately. "Much has indeed been lost, sir, and I intend to neither concentrate on nor to ignore those losses, but rather, to suggest how we can best take advantage of that which we have gained. We have a railroad that reaches from Duluth to the Missouri River. More importantly, no, of inestimable importance, we have title to fifty million acres along the completed track. A great percentage of those acres in Minnesota and Dakota Territory are of such fertility that they can be matched by no other region in this vast country, and, I dare say, on the globe. Now I know," Power put up his hand to stay any comments, "I know that these are familiar sentiments, thanks to the exuberant advertising campaign of Mr. Cooke, and that the days for such exuberance may seem to be behind us, but I say they are not." Realizing that he had lifted his fork into the air to emphasize his point, Power replaced his cutlery onto his plate and set both hands upon the table before him.

"Those days are not behind us quite simply because the truth is not something that can be pulled out and used when it is convenient, and then forgotten when it is not. The truth is as constant as the prairie skies of the Red River valley, and it is that valley about which I want to speak. And," Power hesitated for a moment, "about the great many investors now holding depreciated bonds."

"May we understand, Mr. Power, that you have now moved into the debit column in your accounting?" Septimus Slade looked past Power as he spoke, catching the attention of a waiter. "Bring me some of that 'Alaska, Florida' for dessert," he said to the man who quickly approached.

"The items in the debit column do not require my recitation, Mr. Slade. I am talking, sir, about a plan to shift those depreciated bonds from debit to credit."

"If you have discovered the philosopher's stone that will turn our iron rails to gold, then please continue." Slade lifted his arms from his sides in a gesture meant, Power supposed, to be expansive, but which reminded him rather of a flightless bird flapping its vestigial wings.

"I am aware that there are those on the board who have viewed the

Land Department as little more than a 'necessary evil'. I am proposing that it is precisely this department that will save the road." Power hesitated, hoping for a look of encouragement. Cass nodded briefly. Slade had cocked an eyebrow. Billings appeared to be fully occupied with stroking the hair on the fingers of one hand with the other.

"All of our efforts now must be to hold on to the main line," Power continued. "That comes to four hundred and fifty miles of road through a country destitute of population. If the road is to survive, we need to populate the country alongside the road. We need to carry supplies one way, and goods the other."

"Mr. Power, we know how railroads work." Slade had lost his cherubic expression.

"My apologies. I propose that the Northern Pacific Railroad Company offer a bonds-for-land exchange, not to put too fine a point on it."

Billings lifted his head. "All that will attract is speculation. Speculators do not increase the traffic of a road."

"But if we should reduce the price of land in proportion to the area that the purchaser contracts to place under cultivation? If we should offer from 20 to 60 percent off the list price?"

"You might get some land under cultivation," Billings said. "But even if, say, ten percent of the major stockholders take up farming, which they will not, it would be little more than a drop in the bucket. We're talking about several thousands of square miles. You will not populate Dakota Territory with N.P. investors, I think. You need towns and communities for traffic. You need the entire structure of civilization."

"Our terms will attract men of substance. The bounty produced on the land will be its own advertisement. Gentlemen," Power lowered his voice, as if he were about to reveal a secret meant only for the ears of the men at his table, "this past fall a homesteader on the banks of the Sheyenne River brought into Fargo sixteen hundred bushels of Number One Scotch Fife wheat, the product from forty acres, which he sold for a dollar-twenty-five per bushel. That is two thousand dollars from forty acres. It would be eight thousand dollars from a quarter section. Thirty-two thousand dollars from a section." Power's voice rose a notch with each figure. "N.P. stock originally purchased for a dollar is now worth ten cents. If railroad land, valued at $2.50 to $5 an acre, is exchanged at face value, upon the condition, mind you, that that land be put under cultivation, an acre of land will go for twenty-five to fifty cents. Imagine, one square mile of land purchased for as little as one hundred and sixty dollars capable of producing thirty-two thousand a year!" Power took a breath. "Large stockholders will see value for increasingly valueless stock. The nation and the world will see farms such as they have never seen before, of such size, with such a capacity for production, why, they will advertise the wealth to be had there in a way no mere words can."

"Exhibition farms," General Cass said quietly.

"If you will," Power answered. "But, and this I can not state emphatically enough, the directors of the road must take the lead if others are to follow. Then will come the settlers, and the shopkeepers, and then the churches and the schools and the 'entire structure of civilization'. Gentlemen, I remember my first view of the land. There was not a sign of a living thing on the great unbroken plain, not a sound except that of the whispering wind as it passed over the sea of grass. Dakota is a great, dead space awaiting the occupancy of man to give it life. Gentleman, I say to you, we must all go farming!"

Silence followed Power's speech, a silence during which he met first Cass', then Billings', then Slade's eyes, at which point the little man spooned a last bit of biscuit and ice cream into his mouth, sat back in his chair, and brought his palms together in quiet applause.

"Well put, well put. You have an orator's gift, Mr. Power. And there's even a chance that you may be right. But the simple truth is that we have before us Hobson's Choice. It is this or nothing, and I for one am in your corner."

In the eighteen months that followed that April supper at Delmonico's in New York, J. B. Power's duties as General Agent for the Minnesota and Dakota Division of the N.P. multiplied beyond what even he had anticipated. In the first months most of his time was spent acting as a private land agent for the directors who had been convinced to invest in Power's scheme. For General Cass and another board member, Benjamin Cheney, Power selected eighteen sections of railroad land west of Fargo, arranged with a local man and his crew to begin breaking and backsetting the land the following summer, and then hired an acquaintance from St. Paul to manage the Cass-Cheney farm.

Several other directors took up large parcels along the road, lending their names to the railroad sidings nearby that were certain to become thriving towns. Power wrote letter after letter to these directors and other large bond holders, several of whom were considering parcels totaling over twenty square miles, encouraging them to buy up the government sections that were interspersed among their railroad sections as well. He feared that too much of the government land would be sought after by claim speculators, men who would secure the land by filing Homestead, Preemption, or Timber claims, make the minimum improvements required by law, and then lay off for years until surrounding improvements gave their own land greater value. In a letter to General Cass, Power explained, "I have made an arrangement with the Government Land Officers to hold for me these sections as long as possible. This is somewhat irregular but they are choice fellows at Fargo and will do all they can to accommodate us."

Frederick Billings took up several square miles, but was showing no interest in putting his land under cultivation, behavior that Power found mightily irritating from the chairman of the Land Department. Septimus Slade, despite his pivotal role in persuading the rest of the board to take a chance on Power's land-for-bonds scheme, could not be convinced to take more than five and three-quarter sections. He had chosen for a manager a certain John Bingham, who, Slade said, would be making a trip west soon to take a look at the parcel Power had selected, at which point Bingham would decide for himself if he, too, was interested in trading his own N.P. bonds for land as well.

By the end of '74 Power could report to Billings that land sales were nearing a million dollars, and that he expected 20,000 acres to be a very low estimate of the acreage to be broken in the Red River valley in 1875, which, Power added (somewhat more enthusiastically than realistically) could result in a full million bushels of wheat for shipping east. The world could not fail to take notice of such a bonanza, Power wrote, signing off with the exclamation that he would repeat for years to come: "Every man who locates a Bond is an Emigration Agent for us."

The following April brought about the reorganization of the Northern Pacific Railroad and the end of bankruptcy proceedings. The N.P. had been forced to give up a controlling interest in the St. Paul and Pacific Railroad and in the Oregon Steam Navigation Company located at the projected terminus of the road on the west coast, all in the effort to hold on to the 450 miles of track already completed. The long and short of Billings' reorganization plan was that the foreclosure sale and the following purchase (the 'purchasers' being the very same reorganized Northern Pacific Railroad Company) simply sloughed off the mortgage. N.P. bondholders took preferred stock for their bonds, the Company was ridded of all encumbrances and stood ready once again to raise more money on a good security at the first dawn of good times, at which point the Company could once again begin laying track. J. B. Power was convinced that the Red River valley "exhibition farms" were the herald of that dawn.

It was a rare moment when Power found the time to scribble out a personal note in the midst of his constant business correspondence, but a mid-September letter in '75 to his wife brought him particular satisfaction. Finishing the letter, Power lifted it into the air to give it his usual brief wave to dry the ink, and then, enjoying an unusual moment of leisure, he imagined his wife reading his words.

> *Dear Helen,*
>
> *Your letters are received as a balm in the midst of the daily flurry of business correspondence. I enjoyed your report on the Bingham family. I do not think it so odd that you have never seen John Bingham. There are, I suspect, a great many persons in the congregation of the First Christ Episcopal Church who believe that a certain Mr. J. B. Power is likewise oddly absent. It will not always be so. I can make no promise as to the date, but once the bulk of the N.P. land in the Red River valley is taken up I expect that my long exile in Brainerd will come to a close and I will be able to move the office back to St. Paul. I have been promoted to the position of Land Commissioner of the Northern Pacific Railroad, rewarded it seems for the success of my "land-for-bonds scheme." I am, as always, affectionately,*
>
> *Yours,*
> *James*

CHAPTER V

In Which an Ill Wind Blows Some Good

Percy was home from work much earlier than was his habit, but he had brought with him his usual scent, partly cigarette smoke, mostly whiskey. When Frances had asked him one evening several months earlier, as he emptied the contents of his several pockets onto the bedroom dresser, why he bothered carrying a flask, since he was seldom at any great distance from either the Merchants or the Metropolitan Billiards Hall, Percy had responded that it was a "gentleman's flask." Frances hoped that Percy knew her well enough after almost four years of marriage to understand that she was not deceived into thinking that he had actually answered her question. Or that it had been motivated by a decision to add to her wifely duties the role of watch-dog. In truth, she rather liked the flask, its slender curve both sensuous and tidy. The small cluster of grapes raised on the convex side of the silver container struck her as quite beautiful. Gentlemen's accessories were often such lovely things. She had simply wanted him to know that she knew the flask to be his constant companion.

Frances had been quizzing Mrs. Cook about the salaries of the house staff in other residences in the neighborhood when Percy entered the house through the side door just off the kitchen. The unusual time and manner of entry piqued her curiosity, but Frances was having such success with Mrs. Cook, a great gossip, that she did not immediately seek Percy out. What she had learned thus far was that the Bingham laundresses, who labored for two days each week in the cavernous basement, were paid the same wages as other laundresses on Summit Avenue, as were the gardener and his boy, and the housekeeper as well, but that the seamstresses who occupied the sewing room three mornings each week on the second floor were the highest paid that Mrs. Cook knew. What's more, Mrs. Smythe was known to have been discharged from an earlier position for having too generously helped herself to scraps and remainders of fabric, and Jennie MacFadden, who was Mrs. Smythe's niece—and who had a small child, but, as best anyone knew, no husband, Mrs. Cook whispered—had been forced to leave the same situation at the same time.

"I wonder that Anna did not know any of this when she hired Smythe and MacFadden," Frances muttered as she calculated what the household would save without at least one of the women's services.

"Oh, but she did, ma'am," Mrs. Cook clarified. "But Mrs. Smythe's work was so fine, Miss Bingham said, that it was a shame for her not to be able to put her talents to good use. That's what she said, and she said, too, and this I heard directly from Jenny MacFadden, that the first mistakes were often made in ignorance, and may be forgiven, but that it was repetition that blackened the soul."

That, Frances thought, was quite likely an accurate quotation. Anna had the ability to be simultaneously tender and rigid, a combination as tempting as problematic, for Frances dreamed of making some mistakes of her own. Mrs. Cook, her pump now well primed, had embarked on another tale of disappointing character regarding the man who delivered coal, but this information, Frances saw, could do her no good. As she left the room, Frances wondered aloud if chops for supper practically every night had not grown a bit tedious.

Percy was not in the library, nor the parlor, nor the small balcony off their bedroom where he occasionally liked to hide, so Frances wrapped a shawl around her shoulders and stepped onto the front porch. It was a glorious fall day, a cerulean sky lending distinction to the elms lining the street. Just this week, Frances noticed, the trees had begun their transformation into their autumn buttery yellow. Percy stood with his back to her, his head thrown back like an invalid or a prisoner who has finally gained the sun.

"Hello, my dear," he said without turning toward her. "You have found me."

"Did you come home to be found?"

Percy gave a short laugh and turned. She offered him her cheek and when he bent to kiss it she was able to calibrate his mood as likely to be somewhere between irreverence and petulance, based upon the whiskey on his breath. Frances supposed she should mind, but this was precisely the stage at which she found her husband most entertaining.

"I came home to talk to my wife, wife," he said into her ear.

Frances stepped back to study Percy's face for a moment. "Shall we sit here? The temperature is so pleasant, and the trees are spectacular."

"The leaves change color because they are dying, but by all means,

let us sit and watch them die while you tell me what you have been doing today."

"Why today?" Frances asked, as she settled into her chair.

"Today. Every day. What is it that you do, Frances?" Percy pulled his
own cushioned chair to her side and sat.

Frances felt more than heard the rough edge of Percy's response. It
was increasingly present in his banter with her, and she sensed that it
both frightened and excited him. She had begun to suspect that behind
this faint abrasiveness, lay the violation of that unspoken, unspeakable,
contract into which husbands and wives necessarily entered: to be cou-
pled, exposed, stripped bare of disguise in the intimacy of the bedroom,
and then miraculously transformed into strangers, politely bored and
distant, in the light of day. Sometimes it made her want to laugh aloud,
as she sat in church, or passed a plate of cookies in an acquaintance's
parlor, or looked about while on Percy's arm at the Opera House. She
studied the careful posture of her neighbors next to her in the pew
and could not imagine them turning and bumping under the covers.
She watched her friends daintily lift napkins to wipe away imaginary
crumbs and could not believe that a gasp or a moan had ever escaped
their lips. She looked at the fine dresses and suits and could not picture
corsets coming off, bellies behind the tight waistcoats released, trousers
and petticoats dropped. But these things must happen for they were
happening in her bedroom. A thought brought the slightest blush to
her face. Perhaps her freedom with Percy was completely outside of the
ordinary, and that accounted for her husband's tone. For the first time
as Frances looked over at Percy's half-smile, it occurred to her that he
could be dangerous. Not physically, but... Frances did not know how
to finish her thought.

"I have been most recently talking with Mrs. Cook about some of
the details of the house. Anna and Mother Bingham are taking tea with
the Misses Robertson, this being Tuesday afternoon, so I have been left
to my leisure, and I admit I have made no good use of it."

"Well done. I had forgotten the standing tea of Tuesdays with the
good spinsters. And how is it that you have come to deprive yourself
of the effervescent company of the Misses Robertsons, both of whom, I
take it, are still alive?"

"Breathing, certainly. I complained to Anna of the headache."

"Not as inventive as I would have expected."

"The headache, not a headache. As in, the headache I would have if I were to take tea yet again with Ida and Phoebe Robertson."

Percy threw back his head with a laugh before saying, "You are not nice."

"Oh Percy, I am often nice. I am simply not perfectly nice. And now may I ask, what brings you home this time of day?"

"No. Not yet. The world is too much with me today." Percy made a sweeping gesture, meant, Frances supposed, to encompass this weighty world, but taking in instead the quiet tree-lined street and the spires of the several churches in the wooded city below. "Tell me more about you."

Frances took a moment to study her husband. Just now he reminded her of Mrs. Cook. He had something to say to her, but preferred to have her ease him into it, soothe him with trifles, and then, when he had grown comfortable, guide him to his moment of disclosure. And she would, because she could, because she often enjoyed the moments of unpredictability of his conversations, but mostly because she must. What it would be like to be able to say to Percy, to any man, "listen, just tell me what you think, what you know. Be forthright," without the conversational dance, she could only imagine. So she entertained him for awhile with kitchen gossip and made him laugh with a description of an encounter she had watched from her bedroom window involving old Mrs. Harbaugh, her poodle, and one of the feral cats that had taken up residence in the gorge on the back side of the house. When Percy showed no intention of taking up his part of the conversation, Frances decided to see if she could make better use of her time.

"I was wondering, Percy, did I overhear your father informing Mother Bingham this morning of yet another trip he will soon be taking? I thought perhaps I heard him say 'Dakota'."

"That would be impossible."

"For your father to go to Dakota?"

"For me to confirm what you did or did not overhear, as I was neither with you at the time, nor with mother and father."

Quite impossible, Frances thought, as she tilted her head toward Percy to acknowledge his teasing, all the more so in that such a conversation had not taken place. She would have to find another means by which to sound her husband. A direct question regarding information he may have received from his father would never do, for Percy could not be relied upon for an accurate recapitulation of these conversations. As a result, Frances had been forced to hesitate at doors, pause outside open windows, and, when necessary, glance at correspondence upon John Bingham's office desk. There simply seemed to be no other way to remain sufficiently informed regarding the business of her own home. Just this morning she had taken a cup of coffee in to her father-in-law in his study, shortly after the arrival of the mail, to find him so intently studying a letter that he failed to acknowledge her knock or her entrance. She had waited until John had left the house for the day before returning to retrieve the cup, which he had set not so very far from the letter. There was mention of "bonds" and a couple of names she did not recognize, and a reference to "a trip to Fargo, D. T." A last glance before she stepped away from the desk gave her the name of her father-in-law's correspondent.

Septimus Slade. It was a name she had neither heard nor seen before.

"Quite impossible, of course," Frances said aloud. "I am, it seems, as clumsy in conversation as I was this morning in reality. I tripped against a chair in the hallway outside the parlor and sat to remove the shoe that pained me before I realized that your father and mother were speaking just the other side of the door. Before I could move away I overheard him mention a trip to Dakota in association with someone whose name I forget. September. Septimus. Oh, it doesn't matter, of course."

"Septimus Slade?"

"Who, dear?"

"Did you, perchance, hear the name 'Septimus Slade'?"

"Oh, Percy, I couldn't say. I was up and hobbling away at that point. I'm ashamed to have overheard that much. Is Mr. Slade a friend of yours?"

"Hardly, my dear. I have never met the man; nonetheless, I hold him personally responsible for my servitude as an ink-stained law clerk with the St. Paul and Pacific."

"Your foot is simply on a lower rung than is comfortable for a man of your talents. I do not doubt that you will climb."

For a moment husband and wife studied each other. "Getting and spending, we lay waste our powers," Percy finally said. "Climbing is a matter of definition. Ascent and descent are not necessarily mutually exclusive. Our Mr. Slade and father, for example, have descended to some climbing themselves."

"Is this one of your riddles, Percy?"

Percy sat further back in his chair and reached into his pocket for his cigarette case. Here was another gentleman's item of which Frances approved, as slim and elegant as his flask. She did not know of another man who carried such a beautiful thing. With a nod he asked for permission to light the cigarette and with a matching nod Frances gave it.

"For some years, father owned a significant parcel of land a bit southwest of here, land that he had purchased on the cheap soon after the Sioux massacre of '62 convinced a good many of the settlers there to go farming elsewhere. It was the division and the sale of that land six, or was it five years ago now—? I was back in New Haven, having completed my year of travel in Europe." Percy paused, his thoughts snagged by something in the past, and Frances closed her eyes, concentrated on maintaining an expression of benign disinterest, and willed her husband forward. "Yes, six. So that would have been '69 when father sold the land. Et voilà! John Bingham, thief, lumberman, speculator is transformed into John Bingham, Esquire, a wealthy man of business, a proper capitalist of the first sort, and the Bingham family takes residence in the wilds of lower Summit Avenue."

"With a magnificent view."

"And isn't that a lovely gift to a blind wife? Equally as thoughtful as putting a daughter who walks with a cane on the top of a hill. No, Frances, father is seldom motivated by thoughtfulness. He moved mother from the house she knew well and Anna from the Lowertown neighborhood she loved because he could sell dear, and buy cheap, with the intention of someday selling dear again. It is what he does for a living. He is a gambler."

"Mrs. Patrick tells me that the Walter Ingrahims are to build on a parcel between Rice and St. Peter."

"You have made my point for me, Frances. We are to be neighbors to the fabulously wealthy Walter Ingrahims. Imagine! And when that day comes I fully expect father to sell, and move his family to his next investment, which, if the pattern should hold, will be damned inconvenient for everyone but him. No, the best I can say for father on this account is that he quite possibly recognized the value of his Summit investment completely on his own, which was not the case in regard to his land speculation to the west. That was not prescience. Oh, no. He had some very material help from a very material gentleman in his selection."

This, Frances thought, was new information in the specific, but certainly not in the general, for it had long been her understanding of John Bingham that he was a capable and ambitious man with a talent for using the resources of others to increase his own. Nor was John Bingham the least bit reticent on this point, as one of his favorite and oft-told stories of his past had him, at fifteen years of age, stealing away from his New Hampshire home in the dead of night with nothing but his father's finest sow, which was not long thereafter in his company. Anna had once murmured, in response to the tale, "Your parents must have worried so, father," to which John had replied, "There were nine others to worry about. Don't suppose they missed me much. Missed that sow though, you may be sure," he'd added with a laugh. Exactly how John Bingham had parlayed the profits from a stolen pig into sufficient standing to have married Rhoda Stanton of the New Hampshire Stantons fifteen years later, Frances did not know. Nor did she know if he had the lumberyard in New Hampshire before the wedding, or if it came with his bride. It had been the lumber business that brought John Bingham to Minnesota. Percy could not be led into a recital of the Bingham's early years in Minnesota, and Anna had been just five years old when they had arrived in 1858. Her memories were of noise and mud and a small house near her father's mill in St. Anthony Falls. Then there had been the move to St. Paul's Lowertown and the house on Woodward, about which Anna spoke with so much affection. That move, Frances calculated, would have been around 1865, putting John Bingham about three years into the land speculation to which Percy now referred.

"Perhaps you are too hard on your father," Frances said. "We all rely on others for good advice now and then. There is no shame in that."

"Advice! Ha! He was helped by something far more substantial than that. A map is more like the thing. Father had, shall we say, an invisible partner in his Minnesota land purchase. That partner turned out to be Mr. Septimus Slade, who in 1862 was himself a simple surveyor in the employ of the St. Paul and Pacific Railroad. Seven years later a

branch line of that very railroad passed directly through the property
that father had accumulated. The value of his town lots, as well as of the
neighboring countryside, increased tenfold, and he was able to divide
the property into smaller parcels for sale to the immigrant mongrels
once again flowing in from the east, the U.S. Calvary having long since
hanged any number of offensive redskins responsible for the '62 Massacre and chased the rest west."

"And Mr. Slade?"

Percy sighed, his interest in the story obviously waning. "His fortunes improved in significantly greater measure and he now makes his
home in Philadelphia where he sits on the board of who knows which,
or how many, companies. I think we may assume that his relationship
with father was not idiosyncratic. More to the point, as a sign of his
gratitude for father's discreet handling of his speculative responsibilities, Slade found a position in the bowels of the St. Paul and Pacific
for the son of his former and unacknowledged business partner, a son
who, we may be sure Bingham père had made clear, was failing to show
the proper interest in a career in law, the proper respect for the world
of business, in short, the proper attitude toward the accumulation of
wealth. The answer, it seems, to all that was lacking in the son, were
years of drudgery. End of story."

"Not, Percy, the end of the story."

"Indeed, dear, you are right, for here comes the best part regarding
our Septimus Slade. A newly wealthy, and thus newly important, man,
he soon thereafter bought, I mean to say, secured, a position on the
board of directors of that fine transcontinental enterprise, the Northern
Pacific Railroad Company. I would not be surprised to discover that it
was upon our friend Slade's advice that father put the bulk of his profits
from his successful speculation into N.P. bonds."

Percy leaned forward to crush his cigarette into an ashtray. Then he
crossed his legs, linking his fingers around one knee, and began to hum
lightly.

"I'm afraid I don't see what that has to do with your father now,"
Frances finally said.

"I didn't say it did, dear. Nor am I necessarily privy to the contents
of the letter that father received from Mr. Slade this morning."

Percy's words fell with quiet weight into the day that had gone suddenly silent. Frances felt herself begin to color. Searching for the words that would defuse Percy's insinuation, she found herself in an uncharacteristic stutter before she could say, "A letter? I wouldn't know—"

"But it's an ill wind that blows no good," Percy interrupted as he stood. "The company responsible for the crash, and for the Bingham family's increasingly perilous position in the world, has inadvertently set me free. With the Northern Pacific no longer holding a controlling interest in the St. Paul and Pacific, the latter has taken the opportunity to do a little of its own reorganizing, or to use a more familiar domestic term, housecleaning. As a result I am, as of this morning, no longer in its employ." Percy studied Frances' expression for a moment before adding, "I consider this good news. Perhaps now is the time for us to move east." He reached his hand down to Frances. "I think it has gotten a bit chillier out here. You will want to come inside now."

CHAPTER VI

In Which John and Percy Bingham Head for the End of the Earth

Less than two weeks later Percy was on a train bound for Fargo, Dakota Territory, wondering how his life had moved so quickly from tedious to ludicrous. He had the strangest sensation of having slipped into a nightmare from which he could witness the waking day, but could not rouse himself to join it. In this nightmare every desire would monstrously mutate into a deed he could not have foreseen; every hope would pervert into an opposing action. For here he was, days after informing Frances that his indentured servitude with one railroad company had come to an end, traveling toward a meeting with the Land Commissioner of another. He was not heading east, but west, and his companion was his father, not his wife.

His wife. She seemed to be at the very center of his confusion. Amenable, charming, attentive, she was, to all appearances, precisely what a wife should be. And yet he often felt as if they had entered into a struggle, but for what, he could not say. He could not make sense of his thoughts. Or were they suspicions? But of what could he be suspicious? There was no occasion when he could say, here, I had expected more from her. Or here, she disobeyed me, or disappointed me, or countered me, or was less than a wife should have been. More, perhaps. But if Frances was too much, what was she too much of? He reached up to unwrap his spectacles from his ears, and then began to massage the bridge of his nose. If there were to be a contest, then he was surely lost, for he had no doubt about her strength of will, and no misconceptions about his own.

Frances' support for his father's plan had come as a surprise. John Bingham, at this moment sitting on the hard wooden bench across from Percy, seemingly transfixed by an advertising circular extolling a certain company's harrows and plows, had returned from a brief and sudden trip to Philadelphia to inform his family that not only would he soon be the owner of almost 1300 acres of land in the Red River valley of Dakota Territory, but more importantly, he would be managing the much larger interest there of Septimus Slade. All told, he would be in control of over 5000 acres. Once under cultivation, and the fertility of the region proved, he and Slade intended to divide the land into smaller parcels to sell to settlers. The bulk of the initial capital (for seed, stock, machinery, supplies, labor) was to be provided by Slade. John Bingham would work without a salary, but would take a percentage of the profits from Slade's land.

With his family silenced around the dinner table by this revelation, John Bingham had added that this was all contingent, of course, on a trip he and Percy were to take straight away to see the land for themselves. If they moved quickly there was still time to get some acreage broken this fall in preparation for seeding the following spring.

"Why on earth would I accompany you to Dakota Territory to look at dirt?" Percy had asked, carefully setting his knife and fork down.

"You are not otherwise employed. I was hoping that you would be of assistance."

"I can not imagine how. I know about as much about farming as I know about this trout," he gestured toward his plate, "and am equally uninterested. Anna, how do we come to have fish for dinner twice in one week?"

"It was my suggestion, Percy." Frances spoke. "Fish is so plentiful here, and –"

"It would do you good to take some interest in your family's business," John interrupted.

"If the family business is to be farming, sir, then I must take my family and my business elsewhere. I am no farmer."

"You will not farm. You will not practice law. I have heard often enough what it is that you will not do, but I have not heard what it is that you will do."

"Excuse me, John," Frances spoke before her husband could reply. "Our plans are something we would like to continue to discuss in private before we bring them before the family."

Percy could have kissed her right there and then. Later that evening, alone in their bedroom, however, he found her words less welcome.

"I can not see what harm it would do to travel to Dakota with your father," Frances had said when Percy asked her if she could believe his father's presumption.

"Nor what good, Frances. Surely you do not expect me to support such a scheme, much less participate. It is my intention, rather, for us to leave for New York as soon as possible."

"New York, Percy?" Frances moved her hand to her chest, then let it drop to her lap again. "What is in New York for us?"

"Or Boston. Or Philadelphia. I mean to try my hand at journalism."

"And do you mean to move us there, with no friends, no position, no home, and Percy, no income? Where will we live? What will we live on while you look for this work? This seems precipitate, at best."

"I can go on ahead and find employment, and then you can join me. Let father go to his new Northwest. My world is to the east. And your world, my dear, is with me." Percy watched Frances closely as he said these words. She seemed suddenly far away, her gaze fixed on the items organized upon her dressing table. Then she blinked and turned to him.

"Of course. But Percy, while you are finding your way in the east, I must, as you say, remain with Anna and Mother Bingham. It would be so unpleasant, perhaps even impossible, if you were estranged from your father. Would it not be best for you to make this trip with him just now? Perhaps the time together would allow you to better understand one another. And then, with harmony restored and your father's attention elsewhere, you could begin your search in the east. The opportunities will surely increase in time, as the effects of the Panic lessen."

"So you believe my father is to become a farmer?"

"Five thousand acres is, you said yourself, several square miles. If I understood him correctly, it is more of a business than a simple farm, a business which he is to manage. Investing in agriculture seems to me to be entirely honorable. I do not think you will find your father carrying a burlap bag over his shoulder, casting seed in a plowed field, as he chews on a plug of tobacco." Frances smiled at Percy, drawing a slight smirk from him in return.

"You are right. He is not a farmer, he is a speculator, again and always."

"There is no shame in profit, Percy," Frances said, and to this Percy had no reply.

Their discussions had continued in this vein for the next couple of days. He would speak and she would agree, and then, she would explain to him why his intentions would be best served by doing precisely the opposite of that which he most desired. This was the nightmare that set Percy on a rocking train, facing his father busily reading about gang-plows while he was expected to be likewise occupied in the perusal of a practically blank map. Percy wrapped his glasses back around his face and reached inside his coat to feel the flask warming there.

John Bingham watched his son pass through the door at the end of the car. Only that minor part of himself that could be defined as "father" was surprised at the man Percy had become. Were Percy a stranger, John Bingham would have sized him up and dismissed him as an effete dandy without a second thought. His son's hands were as soft as a woman's. Even his full mustachios, with which he took such care, bespoke an unmanly attentiveness to his person. His eyes, behind his spectacles, seemed too often focused on something far in the distance that no one else could see, when they weren't focused on some confounded book of poetry. John had wanted to believe that Percy toted such a thing around solely for the purpose of irritating him, but he'd come upon his son reading in private often enough to know this was not the case. Condescension and derision were his son's greatest talents, usually directed toward folks who knew how to roll up their sleeves and get to work. Well, progress was messy. Only those who stood on the sidelines gaping could afford to be fastidious.

He had known dozens of men like his son, men whose successes were all in the future, and whose failures were never their own. But John Bingham was not a man to give up on a project before it was brought to completion, and although Percy was a twenty-seven-year-old man and married to boot... and that was the mystery, John Bingham thought to himself, distracted from his silent rant. How his son had managed to woo a woman with the salt of Frances Houghton was beyond him, and whether he knew what to do with her now that he'd gotten her was unlikely, for if there weren't some embers smoldering there, he didn't know his women, and he liked to think that he did. John cleared his throat and brought his thoughts back to heel. Even though Percy was a grown man, there was still the chance that he could be made useful in some small way.

"Hitch young Percy's wagon to that Power fellow," had been Septimus Slade's advice. "The man believes he can turn dross to gold, maybe he can turn your boy to some good. No disrespect intended toward your progeny, of course," Slade had chuckled, and then added, "I'll put in a word, if you like." Well, John thought, he could lead the horse to water but he couldn't guarantee that he wouldn't act like a horse's ass once he got there.

They were to meet J. B. Power at the N.P. offices in Brainerd before traveling on to the parcels southwest of Fargo that Power had selected for their examination. John had hoped to use this first leg of the trip to school Percy in the details of his agreement with Slade, of the land-for-bonds arrangement, on the particulars of the N.P.'s land grant, on the possibilities of taking control of some of the government land proximate to his and Slade's, by homestead, preemption, or timber claim, or by getting hold of Indian or Soldiers' scrip, all in the hopes that Percy would make a good impression on Power. Already that seemed unlikely.

John had allowed Percy a full hour of silent reading before he tried to engage him in a discussion of the days ahead of them. Tucking his watch back into his vest, John had bent to his case from which he produced a Northern Pacific Railroad map of the Red River valley on the Dakota side.

"Have you had a chance to take a look at this yet, son?" John asked. He already knew the answer to his question but was determined to begin the trip on a positive note. He watched as Percy lifted a finger to mark his place in the book he was reading, the only immediate sign that he had heard his father's question. Then after a moment more, presumably finishing the paragraph or verse before him, Percy dropped a ribbon along the spine to save his place, and looked up.

"The opportunity has ever been before me these past few days. A complementary interest, alas, has not."

A simple 'no' would have gotten the job done, John thought. "I would like you to be familiar with this map by the time we meet with Mr. Power. Slade said that Power had several parcels for us to consider. He's a busy man. I'm sure he would appreciate it if we were to meet him prepared to understand and discuss their whereabouts."

Without responding, Percy reached for the map that John had been holding toward him. John suppressed a sigh and again bent to his case beside him. Within minutes of sitting back up with a handful of pamphlets to read, John noticed that Percy had set the map back onto his lap, taken off his spectacles, and was rubbing the bridge of his nose as he stared out the window.

"Well?" John asked.

Percy replaced his spectacles and began to refold the map, his movements and his toneless recitation precise. "On the east bank of the Red River is Moorhead. On the west bank, Fargo. To the north of Fargo there is a settlement by the name of Georgetown, through which the stagecoach line appears to run, heavens knows where. South of Fargo lies Fort Abercrombie. To the west of Fargo the N.P. runs through Worthington, Jamestown, and ends at Bismarck. For good reason, I am sure. There are a number of small rivers tributary to the Red in the immediate vicinity of Fargo. The Maple runs to the west, and the Sheyenne to the southwest. A couple of light scratches on the map represent the Goose River that curls to the northwest, and the mighty, I am sure, Rush River, the mouth of which appears to be a large bog. And that, sir, is the extent of the information one can glean from your map, for it is otherwise little more than a checkerboard of squares on either side of the railroad, each one signifying nothing, distinguished only in that it is not precisely the same nothingness as the nothingness that surrounds it." Percy handed the map back to his father. "You may now consider me schooled and prepared for Dakota. I'm going to stretch my legs."

John studied his son's back as he turned. He would be of no use. There was no getting around it. Perhaps he should blame himself for getting a family off a woman as frail as Rhoda Stanton. He had wanted to believe that her infirmity was limited to weak vision, but he had known better, for she was already sickly when they met. He had hoped that his sturdy Bing stock would be vigorous enough to overcome her natural weakness—for it was Johnny Bing who left the New Hampshire farm that night with a pig in tow even if it was John Bingham who had entered the Stanton household several years later. There should never have been a second child, he had been admonished by that priggish snoop of a doctor. The violence done Anna at birth had injured her spine and hip, leaving her permanently lame. It was a shame to see her limp into spinsterhood, all the more so as there was a comeliness about his daughter, a delicacy that became her more than it did his son.

A blind wife, a dandy, and a cripple. A budding fortune lost in the Panic. A splendid home with a mortgage he was within months of defaulting on. This was what he had to show for fifty-plus years of scrambling. He felt tired. He felt a little like he thought a Johnny Bing might feel. But he had been given another chance, and by God, he would grab it. Some of the capital Slade provided for the Dakota operation could be siphoned off to pay the mortgage on the Summit Avenue house for the time being. As for Percy, if he could make no use of himself on this trip then he would soon discover how far his delicate sensibilities took him without a father's purse to dip into. There would be one loss. What would it have been like, he wondered, to have been a young man with someone with the spirit of his daughter-in-law at his side. Yes, he supposed he would miss having that one around.

CHAPTER VII

In Which Frances Goes Too Far

The morning that Percy was to depart for Dakota Territory, Frances awoke strangely excited, as if it were she, not her husband, who was about to make the long trip to Dakota. Percy's mood, however, was rather more querulous, so Frances thought it best to silence his litany of complaints with a modest indication that she would be receptive to intimacy. It is the rare soul so lost to goodness that it does not feel pleasure in pleasure given, especially when the cost is slight, and Frances descended the stairs later that morning satisfied with her generosity and relieved to be spared the need for more of the same for at least a week. She had lingered at her toilet just long enough to miss the family's hurried "good byes" to the men.

When Frances joined Anna and Mrs. Bingham in the parlor, Mrs. Bingham was already knitting by the window. Anna sat at a small table nearby.

"Your step is especially brisk this morning, Frances," Mrs. Bingham paused at her work as her daughter-in-law entered the room.

"Good morning, Mother Bingham. It must be this glorious weather. Good morning, Anna," Frances bent to kiss the cheek that Anna had lifted to her. "Are you hard at work so soon?"

"Not work, certainly. We have been invited to join the Fredleys for supper tomorrow evening after this month's lecture at the Women's Christian Association. I am writing a short note to accept. May I include your acceptance as well?" Anna's expression held a clear request.

An evening set to the creeping pace of her mother-in-law, followed by supper with the ancient Fredleys was a high price to pay for Anna's company. Nor was yet another lecture on the evils of alcohol likely to match the titillation provided by last month's speaker, a Mrs. Anna Eliza Webb Young ("wife number nineteen," as she called herself). Frances had joined the audience in somber head shakes at the immorality of Mormons, but could imagine the benefits of such an arrangement, too. Still, Anna would need help seeing to Mother Bingham, and old Archie Fredley would be of little use. "Of course," Frances said softly, laying her hand upon Anna's shoulder for a moment before walking to the window that looked past the back yard and onto the ravine beyond. In a more conversational tone, she said, "I must wonder, however, what purpose a public lecture on temperance can serve?"

Mrs. Bingham looked up at the air before her. "You are young, Frances, but you are surely aware of the disastrous effects of an intemperate relationship to alcohol."

"Certainly. But will those thus embraced depart the saloons at seven o'clock to gather for their schooling? I suspect that we who attend such a lecture are generally least in need. We three can not be described, I think, as intemperate. Nor are we likely to deny Percy and John their occasional brandies when they return, no matter the power of Mrs. Davenport's speech. Unless…is it possible?" Frances lowered her voice and turned back to the room, "Have Archibald and Sophie Fredley become entangled in the web of the demon drink?" Frances looked back at Anna who had not, she was pleased to see, suppressed the small smile that Frances had been working to bring forth with her image of these elderly bulwarks of the First Christ Episcopal Church as tipplers in search of reform.

"Frances, no! How could you think–?"

"Frances is in a teasing mood this morning, mother. She does not mean, I am sure, to be unkind." Anna finished her reassurances with a pointed look at Frances and a head tilted toward her mother.

"Indeed, I did not. You must forgive me, Mother Bingham. I will blame my poor joke on a lightheartedness born of this beautiful day. I am determined to take a long walk this morning, and will personally deliver Anna's note to the Fredleys on my way." And, Frances continued in her thoughts, if that decrepit old fool, Archie Fredley, gives my waist yet another squeeze as he guides me into dinner, I will break his bony fingers.

"If you will wait yet another five minutes I will go with you a short ways," Anna said, folding her note. "If, of course, you can tolerate a more sedate pace. You will not mind a morning to yourself, will you mother?"

How quickly good is rewarded, Frances thought.

Lower Summit Avenue saw little traffic and the late September morning, cool and sunny, was perfect for a stroll. When they turned onto Chestnut Street the slope downward increased and Anna slipped her hand into Frances' offered arm, saying, "I wonder, Frances, if I should not turn back now. It would be a shame to spoil your walk, and this incline, I admit, is something of a challenge to me on the return."

In response Frances tucked Anna's hand more securely into the crook of her elbow. "In just a minute, dear, we will be at the Fredleys, where we will certainly be offered the opportunity to sit while we hear the latest news of Irvine Park, which I suspect will not be greatly altered from the last report, and which we will have the opportunity to hear again tomorrow night. When you are rested I will see you back up this hill. And then," Frances spoke before Anna could interject, "if I am not yet sated with exercise, I will disappear for a good long ramble into the ravine behind the house, which Percy insists is wilderness, as you know, but where I have found the most beautiful wildflowers."

A corner turned brought the young women in sight of Sophie Fredley, who was pacing her front porch with a vigor that belied her advanced years. Upon seeing the two young women approach, Sophie Fredley began to wring her hands.

"What am I to do now?" was her greeting. It took Anna's calming questions several minutes to gather that the young man who was engaged each Monday to help her do her errands, had disappeared, a betrayal not the least to be excused by the fact that it was precipitated by the breathless arrival of a still younger boy who claimed to be her driver's brother, and who carried the inconvenient news that their father had been injured in an accident at the rail yard.

"Did they say what type of accident?" Frances asked, to which the elderly lady replied with a fretful double wave in the air, signifying that this was no time to be concerned with trivia.

"I had intended to go to Mrs. Jensson's this morning. She knew I was to arrive. She is a very busy woman, as well am I. Now what shall I do?"

"Mrs. Jensson the milliner?" Anna asked.

"Precisely."

"Perhaps you might send a note explaining—"

"A note!" Sophie Fredley cried, as if the complications had reached their zenith. "Oh dear, I really must sit down."

"And there sits your carriage, with the horse harnessed and ready to go, too," Frances said. "He looks like a very nice horse. A nice, old, gentle horse."

"Butler is a splendid horse, and not that old at all," Sophie replied. "He has been with us for, for, well, I forget now. But a fine horse he is."

"Sophie, I have the solution to your problem. I will drive you to your appointment with Mrs. Jensson. Anna and I will be happy for the opportunity to look at new hats. And then," Frances turned to her friend, "we can let Butler see to your return uphill. It is a lovely morning for a ride."

"Can you drive?" Sophie asked. "Or rather, should you? I mean, it would be so convenient, of course. And Butler is a dear old thing. Quite old, actually," she continued, tying her bonnet under her chin and turning toward the street.

"I was driving a pony cart before I was in school, and buggies soon thereafter. It has been too long," Frances said, and then, dropping her voice and nodding toward the atrocity perched atop Sophie's head, she whispered to Anna, "It does appear to be something of an emergency."

Mrs. Jensson's house and shop were in the crowded but tidy area to the north and east of the bustling commercial district, the latter an area that Sophie reminded Frances every couple of minutes to avoid. There was little danger that Frances would disobey. Although the aged Butler was unlikely to move beyond an amble without encouragement, she would not care to have the reins in the midst of the commotion of Third and Fourth, even now that all the buildings had been ordered to remove their porches so that the street could be widened. This small adventure, she knew, must be completely without incident, for she intended it to be the first of many such excursions to come. Perhaps she and Anna could manage an outing to Lake Como. It would be lovely this time of year. Or better yet, an evening ride in the shelter of an enclosed carriage along the infamous low river dives and dance halls of Bench Street, where Percy said no respectable man walked after dark. Frances let a small chuckle escape at the impossibility of her thoughts as she guided Butler east along Ninth, well to the north of the tumult closer to the river. They soon crossed Broadway and made their way along the increasingly cramped streets and lots that took them to Mrs. Jensson's on Fifth and Kittson.

The good milliner herself came bustling out of her shop to help Sophie from the carriage. She was about to do the same for Anna when Frances suggested that perhaps instead of spending the next half hour looking at hats with Mrs. Fredley, she and Anna might continue the drive just a bit to the north through Lowertown, the Bingham's old neighborhood. "It would be such a favor to Anna," Frances said when Sophie looked startled. "She would not say so herself," Frances laid her gloved hand lightly on Anna's arm, "but she is not able to get about as much as she would like."

At this, the old woman had no choice but to hastily agree with Frances' suggestion, and was still insisting upon it as Mrs. Jensson steered her toward the house, leaving Frances free to encourage Butler forward. Frances had not failed to notice that Anna had quite deliberately, if quietly, withdrawn her arm. She waited for Anna to speak, but her friend's attention seemed to be wholly devoted to the houses they were passing, and the buggies that they met. These streets were busier than Frances had anticipated, and the two women were often carefully studied by passing drivers. Frances was adept at reading the messages of lifted hats, just as she was well schooled in interpreting the nods and small bows of strangers, acquaintances, and shop clerks who attended upon them during their occasional shopping trips. Their attention, Frances had noticed with a strange sensation of concern and pleasure, more often than not rested just a minute longer on Anna. Frances supposed that they saw what she saw. Anna was certainly the more attractive, with her dark brown hair that burnished to bronze in the direct sunlight, a fine aquiline nose, blue eyes saved from appearing too light by large black pupils. Her lips were full, and when they curled into a smile the effect was of a calm and goodness that, for Frances, was like a cool hand placed upon her brow. Seated, there was the elegance of her neck. Standing, in a pose more proper than comfortable, there was the added grace of her figure. Until, that is, she took the step that dipped her shoulder as she leaned upon the cane that Anna had become adept at holding close to her side for the camouflage that her skirt provided. Then, too often, the strangers would frown in dismay, as if a favorite had come up lame just as the race was about to begin. They are fools, Frances would think, furious at the insult, but glad for it.

"I thought perhaps we would drive along Lafayette Park," Frances said as they crossed Grove Street and found themselves in the quieter, more spacious reaches of Lowertown. "Would you like that?" she asked when Anna did not reply.

At first it seemed as if Anna would not speak at all. When she did, it was with a rare edge of anger. "You are a woman of some spirit, Frances, and I see by your delight in the day that you are perhaps too much confined–"

"Dear, I simply–"

"You have laughed aloud at your pleasure today, and I have been happy to see it. I am sure if you were to speak to Percy about a light buggy, he would readily arrange such a thing for you." Anna lifted her right hand just slightly from where it lay upon the other in her lap in a signal that she had more to say before Frances answered. "But you are never again to employ my infirmity as a stratagem for your own gratification."

This was a tone that Frances had not before heard from her friend. Silently, she turned Butler onto Woodward, and then brought him to a halt opposite the home of Horace Thompson, the president of the First National Bank. Another buggy had also stopped to admire the house and grounds, and Frances could tell by the sweep of the young man's arm that he was referring to the graceful towers that soared above either side of the arcaded veranda. She turned toward Anna, who remained facing forward. "I truly believed that a brief ride through these streets would bring you pleasure, too. You did not, after all, demure. But if I have been mistaken, I apologize."

At this speech Anna turned toward Frances, and Frances realized the mistake she had made in choosing to misunderstand her companion's anger.

"It would have been beneath me to call attention to the duplicity of your words, as it should have been beneath you to utter them. Oh, Frances," Anna's tone lost some of its anger. "You are my dearest friend. I love you as I know you love me, but you do me a violence by using my weakness as an excuse to have your own way. For such a thing to come from you, who has been so often my champion … and it was so unnecessary. I should have been delighted to return–" Anna turned her face away, unable to continue.

The women sat in silence for several minutes, Anna as if studying the grand house, Frances watching Anna's profile as she swallowed her tears of anger. Frances longed to reach for Anna's hand, but knew from her friend's rigid posture that any advance would be unwelcome.

"You are right," she said softly. "I am ashamed. I am selfish and willful and thoughtless, and exceedingly sorry. I would give anything not to have hurt you. Darling, please forgive me."

"We will not speak of it again, Frances. Now, we should go back for Sophie, or we may find her once again pacing the streets."

Book Two: This Masterpiece for Common Folk

This flower that runs across the hill
With such unconscious grace,
That seeks some wilderness to fill
And make a heavenly place;
This masterpiece for common folk,
Lit with the artist's joy,
Let no unthinking, wanton stroke,
No ruthless hand destroy.

(From "The Wild Rose" by Marion Lisle)

Chapter VIII

In Which We Meet a Homesteading Mule

Percy was most satisfied with the world when it displeased him to precisely the extent he had anticipated. Although his father had been perfectly satisfactory thus far, much of the trip to Dakota had been decidedly unsettling. Percy had left St. Paul anticipating the ennui of two long train rides, with a period of boredom sandwiched between. And indeed, the first six and one half hours on the Lake Superior and Mississippi north to the N.P. Junction near Duluth, and the following five hours west on the Northern Pacific to Brainerd had been sufficiently tiresome. But J. B. Power had been a surprise. Oh, he was a boomer through and through, but unlike his father and his cronies, whose expressions were so little considered that they might as well have had ticker tape spewing from their mouths, Power, Percy could tell, took real pleasure in the muscle and play of the spoken word.

To Percy's surprise, Power had readily entered into a debate with him over their supper chops regarding a journalist's responsibilities. He did not agree with Percy that it was the newspaper man's duty to expose the whims and caprices (if not the downright dishonesties) of persons of power and the companies they sought to promote, arguing, rather, that the profession would be held in higher esteem when its practitioners learned to report events without opinion, cartoons, and satire. Then, however, the conversation returned to the benefits that the Binghams and Septimus Slade, as "friends of the road," were to enjoy, and Percy's interest waned. He did not care that the cost of their rail passes for this trip would be deducted from the purchase price of the land, that "friends" would have their equipment and supplies shipped east to Fargo (and their wheat shipped west to Minneapolis) at a reduced rate, or that they would not pay storage at the N.P. grain elevator going up in Fargo. So Percy rose to excuse himself for an evening stroll in the small town (which is to say, to replenish his flask), leaving his father and Power to continue their talk about the practicalities of establishing a farm of eight square miles on land now covered by wild roses and prairie grass.

In response to Percy's "good-bye," J. B. Power had replied, "You have the gift of persuasion, Bingham. Joined with the capacity for keen observation, that is a powerful combination."

The seeds that Power had planted in Percy's thoughts took root in the ready soil of his fantasies as he walked along the dirt streets of Brainerd, a town of saloons and boarding houses on the edge of timber country, inhabited, by all appearances, by men alone. The next morning as Percy and his father boarded the westbound N.P. for Fargo, Percy was in a much improved mood. This trip west need not be a waste of time if he only thought of himself as a writer in search of material. He had a sharp eye, he was sure, for the peculiarities of his fellow man, and what more could be needed for a successful career in journalism, beyond a modest understanding of the issues at hand? When he returned to St. Paul he would submit some stories to the *The Northwestern Chronicle*. Perhaps he would have something appropriate for the Chicago *Inter-Ocean* or maybe even for the *Harper's Monthly* piece that Power had mentioned in passing. That would surely lead to a reputation that would allow him to move east.

With a new career now waiting for him upon his return to St. Paul, Percy was determined to face the upcoming privations of the trip in better humor. These privations were not immediately apparent from the upholstered comfort of the N.P. directors' private car, a wood-paneled parlor on wheels, that Power had made available to the Binghams. Percy watched the pine forests give way to the gently rolling terrain of golden stubble and prairie grass, and to the occasional group of workers displayed in all their harvesting quaintness as they gathered bundles of straw under a blue sky dotted with high, frothy clouds (a panorama arranged, Percy smilingly imagined, by the enterprising Power to woo prospective land owners). Then, the field would give way to tawny meadows and autumn wildflowers and sparkling lakes just visible through a fringe of golden-leaved trees. The beauty of the scenery, the pleasure of his daydreams, the rumbling of the train's wheels upon the rails—and his father's throat clearings that signaled his intent to initiate a discussion of those infernal maps of his—closed Percy's eyes, and he was soon asleep.

He awoke in another world.

The trees had fallen away, the lakes had disappeared, and the hills had leveled out so completely that it was as if God had taken a tug at the edge of the rippling and rolling terrain while Percy slept and pulled it smooth.

"Wake up, son, and prepare to look upon a new land of opportunity," John Bingham said, releasing his hand from Percy's shoulder.

The land of opportunity, Percy noticed as he stepped off the train and reached up to keep his hat from sailing away, was windy. Directly in front of him, just steps from the train, rose the Headquarters Hotel, a three-story building that to Percy's surprise equaled many in St. Paul. The lobby was comfortably furnished, the clerk behind the desk prompt and professional, and the rooms spacious and clean. On the second floor Percy looked in on two sitting rooms, one smaller, for ladies only, and the other much more opulent, with plush draperies, and several potted plants. Marveling at the novel sensation of an opinion reconsidered, in this case, about the expected wretchedness of Fargo, Percy walked down the wide steps of the hotel with his father, and stepped back out onto the siding that butted up against the tracks…and into the world he had anticipated. With the train no longer blocking his view, Percy looked across the tracks onto the most desolate streetscape he hoped he would ever witness, if indeed one could rightly call this wide expanse of blowing dirt in the midst of a random assortment of clapboard shacks a street.

"I'm going to the livery to arrange for a wagon for tomorrow," John Bingham announced. "There's plenty of daylight yet. We can hire a buggy to take a look around."

"Take a look at what?" Percy said with a laugh, sweeping his arm before him.

"Fine," John Bingham answered, turning away. He had taken a couple of steps before he paused to call over his shoulder, "We're to meet that McKenzie fellow here for dinner tonight. Eight o'clock." When Percy simply shrugged, John Bingham said, "Mr. Power went to the trouble of setting it up. I want you there."

"I think I will not be otherwise engaged," Percy answered.

And then, because there was exactly nothing else to do, Percy went for a walk. Although a few houses and barns sparsely dotted the prairie to the south of the tracks, Fargo consisted in the main of the shops and occasional warehouses of Front Street. Only a few of these shops extended west beyond the hotel, so Percy turned east, his head cocked and his hat pulled low against the wind as he walked back toward the river the train had just crossed. The buildings soon thinned out and then disappeared completely for several hundred feet before Percy reached the woods that lined the Red River. There he discovered a second Fargo, or, he supposed, a first, an assortment of log houses and huts spread higgledy-piggledy among the trees. Here, finally, were the women who had seemed strangely absent on this trip so far, their open stares offering to do business with the well-dressed stranger passing by. Although few of the shacks in this rough settlement boasted signs, making it difficult to distinguish private homes from public establishments, the bulk of the businesses appeared to be saloons. Climbing to the top of the levee, Percy came upon a half-dozen flatboats bobbing next to a steamboat with the word "Pluck" emblazoned across the bow.

Percy ducked through the doorway of a nearby shack to find himself in a one-room space efficiently furnished with a single rough plank running the length of the room and resting upon stacked nail kegs. There were neither tables nor chairs. Upon a pile of straw in the corner a satisfied customer snored. Percy had just finished wiping the rim of his whiskey glass with his handkerchief when the sound of hooves striking the door jamb lifted his attention. He had a moment to study the man and the mule before both were vigorously escorted back out by the proprietor who had deftly passed under the plank to greet the duo.

"Right to throw out the Norsky, Cyrus," the man on the straw said as he sat up, his face disappearing for the moment into a yawn, "but what you got against the four-legged jackass?"

"Homer's the finer fellow," the proprietor muttered, "but ain't no more likely to pay than Knudson."

The rough whiskey burning in his gut, Percy strolled back to what he had learned in the saloon was still called by some of the "Fargo-in-the-Timber" inhabitants, "Fargo-on-the-Prairie." A few of the shops along Front Street remained open as the day settled into dusk, and a handful of the shopkeepers stood outside their front doors, facing west, as if standing at attention in a ritual salute of the setting sun. It was a sunset, Percy had to admit, worthy of tribute, a fat golden pool of light lapping against the horizon and sending streaks of radiance into the layers of variegated purple, pink, and indigo there. He resisted his amazement. He had not come to Dakota to be amazed. The wind that had practically lifted Percy from the train and into the Headquarters Hotel front

door an hour or so earlier had disappeared. For several minutes Percy
stood beside a stranger in armbands in front of a dry goods store. And
then, as if simultaneously released from their moment of homage, the
men turned toward each other, nodded, and stepped into the store.

E. A. Grant's Dry Goods had the usual eclectic mix of items for sale.
A glass case on a heavy wooden counter to his left held the cigars Percy
was looking for, along with pipes and tins of tobacco. Behind the counter were glass jars of stick candy, bottles of liniment, checker boards,
leather-bound books, stationery, and boxes of various shapes holding
stockings, shirts, cravats and shirt collars. A couple of ornate bird cages
rested next to the counter, against which a half-dozen gilded picture
frames leaned. Three standing glass display cases took up the center
of the long, narrow store. One case remained empty, but the other two
suggested that Mr. Grant had perhaps a too sanguine opinion of his
potential clientele. Percy had yet to lay eyes upon a Fargo inhabitant
likely to part with the exorbitant sum of two dollars for a handkerchief.
Nor could he imagine many who would be interested in the third case,
with its neatly fanned stacks of diaries, ledgers, and journals bound in
soft calf skin.

With cigar and journal in hand, Percy set off in search for what he
hoped would be a more comfortable saloon than the one he had patron-
ized earlier along the river. He had another hour before he had to meet
his father and this McKenzie fellow. The picture he had of himself, an
anonymous observer tucked in a corner with whiskey, cigar, and journal, gave him a great deal of pleasure. He could see his first essay taking
shape. It would be a witty and sophisticated chronicle of the primitive
beings inhabiting this waste land, intended for the amusement of civilized readers to the east.

Percy had just written the words "Prairie Town Inhabitants" at the
top of his first page, and was about to begin his description of a bibu-
lous mule when he was approached by a diminutive figure dressed from
head to toe in buckskin.

"Yes?" Percy asked after a moment of sustaining the buckskinned
man's scrutiny. He was, after all, the one who was to be the observer.

"Sell'n or buy'n?"

Now here was both economy and wisdom, all of mankind parsed
into two categories. Percy restrained the urge to jot down the phrase

with which he would sum up the philosophy of this new prairie town.

"I do not believe that we have met," Percy said in reply.

"Dakota Bill."

"Of course," Percy said, gesturing to the chair across the table, and offering to stand the buckskinned dwarf a drink.

With very little encouragement Dakota Bill commenced a colorful story of his history in the territory. Percy studied his companion as he spoke. He stood five feet tall at best, was beardless, had small eyes and a receding chin. His skin was remarkably pink, his build roundish. Percy would have readily admitted that he knew next to nothing of the customs and habits of the Sioux, who, according to Power, were unlikely to be found east of the Missouri these days. If, however, there had been anything approaching veracity in the little man's tale of a scuffle upon the prairie in which he had so impressed an even dozen Sioux warriors with his fighting prowess that they had honored him with the name of "Dakota Bill," Percy could not grab a hold of it. The point of the tale, beyond the whiskey provided by the listener, became clear with Bill's next statement.

"Yernew. Ought'n see ferself 'n I'm yer only guide'll getcher close t'em Injuns."

"I thank you for the warning," Percy said. "Perhaps you could introduce me to your rivals."

Dakota Bill took a quick look left, then right, before leaning toward Percy.

"Yerain't want'n 'em others. Hell, ain't haf of 'em speak'n English."

"Of that, sir, I am convinced," Percy replied as he checked his watch and then rose with a "good evening."

Stepping out of the saloon, Percy paused to put out his cigar against the side of the building. When the door opened behind him, Percy feared that Dakota Bill had followed him to press his case. Instead, the soft tumbling brogue he heard at his shoulder addressed him in complete and understandable, if not completely grammatical, sentences.

"I see you met Dakota Bill. I hope your first impression of Dakota ain't lasting."

Percy was not entirely sure how to answer the stranger, a big man of approximately his own age, broad-shouldered with drooping mustachios, and eyes so intense that Percy felt as if he had been commanded to stop.

"I do not recall having the privilege of an introduction, sir," Percy answered.

The man's smile in response to his words made Percy yet more uncomfortable.

"Alexander McKenzie. We ain't long on formalities here, Mr. Bingham."

Percy had lifted his hand to meet McKenzie's outstretched arm, but started upon hearing his own name. McKenzie moved his own hand to Percy's grasp. "I was on my way to the Headquarters to meet with your pa when I saw you back there in the corner putting up with Bill's palaver. More convincing as Lord William, what he was when he got here in '72, but I guess the Indian scout getup pays better. I know most of the men in these parts, so felt pretty comfortable in my guess about who you was."

"One simply does not expect to be known in a place as remote as this," Percy said, dropping his hand to stretch and clench his fingers. Nor to hear of one's father referred to as pa, he thought.

"I got to argue with you there, Bingham," McKenzie said. "A man of any consequence hereabouts will soon enough be known by all, for such men are still rare."

It was as unexpected a speech as Dakota Bill's had been, and Percy could think of nothing to say in reply, and so he turned back toward the Headquarters Hotel with Alexander McKenzie now at his side.

Dinner with McKenzie held none of the pleasures Percy had experienced with J. B. Power in Brainerd. Neither his father nor McKenzie was interested in the claret that Percy had ordered (itself a pleasant surprise), neither smoked, and neither paid Percy any attention. And so Percy smoked and paid attention to the claret.

John Bingham, however, was immediately impressed with young McKenzie, who explained that he had recently been through Brainerd himself, where J. B. Power had told him that the Binghams would be coming through on the next train. Power had suggested that McKenzie stay in Fargo an extra day to help them "get organized."

"You work for the Northern Pacific?" John Bingham asked.

"Started laying track in '71. Soon enough got my own crew. Settled in Bismarck where the tracks stopped in '73, so no, I ain't formally employed by the N.P. no more. A friend is more like it. I do what I can for my friends."

Alexander McKenzie spoke so softly that John Bingham found himself leaning toward the big man as he talked. Looked like someone had broken the fellow's nose for him somewhere along the line, and it had been a favor, for otherwise his large, regular features tended toward the bovine. But that rugged break in the natural angle of the bridge gave depth to eyes that never seemed to rest. He had a kind of coarse beauty, in the sense that a new locomotive under full steam was a beautiful machine. John Bingham believed he had the man's full attention, and was equally certain that there wasn't a person who walked into the hotel restaurant who had not been carefully noted.

"Power said you might be needing someone to plow and backset six, seven hundred acres yet this fall," McKenzie said, quite clearly meaning to imply that now he was going to be Bingham's friend, too. "That's a tall order. Can't get Peter Siems, you see. Ain't no one else around like him, but he's spoke for."

"The Cass-Cheney operation," Bingham nodded.

"Been going for over a month already. I'll be hanged if that crew of his don't get two thousand acres ready for spring."

"Do you know of someone else?"

"Breaking sod ain't no picnic, especially when you got all them rose bushes to tear up, but I'll look around tomorrow and get back with you tomorrow night. Then I got to get on to Bismarck." McKenzie pulled his watch out of his vest pocket and studied it for a moment, before adding, "Can get some of the local homesteaders hereabouts to help. For two-fifty you'll get a man and a team to break about an acre a day. They're always needing extra money and got the time now with the crops up. But won't do to rely on 'em, and ain't enough of 'em anyway to do you much good in the long run. Get yourself up to some of them logging camps in Minnesota late this winter, and you'll get your spring crew. Them men know how to work. Bring a beer sled in now and then, but don't let 'em off the place, or you'll lose 'em for good."

"You seem to have given this a great deal of thought. Have you considered going into farming yourself?" Bingham asked.

"What you're getting into ain't exactly farming, Mr. Bingham. More like industry, pure and simple. Someone else, I'm guessing, is going to spend his days studying the hind end of a critter. Me, I ain't holding a fistful of N.P. bonds, and that's a shame. I mean it. Some of them shareholders, if they quit their crying and grow some backbone, could end up with a couple thousand acres for as little as fifty cents an acre. In five years it's going to be worth ten, twenty times that. Them that's got is in a position to get more, and that's the simple long and short of it, you see."

Generally is, Bingham thought, allowing himself a smile at McKenzie's rhetoric. It was certainly less refined than Power's, but perhaps more convincing for its candor. Where Power spoke of "spacious miles of capacious opportunity," McKenzie now talked about an empty land that, cleared of savages and rose bushes, would allow the first to arrive the best chance of turning a profit. Power had asked Bingham to imagine the "villages and cities destined to dot the prairie like buds on a wild prairie rose," but McKenzie talked about the here and now, candidly pointing out that there wasn't a town west of Fargo for another ninety miles deserving of the name and that one made Fargo look like New York City. Power had not mentioned that there had been a shortage of rainfall in much of the territory for going on five years now. The reports of locust infestations, he had said, were exaggerations. McKenzie was more forthcoming, which allowed Bingham to readily believe his reassurances: "If it's real bad, though, it's going to happen west of the Missouri. It ain't going to happen here in the Red River valley."

John Bingham nodded and then asked, "What is it that you do in Bismarck?"

"Running for sheriff just now. Been doing the job on a temporary basis ever since the last sheriff went through the ice on the Missouri in '73. Him and his deputy. Lost the horses, too."

"Are there enough men in Bismarck to require a sheriff?"

"Most of the men in Bismarck require a slow hanging."

McKenzie's response brought a chuckle from Percy who had been lazily studying his glass. McKenzie turned toward Percy, "You got a guide for tomorrow?"

"I will bow to your greater experience, Mr. McKenzie," Percy replied, "but in a land where all things always seem the same, shall we say, how precisely is it possible to get lost? As long as the sun rises in the east and sets in the west, that is."

"You'll get out onto the prairie and you'll get back, too, but that don't mean you'll ever know where you are or where you been. Or if you'll be able to locate them sections Power picked out for you. You got a compass?"

"Certainly," John Bingham spoke.

"Good. You'll need it. Still, it ain't easy spotting them survey posts. Save yourselves some time if you get a guide."

"Dakota Bill?" Percy asked.

"Dakota Bill, Indian finder!" At this McKenzie threw back his head in an unrestrained guffaw, and actually clapped Percy on the shoulder at the joke. Percy did his best to keep from pitching forward off his chair. "Bill ain't never had any Indians to lose, so it ain't likely he'd be able to find any. I first come to Dakota at eighteen years old as an army scout, so I know one or two things about Indians. The only thing you need to know is that there ain't none to speak of hereabouts. Just the same, Mr. Bingham, I think perhaps you and Percy here would be better off with a guide. I'll get someone to meet you at the livery tomorrow morning."

The boy McKenzie had rounded up as their guide climbed over the seat to take a nap soon after John Bingham turned the wagon south onto the stagecoach road that carried Fargo passengers north to Pembina and the British provinces or south to Fort Abercrombie and beyond. "Wake me up when it's time to turn off," he said, curling into a ball with his head cushioned upon his arm.

"And how are we to know when that is?" Percy asked.

"You'll see a house," the boy replied without opening his eyes, and then added, "sort of."

Percy shook his head and pulled a book from his jacket pocket. The directions, vague as they were, probably made sense. With the exception of the occasional claim shanty in the distance there was little else signifying habitation. They were unlikely to miss a house, even a sort-of one, next to the road.

They had been traveling a short time, hardly worthy of a nap, when they came upon a sizeable square of golden stubble perfectly framed by waist-high prairie grass. At the edge of this square a long, narrow mound of sod lifted away from the level prairie. A piece of stovepipe rose from the far end of the mound. The grass nearby was packed and brown.

"A house, sort of," Percy said, reaching behind him to give the boy a shake.

"Gaps," the boy said, sitting up.

"Gaps?"

"James Gaps."

Percy knew the answer to his question before he asked it, but asked nonetheless. "Someone lives in that?"

"Gaps," the boy answered, a little louder, as if discovering that Percy was hard of hearing. Then the boy let out a whistle that pricked the horse's ears, but brought no figure from the dugout entrance. "Hold on a minute," he said, jumping to the ground and crossing to the dugout where he bent toward the door and then disappeared, like a rabbit escaped into its hole.

"Oh, dear. Oh, dear," Percy muttered.

The boy returned quickly, his cheek newly stuffed with tobacco, to report that no one was home but the cat sleeping in the frying pan on the stove.

"But where is his machinery? Or tools?" John Bingham asked. "How—"

"Hires it done," the boy anticipated Bingham's question. "Due west now."

Percy looked back down at his book, and then back up again. "The cat was in the frying pan?"

"Yup. You ever stop by for breakfast, you'll want ol' Gaps to take the first pancake."

With the morning sun at his back, John Bingham turned the wagon off the road and directly into the prairie, setting out upon a land both solid and fluid in which swell after swell of grass rhythmically lifted away from one horizon and rolled toward another. The tall grass, parted by the horse and pressed down by the wheels, sprang up and closed behind the wagon, erasing its passage as thoroughly as waves forgot the passing of a ship. Bingham kept his compass at hand, but soon realized that although he knew how to stay on course, he could not have said if they had traveled two miles or four before they came to a rough but sturdy bridge over the shallow, tree-lined Sheyenne River. Soon thereafter the boy announced that the markers they were looking for should be nearby, and sure enough, within minutes he had miraculously located a stake. John Bingham got out of the wagon, and Percy watched as his father drove a spade into the earth. He worked several large chunks of sod free, and then continued to dig deeper and deeper. Each spadeful brought up the same heavy black loam. The boy watched, too, only he was smiling.

Finally, when the older man had reached a full spade's length deep, the boy asked, "This where you putting your well?"

"How deep does this topsoil go?" Bingham asked.

"Deeper'n you can," the boy answered.

The next stake was quickly spotted, but when the third was nowhere to be found the boy shrugged and said, "Some of 'em is missing. Buffalo rubbed 'em off."

"There are still buffalo here?" Percy asked.

"Gone now. West, what's left. But they rubbed off a few posts on their way out. All's left of 'em hereabouts is the bones, and not much of them no more. But if you ever see a buffalo, look out." The boy gave Percy a sidelong look. "Dakota Bill says if you see a buffalo, one, two there'll be an Indian."

Percy resisted the bait, and asked, "Are they good for anything?"

"Only good Indian's a dead Indian, Dakota Bill says."

"General Sheridan says, rather. I was speaking of the bones."

"Bring eight to ten dollars a ton, but I don't know what for. Grind 'em up for fertilizer back east, I heard. Some feller what took me for a fool told me for sugar. Used to see big piles stacked up alongside the tracks, they say, but the early settlers got the most of it. Around here anyway."

"There will be surveyors to hire in Fargo, I expect," Percy turned back to his father, hoping that this turn of events would end the day's excursion.

"That won't be necessary. Run back there, son," John Bingham turned to the boy behind him. "See if that last post has any markings on it."

Within the half hour John Bingham had located a baseline post from which to work. Then, with his compass in hand, and a handkerchief tied to the spoke of the wagon, he began to mark off the land. It was slow work, and Percy could not share in his father's pleasure when, having placed a stake where the missing post should have been, John Bingham quickly led them to first one surveyor's post and then, directly, to another. Their noon lunch, packed for them at the hotel, was well behind them when John Bingham decided that it was time to return. Removing his handkerchief from the wheel spoke and tying it to the last stake he'd identified, John Bingham climbed back into the wagon and turned the horse back east. When they got to the bridge over the Sheyenne, John Bingham pulled the wagon to a halt. Percy watched his father studying the tree-lined banks and nodding to himself.

"What?" he asked.

"It would have been good to have the sections Power selected run up to the Sheyenne."

"Why does it matter?" Percy asked. Throughout the warm October day he had shed first his coat, and then his necktie, collar, and vest. He'd undone the top button of his shirt and rolled up his sleeves. He was still hot, and was now cross as well. The wind and the sun and the previous night's wine made his head ache. He longed for the flask he had left in his hotel room this morning, believing that there would be no opportunities for an unobserved pull.

"Lumber, ice, water for stock. Power mentioned a slough but I don't see it."

"Other side of the Sheyenne and south a bit," the boy said from the back of the wagon where he rode. "Mostly standing water and mosquitoes. Some Norskies hereabouts on this side. Claim shack back there a bit," he finished with a jerk of his head.

The next day was much the same, albeit without the boy, and the Binghams were able to confirm the boundaries of the eight sections of railroad land John Bingham was now determined to take for himself and Slade, with time to spare to crisscross the government sections hopscotched in between. This latter was an activity that struck Percy as completely unnecessary, for (with the exception of the occasional homesteader's claim shack) there was not one square foot of this land that in any way differed from another. At breakfast on the third morning—at the Fargo House, where John Bingham had discovered meals to cost half of what the Headquarters Hotel restaurant charged—Percy was startled by his father's statement that he had arranged for the use of a handcar for the day, which he proposed they pump down the tracks as a way to see even more of the country.

Percy looked up from the mass of meat and gravy congealing on his plate, a meal he would have had nothing to do with were he not so confounded hungry from tramping around outdoors under a constant sun and unwavering wind. "And when a train comes?"

"There will be no train today," John Bingham answered. "There's only one train to Bismarck a week, and that'll stop come winter. It was McKenzie's idea, and a good one, too."

"Excuse me," Percy said, automatically reaching into his lap for his napkin before remembering that such a thing had not been made available.

Percy was back in fifteen minutes, presenting as his proxy the boy who had been their companion two days earlier. To Percy's surprise, John Bingham readily accepted the substitute, since this, he said, would give Percy the opportunity to stop by the government land office to find out what he could about that parcel along the Sheyenne.

For a couple of hours that morning Percy labored in his room over his "Prairie Town Inhabitants," at first transforming the rabbit-like Dakota Bill into a swarthy and muscular dead-shot with a menacing eye, before realizing that his invention had made his subject predictable instead of singular. It was close to noon before he left the hotel to look for the government land office, hoping to find more material for his story along the way.

The land office, Percy discovered, was a small lean-to attached to the side of a hardware store on a street populated with one other business, a livery, the latter so new that its siding still gave off the smell of pine. The only thing stirring nearby was a mule, harnessed to an odd two-wheeled cart and rubbing its head against the post to which it was tied. The interior of the building, Percy discovered, consisted entirely of one eight-by-ten room. To his left hung a large map of Dakota Territory, and to his right hung yet another map, representing the Red River valley portion of the larger territorial map. The familiar checkerboard pattern of interspersed government and railroad sections ran twenty miles to the north and to the south of the tracks. Behind a desk, itself a plank planed smooth and set on stacked crates, was a floor-to-ceiling cupboard of deep pigeonholes, most of which were empty. Two men were in the room, one sitting on a bench by the door, the other behind the desk. The man on the bench was awake.

"Is the office open?" Percy asked in a whisper.

"Door was open," came the reply in the singsong Scandinavian accent that Percy had discovered was common among the settlers, if not the shopkeepers, in the area.

"Have you been here long?"

"Just about an hour now."

'Yust about an hour now,' Percy repeated to himself, thinking that the fellow's speech scanned like a Longfellow poem. "And he's been asleep all this time?"

"Ya!"

"Are you here for business?" Percy took a closer look at the man, remembering where he had seen him before.

"Ya, vel den, for business."

"Then why haven't you wakened him?" Percy asked.

"It's important business. Don't want to get off on the wrong boot. Better to let him wake himself slow."

"Then I hope you will excuse me. As my business is less pressing, I will risk a precipitous wakening." This said, Percy took the two steps needed to bring him across the room, and rapped twice on the plank next to the sleeping man's head.

"Rise and shine," Percy said as the man snapped awake, reaching for the hat that had fallen off as he slept, and wiping a sleeve across the corner of his mouth. To Percy's surprise the sleeper was little more than a youth. His startled look took Percy in, neatly dressed in suit and waistcoat and not at all likely to be a settler who'd driven in with all of his belongings in a Red River cart. Pulling his hat back off, he jumped to his feet.

"Are you a representative of the government?" he asked.

"No," replied Percy, smiling at the oddness of the question. "I believe that you are."

That response gave the young man pause, but with a shake of his head, he said, "No, no. I meant, are you from the territorial office in Yankton?"

"Let us say that I am a citizen, a citizen who has come to you, the representative of my government, with a question regarding land. But this gentleman, I believe, preceded me. I will stand by for my turn."

Percy stepped aside to study the territorial map while eavesdropping on the conversation. It didn't take long to understand that Mr. Torger Knudson, present, who was currently homesteading 160 acres nearby with his wife and five children, was at the land office as a favor to an in-law, who was scheduled to arrive in Fargo within the next week or two from Norway and hoped to take a homestead.

"Tell him to come in himself when he gets here," the young man stated.

"Ya, sure," Knudson agreed, "but to tell a truth, he can not talk."

"He can't speak English?"

"No. Even *norsk* he can not speak. Not one word can he talk."

"Has he even applied for citizenship?"

"Ya, sure. And with a new American name, too. In New York right off the boat."

"How is he related again?"

"He is my wife's—" Knudson paused. "Brother," he finally said. "He is my wife's brother that is younger. I will tell you a truth. I am to be the," and here Knudson tapped his head, "but good to work is Homer. With me for here," again Knudson tapped his head, "and with Homer and his strong back, it will be fro and to all the day long."

"To and fro."

"Ya, all the day long."

"Come back when he gets here, and you can help him pick out the land, and then he can sign his own name."

"Ya, sure, this is what I think to do. But my wife, she says, 'It will be for Homer too hard, then. He can not so much as sign his own name'. So he will make his X, I say. And she says ... ya, vel den, that is just the talk of man and wife. So to help poor Homer here I am. To tell a truth, he has been a help to me many times. 'So, Homer,' I say to him ... in a letter ... 'if you get into the traces and pull with me, then the money to file for homestead in your very own name I will do'."

Despite Knudson's explanations and reassurances the young land agent clearly remained uncertain about filling out a homesteading claim for an applicant who was not present. When the agent cast yet another concerned glance toward the suspiciously well-dressed stranger listening nearby, Percy gave the slightest of nods. He could have laughed out loud when the young man's brow cleared at the decision made for him. It took a while for Knudson to come up with the eighteen-dollar filing fee from his pockets, but soon thereafter Mr. Torger Knudson had secured a homesteading claim adjoining his own in the name of Homer B. Dragon. He left moments later with his own nod to Percy.

It didn't take Percy long to discover that one of the sections adjacent to the Sheyenne River that his father had asked him to check on was government land, and that as of five minutes ago a certain Homer B. Dragon had claim to a quarter of that very section. The coincidence, and the part he had inadvertently played in the absurd circumstance, Percy found amusing. "What about the rest of the section?"

"The other quarter section along the river is Torger Knudson's. The other half is in the name of a Peter Sondreaal, one hundred and sixty acres as a homestead and another quarter section as a timber claim. That's sort of odd, figuring on there's trees close by along the river, and the law says right out that timber claim land has to be…has to be… just wait now, I got it right here." The young man dug through a loose sheaf of papers, and was clearly relieved to discover the much-handled page he had been looking for. "Prairie land, or land naturally devoid of timber," he read with satisfaction. "A Norsky can get awful clever when it comes to getting land, but I been told," he added, clearly feeling the need to justify his procedures, "that our job ain't to make it hard to get land but the other way around."

"Fine, fine," Percy lifted his palm in reassurance. He had, in fact, regretted his question the minute he asked it, anticipating yet another discourse on the acquisition of territorial acreage, although at least in this company he would not have to hear a recitation on the varying prices per acre for railroad land, depending on whether the transaction were a simple cash purchase, a time payment, or the bonds-for-land exchange. "I have taken up too much of your time already. Thank you and good day."

Percy was adjusting his hat in the doorway when the young man addressed him one more time. "Them other two sections you was wanting to know about. They're railroad. Most likely some big-wig with the N.P. got them, being as they're so close to Fargo."

It was still early afternoon, and too much of the day remained. Percy supposed he could hire a horse and ride out to see more of the country, but he cared little for riding, and less for the country. He was sauntering back to the hotel when he saw Knudson tying up his mule in front of a nondescript building on the other side of Front Street about the same size as the land office, and about as prosperous looking. Knudson turned, and recognizing Percy, waved him over, and then stretched out his hand for a shake. "Torger Knudson, it is," he said. "Are you the man to sell the sulky plows?"

"I am not," Percy admitted.

"Just as well. Into my wife's tin can and the Bible, too, I had to put my hand for Homer's land and for a little drink. Now there is nothing more for the new plow. In the old country the preacher said in the Bible there are to be found...not 'money'...what is the word?"

"Riches?"

Torger Knudson snapped his fingers. "Riches! There are riches to be found in the Bible the preacher says. Ya, sure, he knows just what he is talking about. Riches for Homer's land and maybe even for one or two drinks to give me the *mot* to go home again."

"Won't your wife be grateful for the good service done her brother?"

"My wife is –" Torger Knudson appeared to search for a word, then gave up, shrugged and said, "*motsiende*. She does not always think like I think she is to think. Homer she does not love the way I love Homer." This said, Torger Knudson gave his mule a pat and with a formal bow gestured Percy toward the saloon door. Once inside they both stood blinking for a moment, waiting for their eyes to adjust to the darkness of the room. But they were clearly visible to the bartender.

"Your girl was by here looking you, Knudson. Time for you to get back home."

"Ya, sure. Just one little drink and then to home I go."

"Let's see your money first," the bartender said. "And Homer stays outside."

Chapter IX

In Which We Meet Kirsten Knudson

Ya, vel den, here I am Kirsten Knudson, and that is another new
thing about America. Not so very long ago I am Kirsten Torgersdatter, and Sten is Sten Torgerson, and Ole is Ole Torgerson,
and Haldis is Haldis Torgersdatter, and Guri is Guri Torgersdatter but
from now on we are all to be Knudson, it is like from now on time is to
stand still. But the boot Mor has put down to say, *"No, Astri Hansdatter I was in Gamle Norge, and Astri Hansdatter I will stay, even if I am
lost across an ocean and never to see my father again."* Far he does not
argue with Mor because … because Far he does not argue with Mor. He
just says what there is to be. With Mor there is no need for a name anyway. We call her Mor and to Far she is always *hustru* (or *kjerring*, and
that is not so nice). So, ya, I am Kirsten Knudson and I am good to talk,
except when to hear me there is the family everywhere. Then talk there
is enough. So it was a good thing to have a good long talk and a good
long walk to town with just me for company and no one else, it was
maybe like a *ferie* (this word I do not know in American), but about a
ferie Mor says no one in America knows. Here it is always work, work,
work. Now with Far so loud with the snore and the cart with the squeal
there is not so much of a good thing.

"Go find Far," is all Mor needs to say, and I know just where to go.
Then she takes off her boots to give to me. I am not to put them on
until I get to Fargo. I have boots of my own, but not to wear until there
is the snow that stays. In *Gamle Norge*, Mor says, every single person
wears shoes every day. Here there are the boots for the boys, and boots
for me in the winter, and for the little girls there are *ladder*. If Far hears
from Mor this talk, he says, "Ya, vel den, that's enough. Live where you
are. In *Norge* poor I was born, and poor I would stay." He says this in
norsk first, then he looks at me or Guri or Haldis and says it again in
American. Then he says, "When I come on the boat not one word of
American do I have. Now American I talk. Here everything is possible."
Look at Sten and Ole, I want to say. They are the ones who do not
even try, and they should know better, too, because they are older. But
they are boys and boys can not be told one thing. I think maybe Far

means that in America all things can be learned by all people and that in America to be a *geni* is not an accident. So I am to try harder, because sometimes *norsk* it comes to my mouth when I answer Mor before the American, and I am in America now for seven years. So sometimes I talk in American and sometimes I talk *norsk*, but in my head it is a little bit of this and a little bit of that. Like now. "An immigrant speaks the old language at home and American in public," Far says. "American always we will speak." When he leaves, Mor says, *"Hvilken offenlighet?"* And I say *"Hva? What?"* And Mor says, *"Hva publikum?"* and then she looks at every wall and says, *"Seven strides long is my world, Kirstie. Seven strides long. And out there nothing forever."* And then about her home in *Norge* she talks. About the blue of the *fjord*, and about her valley so green that it made the trees in the mountains look black, but mostly of her Hallingdal village, and of women working and laughing together. *"We were poor, yes, but we were not alone,"* she says. *"Not like this. Do you remember, Kirstie?"*

Ya, sure, I say. I do not say to Mor that what I remember is what Mor remembers. I was a very little girl in *Norge*. Sten and Ole they were older, but they do not say what they remember. "Live where you are," they say now, too. Like Far they are. Haldis and Guri do not remember because they were born here in America, Haldis in Minnesota, where we lived with other Hallings for two years, and Guri in Fargo before it was Fargo.

Only one thing I remember before America for sure, and that is a dream about the boat. Far says, "They are not to speak about, the dreams." Mor says, *"mareritt,"* and Far says, "In American," and Mor then she will not say another word, and I say, "nightmare, Mor." But I do not know if it is a nightmare, or if it is a dream, but this is what I remember.

I am someplace high, like a tree, but for sure there were no trees on that boat. Anyway, I am looking down, but of Mor I see only a little because the women they stand in front of her. I know that she has the baby in her arms and he does not cry now. And every woman has her arms folded over her chest, and together they are saying, like they have just one big voice, "No, no, no." They are speaking to Far who is standing there with his arms out in front of him like he is walking in a strange place in the dark, but really I think he is trying to take the baby, but still the women they just say, "no, no, no."

Maybe it was a dream, then.

We do not talk about that baby here. He is not to speak about, too. Or either. Or both it is, maybe. Sten and Ole they have each other, and Haldis and Guri belong only to this place, but I remember the baby.

It is better now that we do not live in the soddie, but to Mor it does not seem better. When I put my toe to my heel from one end of our new house to the other, it is twenty-eight (if I start where I can go through the door into the room where Far and Mor sleep). Haldis and Guri and I sleep in the big room on the bed that we fold back against the wall during the day, after we shake the straw loose in the mattress and roll it up. Sten and Ole they sleep on boards they have nailed across the center rafters for their bed. When our pallet is pulled from the wall the boys can step onto it and reach up for a rafter and pull themselves up. The boys say that they do not want a ladder because then the girls would go into their "territory." Why would we do that? It is just some boards with a straw mattress for sleeping and some nails for hanging their clothes. Mor says that if they roll out of bed in their sleep they will break their necks. Some nights they wait until Far and Mor are asleep, and then they say "ssssss" at us, and if we are dumb enough up to look then they pretend to make noises like spitting. I hope it is pretend. If Far wakes up he yells, "Go to sleep in there, you *barn*," and I will go to sleep doing my arithmetic. Seven goes into twenty-eight four times.

But it is a good house, you bet, with even a window. Only the Rolfs-ruds and the Norstads have better houses, and that is because they were in America for almost ten years before coming to Dakota, so they have a leg up. That's what Far says, and when he says it the boys laugh, and like a dog by a tree Ole will lift his leg. Most of our neighbors (*"Hva naboer?"* Mor says) still live in their soddies. The Perssons live in a dugout along the river. "High and mighty Swedes living like rabbits," Far says, and Mor says, *"A poor Swede was no better off than a poor Norwegian."* We only lived in our soddie for two years. Now Homer lives there with our two cows. But they are not our cows, Mor says.

This is why. We had a cow but it died three years ago, when we were still in the soddie. It was after the threshing was done and Far and the boys were stacking straw and every day was blue and sweet, not like the summer where it is like a slap with a wet hot towel except when the wind blows to take the wet away but leaves the hot. So then the cow died and we did not have milk or cream or butter, and then Per Rolfsrud, who lives two miles away and preaches in his house on Sunday sometimes and sometimes we go, but not Far, but it is about the cows I was telling, so Per Rolfsrud, who has been to high school and even more in *Norge*, but he and his wife do not have any children, but he does have a nephew who came to live with them and he is almost fifteen years old, and ugly, but here is what I mean to say. Per Rolfsrud has a small herd of cattle and some pigs, and sheep, and chickens, of course, and when he heard Mor tell Ingeborg Rolfsrud that Far said there would be no cow for winter, Per Rolfsrud said, "No cow? You will starve without a cow!" And then Mor began to cry, and Ingeborg Rolfsrud said, *"den mannen!"*, and then Per Rolfsrud shook his head and looked at me, even though it was so quiet I did sit with my *primost* at the table.

Ya, vel den, the very next day here comes Per Rolfsrud in his wagon with a cow tied up behind, and he says to Far that the cow is pregnant and that he is to tend to the cow all winter and see that she is fed and kept warm. And after the cow has her calf in the spring, that he will come to get the calf when it is time for it to be weaned. But the cow Far is to keep because God has seen fit to provide Per Rolfsrud with cows, but not with children, and it has gone the other way with Torger Knudson. And Sten and Ole are to help Per Rolfsrud get his crop in the ground in the spring and then they will call it a fair deal. So we had milk for our porridge until January but not so much of that and then in February Far let her go dry.

So, one day in early March, when so hard the wind was blowing that there was snow inside the soddie from under the door and the stove pipe it did scream like a rabbit in its trap, Per Rolfsrud's cow had not one calf, but two. But the last calf came out a head and a leg and then got stuck for a very long time and when Far finally pulled it out it was almost dead and so was the cow and the calf could not stand, and then it died, but the cow did not. So there was one cow and one calf, then.

One Sunday late in May, when Far and the boys were planting wheat, Mor and Haldis and I came home from the Rolfsruds' where we had gone to hear Per Rolfsrud preach for only the third or fourth time since the snows began in November because Far would not "burden Homer with a walk on ice and snow for no good reason" and it was too far for Mor to walk even though it is only two miles, maybe a little more, because she had been sick almost all that winter with the cough, and anyway it was one Sunday in May that Mor said to Far that it was time to pay back the Rolfsruds and to send the boys over to help Per Rolfsrud and his nephew, Halvor, with their spring planting, and that they could take the calf over with them. So Far said the boys were free to go, but they were not to take the calf.

So you bet it is the very next Sunday and here comes Per Rolfsrud himself after church. And he takes off his hat and says *god morgen* to Mor, and to me he says "hello," and to Haldis and Guri, who are trying to take turns with me churning the butter, but are good for nothing, they are just little, little girls, he says nothing. And then Per Rolfsrud he says that he has come to have a private talk with Far, and Mor points to the field where Far and the boys are working just like every day even though it is the Sabbath, and this Mor does not like, and I hear what happened later that night because Sten and Ole they are laughing and whispering. So this is what Per Rolfsrud said to Far, he said, "Now, Torger, I have done you a good turn because you have a wife and children who deserve better." And Far said something that the boys did not hear, but it made Per Rolfsrud go very red, and then he said, "Never mind decency then. I have come for my calf. I for one will not go back on my word and demand the return of the cow as well." And then Far he said, "The cow had two calves and one died. It is your calf that died."

Ya, so that is why we have two cows now and why we have enough cream for Mor to make into extra butter for me to carry to town because Mor says that she will pay for that calf pound for pound if it kills her. But mostly we trade for flour or coffee or salt pork or, sometimes, fruit in a can. When there is a little to spare Mor puts it in her secret place which is a tin can behind the corn meal sack, but it is not a secret because last week Far and Sten were pounding all the cans flat to fix a leak in the roof, and was Far surprised to see what Mor can save from butter!

It is because of the butter and the tin can that I went to my first day of school two years ago in a new gingham dress. Because Mor said that it was disgrace enough to be going to my first day of school when I was almost ten years old and with no shoes, but that on this day I was not to wear a dress made out of flour sacks. And Far said that it was no school but just more interference from Per Rolfsrud and that old maid Yankee who had nothing better to do than to trot out from Fargo in her fancy buggy to the Rolfsruds three days a week to put ideas into the heads of other people's children, and that it was a waste of time for me because I was a girl, and only boys needed to go to school, but not until the crop was in. So that is why on the first day it was me who went and not Sten and Ole (and not Haldis and Guri because they were too little). And Mor said that Mrs. Harkness was no old maid because she was married to Dr. Harkness, the Yankee doctor in Fargo. But when we got there she was a busy body because she had plenty to do and so did I because the three Norstads were not there at first so I was the only one who knew how to speak English good, and that is thanks to Per and Ingeborg Rolfsrud, and yes, to Far, too.

And after the first day sometimes I took Haldis with me. Sometimes of students there would be four and sometimes fourteen but most of the time somewhere in between. There was me (and sometimes Haldis, and even Guri when Mor was sick, which is sometimes with the cough and sometimes just like being too sad), and the three Norstads and the two Perssons who are Swedes, and I could understand them and they could understand me, but none of us could understand the Sullivans who are Irish. It sounded like they were almost speaking English, but Mrs. Harkness said that she did not know if Irish were capable of being taught anything at all, so I guess maybe it was not, but to tell a truth nobody talks like Mrs. Harkness, and the rest were Germans, Schmidts and Schlaets and a Krueger boy, and sometimes the Germans were there and mostly they were not, and my good friend is Maeta Schlaet now that she knows enough English to be able to have some kind of talking. They are not to speak English at home, Maeta Schlaet says. Maeta Schlaet says her parents do not want her or her brothers to come to the school, but she comes when she can because it sure beats plowing, she says, and that is what it is like to be in a German family where even the girls must learn to plow, and she is only one year older than me and can drive a team at a gallop standing up.

Oh, and for a couple of days there were two Finns, a brother and a sister, and Marit Norstad said that they lived in a dugout right in the middle of the prairie, not dug into a river bank, but just straight down into the earth, and Far said that is how it is with Finns, always digging. And on that first day Mrs. Harkness asked me to tell those Finns something, but I said that they could not understand me, and so Mrs. Harkness asked Lina Persson if they could understand her, but Lina did not know what Mrs. Harkness was asking, so I told her, and Lina looked surprised and said, *"Why would they?"* and when I repeated this to Mrs. Harkness, she said that she thought that if Lina and I could understand each other and Lina was a Swede and I was Norwegian that perhaps it was true that all Scandinavians could understand each other. And I did not need to repeat all that to Lina because that might be true, I don't know, but a Finn is not Scandinavian, and so I said to Mrs. Harkness, "The Finns are Mongolians." That's what Far says, and he grew up in *Norge*, so I guess he would know.

Here is a funny thing that happened at school on our very first day that was almost two years ago now but was a very funny thing to remember. Mrs. Harkness she gave pictures of three men to Per Rolfsrud to put up on the wall right next to a map of the United States of America that was Per Rolfsrud's very own. Then Mrs. Harkness she pointed to the pictures on the wall and said "Can anyone tell me the names of these great men?" It was pretty easy for everyone to figure out what she was asking, but no one wanted to answer the very first question on the very first day of school, but I thought I would try to get started on being a *geni*, so I raised my hand, and when Mrs. Harkness said, "Yes, Kirsten," I said, "Mr. Abraham Lincoln." And Mrs. Harkness said, "Very good. And this one?" But no one knew who Thomas Jefferson was, so Mrs. Harkness she said that he was a President of the United States who could see into the future and saw that there should be farmers all across America, and that people would come from Norway and Sweden and Finland and Germany, and even Ireland, just to farm here. When I told Mor this she said she would have a few things to say to that Mr. Jefferson if he was responsible for setting her down in the middle of this nowhere, but I don't think that would hurt his feelings too much, since he probably did not understand *norsk*, and Mrs. Harkness said he was dead anyway.

So then Mrs. Harkness she pointed to the last picture, and said, "And who is this?" And little Gretchen Schlaet, who was just four years old, remember, got this real happy look on her face, like she had just figured out the rules of a game, and piped right up with, "Frau Krueger!" Oh boy, like Sten says. Right away her sister Maeta and the two Schmidts started to laugh, and that made little Gretchen start to cry, and the Krueger boy was yelling something in German which sounded like it was partly a bad word and partly the noise Far makes when he spits out the door in the morning, and then Maeta was sorry that Gretchen was crying, and got mad at the Krueger boy, and Mrs. Harkness was saying "Children. Children, please." But those Germans could not understand her, and it took a long time for things to quiet down so we could start practicing the alphabet. It was not until that winter when I went with Sten and Ole and Far to help load up the stone boat with ice that Far and the boys were chopping on the river that I saw the famous Frau Krueger because she was there with all of the Krueger boys and their father loading ice, too. And she did look just like the father of our new country, so I felt bad for little Gretchen Schlaet because she has not opened her mouth again in school. Maybe she will do better next year, but maybe I will not be there. Mor is so tired.

And there she is when we squeal into the yard, which is not a yard Mor says, but a place in front of the house where the grass is trampled flat and the dirt is hard, and there is Mor standing by the lye bucket because soap she is making.

"*Did you not find Far, Kirstie?*" Mor asks, and I am sorry to see her even sadder than her every day sad so I am just to answer when Far lifts his head from the cart, and to be true he looks about as sorry as Mor to find himself where he is. "*Have you brought the flour and rice?*" Mor asks, but Far just goes over to the well and pulls and pulls until the can comes up and he pours the water over his head and Mor comes over and looks into the cart and says, "*Skuffet!*" (I don't know it in American, but it is not to be happy for sure.) "*Winter is coming and there is almost no hay put up and plowing there is yet to do and sod to cut for around the house and there you are, three days gone and not one thing to show for it?*"

"*A man's business is not measured in days, wife, and it is a man's business to conduct his business as he pleases,*" Far says, and I think maybe he has forgotten that he is speaking in the old language.

"*Is it a man's business to put his hand in his wife's tin can?*"

Ya, vel den, that is the first that I have heard of Far getting into Mor's tin can, and now even I am worried.

And Far says, "Kirsten, take care of Homer and treat him good. He is now more important than ever. In fact, a house of his own he is to have, I think."

So that is the last that I hear from Far and Mor for right then, and I would like to ask Homer just what it is that is to make him now so important, but he is not a talker is Homer. Not like me.

CHAPTER X

In which Frances is Forced to Behave Badly

Frances read the amusing bits of Percy's letter aloud to Anna, the part about a bumpkin in buckskin, about a homesteading mule, about how he and John would be home within the week. Then, tucking Percy's letter into her skirt pocket, Frances reached for the note Anna held toward her, admiring her friend's smile. She loved Anna, and so it should follow, Frances thought as she glanced at the note, that she should want for Anna what Anna wanted for herself. Yet here was the conundrum, since at the moment what Anna appeared to want was to accept the young Reverend Smith's request that he be allowed to call on the Bingham ladies this coming Thursday afternoon. What Frances wanted was for the Reverend Smith, with his delicate handshake and his thinning blond hair arranged much too carefully about his collar, to stay far, far away.

"I wonder that he has so much time for social visits," Frances said aloud, handing the minister's note back to Anna, and turning toward the parlor window as if to study the dance of the trees that swayed and bent in the ravine below. Silently, she promised herself a long ramble later on in the day. Despite the wind that roughed her cheeks, she loved to walk beneath the dry, pattering applause of the leaves that refused to fall. "Surely there are orphans and widows who could better benefit from his attention. Are there no prisoners to visit?"

"You are teasing now, Frances. I imagine that he sees it as his duty to look in on us, what with father and Percy away. And even a busy clergyman has the right to rest among friends, especially if those friends include the elderly and infirm. Such as mother," Anna quickly added. "She is almost a recluse now. I am certain that she would enjoy the novelty of Reverend Smith's visit." Anna hesitated, and Frances, understanding that she had been asked less for her agreement than for her encouragement, turned from the window to smile at her friend.

"I wonder if we may properly call the third visit in a month a novelty," Frances said. "But, of course, dear, you must say that each Bingham lady looks forward to the gentleman's visit this Thursday afternoon. And when you have finished your reply, we will put our heads together and plan a lunch that does not, once again, include Mrs. Cook's massive molasses cookies."

The spice cake had been perfect and the parlor was redolent with cinnamon. Rhoda Bingham sat nearest to the fire, a knitted afghan resting on her knees. She held her cup and saucer carefully. The wind of a few days earlier had blown through, leaving behind yet another crisply blue autumn day, and Frances trained her gaze on the window just beyond her mother-in-law's shoulder in the attempt to fight off a mid-afternoon torpor in a room that was much too warm. Reverend Smith's recitation of the repairs underway at the First Christ Episcopal Church added to the afternoon's somnolence, and Frances amused herself with an image of Mother Bingham drooped over in her chair, fast asleep, while both Frances and Anna slid insensibly to the floor. Would the reverend, she wondered, notice?

Anna's manners were, as usual, superior to hers, for she had been quietly prompting Reverend Smith for more information about the renovations. In fact, Frances thought, rousing herself to take a closer look at her friend's expression and finding there a liveliness as disconcerting as it was unwarranted, her blue eyes engaged, a slight blush upon her cheeks, her posture just a bit more erect than Frances knew comfort allowed, Anna did not look bored at all. Frances moved her attention to their guest. He seemed nice enough, if unremarkable. He had, over the course of the past two visits, discussed his home in Nebraska, his parents' deaths, his brother's children, his education, and his few years of teaching before he had found his true calling in the church. There had been little of interest in his story, beyond the opportunity for math afforded by his recitation, which allowed Frances to put the "young" minister in his mid-to-late thirties. Beyond the general questions regarding the health of each of the Bingham women, he seemed incapable of imagining that they, too, might have a significant role to play in the conversation, but that, Frances had long understood, was not unexpected from a man of any social consequence.

In short, the reverend should have been perfectly harmless, but here he was, holding forth in the Bingham parlor, and here was Anna, her cane hidden beneath the sofa, acting as if new pews and roof repair were as interesting as the latest catalogue from *Demorest's*. Frances searched for an opportunity to intervene.

"Who, by the way, was the young lady playing the piano this past Sunday, Reverend Smith?" Frances asked. "Watching the two of you before the service at the front of the church I thought perhaps she was your sister. You seemed to know each other so well. But then I remembered that you had not mentioned a sister when discussing your family during your most recent visit."

"You are referring to Miss Olive Hamilton," the reverend answered. "I don't know her well at all. Hadn't met her until that very day, in fact. She is Mrs. Godfrey's niece, in town for a month, and, with Mrs. Godfrey's rheumatism acting up, agreed to take over her aunt's duties at the piano for the service. I'm afraid that Mrs. Godfrey may have to give up the piano altogether soon." Reverend Smith turned back to Anna. "I understand that you play well, Miss Bingham."

"I play a little," she answered.

"Perhaps you would play a little today?"

"Yes, do, Anna," Rhoda Bingham spoke, and without demurring Anna reached for her cane beneath the sofa, stood, and moved toward the piano. Soon the parlor was filled with the hymns each knew, but which, in their modulation and care, were distant things from the martial-like din pounded out by the good Mrs. Godfrey. Although Anna turned the pages of the hymnal as she moved from song to song, her gaze was more often lifted to the window and the back yard beyond, the music she played familiar since childhood.

Idiot, idiot, idiot, Frances berated herself as she listened to Anna play and occasionally cast a glance toward their guest, his attitude no longer simply polite, but suddenly rapt. Of course he thought her beautiful. He'd have to be as blind as he appeared to be self-involved not to have noticed. Certainly he found her gracious as well, for who could not. Here, materializing before him, was the perfect counterpart to the country minister (for the Reverend Smith's temporary assignment to the First Christ Episcopal Church of St. Paul would soon come to an end). A wife with a limp would be a small price to pay for the convenience of a permanent pianist and musical director at his side.

Frances shook her head. She had let her imagination run wild. This was simply an afternoon visit, not a courting call, and yet, here was the Reverend Smith, sitting far too far forward on his chair, and here was Anna, too beautiful and too unaccustomed to attention to be able to imagine the labor and the tedium of being married to a preacher. Married! Frances felt the chill down her spine. Perhaps she was imagining things, but, if so, what harm could come of making sure that what she imagined became unimaginable.

When Anna had finished playing, Reverend Smith reluctantly stood to excuse himself. The afternoon had been a "balm to his weary soul," but he must return to his duties.

"Don't get up, dear," Frances said, standing quickly, and stepping to the piano. "I will see Reverend Smith to the door." Frances bent toward Anna to lightly touch cheeks, noting that the backyard elm was directly in Anna's sight line from her seat at the piano. "Perhaps you could play one last hymn for Mother Bingham in the meantime."

"That would be lovely," Rhoda Bingham said, and then, lifting her hand into the air before her, she added, "Thank you for your visit, Reverend. I hope you will come again soon."

The parting handshakes completed, Reverend Smith followed Frances to the parlor door, where she paused to ask, "I wonder, Reverend Smith, if you would be interested in taking some asters back to the church. The altar was looking a bit bare this past Sunday, and the flowers are abundant this fall by the little stream that runs in the ravine behind the house. They certainly won't last much longer, and I was about to pick some for the house. If you wait just a moment, I will get my shears." The reverend looked as if he were about to demur and Frances quickly added, "What do you think, Anna? Wouldn't asters be lovely?"

Passing through the back yard with her trug across her arm, Frances led the reverend to the path that dipped into the shallow ravine below. The descent was steep for little more than fifteen feet before tapering off to a gentle slope, and Frances declined the reverend's arm. It was a path she followed almost daily when the weather was fine. Even during the spring rains the stream at the bottom was tame, and this late in the fall it had dried to a marshy trickle. The wildflowers were quickly cut and gathered, and Frances once again led the way back up the path, having refused Reverend Smith's offer to carry the flowers. Just as she was about to reach the level ground of the back yard, she quickened her steps, and came up to the elm at practically a run.

The minister, surprised, hurried behind. Frances quickly held the laden trug toward him, as if to keep him at some distance. But just as he reached for the basket, Frances' face took on an expression of horror as she cried, "No!"

The minister paused, stunned, his own face flushed with the exertion of the climb. "What is it?" he asked.

"A spider! On my neck! Lift my collar away! Oh, I will faint!"

Reverend Smith quickly raised his hand to touch Frances' neck. Just as quickly, Frances dropped the trug, spilling the flowers at their feet as she brought her hand to his cheek in a solid slap that stung her fingers.

Startled, aghast, the minister stepped back, and the man who a half hour earlier had been marked by volubility was suddenly unable to speak beyond a stuttered and breathless, "What!"

With one hand gathering her collar tight and the other pointing theatrically to the gate beside the house that led to the front yard and the street, Frances said only, "Go."

"But, but, Mrs. Bingham, you have mistaken—"

"Please, just go," Frances repeated. "I assure you that I will never speak of your behavior to a soul, as I am sure you will not. If my husband knew—" Frances left the sentence unfinished, and looked toward the asters tumbled about their feet. She did not drop her arm until she heard the gate close. Bending to once again collect the flowers, Frances noticed that she could not hear the piano.

Upon re-entering the house through the back door, Frances took the flowers into the kitchen, put them in water, and hurried up the stairs. It was several minutes later before she heard Anna's knock on the door.

"Please do not come in," Frances answered quietly from her side of the door. "I am suddenly unwell, and must lie down for a bit." Frances waited for Anna to speak again, aware suddenly of her heart's pounding. She was about to move from the door when Anna spoke, her voice barely above a whisper.

"Frances. I saw."

"No!"

"Frances, dear, let me in."

Frances slowly opened the door. Her role required that she hang her head, and for this she was grateful, for she dared not look at Anna's expression where she would read her stratagem's success or failure. She did not have to look. Anna's arms wrapped around her, and Frances dropped her head to Anna's shoulder.

"Are you hurt?"

"No. Oh, Anna, I don't know what I did to make the man think–"

"Shhh. It would be unfair for you to blame yourself. It is all too impossible. Had I not seen it with my own eyes I could not have believed it of Reverend Smith. For a man of the cloth, who had been a guest, to reveal himself a monster?"

Before Anna's voice could break, Frances availed herself of a sniff and a shudder. "You must not mention this, Anna," Frances said softly. "I could not bear the humiliation."

"No," Anna said hesitantly, "but would it be right not to–"

"Please, Anna. It would be too awful." Frances lifted a hand, as if to touch her eyes, and then stood back from Anna's embrace. "I must insist. No harm was truly done, and I believe he has learned a lesson he will not soon forget." Frances allowed herself a wan smile. "But I really would like to lie down. Will you lie down with me? I can not seem to shake this chill."

Anna covered Frances with a light quilt and then fit herself next to her friend, her arm lightly draped around Frances' waist. Frances hadn't expected to speak again, but Anna's sighs made her ask, "Are you all right, Anna? You mustn't worry any more about me." When Anna did not answer, Frances said, "Anna?"

"You will always be the strong one, dear. I am afraid that I am feeling sorry for myself. It pains me beyond what I would have imagined to lose my good opinion of Reverend Smith. The world is suddenly a much uglier place, a more dangerous place, than I had wanted to believe."

The sadness in Anna's voice sent a stab of remorse through Frances' chest, and Frances cast about for something to say. But there was nothing to say. Certainly not the truth. She could say that she was sorry, but she was not. Not really. Anna was not meant for a life of labor and tedium as the harried wife of a poor preacher, and she was not meant for a life without Anna. She was about to turn toward her friend to say whatever she could manage, that life was not ugly, that there was still much of beauty in their home, that they would both feel better in a day or two, but Anna's arm about Frances' waist tightened for just a moment, telling Frances that she ought not move.

"Forgive me, Frances," Anna said. "I am thinking of myself when it is you who have been frightened. We will forget this day, as you wish." Anna gave Frances' waist a second brief squeeze. "Now go to sleep, if you can, and I will stay right here."

CHAPTER XI

In Which the Fruit Rolls Far from the Tree

October 26, 1875
John Bingham, Esq.
421 Summit Avenue
St. Paul, Minn.

Dear Mr. Bingham,
Your favor of 18th at hand, I respond herewith to your several concerns.
Regarding the "hopscotch" pattern of land-ownership of which you have spoken several times with some frustration, this is simply the reality of a land grant, which necessarily alternates railroad land with government sections. You may be assured that I intend to keep a close eye on the individuals who file claim on government parcels proximate to those taken up by friends of the road. There is a fine line to be walked here. As you must realize, it is to the benefit of the Northern Pacific to have all land populated and under cultivation as quickly as possible along its line. It is equally true that the company means to show its gratitude to those bondholders

who are willing to invest their resources in proving the fertility of this land for the benefit of the country at large. That said, a settler whose accounts are in arrears in town, or who has failed to make pre-emption payments on time, or who is having difficulty meeting a mortgage taken out on land that he has proved up, is likely to be, shall we say, "receptive" to a reasonable offer made by an interested party.

Now for your interest in the Sections that abut the Sheyenne River, I am going to say some things that are for your ears only. Two of the sections (#7 and #19) are railroad land that has been taken up by the remnants of a Norwegian colony from Goodhue County in Minnesota that had settled along the west side of the Red River ahead of the Northern Pacific surveyors. Whether by insight or dumb luck, they had positioned themselves precisely where the Road decided to cross, in the shadow of what is now the bridge between Fargo and Moorhead. A few of the less savvy squatters simply moved on, but several of the families negotiated for half sections of railroad land as a condition of releasing their claims. The government section in between (#18) is taken up by homesteaders, but frankly, Friend Bingham, these parcels are not of the quality of land that has been set aside for you and Mr. Slade. A significant portion of the river land is quite likely to flood with some regularity, and can be thick with mosquitoes for months at a time. Such property may be appropriate for investment, and should it become available in the future I will let you know, but it is not suitable for the type of farming which you plan to undertake.

In sum, I believe that you are not only sufficiently placed to begin your enterprise, but are also in a very good position to absorb several adjacent government sections, should you desire, as the business grows. Some patience is recommended here. You will be several seasons getting the land you have now into production.

As for your stated interest in developing a small herd of cattle, you will find, I believe, that grazing cattle on this prime wheat-producing soil is not the most profitable use of its ca-

*pacities. If you are determined to raise livestock, however, I
would encourage you to consider the Short Horn breed. Your
homesteading neighbors rely in general on oxen for farm
work, but I believe that a man can do no better than the
Percheron-Norman horse for general purposes on the farm
and for heavy work in town.*

Yours very truly,

J. B. Power

Power wrote 'personal' at the corner of the letter. John Bingham was
proving to be a far more astute businessman than Power had expected.
Unable to get a fix on Septimus Slade—Did he see himself as investor
or speculator? Was he motivated by concern for the railroad, or was he
solely interested in his own fortunes?—Power had been wary of Slade's
choice of manager. Two sharps, Power suspected. Perhaps they should
be wary of each other.

As for the recipient of the next letter he must write, the fruit had
rolled a great distance downhill from the tree. Power pulled Percy Bingham's "Prairie Town Inhabitants" from a cubby hole in his desk, shaking his head in wonder at a grown man's devotion to wasting time. It
hadn't taken a great deal of prompting to discover that Percy had com-
piled a series of sketches of the characters he had met in Dakota, and it
had taken less encouragement still to convince him to share his work.
Power had hoped for better when he had mentioned, upon first meeting
Percy Bingham, that an editor at *Harper's Monthly* had agreed to run a
piece on the Northern Pacific as a personal favor to the chairman of the
Land Department, Frederick Billings. Positive word in print about the
railroad was rare, especially with the bankruptcy and reorganization so
recently in the news, and Billings had directed Power to consider how
best to use this opportunity.

Billings. Power looked up from Percy's "portraits" and searched the
space outside his window, tapping his lips with an index figure. He was
quite likely to be the company's president some day. Power's work as
a personal land agent for the directors was certain to prove profitable,
but Billings was already a tiresome "client," second-guessing Power's
decisions while vacillating between gruff suspicion and appeals for reassurance. Most frustrating, and this Power took quite personally, Billings

was eager to use his N.P. holdings as a means of acquiring a great deal of Dakota land, but unwilling to put any of it into production.

Power shook his head. Neither Billings nor his friend at *Harper's* would see young Bingham's "portraits," for these were not the pictures to disabuse the public of its doubts about northern Dakota as suitable for settlement: a drunken Norwegian filing a homestead claim in the name of his mule (a depiction that was clearly straight out of Percy Bingham's imagination), a buckskinned ruffian going on and on about Indians, a homesteader flipping cats out of frying pans, and an assortment of others, including a foul-mouthed steamboat captain who described the Red River as following a path similar to that of a pig being driven to market. It simply would not do.

Still, young Bingham had a knack for description. He simply needed help in redirecting his talents. The single-most effective piece of Cooke's advertisements for his N.P. bonds had been an oft-published map of the United States highlighting a swooping isothermal line. Lifting over Dakota and into the British provinces it assured investors of not just the habitability, but the overall temperate nature of the lands through which the Northern Pacific was to pass. Unfortunately, it was the newspapers' repeated references to this map and "Jay Cooke's banana belt" following the Panic that had done the most lasting damage. It was now necessary to repair that damage. A direct refutation would simply be read as more propaganda. In fact, the story should not appear to have anything to do with the Northern Pacific at all. What was required was an oblique approach, a seemingly unrelated story placed in the proper forum, written from a detached, yet learned perspective, and filled with the sort of flowery phrases and half-baked scientific presumptions that passed for learning among folks who could afford to waste their time reading that sort of thing. But if it was done right, some of those phrases and assumptions would stick like burdock to trouser cuffs. Percy Bingham could be the right man for the job.

Power sat back and tapped his pencil against his desk as he thought. Realizing that he had picked up the rhythm of the approaching train, he moved to his office window in time to see the '7:45' come to a halt in front of the N.P. offices and depot. The siding, lit by the depot's gas lamps, was quickly populated by several disembarking passengers. A one-armed army lieutenant, traveling with his wife and two small chil-

dren, encouraged his family in an exercise of deep breathing, their in-
halations of the pleasant night air so exaggerated as to be comical, and
Power caught himself taking a deep breath as well. Tomorrow morning
at eight the passengers would once again be back on the train, to be carried further west, some possibly as far as Bismarck.

It had not been so long ago that Power's words extolling the virtues
of the new Northwest had been little more than the tools one used when
making the best of a difficult job. Now that he'd learned the trick of
seeing on the prairie, learned, that is, to draw his perspective in, to focus
on what was immediately before him so as not to feel overwhelmed by
the expanse beyond, he half-wished he could be on that train, too. With
each letter of encouragement he wrote to prospective settlers, with each
party of scouts, sent from Holland, or England, or Iowa or Michigan,
that he guided first to Fargo, and then into the country beyond, he felt
more like he was offering a glimpse into the land of milk and honey.

He had become his own convert.

Earlier in the year, alone and on horseback, Power had ridden the
better part of a day south from Fargo, following the Sheyenne River
until it curved back north again. In the delta thus formed he had come
upon the unexpected sight of hills and trees reminding him of his native
New York. The rich black soil had given way to a sandier loam, but the
grass was rich and prime for grazing. When he returned to Brainerd he
had removed six thousand acres along that delta from the N.P. records
of land for sale. He would call it Helendale some day, in honor of his
ever-patient wife. At no time of the year was the magnetism of the train
heading west as great as these days of Indian Summer, when it felt as if
God reached down to pull away the veil between prairie and firmament.
Power smiled to himself and walked back to his desk. Perhaps he should
be the one to write the flowery phrases.

Power picked up Percy's character sketches. What was it that fraud,
Dakota Bill, had said? Power flipped through the pages until he found
what he was looking for: "Spring ain't no-count here. Goin' from blizzard to blazing heat in 'bout as longs takes a catterflyoffn' a hot stove.
But Indian Summer'll makeup ferit. S'own season. Then winter'll come
and you'll wish you'as dead."

Indian Summer. Like it was its own season. "A fifth season," Power
said aloud. Don't deny and don't repeat, just give it to them a brand

new way. Well, Percy Bingham, here is your opportunity to get your work in a magazine, although we'll have to see to it that there's no name attached. If you do well enough, by George, there's more where this came from. Put that fancy education and European travel to use. Quote your poetry, pontificate, and complicate. You may be useful after all.

"Kindred," Power called.

Power's clerk, C. F. Kindred, was immediately at the door, a stack of letters in his hand. "Yes, sir?"

"Find a copy of Cooke's isothermal map, and enclose it in the letter to Percy Bingham that I will have for you in a couple of minutes."

"Yes, sir. Here is today's mail, sir. Anything else?"

"See to it that the trash is emptied tonight, please," Power said, dropping Percy's "Prairie Town Inhabitants" into the can next to his desk. Then, recognizing the handwriting on the top letter of the stack Kindred had set down, Power reluctantly reached to open it. It was another missive in preparation for a visit by a couple of Dutchmen, who, like the rest of their brethren with whom Power had dealt over the years, would no doubt expect to be burped after meals and cooed to sleep with reassurances regarding blizzards, locusts, and uncivilized (which is to say non-Dutch) neighbors. Billings' letter ended with one of his typically veiled threats: "Secure them all possible facilities, for if these two pioneers are won, you may be quite sure that thousands of Hollanders will follow. Their handling will require a great deal of tact and good judgment. I am relying on you to secure these people to our line."

CHAPTER XII

In Which Two Dutchmen Come to Appreciate Iowa

Mr. Ruurt Okma and Mr. Gerrit van der Meer arrived at Power's office in Brainerd in the company of an N.P. interpreter, Josiah Funk of St. Paul. The Dutchmen, who had been authorized by the families they represented to buy several thousand acres, had just returned from a similar scouting trip in Iowa. Within thirty-six hours the four men were bouncing across the prairie west of Fargo in a wagon Power had hired from Stephens Livery. The early November day, gray and windy, held nothing of the glorious Indian Summer of the recent past, and more than a hint of the winter to come. Several times Power stopped the wagon to get down with a spade in order to dig and dig and dig, his point being that he could not dig long enough or deep enough to come to the end of the topsoil. His guests wore an expression of patience mixed with concern as they watched Power's exertions, and when he gestured for them to get down and plunge their hands into the dirt he had turned over, they smiled and shook their heads.

Pausing to catch his breath, Power let his thoughts wander to Eben Chaffee, the Connecticut Yankee whom Power had escorted earlier in the summer to look at land just a bit to the north. Chaffee had come west as a representative of forty or so stockholders who'd pooled their N.P. stock. He had driven with Power for three solid days, making notes on the plat map he'd copied, drawing in each slough and creek, noting the wildlife he saw, and occasionally jumping from the wagon to dig, smell, and once, taste, the soil. On that trip he had tentatively selected almost 28,000 acres. It worried Power that Chaffee had not yet confirmed the purchase. Returning his attention to his current clients in the back seat of the wagon, Power quietly asked the interpreter at his side what the Hollanders had been talking about.

"They appear to have fixed upon what it is that they are not seeing, to the detriment, I am sorry to say, of what it is you would have them see," Funk explained.

The incredulity and the volubility of Okma and van der Meer (the substance of which Funk translated for Power) grew the further they drove. They saw no towns or villages. No trees, no lakes, no people. It had been a dry summer, and the fall rains had been sparse. The tall prairie grass that only a month ago had continued to bend and wave like the sea so often described in the N.P. immigration guides, now cracked and crunched and fell lifeless to the sides of the wagon.

Still, Billings and the New York office would need to be convinced of the integrity of Power's endeavor, so once again he began to extol his surroundings to the foreigners by way of Funk. Borrowing a phrase from the N.P.'s most popular immigration booklet, the "Guide to the Great Northwest," Power began with a sweep of his hand. "This is the Nile of the North, gentlemen, perhaps the most fertile farmland in the world, *unhampered* by trees or rocks. The civilization to be built here is as yet undecided and will depend upon the men with the foresight to make it in their own image." Power hesitated to let Funk catch up, then added, "Perhaps you look about you and think you see nothing but empty land and beyond that a distant horizon, but I say look again. What you are looking at is the future. What you are looking at is opportunity. What you are looking at is a blank page waiting for a fortune to be writ upon it."

Funk gave him a nudge, jerked his head to the left, and said, "Actually, what they're looking at is over there." In the distance two low mounds lifted out of the prairie's level floor.

Power was surprised to realize that he had followed the wagon tracks out of Fargo this far already. He had intended to turn to the south long before the homestead they were nearing was in sight, for it was not an advertisement for settlement. A look at his watch confirmed what the horses' shining coats should have told him. In his irritation he'd been pushing the team harder than was necessary or wise. He didn't need Funk to translate to know that the Dutchmen were telling him to get closer to those mounds. Finns, Power guessed. Maybe Irish. Seemed like the poorer they were the deeper they dug.

"Haw," Power called, and reined the team into a turn. Within minutes they pulled up to an emaciated horse, still within its traces, its head drooping so low that it appeared to be looking into the taller mound's only window, a top-hinged piece of shiplap, the bottom of which was level with the prairie. It was propped open with a stick, letting in, Power supposed, as much dirt as air. The horse had registered the approach of Power's team with more of a groan than a nicker. A walking plow rested behind. Within the circle of burnt grass around the mound that defined the yard, a steaming kettle hung on a pole, supported on one end by a rain barrel at the corner of the dugout and secured at the other on the spokes of a broken wheel. The smell of burning buffalo chips was powerful. Power had intended to simply skirt the perimeter of the "yard," keeping the detour as brief as possible. He was preparing his commentary on how a large settlement of like-minded families could spare themselves the isolation that they now saw before them, when, from the longer, wider, lower mound a boy of five or six emerged leading a milch cow up from the depths. How a cow had gotten to be so bony in the midst of a fenceless field of grass, even in a dry year, Power could not imagine, but he could deduce from the tones of amazement behind him that his guests were wondering the same thing. A movement from the first mound turned their attention from the unfortunate cow, and as they watched, the tar paper door was lifted to the side and out spilled two tiny and grimy barefoot girls, hand in hand, in dresses of flour sacking. They were followed by a woman with a baby on her hip who slowly lifted her free arm and pointed to the back of the low mound. As if commanded, Power moved his wagon around, and there, sitting on his haunches, with his head in his hands, was the husband.

"Hello," Power spoke from the wagon.

The man lifted his head, sighed, and got to his feet, pulling his slouch hat off his head and holding it before him. Power looked at Funk to see if he could translate the man's reply.

"Can't help you," Josiah Funk said. "Could be an Icelander."

At this the man looked up, his expression more active. Stepping just a bit forward he spoke to Funk. Interspersed in his commentary was just one word in English: "broke." Finally he waved to the men in the wagon to follow him back around to the horse. Pointing at the horse, he said, again, "broke."

"Thinks we're land inspectors, is my guess," Funk said. "Come to see if he's proved up his claim."

Power leaned over the side of the buggy to speak directly to the settler. "Fine. You're fine," he said, and turned the wagon back into the prairie. "Iowa," he heard one of the Dutchmen say.

The wind had picked up, bringing with it a coolness and a smell that the horses registered with snorts and a pull at the reins. Power searched the horizon in the direction of the breeze, but could see no darkening there beyond the steady gloom of the day. Beside him Funk said, "Maybe we should head back to town."

Power nodded his head. "We're almost to the Bingham land I was mentioning. Won't take but a minute to look about."

Coming upon the recently plowed parcel, Power pulled the team to a resistant halt and stood on the wagon seat to get a better view of the sod-breaking crew Alexander McKenzie had put together for John Bingham. The dry summer had made fall plowing more difficult, but the lack of rain also allowed the sod busters the unexpected opportunity to work well into November. A half section of land had been turned over, and Power smiled to see the cross-hatching on his plat maps that indicated railroad land replicated on the land itself. He counted ten men with teams of oxen moving forward in a wedge, finishing the plowing with single-bottom walking plows. Another wedge of workers drove sulky plows perpendicular to the furrows, backsetting the land to prepare it for next spring's harrowing and seeding. Two men in the distance were working independently of the wedges, their mattock strokes practiced and rhythmic as they labored to dig up a patch of wild rose bushes. A sudden gust of wind made Power sit quickly before he lost his balance. As if choreographed, each man in the field lifted a hand to his hat to tug it more securely into place. Power's "Giddup, boys," was superfluous, for the horses had begun to move the minute he lifted the reins.

The first mile of the return trip was alongside the plowed field. The wind that had made itself noticed at the beginning of that mile was soon blowing dirt horizontally, causing Power and Funk to shake out kerchiefs and tie them about their noses. Funk turned in his seat to motion the Hollanders to do the same. By the time the buggy reached grass, Power could taste the grit between his teeth. His eyes stung, and he knew that he and the Dutchmen were covered with the same fine layer of silt as was Funk beside him.

They saw only one other man behind a plow on the return trip to Fargo in the darkening day, and he was not in the field, but was, rather, encouraging his mule as they plowed a circle around his soddie. A fire line was a good idea, given the dryness of the prairie grasses, but the idea had come a bit late in the season, Power thought. It was unusual in a dry year like this, in any year, for that matter, to find a house and barn, no matter how humble, not surrounded either by several overturned furrows or by a wide circle that displayed the results of a controlled burn on a windless day, for once fire got a hold of these grasses, the wind could chase it for a hundred miles. No damage done, really, if the crop was up and the hay stacks and buildings stood secure within their own plowed moats. Otherwise a prairie fire could put a man out of business quick enough.

No worry about fire today, Power thought, giving the horses their heads. Tired as they were, they sensed the stable and picked up their pace against the wind. The sky continued to lower, shading into the blackness that Power had been expecting all along. The first fat drops began to fall as the wagon pulled in sight of the Headquarters Hotel.

"Just in time," Funk said. "Must be our lucky day." When Power didn't respond to his small joke, Funk offered to take the wagon back to the livery.

"I think you'd better see to it that our guests find their way to a bath and dinner," Power said in reply, and then, in the rain that had begun for real, watched Funk and two unhappy Dutchmen, no longer red-faced but black, pull open the door to the hotel.

The walk back from the livery was all that was needed to leave Power soaking and muddied. He had just walked into the lobby when the clerk behind the desk hailed him. "Three telegrams for you, Mr. Power." Pulling his soiled handkerchief free, Power wiped his hands before taking the telegrams. He moved back to the door so he wouldn't be dripping directly in front of the desk while he opened the first. All three were from his office in Brainerd.

The first read simply: "Eben Chaffee. 28,000 acres confirmed. $104,000."

Power hesitated before opening the next telegram, wanting to acknowledge and enjoy the increase in his pulse at the news. He unfolded the second.

"John Dunlop. 10,900 acres. Final. Robert Hadwin. 7680 acres. Tentative. To Dakota in spring."

Now Power looked at the third telegram in his hand. He was hesitant to open it, fearing that some mistake had been made with the first two. Grinding the grit between his teeth, Power opened the third message, and read: "Have a cigar." His first thought was that the telegram had been a waste of money, very much like his assistant, C. F. Kindred, who was too easily extravagant. Then Power reread the first two telegrams. Forty-six thousand, five hundred and eighty acres sold in one day. Seventy-two sections. Seventy-two square miles. The equivalent of two townships. By God, he would have that cigar.

Leaving the door where he had stood and read and dripped, Power walked back to the clerk behind the counter.

"Yes, sir?" the man asked.

"I'd like to have a bath in my room, with plenty of hot water. And a cigar. And a tall brandy."

"Yes, sir, Mr. Power. That's Room 23. But it will be a bit of a wait, I'm afraid. Both of the tubs are in use just now, and Mr. Okma and Mr. van der Meer are next in line. But I'll get one to you as soon as possible."

Power nodded and turned. Then stopped, and turned again, and did a very unusual thing. Reaching into his pocket he pulled out a coin purse. Laying four bits on the counter he said, "I wonder if our Dutch friends, who will leave Fargo tomorrow, never to return, could wait just a bit longer."

"Yes, sir," the clerk said, neither looking at the money nor at Power as he wrote a note to himself. "I think that tub should be free directly."

CHAPTER XIII

In Which Little Norwegian Girls Are Like Grass

Ya, vel den, here comes Ingeborg Rolfsrud. A quarter mile away I see her because in between is just the cow and then nothing but grass and rose bushes, but the grass it is cut for hay and the bushes they are not so high as Ingeborg Rolfsrud, but about as wide, which is right for a rose bush but not for a person because we are all of us just *skin og bein* Mor says. Except Ingeborg Rolfsrud. She is just fat. And another thing is that Ingeborg Rolfsrud is walking. I know that I already said that, and, ya, to see Ingeborg Rolfsrud walk from the wagon to our house or from the kitchen to the room just for eating (ya, in the Rolfsrud house there is a room just for eating) is not a new thing, but for her to walk two miles to our house, that is something else. For me it is nothing at all to walk six miles to Fargo and six miles back. But the Rolfsruds are not like the Knudsons. Maybe they do not walk because they are getting too big for their *bukser* like Far says, but I think maybe that is why they are too big for their *bukser* in the first place.

So down I sit on my stool because the cow is looking at me like to say, "What do you wait for, then?" Instead of putting my forehead into the nice warm place in her side for a little rest while I milk, I lean down and peek behind the bag to watch Ingeborg Rolfsrud come forth, and without even thinking my hands just start to milk. I say, "Kirsten Knudson, Kirsten Knudson, Kirsten Knudson," over and over and each time

I say my name it is two splashes into the pail, and pretty soon the cow is almost asleep because I am good to milk, better than even Mor. Then pretty soon it is about Mrs. Harkness I am thinking, the Yankee teacher that comes for our school to the Rolfsruds' three days a week when the weather is good, but not during the summer, of course, because during the summer it is all work, work, work, and it is not that much different any other time of the year, because when there is planting and haying and threshing it is not for boys and girls to be in school. And anyway, what I am thinking is that Mrs. Harkness she talks about walking back and forth, when here is Ingeborg Rolfsrud walking forth, and then she is to walk back, and so why does Mrs. Harkness say "back and forth," when there is no walking 'back' until you have walked 'forth', and this is just one thing that Mrs. Harkness says that I do not understand, even though I want to understand it all.

To be true, sometimes it is not the words that I do not understand, I just forget to listen when it gets too hard and it is easier just to stare at Mrs. Harkness, because she is always so clean and her hair is so shiny and her skin is so clear and pink that sometimes I think she is maybe an angel, but Far says no, she is just a Yankee, and Yankees all start with a leg up here in Dakota, and then you know what Ole does. And here is another thing about Mrs. Harkness, and it is about her dresses. I asked Maeta Schlaet why do the Yankee women in the pictures in the magazine that Mrs. Harkness brings to school bundle their clothes behind them like that only to sit on, then? And Maeta Schlaet said it was because the Yankees have so much money that they like to show it off by having extra of everything, even extra material on their dresses, and I guess that makes sense, and it is called a bustle, which is why Michael Sullivan said I was supposed to get my bustle in a hustle last week when I was late to school because I had to round up the chickens because Haldis and Guri had left the gate open to the pen, but of course I do not have a bustle, it was like a joke, and I hope Ole does not hear this joke because then it will be "bustle in a hustle," "bustle in a hustle," "bustle in a hustle," over and over again.

So, anyway, here I am just milking and thinking and dreaming in the day and without even noticing I have tucked my head right back into the cow, and the cow does not care one bit, because there is nothing about milking that is to be hurt with a little dreaming, in fact, Mor says to Haldis that she would be better to milk if she did not think about what she was doing so much, and that is just another joke because Haldis thinks only about how to not do what she is doing so she can run away and play with little Guri, and I would just like for Mor to try to find either one of them right this minute because they are nowhere and anyway this is what I am thinking or not thinking about, and then I take another look under the cow, and it is like a big wind has come to lift Ingeborg Rolfsrud up and set her down not so very far away, but like I said before, that is to be a pretty big wind.

Not that the wind is not big here. Mor says that it is enough to make a woman go mad, because it just will not stop. And Far says stop it does because that is how you know that it has started up again, but when it gets started it can really blow. Last winter Ole he got a good strapping from Far because he took Mor's good shawl and tied it to some sticks for a sail, and one long stick he stuck right into his boot, and then he got on the skis that Far made for him and for Sten and off he goes with the wind across the snow, and he said it was worth the strapping, every single minute of it. It was like flying, he said. So here was Ingeborg Rolfsrud right on top of me, and it was too late for me to run inside to warn Mor to cover up the hole that Far dug in the middle of the floor for the buffalo chips and dried cow dung that we burn in the stove and that Mor says no one is to see, and now I know what Mrs. Harkness means when she says that time is not my friend.

So right on top of me or not, I stand up and yell, "Hello, Mrs. Rolfsrud," and she says "*god morgen*, Kirsten," to me, and I sing out very loud, "Is it not a beautiful morning, Mrs. Rolfsrud," just like Mrs. Harkness says, and I even get the "not" right, I think, all short and round like a Yankee, and Mrs. Rolfsrud she just looks at me sort of confused, like Homer when I forget if gee means left and haw means right or the other way around, but sure enough by the time we are to the door, me with my pail of milk and Mrs. Rolfsrud with her cloth bag (which is, I will get ahead of my story here because there is no telling if I will get around to getting behind enough to remember this part, so I will say right now that the bag is filled with some wool for Mor to dye, and this, at least, is something that Guri and Haldis are good for, they are good to fill bags and bags with moss and green nuts and leaves and bark for the green dye that Ingeborg Rolfsrud said was so pretty in Mor's Sunday dress),

and anyway, when we get to the door there is Mor with her boots on
even, and she is standing up in front of the stove that she has rubbed
shiny with newspaper because today is the day to make *flatbrød*, and
the table is over the flour sack that is over the hole.

So there sits Ingeborg Rolfsrud drinking her coffee while I roll the
dough into balls and Mor rolls the balls into round sheets so thin, like
paper, and wider than two pies. Mor is good to make *flatbrød*, she can
lift it onto the top of the stove without one tear and that is not easy, I
know (and that reminds me about how when Ole pretends he knows
something he will say "I know it as sure as I know that my name is Ole
Knudson," and then I laugh because about this he is not so sure). And
now I forget what I was going to say, but anyway, "in the meantime"
as Mrs. Harkness says, Ingeborg Rolfsrud is drinking her coffee and
she says that Mr. Rolfsrud is in Yanktown and she is afraid to be alone.
And Mor asks where is her nephew, then, that big lump with hair like
a haystack? (No, that is not "precisely," as Mrs. Harkness says, what
Mor says, but that is what I am thinking.) And Ingeborg Rolfsrud she
says Halvor goes every day to plow for the big farmer Bingham who
has fields but no farm and that is a very funny way to start I think, and
Ingeborg Rolfsrud says that this Mr. Bingham is paying every man two
dollars and fifty cents to break an acre if he brings his own oxen or
mules, and that Halvor comes back for supper at dark, but she does not
like to be alone all day long.

So instead it is with Mor she is to be all day long but she does not
lift even the one finger to help, and when Mor comes outside to help
me with the washing that is all day rubbing and rubbing and rinsing
and rubbing some more, Ingeborg she brings her chair outside, too, and
that is when she sees that the sky is turning gray and that the wind it is
"picking up." That is a phrase that I like because it is just right, because
the wind is picking up lots of things and setting them down somewhere
else, and Mor she says that we will need to take the clothes off the line if
it starts to rain, and now Ingeborg Rolfsrud looks worried and I can tell
that she is wondering which is to be more the worst, to be alone in her
house or to be walking home in the rain, and it is the rain, because she
says that it is time to go home and I think that she has been waiting for
Far or Ole or Sten to come back with Homer to carry her to her house
all this time. Mor knows this, too, because she says, *"Kirsten, I will*

finish the washing. You take lunch to Far and the boys, that way you can keep Mrs. Rolfsrud company part of the way. Then find Haldis and Guri." Well, to find Haldis and Guri is about as hard as to find Far when he goes to Fargo and does not come back. It is easy is what I mean. They are playing under the bridge I bet, even though Far says that someday they will be eaten up by the trolls that live there, but that is just part of how they play now.

So I carry warm *flatbrød* and milk to the boys and to Far, and Far he just nods his head at Ingeborg Rolfsrud and then spits and tells me to tell Mor that they are not to be home until dark because it is going to rain and he wants to finish thatching the roof and plowing a fire line around Homer's new soddie before the rain starts, except that it is not really Homer's soddie, it is where Sten is to live, even though there is nothing there now but a crate for a chair and a table that is also the bed, and not even a stove, so Sten will not sleep there in the winter, and Far says that is fine because busy bodies from the government land office who come snooping do their snooping during nice weather only, and not during the winter. And as soon as Far says the word "rain" that is when the wind really begins to blow, and it is just like magic, but not good magic, and I think that soon I am to get a good soaking and all because of Haldis and Guri.

Homer's land is very close to the Sheyenne River so I go right to the bridge with Ingeborg Rolfsrud and say good-bye because the Rolfsruds live on the other side of the river closer to Fargo, right beside the railroad tracks, and then I wait until I can not see her because of the trees on the other side of the river, but Haldis and Guri are not hiding under the bridge, so I follow a path back toward home where the grass is broken over and there they are not very far away in a little circle of crushed grass, both asleep, with their bags not as full of moss as they should be and around their necks and in their hair are necklaces they have made by weaving grass together like braids. I am about to wake them when I see something far away, and it is coming near and then I see that it is a wagon and a team of horses, and I do not know why I do this, but I bend low in the grass and just peek up to watch the wagon through the grass, and it is coming right straight at us, the wagon, and then Guri wakes up but I put my finger to my mouth and then Haldis wakes up and Guri does the same and we do not say one word to each other, but through the grass we watch the wagon come closer and closer and closer and then I think, it is going to run right over us, and still I do not stand up, but instead we all fall right back down like this is a game, too.

And that is what happens is all because nothing happens. The horses do not even see us or smell us and I do not know why because we could sure smell them. And in the wagon are four men and they are all dressed up like it is to church they go, and they are in just that much of a hurry, too, and they do not say a thing. And we do not say a thing. And they almost roll right over us, and then they are going away. And then we hear them cross the bridge and that is when we stand up and see the wagon go into the trees, and we all look at each other but do not say one thing, and I do not know what Haldis and Guri they are thinking but I am feeling funny, like when you think that you are on the last step down, but then you take the next step and find that you are wrong and that you have stepped on to air, and your stomach moves right into your chest and for just a little time your body is all wrong. And then it felt like maybe the wagon and the four men in Sunday suits had never been there at all, because all around us there was just to see grass and a field of stubble and a little ways away Homer's new soddie that is really for Sten. I wonder, if when I saw the wagon if up I had stood and Haldis and Guri, too, could the men have seen us? Or are we just like the grass, too, then?

Chapter XIV

In Which the Bingham Family Entertains a 'Fool on the Loose'

The inhabitants of 421 Summit Avenue were in a state of quiet agitation that winter of '75-'76. It was not the weather that made them restless, for it was neither colder nor milder than is typical of St. Paul, there was neither more nor less snow than was to be expected. In fact, each day looked very much like the day that preceded it while giving a preview of what was to follow, and perhaps that was the problem.

John Bingham's anticipation is the easiest to understand. He is daily occupied with the details of commencing farming on an all-but-imponderable scale. Twice he travels to lumber camps in Minnesota to secure a labor force. He corresponds with, and receives visits from, manufacturers and salesmen of farm machinery. He looks over plans with builders and hires carpenters. He is very busy with his ledgers and numbers.

Percy vacillates between dread and (less often) excitement throughout the season. The essay that he has written for J. B. Power is soon to be published in *Harper's Monthly*, an achievement about which he is, being Percy, deeply ambivalent. Power, pleased with Percy's essay on the "Poetry and Philosophy of Indian Summer," has offered to introduce him to E. B. Chambers, editor of the newly created Fargo *Times*. Employment with the *Times*, Power has suggested, could be a mutually beneficial arrangement. Percy could "cut his teeth" in the world of journalism there, while helping out with the occasional N.P. brochure "along the lines of the *Harper's* essay." Power has not mentioned that the *Times*, having absorbed the company organ, the *Northern Pacific Mirror*, is composed in the main of listings of parcels of railroad land available for purchase and of advertising from implement dealers and banks. When Percy reveals his lack of interest in Power's offer, Frances suggests that it is probably not wise to bite the hand from which he has so recently fed. Should a meeting lead to employment—temporary, of course, Frances adds—she would have no choice but to remain in St. Paul for the time being to help Anna with Percy's increasingly frail mother, especially now that John Bingham is to be absent for several weeks, perhaps months, at a stretch. And so Percy agrees to the meeting with Chambers, and waits for the upcoming trip west in the spring with his father, feeling, he suspects, a bit like the condemned prisoner who does not look forward to the morning's hanging, yet longs for the end of the night's anticipation.

Frances is just plain impatient, with everything and everybody, not least of all with herself, since she is well aware that in the increasingly frustrating contradiction around which she has constructed her life, she can pursue Anna best by doing nothing at all. That this paralytic pursuit may be more successfully employed in the absence of her husband is equally illogical, since there is nothing that Frances intends to do that precludes Percy's presence. And yet, Frances very much wants him gone. Her husband's confidence (or is it determination?) as a lover has grown, making him more attentive, more demanding, more likely to linger.

Frances misses the days of haste and awkwardness and feels trapped in her bed. Walking about the house, she resents the confinement of the walls. Driving about town she imagines that the buildings themselves are leaning in upon the Bingham's old carriage. Sometimes she is certain that her own skin has grown too taut and must soon split to reveal to the world the truth that she, Frances Houghton Bingham, corseted and contained and smiling, is in truth a mass of barely contained organs and blood and muscle, tensed and seething.

Even Rhoda Bingham has not escaped the restive malady of the house, not because she is impatient with time — when it is an impending eternity for which one waits, mortal time passes quickly enough — but because she senses the unease of her family around her and wishes they would be still and let her wait in peace.

Anna's brief... what? She must not call it hope. It was never hope. Interest, perhaps. Her brief interest, then, in Reverend Smith's company has passed. Passed away. It is dead, murdered by the man's unconscionable behavior toward her beloved friend and sister. No, Anna is not impatient, for that would suggest expectation. So it is she who best suffers Percy's insistence on a blustery March evening over supper that she and Frances attempt to guess the identity of the acquaintance from out of town whom he has discovered at the Merchants Hotel.

"You must give us some clues, Percy, mustn't he, Frances?"

"Yes, of course," Percy agreed without waiting for his wife's response. "You have met the man."

"Tell us where."

"That would give it away too easily." Percy lined up his fork and knife upon his plate. "And that, in itself, is a hint. But I will tell you when. The summer of '71."

"Is he from St. Paul?" Anna continued.

"No."

"Is he one of your friends from New Haven?"

"No."

"Have we met him more than once?"

"No."

Anna paused in her questioning. "You must help me, Frances. You are much better at riddles than I. Ask a better question."

Frances paused the tapping of her toe under the table. "Will the unveiling of this mystery merit the industry you require for its revelation?"

A chuckle escaped from behind the newspaper that John Bingham had begun bringing to the supper table, much to the distress of Anna and Rhoda Bingham. Percy's color rose, but he smiled as he replied. "Indeed, for I have taken the liberty of inviting the gentleman, along with his wife and two young daughters, to dine with us tomorrow evening."

"Please tell us, then, who our guests are to be," Frances said.

"I will give you one more clue, and if this does not jog your memory, then I shall reveal the name. You met the gentleman while in a row boat."

"I know the man you are speaking of, Percy," Anna said. "You were kind enough to row him across the lake so he could catch his train. It was when we were at the South Shore House." She looked over at her sister-in-law. "But, I do not remember his name. Do you, Frances?"

"Moses Armstrong," Percy said.

"I know that name," John Bingham looked around his newspaper for a moment. "Can't say why, though."

"The Honorable Moses K. Armstrong. He just finished his second term in Washington as the Dakota Territory representative to Congress. He's on his way back to Yankton with his family, but a late blizzard in southern Dakota has left them stranded here for a couple of days before the trains are running again to Sioux City. I thought a new face, or four, at our table would be a pleasant diversion." Percy finished his sentence with a look toward Frances.

When she did not reply, Anna said, "That will be lovely, Percy."

Moses K. Armstrong had a boy's face, trimmed by a neat gray goatee. Few of his forty-three years were writ upon his expression, best characterized as bemused, and the lines around his eyes looked as likely to have been chiseled by laughter as by time. His body told a different story. Rising from his chair in the parlor to move into the dining room it took him a moment to straighten his back. When he walked, a stiffness in his knees shortened his stride. Frances did not carry with her a very clear image of who Armstrong had been four years earlier, but this seemed to be a much older man. Only once during the meal had he indicated the cause for his discomfort, answering a question put to him by John Bingham about his future plans with a humorous evasiveness that was his trademark.

"I return, Mr. Bingham, to the far west with my only remaining stock in trade, consisting of a wagon load of congressional documents, four bushels of garden seeds, my enlarged head, and the chronic rheumatism."

Percy had been quite correct about the diversion the visitors could provide. Maude Armstrong was a quiet, intelligent woman, and the daughters were either very decorous children or else very shy, but Moses K. Armstrong was a guest quite unlike any other to come to the Bingham house. Frances' curiosity was piqued, most particularly by his speech, with its swings from frontier vernacular to statesmanlike locution. When she realized that her father-in-law was not going to follow up on his question, Frances interjected, "I am certain that you could be forgiven for taking your responsibilities and your achievements as congressman-at-large to heart."

"'Congressman-at-large' or 'fool-on-the-loose', I will let others choose their epithets. The fact remains, I return with nothing but empty honors and an empty pocket. Still, I have learned enough in two terms to last me a hundred years." Armstrong finished his speech with a low, pleasant chuckle.

Frances could not tell from Armstrong's demeanor if he were one of those tiresome individuals whose speech was designed to force his interlocutors to compliment him by contradicting his self-deprecations, or if behind the twinkling eyes and easy chuckle lay a man who truly believed that his accomplishments of the past little prepared him for an uncertain future.

"I imagine territorial politics would seem a tame thing in comparison to the U. S. Congress," Percy said, holding the decanter toward Armstrong, and then refilling his own glass when Armstrong shook his head in a negative. "But perhaps you will decide to put that 'learning' to use back in Yankton."

"Territorial politics are hardly tame, Bingham," Armstrong laughed. "I could tell you stories about fisticuffs and knives pulled and guns drawn in the aisles of the legislature, but," Armstrong paused, his glance falling on his wife across the table, who was almost imperceptibly shaking her head, "but I will leave that for another conversation. No, sir, I have already served in Dakota's territorial legislature for more years than I care to admit. Then the good people of Dakota discovered that the only way to get me out was to send me to Washington. In fact, the population is so well satisfied with their success in keeping me out of Yankton, that they would return me for a third term, but I am happy to be quit of it all, and that is the plain and simple truth. I am reminded of the words of my old frontier friend, little Enos Stutsman. After almost a decade of making the 500-mile trip from his home in the Pembina colony in the northernmost point of Dakota Territory to Yankton in the southernmost, as often by dogsled as by horse, Enos announced his decision not to run again for the Dakota territorial legislature with these wise words"—Armstrong sank a bit lower in his chair and pulled his shoulders to his neck in imitation of the speaker that he alone would have recognized—"'I have tried office and find it does not pay, and as a mere experiment, I intend to see if I can not make an honest living'."

"You will be, I am sure, a fount of wisdom within your community," Percy said behind his laughter. "What advice would you give to a young man with political aspirations? For I am sure," he quickly added, "that you will be called upon for such advice upon your return?"

"I would say that if a man intends to run for office he ought to be guilty of one glaring sin, for if not his enemies will load their guns with the whole vocabulary of imaginary vices and will fire at him broadcast, besmearing him with the garbage and filth of suspicion." Armstrong released another of his soft chuckles. "I have washed myself off, eh, Maudie? And I feel better for it, but I got awful muddy in those few days before election."

After supper the two Armstrong girls happily moved to a table in the corner where they proceeded, with their mother's help, to teach Frances and Anna a favorite card game. Rhoda Bingham had gone to bed immediately after supper, as was now her custom. Percy joined his father and Armstrong next to the fire. He was taking an uncertain pleasure in his father's interest in Moses Armstrong, pleased with himself for discovering the interesting lawmaker, but sorry to see the conversation turn toward yet another discussion of farming in Dakota Territory.

"Are grasshoppers such a serious matter as that?" John Bingham asked upon hearing that Congress had appropriated one hundred and fifty thousand dollars to furnish seeds for spring crops to the farmers in the western states and territories whose crops had been damaged by grasshoppers.

"Depends on who you ask," Armstrong settled into his response. "The grasshoppers have been bad three years running in some places and are never seen in others. They'll strip one field bare and fly over the next. On one farm they'll prefer wheat, and on the next it's grandpa's drawers off the clothesline or nothing at all, thank you very much. Personally, I'm in favor of helping the farmer when I can. On the other hand, much as it pains me to agree with Dakota's current thief-in-absentia, our esteemed Governor Pennington, it probably does not do to have the western settlers advertised as beggars upon national charity. But, as I said, the bill passed, and Dakota Territory will get its twenty-five-thousand-dollars."

"How will that sum be dispersed? With the bulk of the territorial legislators, as I understand it, coming from the southern part of the territory, I wonder –"

Armstrong interrupted John Bingham with a laugh. "You will make a fine northern Dakotan, Mr. Bingham. You have not yet, if I understand you correctly, spent a full fortnight in Dakota, and already you are suspicious of your fellow citizens to the south. I predict that you, too, will soon be calling for a division of the territory. I, myself, introduced just such a bill over two years ago in the United States House of Representatives, under the instructions of the territorial legislature in Dakota, providing for a separate territorial government out of that portion of Dakota north of the forty-sixth parallel. The bill was as ill-received as I had anticipated, but I had done my duty as Dakota's representative, and the northern delegates were temporarily appeased. If you will take the advice of an old frontiersman, Mr. Bingham, you will occupy yourself with farming and leave the braying for division to others. It will come to nothing."

"Why is it to come to nothing?" John Bingham asked.

"Because when it comes right down to it, the idea of creating another territory appeals mostly to recently defeated politicians who look to new territories as opportunities for office and patronage. Territories are the dumping grounds for failed politicians with friends in the Federal government. Dakota Territory has been saddled with carpet-baggers and swindlers for governors. The Republicans may control the U. S. Senate, but with the Democrats in the majority in the House, a division bill just is not going to pass. They're not likely to create offices for the Republicans to fill under Grant."

For a moment the men were silent. Percy looked from Armstrong to his father, enjoying the determination of each man to maintain a look of pleasant disinterest while refusing to directly engage the other. "You are a state's rights man, I take it, Mr. Armstrong," Percy said.

"I represent a territory, not a state," Armstrong answered.

"And yet, you resent the role that the Federal government plays in determining who is to guide that territory, if I understand you correctly."

"I am a Democrat, and if I have offended any of the Republican sensibilities of my hosts this evening, I do apologize. It remains, however, a cold, hard fact that year after year, term after term, Dakota has suffered under the graft and incompetence of Republican governors whose allegiance is not to the citizens of the territory, but to their cronies in the Senate or the White House who have given them their jobs."

Armstrong's voice had taken on the tone of bitter conviction, and Percy changed the subject. "Did your wife and daughters enjoy the winter in Washington, Mr. Armstrong?"

Armstrong roused himself from his thoughts and pulled himself straighter in his chair. "They did, indeed, although they were disappointed to find Washington as cold as Yankton. The Potomac itself froze. For the first time in several winters according to my mother-in-law, with whom we were staying."

"Your wife is from Washington?"

"Indeed, I met her in '61. I had come to Dakota a couple of years earlier as a surveyor, but was as handy with a pen as a compass, and had convinced the editor, owner, and sole employee of the Sioux Falls *Northwest Independent* to pay my way to Washington to report on the bill proposing the creation of the Territory of Dakota. As for the coming home, I was on my own, and when I did, it was with the former Miss Maude Grande as my wife, much, I will admit, to the disappointment of the proprietor of Mrs. Grande's Boarding House. My daughters enjoyed getting to know their grandmother better, and have gone a long way toward improving her opinion of their father."

"I imagine that they enjoyed seeing their father at his desk on the Senate floor from the galleries."

"That, I am afraid, I did not encourage." Armstrong lowered his voice and shook his head sadly. "During the sessions of Congress the city is full of gilded females, who flock there like summer swallows, and swarm the corridors and galleries of the capitol. Many a time I have watched, appalled, as one of these females, attired in gay colors, with rose-painted cheeks, crimson lips and dark penciled eye-lashes, dropped her melting eyes upon a gray-haired senator. You know an old fool is the worst fool in the world."

It was an unexpected speech, spoken with a vehemence that seemed out of character. As Percy studied his guest, Armstrong's gaze moved away from the fire and toward the corner table. The young Armstrong girls remained engrossed in their card game, now teamed against their mother and Anna. Frances looked on in profile. Her arm lay lightly across the back of Anna's chair as she leaned forward to point to a card Anna held in her hand. Her foot, Percy noticed, was tapping a quick, silent beat upon the floor. She had begun to paint her eyelashes, too, a development Percy quite approved of, for it emphasized her most attractive feature. As if her name had been spoken, Frances turned toward the men. She smiled a distant smile in response and then turned back to the table, lifting her arm from Anna's chair to touch her hair where it was swept up from her shoulders.

Percy looked at his watch. John Bingham smiled to himself and relit his cigar.

Moses Armstrong cleared his throat, and then said, "Washington, D.C. is as beautiful as it is expensive, but I will be happy to get myself and my family back to Yankton."

CHAPTER XV

In Which We All Need Stories

A soft chime from the grandfather clock across the room woke Moses K. Armstrong from the dream that had him tumbling down a treeless mountainside, each object he grasped to break his fall crumbling in his hands. The lanterns set into sconces on either side of the clock flickered in the path of a nearby draught, making the dial difficult to read. It was the finest piece of furniture in the Armstrong house, purchased for a fraction of its value from a settler who'd dragged his heirlooms across the prairie in a covered wagon, only to sell them come the starving time of early spring. Two o'clock in the morning. With a wince Armstrong stood to give the coals in the stove a stir, a luxury on a damp April night.

Armstrong returned to his armchair and to the nagging question that had followed him back to Yankton. What now? Perhaps the return had been a mistake. Perhaps he should have taken that bank partner-ship he'd been offered in Minnesota. Sure, he could write the occasional column for his old friend, Bud Taylor, the editor of Yankton's Dakota *Herald*. He could start that book he'd planned to write, but these days he didn't feel like he had much ink left in his pen.

He'd been a journalist, off and on, for almost a quarter century, be-tween surveying and politicking. Just fourteen when he left his father's farm in Ohio, Armstrong was eighteen when he crossed the Mississippi in 1850 to work as a pioneer surveyor. Even then he had been able to find newspaper work here and there along the way. He'd settled in what was now southeastern Dakota Territory in '58, writing without pay for the Sioux Falls *Northwest Independent*. It had been a familiar combination of boredom and wanderlust and intuition that took Arm-strong to Washington in February of '61 to cover the bill of organiza-tion that created a territory of 350,000 square miles named Dakota. That's when Moses Armstrong understood exactly what he ought to do. There would be elections and laws and assemblies, land offices, post offices, army camps, and Indian agencies, and he couldn't get back fast enough to throw his plug hat in the middle of the ring with the rest of the hopefuls.

He had rushed his new bride to Yankton, waiting until the final leg of the trip, a sixty-mile ride in a Thompson dead-axle wagon from Sioux City that had his head bobbing up and down like a churn dasher and Maude doing her best to keep from bouncing from one end of the wagon to the other, to admit to a bit of disingenuousness in his mention of the "town" to which they were headed. Yankton in 1861 was little more than a jumble of sod huts and the occasional log cabin. Few of the 300 inhabitants were women, not all of those spoke English, and of that number fewer still were apt to become acquaintances, unlikely as Maude was to frequent Ash's Tavern. Soon after the Armstrongs' return, the news followed that Fort Sumpter in the Charleston harbor had been fired upon. The years that followed were horrible for so many, but they'd been four of Moses Armstrong's best. He had never considered joining the Union forces. His world lay on the frontier, and he was to be a frontier politician in the new territorial capital of Yankton.

Fifteen years later, that frontier was changing, and Armstrong felt as if not only he, but Yankton itself was in danger of losing its central status in the territory. Until recently the only other populated area was an inconsequential string of settlements along the Red River in northeastern Dakota. Despite young Percy Bingham's complaint that Fargo was still little more than an outpost of shacks on the edge of civilization, Armstrong knew it to be a bustling river town, with shipbuilding on the banks of the Red and a fleet of five steamboats running downriver into the new Province of Manitoba. It had a first-class hotel, a handsome courthouse, and church steeples reaching into the blue prairie sky. Armstrong sensed an energy there that once he had felt in Yankton. And it was nothing compared to the commotion developing in western Dakota, in the Black Hills, now that the cry of "gold!" had gone out. A prospector who'd heard the word "gold" would walk into hell itself with a pickaxe and a pan. That, of course, had the Indians buzzing like a nest of mad hornets.

Armstrong wasn't the sort of man to say 'I told you so,' but there wasn't one bit of all that that was unexpected. One of his first acts as the territorial delegate to Congress had been to introduce a bill (unsuccessful) looking to the purchase of these hills from the Indians. They needed to be convinced—with food, annuities, and promises for more—to cede the land they'd been promised in the 1868 Laramie Treaty. Instead, it had all been done backwards. Prospectors rushed in. Indian atrocities followed. Newspapers in the west were soon reporting daily on murders, mutilation, and the usual assorted indignities visited upon white men by incensed Indians. The Chicago *Inter-Ocean* stated the issue with simple cause-and-effect rationality: "There is gold in the hills and rivers of the region, and the white man desires to take possession of it. What, to the roaming Yankee, are the links that bind the red man to the home of his fathers. He is but an episode in the advance of the Caucasian. He must decrease that the new comers may grow in wealth." And *then*, too late, came the offer of a treaty of sale that the Sioux, and now their allies, the Cheyenne, refused. Added to the mix were a number of Sioux roaming in the Powder River country of Montana refusing to return to an agency, despite several messages sent by courier to their leader, Sitting Bull.

Well, Armstrong thought, his head beginning to nod toward his chest in the toasty heat of the room, he could have told them so.

A possible solution to Armstrong's idleness arrived in the post the next week. Armstrong tucked a second letter, addressed to his wife, into the pocket of his jacket and checked to see if the bench outside the general store and post office had dried since the morning's shower before he sat to study the invitation from the editor of Frank Leslie's *Popular Monthly* in New York. Mr. Leslie was interested in commissioning a series of letters from Dakota Territory. As a long-time citizen of Dakota with experience in national affairs, the Honorable Moses K. Armstrong was just the man to pen these stories, provided his "busy schedule permitted and the terms here presented are congenial."

The Honorable Moses K. Armstrong believed that his schedule permitted. As for the terms, they were neither insulting nor very important. Armstrong had not left public office a poor man, having benefited most significantly from his involvement in the creation of the Dakota Southern Railroad, with its terminus in Yankton. Leaning back against the wood siding of the post office, Armstrong reread Leslie's letter. That the magazine was primarily interested in a story on the Indians of Dakota and the situation in the Black Hills was not surprising. Armstrong chuckled to himself at the list of his attributes that qualified him to write upon such a topic, noting that Mr. Leslie had failed to add that no white men in their right minds (and this naturally excluded prospectors and politicians) were riding into the Black Hills these days. Regarding the second suggested topic, the rebirth of the Northern Pacific, Armstrong could thank a serendipitous meeting with young Percy Bingham in St. Paul for an interesting angle. Perhaps he would be the first to report at length on the Northern Pacific's new 'demonstration' farms of the Red River valley.

But, no, Armstrong reasoned with himself, he should not go. Danger aside, the timing was all wrong. He could not leave Maude and the girls so soon after returning home, and for such an extended trip at that. A decision made, Moses stood, stretched his back, and stepped into the street. By the time he arrived at the doorstep of his twice-expanded home, he had decided it would be best not even to mention the offer to his wife, for she would recognize immediately that his first inclination had been to accept. Kicking the wall beside the door to knock the mud off his boots, Armstrong stepped inside his warm and comfortable home and greeted his wife with the second letter that had arrived by coach the previous evening.

"It's from your mother."

"I do hope she is well," Maude said, looking at the envelope.

"I expect you shall find the answer within." Moses Armstrong bent to pull off his boots, dropping them onto the newspaper spread beside the door. With his slippers on, he followed his wife to the kitchen to warm his hands by the stove. Several loaves of bread cooled on the table next to the stove and the kitchen was filled with the yeasty pungency of the day's baking. Through a vent in the ceiling he could hear his daughters' laughter from their bedroom above. What was a story or two in *Frank Leslie's* compared to this, Armstrong thought?

"Oh, Moses, such good news! Mother has been made a good offer for the boarding house and is 'well inclined to accept,' she says. She could be here in as little as three weeks. Oh, this is relief indeed. I had begun to worry about her working so hard still, and now we have the room."

Armstrong heard the chair scrape behind him and knew that Maude had sat down at the kitchen table to read the letter again.

"I am so fortunate," she said a moment later. "So many of the settlers around here have left their friends and families behind, never to see them again, whether they be in Norway or Michigan. It's different for you men. You mean to leave home from the minute you put on long trousers and it seems as if you never look back. But a woman suffers so without…oh, Moses," Maude put her hand toward him as he turned from the stove, "I do not complain about my own situation. My life is so much easier than those of whom I speak."

Careful not to rearrange his expression, which had been most generously misread, Armstrong brought Maude's hand to his lips, turning it over to kiss the palm again before sitting as well. "I am happy for this news, my dear. I am simply concerned about the timing. You see," he reached into his pocket again, "I received some good news myself in today's mail."

Less than two weeks later, Moses Armstrong stepped into the stage coach bound for Fort Sully, three hundred miles to the northwest along the Missouri. Armstrong knew the commander of the fort, Major Henry Lazelle, from the days a decade past when Lazelle had been a captain under General Henry Sibley's command, and Armstrong had spent the summer traveling as the recording secretary with the '66 Indian Commission. He hoped to receive Lazelle's permission to accompany troops patrolling west to the Black Hills, where, in the safe company of the U.S. Army, he would visit a few mining sites, interview a few prospectors, pick his way through the muddy lanes of a few settlements, and then get himself and his scalp, simultaneously, back to Fort Sully as quickly as possible.

Moses Armstrong had chosen the trip by stage coach over the more comfortable passage by steamboat in the hopes of shaving a couple days off his journey. Although the spring melt lessened the likelihood of delays by sandbars and snags, it had also strengthened the Missouri's current, lengthening all river travel north. With no females on board, the pace of the coach had indeed been rapid, making two, sometimes three, relay stations in a day before stopping for a supper of the victuals provided there and a night under the stars. These suppers were crude, at best, with the surprising exception of an unexpected repast of freshly baked bread, tender rabbit stew, custard and pie at old Fort Thompson, a home station on what was now the Crow Creek Indian Agency. The station agent and cook, a diminutive and taciturn bachelor called Little Carl, received no complaints when he charged the travelers a dollar apiece, an exorbitant price for a meal at a stage coach station.

Arriving at Fort Sully a week after leaving Yankton, Armstrong went directly to Major Lazelle's house, which stood separate from the officers' quarters, directly across the parade grounds from a line of barracks. A porch hung over the wide steps that led to two front doors. The door to which he was shown opened directly into the major's office. The other, Armstrong supposed, would take the visitor into the living quarters of the major's family. The commanding officer of Fort Sully who looked up from the many-creased map he was studying had not aged well in the ten years since the men had last met. His words, though soft, were shaded in gloom. His smile of recognition was slight, as if it caused him some pain.

"Moses Armstrong. This is a surprise, sir. Come in."

"I apologize for the intrusion, Major," Armstrong said, shaking the hand the major offered. "I intended to send a telegram from Fort Randall but the man there told me that the line was down. I just arrived by coach, and being informed of your presence at home, I took the opportunity of calling on you immediately."

"This is no intrusion," Major Lazelle gestured toward the chair opposite his desk. "The line worked for a grand total of eleven days in April. I've sent out repair crews four times already this year."

"Indians?"

"Sometimes. For the most part, however, we have simple graft and greed to blame. The line was put up by contract, which specified cedar poles. What we got were cottonwood and ash. Where they aren't blown down by winds, or burned in prairie fires, they are simply rotting away. How long will you be laying over before moving on to," the major spread his hands as if in benediction, allowing Armstrong to finish the sentence with his destination.

Remembering Lazelle as an impatient man, Moses Armstrong explained the purpose of his trip quickly, ending with his request to accompany the next contingent of Fort Sully troops sent out to patrol the Black Hills. Despite his own reputation for plain talk and humor that contained a good deal of self-deprecation, Armstrong was in the habit of getting his way, so when Major Lazelle replied to Armstrong's request with a simple, "That won't be possible," Armstrong was surprised.

"I would not inconvenience your men, Major. I may be a bit longer in the tooth than when we last met, but I assure you that I can still sit my horse and camp—"

"It is not possible," Lazelle interrupted, "because my orders are to suspend patrols into the Hills." The major lifted a hand to forestall Armstrong's next question. "We'll talk this evening." Rising, he stepped to a side door to call out, "Mary." Expecting to now meet Lazelle's wife, Armstrong was surprised when an Indian woman in a gingham housedress arrived.

"Put this gentleman in Edward's room. He'll want a bath." To Armstrong, Lazelle said, "Give the woman what laundry you have. Dress parade is at eighteen hundred hours. You are welcome as my guest."

The interview was clearly over, and Armstrong was left to make yet one more stab at courtesy in the midst of Lazelle's unexpected brusqueness. "I appreciate your generosity, Major. I hope I do not inconvenience your family."

"My wife, Julia, died in childbirth six years ago. The baby, a boy, died the same day. My son, Edward, died of blood poisoning a year ago August. Emily, our daughter, lives with her mother's sister in New Hampshire. You inconvenience no one. Eighteen hundred hours." And with that, Moses Armstrong found himself on the other side of the closed door.

Supper that evening was a modest affair of venison and beets, the former fresh, the latter having suffered through the winter in a root cellar. They were served the meal by the Indian woman.

"Sioux?" Armstrong asked after she left the dining room, having poured each man a cup of coffee.

Major Lazelle nodded. "Sicangu, to be more precise. Brule," he added to clarify, "I was using the Lakota word."

"Well," Armstrong said after a moment's hesitation, "she cooks like a white woman. How did she come to be yours?"

"How did she come to work here?" the major corrected. "She's one of the Reverend Riggs' charges. He and his brother and their wives and one other woman, a teacher, have a Mission north of here about fifteen miles."

"Ah, the 'peace policy' at work. Is the reverend a rich man yet?"

"You have grown cynical since last we met. Is it the effect of Washington?" Major Lazelle raised his hand to indicate that his question required no response. "A story that is true nine times may be absolutely false the tenth," he said. "The Mission in Oahe appears to have been established for the sake of the Indians, and not for that of the missionaries. The reverend is a thoughtful, educated man. I have benefited from his occasional conversation, although I fear that I try the good man's patience. Tell me, have you read Mr. Darwin's *On the Origin of Species*?"

Armstrong was surprised by the turn of the conversation. "I have not."

"It was the cause for much discussion during my days at West Point, and a topic to which Reverend Riggs and I have turned many times. The argument has to do with whether Darwin was saying that species, including us humans, evolved by accident or by plan. On this question the Reverend and I agree, for all of creation is by necessity in the hands of God, and if every species changes and adapts it is because God intends it to do so. Evolution, that fancy word, means nothing more than the path each of us walks with God at our shoulders. Don't you agree?"

Armstrong had just then been in the process of stifling a yawn, and could do no more than grunt his affirmative. He would have liked very much to corner up his host's conversation and get it headed back to the sort of everyday reality that mattered, but until the conversation offered him a handle of some sort, he'd just have to accompany the major while he gathered wool.

"It is only logical, then," Lazelle continued, reaching behind him to open a cupboard from which he retrieved a bottle of whisky, "that the white man, created in God's image, has been placed on this earth to act as the agent of God. God stands at our shoulders directing us in the ways in which to direct the lesser species. That is to say, to help them to evolve."

Lazelle held the bottle toward Moses Armstrong. "A drop of whiskey for your coffee?" When Armstrong shook his head, Lazelle tipped the bottle toward his own cup and continued, "I take this to have been the purpose of the recent war, for example. It was the responsibility of the Union to bring the South forward, to help it to evolve into a civilization that did not rely upon slavery for commerce, and secondarily, to bring the Negro out of bondage so his evolution, stymied by slavery, could continue."

Well, here at last was a lever Armstrong could grip. "Do you mean to suggest, Major, that the darky will some day be the white man's equal? That he has been 'stymied'," Armstrong shot his eyebrows, "by slavery only?"

"There are those who believe that once upon a time all humans had the same origin, and that the children of Adam and Eve, dispersed to all corners of the earth, have been in decline ever since. But that some of the descendents, in particular those relegated to the hotter climes, have degenerated at a far greater rate. This is the position my friend, Reverend Riggs takes. Personally, I hold with the contrary view, that the races were each created separately, given different attributes from the start, with the white man created the superior of the others. But with superiority comes responsibility. It is the God-given duty of the white man to help the lesser races to achieve all that is possible for them."

"And when they 'achieve all that is possible', do you expect these civilized red men to take their place next to the white man?"

"There's next to and there's next to," Lazelle said with a small shrug. "We expect the Swede to live next to the Norwegian, the Irishman next to the Scot, the Finn next to the Dane, and the Yankee next to them all. But there remain distinctions. I mean simply to suggest that if the good Indians are to be civilized at all, it is up to us to recognize those rare moments of commonality, for they may be the rough clay out of which we will form new men."

"Frankly, Major," Armstrong was now shaking his head, "that is strange talk for an Army man. In fact, it is more likely to be the sort of thing a fellow hears in Washington. I'd always understood it to be the luxury of easterners whose only congress with Indians comes from the newspapers and monthlies. It's the damnedest thing. Their most consistent hatred is not for the Indian agent who steals the Indians' money, nor for their elected officials who line their pockets with it. It is not for the Indians who murder the brave settlers who have made their way west to try to make a decent living on the land *that the government has encouraged them to take up.*" Armstrong heard his own voice rise in pitch, and with a breath brought it back down. "No, it is those settlers themselves that the easterner despises. It is the courageous men and women who will break their backs and their hearts in the desperate hope that out of the suffering of their own lives will come a better hope for their children, who will go before telegraph, before train, before roads, before all the comforts and safety of civilization, these are the men and women so easily forgotten by the easterner whose tears and benevolence are all for 'Lo, the poor Indian!'"

"Well, here sir, we come to an agreement," Lazelle said. "The easterner is a problem, but that is where the money is, and we in the west need that money."

For a moment the men were silent. Moses Armstrong swirled a bit of cold coffee around in his cup before taking a last swallow. Major Lazelle added more whiskey to his own cup. When Moses Armstrong spoke, it was with quiet seriousness.

"So the U. S. Army is marching into Montana to help Sitting Bull and his followers 'achieve all that is possible', to borrow your phrase again?"

The look of intense scrutiny that Major Lazelle shot toward Moses Armstrong would have made a less seasoned man squirm.

"What is it that you know, Moses?"

The return to first-name familiarity at last allowed Armstrong to relax. "I received a letter from a friend in Washington just before leaving Yankton. I know that a band of Teton Sioux under Sitting Bull has been ordered to return to an agency, and has refused, and remains somewhere along the Powder River. This," Armstrong searched for the safest word, "this situation, having become the War Department's to resolve, I thought perhaps—"

"You thought perhaps that the resumption of an Indian War following a decade of 'peace policy' is a bigger story than prospectors panning for gold in the Black Hills. Although it is, as you well know, the same story." The major's pained smile returned. "Are you privy to more specific information? To the plan devised by the fearless General Phil Sheridan, for it is little Phil, as you must know, who has developed the military strategy that is even now underway? Can you tell me what he has in mind for these capricious Sioux under Sitting Bull?"

"Not exactly, but—"

"But you were hoping to discover more while visiting your old friend, Henry Lazelle, did you?"

"I presented my plans to you quite plainly upon arrival, Henry. And you, quite as plainly, explained to me why a trip with your troops to the Black Hills would be impossible. An old politician is perhaps not so unlike a military man. When we see the way before us blocked, we don't give up and go home. We look for another route. I have had the afternoon to form another plan, but this one, too, requires your blessing." Armstrong watched the major's face as he spoke, waiting for some indication of encouragement. But this was a changed man, Armstrong had come to understand, and whether that was the result of the loss of his family, loneliness, or a career that seemed to have come to a halt on an outpost in Dakota Territory, he did not know.

"I assume that all action in the Black Hills has been suspended," Armstrong pushed on, "because your troops are to take part in whatever General Sheridan's plan is. In short, I would like to attach myself to one of your units bound for the Powder River. The story that I write is to come from the perspective of one who was there, wherever that 'there' may be. I am applying to you, as an old friend, for permission, to ride along."

Lazelle's expression had gone from suspicion to wonder to relief as Armstrong spoke.

"You will not ride with me, Moses. The 1st Infantry of Fort Sully is not to take part in the expedition, but rather to remain on alert, as will every regiment in every fort along the Missouri…in Montana, Wyoming, and Dakota. And even if I were to lead a company into war, you would not ride along. I have it from General Terry that Sheridan has made it clear that there are to be no journalists in attendance."

"General Terry is at Fort Abraham Lincoln," Armstrong said. "Bismarck."

This time his host's laugh carried its first edge of humor. "You need not work so hard, my friend." Lazelle tipped the whiskey into his cup again, swallowed, and stood. "I will tell you all. You will have names and maps and even the few dates that I know. It will be a pleasure to talk shop with an old campaigner."

"I was never in the army, Henry," Armstrong reminded him.

"Oh, you've been everywhere," Lazelle responded cryptically at the door. "You're Moses K. Armstrong." Lazelle pointed to the sitting room next door. "Wait in there."

When Major Lazelle returned he was carrying a large, creased map, which he soon revealed to contain Nebraska, Dakota, Idaho, Montana, and Wyoming. Handing the empty vase at the center of the low table between them to Armstrong, Lazelle anchored the edges of the map with two lamps from the pianoforte in the corner of the room, and was about to speak when he noticed that his guest was still holding the vase.

"Julia and Emily picked wildflowers every single day it was possible to be out of doors, from spring to fall. They were necessarily accompanied by two or three of my men. Posey detail, they called it. The most coveted detail on the post. Had a private who wanted to keep right on picking those flowers after Julia died. No need." Lazelle took the vase from Armstrong and set it next to the whiskey bottle. "Reason not the need," he said to the bottle as he tipped it once again toward his cup.

"Sheridan's strategy requires no particular innovation, Moses," Lazelle began. "This is a simple snare, a closing noose, at best. Judging from the censuses of the local Indian agencies, there may be as many as 1500 Sioux roaming about unaccounted for. Far fewer than that will be with or near Sitting Bull. How many of those are actually braves capable of fighting? Who knows? But fewer still, to be sure. The forces of Generals Crook, Gibbon, and Terry will possibly triple that number. They will have Napoleon canons, Gatlings, a Rodman or two."

With his forefinger the major traced three paths for Armstrong. The first was that of General Crook out of Fort Fetterman in Wyoming, who was to move north. The second was that of General Gibbon, who was to pick up troops from three separate forts in western Montana and move east. Gibbon's troops had the greatest distance to travel, and were likely to have already been on the march for more than a month. Gibbon was to follow the Yellowstone River until he met up with General Terry, who was moving west from Fort Lincoln. That would put Gibbon and Terry north of the hostile Sioux. To the south General Crook would be waiting. Then it was "surround and squeeze," Lazelle said, nothing very elegant about it at all.

"Will Fort Lincoln's Seventh Cavalry be accompanying General Terry?" Armstrong asked after a minute.

"Custer? What is your interest in him?"

"No interest in the man, in particular," Armstrong replied quickly, responding to the disgust in Major Lazelle's voice.

"Had it not been for the Rebellion he would never have been allowed to graduate from West Point."

"You were classmates?" Armstrong asked.

"No, I was a year ahead," Lazelle said, stepping back to his chair and to the whiskey bottle, and for the first time Armstrong noted that his host's step was unsteady. "Scores of intelligent young men, a few brilliant. And all that energy. Arguments over strategies, and debates over politics that would range through the centuries. I had a friend there, Moses, name of Carruthers. Nehemiah Andrews Carruthers, the third, no less. Mention a famous battle, A. D. or B. C., and he'd look up at you like your forehead was a map, and bang, he was off. It wasn't just memory. It was like the rest of us were looking at a picture when he was looking from inside the picture. The day he left West Point we shook hands, not a word to say. One more year and he would have graduated. He was killed at Wilson's Creek, his tailored gray uniform still clean but for the blood that dripped from his head. Nehemiah Andrews Carruthers, the third. No fourth."

After a moment Lazelle looked up from his cup, and blinked as if surprised to see Armstrong still there. "What was it we were talking about?"

"General Custer."

"Brevet General," Lazelle muttered, almost under his breath. With a gesture toward the door, Major Lazelle peremptorily dismissed his guest with a wave. "Good night, Moses. Sleep tight."

Moses Armstrong came awake to a crash that he could not place in his dream. The second crash, louder, had him out of bed and climbing into his trousers. Barefoot, his suspenders dangling, Armstrong hurried down the stairs, and followed a loud thump into the parlor. Pieces of the vase that he had handled earlier in the evening were lying about the hearth, mixed with the broken glass of the whiskey bottle. Major Lazelle had not heard Armstrong's steps. Turning too quickly from where he leaned against the wall next to the hearth when Armstrong spoke his name, the major lost his balance and once again fell back against the wall. Standing there for a moment, his knees deeply bent, as if this were the only way to remain upright, Lazelle swayed before charging toward Armstrong.

In an act of instinctive generosity, Armstrong did not move, but stood to be caught about the collar by his host.

"You want a story? You need a story? I'm your man, Moses Armstrong. No kiddies to hear stories, but lots of stories to tell. We all need stories. War stories the best. Sit down and let papa give you something for your magazines."

Armstrong let Lazelle shove him toward the chair he had occupied earlier, wondering at the man's capacity for enunciation considering his state of absolute drunkenness. Released, Armstrong waited as Lazelle tottered above him for a moment, then took the step back that immedi-

ately became a stumbling backwards fall. Lazelle's arm caught the side
table and sent it flying, but that slowed his momentum enough to allow
him to drop into his chair.

"Didn't know the word 'Sicangu'. Couldn't find your Mdewkanon-
won from your Yanktonai, and you think it doesn't matter. Think you're
doing damn fine when you can distinguish Crow from Cheyenne, but
mostly it's just Indians. Lazy, stupid, dangerous."

It took Armstrong a moment to suspect that the major's modifiers
were directed toward him and were not in reference to Indians. Armstrong made a slow shift in his chair, in preparation to rising.

"Sit right where you are, private," Lazelle said. "Instruction is about
to begin."

For the next few minutes, Lazelle actually straightened his shoulders
and sat up as he spoke, and Armstrong could imagine who he would
have been, had his life led him back to the classroom, instructing his
beloved West Point cadets. Much of what Lazelle had to say, Armstrong
already knew, or had once known, but hadn't found very important.
The word, 'Sioux', Lazelle began, didn't refer to one homogenous group
of Indians, but covered at least three separate groups that really didn't
have all that much to do with each other, except that their language was
similar. The Santee from Minnesota, for example, the Sisseton and the
Wahpeton, were Dakota Sioux. The Yanktonai and Yankton from Armstrong's area of Dakota were Nakota Sioux. The plains Sioux, Teton
Sioux, some of which Generals Crook, Gibbon, and Terry were on their
way to round up, if the Indians were lucky, were Lakota Sioux. "That's
the language. See?"

Lifting his left hand, and then studying it front and back, as if deciding which side would work better for enumeration, Lazelle continued.
"Take the Lakota," he grabbed his little finger. "You got the Hunkpapa. That's Sitting Bull's crew, but only some of them, because there are
bands within tribes. And Oglala. Red Cloud, Crazy Horse. And Sicangu,
that's Brule. And Itazipcho, that's Sans Arcs. And Oohenonpa, that's
Two Kettle. And—" "How many did I get?" he asked, one hand pulling
back the thumb of the other. "Ought to be seven. Never mind. Take
my word for it. Seven tribes of Lakota. Or Teton. Now where you find
Lakota, you're likely to find Cheyenne, too. But not Crow, which is the
Absanokee, or maybe Absaroka, or more likely, Up-sah-ro-ka. That's

the enemy. Of the Lakota, that is, even though the similarity in their languages suggests that they share a common ancestry." Lazelle sat back and made a noise, which Armstrong figured could either have been a hiccup or a commentary on his next point. "White men love the Crow. Think they're pretty. Beaux hommes. Love them to death."

Lazelle reached beside him for the whiskey bottle, but found neither bottle nor table. He looked about in some confusion before standing and staggering into the next room while repeating: "Hunkpapa, Itazipcho, Oglala, Sicangu, Itazipcho ... missing–"

Armstrong knew better than to try to talk with the man, but here was the commanding officer of a settlement fort along the Missouri talking like some Indian lover from the east who knew nothing about 'Lo, the poor Indian!' beyond queer and exotic names. Softly he said, "What does it matter?" when Lazelle returned with another bottle.

"What does it matter? To the average fellow, like you," Lazelle lifted the corner of a lip, "I guess it doesn't matter at all. Not. At. All. To the warrior, it should matter a great deal. Has the Honorable Moses K. Armstrong ever killed a man?"

Armstrong sat forward in his chair at the unexpectedness of the question, deciding then and there that it was time to leave the room, if not the house. But Lazelle in his drunkenness seemed to anticipate Armstrong's intentions. "Just sit right there, my friend. I didn't think so. So much easier to wield a pen and to say who ought to be killed and who ought to do the killing. Well, I couldn't even tell you how many men I have killed. Not as many as I shot at, to be sure. I was at Wilson's Creek myself. Killed as many as I could get in my sights, and sometimes I just closed my eyes and pulled the trigger knowing that with that many men nearby in gray, surely the ball would strike someone. Who knows? Maybe I killed Nehemiah Andrews Carruthers, the third. For his sake, I like to think I did. Shakespearean, rather. I'd like to think that I knew the name of at least one man that I killed. You shake your head–"

(Armstrong was quite sure he had not.)

"–but you know I'm right. Who will we say we are killing now? Maybe the Sioux. More likely the Indian. But even that is too dangerous, so we call them savages, demons, red devils. And the most cowardly of all will call the enemy simply 'evil'. That's when the man leaves the battle field and the murderer takes over. No, I say give them a name and make it impossible to lie to yourself about what you are doing. Give them a name and then kill them. Acknowledge your own role in adding to the decay and carrion in the world. And then kill, kill, kill, kill, kill, kill. And then hope, in the moment before your own scalp is lifted and held aloft, that you will have breath enough to whisper your own name to your killer."

Armstrong swallowed. His mouth was dry. "Call them what you like, Henry. Give every damn one a name. That doesn't make them white. And if you're going to tell stories, then how about whole families murdered. Women and children mutilated, disemboweled, dragged across the plains until their arms and legs pull off."

Armstrong's voice appeared to startle Lazelle. The major pulled himself up in his chair before answering. "Yes, of course. But they are the savages, remember. We are the army of the United States of America. We are supposed to be different. Now, Moses," Lazelle held up his hand to stop whatever else his guest might say. "I see that I have upset you, and I find, as well, that I can no longer tolerate your company. Please do not be offended. There is not a human being who walks the earth in whose presence I care to be, least of all mine, but there is little I can do about that as long as my Emily remains, albeit far away. Here, sit here, and act as my secretary for a moment before you retire to your dreams. My hand appears to be a bit unsteady this evening."

And so, while Lazelle dictated, Moses Armstrong wrote out an order to the company's second in command, turning over the command of the fort to him until Major Lazelle returned. When the message was completed, Lazelle swayed to his feet, signed the order with the deliberation of a drunk with one last task to accomplish, shook Armstrong's hand, and reached for the whiskey bottle. Lazelle was to the door when he said, without quite turning, "Enjoy your trip to Fort Lincoln and be damned, Moses. You'd be better off going home."

As it turned out, Lazelle had been right. It hadn't mattered that the stage coach continuing north had made good time, the weather dry, the road clear and no bumpier than it had a right to be. They were still at the station inn across the river from Fort Rice, twenty-five miles from Bismarck and Fort Lincoln, when word arrived that General Terry had marched a thousand men, a battery of Gatling guns, Ree and Crow scouts, and a beef herd out of the fort almost a week earlier on May 17. Armstrong's mood hadn't been improved by his company on the last leg of the trip. He'd kept his hand on his wallet, packed in as he was with five other passengers, including a professional gambler (who was good enough to stick his fashionable cane in the top of his boot) and two painted females. Something about meeting Alexander McKenzie within fifteen minutes of registering at the Merchant's Hotel in Bismarck made him want to reach inside his jacket to check on his wallet again.

Armstrong had just finished tightening the ropes under the cornhusk mattress of his bed when a knock on his door brought him face to face with the big man, his wide face of a prize bull made unnaturally handsome by sea-blue eyes and long sandy lashes. Armstrong knew from his friend Bud Taylor of the *Herald* that McKenzie had been at the territorial assembly in Yankton this past winter, not as a delegate but as one of the many "interested parties" who could be found in the saloons and hallways while the legislature was in session. It was rumored that he was unofficially associated with the Northern Pacific Railroad, but Taylor thought it more likely that he simply represented the saloon faction in Bismarck. Someone to keep an eye on, though, Armstrong's friend had added. Not so long ago there was little need to pay much attention to anyone or anything in north Dakota, but the Northern Pacific Railroad had changed all that.

"Hope you don't mind the intrusion, Mr. Armstrong," McKenzie said. "But it ain't every day that the Dakota delegate to the United States Congress comes to Bismarck." McKenzie held his hand toward Armstrong as he added, "Hearing you was here, I took the liberty, as sheriff, to make sure you got a good welcome."

In the twenty years since he was McKenzie's age, Armstrong had slept on frozen ground, forded icy streams, guided a loaded stage coach through a blizzard by walking next to the lead horse, lived in the same clothes for thirty days while running a survey line through Indian country, stood in front of more than one man waving a gun at him in the territorial assembly, and addressed the most distinguished men in the United States in the halls of Congress, all without a whine or a stutter. He was unlikely to give this husky brute the satisfaction of a wince. Still, he was relieved when McKenzie released his grip.

Armstrong held his smile steady as he replied, "Former delegate. And it's my pleasure, sheriff."

"Once you get yourself settled in, get a bath and a shave, maybe you'll feel like joining me for supper. Chops at the Capitol House are better than here. If there's anything I can help you with during your stay, you just let me know."

This, Moses Armstrong understood, was the sheriff's invitation for Armstrong to explain the purpose of his visit. But having failed to make the trip he had planned to the Black Hills, and then having missed the opportunity to accompany the Ft. Lincoln troops west (for despite Sheridan's instructions that there were to be no reporters allowed, Armstrong had been counting on General Custer's well-known love of publicity), his purpose was no longer clear.

"You can tell me when the next train for Fargo leaves," he said.

Chapter XVI

Scooped

In July of 1876, men of optimism and industry, such as James B. Power and John Bingham, and men with deep pockets, such as Septimus Slade, were not only weathering the uncertain times following the Panic of '73, but had found within the crisis opportunities for profit. For others, the Panic continued to play itself out in an endless variety of dreams lost and hopes dashed. The public had read in the newspapers about the spectacular suicides of a few capitalists who chose death over the dishonor of accompanying their families into financial embarrassment. Less dramatic stories were read in the faces in the streets. Six thousand businesses went bankrupt in 1874. More in 1875. More still in 1876. Jobs were lost. Savings disappeared. For the citizens in the hamlets of the new Northwest, however, there was work for those who would and hope for those who could. There, the dream was too new to have gone too badly wrong.

Celebration of the one-hundredth birthday of the nation in Bismarck may have been a small thing in comparison to the Centennial Exhibition in Philadelphia, but the participants were no less enthusiastic. All morning wagons pulled into town under a cloud-dappled blue sky, like so many boats that first appear upon an empty horizon and then gather to sail into port. The general mercantile and hardware store and blacksmith shop did a brisk business, for the next trip into town could be weeks away for most, months for some. With the shopping done and the wagons loaded, the women began to set out the noon meals, pulling gingham cloths off pails and unwrapping parcels. Here and there a farmer slept in the shade of a wagon. A judging committee strolled through the tents that lined the street, examining garden vegetables, homemade articles, and livestock. A young deputy, inordinately conscious of the star upon his chest, kept up a nervous patrol from saloon to saloon, surprised to find himself in charge of maintaining the peace on this busy day. Sheriff McKenzie had left town before daybreak in the company of one of the soldiers who had remained behind at Fort Lincoln. He hadn't said where he was going, but then, he never did.

Then, like the first cool breeze that caresses the skin before the rain cloud can be seen on the horizon, felt more as difference than significance, anticipation begins to stir the crowd. Children, sensing their parents' shift in attention and hoping the festivities are, finally, about to begin, look toward the hay wagon decorated with elm and ash branches positioned at the upper end of Main Street. The adults cast glances in the opposite direction. Rumor that the cross-river ferry has docked, bringing the officers' wives and their children from Fort Lincoln to join the celebration, drifts through the crowd.

But it is Alexander McKenzie alone who strides into view. Approaching the Merchant's Hotel he catches the eye of his deputy standing at attention there. A tilt of McKenzie's head toward the *Tribune* office pulls the young man across the street in his wake. They discover the newspaper's editor, Colonel Clement Lounsberry, seated at his desk in conversation with Moses K. Armstrong, who is newly returned to Bismarck after a month's visit to the Red River valley to document the first season of planting at one of the N.P.'s new demonstration farms. "Bonanza farms," he has called them in his piece for Mr. Leslie's magazine.

"General Terry's troops are not the only army on the move in Dakota Territory," Armstrong is saying when he hears the steps approaching Lounsberry's office. "To watch the laborers seeding the fields is to watch a battalion sweeping along in grand–" Armstrong is silenced, mid-sentence, by McKenzie's expression as he steps into the office without a knock.

Together the men agree that McKenzie's information is not to leave the room. Lounsberry suggests that they search out Charley Blackhorse, the Ree half-breed, to see what he knows, but McKenzie stops his man, who has turned to go. He will not find Blackhorse, nor any other Arikara in town, or at the Fort, or anywhere near, for that matter. The few Indians who had remained behind in May with the families of the Ree scouts had refused to share the news (or how they had come about it) that had them packing up their ponies this morning, but the wailing of the women throughout the night left little doubt as to the tone, if not the content, of what they knew.

"Wait," McKenzie says to the other men. "We don't know nothing. So we don't do or say nothing."

Moses Armstrong is the first man to leave the office. He crosses through the alley to the railroad tracks and approaches the N.P. depot and the telegraph office there. Rounding the corner he sees Alexander McKenzie already speaking to the operator.

Armstrong covers his surprise, and asks, "Any news?"

"Ain't a telegraph office between Bismarck and Bozeman," McKenzie replies.

"I was about to wire my wife with the news that her errant husband is on his way home at long last."

The look McKenzie gives Armstrong is cold, appraising. "We got to keep the line open," he says. "Just in case." Then he turns to the operator. "No messages go out 'til I tell you different, Seth. Someone gives you trouble, you send him to me. You hear anything important, you come get me. You can't find me, you get the Colonel. Understand?" McKenzie turns to leave, his nod toward Moses Armstrong an afterthought.

Now the afternoon moves slowly. Moses Armstrong finds a seat on a barrel on the shaded side of the street with a view of the telegraph office. More of the men, he notices, have disappeared into the saloons. Others carry jars of their own homebrew. A fight breaks out behind the livery and several young boys clamber onto the low lean-to roof to watch. They are rewarded with the sight of Alexander McKenzie stepping into the fray to knock down the larger man and then, to the surprise of the other, turning to knock him down as well.

"Go home or go to jail," McKenzie says. "Your choice." Without waiting for an answer he turns away. "Get down before you fall down," he says to the boys as he passes without looking up.

The cotton ball clouds stretch, merge, evaporate as the sun grows hotter. Tanned faces of the country people grow redder. Babies cry and then sleep. Colonel Lounsberry's wife asks him, again, if he is well before he steps onto the hay wagon to pass out certificates for first prize winners, for cakes and quilts and shawls, for best heifer and best sow. A small pig, washed and brushed and noosed with a pink ribbon, breaks away from him as he is about to turn it over to the winner of the drawing and is chased through the gathered crowd by a gang of gleeful children. Lounsberry opens the pages of the short, patriotic speech he has prepared for the occasion. He wishes there were a breeze. He wishes it were later in the day. In the distance he sees Moses Armstrong's head nod along with his words, and Lounsberry wonders if he is agreeing, or fighting sleep. The speech over, a man with a fiddle and another with a harmonica climb onto the hay wagon.

The fiddler makes one run of his bow across the strings when someone at the river end of Main Street comes running into sight, his yell preceding him. "Steamboat coming! Steamboat coming!" The cry is carried through the crowd, and then comes the added news: "It's the *Far West!*" A cheer goes up, and the crowd moves away from the hay wagon as a unit and flows down the hill toward the landing. The excited chatter drains into silence as the steamboat draws near, its lower deck enclosed in canvas.

The steamboat carries no dead. They had been hastily buried in the Little Bighorn valley. These were the wounded survivors of Major Reno's command, they who had been ordered by General Custer to cross the Little Bighorn and attack the Indian village that Custer's scouts had located, a village that Reno's soldiers would insist extended well beyond what could be seen by the naked eye. Another three companies, under the command of Captain Benteen, had been ordered to search the badlands to the west. One company was to stay behind with the pack train. General Custer had taken his remaining five companies to the north of the Indian camp, where, because of the size and configuration of the valley and the bluffs around the rivers, he would not have been able to see Reno's troops, and so could not have known that the major's attack had quickly become a retreat, first to a stand of timber and then to a bluff nearby. For two days Reno's men remained surrounded. They were saved, those who survived, by the arrival of General Gibbons' forces.

Beyond these facts, the stories of what had transpired seemed to vary with each litter carried off the boat. There were 200 dead. There were 500 dead. There were 2000 Indians. There were 5000 Indians. On one point, however, there was no disagreement. General Custer and the five companies under his immediate command were, to a man, dead. The story may not have made sense—why Custer had commenced the attack without waiting for General Gibbons' forces, as he had been ordered, was unclear—but it was now the editor of the Bismarck *Tribune's* to tell. Slowed by a hip ruined in the Battle of Spotsylvania, Colonel Lounsberry began to compose his words as he limp-hopped toward the telegraph office. He would not repeat, but he could not forget, his own last words to Mark Kellogg, the young correspondent who had ridden out with Custer in Lounsberry's stead, once the editor and old warrior reluctantly admitted that his wife's fragile health made it impossible for him to accept the General's invitation. "This is the opportunity of a lifetime," he had proclaimed to the wide-eyed young man as he ceremoniously handed over his own blood-stained holster. "I envy you, Kellogg."

With first one of Major Reno's junior officers at his elbow, and then, as the night progressed, in the company of other soldiers and scouts who were well enough to tell their stories, Colonel Lounsberry took up a desk at the telegraph office to compose and send the story to the New York *Herald* that would result in a fourteen-column account of the "deeds that shall go sounding down through the ages, hot from the field of battle and dropped from the lips of those who saw the dead."

The first signs of light were just apparent the next morning when Colonel Lounsberry shook hands with an equally exhausted Seth Rogers at the telegraph office, and limped toward his home, his aches giving notice that he would pay for his hours of labor in a chair. From the window of the stage coach in front of the Merchant's Hotel, Moses K. Armstrong watched Lounsberry pass by. The relief he felt at his own "missed opportunity" to travel with General Custer's troops did not lessen the disappointment of being scooped out of the story of a lifetime by another newspaperman. It was time to go home to Yankton.

CHAPTER XVII

In Which the Women Go West

Fatigued by her mother's final illness, death, and funeral, by the business of closing up the Summit house and packing for a two-week visit to Fargo, by the almost twenty-hour trip (eased by an initial night's sleep in a Pullman Palace sleeping coach, but lengthened by delays at both the N.P. Junction and Brainerd), Anna had finally given in to the locomotion's lulling rock. The colorful bird that completes the red and black silk trim of her small chip hat cushions her head against the window, as if there its flight has tragically ended. As Frances watches, Anna's lips part, but immediately, with the rigor of manners that the barely asleep will maintain, she brings them together again. Frances waits, pleasantly aware of the pulse beating in her own throat, of the heat that flushes her skin, and then, as she had hoped, Anna's lips part again, just enough to show the tips of her teeth. A tiny thread of saliva appears as Anna's jaw relaxes. Anna's tongue darts between her lips before they close again.

Even now, as Anna sleeps, rocked into somnolence by the train's rhythm, she maintains the air of serenity that she has cultivated in response to her body's aches. The effort of this composure has painted a patina of maturity upon Anna's face that heightens her beauty beyond the promise of her early conventional prettiness. She is a beautiful woman suffering beautifully, and Frances loves her for it.

Odd, Frances thinks, relaxing into a more leisurely study of Anna's figure, how the absence of the other Binghams—consistently, of John; frequently, of Percy; and now, permanently, of Rhoda—has made it less easy for her to openly observe her beloved. Whereas triangulated conversation allows for the casual study of another, particularly when that other's attention is directed toward a third figure, a *tête-à-tête* calls for strict policing of the gaze, directed toward the eyes always, forbidden to drop to the full lips, the swell of the breasts, the curve of the hip, the ankle. So here, on the final stretch of the long train ride on a warm August day, Frances takes advantage of the opportunity to look. Just look.

And dream. Rhoda Bingham's death had cemented the women's relationship in a way that Frances could not have anticipated. With the exception of his brief return for the funeral, John Bingham had been entirely absent from St. Paul since the previous April, and was not expected to return again until late October after fall plowing was finished. (He had been overseeing his first season of planting on a quarter section of newly broken Dakota sod, a neat black patch where recently there flowered an abundance of wild prairie roses, when he received the telegram brought out from Fargo announcing his wife's death. Bad time for a funeral, he had thought, proving that he had truly taken to farming.)

Percy's new position with the Fargo *Times* made him likewise absent, although he had been able to visit his ailing mother twice before she died. "Do not tell me how you feel about your work, Percy," Frances had said to him in a moment of exasperation one evening during his first return to Summit Avenue when he had lamented that he feared he had sold his soul in his new position. "Say, rather, what you plan to do about it." Good advice, perhaps, but spoken more out of irritation than in the service of heartfelt counsel, for Frances appreciated both Percy's new position, which kept him often away, and his insistence that the position was temporary, which kept her from joining him in Fargo. And so, with father and brother, and now, much beloved mother, gone, Anna had come to rely entirely on the intimacy that Frances encouraged. They were constantly in each other's presence, except for those hours when Anna would lose herself at her piano until the ache in her hip crawled up her spine and forced her to the sofa.

And still, Frances thinks, her focus for the moment on Anna's hands primly folded on her lap, she is not satisfied. She wants more than the love and affection that Anna so willingly offers her friend and sister-in-law. She desires the unknown, and that is hard to come by. This, Frances thinks, silently addressing her sleeping companion, is where we differ. You, Anna, are satisfied to be, and I am desperate to become. But become what? Frances chuckles to herself, thinking, I am become like Percy, that's what, with my head in the clouds and my mind filled with if, if, if. Well, then, if what?

Despite the very visceral pleasure Frances takes in her appraisal of Anna, she is not such an aberration of her sex that she believes in her power to effect great change. She is not a wealthy capitalist, a Frederick Billings whose plan for reorganization, she has heard, has saved a railroad intact. She is not a professional man, a J. B. Power, say, whose vision has set in motion an advertising campaign of such sweep and breadth that it promises to dot a wilderness of wildflowers and grass with farms and hamlets. She is not even an Alexander McKenzie, described to her by Percy as uneducated and illiterate, but of unabashed ambition, for he believes that a man can begin with nothing and build a kingdom out of nowhere. Percy says he has chosen Bismarck.

No, Frances can not build, she can not bank, she can not broadcast, buy or bully. Those are things for a man to do. A woman's desires must be subtler, she knows, and it will cause her naught but pain should her reach exceed her grasp. Still, if she has been taught to want less, it does not follow that she will want less desperately. So Frances waits. The frog, camouflaged in stillness, is as intent upon the fly as the fox, in full pursuit, is upon the hare.

A gradual northward shift in the direction of the tracks turns the window against which Anna's head rests a burnished red as it catches the edge of the lowering sun. The change in the light emphasizes the outline of Anna's lifted jaw and cheek, defining the outline of her neck in silhouette. As the train curves westward again, the sun's glow lends to Anna's skin a fleeting impression of health. Although the shift and correction of the road have been gradual, Anna's eyelids flutter, and Frances looks down to turn the page of the book upon her lap.

"I believe I fell asleep for a moment," Anna announces.

"Did you?" Frances replies, looking up with a smile.

Percy Bingham pulled his watch from his vest pocket. It was approaching seven o'clock already. The train was several hours late, almost unheard of for the Express, although the station agent said it had left Brainerd at just after one, so it should be arriving any minute. The saloon in which Percy stood was itself just one block east of the Headquarters Hotel and Fargo depot. He would hear the train's whistle in plenty of time to finish his drink before strolling to the depot to meet his sister and wife. Percy patted another pocket for the hard liquorice sticks he kept there.

Percy was not looking forward to the visit. He made the trip in reverse to St. Paul whenever given the opportunity, but to see the women of his family here—no, to be seen by them—in this place, would somehow make his own presence too real. A combination of cynicism and disbelief and whiskey (and occasionally, one of the "sisters" in the simple clapboard house nestled in the trees by the river) kept him company. Once a week Percy had supper with his father, who contributed to the fantastic nature of Percy's life by talking as if his son could possibly care about the quantity of dirt that had been disturbed the week before, or which buildings on what John Bingham had taken to calling the "headquarters" were underway. These "headquarters," Percy liked to remind his father, consisted in the main of a small village of tents thus far. The one building completed was a barn for the livestock. The next was to be for machinery.

Percy's one consolation (other than his flask and the five sisters) was the carrot that J. B. Power had offered, the essay on the "Poetry and Philosophy of Indian Summer," for *Harper's New Monthly Magazine*. Donkey that he was, the promise of seeing his words so prominently displayed made the stick that was his daily employment with a prairie newspaper bearable. The ten-page essay's transformation in Percy's mind—from distaste at his participation in what was clearly railroad propaganda; to an impersonal pleasure in his own power of obfuscation as he yoked half-baked science to the musings of Coleridge and Arnold and Thomson; to an investment in the success of the project; to (most disastrously) pride in the final product—in effect recapitulated the signs of a slow reversal of the public's opinion about the new Northwest itself. Percy understood that this one essay had not made all the difference, and that it was the stories (such as Moses Armstrong's contribution in *Frank Leslie's Popular Monthly*) about the new "bonanza farms" that had likely begun to fire the nation's imagination. And yet, Percy returned to his words over and over, imagining how his glorious closing descriptions of the "tinted beauties of the Indian Summer" were at this moment compelling a man, a family, a community to ponder the essay's accompanying map of isothermal lines that appeared to drag warmth (not to mention "fertility, verdure, and health") north through Dakota Territory.

The essay had pleased J. B. Power, and he showed his approval by soliciting Percy's help with his next Land and Immigration Department brochure, which, translated, would ultimately reach Scandinavia and England and Germany. It is work, Percy has learned, that requires the perfect combination of deception and accuracy, exaggeration and understatement. It must inspire the sort of enthusiasm in a man that will cause him to cross an ocean and roll his family half-way across the country in a prairie schooner, or to load up all he owns—animals, tools, children—in a supply car on a westbound train. Percy must tell the potential settler what the settler wants to hear, but it will do no good, Power has explained as he hands over great fistfuls of facts and figures, to attract a man only to have him fail. It is the most delicate of hackwork, and Percy is a natural, and it is breaking his heart.

For Percy Bingham is increasingly conversant with his own limitations, a rare and devastating disability for any man. Great or small, what failed dreams have in common is disappointment too keenly felt. And it is in this disappointment that the disappointed become pathetic. Percy's distress is all the more regrettable in that what he wanted need not have been beyond his grasp. If he lacks the precision and the intellect to be an essayist—he is certainly without the humor or wit of the gentleman from Hannibal who is doing so well these days with his homey and piercing observations of his fellow man—Percy is, nevertheless, as talented as the average newspaperman at the *Pioneer-Press* of St. Paul, or the *Inter-Ocean* of Chicago. Had he dared to refuse to study law, when law held no interest for him and he no talent for it, had he tried to make his way, alone, in one of the eastern cities he dreams about, instead of lazily stumbling back to St. Paul, had there been some accident or initiative along the way to set him on a clearer course, he would not, perhaps, have given in to a paralyzing cynicism. Perhaps he would not now find himself guided by several personalities several degrees stronger than his. He would have been otherwise, and he would have been otherwhere, and not about to call for yet another whiskey when he hears the whistle of the Northern Pacific as it crosses the bridge over the Red River.

Anna, Percy could see, was clearly exhausted by the trip, and would have preferred to lie down in her room before supper, but the dining room at the Headquarters Hotel closed too early to allow for such civility. As for Frances, her comeliness had always been about a certain force of personality and those singular eyes of streaked steel. She had borne the journey well. Both women were pleasantly surprised by the fineness of the hotel and the table set before them, and Frances cheerfully announced her excitement about the coming day and the opportunity it would bring for seeing more of this new land.

"There is precious little to see," Percy warned, "in a hamlet of five hundred persons."

"There is the farm, the 'bonanza farm'," Frances widened her eyes for a moment, "as the papers are calling it."

"You may be a bit disappointed, my dear. There is actually no farm just yet, never mind the bonanza. There is farming, in the sense that there are men and beasts laboring in fields, but there is very little of civilization, to use the term loosely, that one might expect."

"I'm sure father plans several fine buildings for the future," Anna said.

"Just pray that his plans do not include one for you."

Anna and Frances looked up from their plates in unison at this comment. Frances spoke first. "Why would he build a house for Anna? Her home...his home is in St. Paul. Surely he would not consider living out here during the winter? What would be the point?"

"I did not say he has such a plan. He has not mentioned such a thing in my presence, anyway. But I have noticed a, shall we say, deepening of affection for his new vocation."

Frances reached across the table to give Anna's hand a reassuring pat before changing the subject. "There is a closeness to the air here. Is that typical, Percy?"

"The humidity is a recent development. The heat is not. Generally, the incessant Dakota wind lessens this 'closeness' to which you refer, my dear, while coating everything in its path with silt and dirt lifted from the nearest plowed field. For the past week, however, the temperatures have steadily risen and the wind has disappeared and the result is this muggy, mosquito-infested, pestilential, God-forsaken–" Percy's voice trailed off, until recollecting himself he began again. "Each night the clouds gather, the skies darken, and I prepare myself for a thunderstorm, the drama of which, I must say, exceeds anything I have before seen. Standing in a doorway watching a storm approach has been quite my favorite Dakota experience thus far. Each time I fully expect to be blown back into Minnesota."

"Shall we have such a storm tonight?" Anna asked.

"I hope so. I find this humidity completely enervating."

"But you shall gather the strength to show us around tomorrow, I am sure," Frances smiled at Percy. "I am looking forward to a stroll through the town."

"Wet or dry, I think you will be more pleasantly situated in a buggy, my dear," Percy replied. "The sidewalk in front of the hotel runs out pretty quickly, making for a dusty walk, and if it does rain you will be dragging several inches of your skirts in mud just crossing Front Street."

"A buggy it is, then. And when do we drive out to see this bonanza farm of John's?"

"Should he be able to tear himself away from harvesting, which, I understand, has just begun, he will ferry you across the prairie himself. I may be unable to get away from work."

"Is it quite safe?" Anna asked, a bit hesitantly, as if she were embarrassed by her own question.

"Safe?"

"It's just that the horrible news of this past month–"

"Ah, Custer," Percy said. "The Montana valley where he and his brave men fell is far removed from Fargo. You need fear only bloodthirsty mosquitoes here. I do have one bit of happy news, however. There is a local doctor and his wife for you to meet. She is a lovely woman, from Philadelphia, I believe, who is much out of place here. Dr. and Mrs. Harkness. She has taken the remarkable step of teaching some of the local immigrant children how to spell their names as a means of alleviating the boredom of her new home. It is a course of study made easier for the bulk of the children by a certain Scandinavian economy of nomenclature. Ole Oleson, meet Thor Thorson. Anders Anderson, meet Sven Svenson," Percy engaged in a pantomime of introductions. "It can, however, get more complicated. Ole Thorson, meet Thor Oleson. Anders Svenson, meet Sven Anderson."

With Anna settled in her room after dinner, Percy escorted his wife to the suite he called home in the new annex of the hotel. It was an expense he could not afford, the cost of room and board almost equaling his Times salary, but Percy had discovered that credit was readily extended to the son of the area's new bonanza farmer. His boss, E. B. Chambers, was just now completing a new house, and had offered Percy the rooms above the Times he would soon be vacating, the window to the north looking out upon the Fargo settlement, and the one to the south upon nothing at all. Percy had hesitated to accept, preferring the fantasy of transience he enjoyed by staying in a hotel. And he could not for a moment imagine Frances living with him there.

Percy had expected to see his wife comfortably situated in his suite before excusing himself for a last cigarette, which he would roll and smoke on the wooden platform in front of the hotel. Or perhaps, crossing the tracks, he would stroll through the new "park," a fenced rectangle of grass on Front Street, complete with a gazebo and saplings planted about the perimeter. To his surprise, however, Frances asked that he excuse her for a half hour only as she completed her evening toiletry, adding that perhaps Percy would care to brush her hair for her before she turned in.

"Of course," he said, closing the door behind him. He still had time to smoke, and time to wonder about the odd sense of resentment that had come upon him at his wife's coded invitation. He believed that he had been in love with his wife when he married, and was content to assume that the condition remained. Still, he could not deny that there had grown between them a coolness of the sort that Percy expected was common to all married couples after the novelty of the union had worn off, although he had previously assumed that the easy neglect of husband and wife came about with the appearance of children.

Children. Here was a topic not easily discussed, and yet, on this one point, Percy was not the least bit ambiguous. His sojourn in Dakota had convinced him that he wanted a family. Not that he was eager to support a wife and children under a roof of his own; rather, he wanted to see Frances restrained. Percy had once enjoyed his wife's intelligence and independence, her private impertinence, all of which made her seem lively and exotic in the midst of the Bingham household. It had been his fondest secret to know that the woman who smiled and nodded to guests so properly in the parlor could dissect them with wit in private. But as his own insecurity grew, so did his irritation in Frances' confidence. She needed to be more passive, which is to say, more womanly. She needed to be pregnant.

Percy put his cigarette out with his boot, his resentment at his wife's initiative become determination. From now on there would be an end to distasteful strategies. The male safes that he had tried at Frances' bidding were completely unsatisfactory and he would have nothing more to do with them. Nor would he longer allow her to spring from their bed to douse herself with syringe and alum. She had mentioned, once, something he believed she had called a womb guard. No, that was not quite it. Womb veil, perhaps. Some vile contraption, he supposed. It would be unpleasant, perhaps, to speak of such things, but it was none-theless his responsibility and his right to do so.

CHAPTER XVIII

In Which the Impossible is Seen and Done

The next morning Anna and Frances took stock under a color-less sky of the unlikely town that had become Percy and John Bingham's home away from home. After pretending surprise at the determination of his wife and sister to set foot outside the singularly civilized environs of the Headquarters Hotel, and even to forego the buggy ride, Percy snugged his hat on securely, gave each woman an arm, and led them across the tracks, through the small park, and onto the boards laid end-to-end across the wide, dusty expanse of Front Street, where they were forced to walk single file. It did not take the party long to run out of stores to explore. When they ran out of sidewalk as well, in front of the Fargo House, the women turned their attention to the half dozen large freight houses across the street, their raised platforms abutting the train tracks. Rising from the curving river of trees that lined the Red was the train trestle, and just beyond, a plume of smoke, which Percy said was from the Belle of Minnesota flour mill on the Moorhead side of the river. An assortment of businesses and houses sparsely dotted the plain between.

Retracing their steps, the Binghams passed their hotel to take in the remainder of what Percy enjoyed calling "upper" Front Street, which unlike "lower" Front, had a wooden sidewalk (rising as much as fifteen feet over a small slough thick with mosquitoes) but no buildings.

"And that," Percy said, taking out his watch yet again, "is the total sum of Fargo."

"Are we keeping you from your work, Percy?" Frances asked.

"Such as it is."

"We will walk with you to your office, and then," Frances turned to Anna, "we will return to the hotel where we will comfortably entertain ourselves."

"No, no, no," Percy replied. "The Fargo *Times* is housed in yet another rectangular clapboard structure, albeit with the anomaly in these parts of two several-paned windows. If it is more walking you require, the courthouse alone is worth the visit." He pointed, unnecessarily, to the large brick and limestone structure in the near distance that looked oddly out of place, standing as it did in the midst of the prairie, its ornate cupola overlooking a small stable.

"The courthouse it is," Frances said, offering Anna her arm and then patting the gloved hand Anna placed there. "If you feel—"

"I feel fine," Anna said.

Percy watched his sister and his wife for a moment, and when he was certain that neither would turn for a wave good-bye, he reached into his vest for his flask.

In the late morning the women retired to their separate rooms, Anna for a nap and Frances to study the ledgers and notes that John Bingham continued to insist upon leaving with his son. When she was finished with these she turned to the Fargo *Times*, which consisted almost entirely of advertisements for land, equipment, animals, services. Here, it occurred to her, people were buying new lives, filling up the Dakota void purchase by purchase.

Frances and Anna were reading in the ladies' parlor that afternoon when the doctor's wife, Mrs. Harkness, called, offering to take them for a buggy ride into the prairie to collect wild flowers. Returning the call the next day, the friends discovered a fine upright piano in the Harkness living room, and Anna was persuaded to play from the impressive collection of sheet music Lydia Harkness produced. It was not until the late afternoon of the third day of the Bingham women's visit that John Bingham arrived at the hotel, explaining, if not exactly apologizing for, his tardiness with the news that harvesting had begun on his first crop of wheat. At dinner that evening, they agreed that Frances and Anna would ride into the country the next morning with John, after he arranged for the delivery of a half-dozen self-binding harvesters that had finally arrived on the previous day's train. Intermittent showers that evening were all that came of the long awaited rain, enough to cool the morning and temporarily return the sky to a pasque flower blue, but not, John predicted, enough to keep the sweltering humidity from returning.

Seated next to her father-in-law in his buggy, Frances took note of the bay horse that John clucked into a trot out of town. Frances would have thought that this gorgeous beast was a rare extravagance of her father-in-law's, perhaps meant to broadcast his status as one of the newly important bonanza farmers, had she not seen a couple dozen equally magnificent horses pulling buggies down Front Street during the past three days. The citizens of Fargo, with so little else to show for their labor thus far, appeared to be determined to outdo each other in horseflesh.

Although the bay was soon following a track worn into the prairie, Anna wondered aloud whether there were danger of getting lost, with no markers to follow, no trees, no real crossroads.

"You'd be surprised," John Bingham replied, looking across Frances to address his daughter. "After awhile you start to notice different things here and there. A small rise where the grass is just a little shorter, a depression that holds some stones, rose bushes bunched together a certain way. Pretty soon instead of everything looking the same, it all looks particular. You just have to learn to see in a different way. Over there, for instance," John nodded his head to his right. "You can just make out where the train tracks rise up out of the prairie. Looks like a dark line run across the horizon, but when you know what it is, it becomes a sign of sorts."

Frances turned toward Anna to wait for her reply to John's comments, and in the process removed her arm from the press of her father-in-law's.

"Well?" John Bingham said after a moment's silence.

"It is like...like expecting to see a new piece of artwork," Anna spoke slowly, "and then being presented with a frame surrounding a blank canvas." She laughed a little nervously, afraid that she may seem contrary. "Not precisely blank, of course, for there is much to see, but too much of the same thing is not easily discerned from too much of nothing."

"You sound like your brother," John Bingham said.

"But the colors, Anna?" Frances said.

"Yes, but that is my point. There is solid blue, and then there is solid green, and they meet as if in a straight line, somewhere there, before us, on the horizon, like, like—"

"Like a flag," Frances said and then laughed, and for a moment looped her arm into Anna's, "and we are riding into the flag of this new land, blue on waving green, guiding us on while it passes beneath and behind."

"Not green for long, though," John Bingham said. "You will have to put some gold on that flag of yours." He pointed toward a field of wheat that they were approaching.

Frances had never heard her father-in-law edge quite so close to casual banter. "Anna," she said, "you must stitch this flag some day. You alone have the skill."

"But leave the other side white," John Bingham said. "For winter."

And then they were silent. Frances assumed that John Bingham, his conversational duties attended to, had returned to thinking about his work. She was wrong, but only for the moment it took him to mark once again the pleasure of her company. Despite the trim severity of her dress, Frances was giving the impression of someone about to swing her hat free to let her hair fly in the wind.

The openness of the country and the morning air were indeed giving Frances pleasure, although the small smile she wore had more to do with a seldom-summoned memory of long-distant rides she had enjoyed as a little girl. Always, in these memories, she rode at a gallop with her arms clutching the body before her. She had not been astride a horse since. Frances was far away when Anna spoke, softly, her words directed to her sister-in-law only. "I am sorry that Percy could not join us today. Do you think he is perhaps working too hard?"

With a quick squeeze of her friend's arm, Frances assured Anna that Percy seemed to her to be perfectly happy. Anna did not seem convinced, but let the conversation drop, occupying herself with a veil she had attached to her bonnet for protection against the sun that was becoming increasingly oppressive.

Percy working too hard? Frances wondered if Anna could possibly know her brother so imperfectly. If so, Frances had no desire to disabuse Anna of her assumption, nor to share with her the details of the argument that had continued between Frances and Percy since their first night together in Fargo. Even though Frances had woken this morning ready to make amends, Percy had offered a hasty excuse at the breakfast table and begged off the trip.

"I believe he is at work on another project for Mr. Power...oh, my goodness, what is that?"

Anna and John Bingham, too, looked toward the approaching spectacle that had burst forth from a stand of scrub trees that stood at the edge of the slough they had been skirting for the past half mile as they neared the Sheyenne River. Seeing that the apparition was itself on a dirt path precisely perpendicular to their own, John Bingham pulled the bay to a stop. Silently, the Binghams watched the cloud of dust clarify into a team of four workhorses pulling an empty farm wagon at a dead run, piloted by what proved to be a young woman who drove the horses forward while standing on the wagon's seat, reins held tautly in her left hand, whip cracking regularly from her right. Without so much as a glance at the tidy buggy, with its fancy bay crow-stepping in agitation, the wagon's driver hurtled the team forward and past. Within moments the spectacle had diminished into a receding line of dust.

When John Bingham allowed the bay to step forward, Anna was released to speech, but she did not get beyond the obvious.

"That was a woman." Anna's incredulity was clearly mixed with horror.

"A pretty young one at that," Bingham added.

"She wore no hat," Anna summed the impossibility of what she had seen.

"Shame to see a team driven like that for no good reason," Bingham said. "Most of the settlers around here, immigrant or not, don't really have the leisure for a fine distinction between masculine and feminine duties. I don't suppose you'll find too many men baking cakes," John Bingham chuckled, "but I've passed more than one field with the womenfolk working alongside the men. This is the Sheyenne River, by the way," he said, changing the subject as they crossed the short wooden bridge.

As John Bingham spoke, Frances let herself see again the young woman and her team as it flew past. The brownness of the girl's face was unfortunate, to be sure, and the thin ropes of muscle that stood out upon her forearm as she grasped the handful of thick reins had been unsightly. But the hair that had come loose and flowed wildly behind her, the calico dress opened at the throat to sun and breeze, the skirt pressing against long legs that bent and moved with the bouncing of the wagon upon the rough track like agile springs, why, it had been a breathtaking display, as much for its grace and force as in its inappropriateness. Frances shifted in her seat to rearrange the coils of her bustle and relieve the press of her corset into her side that a moment ago she had not noticed. The pads so recently pinned into the sleeves of her dress were already moist. Again, she imagined the girl who had flown past. What, she wondered, must that feel like? And what was this place from which such impossibilities could spring? Perhaps Anna's analogy of the empty frame, the unpainted canvas was apt. Perhaps here was a place in which Frances could paint herself into a sensible world. Perhaps here, in this world of the known and the necessary, of men involved in industry and agriculture and railroads and politics, of settlers and storekeepers, Yankees and immigrants, capitalists and laborers, there would be space for a new life, heretofore unknown. She could happily dot her canvas with these horses, oxen, machinery and men that she could now see moving upon the expanse of gold they approached, for they all struck her as strangely beautiful in their purpose and energy.

She was about to ask her father-in-law to stop the buggy so she could better study this bustling tableau, a rectangle of labor surrounded by an expanse of untrammeled prairie, when he did just that. Individually, each team of harvesters followed the trajectory of a straight line; in unison they formed a wedge of progress. Yes, there, Frances thought, not in the center, but well in the background, perhaps at the vanishing point on the horizon toward which the wedge's line directed her eye, there she could paint her life with Anna.

Skirting the edge of the field for another half-mile brought the trio to a small tented town, the farm's "headquarters" of which John and Percy had spoken. John escorted Frances and Anna to the welcome shade of a surprisingly cool tent, open to cross breezes and smelling deliciously of the loaves of freshly baked bread that had been piled onto the long plank tables that spanned its length. Behind this tent could be seen another, smaller tent, this one with each side rolled up. Moving about several large tubs, kegs, barrels, sacks and tins, and a large wood-burning

cook stove, were a pair of stout women speaking in the bouncing cadence of Scandinavians. The cooks were preparing the evening meal still
eight hours away, John Bingham explained. The noonday dinner had
already been loaded into a wagon to be taken to the men in the field,
and if Frances and Anna would excuse him, he needed to check with
the foreman there, too. The cooks, John Bingham gestured toward the
tented kitchen, would see to their noon meal.

The moment Frances and Anna took the last sips of their coffee,
the larger of the cooks beckoned from the end of the tent with a "You
come," that probably sounded like more of a command than the speaker intended. Frances and Anna followed their guide to a small tent that
turned out to be John Bingham's temporary home, recognizable by his
trunk and familiar ledger. A sturdy camp desk stood in the corner. A
kerosene lamp sat nearby upon a pair of stacked crates. An extra cot
had been placed against one side of the tent, and both cots were covered with quilts of extraordinary and intricate design. The look upon
the large woman's face indicated that this was her handiwork as well
as her contribution to the comfort of the visiting ladies. Anna's honest
appreciation of the workmanship, and the large woman's pleasure in
receiving the compliments, did not require a shared language.

Frances helped Anna loosen her corset, but declined to rest, and
was soon strolling from tent to tent, her parasol providing scant protection against the midday sun. She was about to explore the massive
barn when a short parade of heavy wagons, pulled by teams of lathered
workhorses and weighted by the iron and wood of some previously unseen machine, approached the Bingham headquarters. Frances watched
from the barn door as John Bingham, who had followed the wagons in,
gestured toward the second wooden structure on the place, roofed, but
still lacking its walls. He gave no indication of seeing Frances, but when
he moved away from the men beginning to unload the harvesters from
the wagons, he walked directly toward her.

"I expected to find you and Anna resting at this hour."

"Anna is lying down in your … quarters. That's not right, is it? But
there is something here that makes me think of what I imagine an army
camp to be. The emptiness. The tents, I suppose."

"The manager of the Cass-Cheney operation I was talking about
over supper last night has instituted precisely that terminology. His su-

perintendent is a 'Captain', the foremen under him are 'Lieutenants'. Pretentious, but effective."

"And the men driving the teams? Are they privates?"

"For the most part, as with the men you saw in the field we passed, they are area settlers who are waiting for their own crops to ripen and are taking this opportunity to earn some extra money. I'll need to find more next year when I have another two thousand acres of sod turned. But I apologize, Frances, this must be tedious for you."

"It is not," Frances turned toward the interior of the barn, as if to take a pleasant promenade down the long central aisle redolent of hay and ammonia. John Bingham had no choice but to follow. "Percy has been sharing some information about the operation with me, some of the expenditures and projections." Frances hesitated, then added, "I hope you don't mind."

"It is family business," John Bingham answered, leaving Frances to guess whether that was approval or reprimand. "I will say that I am surprised, both that Percy would care to share the information and that you would care to read it."'

"My husband, I believe, takes some pleasure in remaining a mystery to those who should know him best."

"Well, then," John's tone took on a edge, "I would say that he has been successful as far as his father is concerned."

"I believe that Percy's true talents are yet to be realized. I very much hope that the day will come when the son will take his place at the father's side."

They had reached the far end of the barn that opened onto an empty paddock. Frances busied herself with her parasol, knowing that John was openly studying her. When she looked up, she looked into a face of some disbelief.

"I am surprised to hear that Percy has so much as looked at the information I have given him." As John Bingham spoke he took off his coat and laid it over the top rail of the fence. "I would be an unnatural father, Frances, not to wish for my son's interest in what I am doing here. I find, somewhat unexpectedly, I will admit, that I like this," he gestured forward with his arm, "very much."

And it would be an unnatural son who did not take advantage of his father's progress, Frances thought.

"And you, Frances," John Bingham said after a moment's silence. "Can the details of an agricultural operation such as this possibly interest you? If you have forgotten to bring one of your novels with you from the city, I have seen a shelf-full at E.A. Grant's."

Frances responded to his teasing in the same tone, although her words carried less humor. "You need not condescend, John. I am well aware of how much I do not understand about the world of business, but I am not completely unfamiliar with country life." Frances turned to face her father-in-law before saying, "As you know."

After a moment's silence, Frances let her lips lift into a very small smile, allowing John to answer, albeit cautiously, "Well, yes, yes, of course, I did feel that it was best to know, well, to know something about your people before you and Percy married, and of course—"

"It is fine. It is what I expected you to do. And you found, I trust, no skeletons in my family closet, beyond those buried in a Rebel graveyard."

"I found, Frances, that the Virginia Houghtons were a respected family. I did not need to be schooled on the fact that men of honesty and integrity died in gray as well as blue. Come, I have asked the cooks to prepare one of their Swedish treats for a very civilized tea for you and Anna before I have my foreman's son carry you back to Fargo."

As they walked back through the barn, Frances, lifting her skirts and stepping with care, wondered if her father-in-law's informant had indeed been so kind, or if her own memory had simply become less so. She did not doubt that there were fine Houghtons everywhere, and it was possible that some came from Virginia. But it was equally as likely that her father had been a distant drunk. Her mother had disappeared when Frances was small. Run away, or taken away, she never knew. And the aunt to whom Frances had been sent in Chicago had been rarely present or pleasant.

Frances was not yet eight years old when she last saw her father and brothers, each already a grown man. It was these brothers that she remembered with pleasure, the hours of being tumbled about like a doll, often passed from brother to brother as they rode down a shady lane without their horses breaking stride. It was the oldest, Nathan, who had built the dog cart for her, and taught her how to drive the pony. That much she was sure of. The big house she remembered in her dreams was at times magnificent, at times a ramshackle ruin. What remained constant was her image of a father, sitting in a chair on the front porch, a bottle nearby from which he poured whiskey into a pewter cup day after day, hour after hour. The eyes that occasionally looked blankly past her had been pewter, too.

All that was memorable about her four years in Chicago were the series of letters, each carrying the news of another death. She was twelve years old when she waved good-bye to her aunt from a train bound for St. Paul and Miss Ardwell's Female Institute, where she was to remain for another four years. Having been placed twice on trains by family members who were never again to be seen had been enough to convince Frances that from there on out her destiny was in her own hands.

Frances turned to John Bingham as they neared the cook tent. "I suspect that such a heavenly aroma has already wakened Anna. I will go see if she needs my assistance." Frances took a step away from her father-in-law, but then hesitated. As if musing aloud, Frances spoke into the distance, "It has been such a pleasure to watch her improve in the past few days. She has not been well since Mother Bingham passed. There must be some truth to the claims made of the healthful climate of Dakota."

They rode back to Fargo under a lowering sky. The muted, rumbling thunder was too distant to be frightening, too constant to be ignored. Frances noticed that Anna often needed to bring her handkerchief to her face to touch away the beads of sweat upon her upper lip and brow. The day had become as sweltering as John Bingham had predicted, but Frances understood that Anna's discomfort was as likely to be from the pain of the second long buggy ride of the day as from the heat. Back at the hotel, Anna immediately returned to her room, but Frances remained too agitated to consider resting. The precise cause of her agitation she could not quite identify. There was in it the old, constant component of excitement and frustration in Anna's company, exaggerated by the proximity of her friend's body pressed next to hers in the buggy. But there was more. It felt like a plan taking shape. It felt like hope.

Frances did not try to contain her enthusiasm that evening for all that she had seen during the day, despite Anna's more guarded opinions and Percy's incredulity. Her excitement ultimately won her companions over, not to her estimation of the Dakota prairie or of the magnificence of John Bingham's undertaking, but rather, to the pleasures of her personality plain and simple. Frances excited, Frances passionate, was a force neither brother nor sister could entirely withstand. To her passion Frances added humor, and soon she had brought a treasured laugh to Anna's lips, and the opportunity for wit to Percy's. A magnificent storm had finally broken loose with all of the fury of chaos unbound, and they grew a little giddy with the smug well-being of the lucky, safe and dry, excited by the broken flashes of lightening that revealed the rain dashed against the windows, by the thunder that shook the chandeliers. They were an attractive threesome that night in the restaurant of the Headquarter's Hotel, smiling, young, handsome, any one likely to reach out to touch the hand of another.

Later, as Frances finished her toilet, and let down her hair for the evening, she had every intention of continuing to please her husband. The arguments of the previous nights would not be repeated, and if she were to become with child, then children would become part of her plan. She was a little surprised that she had been able to escape pregnancy up to this point, and not at all surprised that Percy had begun to complain. And perhaps, Frances thought, if Percy believed that their love-making was now for the purpose of reproduction, he would be quicker about it. Not that she disliked the act itself. Her invitation to Percy to "brush her hair" the other night had been real, for, as the passage in the Bible stated, it was better to marry than to burn. Frances' interpretation of the command, responding to her desire for Anna while in Percy's arms, was as unsatisfactory as it was creative, but she could see no alternative. She had been sorry for the passing of the brief period during which Percy's rather precipitate needs seemed to most closely match her own, when her pent up longing for intimate touch brought on by hours in the company of Anna could be at least addressed, if not assuaged, by penetration, by the pleasure of punctuation, full stop. But this period of what she had believed to be mutual satisfaction had not lasted, and for some time now, in Frances' opinion, Percy's love-making simply went on much longer than was quite necessary. In short, where Percy now began, Frances finished.

So Frances prepared herself for Percy's return to their room after his "evening stroll" by closing her eyes and remembering Anna, asleep on the train, her tongue making its delicate sweep across her lips. She imagined Anna laughing again, and watched her friend's lips part to reveal the strong, white teeth there. She felt Anna's breasts graze against hers as they kissed goodnight and let her imagination continue the embrace. When she heard Percy at the door, Frances lifted her hand from her chemise and calmed her own breathing. Her gaze drew Percy across the room and she imagined herself reaching toward Anna as she stood to meet Percy's kiss. He put his hands on her shoulders but Frances gently drew them back to his sides. Percy's blue eyes were puzzled, his shoulders and head tilted toward her in question, but he remained silent as she unbuttoned his shirt. But when she moved to unbutton his trousers, Percy, startled, put his hand upon hers and nodded toward the bed. Frances understood that she was expected to quietly slip under the sheets, but instead she chose to watch Percy as he turned to fold his clothes and carefully hang his shirt and trousers in the wardrobe before shrugging into his nightshirt. He was clearly surprised when he turned again to find her still standing there, and self-consciously dropped his hand to hold his nightshirt away from his body. "Are you coming?" he asked, his voice dropped to a whisper as he pulled the bedclothes back and climbed in to wait for his wife. Frances undid the top buttons of her chemise, but remained standing. Percy swallowed, and said, softly, "Your eyes. They're almost black."

Frances was not surprised. She could believe herself to be in some unforeseen way transformed for she felt at that moment as if she knew neither herself, nor the man before her, his body both strange and familiar. The eyes she looked into held Anna's blue, made strange by Percy's broader face. The lips were full here, too, but widened, coarsened by a square jaw, disguised by the neat mustachios. She took the hand Percy reached toward her and brought his fingers to her lips before easing the hand to her breast. Percy reached to pull her toward him, but she was excited by the little bit of control that she had taken, and was loath to lie down. Slowly, Frances leaned over to kiss him, dropping her hand to his chest, and then, under his nightshirt. Upon hearing his soft moan, a genderless sound of intimacy, Frances closed her eyes and worked to hear the moan again. And that is when she did the impossible thing, a thing she had never imagined, a thing she did not know was done. A thing which was perhaps not to be done. Her finger had found the place to enter and she pushed against his body with all the force she dared. Percy gasped and lifted toward her and she watched, amazed, as his seed dampened his nightshirt.

Percy woke the next morning aghast at the form of the previous night's sexual congress, disgusted by the stain upon his shirt, furious at the vulgarity of his wife's actions, and horrified by his unexpected, unprecedented and immediate excitement in response. And by his arousal at the memory.

It is the fury, he believes, that he will save him, and with no gentle stirrings or words to waken his wife, he pulls her beneath him and lets her come suddenly awake to his rapid and thoughtless thrusts and quick ejaculation. Then, without comment he moves away. Minutes later he leaves the room.

That evening is the same, and for a week, Percy walks about with the excitement of a man who is making the woman who has embarrassed him feel like a whore. There are no words of tenderness before, no questions of concern after, no conversation between. Then comes a slow realization, more of an incredulous intuition than understanding: Frances is enjoying this change in his behavior. So Percy removes himself as completely as he can, lying next to her without touching, or staying away altogether at night. And finds no sign of disappointment in his wife. Soon, but not soon enough, he is simply relieved to say good bye as he puts his wife and sister on the eastbound N.P.

Book Three:
The First Low Wash

I hear the tread of pioneers
Of nations yet to be;
The first low wash of waves, where soon
Shall roll a human sea.

The rudiments of empire here
Are plastic yet and warm;
The chaos of a mighty world
Is rounding into form!

(From "On Receiving an Eagle's Quill
from Lake Superior" by John G. Whittier)

CHAPTER XIX

In Which J. B. Power Harvests Gold

News about the bonanza farms "in the land of golden grain" had begun to advertise Dakota precisely as J. B. Power had planned. Throughout the upcoming summer and fall he intended to outfit several excursion cars for the pleasure of newspapermen and potential investors, who could thus combine hunting for pheasant and prairie chicken with sightseeing in the new Northwest. Just this past August, Power had been on his way to Bismarck to see to one of Frederick Billings' speculative concerns when a woman sitting behind him on the train had exclaimed upon watching men on the Cass-Cheney farm sacking wheat as it poured from the separator, "Why, it's as if they are harvesting gold!" Power had repeated the phrase to Percy Bingham, who had put it to good use in a special edition of the Fargo *Times* cooked directly to immigration. Power had sent a thousand copies of the *Times* to each N.P. immigration agency in Europe. From the bulk of the correspondence that Power and his assistant, C. F. Kindred, were receiving daily, and from the reports of his friends in the government land offices in Brainerd, Moorhead, Fargo, Jamestown and Bismarck, Power could confidently predict that the low wash of settlers entering Dakota was about to become a tidal wave.

And what did he get from most of the directors for his good work? What did he hear from Frederick Billings, for example, for whom he had secured over forty-six square miles of land most likely to appreciate rapidly and whose holdings Power was constantly involved in managing: finding buyers for the land, setting terms, arranging for collections, adding to his already heavy correspondence load? What was Billings' response? Suspicion, parsimony, and impatience.

Power continued to fume over the most recent letter, marked "Personal," of course, in which Billings expressed his reluctance to write the terms of Power's commission into a legal contract, while as much as accusing Power of—what were his words, now?—of making a "life case" out of his work as personal land agent for Billings, as if Power were a common sharp intent upon milking the wealthy director. Power had been so offended that he had replied that very day, and now worried that he had allowed his growing antipathy for Billings to color his reply.

Power fitted his glasses around his ears, sat forward, and flipped his letterpress book back a few pages to check the paragraph that had him worried. No, he could rest easy. The letter had been blunt, but professional. Turning a few more pages of the letterpress book, Power noted that a full half of the letters of the past week had been written to N.P. directors and "friends" of the road. He had warned the directors that obvious speculation would look bad for the railroad, and had received in reply several variations on the same theme: It was their right, as the bearers of the greatest risk, to make the greatest profit. They did not "speculate"; they invested. Power did not disagree, but he could imagine a day, and it not too far in the future, when the growing communities of settlers in Dakota would fail to make such a nice distinction and would begin to cry "favoritism." It was all so unnecessary. With a little discretion and patience, this was one business in which a man could have his cake and eat it, too. Power had already picked up several quarter sections of farm land and a number of city lots in various counties and towns. These he rented on liberal terms, enough to make a small, steady profit and to encourage development. He held the mortgage on another two dozen farms. And when he did purchase those 6000 acres well to the south of Fargo that he had held off the market thus far, it would not be for speculation, but for cultivation and for raising stock.

He could say that much for Cass and Cheney and Slade and a few of the other directors. A recent letter from Septimus Slade expressing concern about his "Dakota investment," however, promised to make still more work for Power. Evidently John Bingham was calling upon Slade to provide twice the capital for the upcoming season than had been required for the first, a situation Slade found most unsettling in light of Bingham's assertion that all profits from that first season had been necessarily "plowed back into the business." If the rumors circulating in the lobby of St. Paul's grand Merchants Hotel were to be believed, Power thought, Slade could well be about to pay for a fine new house, the likes of which had yet to be seen on the Dakota prairie.

Power closed his letterpress book, pulled out his watch and, barely able to read the time on the dial, realized that the early winter dark had already begun to fall. Directors be damned, he thought, there was still much about his position to his liking. Beyond his own growing wealth was his determination to be recognized as the savior of the N.P., which, despite its reorganization following the bankruptcy proceedings, remained a financially tenuous enterprise. The massacre of General Custer and his troops had been a boon to the road, requiring fully five hundred cars to carry freight west to supply the U.S. Army as it continued to chase Indians, but that would not last. Power supposed he should walk over to the Merchants to spend an hour or so in the company of the city's businessmen as they read their newspapers and discussed the events of the day. One of the reasons for reopening an office in St. Paul (leaving the Brainerd office in C. F. Kindred's capable hands) had been to encourage these businessmen to invest in N.P. land in Dakota, and already several casual conversations had resulted in more serious letters of inquiry. But the sky was threatening snow again and there would be a fire waiting in the parlor of his Rice Street home and the talk at the Merchants was certain to be about the presidential elections. The whole business had been a long, drawn-out mess, but the fifteen-member electoral commission appointed to make a decision, one way or the other, now consisted of eight Republicans and seven Democrats. So, popular vote notwithstanding, Rutherford B. Hayes, and not Samuel Tilden, would become the new President. That, at least, was good news. A Republican administration would be more congenial to the N.P., which still needed all the help it could get.

Odd, Power thought, standing to reach for his coat and hat, how so much of the hubbub seemed to him to be taking place in a distant land. And now there was talk of increasing unrest among workers in the east, which could easily get worse if some of the speculation and suggestions regarding wage cuts that he had heard in the N.P. board room during his last trip to New York bore out.

Look east, Power thought as he stuffed a few more letters needing responses into his case, and all you will see is trouble. Look west for hope.

Chapter XX

In Which Kirsten Begins to Learn About Love

Kirsten Knudson. Kirsten Knudson. Kirsten Knudson. That is my name still, and I hope it always is to be. Mor says it is different I will feel someday, and all I can say is that I will have to feel very different than I feel now if I am to feel different about that someday. And if I do feel different (and that is, as Mrs. Harkness said last October when I asked if the Sullivan boys would be coming back to school, "to be neither encouraged nor anticipated") I do not think that I will feel like being Kirsten Rolfsrud. That is the name that is on the paper that I am putting into the firebox of the stove when Mor comes through the door with a load of kindling that Haldis and Guri and I are all the time to pick up in the trees by the river.

Now why do I have such a piece of paper? Did I write it myself? Ya, vel den, you would not ask such a thing if to look at the writing you did. Mrs. Harkness says that for writing I have the finest something (it is a long word) of all of her students, her students no more, that is, although some will be, but not me, because this year Mrs. Harkness is to teach in her own home in Fargo, and that is too far for me to go every day, and of school enough I have had Far says because I am a girl and almost fifteen years old. Ole he says that it is not a real school anyway, and that there is a real school in Fargo now with a real teacher, a Miss Giddings, and that Mrs. Harkness is just *en gestkjefig person* with her nose in everybody's business and...oh, never mind what Ole says, it is not always so nice and that is not the point. The point is that the name Kirsten Rolfsrud on the paper is like one of Mor's hens got a pencil in its beak and then tried to stab a bug with it and kept missing, and I am saying right here and right now that every single one of Mor's hens is with more sense than Halvor Rolfsrud, who is the one to write that name and then hand it to me when I am walking out of the door after hearing Per Rolfsrud's Sunday morning sermon, and that is, as Mrs. Harkness would say, taking the un-do advantage (and that means, I think, to do something that the done-to would like to un-do).

I will be careful not to look at him next Sunday, and that is not so easy to do, since there are only to look at Per and Ingeborg Rolfsrud, and their simple nephew, Halvor, and the Norstads, and the Stakkes, and Osten Sondreaal and sometimes his brother, Peter, who has one eye that looks at Per Rolfsrud as he preaches, and one eye that is all white and just rolls around and around like an egg that has been boiled and peeled and then begins to roll on the table, and you just hope that when it comes to a stop it is not to look at you. And sometimes Mr. and Mrs. Solheim and their three little ones are there, too, but not very often is it that they are all well enough to come to church at one time. And Mor she says that the little girl, Gunhild, is their second Gunhild, because the first one died. And we are all in the room with the Rolfsrud's big table in the middle, and there Per Rolfsrud stands at the end of the table to read a sermon from *Lars Linderots huspostil*, and it is a big room, almost as big as our house, but when it is the Sunday service even that room is full, on the chairs are the grown-ups (really, that is a word in English and not just a made-up word like what Guri and Haldis do), and the children sit on the Rolfsrud's big *tine* or on the floor or on their parents' laps. Now that there are more people from Norway coming to farm here in Dakota all the time, soon, Per Rolfsrud says, we will have need for a real church and a real minister. Far says that Per Rolfsrud says this because he is tired of just telling a few poor Norwegians what to do, and that now that he is a big man, too big for his *bukser*, and is a delegate of the territory he goes to Yanktown to tell someone else what to do, and good riddance. When I asked Far what Yanktown is, he said it is a place where Yankees live and make the rules, and I guess that makes sense. But I will be sorry not to hear Per Rolfsrud because he is good to read, his words sound so nice. Mor says that is because he is from Gudbransdal in Norway. But when the Solheims talk it is very funny, their words all tumbling out so fast and funny. Far says what do you expect, they are Sognings. But Mor says that they are *norsk*, too, and Far says there are Norwegians and there are Norwegians.

Osten Sondreaal is a Halling like us. He is the last most new person to come to be a neighbor and he is homesteading the land between our place and the big Bingham farm that is more than a farm, right next to the homestead of his brother, Peter Sondreaal, who was on the boat from Norway with us, Mor says, but I do not remember him, or his wife or their baby. Mor says it is very sad because the wife and the baby died their very first winter in Minnesota, and that is where we were with other Hallings for two years before we came to where now it is Fargo and then it was not even yet Centralia what it was for not very long and then the train came and then it was Fargo, but when we lived there it was no town at all. Sten says it was called the Crossing, and that makes sense, too, because that is where people cross the Red River from Minnesota, but really, they could cross anywhere, and Sten says we crossed at Frog Point, and then Ole he says that we hopped over and then he and Sten laugh again. But it is now an old joke. So it is the railroad that moved us out to here by the Sheyenne River, but not really, because we did not ride on the train.

This is how Mor says it. The railroad wanted to own the very land that we were squatting on, and that is the word that Ole likes to hear because then he acts like, well, never mind what he acts like, it is a boy that he acts like, even though he is big like Sten now, and a man. So anyway the railroad said that we are to go and so go we were gone. Far took a homestead right where we are, but Per Rolfsrud did not go so easy and the railroad gave him 320 acres in a trade just for moving, and then he took another 160 acres for a homestead, too, and that made Far hopping up and down mad, but now he is happy again because of Homer and his homestead. That is America for you. And now Sten, he says that Per Rolfsrud is to take another quarter section by preemption, so I looked that up in the dictionary that Mrs. Harkness says I am to read and then give back to her when I take in the butter some day, because not one other student did she ever have with my "potential" (and you bet I looked that up right away, too), but I am not going to get forever out of the "A's" and so I will have to be for Mrs. Harkness a disappointment. Anyway to preempt is to do or buy something before someone else can do or buy it, I think, but Sten, he says it just means to buy a quarter section of land from the government and then promise to farm it. There is a ready-made gingham dress at E. A. Grants in Fargo that I would like to preempt but that is just to dream.

But I was talking about Osten Sondreaal. Except that I do not have much to say about him, except that he has lost almost all of his hair, and both of his eyes go in the same direction, and he has a smile that is like he is sad, and he is new in church, and so I look at him most. And one more thing. Every Sunday he comes up to Mor after church and says, "*god morgen, Astri. I have something for the children.*" And then he goes into the pocket of the good broadcloth coat that one Sunday he wears and the next Sunday it is Peter in the coat, so if it is this Sunday Peter's turn with the coat it is into the pocket of his *bukser* that Osten Sondreaal goes, and out he brings a little buffalo bone that he has cleaned and shaved into the shape of a cow or a pig or a horse. Once he had a piece of charcoal stuck into the end of a hollowed-out stick, for drawing, and once, he had a lemon, which was a new thing and I have not seen another one ever. I think that it sounds very funny to hear Osten Sondreaal call Mor 'Astri' because not even Far calls Mor like this, and the Rolfsruds call each other 'Mr. Rolfsrud' or 'Mrs. Rolfsrud', but here is this Osten Sondreaal calling Mor by her Christian name, and here is Mor smiling the same sad smile that is from the face of Osten Sondreaal.

What Far would say if he heard a man call Mor, 'Astri', I do not know, but maybe he would not care if that someone is Osten Sondreaal, because Osten Sondreaal has a pair of oxen and they are stronger than even Homer and so first Far said to Osten Sondreaal that Sten and Ole are to help him to dig a well in return for the use of those oxen and then Osten Sondreaal will not have to go to the river for water, but Osten Sondreaal and his brother, Peter, had already dug his well. So Far said that Sten and Ole are to help Osten Sondreaal get up his hay, but Osten Sondreaal said no, *takk*, but that would not be necessary, and Far said to Mor that the Sondreaals may have thought they were better than everyone else in the old country but now they are in America where everyone is equal and that means that they are as low as the rest, so who is Osten Sondreaal to turn down Far's offer of his sons' help.

That is when Mor said that maybe those men needed more help inside the house than outside, and that is how Mor and I are now to do the *husarbeid* (that is called *huskeeping* here in America) once a week for Peter and Osten Sondreaal, and that is not a hard thing to do, because they are already so clean. Even the pig that lives in Peter's house when it rains gets a scrubbing every night and is as pink as a wild rose, which is what Peter calls her, "Rose," which is a nice name for a pig, and I am glad that she has such a nice life, because pretty soon Rose will still be in the house, but she will be in pieces in a barrel. But until then she just watches and smiles when Mor and I scrub Peter Sondreaal's chair and table and the pails and the churning bowls and milk buckets with sand and water until our brushes that we made from the rushes and reeds that grow in the slough finally fall apart. And then Mor she says to me, *"Kirstie, water down the floor to settle the dust before you sweep, and then meet me at Osten's,"* and then there she goes walking across the prairie toward the next shanty, and so there I am sprinkling the water and I am saying to Rose, "Osten? It is Osten, too, and not Mr. Sondreaal?"

So that is how it is that Far gets Osten Sondreaal's pair, and when Far leads them into the yard I see that the skin on Mor's forehead starts to wrinkle like when Far is to go to Fargo without the company of Sten or Ole. And Far he says at supper that night that Osten Sondreaal just about gave each ox a kiss before he let them out of his eyes, and then Far said something in Norwegian that I did not understand, but that Ole and Sten did, because Ole he laughed, and Sten frowned, and Mor said, *"Torger, for shame!"* Ya, vel den, in the morning Far he hitched the oxen to the big wagon with the tall sides that he borrowed from the Rolfsruds and that was piled high with hay to sell to Mr. Stephens at the livery because for hay it is a good year and more than Homer and the cows need. Before he is to go Mor says to him again for maybe four times or five about the flour and the fruit in cans to bring home, and I put the butter and eggs under the seat, packed in straw and the last of the ice from the dugout and like Mor I say, please, Far, do not forget to go to Mr. Lindstrom to get my very first pair of shoes to be just for me. Because with this load of eggs and butter we are to be square, as Sten says.

But Far he did not come home that night, and he did not come home the next day, and then we knew that Far had escaped again, and so I said, "I will walk to Fargo, Mor, and find Far," and Mor just said, *"Far you will be able to find, Kirstie. It is Osten's oxen that I am afraid are lost, and then what are we to do?"* Sten said that he would go find the oxen and Far, but Mor said, no, we were to get back to our field work, and she would go herself, and that was a surprise, because Mor does not leave the yard, only to go to church or to a neighbor if there is someone there sick, and never to go into Fargo at all. I think she did not want Sten to go because he and Far are more and more ready to fight now that Sten is a grown man, and then in come Haldis and Guri, and they are yelling about the man with the bones coming and he is with the oxen, but no Far.

And sure enough, it is Osten Sondreaal, and here is what he says, more or less, as Mrs. Harkness says, because he and Mor talk all *norsk*, and the more it is English I know the less room there is for *norsk* in my head.

"*Morn*, Astri," Osten Sondreaal said, which means, "hello, Astri."

"*Ver saa god og gaa ind*," Mor said, which means, "Please come in." And now I'll just say it all in English, since it is too long the other way, and sometimes I have trouble getting to the point anyway, at least that's what Maeta Schlaet said at school, and Mrs. Harkness said yes, it is true, Kirsten Knudson is "not a model of concision," and that is something that I do not exactly understand what it means, even though I looked it up, but I think it is that I do not make a long story short, which is what Ole is always saying that I am to do, but you can just bet that he did not make that up, and I do not think he even got it from Sten, who is the one to think for Ole. But back to the concision of Osten Sondreaal.

He says that he walked into Fargo (he has a pair of oxen but he does not have a horse or a mule) to do some business, and he was halfway there, and that is about three American miles, when there he sees a wagon and a pair of oxen by the side of the road that is not really a road but more like a pair of wagon tracks, but I will remember the concision, so anyway Osten Sondreal he says that he can tell by the way one of the oxen is swinging his head as he grazes that it is his Washington and Adams and so into the prairie he goes, thinking that Far has had some sort of trouble, and there he finds his pair eating their way toward a cornfield, but they had not got into it yet ("*Love Herren!*" Osten Sondreaal says). But no Far. So he gets on the wagon and heads the team back into Fargo, where he does his business, and then finds Far—and here he looked even sadder than before—in a saloon and not one bit ready to come home, and some words there had been about Washington and Adams. So here was Osten Sondreaal now and he had returned the wagon to Per Rolfsrud, and he was sorry to be the one to bring a bad report to Mor and was there anything he could do to help?

And now Mor she does not look at Osten Sondreaal. She just looks over his shoulder like she is to see Far sitting in that saloon drinking the hay money, and she looks so hard that I look, too, because once, it was in the middle of last winter, and there had been so much snow and everything was all white, I don't just mean that there was a lot of snow, I mean that everything below the sky was white and even the sky was the sort of blue that is mostly white, and the little bit of the sun that was shining in the almost white sky was white like it was behind a cloud but there were not the clouds, and it was as calm as a winter day can get, and that means dead calm, and here in Dakota a day without wind is not a thing that happens very often. Mor she was outside to break the ice off of the laundry with a stick, and then in she came running back to the house so excited and said, *"barn, komme fort!"* so out we came forth, and there, I swear on the Bible and on *Lars Linderots huspostil,* was the Northern Pacific Railroad train sailing through the sky, and behind the train there was the church steeple of the new Yankee Lutheran church, too, just floating off the ground, and that is six miles away, but there was no sign of the Rolfsruds' house that is in between our home and Fargo. Not that we can see the Rolfsruds' house from here, but neither are we to see Fargo and no one is to see a train fly through the sky, but there it was. When I told Mrs. Harkness what I saw, she did not even laugh, but said that it was a "mirage" and that it happens in Dakota sometimes when "atmospheric conditions" are just right. So here was Mor with that same look on her face, so I took a good look, too, expecting maybe atmospheric conditions again, but all I saw was Sten and Homer like little dots far away plowing around Homer's shanty because it has been awhile now and no rain and there is the fear of the prairie fires again, and even farther away just more grass starting to get brown, but no trains in the sky.

And then Mor she looks back at Osten Sondreaal and just says, *"tusen takk."* Which I am to say sounds funny because that is what you say when you leave a house after you have had a nice time there, and this was not so nice, and one or two thanks would seem like enough, but a thousand is a lot, and then Osten Sondreaal he smiles and looks sad, and Mor she smiles and looks more sad, and I think maybe I had better say something because if there is any more smiling everyone will start to cry. So I ask that Osten Sondreaal if maybe there was a one-hundred-pound bag of flour and some cans of apples or maybe some shoes in the wagon that he left back at the Rolfsruds, and Osten Sondreaal he kind of wakes up and turns around and unties a pair of shoes hanging there on the yoke, but about the flour and fruit he had to say 'no' and then away he goes with Washington and Adams.

And even that is not the end, because the next morning when I got up (but did not put on my new shoes because they are for the snow) and went outside to empty the slops before setting out the bread and butter and milk for breakfast for Sten and Ole, there was a bag sitting by the door, and it had almost ten pounds of flour in it. When Mor came out of her room I just looked at the corner where I put the flour, and then Mor looked at it, too, and then she just shook her head a little shake, like to say 'do not say anything'. And when she put the flour away after the boys had gone outside for the morning chores I could see that now she did cry, but just with her eyes and not with one sound.

CHAPTER XXI

In Which We Consider Perspective

It was another gorgeous day in "the fifth season of the earth's temperature," a continued respite from the dispiriting wind that Percy believed would one day drive him mad. Feeling slightly foolish, Percy pushed an empty perambulator, decorated with dozens of tasseled balls of brightly colored yarn that merrily bounced and swayed as he crossed Front Street. The train carrying the Bingham women was due in soon, Percy's warning jest of fourteen months earlier become a reality. Construction on John Bingham's bonanza farm had continued apace, and did indeed include a new home for his family. "Father's Folly," Percy preferred to call the structure. Set alongside the mansions of St. Paul, it would have been a modest affair, but rising from the Dakota prairie the house—three stories high with an octagonal turret, bay windows and gables, a wide front porch and above that a second-floor balcony, and all topped by a small look-out surrounded by an ornate iron fence from which his father could survey his domain—was simply monstrous.

And unfinished, an inconvenience that had not prevented John Bingham from selling the St. Paul house "out from under Anna's feet," in Percy's words, when a buyer appeared with cash and a vision that complemented Bingham's own regarding Summit Avenue's certain destiny as the location of choice for St. Paul's wealthiest businessmen. Percy knew that his father had spent several hours during this past winter in St. Paul in the offices of Abraham Radcliffe, a master builder cum architect, and carpenters had begun work on the new Bingham house as soon as the ground began to thaw in early spring, but it was not until Frances gave birth in late May that John Bingham informed his family of their new Dakota home, and of the sale of the Summit Avenue house from which they had five months to move.

The Headquarters Hotel in Fargo would be their home until the new house was completed, which John Bingham had been assured would be before the snow flew. On an Indian Summer day like today, Percy thought, snow felt months away. But that could change quickly. Snow in October was a distinct possibility.

Despite Percy's scorn for the ostentatious proclamation of wealth that was his father's new home—wealth that Percy knew was all in John Bingham's plans, and not a bit of it in the bank—it had, at least temporarily, solved the problem of just how Percy was to reunite his own family, which now included a five-month-old son, Houghton Oliver Bingham. Frances and the baby could not be expected to make a home with Percy in his two rooms above the *Times,* nor was Percy inclined to build a house of his own in Fargo, an acknowledgment of permanence that he continued to resist. The point, Percy understood, was moot. He made very little money, and saved less. Local store owners were more than happy to extend credit to the son of a bonanza farmer, but the owner of the Fargo bank—a twelve-by-fourteen-foot shiplap shack lacking only, Percy believed, a sign that read "Rob me"—was evidently less sanguine regarding the younger Bingham's promise, and insisted upon John Bingham's signature on any loans to Percy. And so, Frances and Houghton were to continue to live under John Bingham's very substantial roof. Percy would keep his rooms above the *Times,* spending the bulk of the week in Fargo, and making the six-mile trip to the farm "whenever possible," which is to say, whenever convenient. It would be an arrangement that suited Frances precisely to the degree that it suited Percy, and for that he was already resentful.

Percy parked the gay perambulator, which Lydia Harkness had been kind enough to pick out for him, against the wall of the hotel, and then walked to the edge of the platform to peer eastward along the tracks.

He was unaccountably nervous. That his role of husband had turned out to be far more complicated than he could have imagined did not bode well for his new status as a father. He had returned to St. Paul just twice since his son's birth, itself an excruciating experience for Percy. On that day he had arrived just in time to be greeted by the commotion of the delivery, and was horrified by his wife's lack of inhibition and decorum, for her angry cries of pain carried throughout the house. With the exception of the doctor attending Frances, it had become a house of women. Even the cook and the housekeeper bustling past him were more comfortably at home there than he. The results of Frances' labor, a red, wrinkled simian-like creature prone to leakage, had been equally disconcerting.

The next day, when he first came upon his wife in their room, she was cradling the sleeping baby in the crook of her arm as she stared out the window opened a crack to the sounds of the birds calling from the wooded ravine. Frances looked fairly beaten by her experience. Her long hair was lacking the shine to which Percy was accustomed, beneath her eyes were dark circles, her skin had none of its typical healthy flush, and she lay unnaturally still. And yet, there in her eyes remained the singularity that was Frances. She had taken her gaze from the window to acknowledge Percy as he entered the bedroom, her small smile less a greeting than the continuance of the expression of her eyes. Then she had looked down upon the wizened creature next to her, and Percy understood that there slept Frances' newest ally. As if looking into the future, Percy imagined the child's growing allegiance to his mother, and a phrase, unbidden and unspoken, entered into Percy's thoughts: "I have populated the opposition."

The thought had brought him up short. At what point had Frances become the enemy? Over what did they war? Behind him a gentle tap at the door had rescued him from his thoughts, and when Frances responded with another quiet "Come in," Anna had entered. Touching Percy's sleeve as she passed him, Anna had gone immediately to the side of Frances' bed, bent to kiss her forehead, and then looked down with absolute adoration at her new nephew. That is when Percy realized that he had not yet moved toward his wife and son.

He had stayed for two weeks in St. Paul after the birth, able to work on a new brochure for Power from there, and to manufacture several letters to the editors of agricultural periodicals, choosing a different persona and name for each. He was an old farmer who, with his wife, had made a visit to his son's new homestead in the Red River valley, and who marveled over the opportunities afforded settlers by the fertile open spaces waiting to be claimed. He was a salesman for a St. Cloud manufacturer who had passed through Fargo by stage coach on his way south, and waxed poetic over the energy of the boom town and its inhabitants. He was an eastern businessman who had taken a pleasure trip through the new Northwest on an N.P. excursion car and had been moved to express his wonder over the bonanza farms that he saw there.

During his two subsequent visits to St. Paul, Percy had grown a bit more comfortable with his status as new father, although the topic of conversation in the parlor was as likely to be about carpets, curtains, and fixtures for the new Dakota house as about the baby's daily alteration. A letter from Lydia Harkness had recommended that their carpets be dark, as it was simply impossible to keep the fine silt, raised by a multitude of plows and blown across the prairie by a too-constant wind, out of the house. On particularly dry years, she warned, the dirt would insinuate itself into every part of the house, under the doors, on windowsills, even in closets and cupboards. Frances had assured Anna that this must be hyperbole on Lydia's part, looking at Percy for support, who resisted for a moment before saying that dark green carpets would be quite elegant.

It would *all* be quite elegant, Percy was certain, and, if Septimus Slade could be kept at bay long enough, and if there were a succession of good crops, and if his father's latest scheme—of securing several quarter sections of government land to be homesteaded under the names of his year-round laborers on the farm—was successful, then perhaps the Bingham family would not find themselves dunned out of Dakota Territory before the sawdust of the new house settled. It was with this prospect before him that Percy finally heard the train's approaching whistle.

Although the westbound '2:05' that carried Anna and Frances and Houghton to Fargo was a through sleeper, both of the women were clearly fatigued by the journey. The baby was either more or less tired than the women, Percy could not tell which, but whatever it was expressing, it was doing so loudly.

"He has been like this for the better part of the last hour," Frances explained, handing the baby to Percy so abruptly that his choice was either to accept the bundle quickly or see him dropped onto the platform. "He has been fed, and changed, and bounced, and rocked, and he is inconsolable. And I," Frances added, "am exhausted. We, I should say, are exhausted." Frances offered a faint smile to Anna whose face was drawn in concern.

"Maybe this will help," Percy said, carrying Houghton the few steps to the colorful perambulator abandoned nearby. Holding the baby as if it were composed of discrete and unattached pieces that could slip from his grasp if he were not careful—an arm dropped here, a leg slipping between his fingers there—Percy lowered his package into the carriage. And then started back in horror when the baby's wails increased in force. With a jerk Percy pushed the contraption toward his wife and sister, at which point the baby fell silent. The moment he stopped, however, Houghton resumed his screams.

"Perhaps you should see to our luggage, Percy, and get Anna settled in her room, while I push the baby about," Frances said. "Forward motion alone seems to serve."

When Percy returned to the platform fifteen minutes later Frances was no longer there. He discovered her slowly pushing the perambulator along the northern boundary of the small grassy rectangle on the other side of the tracks. To his relief no infant caterwauling emanated from the depths of the baby carriage.

"Is he sleeping?" Percy asked as he joined his wife.

"He is waiting for me to stop, at which point the wailing will resume. Please," Frances gestured toward the handle of the carriage, and Percy began to slowly push. The turf on which they walked was uneven enough to keep the balls of yarn swaying, and Houghton appeared to be fascinated with the movement.

"You look tired," Percy offered.

"I am, and so is he. He is putting up a good fight to stay awake, but I would wager that he will be asleep with one complete turn around the perimeter of this park."

"What would you wager?" Percy asked.

"What do I have that you want?" Frances replied.

His wife's expression was completely unreadable to Percy, and he felt a moment's confusion, unable to answer her question even to himself. They had just come opposite the gate of the park from which they had entered, and were next to the gate that stood open to Front Street. A front wheel of the perambulator struck an uneven mound of sod there, causing the carriage to rock on its springs, bringing the dozens of balls of yarn suddenly alive and bouncing. Houghton's drooping eyelids sprung open, but then drifted closed again. A sudden commotion immediately to their right in the street brought Percy's hand to Frances' elbow, and together they turned to see a half-dozen wide-eyed men and women pulling themselves upright in a small farm wagon that looked as if it had run aground, its tongue driven into the dirt. A team of skeletal horses in broken harness bolted down Front Street, slowed only by the determined grip of a man bouncing and twisting lengthwise in the dust behind them.

"Why doesn't the fool let go?" Percy asked, releasing the baby carriage and stepping out into the street in time to see a handful of men in the distance leap from the opposite sidewalk and throw their hands in the air while hollering a "ho-there" chorus that slowed the team to a nervous stop. This seemed to release the occupants of the wagon into motion. The women began to wave their hands and exclaim. The men jumped out of the wagon and raced down Front Street toward the unfortunate driver.

"What is it that they were speaking?" Frances asked as Percy stepped back to her side and resumed his pushing.

"Whatever it is that Jews speak."

"Jews? Here?"

"Not too terribly far from father's very own esteemed operation."

"They did not appear to be prospering," Frances said. "It was my understanding that Jews were good at making money."

"People with money are good at making money. Father, for example, has entered into his, nay, let me say 'our' endeavor with a great deal of Septimus Slade's capital as well as the best wishes of any number of bankers. These poor beggars came with the clothes on their backs and just enough capital to see to it that they starve slowly instead of quickly."

"Supplied by whom?"

Percy leaned forward to look at the baby. "Sleeping?" he softly asked.

"Sleeping," Frances answered, before repeating her question. "In whose interest could it be to see Jews settled here in Dakota?"

"Ah, you will find me conversant with all of the gossip of our little burg. They are Jews from somewhere in Russia. On that point, I can be no more precise. They have been settled here by a Jewish congregation—is that the right word?—in St. Paul, a congregation that is showing gratitude to God for their own considerable material comfort by transporting handfuls of peasants from Russia to Dakota Territory. Having seen the condition of the beneficiaries of this philanthropy, I will let you form your own opinion as to the favor that has been done them."

"You are sympathetic, Percy."

"On the contrary, I am horrified. You have remarked, my dear, that I am an orderly man. In my wardrobe drawers you will not find my stockings consorting with my collars, nor my cufflinks with my cravat pin. On my bookshelf Shakespeare will have nothing to do with Homer, and neither associates with Mr. Twain. And on my plate the potatoes do not touch the meat, nor the vegetables the bread. I prefer to have a place for everything and everything in its place. That is one reason why I can not share my father's enthusiasm for Dakota Territory. You can not walk down the street of this town for ten minutes without hearing a half dozen vulgar languages. There are Norwegians, and Swedes, and Danes (they all sound alike), and Scots and Bohunks, and Germans, and Russians, and Icelanders, and Finns, and, I did not tell you this, but this past spring there was a Negro arrived here, on the eastbound train. I can not imagine where he could have been. He took a quick look about and wisely continued east. And now Jews. And Irish. I simply can not believe that such a stew can be healthy."

"But we need not mix."

"My dear, we always mix sooner or later. It takes constant vigilance to keep the gravy from seeping into the beans."

They had arrived back at the gate in front of the Headquarters Hotel when Frances spoke again. "Percy, you said the Jews were on land near your father's. How can that not be fertile land."

"Shall we risk bouncing him over the tracks, or do you want to pick him up?" Percy said in reply, and Frances leaned toward the perambulator to lift her sleeping son into her arms. "Watch your step," Percy said.

"That board is loose. It is not a bad thing to farm near a river. There are trees, which, as you have noticed, are not overly abundant here, and there is water. It is quite another thing entirely to homestead in a slough between two rivers, in this case, between the Red and the Sheyenne. It is regularly flooded during the spring thaw, and is thick with mosquitoes all summer long. J. B. Power told me that the St. Paul congregation first intended to buy railroad land, but could not agree with Power on the terms. That was their first mistake. It is no secret that Mr. Power keeps the best railroad sections for his N.P. cronies, but he is not the least bit interested in seeing any of his buyers fail, for, as he insists upon repeating ad nauseum, 'every satisfied settler is an emigration agent'. The second mistake those Jews made was to select a local land sharp as their agent, and to trust him to locate the government land to be taken by homestead and preemption sight unseen. He made his commission, the Jews in St. Paul can go to sleep at night thinking well of themselves, and our neighbors," Percy tilted his head back toward the wagon across the park, "wake up each day a little closer to hell."

"Do Jews believe in hell?" Frances asked as they stepped onto the platform in front of the hotel.

"They do now, I expect."

Four of the five freight cars that had been attached to the westbound train in Brainerd were quickly unloaded at the warehouses that lined the north side of Front Street leading up to the Headquarters Hotel. It was not uncommon for a freight car to contain a family or two of settlers and all they owned, livestock and material goods, accumulated in a life elsewhere and brought to Dakota in the hopes of multiplication. So it was no surprise to the warehouseman to discover, upon sliding open one large door, a family of five eagerly waiting to step off the train and into a new life. A few moments later another man, blinking into the late afternoon sunlight of the mid-October day, carefully walked down the ramp that had been hastily placed between the car and the warehouse platform. The man was dressed in the workingman's uniform of the day, broadcloth pants and work boots, collarless white shirt and dark vest. His hat sat high upon his head and appeared to be a full size too small. He reached forward to tap the shoulder of the settler who had allowed him to travel with his family in the freight car from Brainerd. "Thank you," he said in English, smiling as if the German man from Michigan had done him a favor, as if he had not paid two silver dollars for the privilege of riding with cattle and chickens and pigs. "'Luck, Isaac," the German man nodded in reply, and turned away.

Isaac. This is who he had become while in New York for five years. Not Yitzchok, the best scholar in his village yeshiva near Kiev, the grandson of a rabbi, but Isaac, a man with grease worked into the creases in his hands that no washing could remove. In America, Isaac believed, a common laborer may be a rich man one day. In America, a Jew must work with his hands if he is to be accepted.

"*Accepted?*" he could hear his grandfather reply. "*Who is Yitzchok Chavinitz to be accepted by goyim?*"

He was a man good with machines, and that meant that he would have work wherever he went. When he read the newspaper advertisement from the *Yiddishe tseitung* that had been placed there by the Jewish Agricultural and Industrial Society of St. Paul, announcing their program to help immigrants from Russia settle in Dakota Territory, he was eager to leave New York to join the community just established near Fargo. A letter in his pocket promised him that someone would meet him at the train. While he waited he read the handbills posted on the side of the closest warehouse. Most of the sheets there advertised programs at the Reynold's Variety House, many of which did not seem very nice. He had just begun to work his way through a notice that looked more promising when a stranger asked over his shoulder, "You looking for work?"

"I am a mechanic," Isaac said.

"Too bad," the man replied, pushing a large, soft-brimmed hat back from his forehead. "I'm looking for carpenters who can work for three dollars a day."

"Yes, a carpenter, too," Isaac replied quickly.

"Thought you might be. Lots of men remember that when they hear about the three dollars a day. Be in front of Henderson's Hardware at seven tomorrow morning if you're still interested. Put your John Hancock here."

For a moment Isaac stared at the sheet of paper and pencil that the man extended toward him.

"Your name."

"Yes. Yes," Isaac said, but even then he paused for another moment before writing a new name on the list. His new friends, he hoped, would help him put up a claim shack. It was October, so there would be no field work to do until spring. In the meantime, he would make three dollars a day as a carpenter, or mechanic, or as a well digger, if necessary.

When the train pulled away, the new arrival turned to look over the wide span of Front Street now revealed on the other side of the tracks. Directly in front of him three women stood about a small farm wagon. They were dressed in rough-looking garments of the sort that only the poorest of peasant women in Russia would wear. On the feet of all three were the work boots of men, several sizes too big. Two men appeared to be working on the horses' harness and did not look up. A third man stood at the head of the sweating, and certainly starving, team. Another man wiped his hands upon his pant legs and began walking toward Isaac. His coat sleeve was torn away at the shoulder and a dirt smear ran from his knees to his chest. As he came closer Isaac saw the seeping wound on one side of his face.

"Are you Isaac Chavinitz?" the man asked.

The former Yitzchok Chavinitz, more recently known as Isaac Chavinitz, nodded, held out his hand, and said out loud the words he had written on the floppy-hatted man's paper. *"My name is Jack Shaw."*

"Ya, vel den, here is Kirsten Torgersdatter with her hair as yellow as butter and eyes as wide as the eggs she brings to town just for me, then."

It is the same thing Mr. Jonsson is to say, every single time I come to Fargo with the eggs and butter, and why I do not know. Over and over I tell him, it is Kirsten Knudson I am, and about the butter and eggs just for him, well, that is wrong, too. Already there are the eggs and butter to Doctor and Mrs. Harkness, and to Mr. Lindstrom, the shoemaker, and to Mrs. McDougall because her husband is to fix the harness for Homer. But this I do not say, because I am watching Mr. Jonsson dig through the straw to see if any of the eggs are broken, and then he says, and this is *every single time*, "but Kirsten, there is one missing!" And then he puts his hand behind my ear and acts like it is an egg that he did find hiding there, and says, "Here it is!" And then it is the other ear and another egg. And then it is, "What is this in your nose, Kirstie?" and there is another egg, and then it is from the mouth, and then I see him wink at whoever stands at the cigar case or sits with his feet up against the stove in the middle of the store, and that is when I think, ya, vel den, I had just better put a stop to where those eggs are to come from next, and so I hand him the list because it is a long time now that we do not get money for the eggs because it is always the supplies from last week or the week before that we are to pay for today. And then it is a piece of hard candy that comes from behind my ear for while I wait.

So you will say, Kirsten Knudson, you are fifteen years old now and that is too old to be teased in public and too old to sit on the sidewalk in front of Jonsson's General Store sucking on a piece of hard candy. Get up and take your supplies home and get back to work.

And I will say to you. I am good to work. I am good to cook and to milk and to feed the chickens and to cut hay and to make soap and candles and butter, and to do the washing, too. And that is just to begin what I am good to do, from first I wake up till last I sleep. It is work, work, work with me all the time, and I am not to complain, but when it is to Fargo I can go, then go I am gone. And if I am to rest my *bak-ende* for ten minutes while the candy gets to be small in my mouth, the work is still there to do when it is home I go. And if you ask Homer if he minds the wait, he will tell you he does not. And there is one more thing. If I am just right with the time then I can see the train, and that is a thing I am never to be tired to see. And that is just what happened, but to look at there were many things and not just a train.

The first was a Jew. I did not know about the Jews in Dakota, and to tell the truth, I did not know if there were any anywhere anymore. They are in the Bible because they were living where Jesus was born, and they killed Jesus because he was a Christian, and the picture of Jesus in Per Rolfsrud's Bible shows that Jesus was as blond as a Halling Norwegian, but the Jews in the pictures are very dark. And well, I guess I was just plain dumb (no, that is not right, just plain ignorant, as Mrs Harkness says) about those Jews not being around anymore, because where would they have gone? Well, to Fargo, then, some of them. Not that I would have known that they were Jews just by looking at them, but I knew because Mr. Jonsson came out onto the sidewalk just as I was sitting down right there on the edge of the boards with my feet in the dirt, and he said to the man from the cigar case that had come out, too: "Jews." And then he spit, and that is not a nice thing to look at when it is candy in my mouth, so I looked back at the Jews.

Well, they just looked like anyone would look if they had the same luck as, for example maybe, the Solheims, who have not had a Gunhild to live yet and Mor says that if there is another baby there will not be a Birgit Solheim either, and it is not just the Solheims with the bad luck, which is for us some the weather and some, I will just say it, Far, and there are rags for our feet, too, when it is too cold to go in bare feet, but not yet snow, but not to Fargo. There are always boots for Fargo, even if they are from Ole or Sten, and that is how I knew just where those boots came from on the women Jews and I thought it was nice of the men Jews to give up their boots for the day so the women did not have to come to town with their feet in rags. But the men had rags hanging from under their jackets, too, and this is a bad thing, because it is one thing to be poor but "another matter entirely," as Mrs. Harkness says, to be sloppy.

And it was for one of the Jews to get even worse, but that is later, because it was not the Jews that I was watching for very long because they were just sitting there in the wagon in the street right beside the gate to the little pasture in front of the big hotel like they were waiting for something, and then the very thing that I was waiting for happened, and there was a whistle and there was smoke coming from the river and then there was the Northern Pacific train rumbling right in front of me and that is just plain wonderful. Sometimes I get myself to the other side of the street in time to watch the freight cars unload because there is never to know just what will be behind those doors. Once it was a load of pigs that came tumbling out so fast that the boards underneath them broke and then it was pigs up and down the street everywhere you looked and men trying to catch them but that is not easy to do and one man on his horse even caught a pig with his rope, and that was the best, you bet.

Ya, vel den, that is when it was time for me to get up, but I could see that Mr. Jonsson was talking to another customer and had not even started to put the things on Mor's list into the empty egg box, so I just sat there and hoped that he would take his time slow and then maybe I would get to see the train leave Fargo, too, but that is twenty-five minutes just to sit and do nothing and that is not a thing to do. But there is a first time to do everything, as Sten says, so I decided to look around some more and that is when I saw the man and the woman, but really it was the woman to look at because for beautiful I have never seen such a dress. Mrs. Harkness has dresses that make her look just like that from the side, all tight and tiny from shoulder to waist and then with that pile of material bunched up like it is a cloud sitting on her *bakende*, and on her feet those pretty boots…no, elegant, that is the right word…with a half dozen little buttons for hooking and with a heel that is an inch off the ground so that it looks like she is walking always into a good stiff wind, which she is most of the time like everyone else, I suppose, but Mrs. Harkness I have never seen with such a dress like this one. Oh, I would have given every bit of candy from Mr. Jonsson for a year to touch just once such a thing. At first I thought the dress was dark brown. But then I thought, it is maroon (which is like a purple—I have not been reading that dictionary for nothing I want you to know, although I skip around because it is not for me to care about flora or fauna or this or that chemical). So I will say both brown and maroon, because when the sun was behind one of the little puffy clouds it was brown but when out the sun slips again, there it was shining and maroon. And even from across the street I could see that there was embroidery all across the collar and maybe even down the front of the jacket, but she was on the other side of the man so I can not say for sure.

But what I really wanted to see was the little baby buggy that the man was pushing because it looked like there were balls or something hanging all around it, but I could just barely see it in between the boards of the fence of the tiny pasture that is where they were walking. And so I just stared and stared and waited for them to get to the open gate so I could get a good look and I said to myself, "Come on. Come on. Come on," and then just like that, when the man and the woman got to the gate the man tripped on something that made the balls that I do not know what they were but they were like they were each and every one alive and like they were dancing, and the sun peeked out from behind a cloud turning the dress all purple and shiny, and I could have laughed with surprise if the next thing had not been even better.

Because the team of horses harnessed to that little wagon of Jews that had looked like they were half asleep a second before and had not even moved when the train came in with its whistle and its rumble and its smoke, well, they came right up out of their skin when those little balls started to dance and when their front hooves came down they were a good six feet in front of where they had been before and the Jews were all tumbled about in the wagon, and then up go the horses again, but this time not together like the first time, and the man who grabbed the reins was yelling the one word of English that everyone seems to know and that is a good and simple "Ho!" but there was no 'ho' in those horses now and the third time they went up it was in a tangle and when they came down they were no more with the wagon and down the street they go, but not without that man who flew right off behind them and when he hit the street it was with a thud that made the candy go bad in my mouth.

"Let go!" I heard Mr. Jonsson yell behind me, but the man did not, and that is when I saw some men come running out of the meat market down the street and jump off the sidewalk and they just ran right into the street in front of the horses with their arms up in the air. Those horses just sort of zigzagged (that one I got from Sten who is getting pretty good with the English, too) down the street until they came up to the men with their hands in the air yelling, "Ho there, boys," and then those horses stopped. And that is not a surprise, because if you have ever seen a run-away team you know that they are just plain relieved when they can stop acting like fools. This I can not say is always how it is with people, or "human beings," as Mrs. Harkness says, or else we would have all learned to throw up our arms in front of Far as he is about to escape to Fargo, and say, "Ho there, Far."

So back to the baby buggy and the beautiful dress I looked, but the woman and the man were gone and so the fun was over and it was time to get the supplies and turn Homer back home, and as I was standing up I saw that the Jews had all left that wagon and the women were standing around the man that had been dragged by his horses and they were brushing his clothes and using their rags to wipe his face, and some of the men Jews were with the horses, and then the train pulled away and they all looked up and so did I, and there was a man standing on the platform in front of the warehouse right across the street. Now that is a lot of people to come to town to pick up just one man, but who am I to talk about the wasting of time. But I don't care. To see such a beautiful dress and a man dragged down the street by a team of horses, well that is pretty good luck and better than pigs on the loose any day, and

as Mrs. Harkness says, we must each take a little time out to smell the
rose.

Chapter XXII

In Which We Study the Intricate Geometry of Frost

Anna missed St. Paul, Frances knew, and the long stay at the
Headquarters Hotel, followed by almost three winter months
cloistered in the rather Spartan surroundings of their new
home, had not made the transition to life in Dakota easy. Throughout
December and January, and now, much of February, the women had
listened to the continued blows of hammers and the rhythmic crunch-
ing of saws throughout the house, as the rooms on the third floor were
completed, and trim and detail throughout were fitted into place. The
sturdy joists and beams occasionally rang out with gunshot-like reports
as they contracted in the cold. The intricate geometry of frost lacing the
windows would have been quite beautiful had it not introduced within
the frozen world without. The carpets and drapery ordered in St. Paul
during the fall waited in a warehouse on Front Street in Fargo, as did
much of the furniture from the Summit House, including Anna's piano,
and there it would all sit until the weather cleared long enough to allow
delivery, by sled or by wagon.

In the meantime Frances was doing her best to keep her friend's
spirits up as they waited for whatever release spring would bring. Today her plan was to encourage Anna to imagine how the house yard
could be transformed with trees and shrubs and flowers. As soon as the
farm supervisor's wife, Mrs. Johnson, whose third child was just a few
months older than Houghton, made her trip across the yard to nurse the
baby, Frances intended to settle in next to Anna on the couch. Pencils
in hand and a large sheet of heavy paper before them, they would begin
gardening.

"Are you certain Mrs. Johnson is...is...well, is the right sort of wet-
nurse for Houghton?" Anna asked as Frances walked into the parlor.

"The right sort of person?" Frances laughed. "She has milk and she
lives across the yard. That makes her the perfect sort of person. And

just this morning I discovered that one of our carpenters not only understands the mysteries of steam heat and the forty-gallon copper boiler in the kitchen, but was able to explain how it operated in a way that I could understand, too. We are surrounded, it seems, by the right sort of people."

"Which carpenter?"

"The one with the hat that is too small."

"I wish he would take it off in the house."

"Do you? I will speak to him, if you like."

"Oh, no," Anna said. "He will be gone soon enough. They will all be gone soon enough."

Anna's sigh, Frances knew, was not for the impending absence of strangers in the house, but rather, for the general tendency of loved things, of parents, homes, friends, to disappear over time. It was a lesson Frances had learned very early, but it was a mood for which she had little patience. "And then it will be spring," Frances said as she bent to retrieve the scrolled parcel she had earlier placed upon the room's lone side table. "And we will have all of our old things around us, and the roads will be fine, and we will have friends to visit, and you, dear, will be happy once again."

"I am not truly unhappy, Frances, just a little melancholy today. I know that my blue look-out must be very tedious for you, for your spirits are never low. It is something I have always admired. There, I'm afraid, I am not your equal."

"No, you are not my equal. You are in every way superior, and it is your company that keeps my spirits high. That is why I have brought this for us to study." Frances lifted the tube, and settling in next to Anna on the sofa, unrolled the architect's drawing of their new home. She and Anna had studied the drawing for hours in the Summit house parlor in anticipation of their move west, and although Anna had never spoken of her dismay upon first seeing the real house this past October from her father's carriage, Frances had understood. Abraham Radcliffe's sketch had included a yard dotted with several full-grown trees that softened the contours of the large building. His lightly penciled picket fence, laden with flowering vines, was suddenly revealed as a bit of cruel whimsy. Although the very real prairie grass surrounding the house had been mowed by some crude implement that left the vegetation heaped in browning swaths, this was no more a yard before them than was the sea that surrounds a ship. There was not a tree in sight.

"Let's start with the trees," Frances said, tapping the drawing. "What do you think about the ones Radcliffe has drawn in?"

"I think that they are at least thirty to forty years old," Anna said, favoring Frances with an unexpectedly wry smile.

"I actually meant, what do you think of the placement?"

"I think that they are perfectly placed, and that as soon as possible we should have some saplings planted this spring, but while we are waiting for trees to grow, we must put in a hedge, or a fence."

"To keep the gravy from seeping into the beans?"

"I beg your pardon?"

"Nothing, dear, just something that Percy said to me once. You two are very much alike sometimes. A hedge, then. Where will you have it?"

As Anna began to lightly trace in the hedge that would separate her world from the random space of the surrounding prairie, Frances settled back into the cushions to enjoy her daily allotment of pleasure in Anna's nearness. Within minutes she would not be able to distinguish where her warmth stopped and Anna's began. She was about to close her eyes when Anna spoke.

"This weather has been hard for the two of you."

For a moment Frances could make no sense of Anna's words. The "two of you," Frances assumed must refer to her and to Houghton, but that made no sense. Then Frances realized that Anna was talking about Percy, and that this was Anna's quiet form of interrogation.

"Yes, but it can not last," Frances said, noticing that Anna's hedge was taking the shape of a perfect square, each side equidistant from the house. The severity of the winter had indeed made Percy's trips to the farm rare. These visits were congenial, if unremarkable. They had not resumed their conjugal intimacies, nor had the absence of such attentions been remarked upon by either husband or wife. Their days of playful camaraderie had quite simply evaporated, and Frances had all but forgotten how her mind once hungered for all that Percy knew, for all that he could tell her of the world beyond her ken. Now, her intuition told her, there was a better world for her about which Percy felt nothing but contempt, and that world was right here. Although she could not put her expectations precisely into words, she had the sense that what she waited to enter depended almost entirely upon what she had the will to imagine, or perhaps more accurately, the imagination to will.

"I love seeing him with the baby," Anna said. "There, what do you think of that?"

Frances sat forward to look at the sketch. "Very neat. And now the garden. We are to have flowers, surely. And maybe more trees on the north side of the house."

"What will grow here, do you think?"

"Whatever grows in St. Paul, I imagine, but perhaps you should start with the outlines of the garden itself."

Percy was getting better with Houghton, although Frances was careful to check her husband for signs of inebriation before placing the baby in his arms. She had come to recognize a certain erectness of carriage and a greater deliberation in his manner as tell-tale attempts to disguise his condition. He consistently smelled of the hard liquorices he sucked upon, and his tongue appeared to be permanently blackened. Still, Anna was right. It was good to see him with the baby, and that surprised her a little. Everything about her child was surprising. She had looked forward neither to pregnancy nor to the child it would produce, and yet she was daily amazed at her capacity for devotion. Seeing Anna with Houghton was at times almost unbearably stimulating.

Frances picked up her own pencil and began to trace in the outline for the flower garden on the side of the drawing closest to her, for she could see that it, too, was to have edges that were straight. There would be no flowers on the north side of the house, but the other sides would be surrounded by a U-shaped garden, perfectly symmetrical and divided in two by a sidewalk leading up to the front steps.

"What are those?" Frances asked, pointing to the fountain-like images Anna was now drawing next to the house's foundation, on either side of the front door, and then, once again evenly spaced, on each side of each of the windows that looked out to the east and the west.

"Lilacs."

"So close to the house?"

"No?"

"I don't know. I guess that would work. It would be a lovely way to greet friends who come to visit."

"Which friends are those?" Anna asked without lifting her head.

The tone surprised Frances, for it held a note of irritation not at all typical of Anna's quiet reserve.

"Anna, dear," Frances said, reaching over to place her hand on her Anna's arm.

"Oh, don't mind me."

"You are fond of Lydia Harkness. You have called her 'accomplished', and that is approbation that you reserve for a very few."

"I hope I am more generous than that, Frances. I am, indeed, fond of her."

"I am surprised that such an *accomplished* lady finds it agreeable to spend much of the year trying to educate immigrant children."

"Is that so unlikely? She is a trained teacher, married to a man whose business is also to tend to others. She works with the mind, and he, the body. They are, I think, a good match."

"What I meant was that it must be hard for someone of her sensibilities to be in the presence, not of children whose inquisitive minds she can train to culture, but rather of children from whom she can expect little more than that they might learn to speak something approximating English. Now what are those?"

"Rose bushes. They're everywhere, so why not? That would be hard, but do you not think, Frances, that she does it for the sake of the occasional diamond in the rough. I am thinking of the Norwegian girl she told us about for whom she had such high hopes." Anna hesitated and then added, "If there is a wonder, it is perhaps to be directed at ourselves. What are we to do here?" And then, as if surprised by her words, she corrected herself. "I do not mean 'we', of course, for you have Percy and Houghton, and—"

"Anna, darling," Frances interrupted, "you are needed here precisely as you were needed in St. Paul, by every single one of us. In fact, now you are needed more, for it is already clear that you have become indispensable to my son's happiness."

"Mrs. Johnson must have left some time ago," Anna said after a moment's hesitation.

"And that means Houghton is fast asleep in his crib where she puts him when he has had his fill. I'll go take a peek."

Anna set her pencil down and slid the sketch from her lap as soon as Frances was out of the room. She shifted her weight to her good hip, repositioning the sofa pillow behind her. It wasn't like her to complain so, and yet each day her nostalgia for St. Paul grew into something closer to mourning. Sometimes she even felt the tiniest bit of resentment rise toward Frances, whose good cheer, Anna could tell, was not an act put on for her benefit. She was finding this whole Dakota experiment interesting. And now here she was, giving Anna's hand a squeeze while insisting that she was still needed. It was patently untrue, Anna knew, and it was insulting to be lied to in the form of a compliment. No, she wasn't needed, but she would be dutiful, nonetheless. If her father wanted his family about him in the new life he was constructing in Dakota, then so be it. He was a widower, with no wife to see to his comforts. She was a cripple, with no husband. She would do, she must do, as her father requested. Her greatest fear was that the day would come when she would have to do so alone, when Frances and Percy and Houghton would make their home elsewhere, as someday, she believed, they certainly must.

Anna glanced at Radcliffe's drawing next to her, its professional lines now marred by her amateurish and oddly proportioned additions. There had been lilacs in the front yard of the Summit house. A lovely way to greet friends who come to visit. In St. Paul friends had often called for an evening of cards or to listen to her play. Neighbors were kind enough to stop by in sleighs on pleasant winter days, in carriages during the summer, encouraging her to join them for a ride.

But here, there were no neighbors, and so far, just one friend.

Not counting Frances, that is.

CHAPTER XXIII

In Which To Go is To Be Gone

Everything is growing and changing now, and it seems like only for the Knudsons is the change not so good, then. Sten is gone. It is one day that he is busy with the newspaper and plaster for between the boards of his new house on Homer's land and then the next day it is only a note and no more Sten. The note is some in English and some in *norsk* but it is not one bit of it good. Ole he tells to be the man of the house, and to me he tells to "lift the work on Mor," but I know what he means. For Guri and Haldis he has no thing to say, and they are the ones who cry. To Mor he says only *"om forlatelse"* but sorry or not, go is gone. It is the worst for Ole, because he has a strong back, but before, not one decision did he make. No, it was Sten. When Far is here Ole is fine, but when Far escapes, then Ole he is like he is lost.

It was the last escape that brought Sten to go. Far had a load of potatoes to take to Fargo, and I can tell you that two acres of potatoes is a lot of potatoes to dig and we were glad that we did not eat the seed potatoes in the dugout last winter like we thought we might have to, but it is not potatoes that I am talking about, it is Far, and this time he was gone for almost a week and then here he comes walking home and if I did not know it was Far I would not know it was Far, with his beard sticky with straw and blood, and one eye closed and covered with a crust of yellow like the little hen that we ate last week because the other hens were trying to peck it to death. And now that I think about it, Far was walking like that hen that could not see, too, and he had no shoes on and there was a smell that I will not say what it was. And you will ask, why would Sten and Ole and Mor let Far go to Fargo alone with a load of potatoes when it is to escape that he might do. And maybe they would answer that Far can go to Fargo and back nine times in a row with no trouble, so who is to know that on the trip that is ten he will escape? And maybe they would say that there is too much work to be done to send a son along to act as a chaperone. (That is a word from a book that Mrs. Harkness gave to me, so it is not what Sten or Ole or Mor would say, but it is what they would mean.) But I will say that it is because Far is a man, and he is the father, and what he says there is to do then that is what there is to do.

The potatoes they were the last of what there was to sell. The money from the wheat had all gone to pay the debts in town, with not one thing left over because it was only ten bushels to the acre and that was too bad because it had come up so green and full but then there had been the hail and so it was up to the eggs and the butter and the potatoes. Now here was Far with no flour and no cornmeal and no barrel of pork and no maple syrup and molasses and no coffee and I thought about the potatoes and the turnips in the dugout and the eggs that Mor had been packing in salt all fall and I knew that was our food for the winter, that and what the cows could give us, and I hoped that we would not have to butcher one of the cows because to lose the cow is to come to the end of the rope. I do not know what rope that is, but the end is not so good, you bet. Guri and Haldis started to cry again because there would be no shoes for them again this winter. But even this was not the bad news, and it was not until Sten came home from the big Bingham farm from the plowing there that he said the words that no one had said right out loud, he said, "Where is Homer?"

Far he just looked at his supper of bread and hot milk and did not answer, but made a sort of growl in his throat, and even though he had dunked his head in Homer's trough to clean up the blood, there was still the eye shut, and so the growl was to take serious and no more there was to say. Well, Sten he just walked right back out the door, and we knew that it was to Fargo he would go and that is five miles as the crow flies but it would take that crow a lot longer on his feet like Sten, and after a full day behind a plow, too, and already it was suppertime and when it was breakfast there he was at the table. But Homer was not in the barn because Homer was now the property of Mr. Stephens at the livery. Sten said that Mr. Stephens said that Far sold Homer to him five days before, and he had a bill of sale signed by Far to prove it, and so Sten said that it was not right to buy a man's mule from him when he was drinking, but Mr. Stephens told Sten that the conversation was over unless Sten was there to buy that mule back. Well—I know that I am not supposed to begin sentences that way because it is "vulgar," as Mrs. Harkness would say, but that is a funny thing because it is Mrs. Harkness who told me to say "well" in the first place instead of "ya, vel den" (so really the "well" is in the second place), but sometimes it just does not seem right to start out without one or the other, it is like trying to walk out of the house before you open the door. Sometimes when I start out with a "well," Ole he says, "That's a deep subject," and then he laughs and laughs like it is a thing that he made up and has not said a hundred times before. So anyway, Sten did not have the money, of course. In fact, there is not one thing we have that is worth so much as Homer, except our quarter section that is now proved up but land can not produce without a Homer, even if Per Rolfsrud and Osten Sondreaal let us have a team now and then to help out.

Far was still sleeping when Sten told Mor and Ole and me the news, and just like that there was a cold feeling on me, like when you are just sitting there and all of a sudden your skin does a shiver, like Homer when a fly lands on his shoulder only all over. Once when I was in school and this happened to me, Molly Sullivan said it meant that someone had walked on my grave, but the Sullivans are Catholic and so I did not listen to her superstition, but when I was listening to Sten I thought maybe what Molly Sullivan said could be true, because right then and just like that I understood that my grave really is somewhere right now, even if I am not in it yet, so it is not really a grave, and maybe it just looks like another piece of grass waiting for the plow, but it is only me to plant and then it is a grave. And that is when I took a good long look at Mor and I saw how worn out she is, and there in the bed on the wall were Haldis and Guri and so thin they are, they are like wrinkles in the quilt on top of them. They are not any more the little girls who run from work to pick wildflowers for necklaces. With them it is always crying and coughing and drip, drip, drip from the noses, and I thought, it is like they are turning into water, but if the tears and the drip, drip, drip dry up then they would just blow away. Ole and Sten they both looked strong and healthy, like young men, but what did I look like? Maybe I looked like I could slip over into my grave, too.

Because without Homer there is no plowing and no planting and no haying and no no carrying and no doing. There is no nothing at all.

So no more was there to say and we went to our chores, and I do not know what the others were thinking, but I was thinking that the winter would be the time for me to work out, to be the *hushjelp* for one of the Yankee families in Fargo, and that would be hard on Mor, because Guri and Haldis can not do what I can do, but I would be one less mouth to feed, and I could earn money to give to Mor. And maybe the same would be true for Ole or Sten, maybe they could go to the trees in Minnesota and maybe a man's winter of logging would be worth a mule. And this is what I am thinking and I am again in the potatoes, digging and digging, when up I look and here is Osten Sondreaal walking toward the house with Homer on a rope, and my sacks are not full but I bring them to the yard in time to hear him say *god dag* to Sten who is stacking sod up against the sides of the house to get ready for winter. He was in Fargo, says Osten Sondreaal, and there he did see Homer in the pen behind the livery, and Mr. Stephens owed him a favor and is not really a bad man, so he was able to get a good deal on Homer, and Far and the boys are to repay him with plowing and backsetting this fall as long as the weather holds and again in the spring with planting, and so on and so forth (as Mrs. Harkness would say and not really what Osten Sondreaal said) until the debt it is worked off. And that is all very fair, even if there is never one extra minute for Sten and Ole and it would mean not as much time for Sten to work on Homer's land, but at least there was not to be so much the stepping on our graves now.

Well, Sten he just pulled himself up tall like the big man he is now and held out his hand to Osten Sondreaal and that would have been that, except now there is Far charging out from the house, and it is like the words that come out of his mouth are yellow and green with pus like his eye, and now it is not the English that he is so proud to speak, so I will not say his exact words, and I am glad for it. Far said that he knew what Osten Sondreaal was doing, and Osten Sondreaal said that he was trying to help a Halling friend who had gotten into some trouble, and father said he knew just who that Halling friend was and she did not want anything to do with Osten Sondreaal either and so Osten Sondreaal could keep his dirty tricks to himself. Well, that is when Osten Sondreaal he pulls his shoulders back and puts his hands on his hips, so that he looks like a grasshopper standing up, and he is close to Far now so he has to bend his head back and he says, *"Dirty? Here is Torger Knudson, stinking of the gutter, telling Osten Sondreaal that he is dirty?"* And then Mor was at the door, and we all had to turn and look at her not because so soft she was speaking, because this is always her way, but because her voice was quiet like when the wind has been howling through the window and under the door all day long and then it just stops.

"Go now, Osten," Mor said. *"We thank you with all our hearts. Go now."*

Far he looked like he had been knocked over the head. He just stood there with his mouth open, and his one eye all popped out, but it wasn't until Osten Sondreaal was walking away, right through the potatoes, that Far turned and said to Mor, *"Hore."*

That is when Sten he just stepped up to Far and hit him with his fist right in the nose, and Mor yelled, "Sten, no!" But the words were done

and over, and so was Sten because even if he is a full-grown man now
with his own thick brown beard just like Far, and Far was with one eye
looking like the scum that is on the slough pond in the middle of August, pretty soon it was Sten that was not to get up. And when he did get
up he walked to Homer's trough and washed the blood from his nose,
and then he turned and walked to his new little house on Homer's land
that is still half with tar paper and half with the boards and plaster, and
now he is gone. Far says that Sten will be back soon enough, and then
he tries to make a joke, but there has been a long time here with not one
thing to make a laugh.

And then the snow was here and I will tell you now that the winter
is not hard because it is cold or because it is windy, even if the cold is
more than you can think is possible unless you, too, have tried to milk a
cow with hands so frozen that they can not squeeze or when you bang
a stick against the cart wheel to break off the ice and straight back at
you comes the stick and you think that maybe your fingers will break
before the ice, or if you have ever come inside with your feet frozen
like blocks of wood and you think it is not so bad until you begin to
unwrap the rags as you sit by the stove and then little by little the feeling comes back, but the feeling is now like a fire, and it makes you hold
your breath, but you can not hold it long enough. For Guri and Haldis
winter is the worst and they cry and cry when Mor sends them outside
to feed the chickens, and over and over I say to them, do not cry outside,
but they do not stop and then there are the sores, on their faces and on
their hands and on their feet, arms, legs. Chilblains. That is the word.
Mor put thick cream on their sores, but still there were the tears.

But I forgot to say why winter is hard, and it is because we are all
in the house at the same time, except for Sten who is gone, and we are
all getting bigger and the house is getting smaller, it is now for me just
seven strides long, too, and only that because I have to walk around five
people to get from one end to the other, and around the spinning wheel
that Far lifts down from where it hangs from a hook on the rafters. I
know that it is necessary the spinning, but every day I look at the bag
of wool on the wall and wish that Mrs. Rolfsrud would take it to someone else. Guri and Haldis are at least good to separate the wool and
untangle the long strands. I am best to card it into fluffy rolls, but it is
Mor who is good to spin and it is Mor who is good to knit.

Only on Sunday morning does the working stop. The new church with its steeple pointing straight up at God sits so pretty and white on the only thing like a hill nearby. There was some fun at first because although we are all *norsk*, or Norwegian, as Mrs. Harkness says I am to say, and Lutherans, of course, not everyone was used to the same kind of church in *Norge*. Pastor Fedje is Norwegian Synod like the Rolfsruds and that makes sense because it was Per Rolfsrud who got together with some of the folks in Fargo to bring him to Dakota, and that is why Pastor Fedje preaches in Fargo and at our church, too. Mor says Norwegian Synod is fine with her and that it is not so different from what she and Osten and Peter Sondreaal grew up with, but some of the new families farming nearby were Lutheran Brethren and they can be just silly. Once when our heads were bowed in silent prayer Ole Lavik he stood up and started to pray out loud, just like that, like it was anyone else's business what he had to pray about, and Pastor Fedje he turned so red it looked like he was being choked by his collar that makes it look like his head is sitting on a plate, and sometimes the new Ericsons and Siversons would get to nodding their heads during the sermon like they were riding on a trotty horse and not in the house of the Lord, where it is only right to be with more respect and that means to sit very still and to look sad. So it was not very long before some folks decided they needed a church of their own and some other folks said good riddance. Now and then Marit Lavik comes to our house to trade her preserves for a chicken and every time she tells Mor about the *afholds foreninger* that her church has started to protect Norwegians from the evil effects of American society, and Mor smiles and is polite, but I do not think she needs a Lutheran Brethren to tell her about the dangers of the saloon.

Pastor Fedje he preaches three Sundays in *norsk*, and then there is one in English (and that was the thing that finally brought the Lutheran Brethren families to go start their own church) and here is the proof that things are easier for natural-born Americans, because even hell sounds not so bad when Pastor Fedje talks about it in English, but on the other three Sundays, by the end of the sermon the hair is standing right up on the back of my neck, and Guri and Haldis are holding hands and their eyes are wide open like they are looking right into the fire in front of them, and even the boys are swallowing hard.

Far does not go to church, and we do not tell him that Mor talks to Osten Sondreaal there, and that is how we know that Sten is in the pine trees of Minnesota, and each month he sends three dollars to Osten Sondreaal to pay him back for Homer and three dollars to Mr. Jonsson at the general store for our supplies, and Osten Sondreaal looks sad at Mor and says that he wished Sten would send his three dollars to his mother, but Mor just says, *"Sten is a good son."* And Osten Sondreaal says, *"He is a good man, Astri."* And then Mor smiles, and that is not too often to happen.

Guri and Haldis were sad that they could not go to the church school that Pastor Fedje started during the winter, but I am glad. There are times when I wish I could stay home with Far. I do not like the way the Norstads and the Nielsons look at Guri and Haldis in their *ladder* and at the boots I have because Ole has grown out of them. Mor says there is no shame to being poor if you are working and you are clean. Well, I will just say it now. I have shame. I have shame that Guri and Haldis wear mittens on their feet, and that our dresses are made out of flour sacks, and that shame is not even half of why I do not like to go to church.

The other half is Halvor Rolfsrud. He is big and he is ugly and he says he is going to marry me. First, about the big. He does not just seem big because I am small, which, in fact, I am, but I was not always. When I was thirteen years old Mrs. Harkness measured us all against the Rolf-srud's door, and I was the tallest girl except for the Schmidt girls and they are almost giants. No, giantesses. That is what Mrs. Harkness said to Marit Norstad when she said that about the Schmidts, and then we repeated after her, "The German girls are giantesses," and wrote it on our slates, and that was when I was five foot and two inches, and I came home and made a mark with a nail on the wall outside by the lye bucket so I could see if I am growing, and it is not even an inch different now and I am soon to be sixteen years old, so I am growing, but I am not five foot three yet, so not much, and here is my point: Halvor Rolfsrud is six foot and two inches and as strong as an ox, he says. And like an ox is exactly right.

Because he is ugly, too. Here is a story about Halvor Rolfsrud. One day early this winter when Mor and I were all day making candles, so all day it was dip the sticks with the strings into the tallow and then into the pail of snow water and then the tallow and then the snow water, and over and over and over and forever it seems, well, it was then that we heard a jingling from a sleigh. I scraped the ice from the window and looked outside and there was Mr. Norstad bringing his team into the yard, and Marit Norstad and Lena Nielson were in the sleigh and all under a buffalo robe, and they were stopping to see if anyone wanted to go for a ride. And that is just like Marit Norstad, sometimes mean and sometimes like a friend. Mor would not let the little girls go because there was not room for everyone and besides they had been all day complaining, and if I had been Mor I would have pushed them into the sleigh just to not have to hear it any more. But I was to go.

We went straight from our place to the Norstad farm that is just on the other side of the river and right on the way to the Rolfsrud place that is not much more than a mile beyond as the crow flies (or as the sleigh rides on the prairie). Sometimes the Norstads are with their noses in the air because Mr. Norstad went to high school in *Norge*, and they had already been in America for fifteen years in Iowa before they moved to Dakota, and Marit and Jens Norstad go to the new school in Fargo and Marit Norstad is sure to marry Sven Nielson. So pretty soon there is the fine Norstad house that has two stories, and we go to the room that is just for Marit and her two sisters, and on the wall is hanging a big mirror, just like that. Pastor Fedje would have something to say about that, I think, but he was not in the room with Marit and Lena and me, so I just took a good look. And I looked and looked. Because we do not have a glass at home, not a real one anyway that shows more than a little bit of this and then a little bit of that, so as far as I knew I had one blue eye and then another blue eye and a nose that looked pretty regular and a mouth that looked pretty regular and so on and so forth, as Mrs. Harkness would say. But this mirror was stuck right to the wall, and if I stood back about two feet I could see from shoulders up, and well, there I was, the whole thing, top to middle. My hair is the color of Mor's and Guri's and Haldis', but mine is full and thick and almost to my waist. I braid it up so that is not special, but all put together, the eyes and the nose and the mouth and the hair at once, if you saw it on someone else you might say, 'What a pretty girl,' and I know that this is a sin for me to say it, but that is what I was thinking when I stood in front of the mirror. It came on me as sort of a surprise, so I think "we must make some allowances," as Mrs. Harkness used to say to be nice when Michael Sullivan would try to read. But then I heard Marit whisper something to Lena that made her laugh and it sounded like she said, "Kirsten *ga i giftetanke*," but I did not think that anyone would say that I went in wedding thoughts just because I was looking in the mirror.

Then Mrs. Norstad called us into the kitchen for our hot cider, and I saw that they had been plucking the bristles from a boar's skin that had been boiled, and I thought that it would have been nice to have had some nice fat pigs to butcher now and then. Marit she picked up a bundle of the bristles that had been tied together and set it onto her head and said, "Who am I?" And I laughed and laughed when she said, "Halvor Rolfsrud," because that is just how his hair looks, sticking straight out every way, and then a tuft at the top sticking straight up. And then Lena said, "Halvor is sweet on Kirsten," and I stopped laughing.

Because it is true. He tells everyone, and to me he says, "I am going to marry you, Kirsten Knudson." One day last fall I was out to stake the cows after we had cut the hay, and here comes Halvor on that big horse of his, and he gets off the horse and he says the terrible thing right out loud, and I say, "Back up, Halvor Rolfsfud. It hurts my neck to talk to you so close. And don't say that. I am not going to marry you." So he gets all red, and when he gets red his hair seems to stand out even more, like he has been sleeping in the straw and it got stuck to him every which way. And he says, "Who are you going to marry?" And I say, "I am not going to marry anybody. I am fifteen years old." And then he smiles and says that lots of girls get married at fifteen or sixteen. And I say, well, not me. And he says that maybe I need to have a reason to be married, and that is when I decided that maybe I should be paying not so much attention to how ugly he is and more to how big, and I say, "No thank you." And that is what I said to Lena Nielson and Marit Norstad. "No thank you."

I was glad when Jens Norstad came in from his evening chores feeding the cows and hogs and sheep and asked if he should unhitch the team, and Mr. Norstad said, no, he guessed it was time to carry the visitors home. I was glad because that meant that Jens Norstad was not in the room to hear Lena's silliness about Halvor, and then I was especially glad because Jens said, "I can do it, Far." And then, best of all, Marit Norstad said she would say good bye in the house because it was too cold now for any more sleighing, and that meant it would just be me and Lena Nielson and Jens Norstad. So I said, once we got going, was it not a beautiful night with shining so bright the stars, and how I just never got to go sleighing just for fun, and how it was not cold at all under the buffalo robe, and if Lena wanted to go home first, that would be fine with me. Because Jens Norstad is a good-looking boy, with a nice smile and hair that looks like hair and not a haystack, and he is the only Norstad boy, too, even if he is only fourteen, and Mr. Norstad bought a whole section from the railroad, and has a 160-acre timber claim as well. But Jens Norstad said he could not do that, because Halvor Rolfsrud said to every boy around that if he saw any one of them with Kirsten Knudson he would swing them by the ankles until they threw up.

"It was for him a joke," I said.

"No," Jens shook his head. "Ole Dahl laughed at him, and Halvor he picked him up and did just that and we did scatter then."

So Halvor Rolfsrud, dumb as an ox, had outsmarted me, never mind my potential, and pretty soon there I was standing in front of our house with the snow shining with Dakota diamonds under the moon all around me and there was Lena Neilson just jingling away with Jens Norstad. Well, I suppose she knew about the timber claim, too.

That was the nice start to the very worst winter yet. Soon there was sleighing enough because there was no other way to go from here to there, not that any of us had much of a there to go to, although of the here there was plenty. And really it is not a sleigh we have but a stone boat for hauling rocks, but it hauls people, too, although it is not easy for Homer. And all winter long Far said that come spring it is another team of mules we will have, and a mower and a sulky rake, too. How could that be when even for shoes for Haldis and Guri there was not enough, I wanted to ask Far? I thought maybe it was only too much snow that made Far say those things. Blizzards and blizzards and blizzards and Mor said that with the snow blowing straight over the prairie and none coming from the sky you would not think there could be so much snow right where we were.

Once the blizzard went on for four days and Far tied a rope between the door of the house and the outhouse so we would not get lost going forth and back, and when it was time to do the chores Far tied the rope to himself to go to try to find his way to the soddie where Homer and the cows are, and he had to follow the rope back to the house two times before he found the way. And every day it was more than an hour with the shovel for Ole and Far to open a path from the door, and on the fourth day it was no more a path but a tunnel (and that is the same word in *norsk*, and that is nice when that happens) and then we knew what it was like to live like a Finn. When that blizzard stopped we all were happy to go to church, even Far wanted to go to hear the news, and the news was not one bit good. Everyone we knew was alive, but there were others who were not. Mr. MacLeach, that Ole had husked corn for last year was found frozen to death not even fifty feet from his house, and the Solheims had lost all of their chickens from the cold, and Ingeborg Rolfsrud had an English newspaper from Fargo, and there were stories and stories about people lost and having their fingers and toes and noses frozen off. And even the trains could not get through to Fargo with three engines pulling. Or pushing. Because they are trying to push the snow but they are trying to pull the train.

And that was just one storm, and it happened over and over again, and it was very hard on people, especially on a Mrs. Emily Smith from north of Mapleton that Pastor Fedje talked about in church, because during one storm when Mr. Smith and their twelve-year-old son went out to bring in the cows that had wandered away, Mrs. Smith cut the throats of their four little children and then cut her own throat as well, and the Pastor Fedje said that we were to pray for the souls of the little children, but as for Mrs. Emily Smith she was lost to eternal hellfire, and Ole he leaned over to me and said, well, at least she was warm, but I did not even smile because it seemed like things had been hard enough for Mrs. Emily Smith whoever she was without being talked about behind her back from the other side of the grave, and sometimes I just wish Pastor Fedje would preach only in English.

So we waited and hoped for spring to come, but it turned out that there was something worse than blizzards to come first. It started in March with the Sullivans, and what we heard was that there were three of the little children that died in just two weeks. Then we heard that Frau Krueger, who Greta Schlaet had called the father of our country, had died on the same day as two of her children, and in church we heard that the sickness was in Fargo, too, and that there would be no more church until it had passed. And then we were not listening for who else was sick, because it was in our house, too. First it was Guri and Haldis, and then it was Ole, and that was a very bad sign because he is a grown man and strong. And Mor and I were busy with the rags soaked in warm vinegar and putting hot cups and plates on their backs and chests and they all did sweat and sweat but the fever would not stop, and for two days not a one of them knew if it was night or day, and it was not so very different for Mor and me, we were working that hard, and then first Ole and then Haldis and Guri started to get better, and that is when Mor just fell down. One minute she was standing there with her arms full of sheets for the washing and the next she was on the floor and I wanted to think that she was just plain tired, but she had the sickness, too. Ole he was sleeping on a pallet beside the stove because he was still not with the strength to get into the rafters, and Haldis and Guri were in their bed on the wall, and Mor we made a bed for on the table in the middle of the room because it was too cold in her room with Far, and all day long Far and I were wringing out rags and putting them back, and I was scrubbing the laundry and hanging it out in the wind that was so cold that my wet hands were raw and stiff like chicken claws. Far he killed a chicken and I plucked it for soup but we were the only ones with any appetite, and plenty of that because there was still the milking and the chores and only Far and me, and then I got the headache and then it looked like our little house was very big and everyone was very far away from me, and then I knew that if I did not lay down I would fall down like Mor, and then I thought, good, I would like to lay down now, and the next thing I knew it was almost a full week later, and there I was on the pallet by the stove, and everyone was weak but getting better, except Mor, and Far was gone to Fargo to get Dr. Harkness, Ole said. And I said, "Oh, Ole, he has escaped for sure, then."

But Ole said, "no, here he comes into the yard now, sitting next to Dr. Harkness in his little sleigh and Homer trotting behind." And Dr. Harkness looked at Mor and said, "Why was I not called earlier?" and then he checked on me, and said, "So you are Kirsten. My wife has given me very precise instructions to make you well again." And he gave Mor some quinine to swallow and left a jar of syrup for the two of us and he said I was not to get up for one full week, and Mor was not to get up until he had seen her again, and when the doctor went he said he would send someone to help us out until Mor and I were back on our feet. And the very next morning in comes a Miss Jena Olafsdatter that is the nurse for Dr. Harkness and what do you think, she is *norsk*, too, only from Oslo, and she had been a deaconess nurse there, and that is using your potential, I think. She was taking medicine to many Norwegian families, and she had brought with her Olaug Berg who is a cook at the Bingham farm during spring planting and fall harvest and in between is *hushjelp* at the big hotel in Fargo.

Well, that Olaug Berg she had a beautiful voice when she was to sing, but for talking it was not so nice, and what she said was that Miss Jena Olafsdatter is for sure sweet on the doctor, and that last Sunday a man and a woman were *kjerketukt* at her church and we could just guess why they had been kicked out and they were both married, and her with little ones at home, and that there were two new Irish girls to cook and to *huskeep* for the men at the second Bingham farm (really, what she said was *"the Number Two Bingham farm,"* and that is because Mr. Bingham is with so much land now that he needs another home for the men and the stock) and that those Irish girls had been working as *husjelp* at the Fargo Hotel ever since arriving in Fargo on the train with not a father or brother or husband and you just needed to take one look at them to know each one was a *sjusket kvinne* and up to no good, and that there are already six families of Jews living in Cass County, and not even a stone's throw from the bridge across the Sheyenne, and what did we need with Christ killers here in Dakota, and that is when Mor says her first words and they are, "Please sing now, Mrs. Berg," and the next day Mor gets out of bed (which is exactly what Dr. Harkness told her not to do) and thanks Mrs. Berg and promises her a pair of new wool mittens to be made as soon as Mor has the strength, and then she tells Ole to take Mrs. Berg back to Fargo.

Then it was April and all that snow was now water and the rain came down on top of the snow and then it all froze again and the Red River started to flood and Far said that for a river to run north so that what thawed to the south ran into ice downstream was just plain backwards, and so much for American progress. Even the little Sheyenne was running fast and wide, and every single thing was either dirty or wet or both and everyone was cold, but we were all over the sickness, and only Guri and Haldis were still with the sore throats and coughs (but it was Far who drank the syrup that Dr. Harkness left).

And then Guri died.

I am sorry to say it just like that, but that is how it happened, just like that, like when the thunder claps right on top of the lightning without even a second for holding the breath with no time to even worry or pray. Even when I say it I think that it can not be possible, because we had all been sick, except Far, each one of us, and when we were sick it was almost like we were dead because of the fever and the choking and we did not know one thing, and then one by one we woke up, and we were weak, yes, and with Guri and Haldis there was still the cough, but we all got stronger and then we got out of bed and then we got well. But Guri just died. She got sick. And then she got better. And then she died. I am sorry to repeat myself, which is what Mrs. Harkness says is a thing I do, I say the same thing over and over even if it is in a different way, but how can you make sense out of that? How can you explain it? How can you say, well first this, and then that, and then that is why this? Because that is logic. That is what it means, Mrs. Harkness says, to be rational. You can make sense of your world, Mrs. Harkness says, if you can just understand one plus two equals three. Put things in order. Think about cause and effect. Be curious first, then be logical, and always follow a system, and then you will have understanding. But I tell you this is what happened. Guri got sick and then she got better and then she died. That is one plus two that does not equal three, and it is not logic and it is not right and I do not understand it one bit.

That is when Mor she went back to bed and she took Guri with her and I could not get Mor to let her go and Ole he was no help at all and Far I could hear in the yard pulling the planks from the old Red River cart to make a box. When he came inside I was in the rafters to get Ole's shirt to mend, and I saw Far try to take Guri from Mor. And there was my old dream right there in front of me only I was wide-awake for sure. Far he was standing there with his arms straight out in front of him and Mor was holding onto Guri like she was just sleeping and for once in peace and without the cough that you could hear all the way to the soddie barn, and Mor was saying "No, no, no." And then she said the thing that was like the walking on the grave again, she said, *"He sinks and he sinks and he sinks. Oh, Torger, what have we done? With no gravestone and no grave, where will I find my baby?"*

That is when Far left and when he came back he had Ingeborg Rolf-srud and Mrs. Norstad with him. They told me to take Haldis to go to sit in Homer's shanty that Ole lives in now that the weather has warmed up. That is when I took a good look at Haldis because there was no crying and no drip, drip, drip, just a little girl staring with big, blue eyes. So I reached across the table and put my hand on her hand and it was like there was nothing there. Not because she was so thin, but because it was like when Guri died Haldis was the shadow that stayed behind. So Guri we buried in the graveyard behind the new church that is not any more new because when it was new there was not one grave and after the sickness there are now six.

But then a good thing finally happened, even though I did not know it was happening, and I hope it is not a sin to speak of good so soon after poor little Guri did leave us, but how it happened is this, and I have to thank for her good opinion of my potential Mrs. Harkness. It was on May 17. Far and Ole had gone to the Norstads to "lift a glass to *Gamle Norge*," and Mor had not said one thing, not even that there was field-work to do, or that it was a shame that Far's own son had to lose a day of work as well just to make sure that Far would come home, or that if Far was going to celebrate the Fourth of July in a couple of months then he should stop celebrating the Seventeenth of May, because one independence day celebration a year was enough, which is what Mor did say every other year on *Syttende Mai*. So, anyway, Far and Ole had gone to the Norstads on the new team of mules that Far had brought home just the week before, and let me tell you about that day, too, because right behind Far is a stranger, all dressed up in a store-bought suit and he is driving a big wagon with a new mower in it (but no sulky rake, and I could not have been any more surprised if there was a rake and even a new threshing machine coming down the road, too), and when I asked Ole how Far could afford such things, Ole said that Far had gotten something else, too, and it was a mortgage, and that was a new word for me, too, and I guess there are still a lot of English words to learn. And even about this Mor did not say one word. But about the mules and the mower and the mortgage I am not talking.

So I will start again. It was on *Syttende Mai* that I went with Homer in the cart to town with eight pounds of butter for Mr. Jonsson at the store. The cart was without the planks along one side and the back, but that did not make it look so much worse than ever, and that it is ugly is not the problem, it is the sound that is just like a pig strung up by its feet that is hard. At first Mor wanted Far to please grease the wheels, but he just said, "There is nothing to grease on a Red River cart," and he is right, because every single thing on that cart is wood, and there is no point to oil a thing that is not metal. And that is when Mor said, "*primitivt*," and so it is, but now it is like Mor does not even hear the squeal. But I think that it is the worst for Homer because of how big are his ears.

So anyway, even though I was in the squealing cart that Far said he bought from a half-breed (which is like an Indian, but is not quite), I was still glad because when I am in the cart it is not so dangerous to go past the Rolfsrud place. No matter how fast I try to walk, if I am alone for sure Halvor will see me and will catch up to me when I am out of sight of the house. And every time he says, "Hello, my little Kirstie," and every time I say, "Halvor, go away." And the last time Halvor looked like he was thinking about getting mad, but I don't even know if he can think, but anyway he looked mad, and then he said, "Someday I will not ask," and I said, "good," and then he said, "Someday I will take what a man deserves." So Homer and I try to go by the Rolfsruds as fast as we can, and sometimes I wish the Knudsons did not owe the Rolfsruds so many favors, but Mor says that we would all be dead of starvation long ago if it had not been for Per and Ingeborg Rolfsrud. Or at least that's what she used to say, because ever since we buried Guri she does not talk that much. And the only person she has the smile for is Osten Sondreaal at church, but it is that sad smile.

But I can see that I have not even started to talk about the good thing that happened to me that I did not know was happening. So I'll just have to get past the sight and sound of me and Homer coming into Fargo. And when we go past Stephens Livery, Homer he slows down, but Per Rolfsrud and some of the other men from the church board talked to Mr. Stephens and asked him to please stop buying Homer from Far, because it is to take the un-do advantage, or at least that is what Ole said. Mor and I have a new place to hide the butter and egg money and there is no one around any more who will lend Far money, but we did not know about this thing that is a mortgage. This time Homer and I went to Jonsson's General Store first because the day was warm and the ice that Ole and Far cut from the river and covered with straw in the soddie dugout melts fast in the sun. So I did not waste any time there. I did not even give Mr. Jonsson a chance to do his tricks, I just went right on to the Harkness house in a hurry. And there was a fancy carriage in front of the door and the bay horse that was standing there did everything but come right out and sneeze at Homer when we went by, but maybe it was just the noise that put his ears back and made him snort. So I went around to the back, because I know where is the ice box, and I was disappointed because there would not be the chance to say 'Thank you' to Mrs. Harkness for the book that she had sent with Miss Jena Olafsdatter for me to read when we were all with the sickness.

So I put the book on the table and was going back out when Mrs. Harkness came around the door from inside the house, saying, "Is that you, Kirsten?"

And I said, "Yes, ma'am. I am sorry to disturb you," because when I am around Mrs. Harkness I try to talk like her, and that means not saying absolutely everything that comes to mind, but just choosing the polite things.

"Please come into the parlor, Kirsten," she says, "I have guests I would like you to meet."

Well, you could have knocked me over with a feather, I was that surprised, but I followed, because if Mrs. Harkness said, "Kirsten, please jump off a cliff now," I suppose I would smile and say, "Yes, ma'am," and then I would not be at all surprised to find out that jumping off a cliff was a good idea, except that there is no such thing as a cliff around here.

So I followed Mrs. Harkness into the parlor, and there were two women in the prettiest bonnets, I think the right word is 'tidy,' and they were made of exactly the same cloth as their dresses, really, just exactly the same! And Mrs. Harkness said to them, "This is the young woman about whom I was speaking. Kirsten, I would like you to meet Miss Anna Bingham and Mrs. Frances Bingham." The one named Anna lifted her hand toward me, and I just felt like a panic because I had been driving Homer and then handing out butter and I did not think that my hand was something to put next to that glove, because it was—I looked this word up when I got home so I know it is right—it was lavender. It was a lavender kid glove and it was exactly the same color as the ribbon on her hat, but there she was with her hand held right out to me and I knew that she was being really polite, so I just took a quick swipe of my *bakende* with my hand as secret as I could and hoped for the best, but she did not even look at my hand, which is good manners, you can't beat a Yankee for it. And her smile was so sweet that I just smiled right back, and I would have liked to just stand there for awhile, because she was so pretty and she looked so cool and clean, but then she took her hand away.

And then the other one said, "How do you do, Kirsten," and I looked away from the Anna one to the Frances one, and all of a sudden I got this shiver that ran straight up my backbone, because I had never seen eyes like those before. And I looked right away from her to Mrs. Harkness to see if she would give me a clue about what to do, but she was still with the same polite Yankee expression, which tells you not one thing. So I took a deep breath and looked back at Frances Bingham, and she had this little smile on her face that did not make even one hair on the back of my neck sit down. And then I figured out that she was not blind after all, because that is what I thought those eyes must mean, because they were mostly like the color of the sky just before you get the kind of summer storm that is probably going to blow someone's claim shanty into the next county, except that they were really bright. They were dark and bright at the same time, and they had almost no color at all. I know that can not be possible, but there they were and at first I could not look at them and then I could not look away, and then I noticed that she had not put her hand toward me like the other one. So I just said, "I am well, thank you. I am pleased to make your acquaintance," just like Mrs. Harkness had taught us to say. And then all three of the Yankee women smiled and I supposed that I had done the right thing.

"How is your mother, Kirsten?" Mrs. Harkness asked, and I said, "She is fine, thank you," except she is not, but I do not think Mrs. Harkness really wanted to hear about that, and what was I going to say anyway, something like, well, she does not seem to want to talk to anyone much anymore and she still works all day long, but it is like she is not really there, and if Haldis or I do not keep watch she will just spin and spin and spin and never with one thought about when to quit, or what she is spinning for? No, better just to say, "Fine, thank you." And then

Mrs. Harkness said, "Please say hello for me." And I knew that meant that I was excused, so I said "Good-bye" and took one more look at the pretty woman's hat and a peek at the strange eyes of the other one, and she still had that little smile that seemed like she was reading all of my secrets inside my head while she looked at me, except I do not have too many secrets, except that Mor is losing her mind and Far drinks too much and Halvor Rolfsrud is threatening to do something that will make me marry him.

Well, Homer and I were just coming around to the front of the house and back onto the street when the two ladies came out onto the front step saying good bye to Mrs. Harkness, and what a shame, that pretty one was leaning on a cane, and then she took the arm of the other one as they walked down the steps. And I was barely asking Homer to move because I did not want to attract attention with the squeal, and maybe I wanted to watch them a little more, too. O.K. And the one with the eyes, Mrs. Frances Bingham, helped the one with the limp into the carriage, and it was like she was helping a child, she was just that gentle, and I thought well, maybe they must be sisters, even though they did not look at all alike, except they looked healthy and clean, like Yankees. And then the Anna Bingham sister smiled such a nice smile like she was saying thank you, and the one with the gray eyes smiled back, and it was just so different that smile that all of a sudden the chill that had gone up my back just melted.

So that was the thing that happened that I did not know had happened. It turns out that those two women are not sisters, but one is the daughter of Mr. John Bingham and one is married to John Bingham's son, Mr. Percy Bingham, who Far says is his friend, but that can not be, because Mr. John Bingham is the big bonanza farmer who is sort of a neighbor, but not really since all that is near to us is his land, and they are not the sort of folks that would have anything to do with settlers like us anyway. Per Rolfsrud says that John Bingham and Oliver Dalrymple and the Grandin brothers and the other bonanza farmers are not really part of the community, but why would they be. They are not Norwegian.

Anyway, it was just last week that here comes Mrs. Harkness, and she says she has a "proposition" for me to consider. Well, you would never guess what it is, and I am going to say just as soon as I fill in the details. Cause and effect, Mrs. Harkness says, so here is the cause. Mr. John Bingham built a big new house that everyone I know has found a reason to drive by to see, but I have not because it is not on the way to church and it is not on the way to Fargo, and they say it is not like a house but a hotel and more beautiful and so now here is his family, too, and oh, yes, there is a sad thing, and that is about how his wife died not too long ago, but here is the good part. Those Binghams need *hushjelp*, I mean, a *huskeeper*, and so the "proposition" of Mrs. Harkness is, would I be interested?

Would I be interested in living in a house in a room that is maybe to be my very own, where I do not milk the cows or stack the hay or make soap or candles, but I am to make two dollars a week to send to Mor so that she will not have to kill herself over a butter churn. And here is the other thing, but not a thing that Mrs. Harkness would know about, and it is that at the big Bingham house I am not to run into Halvor Rolfsrud except in church on Sunday, because I am not to work on Sundays and of course I am to go to church, and the not running into Halvor is a good thing because just the day after I took the butter to Fargo and met Miss Anna Bingham and Mrs. Frances Bingham I was down by the river picking gooseberries and that is a terrible job. There are the mosquitoes to slap and the needles on the bushes to watch out for and then when I get home there is for each berry the tiny black tail that needs to be pulled off, but Mr. Jonsson will give me ten cents for every quart, and so if there are gooseberries to pick it is gooseberries I pick and mosquitoes I slap, and so anyway there I am and here comes Halvor on his horse, and he gets down from his horse and walks over to me, and I just keep slapping and picking, and then he grabs me by the arm and pulls me next to him, and then he lifts me up while I am trying to push him away and then when he lets me slide back to the ground on my feet he holds me against him, and says, "You see, little Kirstie, that I am a man who knows what he wants," and I could not see, for that much I can still give thanks, but I could feel, and then he laughs and gets back on his horse, and if he will do that in the light of day, then there is no telling what he will do if he catches me alone at night. But he will have nothing to do with the home of Mr. John Bingham.

So there I am, listening to what Mrs. Harkness has for the proposition, and I am thinking about all the reasons why I am wanting to say

yes, yes, yes, yes, even though I know that this would be so hard on
Mor, because Haldis can not do one half of what I can do, and then
I think about a 'no' and I say, "but I do not know how to make those
cakes and puddings that Yankees eat," and Mrs. Harkness just laughs,
and says, "They have their own cook, dear." A cook and a housekeeper.
Well, that keeps me quiet for a minute, and then Mrs. Harkness says,
"I will leave you to discuss this with your mother and father," and here
Mor speaks right up, and it is like she is her old self again, and she just
says (and in American, too), "She is to go. Kirsten, you go."

So go I am gone.

Chapter XXIV

In Which There is No Shame in Profit

"She is pretty enough, in a common sort of way. We will need to
provide her with some decent clothes."

"And shoes. Did you see the shoes, Frances? Poor thing." Anna
shook her head and then turned her gaze toward the window.

"It might be wisest to deduct the cost of a calico dress or two from
her pay. Otherwise we may discover ourselves clothing the local immigrant population girl by girl."

"Mrs. Harkness spoke quite highly of her. I believe we may trust her
judgment."

A clatter from the kitchen, followed by a woman's raised voice,
brought Anna's attention back from the space beyond the window.
Frances looked up from the crate she was unpacking. It had gone missing during their move from St. Paul the previous fall, and had recently
been discovered in a storage warehouse at the Northern Pacific Junction
outside of Duluth. An assortment of candlesticks, picture frames, and
figurines lay about her feet. "Shall we investigate?" Frances asked.

"I shall not," Anna said. Seated on the sofa with a breakfast tray
on her lap, Anna carefully worked the corner of a rag about the fragile
edges of a porcelain figurine of a girl holding a bouquet.

"Mrs. Berg is temporary, Anna. The Ford widow is to arrive within
the week." Frances waited for a moment for Anna's reply before bending

to reach into the crate again. She understood that it was not dedication to the work before them that kept Anna from the kitchen, or from the afternoon tea she was in the habit of preparing there. Rather, it was for fear of what she might discover in the hands of Olaug Berg, their third "temporary" cook. Just yesterday they had chanced upon her cheerfully scooping out the contents of a calf's stomach in preparation for a delicacy neither had been able to bring themselves to eat later that evening, but which Houghton, to the dismay of his mother and aunt, gleefully accepted spoonful after spoonful. "We must find a nanny," Frances had said to Percy as she slipped into bed beside him that evening. When Percy pointed out that their son was as likely to accept immigrant food from a nanny as from his mother, Frances had replied, "Yes, but I would not have to participate in the barbarity."

"Here it is at last," Frances exclaimed, her voice muffled from within the crate. Sitting back on her heels while carefully unwrapping a soft cloth, Frances revealed a tray of inlaid wood and ivory, one of the few Houghton family pieces she had brought into the Bingham home. It had been her great-grandmother's, a gift from a cousin in British India. Not long after Frances had been sent to live with her aunt in Chicago, a crate similar to the one she now emptied in the Bingham parlor appeared, and Frances remembered watching her aunt pull wonder after wonder from within the box, this tray, a sapphire ring and a horseshoe-shaped brooch, several formal photographs in gilt frames, and a full set of silver. Frances had never before seen the ring or the silver, but that the items were meant for her, she was certain. At eight years old, however, in the new home of a strange woman whose pewter eyes alone were familiar, she had no words with which to make the claim, and only the brooch was placed in her hand. When Frances became engaged to Percy she had written to the aunt—whom she had not seen since she herself had left for St. Paul and Miss Ardwell's Female Institute—asking that the tray, the photographs, the ring, and the silver be sent to her. The response was a letter in an unfamiliar hand, saying that Miss Evaline Houghton was no longer at that address, and that her whereabouts were unknown. And then, a month after the wedding, the tray alone arrived, with no accompanying letter and no return address. Frances felt little curiosity regarding her aunt's situation, but she would have liked to know just where that sapphire ring and the silver had gone. The photographs would have been nice as well.

Another bang from the kitchen, followed by a duet of hissing, brought Frances fully upright. "They will wake Houghton," she said, standing.

In the kitchen Frances came upon an unlikely tug-of-war between Olaug Berg and Little Carl, the new crew cook who was seldom to be found outside his cookhouse, where he slept as well as prepared meals, and whose last name Frances had yet to hear. Mrs. Berg had the weight advantage, but Little Carl was her equal in tenacity, and could not be shaken loose from the large fire-blackened cast-iron pot that they held between them. When they saw Frances, both stopped pulling, but neither let go.

"I must ask you to stop this racket before you wake my son from his nap," Frances said. "What is this about?"

Olaug Berg launched into a lengthy explanation, not a bit of which Frances understood until the final words, "It is me!" directed with a hearty nod toward the pot on which she maintained a firm grip.

"It looks like you, you old so-and-so," Little Carl mumbled, "but it ain't yours. I've carried this here pot with me from Ohio, into the logging camps of Michigan and Minnesota, and to a station house or two along the Missouri, and a few other places I'd like to forget, and there ain't another pot as perfect for rabbit stew, and I'll be god-damned, begging your pardon, Mrs. Bingham, if this old Norsky is going to pinch it from me now."

If Olaug Berg understood Little Carl she was not convinced, and for a moment Frances stood looking back and forth at the dueling cooks, not quite knowing what to do.

"Is there some sign, perhaps, Carl, on the pot by which you can identify it."

At this suggestion Little Carl brightened. "It's pretty beat up on the bottom."

"That is not unusual for a cooking pot, and may not convince Mrs. Berg."

"That may be, Mrs. Bingham, but when a fellow uses an iron pot as an anvil for pounding a hot horse shoe on, I can tell you it leaves some peculiar marks. Just like I left on that fellow who done it."

Frances studied Little Carl for a moment, trying to imagine this oddly shaped man, whose voice was the hoarse high hiss of catarrhal laryngitis, bettering a blacksmith or farrier, or any grown man at that, in a fistfight. Reaching for the pot, reluctantly released by the contestants, Frances turned it upside down on the table behind her, and there, indeed, were several deep indentations, one of which clearly bore the partial imprint of a horseshoe.

"You may take the pot, Carl," Frances said, handing it to him and causing Olaug Berg to launch into an energetic response, some of which was directed toward Little Carl, and some toward the apron that she was pulling over her head.

"Do you understand Norwegian, Carl?" Frances asked.

"Little bit."

"And what is Mrs. Berg telling us."

"She's apologizing," Little Carl said with a rare smile that made his pinched face almost youthful, and Frances could not help but smile in return.

"You took the side of your champion, did you?" Anna said, after Frances recounted the details of the kitchen fray.

"He is attentive, but I do not think that slipping a few biscuits, heavenly though they may be, past Mrs. Berg for me to eat on my rides quite makes him my champion."

"I was thinking of the dressing down you said he gave to that young man you had asked to saddle your horse yesterday," Anna explained as she set a polished candlestick on the table beside her and began to work upon its mate.

"Little Carl reminds me a bit of Sophie Fredley's rat terrier. Remember how he would catch at Percy's trouser leg and refuse to let go? But that young man," Frances added after a pause, "was absolutely right, even if his comportment could stand improvement. He was hired to tend to the farm stock, not to saddle my horse, which is something I must learn to do for myself."

"Really, Frances? Is the saddle not too heavy?"

"No heavier than Houghton, and we each pick him up a dozen times a day. What?"

"I did not say anything."

"Indeed you did. You said that you disapprove of something. You gave me one of your steady looks, you let it rest upon me for approximately two to three seconds, and then you sighed and looked down again. I can not tell if it was the look of absolute disapproval or simple concern. The 'Anna look' can be either. Please clarify."

"And that we shall call the 'Frances strategy', in which with a dose of wit or humor you deflect any possible criticism that might come your way," Anna said, laughing.

"Then, for the moment we will leave dissembling aside and strike right to the point. Which is?"

Anna set down the candlestick and shifted her weight to slowly straighten her back. "I simply wonder if these rides of yours are safe. You have convinced us all with your competence, and father assures me that the bay horse—"

"Raleigh."

"—that Raleigh is perfectly trustworthy, but what if something should happen to you? How would we know where to look to find you?"

"What could possibly happen? I ride only when the weather is pleasant. There is simply nothing to cause me danger, unless I am to fear rose bushes and tall grass."

"And Houghton? Is he safe as well?"

Frances looked up at Anna, her expression of surprise admitting that she had not believed herself observed as she gave her son of fifteen months his first ride. His wet nurse, Mrs. Johnson, had come out of the supervisor's house with Houghton just as Frances trotted into the yard a few days earlier, and at Frances' request had handed him up to her where she sat. Mother and son had simply taken one slow turn about the farm yard before Houghton was returned to Mrs. Johnson's arms, a ride of no more than three or four minutes.

"He could not have been safer, Anna, tucked into the saddle in front of me with my arm around him. And he loved it."

Anna shook her head. "He is to be perfectly wild, I fear. There is Percy throwing him into the air as if he were a bag of flour, and you… Frances, you do not canter, do you?"

"You saw all there was to see."

"But when you are alone?"

"I do not," Frances lied with ease, thinking for the moment of how readily Raleigh moved from an easy canter into a full gallop.

"I suppose I am afraid that with all of the excitement that is available to him here, Houghton will grow up quite ignoring his feeble aunt."

"He has no feeble aunt, darling," Frances said, "and he needs you as we all need you when we come to ground."

Although the early months at their new home in Dakota had been marked by the unsettling sounds of construction in a space made too large by too little furniture inside, and too confining by incessant winter storms outside, spring and summer were taken up with the reassuring process of restoring order. Frances and Anna unpacked crates and conferred over decorating choices. They guided the placement of the Summit house furniture that arrived piece by piece, and then they made trips to Fargo to Ferdinand Luger's furniture store, where they ordered several more pieces as well as fabric for pillows and curtains, and wallpapers for several rooms. Some of these trips were made in the company of Percy or John, but often enough it was Frances with the reins. They regularly surveyed the contents of E. A. Grant's for the chance treasure. By August much of the house was satisfyingly and completely decorated, and there appeared to be a settling of the family's routine. Better weather allowed Percy to be home more regularly on the Bingham farm headquarters, although he still lived in his rooms above the *Times*. John Bingham was, for the first time in his family's memory, regularly home in the evenings, and seemingly pleased to have his family about him at the dining table once again. His fondness for his grandson was well beyond what anyone had expected, certainly exceeding any affection he had shown for his own children, and even his impatience with Percy had appeared to diminish. Frances, discovering a freedom heretofore unimagined, spent hours at a time in the new riding habit that she and Anna and Lydia Harkness had worked on together.

As for Anna, she was doing her very best to be reconciled to her circumstances. She had many of her old things about her, including her piano. A friend had been charged with seeing to it that the latest books to arrive in St. Paul were forwarded to John Bingham's post office box in Fargo, where Anna's subscriptions to *Godey's* and *Peterson's* followed as well. The First Methodist Episcopal church, populated with the families of some of the leading businessmen of Fargo, was something of a mixed blessing. On the one hand, Anna was grateful for the community of fellow worshippers on a Sunday morning, while on the other, she was aware of the degree to which these others were not quite her "community." Fortunately Dr. and Mrs. Harkness were members of the church and were frequent dinner guests as well. In short, Anna believed that if she could learn to ignore the rattle of the windows (for even the finest house in the state, as her father had referred to their new home, was not impervious to the Dakota wind) and if she could keep her mind occupied on some immediate thought or object on her occasional trips to and from Fargo so that she did not become lost in the monotony of the terrain about her, and most importantly, if she could teach herself not to compare her days on this bonanza farm in Dakota with the congeniality of city life in St. Paul, then she could be content. It was a matter of perspective, she was learning, like finding pleasure in bits of pretty seashells while marooned on an island in the midst of a vast, impersonal sea.

The same day that Frances settled the kitchen tussle in favor of Little Carl, Olaug Berg packed her bag and was last seen striking a line west across the prairie, leaving behind several loaves of bread dough to rise, a roast surrounded by potatoes and carrots in the oven, and two days' pay.

"West?" Frances asked Little Carl, who had made his second trip to the big house that day to report the house cook's departure. "That seems odd if she were leaving for good. Perhaps you are mistaken, Carl. Perhaps there is some friend in that direction whom she intends to visit."

"She's gone, Mrs. Bingham. Had her bag with her. Gone to the Dalrymple place, my guess."

"The Cass-Cheney farm?"

"Same thing."

"Do they have a position open for a cook?"

"Operation that size, they got a position open for an anything. Got posters up all over town advertising jobs for anyone with two arms and two legs."

"I see. Thank you for your information, Carl. I will let you get back to your work," Frances stood back from the door, but Little Carl did not turn to go.

"Especially now," he said.

"I beg your pardon?"

"They need all the help that they can get, especially now," Little Carl clarified.

Frances hesitated. She was not inclined to gossip with her father-in-law's farmyard help, but she had become fond of Little Carl in a very short time. There was something about the way he watched her that felt neither intrusive nor insulting. There was no explaining it, she just felt approved of. So she said, as she was meant to, "Why, especially now?"

"On account of the President of the United States."

Supper that evening was unusual in that it was served by Frances, who had every intention of enlisting Percy's aid in the cleaning up, and to take that opportunity to give her opinion of a day without a house-keeper (who would not arrive until the end of the week), a cook, or a full-time nanny. The meal had in common with several others in the area a singular topic of discussion: President Rutherford B. Hayes was to be among a large party on one of the N.P.'s excursion trains, set to pass through in late August or early September, to see for himself a bonanza farm in this new Northwest. Percy brought the news to the table and Frances did not immediately spoil his moment by telling him that word of the President's visit had already reached the house by way of the farmyard. Percy could add few details to Little Carl's report, except that there was to be a grand subscription ball in Fargo for which gentlemen's tickets would be $25, although there could be no guarantee that President Hayes would attend, and that General George Cass and his wife were expected to be among the President's party, making the Cass-Cheney farm the logical focus of his visit. "I can't imagine that he will stay the night with Dalrymple," Percy concluded. "It isn't much of a house."

"They would stop over the night before at the Headquarters Hotel, don't you think? And I am sure that the President will have his own car," John replied.

"There is to be quite a feast, too," Frances said, and when the others looked at her with their question, she continued, "My informants are everywhere. There is to be prairie chicken and pheasant and several hogs roasted whole. Gardens will be raided throughout the countryside, and there will be several dishes made solely out of cream by Norwegians and Swedes."

For a moment no one spoke beyond John Bingham's "hmm, is that so?" Frances could feel Percy's stare, which he broke himself by reaching for the decanter of claret that he had brought to the table. "And lemonade, I imagine," he said. "In honor of Mrs. Hayes."

"The President?" Anna said quietly, her words hovering between question and wonder.

"Indeed," Percy said. "I ran into the N.P. photographer, Jay Haynes, this afternoon at the bank. He will be there, of course, to document the occasion. He told me Dalrymple expects to have upwards of 400 men and forty to fifty self-binding reapers during harvest this year. That will make a picture to impress the investors back east."

"If the weather holds harvest will be well over by September," John said. "Frances, this roast is excellent. Please give my compliments to the cook."

"I would pass them on to her, but she, too, has gone to the Dalrymple place, it seems."

Percy reached into his pocket and set a large coin upon the table with a slap. "Harvest may be over, and every boxcar east filled with wheat, but here's a brand new silver dollar that says Dalrymple has a section shocked and waiting for a dozen steam-powered threshers to go to work on the day that President Hayes arrives."

"He'll see to it that the fields are harvested the moment the wheat is ready and he can get a crew onto it. No decent manager would do otherwise. Nor would he put twelve threshing crews in a single field. But let's see that coin." John Bingham rubbed his thumb appreciatively across the profile of Lady Liberty before turning it over. "Looks like that eagle has missed a few meals," he said as he handed the coin back to Percy.

"Wags in the east coast newspapers are calling it the buzzard dollar. I'll wager another buzzard," Percy said, "that this field of Dalrymple's, shocked and waiting, just happens to run directly along the train tracks."

"Keep your money in your pocket, son," John said. "I have enough to worry about getting my own crop up. But a picture like that could bring another trainload or two of settlers to the Red River valley, and that is all to the good. The faster they come, the more valuable our land becomes."

"And the higher the taxes," Percy added.

"The new land tax is unfortunate, but not unexpected. The speculators will sell now, and the large farmers who can continue to come up with the capital will stay."

To everyone's surprise, Percy clutched his lapel and threw an arm forward in an orator's gesture. "Those who labor in the earth are the chosen people of God." Percy looked about the table in anticipation of a response. When no one spoke, he brought his hand back to his wine glass and said, "Thomas Jefferson."

"I will never understand your sarcasm," John Bingham said, setting his napkin down beside his plate. "Farming here, like this, is good business, and it doesn't necessarily involve God one way or the other. No shame in profit."

In response to his father's words, Percy turned toward his wife with an odd look of searching recognition, and Frances was grateful for Anna's repeated interjection of amazement.

"The President of the United States? Here?"

After a moment John Bingham spoke again. "Anna, would you like to meet some of the members of the President's party? I will speak to Dalrymple tomorrow, if you like."

As the family turned to their dessert of tinned peaches that Frances had discovered in the pantry earlier in the afternoon, John Bingham took stock of the room, and began to nod to himself. The stamped copper ceiling shone in a rich warm halo above the gasolier that illuminated the table and sideboard. To his left was the hearth with its colorful tile inlay (which he had insisted upon for the formal dining room, despite his architect's attempts to convince him that the fireplace was not only unnecessary, but impractical in a land largely devoid of trees). To his right flocked wallpaper gave way to paneling, a small door cut perfectly into the panels all but hiding the entrance from the kitchen. Percy was right, the Dalrymple house might be comfortable and pleasant on the inside, for all he knew, but it was not the home of a capitalist of the first sort. Success was about more than the accrual of money. It accounted for nothing without the appearance of wealth, too.

True, after a couple of good harvests and the prospects for another before him, John Bingham's bank account was no healthier than it had been on the day that he first dug into the Red River valley soil with a borrowed spade, whereas his debts had increased exponentially, but any new enterprise necessarily required the greatest input of capital in the early years. He'd explained this to Septimus Slade each time he'd forwarded to him bills for machinery or seed or requested an infusion of capital to pay for labor or for "miscellaneous costs." So far Slade had responded with the necessary funds, although his letters had grown increasingly suspicious. And now he'd written to say that he had asked J. B. Power, as a disinterested party, to "take a look" at Bingham's book-keeping. John Bingham intended to resist Power's prying. He knew that Power had "taken a look" into Dalrymple's accounts as well for General Cass and Benjamin Cheney, and the result had been one Israel Lombard, sent from the east to take over Dalrymple's books. John Bingham did not intend for a moment to have someone working just for Slade snooping into his financial records. Fortunately, Slade had shown no interest whatsoever in actually making his way to Dakota to set foot upon his investment there, and that made the "miscellaneous costs" easier to keep vague. Not that there was anything truly amiss in his records, of course. There were simply too many intangibles to account for. Farming on this scale, where machines and men were working in the morning on Slade property and in the afternoon on Bingham land, simply did not allow for the sort of precise credit and debit figuring that Slade was suddenly asking of him. Power ought to understand this, but then again, John Bingham thought, they both knew which side the "disinterested" Power's bread was buttered on.

"You are spending too much capital too quickly," Septimus Slade had warned in his last letter. "Be more circumspect, more cautious." Damn it all, Bingham thought, caution was no way to build a fortune. Leave it to the younger men to scrimp and save. He had been that young man once. Then the panic of '73 had taken the bulk of what he had accumulated over the years. But it had not taken his understanding of what it meant to be wealthy. As long as the rains continued, the grass-hoppers stayed away, and the hail fell elsewhere, this bonanza farm was going to be a success, that much was clear. And the larger the operation, the safer it was, for no natural disaster was likely to take out several thousand acres at once. The time would come to put the money in the bank, and a good portion of it back into Slade's pocket. Now was the time, however, to plow it back into land and machinery, and, equally important, into an image of success that made Bingham an easy man to lend even more money to. He had been busy with the farming. It was time to get busier with the image. The house was just the start.

Again, John Bingham looked around the richly decorated room, and then brought his attention back to the large oak table at which he sat. For the first time since his family and furniture had arrived it was the eight empty chairs that struck him. To his left Anna placed a hand brief-ly upon his arm, her signal that she was about to leave the table. She was quite pretty, he thought, if at twenty-five well beyond the bloom of youth. Despite her infirmity, she would make a charming hostess. The sound of a cry from the room above brought Frances to her feet as well, and John noticed, not for the first time, the grace of his daughter-in-law's figure. A man would have to be dead not to, he thought. She was a handsome woman, more so than a first glance might suggest, and he'd seen a dozen men move toward her in conversation as if those eyes were magnets. And Percy? Percy was a fish out of water on a farm, although he'd proven surprisingly useful to J. B. Power in writing those emigra-tion brochures—his "foray into fiction" as Percy insisted upon refer-ring to the work. His work at the Fargo *Times*, as far as John Bingham could tell, was of little consequence. But put him in the parlor and let him hold forth about politics or books or the political events of the day, and he would be right at home.

I have planted this, too, Bingham thought. Might as well cultivate it and see what will grow. Other investors, perhaps. Certainly he could only benefit by a friendly relationship with the N.P., and now, especially, with J. B. Power. Out loud he said, "I have been thinking. J. B. Power generally gets up a half dozen hunting and excursion parties on the N.P. through here in the fall. Perhaps we should open our home to some of the businessmen and dignitaries passing through, too."

Anna and Frances paused at the door as John Bingham spoke.

Percy lifted his glass. "To Squire Bingham," he said.

CHAPTER XXV

In Which Peter is Robbed and Paul is Paid

It had not been an easy year for J. B. Power, and by the looks of his correspondence it was not going to get easier. Sometimes he wondered if he were the only Northern Pacific man who truly understood the delicate nature of the Land Department's work. Certainly his land-for-bonds scheme had been a success, and the stories told of the gold that bonanza farmers were harvesting from their fertile fields had already lured thousands of settlers to the Red River valley and beyond. Now here was the Executive Committee of the N.P., led by Frederick Billings, the new president of the road, suggesting that railroad land be increased from the current $2.50/acre to $5/acre, regardless of a parcel's distance from the road. Evidently the Committee feared that the road was in danger of losing its transcontinental land grant should it not make greater progress with construction, and so it was looking for ways to boost revenue.

It would be a mistake, Power was certain. The result of this increase would have quite the opposite effect by slowing sales, never mind the way in which the increase was likely to send business over to the land department of the St. Paul, Minneapolis and Manitoba Railroad that had moved into the valley. Potential buyers were well aware that transportation costs necessarily made distant land less valuable than land closer to the tracks, and to the sidings and elevators located there.

And there was another twist to the situation. Billings had begun negotiations with several banking houses in the attempt to secure loans toward continued construction, and that meant that Land Department records had come under scrutiny. There was absolutely nothing about the Dakota and Minnesota bookkeeping practices that Power could not readily justify, of course, but he resented the "concern" that Billings had recently expressed regarding a discrepancy between the Brainerd office's estimation of unencumbered lands and the records at the New York office. Billings knew quite well what that "discrepancy" was all about, so his professed ignorance was worrisome. The fact that railroad land had been sold before official patents had been filed was simply a matter of the bookkeeping not quite keeping up with sales, and in fact, the office in New York had been in tacit agreement with this tardiness (restricted to the less desirable land some distance from the road), since it allowed settlers to use money they would otherwise be paying in taxes to offset their necessarily higher transportation costs. It had made this less-attractive land more appealing to large investors, as well. As a matter of fact, more than one N.P. director had been the beneficiary of these delays.

Billings had even suggested that this "arrangement" (which Power had been quick to reply was nothing as formal as that) could inspire a criticism regarding unequal taxation. This, from Billings! This, from the man who had happily taken Power's advice not to pay his tax bill at all! Power remembered quite clearly his personal note to Billings recommending a strategy of "contest and delay" as long as there remained some ambiguity in the wording of the tax laws regarding just when land grant property should become taxable. He could not, however, remember getting any indication of gratitude for his advice. Well, if the directors of the Northern Pacific truly wanted to get the citizens of Dakota buzzing like a nest of disturbed hornets all they needed to do was double the minimum price of railroad land. Then would come the claims that railroad officers, known to have invested heavily in Dakota, were trying to enrich themselves as they began to sell.

And there was more. But just what that 'more' was, Power did not know. Since Billings' rise to the position of president, his letters had become simultaneously more aggressive and less specific, the most recent suggesting that Power's "personal business affairs" had not been at all times "consistent with his responsibilities and duties for the Northern Pacific." Power had no idea what the man was talking about. That his official duties had been punctuated with activities as the personal agent for various directors of the road, including Billings, was true, but that was not uncommon in the world of business. That he, J. B. Power, had prospered in his role as Land Commissioner for the N.P. was also true, but there was no reason to believe that the benefits available to the directors should be denied lesser officers as well. Power expected his work for the railroad to keep in him in St. Paul for several years to come, but when those days were over, he could look forward to a pleasant life on the six thousand acres he now owned south of Fargo, and there was no one who could tell him that he had not earned the privilege.

At least some of the directors recognized the personal time Power had labored in their interests. He had spent untold hours in '78 going over Oliver Dalrymple's accounts for General Cass and Benjamin Cheney, and they had been generous in their expressions of gratitude. Now here was Septimus Slade insisting, once again, that he "take a look" at his manager's books. John Bingham's correspondence in reply to Power's questions had been less than forthcoming, leaving Power little choice but to add a visit to Bingham's farm to his next trip to Fargo. It was likely to be a hot and dusty buggy trip into the countryside in August, but it would give Power the opportunity to see some of the harvest of '79 up close, and that was always a pleasure.

John Bingham's lack of preparation for this meeting was not a promising sign, J. B. Power thought, as he watched the other man collect ledgers, letters and scraps of paper from various drawers and pigeon-holes of his desk. In previous meetings Bingham had presented himself as a competent and careful businessman, and this disorder struck Power as carefully considered.

"Ah, here they are," John Bingham announced, unearthing a sheaf of invoices from beneath a stack of letters to his left. "That should clear things up."

Power added the papers to the stack of invoices and receipts before him, took out his pencil, and began his calculations. Within minutes he looked back up. "The amount in question, the amount that has been requested from Mr. Slade, is $6862.50. These vouchers amount to $4626.10. That leaves," Power looked back at his figures, "$2236.40 unaccounted for."

"That is the amount paid to the Moline Wagon Company, the Buffalo Company, and Peterson & Thompson. You have those figures before you as well."

"I have your note to that effect, but Mr. Slade must have the receipted bills. A simple statement of expenditures will not do."

"Surely, Mr. Power, you must understand that the bookkeeping for this operation is not as simple as all that," John Bingham explained. "I may need to order a half-dozen harrows from Peterson & Thompson, for example. Two may be for me and one for Slade, and yet there is just one invoice, one check, and one receipt. Here, for example," Bingham said, as he began to search yet again through the pile of papers by his side, "here is that receipt from Peterson & Thompson. Although I must insist that my personal accounts remain private, I can assure you that it is recorded in my ledger, and that the amount I am due from Mr. Slade is as you have it before you."

"I do not doubt that this is true, Mr. Bingham," J. B. Power said, measuring his words carefully. "And I am well aware that your position here as both owner and manager complicates the accounting on an operation of this size. But, and here I use Mr. Slade's words exactly, your accounts suggest that there is a bit of robbing Peter to pay Paul going on."

"Peter and Paul are in business together, Mr. Power."

"There have been three years of harvests from this farm now, and Mr. Slade has yet to see a return on his investment."

"Surely I do not need to lecture you on the capital needed to get an operation such as this off the ground. The machinery alone—"

"I understand this," Power interrupted. "As does Mr. Slade. And yet—"

"And yet, Mr. Slade would be more comfortable taking his profits as soon as possible. But that is simply not good farming."

J. B. Power knew well what the next sentence was going to be, so he spoke the words for Bingham. "Yes, yes, I know. Now is the time to plow the profits back into the farm. It is not your management of the business that concerns Mr. Slade, Mr. Bingham. The farm is producing admirably. It is your system of accounting that leaves something to be desired. This disclosing in part only is necessarily worrisome. Now," Power spoke the word with emphasis to keep Bingham from responding, "I am certain that this is neither negligence nor deception on your part, but rather, the result of simply having too much to do. Managing several thousand acres does not leave a great deal of time for precise bookkeeping."

"You are right that I am a busy man," John Bingham said, straightening the sheaves of paper before him. "And the last thing I need is to have one more man to check up after, so if you are going to suggest that I take on an accountant simply to keep track of Mr. Slade's interests, I must tell you that that is a suggestion I mean to resist."

"It has been Mr. Slade's suggestion."

"That will be unnecessary, I assure you. As for profits, '79 is shaping up to be the valley's best harvest so far. I will see to it that our mutual friend receives the revenue he has been expecting."

And so the afternoon continued on. John Bingham remained courteous and for the most part, unhelpful, doing little to change Power's understanding of his bookkeeping system, which was practically that of using Slade's capital to employ first class men and machinery, taking one-half of the net profit if there were any, and if not, charging for his time, which, if rumor were true, was generally spent in working up a scheme to get more land. The system was further complicated by the fact that accounts for Bingham's personal holdings were inextricably interwoven with Slade's. As for the plowing back of profits, Power suspected that the plow as well as the profits were Slade's, and the land, Bingham's.

All of this, Power would report to Septimus Slade, but he would not recommend legal intervention. Not at this point. Power hoped that this personal visit would serve as a check upon Bingham's accounting irregularities. And the truth was that Bingham was proving to be not only a top-notch farmer, but a valuable friend to the road as well by opening his home to prospective investors as they passed through the area. And his son, Percy, had a knack for writing advertising brochures, although his flights of fancy occasionally marred his workmanship. So Power's report to Slade would advise patience. If they could untangle the bookkeeping snarl, Slade's investment was sure to produce. If not, and Slade decided to end his arrangement with Bingham, he would discover that improved land near the line close to Fargo would bring top dollar.

The open windows in John Bingham's office had done little to relieve the closeness of the August afternoon, so it was with genuine relief that Power turned to see a woman entering with iced tea after a quick knock. Power quickly stood for the introduction. He had assumed the woman was John Bingham's daughter, and hoped that his surprise had not been obvious upon learning that this was Percy Bingham's wife.

"It is a pleasure to meet you, Mr. Power," Frances said, setting the tray upon the desk. "I have heard your name so often in this house that I feel as if we are friends already." She slipped her hand from Power's and bent to pour the iced tea. "I apologize for the intrusion, gentlemen, but the day is so warm that I thought perhaps you would appreciate a cold drink."

The men muttered their assurances of "very thoughtful" and "thank you." Turning to J. B. Power with a glass that had already begun to sweat, Frances lightly asked after the two gentlemen from Vermont who had recently dined with the Binghams. "They had spoken of—what was it now, John?—sixteen hundred acres each that they were interested in, I believe. Please sit, Mr. Power, I will be out of your way in just a minute."

"I am pleased to say that they have made their applications," Power answered. "They spoke highly of your hospitality."

"I know I speak for the family when I say that we take a good deal of pleasure in meeting and welcoming the guests of the Northern Pacific who are here to take a look at our home," Frances lifted her eyes to meet Power's, let them hold for a beat, and then, with a warm smile finished, "that is to say, at Dakota. It is very satisfying to be able to assuage those fears of isolation that are not uncommon to first-time visitors to the territory. Do you take sugar with your tea? The Vermont gentlemen, I believe, were quite relieved to see a family happily at home on the plains, for they were under the impression that the owners of many of the larger farms kept their families behind in the east, and they were loathe to face years of separation."

"I believe they did mention that their intentions were to bring their families west."

"Oh, I am glad. We were fortunate that evening to have Dr. and Lydia Harkness of Fargo with us as well. Do you know them? And of course my sister-in-law, Anna, played the piano for us all. To find a talent such as hers anywhere is remarkable, and so many guests have expressed their pleasure in hearing her play. I hope you have the opportunity yourself some day. Now, I won't keep you from your work any longer. I'll leave the pitcher here." Frances moved the tray to a table by the door.

"Perhaps that will be sooner than later," J. B. Power said, causing Frances to pause with her hand on the door knob. "I received a letter from a Scotsman by the name of Finlay Dun the other day–"

"Finlay Dun?" John Bingham interrupted. "I have a couple of his books on agriculture here."

"He's in the country to make a first-hand study of American agriculture, and has expressed interest in seeing our Red River valley farms. He will be joined by two members of the British parliament who are conducting their own study for the Royal Commission on Agriculture. I have secured private cars for the gentlemen and plan to accompany them through the valley, and perhaps into Bismarck. Our plans are to arrive, let me see–" Power reached into the inner pocket of the jacket that he had placed across a nearby chair, and retrieved a notebook. "The 25th of next month. Would you be so kind as to extend your hospitality to these guests on the 26th?"

"Of course," John Bingham said.

"I will talk with Anna about the menu," Frances said, adding, "Now, John, don't worry, I will not be extravagant." Frances bent slightly toward where Power sat in his chair and spoke quietly, as if she were including Power in a secret. "It is a great temptation to want to impress these special visitors of ours, knowing that the impression we leave may influence their opinion of the new Northwest. Good-bye, Mr. Power. I look forward to meeting again in September."

Frances returned to the door, pausing as she stepped out of the room to return her father-in-law's slight smile over Power's shoulder.

Chapter XXVI

In Which Frances Finds a Match

It began as their third argument of the month, and was like the first two in that it grew out of nothing more specific than a general irritation in the presence of the other. Precisely when Percy had become demanding, Frances unreasonable, and both intractable was unclear, but the exasperation was now mutual. Percy's most recent grievance had to do with Frances' morning rides about the countryside. At first he had phrased his complaint as concern over her safety, but upon discovering that Frances had tucked Houghton, not yet two-and-a-half years old, before her in the saddle on a couple of short rides, Percy had donned a father's mantle of indignation and insisted that his wife cease "this gallivanting about." What was she thinking?, he wanted to know, especially with the recent outbreak of Red River fever, caused, Alfred Harkness said, by the unhealthy vapors released by acres of newly turned sod. Frances could ignore Percy's protests and pronouncements, but the suggestion that she was an irresponsible mother infuriated her, and so she retaliated with the observation that Percy's long absences gave him little right to question her care of their son. And that, of course, led Percy to grumble about his work with the *Times*, for Power and the N.P., with life in Fargo, specifically, and in Dakota Territory, in general.

There were variations, of course. Percy also did not like to see Frances talking so freely with the laborers about the farm. When she insisted that she did not talk with the transients, but could see no harm in being friendly with the regulars, with Little Carl, the crew cook, for example, or Jack Shaw, who had turned out to be a genius with machines, Percy would repeat his opinion about the need to maintain boundaries. Frances would then ask if such an injunction against mixing extended to his choice of company while in Fargo. This was always a mistake, for Percy's response to this was unassailable: he was a man, and must necessarily mix with any number of other men, gentlemen or otherwise, whereas she was a woman, well-taken care of in a fine house, with no good reason for chasing about. As frequent as their disagreements had become, they were careful not to directly refer to their own troubled relationship or to strike at the real problems therein. They had been long enough in each other's company and, once upon a time, sufficiently relaxed in their mutual disdain for others, to know full well the other's ability to inflict real damage during an argument. So Frances' references to Percy's drinking were seldom and oblique, meant to let him understand that she knew what he was doing, but not to corner him with a direct confrontation. In return, Percy's hints that Frances would be more content with her duties about the house if she were to have another child were phrased by way of supposition, for he did not want to face a direct refusal.

Frances understood that she had more to lose than to gain in these skirmishes. Certainly she had grown weary of Percy's theatrics, of his cynicism and litany of opportunities lost by entrapment here in Dakota, and yet her own happiness depended on his remaining. To live elsewhere would be to lose the freedom she had discovered and to be taken away from Anna (and, almost inconceivably now, to live permanently by her husband's side). For his part, Percy feared the moment when

Frances would challenge him to provide for her and their family were they to no longer be a part of the Bingham bonanza farm. So they argued and they picked at each other a bit when no one else was around and discovered as the days wore on that they had less and less in common. The one thing they would have agreed upon remained unspoken: they were happiest when apart.

On this late September afternoon Frances looked up from her dressing table as the door to their bedroom opened and Percy stepped in, his jacket across his arm, his vest open and a soiled collar in his hand.

"Where have you been, Percy? Our guests are expected any time now and you have yet to dress for supper."

Percy ignored the question, knowing it to be no question at all. What matter where he had been or what fascinating story he had been working on for this week's paper as E. B. Chambers stalked about muttering complaints, today's having to do with Percy's planned early departure from the office. But the editor's grumbling had been half-hearted at best, for next week's *Times* would contain a first-person account, by Percy Bingham, of an evening in the company of two members of the British parliament, a story that neither the Fargo *Republican* nor the newly established Fargo *Argus* could match. So Percy did not explain to Frances that he had ended his day composing a dithyramb to the self-binding reapers that used twine over those that used wire. Were he to complain of the day's tedium, she would, he supposed, say that everyone had to work and that it could not all be pleasant. Or worse, much worse and more likely, she would want to know about the twine.

Tossing the collar onto his dresser, Percy poured water from the jug on the washstand, unfastened his cuffs and bent to the bowl. "Who is it to be this evening? I have forgotten."

"You know very well who our guests will be."

"I know of Messrs Pell and Read, and of the Scotsman, whose name I can not–"

"Finlay Dun."

"Of course. But I do not know if there are to be others for us to charm around the table before they are turned over to Oliver Dalrymple so they can witness the glories of a real bonanza farm with its fields full of men and beasts laboring to make money for someone else. Where is the towel? Oh, here, never mind."

"The laborers are paid, Percy. They are not slaves."

"Ah, the good old days. Well, are there to be others? And do not sigh so, my dear. It is not at all attractive."

"J. B. Power."

"Yes. I knew that, too. No others? That leaves four spaces unoccupied at the table. Not very efficient of father. I see a lovely evening before us," Percy spoke with his back to Frances as he stepped out of his trousers and reached for the pair that Frances had laid across the bed for him. "It will begin with a toast to wheat, 'to Number One Hard,'" Percy proclaimed, holding his trousers up with one hand and lifting a fresh pair of cuffs above his head with the other. "Over dinner, we shall plow and backset and harrow and seed and reap and thresh. When you and Anna excuse yourselves from the table, we will move to more manly topics and perhaps debate the merits of the straw-burning engine. Returned to the parlor we will resume a sociable conversation—the call of the meadowlark, the plover, the curlew, I think. Not until the clock moves toward midnight and the last brandy is poured will the true mysteries be dared. Then, perhaps, perhaps, we will confront the wonders of twine and the self-binding reaper."

"I thought the reapers used wire?"

Percy released a low groan and walked toward Frances with his arms outstretched. "Help me with these cuffs, will you?"

Frances watched him through the mirror for a moment before turning from her dressing table. His movements were deliberate and careful as usual, if only a bit more precise with drink. He had not needed to bend toward her for her to smell the whiskey behind the liquorice on his breath. Glancing up from his cuffs she noticed that Percy's eyes had taken on a reddened squint. His face had lost its boyishness and Frances wondered for a moment if other women found him handsome. She herself could no longer tell. As she moved to his left cuff, Percy reached toward her with his right hand and lightly traced the outline of her breasts above her corset.

"Don't."

"Don't now or don't ever?"

Frances pulled her wrapper closer and turned back toward the mirror. "I would think that you would enjoy these evenings, Percy. You complain incessantly about the tedium of your days, and then, when you are given the opportunity to socialize with men of substance whom you consider to be your peers, you complain as well."

"We are not their peers, my dear. We are the entertainment. We are the railroad's whores."

"Oh, Percy, really."

Percy finished buttoning his vest, a fancy silk jacquard of rich burgundy that he wore for these dinners of his father's, undermining his affect of disinterest, and sat back on the bed to pull on his boots. "The peers of the capitalists who pass through the Dakota underworld in search of yet another industry by which to multiply their wealth, my dear, are the owners of far more acreage than father can boast of. I am speaking of General Cass, and Benjamin Cheney, and the Grandin brothers, and even that sad excuse for a rich man, Septimus Slade. We, my dear, are the exalted hired help. But, that said, we have something the others do not have. We have what passes in this benighted country for a mansion, which, by the way, as of this week has a second mortgage, courtesy of our very own J. B. Power, if I don't miss my guess. We have two fine carriages, a supply of palatable brandy and claret, and a table laid with linen and silver. Our job is to put the visitors at ease, soften them up, if you will, so that they are in the best possible frame of mind when they move on to size up the real bonanzas tomorrow. And in return, we receive…what? The gratitude of J. B. Power and the Northern Pacific Railroad, I suppose. Just what good that will do us, I admit I do not know. But I am certain my father has his reasons. Quid pro quo is how we go. Oh, and most importantly, we have two beautiful women, one who behaves like a lady and one who entertains the gentlemen."

Frances' arms froze in mid-air, the perfume atomizer directed toward her neck stilled. Slowly Frances set the bottle down and turned in her chair. She could feel the heat that had risen to her cheeks and knew by her husband's small smile that he was pleased with himself for the obvious shock of his words and the anger they had inspired. To rise to the insult would be to give him his victory, but she could not resist.

"I beg your pardon?" Frances' voice had dropped to a whisper.

"As well you should, dear wife. Did I not quite specifically ask you to cease your intimacies with the hired help, and yet, there you were, just this past week when I drove up, in a *tête-à-tête* with that clever Jew, Jack Shaw?"

"He was simply telling me about an idea he has for the machine storage. It's based on much the same concept as a railroad's roundhouse. He–"

"I do not care what he was explaining," Percy interrupted. "It can be of no importance to you, and it disgusts me to see you so friendly with strangers. And while we are at it, the same holds true for our more distinguished guests, who may be counted upon at some point during the evening to hover over you and your not unimpressive décolletage, with, I must assume, your tacit permission. Tell me, dearest," Percy held up his hand to stay Frances' retort, "have I no right to be offended? Did I not see that brute Alexander McKenzie actually put his hand upon your waist as he led you in to dinner last month? In sum, am I not perfectly within my rights, my dear, to ask my wife to not play the barmaid in her father-in-law's home?"

"Lower your voice. McKenzie is indeed a brute and had you truly been paying attention you would have seen me remove his hand immediately. What you are saying is hateful. Perhaps if you were less sodden with liquor in the company of our guests you would not be imagining these specters of indecency." This was not oblique, nor was it wise, but Frances was furious. "And if I am too lively in conversation, perhaps it is to cover the embarrassment you threaten to become to your family."

"An embarrassment, Frances?"

"Is this moment itself not shameful?" Frances hissed. "Would you insult me so hideously were you not drunk?"

Percy's countenance had darkened to match Frances' anger. "Drunk? Now? I do not think so. Perpend. If I were drunk, would I be able to do this?" Percy reached into his vest pocket for the small flask there. Pulling the cork free he set the tidy silver container on the tips of his thumb and middle and index fingers and let it balance there for a moment before letting it slide into his palm. Then, lifting the flask toward Frances in a silent salute, Percy took a long, deep pull of whiskey.

Frances did not hide her contempt as she turned away from him and stood to reach for the evening dress that hung from the door of her wardrobe. When Percy stood as well and touched her arm, she tried to pull it away, but Percy's grasp was hard.

"Or this?" In a sudden gesture that made her catch her breath Percy swung his free hand toward Frances, stopping it just in time to let it caress her cheek.

"Save your tricks for your whores by the river. Let me go."

Their eyes locked and Percy said, "Speaking of whores, if I were drunk would I be able to do this?"

For a moment Frances did not understand what Percy meant, and then she realized that he had dropped his free hand to unbutton his trousers.

"Stop it. Now. Are you mad?"

With the precision that marked his general inebriation, but with a force completely unexpected, Percy pushed Frances back onto the bed. Frances struggled to push Percy away, but to her shock found herself held down with a forearm across her chest. "Percy, stop. I insist."

"Shhh." Percy's whisper was hoarse in Frances' ear. "You do not want to startle the rest of the house."

Frances' wrapper had fallen open in her struggle and Percy now used his free hand to lift her petticoat. Frances heard one of the petticoat's ties rip free from behind her thigh, and the damage increased her fury. Her long, buffalo-horned corset further restricted her movements and the combination of indignity and helplessness brought her close to tears. It cost her greatly to plead, "Stop. Please. I am begging you."

It was as if these words were precisely what Percy had hoped for. The moment he entered her, Frances ceased to struggle. She felt her hair come free from its pins with the impact of Percy's recitation above her.

"You will do as I say. You will *not* spend your mornings chasing about the country. You will *not* spend your afternoons talking with the stable hands and cooks. You will *not* insert yourself into discussions about the farm. You will *not* act the hussy around visitors and guests. You will *not* argue with me. You will *not* insult me. You *will* do as I *say*. You *will* ... You *will* ... Be. My. Wife."

When Percy backed away from the bed, Frances kept her face turned toward the wall as she reached down to pull her wrapper back across her legs. She could hear him at the washstand and waited for the door to open and close. But his footsteps came again toward the bed, and she felt his hand upon her arm, pulling her upright.

He had fastened on a clean collar, and was holding his necktie before her. To keep him from speaking, she took it from him and tied it in the low, loose knot he favored, dismayed to see her hands tremble so.

"I will tell Anna and father that you are not feeling well of a sudden and will not be joining our guests for dinner. I will send that girl up in ten minutes to see to you."

I float.

They turn to stare at me as I enter, and I do not wonder at their amazement, for I have passed through the solidity of the parlor door, like a spirit come to a séance, beckoned but unexpected. The gasolier radiates with unearthly brilliance, each prismed crystal afire. The room is struck with clarity. A deck of cards toppled upon the card-table is a tiny curving staircase. The marquetry upon the pedestal of rosewood and walnut by the door is lively in its design. The old-man Anna has picked and placed in her mother's favorite aquamarine glass vase to dry there trembles with the gentle breeze my floating creates. I laugh to see each fleur-de-lis gaily pulsing from the wallpaper. My husband turns toward me and the aura of red heat about his head crackles. It is shame. When he takes my arm his touch brings my feet to the floor. He leans and whispers, "What is wrong with you?" and I put my mouth to his ear and say, "I am ice. See?" I widen my eyes to let him search for the cracks there, but he turns away, makes his lips smile, and pulls me toward the strangers to whom I am not to speak. I do. I extend my hand and I say what an honor it is to receive such distinguished guests in our home, and yes, I am feeling much better. It was a headache only, now gone. To Mr. Power I say that it is a pleasure to see him again and ask after his wife, who is, I am told, not yet well enough for a visit to Dakota. I say that perhaps it is Dakota that would make her well, and his expression tells me that I have spoken his own thoughts aloud. My voice sounds like a tinkling bell and I am excited to speak more. To the Scotsman, Finlay Dun, I remark upon the privilege of meeting the man whose works on agriculture I have seen my father-in-law read with enthusiasm. He demurs, saying that farming on the British isles is a primitive thing compared to what he has seen since coming to the Red River valley. As he speaks he leans forward to stare at my bosom and I wait for my husband to strike me. When he does not, I shake my head at Mr. Dun as if to say "no," and place my hand upon my breast. My husband leads me to the divan where I am to sit next to him.

You have been watching since I entered the room, Anna, your gaze like a caress. That you are seated at the piano tells me that the dinner is over. I do not know how this can be; just moments earlier you left my side in my bedroom above. You open a sheet of music and turn to face me alone. The motion transforms the men to stone. Mr. Dun's hand is suspended over his glass of brandy on the side table next to the chair he has taken for your recital. Mr. Pell leans against the mantle as if stunned by the words of my father-in-law, whose mouth will not close. Mr. Read holds a pencil fixed against the page of a pocket journal. Mr. Power's head is dipped in a nod that holds his gaze to the carpet. Percy, too, is frozen. His hand is no longer upon my arm, and once again my body rises in weightlessness. My mind is of such lucidity that I read your cryptic message to me with ease. Our eyes meet, and I answer, "I love you, too. Oh, my darling, why do we wait." Your eyes speak in reply. "I am waiting for you to make me possible," they say. Then you place your hands upon the keyboard, and the very first note brings Mr. Dun's hand to his glass. Mr. Pell nods to John, who turns and gestures toward a chair. Mr. Read tucks his journal into his vest. Mr. Power moves his gaze from the carpet to the watch he pulls from his vest pocket, and Percy leans toward me and hisses, "Why did you come down at all? I told everyone that you were not feeling well. Anna said you had taken something to help you sleep." I whisper in reply, "Indeed, I am not well. I have been assaulted by my husband. Shhh. It is Chopin. She is brave tonight."

Frances slept late the next day, and when she woke and dressed, it was with a languor quite foreign to her. Percy, Anna said, had returned to Fargo several hours earlier, citing "business" that made it impossible for him to spend the weekend on the farm as usual. John was going over accounts in his office, having seen Power, Dun, Read, and Pell off to the Dalrymple farm, where they were expected to spend the day. J. B. Power had promised to "stop by" again this evening to meet privately with John. The plans of the foreign visitors were unknown, although Mr. Dun had expressed interest in continuing on to Bismarck, hoping to see some authentic wild Indians. This comment by Anna stirred Frances' memory of the previous evening's conversation, much of which remained unusually vague. There had been a moment after Anna's brief recital when, at the behest of Percy, Finlay Dun had delivered his opinion of Fargo and the other "primordial cells of towns" nearby. He had especially enjoyed his evening at Fargo's Opera-Comique, although the Indians he had seen there, in company with half-breeds and farm-fellows with slouch hats, had been a disappointment. The entertainment itself he commended. The representation on stage of an imperturbable, irrepressible Irishman could not have been improved upon at the Haymarket or Olympic.

Reclining on the sofa in the upstairs sitting room throughout the afternoon, drifting in and out of a light sleep when not occupied by Houghton (who had mercifully taken to toddling after Kirsten as she moved about the house), Frances worked to reclaim bits and pieces of the previous evening. Her husband's violence she retained with perfect clarity. Despite her revulsion and anger at his brutality and her helplessness, the act itself slowly transformed in her mind as the day wore on from an experience of entrapment to one of potential emancipation. The rules of their relationship were, from that point forward, forever changed. Although Frances hadn't the energy to imagine quite what they had changed to, she understood that the Percy who left their room the evening before was not the husband who had entered. It followed that she, his wife, must necessarily be altered as well.

It had not been Kirsten, but Anna, who, upon hearing of Frances' sudden illness and inability to come down to dinner, had slowly climbed the stairs in concern. Frances had been prepared to refuse entry to Kirsten. She would not undergo the further indignity of having the housekeeper witness her distress, but when she heard Anna's voice she found she could say nothing at all. And when Anna stepped into the room, Frances had begun to cry again, leaning her head against her arm that rested upon the marble-topped vanity table. For a moment she could not respond to Anna's questions. But when Anna asked point blank,

"Have you and Percy quarreled?" Frances lifted her head and turned toward Anna and nodded her head.

"Was it about his drinking?"

That Anna was even aware of this as a problem was a revelation. Frances turned her head aside, considering her response, and Anna placed a gentle hand upon her shoulder.

"There is no cause for shame on your part, Frances. If you have confronted Percy about his habit, then it was just as it should have been. Although I do wish that father would not insist upon serving wine at dinner when there is company. No," Anna said, as if Frances were about to argue, which she was not, "I am not blaming father for Percy's problem. Still, I must wonder if this is the proper place for a sensitive man such as he. I think I understand a bit of what he is going through, even if it is different for me. Easier. I am a woman, and may take solace within the cocoon of family comforts, whereas he must be daily offended by the roughness of his environment and his companions. It would break my heart three times over, but sometimes I think he must take you and Houghton away from here, to make a new start elsewhere, to save himself."

Frances did not have to think about a reaction here. Her exclamation of dismay was quite real. To have been first brutalized by her husband, whose every action she had come to believe she could control, and then to hear the woman for whom she had schemed and worked so hard in an effort toward intimacy and permanency suggest that they be parted, it was all simply too much, and again Frances laid her head upon her arm, giving in to a fresh flurry of tears.

"Oh, my dear. Oh, my dear." Anna leaned down to place her cheek against Frances' head. "I am thoughtless. Here you are, in true distress, and I am thinking about what would be best for Percy, and how that would pain me. I am all selfishness. Forgive me."

No amount of "there now" and "come, come," could bring Frances relief, so Anna retrieved the cane she had set aside and left with a promise to return immediately. When she did, it was with a small brown bottle that Frances had never seen before.

"Dr. MacNeil prescribed this for my hip pain just before we left St. Paul," Anna explained, seeing Frances' surprise. "I took it twice, and although it did indeed make the pain more bearable, it also made me quite light-headed and, in fact, a little nauseated, so I chose not to continue. Dr. MacNeil did say that individuals would react differently to the medicine, depending on their constitutions. It was not inexpensive, so I kept the bottle."

"Laudanum?" Frances finally spoke. "It is my heart, dear, and not my hip that hurts."

Anna cupped Frances' face in her free hand for a moment. "You are not alone in your distress. We will put our heads together to find a plan that is best for our dear Percy. But I am afraid that we will solve no problems this evening. Now you must get into bed. Shall I help you with your corset?"

"Thank you, no. I can manage. But I do have a headache," Frances said as she stood.

"Then this will help. Just ten drops in a glass of water. It will relax you, too, so you can sleep. That is what Dr. MacNeil said when I confessed that I was quite anxious regarding our move to Dakota. He spoke of it as practically a cure-all." The chime from the grandfather clock in the front entry sounded from the room below, and Anna stepped toward the window. "Here are our guests now. Rest, dear. I will send Kirsten up later with a tray."

The laudanum had not been the least bit relaxing. In fact, the response was quite definitively one of nervous stimulation and an astonishing rapidity of heartbeat. Sometime later, when Kirsten was allowed to enter the bedroom with a bowl of broth, she discovered Frances not in bed, but busily pacing from one end of the bed chamber to the other. To Kirsten's polite, "Are you feeling any better, then, ma'am," Frances replied that she was feeling like crawling quite out of her skin, thank you. The unexpected reply brought Kirsten to a halt at the door, where she stood rocking from one foot to the other.

"Yes? What is it?" Frances asked when it became clear that, atypically, the Norwegian girl could not quite decide to speak.

"Well—"

"Yes?"

"When Mor was so sick... not with the fever, but after we lost poor little Guri, who was my little sister, not the one that was with me for a few days when I was first here in this big house to help with the washing down of each room. That is Haldis, who is to try so hard now—"

"Kirsten, please."

"I am sorry, ma'am. I will hurry with the concision. When Mor was sick, after Guri died, Far brought home some Winslow's Soothing Sirup, and Mor would not take it, but Far must have thought that he could use some soothing, too, so he drank it, and then the next time he came home from Fargo, there he was with another bottle, and Mor said to me, 'Kirstie, I do not know what is in that bottle, but if your father wants to drink it, it can not be a good thing. Throw it away'. But I just could not throw it away, because such a pretty bottle it is and here is what I mean to say—"

"But can not, evidently," Frances interrupted again, but this time the edge was gone. "You mean to say that perhaps your employer pacing before you with her hair streaming about her shoulders and acting like Bertha Rochester come down from the attic to look for a match could use a taste of Winslow's Soothing Sirup."

"I don't know many of the Yankees around here, ma'am, but I would run get that bottle for you."

In retrospect, Frances remembered taking at least one draught of the Winslow's and then handing Kirsten the hair brush. Whether it had been her idea, or Kirsten's, to style her hair in a new manner, complete with several twists and braids worked in to support the heavy upsweep, Frances could not say. At some point as Kirsten worked and chatted away, Frances became entranced with the way her own image had come alive in the mirror. Like cracks in a diamond, Percy had once said about her eyes. Never again, she thought. Never again. Everything changes now. It gave her a small shiver to see one eye in the mirror wink quite independently of her own. The mirror, Frances understood, was itself a passage through which she had stepped, only to come face to face with a stunning image of herself. Her hair, piled upon her head, made her look positively regal. The tears were long dried, but her cheeks retained a heightened pink. It is a shame, she thought, to be shut up alone all evening. Aloud she said, "Why should I pay the price of another's cruelty?"

"Ma'am?" came Kirsten's voice behind her.

"You have done such fine work with my hair, Kirsten, that you shall help me dress as well."

"Help you with your dress, ma'am?"

"Would you have me go below thus?" Frances laughed, stood, spread

her arms and twirled once in her wrapper, revealing a chemise trimmed
with lace.

"No, but–"

"But?"

"But your shimmy is prettier than most dresses I've seen, ma'am."

Although the corset's laces and stays were a novelty to Kirsten, she
was an energetic learner, causing Frances to exclaim, "That will do. I am
a twenty-six-year-old mother and need no longer risk internal injury for
fashion. The gown, please. No, not that one on the door. I have changed
my mind. The emerald taffeta in my closet. Yes, yes, open it up. We will
make you into a lady's maid yet. Where is that Winslow's, Kirsten? Perhaps I shall require more soothing still. You may leave it here for now.
Bring me my case. There."

Frances touched the necklace that Kirsten fastened about her neck.
The pendant felt pleasantly heavy and cool against her skin. She reached
forward to tilt the dressing table mirror, and then stood back to appreciate her standing image. She had turned quickly and was at the door
before Kirsten's voice came from behind.

"Your shoes!"

"Ah, yes! Of course," Frances laughed, returning and placing a hand
on Kirsten's shoulder as the young woman worked each buckled shoe
over Frances' black silk stockings. When Kirsten stood, Frances said,
"You may give me a kiss now for making me beautiful." Lifting the
Norwegian girl's chin with a finger, Frances kissed her full on the lips,
and then swept through the door.

What Frances remembered of the evening from that point forward
followed the contours of a fabulous dream, in which images were remembered with clarity, but the sequence of events and conversations
was unclear. The playing cards had been delightfully alive, and it was all
that she could do not to giggle at the ways in which they insisted upon
arranging themselves in her hands. As she set down a queen of diamonds to lose the last trick of the evening, bringing to a close the game
of euchre that she had been playing with Anna and the two Englishmen,
Frances noticed that Percy and John and Finlay Dun had become quite
animated in their discussion nearby. J. B. Power looked on uncomfortably, his glance toward the watch he had once again removed from his
vest no longer discreet. John Bingham was leaning toward Finlay Dun,

using the fingers of one hand to clap against the palm of the other to make his points. Frances could tell by Percy's expression that he was taking pleasure in his father's animation. His smile seemed an exact replica of the one she had seen earlier.

"You will see for yourself, sir, with the aid of an auger and a bit of sweat, that the topsoil here is, for all intents and purposes, limitless. I expect to plant twenty wheat crops in twenty seasons and see no diminishment in yield."

"I will agree, sir, to the land's fertility," the Scotsman replied, his heightened color reflecting his enthusiasm for the topic. "In my lifetime I have never set foot on soil so rich in vegetable fiber. Nonetheless, I hold that these soils can not go on yielding wheat indefinitely without the return of the more important elements of fertility. Just ten years' continuous corn-growing will exhaust even the best of virgin soils, leaving you with reduced, starved crops that will not pay."

"Speaking as an enterprising capitalist, then," Percy broke in, directing his comment toward Power, "the question simply comes down to when to sell. If father is correct then the time to sell would be during year nineteen. If you, Mr. Dun, are correct, then the time to sell is after the ninth harvest. The only uncertainty is deciding when to walk away."

Did Frances speak then? Would she have inserted herself into the conversation with such a word? Trying hard to remember the rest of the events of the night before, Frances thought to herself, 'no', it was unlikely that she had spoken. Perhaps the men had risen just then to bid the ladies good night. Perhaps Percy's grasp upon her arm, as he slid her hand into the crook of his elbow to lead her from the room had been no more deliberate than usual. Perhaps Anna's look had not been as shocked as it was concerned. No, certainly not. Certainly she had not said into the moment of quiet that followed Percy's remark, "As a man would walk away from an assault upon his wife."

Surely, she had not.

CHAPTER XXVII

In Which Frances Gets to Work

Frances woke the next day to the sound of the blacksmith across the yard striking an anvil with the regularity of a church bell. With harvest over, the farm's laborers were welcome to take Sundays off from plowing and from farmyard chores, but there were always a number of men who refused to rest, the blacksmith among them. A breeze lifted the curtains away from the window that Frances had opened to the evening air the night before, as she often did when Percy was not there to insist that it remain shut against dangerous night vapors. Reaching for her wrapper Frances was grateful to discover the heavy languor of the previous day gone. She longed to saddle Raleigh for a ride in the crisp fall morning, but needed to dress for church. Anna was likely to be already dressed and waiting at the breakfast table. John would be otherwise occupied, and Percy... well, Percy was long gone. It would fall to Frances to drive the carriage to church in Fargo, in the company of Anna and Houghton, whose delight in the carriage ride and boredom during the service to follow very closely mirrored his mother's. Ordinarily Frances would have taken pleasure in Anna's and Houghton's company, but today she felt the need for thoughtful solitude. Along with her renewed energy came the understanding that she needed a plan. She had been content to dream and imagine for too long, as if the future would magically unfurl itself in a parade of events to her liking if only she were patient. But she had been a fool, believing that this new and open stage of Dakota would necessarily alter the drama into which she had put herself. Waiting had accomplished nothing.

The story of the prairie was not that rich men could become richer through the investment of capital and the physical labor of poor men—that was simply the story of the world. No, the lesson she had failed to heed had hurtled before her when the young immigrant woman (the daughter of a German neighbor whose cattle had a tendency to stray into John Bingham's wheat fields) drove her team of four past Frances at a gallop, standing on the buckboard seat with her hair flying in the wind. The lesson was there in a man like Jack Shaw, whom her husband would not have her talking to because of his accent, because he came from a place with an unpronounceable name, because he was a Jew. But he was a man with an eye for opportunity. Just this last week John Bingham had spoken at the dinner table of the trolley and pulley system Shaw had designed to help the stockmen clean the barn stalls.

The lesson waiting for Frances to learn, she decided, had come with each trainload of immigrants who made their way to the government land office to claim a quarter section to homestead, and again when these same immigrants, citizens now, claimed another 160 acres by pre-emption, and then another 160 by planting ten acres of trees. Within a lifetime these people would go from having nothing to being landowners with a legacy for their children.

Even single women were taking homesteads.

A surge of excitement, unformed, unnamed, irresistible, rose in her chest. She parted the lace curtains with a finger and peered into the distance where the line of the prairie met the cool cover of the sky as if something important waited for her there. She was not wrong and what she desired was not impossible. Here people were breaking rules, doing the unexpected, filling needs as they saw fit, and all because there was the space for it all. It just made sense. Convention was necessary in small, tight places, but a hindrance to progress in a land as open as this. Now, Frances thought, was the time to act, to re-imagine her life, to move forward. But she would have to move quickly. Dressing hastily, Frances thought, I must begin. I must start right now. I must... what? What was it that she wanted? Anna, of course, but not Anna alone, not precisely. There was something more waiting for her, of this Frances was certain. "Freedom," she murmured, thinking, what good is space without freedom? What good is imagination without independence? What good is desire without fulfillment?

Frances sat at the edge of the chair at her dressing table to begin hastily fixing her hair. The excitement in her chest had dropped to clench her stomach in that hybrid of fear and anticipation. It was a sensation that always brought to mind the time that she had peeked through a loose slat in the barn to watch her brothers kill a sow to butcher. She had known that she was about to see something horrible, but the impulse to witness a new and forbidden thing was stronger than her fear. It had been perfectly awful, what she had seen, but it had made her feel strangely alive, excited and brave. Today she would begin to cut herself free from her husband, Frances thought, pinning her silk bonnet into place and reaching up to fluff the short bangs that rimmed her forehead. J. B. Power had spent the better part of the previous evening with John Bingham in John's office, and his buggy remained in the yard this morning. Frances suspected that despite the civility of both men, the length of Power's visit was not giving John much pleasure. He would be in need of a confidante, a helpmeet, an associate, all that a son was expected to be, all that Percy had refused to be, all that Frances was determined to be.

She would not divorce her husband. She would replace him.

Over the next few months Frances' measured offers to help her father-in-law with his correspondence (a duty, she said, that would assuage the tedium of her afternoon hours while both Houghton and Anna took their naps) slowly moved John Bingham through the stages of reluctance to benign acceptance to expectation. More than one gruff implement dealer softened his demand that bills be paid in a more timely fashion, now that the letters explaining the delays were couched in more civil terms. The occasional mistakes in goods ordered, due to John's careless penmanship, became a thing of the past. He did not seem to be the least bit surprised when he entered his office one winter afternoon to discover Frances sitting at the small writing desk she had lugged into the spacious room earlier in the day.

Conversation during the hour or so that Frances spent daily in John Bingham's office rarely extended beyond John's instructions, Frances' occasional questions, and her offers to fetch a cup of coffee for them both. So it startled her one January afternoon, as she paused between addressing envelopes to blow a little more warmth into her hands, to discover John's gaze resting upon her. When he spoke it was as if to continue a conversation that had he had been having with himself, the particulars of which Frances quickly imagined.

"I saw Percy yesterday in Fargo," John Bingham said. "When I sked if we could expect him for dinner after the paper is out on Saturday, he said business would not allow him to get out of town this week."

The length of John's pause told Frances that she had been asked a question.

"Yes. He mentioned as much last Sunday."

"For the life of me I can not see how his responsibilities at that little newspaper are so vast as to prevent his spending more time with his family." John's voice had taken on a gruffness that Frances suspected was meant to disguise the discomfort he felt with the intimacy of the conversation.

"There are many times," Frances spoke hesitantly herself, "when I am sure that Percy would choose to be with us if he could, but inclement weather forces him to remain in Fargo. Six miles is not a difficult journey in fine weather, but–"

"A man can ride in the rain and snow," John interrupted. "He will not melt."

Frances did not reply and for a moment the two of them listened to the rattle of the window panes and the moan of the wind without. Although the house was sturdy, a couple of winters had proven the many-paned windows that lined three sides of the octagonal office to be a mistake. Heavy draperies, added the second year, lessened the draft, but darkened the room considerably, making the gas lamps a constant necessity. Frances allowed herself a small nod that acknowledged precisely nothing and then returned to her work, but John Bingham had more to say.

"I am surprised that he continues to be interested in the *Times*. I had hoped, I will admit, that in time he would take an interest in operations here. There is talk, Percy says, of Chambers selling the paper. Perhaps then–"

This time the question, although unspoken, was obvious, and Frances answered directly. "No, I do not think that is likely."

"Then, and I hope you will excuse me, Frances, for the personal nature of my question, but I have a grandfather's interest here, has he made plans to bring his family together in Fargo? I know," John Bingham hurried forward at this point, "that he can not be making much of a salary, but if–"

"I do not think that is possible," Frances interrupted. "I do not know…that is, Percy does not say precisely–" Frances looked down at her hands, and brought them together in a clasp upon her lap. "I do not think that there is money saved. I am sorry, John. I am sorry if Houghton and I have become a burden on you."

"Not at all," John Bingham answered quickly, his voice registering surprise at the direction the conversation had suddenly taken. "I simply meant to discover if you and Percy had any plans that I should know of, that I could perhaps—" John Bingham let the sentence trail off and then, with a throat-clearing, and a "well, then, enough of that," returned to his work.

Frances felt the old sensation of fear and anticipation quicken her pulse. She had not expected to speak so frankly to her father-in-law, but an opportunity had presented itself, and she must take advantage of it.

"I, too, had hoped, for some time," Frances spoke slowly, quietly, without looking up, "that my husband would take a greater interest in the farm. And then, when he did not, I learned to hope that his work as a, a newspaperman," Frances let the inflection of her voice display a resigned, if reluctant, disapproval, "would grow into, oh, I do not know what, but Percy has such a fine intelligence and such a mastery of words that I believed...I believed...I believed in him, I guess. But for some time now—"

The reluctance of John Bingham's "yes?" was obvious, but it allowed Frances to continue.

"Percy has changed, and I am worried, and a little frightened."

"Frightened?" John Bingham asked. "Of what are you frightened, Frances?"

"I am frightened for him, and maybe, oh, John, I do not know how to say this. I have longed to speak with someone, but I simply do not know how."

"Just say it." And then, as if hearing the impatience in his own voice, John Bingham repeated, more softly, "Just tell me what it is that you fear."

Frances dropped her head toward her lap and spoke softly. "He is drinking. More. Too much. And sometimes, when he has been drinking, there is...violence."

That his son could not hold his liquor was not news to John Bingham. Nor would he have been surprised to learn that Percy spent several hours each evening in Fargo saloons. That his son, who had never, as far as John knew, even been in a childhood fistfight, could sink to the disgrace of brutality toward a woman, however, shocked him. The revulsion he felt did not completely spare Frances. He did not want to know more. He did not care to be privy to the intimacies between his son and his son's wife. He did not want what should rightfully remain private to be stated aloud, for once articulated it would become in some way his responsibility.

"Perhaps you could convince Percy to speak with Dr. Harkness."

"I have tried, but it is no use. I am afraid to raise the subject again, it makes him so angry, and he does not know his own strength when he is angry. For my own injuries I care little, but—"

"Injuries?"

"Nothing to speak of. Really. Oh, please, John, do not say anything to Percy. He does not mean to hurt me, I am sure. It is simply, as I said, that he forgets his own strength when he has had too much to drink. Oh, I have spoken too freely. Here I have intended to be of some help to you, and instead I have added to your burdens. I beg you, please do not repeat what I have told you to Percy. It is not so bad. I just…I just—" Frances reached into the pocket of her dress for her handkerchief. "I just can not imagine a home away from here. I can not imagine taking Houghton away from you and Anna until Percy is better, for he must come to his senses, of course, and then, surely we will be able to be a family together. Then, perhaps, we will have our own home, but until then—" Frances turned her head aside, offering her father-in-law the profile of a woman suffering in dignified silence. John Bingham, she knew, was not a man to appreciate a woman's sobs.

"There, there," John Bingham said, but did not rise, his voice taking on its embarrassed gruffness again. "I shall say nothing to Percy about, about anything other than the drinking, but that, I feel, is my duty. Now why don't you go rest. I can finish those letters."

Frances was not sure exactly what she had accomplished with her revelation, which was not precisely a lie, but was not precisely truthful. There had been that one act of violence by Percy, an act which, Frances suspected, most men would consider ungentlemanly, but nothing worse. She was, after all, his wife. Percy had not touched her in the five months since, and took care not to retire to their bedroom on those nights that he was at the farm until long after Frances had fallen asleep. She hoped that her conversation with John had nipped in the bud any idea that she and Houghton should at some point join Percy in Fargo, given that Percy showed no intentions of moving to the farm. If she had hoped that the confidence she had shared with John would draw them closer, at Percy's expense, she discovered quickly that the effect had been quite the opposite. For several days her father-in-law's bearing toward her was decidedly cool, as if he felt tainted by what she had said, and did not want to be reminded of it by her presence. It took her weeks of patient, quiet diligence at her desk before the silence between them was once again that of comfortable disregard.

Although Frances was good with figures, and had proven herself to be of orderly and precise habits, her occasional suggestions that she help with the accounting had met with little success, and Frances remained patient throughout the spring and into the summer, careful not to jeopardize her modest gains as her father-in-law's assistant. She hoped that the flurry of activity that accompanied spring plowing and planting would provide her with an opportunity, for John Bingham was very much a hands-on manager who preferred to spend his days riding from one field to another to check in with his supervisors and foremen.

A letter received in early June made the difference. John Bingham's exasperated complaint of "I do not have time for this now," lifted Frances' attention from the envelopes that she had been slicing open. "Time for what, John?" she said. "Perhaps there is some way that I could help?"

John Bingham did not immediately reply, but allowed a soft growl to escape as he swiveled his chair toward the bank of windows behind him that framed a farmyard of activity. In the foreground Little Carl loaded a wagon with the noon lunch for the field hands. John Bingham's growl, Frances understood, was meant to dismiss Frances' question. She returned to the remaining letters, but upon hearing John mutter again, said, "I beg your pardon?"

"Nothing, nothing," John Bingham said, and then added, "except that the man's interference has become a damned nuisance, begging your pardon."

"J. B. Power?" Frances asked, knowing full well it was Power's letter John held in his hand.

"The same." For a moment Frances thought that John Bingham would not speak again, but then he added, "With all that he has to worry about now, I'm surprised he has time to bother with matters as petty as this."

To Frances' surprise John turned to hand the letter to her. Short, and to the point, it stated that once again the receipts that Power had requested of John Bingham regarding business transactions made in the name of Septimus Slade did not precisely correlate with the credited amount. No longer convinced that the "irregularities" could be resolved by correspondence, Power stated that, as a "personal favor" to Slade, he must insist that a full-time bookkeeper be positioned at the Bingham headquarters farm in order to "end all confusion" regarding Slade's accounts and interests.

"A full-time bookkeeper?" Frances said softly, as if musing over a complicated riddle. "Would that be … inconvenient?"

"Of course it would be inconvenient. I do not care to have a stranger sitting in my office, going over my books, inserting himself into my business. If, however, you mean to ask if I have something to hide–"

"John!" Frances interrupted. "I certainly do not question–"

"I do not," John interrupted in return. "But that does not mean that I intend to explain every business decision that I make to some ink-stained clerk with no comprehension of what it means to operate a business of this scope. Of course we're making up the rules as we go along. Solutions have to be invented as quickly as problems are discovered. We are not buying and selling neckties here."

This was a very long speech for John Bingham, and Frances feared that this was to be the end of the discussion. "J. B. Power aside," she asked, "what is it, do you think, that Septimus Slade has in mind?"

"Say two men buy a mule to use on their separate farms. One of the men, dissatisfied with the arrangement for one reason or another, wants his investment in the mule back. What does he expect? That the other man will send him either the front legs or the hind? Septimus Slade is proving to be an impatient man, Frances, more so than I had expected."

"He is unsatisfied with the returns on his investment?"

"He can not be dissatisfied with his profits from last fall's harvest. His complaints all have to do with the accounting of the first three years. He would like to see a clear and absolute distinction between his costs and mine."

"Which would be practicable, perhaps, if you purchased different machinery and used different crews for his land and for yours," Frances did her best to complete John's thought, "but that would also be a very great waste of money, it seems."

"Precisely. Now if a woman can understand that, why can he not?"

Frances could very well imagine why a wealthy and successful capitalist was unhappy to be providing the lion's share of the capital for his manager's private operation, but she had no intentions of contradicting her father-in-law. "What did you mean earlier, John, when you spoke of all J. B. Power had to worry about now, if I may ask?"

"Men's gossip, my dear. While the ladies are discussing hem lines and…whatever it is that ladies discuss over tea, the men prefer to speculate over the rise and fall of their fellow man."

"And is Power rising or falling?"

"Oh, I don't know. The gentlemen to whom he so generously offers fares upon his excursion trains through Minnesota and Dakota are occasionally equally generous with their gossip. Our last guests—you remember the Ford brothers, the bankers, who were in the party that visited this past spring?"

"Very well."

"They were quite interested in any information I could give them regarding J. B. Power's methods of selling railroad lands and town sites. I answered that I could speak only for myself, and peripherally, for Septimus Slade, but that we acquired our land by way of the N.P. Land Department in precisely the same manner as had, I believed, General Cass, Benjamin Cheney, Robert Hadwin, Eben Chaffee's Amenia-Sharon Company, and so forth, by exchanging bonds for land. Had there been any indication, they asked, of 'personal speculation'? Those were Eben Ford's very words, and they are dangerous words at that. 'None that I knew of,' I said. That ended that, but it didn't sound good for Power."

As John Bingham finished speaking he returned his attention to the papers upon his desk. He appeared to have finished with the conversation, and for several minutes the room was silent as he read and as Frances went over the list of supplies that Little Carl had requisitioned for the cook house, although her thoughts for the moment were more concerned with the fortunes of J. B. Power, and the mortgage he held on the house in which she sat.

It took John Bingham a moment to lift his head and then lift an eyebrow in question when Frances unexpectedly spoke aloud, but did not take her gaze from Little Carl's list before her.

"Given what you have said, John, perhaps Mr. Power's letter indicated more of a desire to be excused from Mr. Slade's business than a determination to rectify accounts that are ultimately of little concern to him."

"Perhaps." John pushed the last letter aside, and reached for the ledger to his right.

"In which case, he could be easily assuaged. And if he is assuaged, then so, it appears, is Septimus Slade, at least temporarily."

"Your point, Frances?"

Frances could feel John's eyes upon her. Looking up she forced a gay smile and said, "Frances Bingham, amateur bookkeeper at your service." Dropping the smile, she continued, "Before you say no, consider this for just a moment. Perhaps I could help with payroll and with some other minor accounting matters, John. I know how much of your time is occupied with these things, and I know how busy you are." Frances held up her hand to stay John's comment, and continued. "You need not mention the name of your new bookkeeper, or if you choose, you may inform Power of an F. L. Houghton in your employ. It is true that the accountant was to have been one of Mr. Slade's or Mr. Power's choosing, but given what you have said about J. B. Power's current concerns, I suspect that he would welcome the opportunity to wash his hands of Septimus Slade's business. For his part, Mr. Slade will perhaps relax his scrutiny into the accounts of the first couple of years here for the time being."

"That would be a pleasant conclusion, Frances, much more so than a go-round in the courts."

"In the courts!" Frances was clearly startled. "Has litigation been mentioned?"

"No. No. It has not. Of course not. And it shall not. This is all a storm in a teacup."

"Then you will consider my little plan?"

"Let me think about it."

The very next day John Bingham asked Frances at the breakfast table to step into his office for a moment to take a letter. Standing beside the small desk where Frances seated herself, John Bingham began to dictate: "Dear Mr. Power. In response to yours of the 3rd, I am pleased to inform you ... well, you know what to say, Frances. Write a draft out for me to read over this evening and we'll go from there. I'm going over to the Number Two Farm to speak with the supervisor there. I'm not at all pleased with the new plowing foreman he hired. We'll go over the payroll accounts together tomorrow, unless, of course," John Bingham favored Frances with a rare smile, "you have any other ideas."

"None at all." Frances smiled in return as her father-in-law nodded and stepped out of the door. The previous Sunday's gossip on the lawn of the Methodist Episcopal Church, that the Grandin brothers were to install a telephone line between their farms so they could discuss the day's plans with the responsible supervisors without traveling several miles each day, was an improvement she could mention another time.

CHAPTER XXVIII

Two Rocks, a Prairie Fire, and an Inquest

Osten Sondreaal dipped his head and hands in the rain barrel and shook the dirt off his trousers as best he could. He did not like to go to town like this, but there was no time to do better. With his wheat threshed, bagged, and sold, and several stacks of hay already standing in his yard, this should have been a time to relax just a little, a time to rest and give thanks to God for the good fortune he had found in this new land, but just now he could not. He turned once again to look at the distant smoke to the northwest, lifting like a pale cloud from the earth to join the overcast sky where it belonged. All morning Osten Sondreaal had kept one eye on this haze in the distance as he plowed firebreaks, first around Peter's shanty, then around his own soddie. He had made just one circuit around the animal shed when the plow struck a rock, neatly shearing off the front shovel along a hairline crack in the iron he had worried about for a year. For a moment he had just stood there, shaking his head. Rocks were few on his land, and yet there one had been, perfectly placed to break his plow. This was God's will, he knew. Another trial. Another test.

There had been plenty of those since coming to Dakota, but there had been good, too. This he needed to remember. In just three years or so his homestead claim would be proved up and the quarter would be his, free and clear. Peter's claim was proved up already. Once again the brothers were land owners, just as they had been in *Gamle Norge*, where three older brothers remained with their wives and families. Peter had been the first to leave, striking out for America with his wife and baby boy in a small group that included Astri Hansdatter and Torger Knudson, all of them excited by the stories they had read of free land. Osten Sondreaal had followed, persuaded less by Peter's assurance that the stories were true than by the loneliness his closest brother could not keep out of his letters after the loss of both wife and child. And it was also true that there was simply no room for him on the old place. These were the reasons for Osten Sondreaal's move to Dakota Territory. That is what he said then. It is what he tried to tell himself now. To think of his real dream, to think of Astri as his own, Osten Sondreaal knew, was a sin.

At first that line of smoke had been little more than a faint smell upon the light breeze, a reminder of the work Osten Sondreaal had yet to do, and not a great concern. It was a common smell this time of year when the big farmers burned off their fields after harvest. Then the wind picked up, covering his face with the silt lifted by his plow and turning it to mud in the creases where his sweat ran. Then the plow share cracked, and Osten Sondreaal began to worry. But he had a horse now to hitch to his wagon and it was only a five-mile trip to Fargo. He could be back plowing in two, maybe three, hours.

Osten Sondreaal was within sight of the Sheyenne River when he spotted Torger Knudson on the other side, about to stumble onto the bridge. He knew from the few words he had spoken with Astri in church that Torger had been gone for almost a week. It made him sad for Astri that Torger had escaped again. It made him sadder to see Torger on his way home. Things were not so good these days for the Knudsons. Astri would not say, and it was not for Osten to hear, but still, everyone knew about the "mortgage." It was a terrible American word, Osten Sondreaal thought. Per Rolfsrud had done what he could as a good neighbor, taking the new mower from Torger and signing for the remaining payments when Alf Peterson of Peterson and Thompson had come to repossess it. He and Peter had helped Ole get the crop in, and Ole hired out with Torger's new team of mules to the Bingham bonanza farm whenever he had a day to spare. Osten could see that Astri was working her fingers to the bone with her chickens and her milking, but all together they could not keep up with Torger. It would be better for everyone if Torger

Knudson would fall right off the bridge and drown in the Sheyenne River right now, Osten Sondreaal thought, and then quickly asked God to forgive him for his evil thought, silently pointing out to the Almighty that the Sheyenne was so shallow just now that Torger would have to lie down to drown anyway. And if Torger Knudson did fall face down into the river, right in front of him, Osten Sondreaal knew, he would wade in and fish him out.

It took Torger a while to cross the little bridge because there were no straight lines left in him, but when he recognized Osten Sondreaal driving toward him, he did straighten up enough to call out, his slurred words an insult to the old tongue.

"I see you there, Osten Sondreaal!"

Osten Sondreaal looked about. On either side of the rutted track the flat fields had been harvested leaving a neat landscape of golden stubble. Further to the north the train tracks rose from the plain, cutting off the horizon. Behind him a small depression that was always the last to dry out for planting in the spring was alive with wheat that gently flexed under the breeze. Well behind this field, the line of smoke was unchanged. There were a few houses within sight, and a couple of claim shanties, dots on the prairie, but not another human. A hawk screamed almost directly above, banking and floating. On his wagon, Osten Sondreaal would have been the tallest thing within Torger's view.

"Ya, vel den, so you see me, Torger Knudson."

"I will tell you what I see!"

"Tell me as I drive by. I am in a hurry."

"I see a thief and a sneak, Osten Sondreaal. I see a man who is no man."

Torger Knudson had planted himself squarely, if unsteadily, in the center of the track, his hands on his hips. Osten Sondreaal pulled the horse to a stop for a moment, and looked at the man swaying in his path. Torger Knudson had been a fighter as a boy in their village in Norway, and now as a drunk he was a fighter again. Osten Sondreaal was not. He turned his horse off the track.

"And a coward!"

With this exclamation Torger stumbled toward the horse in time to grab the harness. Osten Sondreaal slapped his reins upon the horse's rump and yelled a fine American "Get up!" that sent the horse forward.

"Let go," Osten Sondreaal yelled, just as Torger did just that, tripping and falling as the wagon passed.

Osten Sondreaal stopped his wagon and looked back at Torger, motionless, on the ground. *"Get up now, Torger,"* he said. When Torger Knudson did not move, Osten Sondreaal tried English, calling out louder still, "Get up, then," causing his horse to start forward again. Osten Sondreaal pulled back on the reins and got out of the wagon to stand over Torger. A smell of whiskey and barnyard and slop jar met him when he bent to give the drunken man a shake. *"Get up and go home,"* he said.

"You go to hell," Torger said, his eyes suddenly wide open, and before Osten Sondreaal could straighten his back, Torger grabbed Osten Sondreaal's collar and brought a fist to his nose. Osten Sondreaal had not once struck a man, and he would have liked to have seen some other choice now, but there was Fargo to get to, not to mention that line of smoke behind him, and so he brought his fist back and struck Torger Knudson on the jaw. It felt just as bad as he had thought it would. His knuckles stung and the noise they made in contact with Torger's bones made him feel sick to his stomach, but at least Torger released his grip on Osten Sondreaal's collar and did not strike back. Osten Sondreaal quickly stood up and scrambled to the wagon before Torger could get to his feet. A look back showed Torger still lying by the dusty track. As he crossed the bridge, Osten Sondreaal lifted his bruised hand to his nose and wiped away a small slug of blood from under one nostril.

The blow to his jaw had surprised Torger Knudson, and by the time it occurred to him to sit up he had long since missed his chance for a second swing at Osten Sondreaal. Remembering something far more important, Torger reached into the back pocket of his pants, and there, like a miracle, was the bottle, unbroken. He brought it to his mouth for a long drink, and then thought some more about getting up. He drank again, and thought, and then drank and stopped thinking as he lay back down with his eyes closed. It was the smell of smoke that woke him up and brought him onto his knees and then, unsteadily, to his feet. The wind that had been blowing over him as he lay by the side of the wagon track hit him with surprising force when he stood, and for a moment he tottered against the pressure until he found the right lean forward. In front of him a dirty haze approached at eye level. The air that entered his nostrils was hot and dry. Peering toward the darkness that was closing the day in reverse, like a curtain drawn from west to east, Torger could just make out a low line of red spread across the horizon. Torger looked at the bottle in his hand, took a long last pull to finish the whiskey, dropped it to the ground, and then struck off across a field in the direction of his farmstead nearby. Ole had plowed a fire line around the house and barn early in July. He would be safe there.

Several minutes passed before Torger realized that he had misjudged the fire's advance: it was already between him and his home, and it was ash, not smoke alone, that stung his eyes. Now that the blaze was closer it was hard to distinguish between the fire line and the smoke that rolled before it. The air was closing about him in a hot dry suck. Torger changed his direction, this time stumbling parallel to the fire's advance. There was an abandoned soddie less than a quarter mile to the south, just on the other side of the standing wheat field. He would be safe there. He had staggered no more than fifty yards when a wave of heat hit him and live cinders swirled over his head. The hairs in his nose felt as if they had caught fire and his throat began to burn. Torger turned in surprise to face the magnified wind that seemed to be propelled by the fire itself. And then, as if springing up from the earth below, the flames transformed from a color in the distance into a living blaze that burst through the dense curtain of smoke. Torger spun around, and dizzied, fell to his knees. He was on his feet immediately. He made two complete revolutions before he began to run back toward the Sheyenne. Again he fell, and again he got up to run. He was almost to where he and Osten Sondreaal had scuffled when he tripped over a pile of rocks that had once marked a section corner and struck his head against a stone that had rolled a few feet away. Torger Knudson did not lose consciousness, but he could not clear his head to stand. Crawling through the grass alongside the wagon track, Torger worked to catch his breath in the smoke that approached, surrounded, passed him. He could feel the bottoms of his boots scorching the soles of his feet. A patch of burning straw blew against the back of his neck, and Torger swatted it away and continued to pull himself toward the river. The popping and crackling of the fire had been replaced with a muffled low roar. He could not breathe. Pushing his nose close to the earth Torger felt a momentary coolness waft up from the earth. He began to claw at the ground. He would cover himself with dirt. And then an astonishment of pain embraced his body, and the fire was upon him.

The inquest was held that evening on the blackened prairie where Torger lay. A lone woman sat in a buck-board a short distance from the four men silhouetted against a sanguineous moon resting heavily upon the horizon. At their feet lay the corpse, tightly curled into itself, the man's forearms stiffened against his face in a final, futile protective gesture. With each movement their feet stirred up a fine silty soot. They had tied handkerchiefs over their noses to filter out the smoke and ash that lingered in the air. All about them patches of burning stubble continued to glow. Voices could be faintly heard calling to each other in the distance where a Northern Pacific crew worked to stamp out the embers that smoldered along the railroad tracks. Although the wind had gone down with the sun, no rain had come in its place. The fire had not crossed the Sheyenne River. Moving rapidly, it had done little damage to the trees that lined the west side of the river, devouring instead the brush and shrub and grasses before sizzling to a halt in the shallow water. The few patches of grass singed by burning brush blown across the narrow river had been quickly attended to by a troop of farmers armed with spades and shovels.

Osten Sondreaal worked his soft felt hat between his hands. Before him Dr. Harkness kneeled beside the burned body of Torger Knudson. Sheriff John Haggart and John Bingham waited by his side.

"Well?" the sheriff asked.

"He has a nasty cut on his forehead. Here. Struck by a blunt object of some type. Given his condition, it's hard to say just how old that bruise is, but I'd say it's pretty fresh."

"Could the blow have killed him? And the fire come along and burned him where he fell?"

Dr. Harkness shook his head, and gestured to the sheriff to come closer. "That's unlikely. The injury looks severe enough to have stunned, but I am feeling no instability in the bones surrounding the wound. Judging by the way he's drawn himself up, I believe he was conscious when the fire reached him."

"But the blow to the head could have made it impossible for him to get out of the way of the fire?"

"It's possible, but it's also possible that he was in a condition, as Mr. Sondreaal has suggested, that would have impaired both his judgment and his mobility."

"So he burned to death," the sheriff said.

"I expect that he suffocated due to lung spasm," the doctor clarified. "The burning could have followed, or it could have been simultaneous, and horrible. He would surely have died of its effects sooner or later. In my opinion, we may safely say that the fire was the direct mechanism of death."

The sheriff turned to Osten Sondreaal. "Is this where you last saw him?"

"No, no, no." Osten Sondreaal moaned, and then slowly began to pick through the words he knew in English to try to explain where he had tussled with Torger Knudson on the other side of the wagon track. He had made very little progress when Dr. Harkness stopped him.

"Sheriff Haggart, I asked my nurse, Miss Olafsdatter, to come along to interpret for Mr. Sondreaal, if she may."

"I don't see why not." The sheriff turned to see that the woman had stood upon hearing her name and was about to climb out of the wagon. "No, no, ma'am, you stay up there," he said. "We'll come to you."

When the men were grouped around the wagon, the sheriff nodded to Osten Sondreaal. Standing like a penitent with his hat in his hands, he began to speak, softly and with the occasional gesture toward the body behind him. Occasionally, Jena Olafsdatter would hold up her hand to stop the steady flow of Norwegian from the man standing below her, and then she would repeat what he had said in English. At one point she stopped Osten Sondreaal and gestured for the sheriff to come closer to the buggy. In response to something she said, Osten Sondreaal lifted the corner of his kerchief and the sheriff moved the kerosene lamp he held closer to the man's face. Unbidden, Osten Sondreaal lifted his right hand to show it to the sheriff as well. The rest of the story was told quickly. Once in Fargo Osten Sondreaal had gone directly to Henderson's Hardware. He had loaded the new plow share into his wagon and was about to turn back home when the cry had gone up and down the street for all men to grab a shovel and get themselves to the western outskirts of town. Looking up from his wagon Osten Sondreaal had seen A. E. Henderson himself wrestling several new long-handled shovels and spades out onto the sidewalk. He had grabbed a shovel and followed the running crowd out of town. There he had discovered a number of men with teams widening a firebreak in the smoky haze that had crossed the Sheyenne ahead of the fire. He had joined the line of men standing by with their shovels, should the fire leap both the Sheyenne and the firebreak. When it was clear, late in the afternoon, that it would not, he had returned his shovel to Henderson's, checked to see that the plow share was in the back of his wagon still, and encouraged his reluctant horse west into the smoke to see if his homestead had survived the prairie fire.

"And?" the sheriff asked when the nurse stopped speaking.

"And?" she repeated in English.

And when Osten Sondreaal came to where he and Torger had exchanged blows, he was relieved to see that Torger was no longer there. He had gone just a few yards further when something made him look to the other side of the wagon track. That's when he saw the little mound that was Torger Knudson. Like a big lump of coal.

"Very poetic," the sheriff said when Jena Olafsdatter was through translating. "And then he turned around and came back to get me?"

The nurse spoke again and Osten Sondreaal nodded yes.

"Did he get down from his wagon? Did he move the body?"

This time Osten Sondreaal shook his head in a negative without waiting for the nurse to translate.

"Tell him to lead us to where they fought," the sheriff said, but again the nurse did not need to speak, for Osten Sondreaal was already striding away. He had taken just a few steps before he tripped over a rock, and fell to his knees. A cloud of disturbed ash rose about him, but Osten Sondreaal was quickly up again. After a moment he turned to face the Sheyenne again, gauging its distance, and then said, "Here. Ya, it is here."

John Bingham bent over to pick up the bottle that his boot had struck, and handed it to the sheriff, who nodded and said, "It's a wonder the Norsky didn't explode when the fire got to him, soaked in alcohol like he was. My deputy dragged him out of the Red Light last night and told him to go home. Don't know where he was after that, but it won't be hard to find out. He usually ended his toots down by the river."

"It is to jail I go, then?" Osten asked.

"Go home," Sheriff Haggart said, adding softly, "if you still have one." To Jena Olafsdatter he said, "Explain to Mr. Sondreaal that he is not to leave his place until I have a chance to talk to him again." No one spoke as Osten Sondreaal climbed into his wagon and turned toward his homestead.

"That man is about as capable of murder, or of landing a blow that would render a fellow unconscious, as my wife. Less so," Sheriff Haggart added upon reflection. "Torger Knudson's was an accidental death. He was overcome by the smoke, and then the blaze itself. Do you agree, Dr. Harkness?"

"I do."

"Then I will need you all to stop by the office within the next couple of days to sign the official report. Thank you, Mr. Bingham. I appreciate you taking the time to act as a witness to these proceedings. Now if you will excuse me gentlemen, I have to pay a call to the widow Knudson." The sheriff handed the lamp to Dr. Harkness and walked to the back of the buck-board and his horse tied up there, but then stopped and turned around. "I'll help you get him into your wagon, Doctor. If you would be so good as to drop him off at Lugers."

"It's my wagon, sheriff." John Bingham spoke for the first time. "You go on ahead. The doctor and I can take care of Knudson."

"Pull the wagon closer, if you will, Miss Olafsdatter," Dr. Harkness said to his nurse as the sheriff's figure disappeared into the dark along the wagon track. Walking back to the body, Dr. Harkness spoke quietly to John Bingham, "We had not, I believe, concluded our conversation when the sheriff arrived at my office. Was there something more you had wanted to speak with me about? Beyond your son's…situation?"

"No, and I thank you for your advice. And for your discretion. I will speak to Percy, but I do not expect him to appreciate my interference. If it is total abstinence alone that will do the trick, I am not optimistic." The men slowed their pace as they approached the coiled body before them. "I have read advertisements for sirups that are purported to have a calming influence, and can be used precisely to wean–"

"By no means!" Dr. Harkness' voice lifted into the night. Although his next words returned to the soft pitch that kept his advice out of ear-shot of his nurse who had pulled the wagon next to the men, his tone was no less emphatic. "These so-called 'soothing sirups' are each and every one but a preparation of opium and not to be trifled with. As a physician I naturally find occasions to prescribe opium or its alkaloids. But it is a medicine that, in incautious hands, becomes very quickly dangerous. The curse of alcohol in its worst stages allows its victims intervals of rationality, but the curse of opium is never-ending. It will make a man its slave. Every druggist in Fargo knows that a prescription for opium or morphia is never to be refilled without my approval. If I had my way, anyone who sold laudanum, paregoric, or sulfate of morphia as a means by which to relieve a dependence upon alcohol would be tarred and feathered."

John Bingham nodded and then gestured toward the charred body at their feet. "I keep a tarpaulin in the wagon. We can roll and lift him in that. His daughter is our housekeeper, you know."

"Kirsten Knudson. I had forgotten. She is a great favorite of my wife's. Poor girl."

"She has become a favorite of Anna's, too, and even more so of Frances'."

CHAPTER XXIX

In Which Far er Død

So terrible a thing I was without the words. At first.

And now Far is in the graveyard with Guri and in a box almost no bigger. Ole he was hopping mad, but Mr. Luger from the furniture store said that he thought he was doing the right thing to save the Knudsons some money because here lumber is not cheap and Far would not go straight no matter how hard he tried.

The fire was only one week ago and since then so much has changed, and I will try to tell it with the logic of cause and effect, but it is never so simple as one this and one that because sometimes it is like it is two of this to make one of that, but in this case there are so many thats and then each that becomes a this to make at least one more that, and I tell you I am now a grownup, too, almost eighteen years and I am still with no concision about cause and effect. But I will start with the first cause, and that is the fire. Except there is also Far's escape and then the way Osten Sondreaal looks at Mor in church.

First about the fire, then. It was laundry day and I was busy taking the sheets off the line before the smell of the smoke got into them, even if to me it is...was...a nice smell. It comes when there are the barrels of apples and the pumpkin pies, and here at the big Bingham farm it is the time for pheasants and prairie chickens because now is when the rich people come through on the train to shoot things, riding in cars that are their very own, and sometimes they do not even leave their cars to shoot, but send their dogs and boys to bring back what is dead. Then at night they get all dressed up and come to this very house and when there is pheasant left on the plates that come back into the kitchen, then it is pheasant that I have for supper. Mr. John Bingham burned his fields all around our headquarters farm the week before so I knew that the fire was not near. Little Howie, that I am to call Houghton when Mr. Percy Bingham is home, was helping me to gather the clothes pins into a bag and when a three-year-old boy helps every job takes just that much longer, but he is a good boy is Howie. So after I set the laundry inside the back door by the kitchen I said to Howie, "Do you smell the smoke?" and he said, "yes," and I said, "do you smell anything else?" and he just looked up at me with those big blue eyes that are like Mr. Percy's and Miss Anna's, so I said, "I think I smell someone making pumpkin pie. Let's go see." So hand-in-hand we crossed the yard to the cookhouse and sure enough, there was Little Carl pouring pumpkin cream into two pie crusts. There were pies in the oven and a half dozen already there by the window to cool. Little Carl winked at Howie because that makes Howie laugh and pretty soon there we were, all three of us, wiping out the bowl with our fingers. Little Carl is a funny man. With every woman he is all smiles and politeness, and Howie he is always spoiling, but if it is a man that comes through the door he just curls up his lip and starts to grumble.

So there we are, taking a rest from work, and not a soul is to blame us. Laundry day is a long day, and there are about three laundry days a week. Little Carl he makes twenty loaves of bread and half as many pies before the morning is over and come noontime there is dinner for all the men ready, too. The threshing crew that comes has its own cook and cook wagon, but a working man would starve on what they serve, Little

Carl says. Some of the men are gone to the Minnesota woods already, but most are still here for fall plowing. Anyway, there we are having a little afternoon party, when here comes Miss Frances into the yard at a dead gallop, and if I was to stop here and tell you what Mr. Percy Bingham has to say about Miss Frances and her rides I would never get to what happens next, except maybe I would because there is less of the arguing now, which I am not to know about because it is not my business but I will tell you that the *hushjelp* gets to know a lot of things in a big house, and I know even more because now I help Miss Frances with her hair and with her getting ready for the suppers with the rich people and she says that she likes to hear me talk. Sometimes she says things, too. So here is Miss Frances with her hair starting to come all undone and she sees Little Carl and me and Howie come out of the cookhouse, and she stops so fast it is like that horse just about sits right down on his *bakende*, and she says to Little Carl, "Have you seen Mr. Johnson?" And Little Carl says that Johnson, who is the farm's supervisor, went out with the plowing foreman. And Miss Frances says that a field burn just west of Casselton has gotten away from the crew, and Little Carl is to get to the house and tell Miss Anna to use the telephone to "alert" the other farm that the fire might be coming their way, and about this telephone I will not even try to explain. And then Miss Frances is just about to fly out of the yard to find Mr. Johnson when it is like she sees me and Howie for the first time, and she says, "Kirsten, get Houghton to the house and do not let him out of your sight until I return."

Well, that was a lot of excitement, and Miss Frances she looked so grand there on that horse that I just looked and looked at the trail of dust she left behind for the longest time, even though Howie had started to cry because he wanted to go with. But that was all the excitement there was going to be, it seemed like. And I wish it was. I wish I could go back and stop everything right there. Because the fire did not even come near the yard. Everything around us is either already burned off now or under the plow, and only about the smoke getting in the house did we have to worry. So that was that.

Until there was the tapping at my door when I was in bed and sound asleep. Mrs. Ford, who sleeps with me and snores like Far...like Far used to, did not wake up, and the new girl, who is here to help me and Mrs. Ford, whoever needs her most, just turned over on her cot in the corner, so I got up, and there was Miss Frances again. "Put on a robe, Kirsten, and come to my sitting room," she said. Well, I do not have a robe and I could not go down in my shimmy, so I put on my housedress and went to the pretty room on the second floor that is really for nothing but sitting where the men are not.

What do you think but Miss Anna was there, too, with Miss Frances, and they both were with their hair down and Miss Frances was wearing the most beautiful night-gown, silk it was, I think, and as blue as the sky in Indian Summer. It was pretty enough to wear to church, with a gold belt and trimmed with gold braid. Miss Anna's was very plain, but shiny, too. Miss Anna was sitting on the sofa but Miss Frances was standing by the window. There was burning only one light by the door and a lamp on the table next to Miss Anna and it seemed very strange to be there, like I was in a dream. What time is it, I thought, and just then the big clock in the hallway downstairs began to strike, and all the time that I was counting to twelve not one word did anyone say, and then Miss Anna said to me, "Come here, Kirsten. Sit here," and she patted the sofa beside her.

Well, let me say right now that Miss Anna and Miss Frances are very nice to me, and sometimes Miss Frances will even laugh a little when I am doing her hair, although I do not think that I have said a funny thing, but I do not sit down on the sofa with them, so I was thinking, well, maybe this really is a dream, so I reached behind to give myself a good pinch on my leg, and sure enough I was awake. "Come," Miss Anna said again, and so I sat right on the edge of that sofa. And Miss Anna looked over at the window at Miss Frances like she was waiting for her to say or do something, but Miss Frances just turned and nodded her head, and then Miss Anna said, "We have some difficult news, Kirsten. There has been an accident. It is your father, dear. He was caught in the fire and perished."

I did not move. Perished? All I could say was, "Far?" And Miss Anna reached over and patted my hand a little, and still I just sat there, and said again, "Far? What is it about Far?" And then I was standing and I did not know what to do, because I thought maybe that Far was dead, but there was no one there to say to me, plain and simple and true, "Far er død." And so I said it, but like a question: "Far er død?" I did not know what I was supposed to do or where I was to go, and I could not get one single thought straight in my head, and then all of a sudden there was Miss Frances, and she did not pat my hand or tell me about the perish, she just put her arms around me and held me so close, and she put my head right to her shoulder and held it there, and then she said, real quiet and right in my ear, just like I had said, but like an answer, "Yes, Kirsten. *Far er død*." And so I just cried and cried right on that beautiful night-gown and all the time she did not let go.

Downstairs Little Carl he was waiting to carry me home to Mor under that red, red moon so alone in the sky, and there in the middle of the night was Per Rolfsrud and Pastor Fedje and Peter Sondreaal with Ole, all around the table, but no Osten Sondreaal. The fire had come right up to the house and barn, but Ole's plowing had saved everything. Peter Sondreaal had lost his house even though it had a firebreak plowed around it, and he said it must have been because he was not home to put out a little cinder that blew across the break, but it had been worse for Osten Sondreaal because he had lost his barn and all of his hay. Inside Mor's bedroom it was Ingeborg Rolfsrud and the pastor's wife and Haldis sitting so quiet in the corner, and the next day there were more and more of the women from church but for Knudsons there is now just Mor and Ole and Haldis and me. And with the women it is about God and heaven and praying for forgiveness, but when it is the men I hear then it is only "mortgage, mortgage, mortgage."

It was after the funeral that I said to Ole, "tell me now about this mortgage," and poor Ole he looks like he is about to cry, and he says, "It is bad, Kirstie. There is no money." And I say, "Are we to give the farm to the mortgage, then?" and Ole he just shrugs, and so I say, "Homer's, too?" and Ole says, "I don't know. But, maybe... Oh, Kirstie, I do not know what to do." Ole he is not easy for a brother. He is always to tease and make fun and then to tell me or Haldis to do this or that for him, but for Ole I must make the allowance because he is not with Sten's mind, and not Far's either, so here he was, the man of the family, and lost like a little boy. So all on my own I walk to the Rolfsruds' and I go right up to Per Rolfsrud where he is in the barn, and I say to him, "Per Rolfsrud, you know about the mortgage. What is to happen?" And he says to me, "That is for the men to take care of," and I say, "But Ole does not know what to do," and Per Rolfsrud says to me, "Then it is for the men to help him. Wait here," and when he comes back it is with Halvor, and I swear that I was so busy thinking about Far and the mortgage and Mor and Ole about to lose the farm that I did not even think that I was walking into a Halvor trap, but there he was, and Per Rolfsrud says, "Halvor will walk you home, Kirstie." And just like that, big Halvor takes my hand in his and starts to lead me home, just like he is my *ektefelle* already.

Well, even Halvor Rolfsrud knows enough not to do just what he wants to do right after a funeral, but that is about as far as his good manners are to go, and you will not even guess what he said to me, he said that since I had not been able to make up my mind about marrying him (that is not true, I have been as clear as the bell, as Ole says) he had gone to Far, and Far had said that of course I would marry Halvor Rolfsrud. Now Halvor Rolfsrud is not smart enough to make up such a thing, and I am sorry to say that I think that is exactly what Far did say, even without asking me for my opinion. So I said, Halvor, please. Far is dead not one week, and Mor is sick with the mortgage, and this is not the time for such talk. And Halvor said, yes, but the time is to be soon.

So all of that is why one week after Far came to perish I am back in Miss Frances' room to put her hair up in the braids and twists that we have learned to do together, because there is so much of the dark, dark hair, and well, I just take a big breath and say to her, "I am sorry to bother you with my problems, Miss Frances, but may I ask for advice, please." And she says, "Of course." So I tell her all about the mortgage, and that is all I mean to say, but then I tell her about Osten Sondreaal and the way he looks at Mor, and how, now that I am all grown up, I can see the way she looks at him, too, and then I tell her what Per Rolfsrud said, and she listens and listens and listens, just like what I am saying is important, and then she says, "I will see what I can do, Kirstie," and just like that I feel a load to fall off my shoulders, because now I am Kirstie here and Kirsten no more.

Chapter XXX

In Which Frances Gains a Little...

The day after Kirsten had spoken to Frances of the mortgage and of the 'relationship' between Osten Sondreaal and her mother that threatened to color the circumstances of Torger Knudson's death (if not in the eyes of the law, then, perhaps more importantly to Osten Sondreaal, in the eyes of his community) Frances entered John Bingham's office to find him staring out at the rain that was slapping against the windows.

"I thought you might like a cup of tea on this dreary day," Frances said, placing a cup of her own upon her desk before handing the other to John.

"Thank you, Frances. Dreary, perhaps, but this rain is good. It will settle the ash that we have been chewing on with each breeze for a week now."

"Perhaps, but I will miss the sunrises and sunsets we have had as a result. The sun has been like a fireball set in a sky streaked with scarlet and turquoise, indigo and gold."

"You have caught Percy's poetry bug." It was a harmless statement, but it closed their pleasantries with a clap. "Well, thank you for the tea," John Bingham said after a moment, setting his cup down as he returned to his desk. "I should get back to work."

This was John's signal that the conversation was over. Frances could leave the office, or she could busy herself with receipts and ledgers at her desk, but she was not expected to speak again. So she was not surprised by John's scowl when she did.

"I know you are busy, John, but I have something I would like to speak with you about, if I may."

"If it is about Percy, Frances, then you should know that I have spoken to Dr. Harkness about his...problem. He has no anodyne to recommend, nor, it seems, does he place much hope in a sanatorium. He did suggest," and here John Bingham released a small cough of discomfort, "that perhaps the amount of time that Percy spends alone, away from his family, is not helpful."

"It was about something else," Frances hurried to assure John. "I have become privy to some information by way of our housekeeper regarding Torger Knudson's land. The situation may represent an opportunity, although I do not pretend to understand the details."

"You understand a great deal, Frances. Say what is on your mind."

As concisely as she could, Frances summarized Kirsten's tale, arranging the separate pieces to form a quilt of potential: Torger Knudson's mortgaged quarter section and a family increasingly desperate; another quarter section homesteaded in the name of a mule; a neighbor on an adjacent quarter section who had just lost his barn and hay and was the last man to see Torger Knudson alive, albeit lying insensible upon the ground after a blow he had delivered.

"Torger Knudson's death has been ruled an accident," John interrupted. "And Osten Sondreaal is accused of no wrong-doing. I believe I said as much on the night of the fire when I woke you and Anna to speak to the girl."

"Osten Sondreaal is, I understand, somewhat less clear on his status. According to Kirsten, Sheriff Haggart told Mrs. Knudson only that her husband died in the fire. For whatever reason he has not since spoken to Osten Sondreaal, or had not, at least, during the time that Kirsten was with her family. She says that Mr. Sondreaal has been waiting in some trepidation ever since the inquest." Frances paused for a moment, tempted to smile at the memory of Kirsten's pride at bringing forth this very word. "As you said yourself, his English is limited, as is, I suspect, his understanding of the workings of the law here. But there is more." Frances could see that John was becoming impatient with her story so she hurried on to explain how another neighbor, Per Rolfsrud, whose farm on the other side of the Sheyenne they passed on their way to Fargo, seemed poised to take advantage of the situation. He was one of the more prosperous of the Norwegian settlers in the area and, much to Kirsten's surprise, had arranged with Torger Knudson for a marriage between his nephew and Kirsten. It was meant to be, Frances believed, a foot in the door to Torger Knudson's land for the Rolfsruds.

"So you are about to lose your housekeeper?"

"Not if our housekeeper has anything to say about it, although the situation does seem rather desperate to her. That is why she came to me for my help."

"Frances, you have spoken to me of an opportunity, but thus far, what I see is one settler about to take advantage of the misfortunes of another. What does this have to do with me?"

"There is one more piece. There appears to be an attachment between Mrs. Knudson and Mr. Sondreaal that goes all the way back to Norway."

At this, John Bingham sat back in his chair with an exasperated smile. "This is directly from one of your novels, Frances. I do not doubt that there is intrigue here deserving of a lady's rumination on a rainy afternoon. But if you will excuse me—"

So like a man, Frances thought, not to see how hard cold facts could be transformed into something quite other by desire. Instead she simply said, "There are four contiguous quarter sections, directly between Bingham land and the Sheyenne River that will change hands soon. I am suggesting that the hands they come into could be yours."

"Indeed?"

"I suspect that this Rolfsrud plans to get both of Torger Knudson's quarter sections for a song. I do not think that he is aware of the more personal details about Mrs. Knudson and Mr. Sondreaal. From what Kirsten says it seems that their church quite regularly ousts members of the congregation for so much as a look sideways. Nonetheless, we have Osten Sondreaal fearing that he has come under a cloud of suspicion regarding the death of the husband of the woman he loves. Even if he were assured that the law had no further interest in him, from what I understand about these Norwegians, any gossip speculating upon a motive he may have had for wanting Knudson to be dead would put the widow as far out of reach as she had been with Torger Knudson alive. Wait a minute before you speak, John. I know this all sounds quite labyrinthine, but I think it could be quite simple. Preempt Mr. Rolfsrud. Make an offer to the Knudsons and to Mr. Sondreaal. Mrs. Knudson is quite desperate. There is an older son, but he is, I understand, of no help. About the mule's quarter, I believe that if we…if *you* let Mrs. Knudson understand that you have known all along about the illegality of that homestead—remember, it was Percy who told us of this long ago—but did not want to interfere, and then convey your concern that the family may now face the penalties for fraud involving federal law, well, then I think you may find that Mrs. Knudson will take whatever you offer. The third quarter, Osten Sondreaal's, is less of a sure thing.

I am hoping that he will decide that this is simply the best time to sell cheap and to head west, where he and his wife-to-be can start anew."

"His wife-to-be? You move your story along at breakneck speed, Frances. I have met Osten Sondreaal. I expect his imagination travels at a much more sedate pace." John Bingham looked at Frances for a moment, and then swiveled in his chair to once again study the sheets of rain beating against the windows. "You have given this a great deal of thought."

There was no reason for Frances to deny this. "I remembered that you had asked Percy to look into that very piece of land when you were deciding to begin this enterprise. It is good land. It is contiguous with ours. And it will give us direct access to the river."

"You mentioned a full section, and have spoken of three quarters."

"The fourth quarter is owned by Sondreaal's brother, Peter, who lost his house in the fire. Perhaps he will not be interested in selling, or at least not at the price that I think you can get for the other quarter sections. But they are a dispirited lot, and now is the time to make an offer." With that, Frances excused herself and left the office, pausing for a moment on the other side of the door to take a deep breath.

There were, Frances knew—now that she had access to the farm's accounts, and increasingly, John Bingham's confidence—several reasons why her father-in-law would perhaps choose not to follow up on her suggestions. Despite yet another successful harvest, the Bingham's financial resources were stretched thin. Each year John Bingham had continued to add to his land holdings, determined to absorb as many of the government sections contiguous to his own land as he could, working toward the day when a map of his land represented a solid block, and not a series of squares on a checkerboard. His scheme of taking quarter sections as homesteads in the names of his transient laborers had worked well for awhile, but a couple of the laborers proved to be surprisingly savvy, costing him more than he had anticipated. Much of the land he coveted, made all the more valuable by the proximity of his own farm, had been quickly taken up by settlers with ambitions of their own. And now there was the added difficulty with Septimus Slade, whose patience with the return on his investment was running out.

There had been a time, Frances understood, when John Bingham had hoped to purchase Slade's holdings as well, but that was no longer within the realm of possibility. The best he could hope for from Slade now was patience. Threatened with litigation, John Bingham had finally agreed with J. B. Power on a sum due to Slade to rectify the "discrepancies" in the accounts for 1876 through 1878. There were bank loans as well, and debts owed to several implement companies, and finally, the mortgage on the headquarters section, held by J. B. Power. Frances had discovered each of these concerns of John's, and yet she understood as well that he did not believe for a moment that he had taken on too much, for taking on too much was precisely how an industrious man became wealthy. He simply needed more time. So perhaps John Bingham did not need, just now, to purchase another square mile of land, but Frances had come to recognize in her father-in-law a man for whom opportunity trumped need. If he could gain the section that he had wanted since first setting foot onto the Dakota prairie five years ago, for a price well below market value, then, Frances expected, John Bingham would feel an obligation to the future of his business to do just that.

As it turned out, the arguments for and against making an offer to the Knudsons and the Sondreaals that occupied John Bingham for two straight days were much more complicated than the actual transactions. The Norwegians seemed almost relieved to have been offered so neat a solution for their various troubles, although both Osten and Peter Sondreaal drove a much harder bargain than either Frances or John had anticipated. It was the news about the mule's quarter section that held the biggest surprise for everyone. What John Bingham had discovered, first at the government land office, and then, in the company of Osten and Peter Sondreaal at the court house, was that a Mr. Homer B. Dragon had proved up his claim the very week of Torger Knudson's death, and on that day had signed his 'X' on the deed of sale to Torger. This was not the surprise. The story of Torger Knudson's homesteading mule was evidently a favorite among the local Norwegians. The timing of the proving-up and the immediate "sale" explained what Torger had been doing in Fargo in the first place (although it did not explain where he had found the money to pay for a full week's binge). The unexpected revelation was that Torger Knudson had no sooner legally taken possession of Homer's quarter section than he had turned around and deeded the land over to his eldest daughter upon her eighteenth birthday.

There was simply no making sense of Torger's action. Perhaps he had meant to protect Homer's quarter from the lien against his mortgaged quarter, but still, to put land in a daughter's name was simply not done when there was an older son at home. The Sondreaals were shocked, but Ole Knudson was outraged. When Kirsten paid a visit to her family soon after the news reached her, ready, she explained to Frances, to share the land with her family, Ole would not even talk to her. When he did speak it was only of heading west to take a homestead of his own on the other side of the Missouri. Although John Bingham had made it clear that the Knudsons and the Sondreaals were welcome to remain on their parcels until spring, within three weeks of Torger Knudson's funeral a small procession of laden wagons and farm animals made its way westward against a steady cold wind that had more of winter than fall in it.

The Binghams were better equipped to understand Torger Knudson's motivation following a visit from a very perturbed Per Rolfsrud less than twenty-four hours after John Bingham had secured the Knudson and Sondreaal land. With his nephew, Halvor, lurking at his side, Per Rolfsrud carefully explained to John that Homer's quarter section, which was now legally Kirsten Knudson's quarter section, was to become part of the Rolfsrud farm upon the marriage of Kirsten and Halvor. Torger Knudson had promised as much, in return for several favors from Rolfsrud, including taking over payments for some farm equipment and a team of mules. Knudson had been allowed to continue to use the machinery and the team, and had been given a small cash settlement that Torger had extracted from Per Rolfsrud on the very day that he was to see to the transfer of deeds. That explained Torger's week-long binge, but it didn't explain why Rolfsrud and his nephew were standing on John Bingham's front porch explaining their business to him. That became clearer when Kirsten was called to the porch as well.

That Kirsten was already aware of her father's promise to the Rolfsruds was quickly ascertained. That she had no desire to fulfill her father's contract was equally clear. Saying this to her elder, however, a man who was a leader in the Norwegian community, who had read sermons in his house for years before there was a church and a pastor, who had over and over again come to the rescue of the Knudsons, was almost beyond Kirsten's abilities. Her meek, "but I do not want to marry Halvor," was about to be waved aside as incidental timidity when Frances, who had accompanied Kirsten to the porch, spoke up.

"Excuse me, Mr. Rolfsrud, if I may I would like to ask Kirsten a few questions." Frances did not wait for a reply before she turned to face Kirsten. "Has this young man asked you to marry him?"

"Well, he did not exactly ask—"

"What?" Halvor could not contain himself. "Have I not said twenty times, thirty even, that you are to be my wife, then?"

"Yes, but—"

"But he has not asked, has he?"

"No." Kirsten was looking more and more uncomfortable.

"Then perhaps this could all be settled with a simple courtesy on your part, Mr. Rolfsrud." Frances looked toward Halvor, who reddened with the attention, pulled his hat off his head to reveal an alarming stack of hair, and stepped forward.

"Ya, vel den, Kirsten Knudson. Will you marry me?"

Kirsten's eyes had widened in consternation as Frances spoke. Halvor's proposal had her scanning the porch as if she were considering a dash into the prairie.

When she did not speak, Frances smiled and placed her hand upon Kirsten's shoulder. "It is really a simple enough question, Kirstie. If you want to marry Halvor, then say 'yes'. But if you do not want to marry Halvor, say 'no'. One word is all that is required, but it is your word to choose."

For a moment Kirsten remained with her head down, but then she began to shake it from side to side. "No," she said. And then again, "No. I am sorry, Halvor, but this I have told you before. I do not want to marry you."

Halvor's face grew dangerously red. He had begun to stammer when Per Rolfsrud stepped forward to speak to Kirsten. "That is enough of that, Kirsten," he said, his voice neither gentle nor rough, but certain, the voice of authority. "Your father has given us his word and it is time for you to make your own home now. Be a good girl and do as your father expected. We are all busy men, and do not have the time to wait for you to be shy. You are to marry Halvor and—"

"Mr. Rolfsrud," Frances interrupted. "The laws of the country and of civilized men extend to Dakota Territory. Fathers do not sell their daughters...no, please let me speak. If Kirsten does not wish to marry now, then she shall not marry. And until she changes her mind, she shall have a home here as our housekeeper."

"But the land—"

"The land is Kirsten's to do with as she pleases. Good day, sirs."

Kirsten owed her next decision to Frances, too. Her quarter section was to be farmed as part of the Bingham bonanza farm. She would receive one-fourth of the profits. This sum would be put in a savings account for her at the First National Bank in Fargo, the two-story brick building with floor-to-ceiling arched windows that had sprung up on the corner of Broadway and First to dwarf its first tiny clapboard home next door. Were she to decide to sell, the Binghams would have first rights of purchase.

Clearly dumbfounded by the many turns of events, Kirsten was grateful to have those decisions made for her. Everything had happened so very quickly. Far was dead. There was no guarantee that she would ever see Mor or Haldis or Ole again. Sten had disappeared long ago. Her father's land as well as Osten and Peter Sondreaal's were to become part of John Bingham's bonanza farm. And then, grasping onto the known in the midst of so much that had become strange, Kirsten informed Frances that on her day off, as long as the weather allowed, she would walk to Homer's place to tend to the house that Sten had built. But, she was quick to add, she was grateful not to have to give up her job as housekeeper. She would be too lonely at Homer's all alone. Saying this, she had once again been unable to keep her tears to herself. But Kirsten's was a naturally cheerful disposition, and her tears as the days passed were less and less frequent, and for this Frances, who had little patience for sorrow, was thankful.

CHAPTER XXXI

...And Loses More

The Bingham family gathered in the parlor in the somnolent aftermath of a noon dinner of roast duck, mashed potatoes, cranberry sauce, fruitcake, and pumpkin pie, the latter Little Carl's contribution to the Thanksgiving dinner. His own cooking duties were much reduced now that only a half dozen men remained on the headquarters farm to tend the stock throughout the winter. Outside, the second major blizzard of November whistled and moaned; inside, the sturdy house creaked and the radiators clanged and hissed. Over the percussion of their environment, Anna read aloud from Gail Hamilton's *First Love is Best*. It had been the women's good fortune to discover several novels from the Cobweb Series in the traveling book agent's possession just two weeks earlier.

The Binghams had hoped to constitute a much larger gathering for the holiday. A party of old friends from St. Paul had been expected, but the railroad tracks between Brainerd and Fargo had been closed for over two days with this current storm. Nor had Alfred and Lydia Harkness attempted the six-mile trip into the prairie. Just to walk from the cookhouse to the Bingham kitchen earlier that morning to deliver a pie had been an act of either bravery or foolishness on Little Carl's part. There he had found Kirsten stuffing the birds alongside Mrs. Ford, who, unlike her predecessor, was not inclined toward territorial jealousies, and welcomed Little Carl's contributions.

Mrs. Ford often wondered just what prompted the little man to offer up his gifts with some regularity. She knew it was not her own charms that drew him to the house. Although she had put aside the black of mourning, worn for over a year following her late husband's fatal goring by a bull, she had yet to meet the man who could replace either Mr. Ford or the pleasurable orderliness of widowhood. She could imagine that the day would come when she would once again marry, but her new husband was likely to be a bit more robust than Little Carl. Between Little Carl and Kirsten there was a teasing familiarity, but to imagine the pinched little man of indeterminate age—he was as likely to be sixty as forty—approaching the healthy blond youth of the Norwegian girl was to stretch credulity. He was probably just lonely.

In the parlor Anna read on, undismayed by her audience's apparent lack of enthusiasm for her story. After several minutes of playing with an intricate necklace of metal objects that Jack Shaw had presented as a puzzle to be taken apart piece by piece, Houghton had given up, choosing to use the necklace as a tornado come to disperse a regiment of Rebel soldiers assembled just inches from his Union line. Houghton very quickly sent soldiers of gray and blue flying and was summarily called to his mother's side on the sofa. He was soon fast asleep on Frances' lap. Percy dozed on the opposite end of the sofa.

When Anna paused between chapters, John Bingham rose from his chair to excuse himself for a few hours' work in his office. He offered to take Houghton upstairs to complete his nap. Frances smiled at the rare personal gesture from her father-in-law, which she believed was as much due to their own growing camaraderie as it was to his obvious affection for the boy. Kirsten's confessions had given Frances precisely the information she needed to prove herself a worthy ally to John Bingham. And really, no harm had come to anyone as a result of her suggestions. Frances was about to shift Houghton from her lap when she froze upon hearing Percy's words.

"Let the boy take comfort in his mother's arms while he can. There will be precious little of it soon enough."

Percy had spoken without opening his eyes. He had been quite animated at the dinner table, entertaining his family with bits and pieces of random news items that he had gleaned from out-of-town newspapers that crossed his desk. When next they journeyed to New York, should such an excursion be in their future, they would find the streets there lit by electric lights. A new lotto game was reported to be all the rage in St. Paul and E. A. Grant was sure to have it in his store soon. The recently appointed territorial governor of Dakota was frustrating Yankton politicians with his gentlemanly comportment and sensible statements; even the irascible editor of the Dakota *Herald*, Maris Taylor, had been unable to find something to criticize. J. B. Power had been spotted in the company of Jim Hill in St. Paul, fueling the rumor that he was about to jump ship to the Northern Pacific's rival, the St. Paul, Minneapolis and Manitoba Railroad. This latter bit of gossip, Frances noted, gained John Bingham's attention, but Percy had nothing more of substance to report. Not until the end of the meal had Percy gaily announced that his boss, E. B. Chambers, had indeed sold the *Times* to a fellow Fargoan, who was expected to rename the paper the Fargo *Weekly Times*. Little else was likely to be altered, Percy added, except that a certain Percy Bingham was to no longer be in the paper's employ. "And that," Percy had concluded, looking into the startled expressions of his father, sister, and wife, "is that. We shall speak no more on such a dull topic."

Now in the warm parlor, without his wine glass before him, Percy slumped against the high arm of the sofa. But the intentional unpleasantness of his words that had clearly been directed toward his wife could not be mistaken. Anna looked uncomfortably at Frances, then found her place on the page again. John scowled. Frances lowered her head to graze the top of Houghton's head with her lips.

"Yes, well," John cleared his throat. "I'm afraid I must excuse myself for the remainder of the afternoon. There are letters—" Leaving the sentence unfinished, he strode out of the room.

"Please continue, Anna," Frances said, forcing a lightness into her tone. "You and I alone, it seems, are to discover how Mrs. Hamilton will save her heroine from—what was it she promised in the preface?—years of misunderstanding and misery, I believe."

Despite the author's promises, the heroine had not been spared the requisite hardships and heartbreaks. But it was a short book, and with just one more pause—allowing Frances to take Houghton into the kitchen to Kirsten when he woke from his nap—the trials were swiftly overcome for the happily-ever-after.

"Well, that was pleasant, wasn't it?" Anna said, closing the book. "Did you enjoy it?"

"I enjoy listening to you read, dear, although it makes me feel very lazy. Perhaps tomorrow, if this storm continues to hold us hostage indoors, we could will our imaginations into spring with your new *Demorest's*. We really should be ready to order our patterns as soon as this atrocious weather allows us a trip to the post office. And then we will turn to something new. I am thinking of the short stories by Charles Reade I acquired from the agent. Or the Collins novel."

"Charles Reade and Wilkie Collins. Your tastes and mine there diverge, Frances."

"Things happen in their novels."

"Yes, but such things."

Frances laughed. "I understand. I shall enjoy Mr. Reade on my very own. You need fear no confrontations with corpses on rafts in the middle of the ocean and lion attacks in deepest Africa. Shall you lie down now?"

"I believe so."

Each afternoon Anna retired to her room for a couple of hours before supper, having discovered years earlier that the pain in her hip and back was significantly lessened if she punctuated her day with rest that did not involve sitting. Anna had assured Frances several times that she could manage on her own, but was equally consistent with her gratitude when Frances helped her undress for bed.

Although their friends from the city had not been there to make the Thanksgiving day celebration more formal, Anna had chosen to dress in her finest, and Frances stood by as Anna unfastened the dozen polished buttons of her new basque of green silk, and then unfastened the silk scarf she had fitted around her neck frill and draped over a jabot of white lace. Standing behind Anna, Frances unbuttoned the matching overskirt and then bent down to keep it from dragging on the floor as Anna, leaning upon Frances to keep her balance, stepped out of the skirt and the matching underskirt of pleated flounces. Anna unfastened her silk corset cover while Frances unbuttoned the several straps of her friend's shoes. Released, finally, from her hip-length corset, Anna stood before Frances in her chemise. But only briefly. The room was chilly and Anna quickly wrapped herself in the dressing-gown that Frances handed her, and then, as was her habit, leaned forward with a kiss of thanks.

The women had been constant companions now for over a decade, and their intimacy had become second nature. They were comfortable speaking in endearments, a "darling" or "dearest" passing between them as naturally as between the best of friends in parlors, dining rooms, and bedrooms across the country. On those occasions when Anna was not well—neither could think of a time when Frances had been ill, excepting the distress of her pregnancy—it was Frances who sat by her bedside. Should Anna be taken with a chill, it was Frances who would lie next to her to lend her own body's warmth. In their moments of quiet familiarity they made their week's plans, smiled at girlhood memories, or, less often, shared fears and expectations. In this, they were not unlike so many other women of their day and social class who found the intimacies of soul described in romantic novels between a man and a woman to be more readily available off the page between best friends. Nor were their kisses infrequent. Meant to indicate a thank-you, a punctuation of pleasure, an acknowledgment of trust, or a simple good night, they were readily dispensed in a gesture that announced the other as cherished.

This was precisely why Frances had married into the Bingham family, and for several years she had worked to convince herself that Anna's affection was sufficient to her needs. She did not think of the pleasure that she took in these intimacies as wrong, nor did she feel dishonest when indulging in the fantasy that Anna's endearments reflected her own desires. She was a good friend. She was devoted. She was loved, and she loved in return, and she would leave it to Percy's poets to quibble over the shifting definitions of the word. Her private interpretations did no harm.

Anna leaned forward with a kiss of thanks, her hands on Frances' shoulders for steadying. Frances met and returned the kiss, and then circled her arms around Anna's waist. The kiss did not last more than a second longer than the hundreds of innocent kisses that had preceded it. There was very little increased pressure between their lips. The women's mouths did not open wider than friendship allowed. And yet all was changed. Frances opened her eyes to a new Anna, flushed and confused, and unhappy.

"You are too warm, Frances," was all she said, taking one awkward step back. And then she looked away, and in that moment Frances understood how different a life of hopelessness would be compared to one of anticipation.

"Anna," she said, and watched as Anna took a deep breath and turned back to face her. Her eyes, blazing blue in contrast to the pink that had come to her cheeks, bore an expression Frances had never before witnessed, and she labored to read the messages written there: anger, confusion, maybe simple wonder. And more than all, there was defiance. Not the defiance of a challenge, but of resistance. The passion they signaled, the tumult that replaced the calm that Anna embodied, filled Frances with a desire that she did not believe she could tolerate. She felt as if she must either weep or beg, and she knew that to do either would be futile. Frances held out her hand to Anna, a supplicant, waiting for Anna's response to define the gesture's request.

Even that simple motion startled, and in her haste to step further away, Anna stumbled and winced. Before she could refuse Frances' help, Frances was by her side. Together they walked to the bed, and as Frances helped Anna under the covers she noticed that the moment of pain had stolen the pink once again from Anna's cheeks. Frances stood by the bed, still holding the hand she had grasped when Anna faltered. But the stern look that Anna directed toward Frances forced her to let go.

"Are you O.K.?" Frances asked, and then winced at her choice of a vulgarism picked up from the farmyard that made her question sound even more ludicrous. When Anna did not reply, Frances spoke again. "Anna, let me explain." But what was she to say in explanation? Certainly not the truth. Exhaustion and worry about Percy, perhaps, Frances thought, her mind racing.

"I have often stood in amazement at your resourcefulness, Frances, but even you, I think, can not make sense out of the impossible. Tell me, rather, that I have imagined your warmth. Yes, I am certain that is it. Forgive me. Perhaps I am coming down with a fever."

Frances felt her own face flush with unexpected anger. For the first time in their friendship, instead of marveling over Anna's stoic calm, Frances felt an impatience with her friend's insistence upon absorbing the wrongs of those about her. It was meant to be a gift, a solution, but surely Anna recognized that it magnified her role as an invalid to thus excuse the foibles of others. Frances swallowed and looked fully upon Anna. She needed only to pat the hands that Anna had clasped in front of her upon the coverlet and mouth a bit of nonsense, something insipid and empty, a "There, there. Don't give it another thought." Then she was to feel the invalid's forehead and offer to send Kirsten in with a small brandy and water.

Instead she said, "Why call impossible what has happened so naturally?"

For a moment Anna looked as if she had been slapped. Frances' rejection of her offering was clear. "Naturally?" Anna drew herself up against the bed's headboard. "Will you insult God as easily as you insult me?"

"I will insult neither with lies. Anna, you kissed me, as I kissed you."

"Well," Anna reached up to tuck a curl behind her ear, and Frances could see that her hand trembled. "In truth, we have kissed often. I think of you, my beloved brother's wife, as my sister. I would be sorry –" Anna hesitated and then looked straight in front of her, refusing to meet Frances' eyes as she continued. "I would be sorry if our friendship were to be altered. Or lost."

"I would never hurt you, Anna."

"On that subject I will be the expert. I have learned over the years that unintended pain is no less piercing than that which can be anticipated." Anna paused, and then said, "I have been thinking of late of the invitation I received this fall from Sophie Fredley to spend the winter with her in St. Paul, now that dear Archibald has passed and she is so alone. I have changed my mind and will accept. It will be good to see old friends again. I will send a telegram announcing my decision as soon as the weather allows, and leave immediately thereafter."

BOOK FOUR:
A STRUGGLE WITH DIRT

With mud and with grime from corner to center,
Forever at war and forever alert,
No rest for a day lest the evening enter;
I've spent my whole life in a struggle with dirt.

(From *The Checkered Years: Excerpts from the*
Diary of Mary Dodge Woodward, Written While
Living on a Bonanza Farm in Dakota Territory
During the Years 1884 to 1889)

CHAPTER XXXII

In Which Alexander McKenzie and
Governor Nehemiah Ordway Meet, Dance, Embrace

A man who is precisely what he needs to be precisely when he needs to be just that may be either hero or scoundrel. There was some disagreement as to which category Alexander McKenzie belonged, although he would have dismissed the distinction as the sort of quibbling best left to men who sat around and philosophized while they watched men like him act. Sheriff McKenzie's foremost policy was to make people grateful. There were businessmen who had stocked their shelves on McKenzie's capital, farmers who tasted their monthly ale at McKenzie's saloons on credit until the harvest was in, and widows who opened their cellars to loads of coal purchased and delivered by McKenzie's orders. He was not particular about whom he helped, understanding that there was no telling who would be useful in the future. More useful in the long term than the helping hand extended to the businessman short on cash or the widow in distress was the favor bestowed upon a man well before he understood his own desires. Prop a man up before he needed support, McKenzie believed. Encourage him to lean. Give him something he will not want to lose. Then, should he become disagreeable, let him know who has the power to kick his foundation out from under him.

In his official capacities as both Bismarck's sheriff and now deputy United States marshal, McKenzie made it a practice never to insult with physical force a proper citizen discovered to be operating in a manner not entirely consistent with the law. It was much better for the community, and for all parties concerned, to work out a private arrangement with the malefactor. As for transients, railroad workers, hired farm hands, and lesser folk, force was generally more efficient. And the force of the man of not-quite thirty and affectionately referred to as Big Alec was substantial. Quiet and soft-spoken, the man's physical courage in pursuit of the murderer or horse thief was a subject of local lore. McKenzie's friend, Colonel Lounsberry of the Bismarck *Tribune*, editorialized that "the sheriff knows the methods and faces of every crook on the N.P. line, and is able to spot any new arrival almost instantly."

He knew the "methods and faces" of a number of powerful men as well. Information from his friends at the Northern Pacific had him buying town lots in Bismarck practically before the town itself was platted. Sharing a bit of that information brought him into a silent partnership of the tri-weekly stage line to the Black Hills, which was soon thereafter awarded the government contract for mail delivery. It was good information that opened the doors of any number of judges and politicians. And it was good information that made him a valuable lobbyist for the Northern Pacific Railroad Company when the territorial legislature was in session in Yankton.

As a voice (always in the background, always unofficial) of northern Dakota interests, McKenzie was still part of a minority when in Yankton, although no longer a welcome minority. The days when the northern delegates were looked upon with some merriment by the territory's southeastern politicians were gone. Only four years earlier, in the Twelfth Legislative Assembly of '77, the north Dakota delegates constituted a scarce fifth of the territorial seats. Since then the Yankton faction had suffered the indignity of watching the small settlements of the Red River valley double their populations yearly as the Northern Pacific Railroad continued its transcontinental way westward. One-third of the delegates to the upcoming legislative assembly would be from the north, all but one with connections to the N.P. The Yanktonites did not like this one bit, grumbling that they now had the N.P. (as well as the federal government) to contend with as an absentee power, with railroad attorneys in the east writing the laws regulating all railroad activity in the territory. This was a charge that Alexander McKenzie knew to be absolutely correct.

So it was a surprise to no one that, come January of 1881, Sheriff Alexander McKenzie's decision to transport a prisoner from Bismarck to the insane asylum in Yankton happened to coincide with the beginning of the Fourteenth Territorial Assembly there. It would be a busy legislative session. The tide of immigrants flowing into the territory continued to rise each year, and even the reports making their way into the eastern papers of the exceptionally harsh Dakota winter seemed unlikely to check the flood. Territorial newspapers were predicting upwards of several thousand new arrivals daily, come spring. Towns were popping up across the prairie almost overnight, creating new sources of wealth for land agents, merchants, lawyers, and newspapermen. With this great influx of population came the opportunity for taxation. Towns and counties that could prove that they could build and support an insane asylum, for example, or a penitentiary, or a university, would capture a significant portion of the territory's treasury, not to mention the commerce that would necessarily follow the town's elevation in importance.

McKenzie meant for Bismarck to have a piece of this pie, although it was not a slice as small as an asylum, or penitentiary, or university that he had in mind. His plans would require the friendship of Nehemiah Ordway, the new governor, whom he had not yet met. There had been little to gain by rushing down to Yankton to stand empty-handed before the man who now largely controlled the territory's coffers. But he had not been idle. For seven years, since he had first become sheriff, McKenzie had been quietly spinning a web of influence that radiated out from Bismarck. Through the eyes of his minions throughout the territory, McKenzie had watched as Governor Ordway, within months of arriving in Dakota, created a newspaper with his personal secretary as editor. When that paper failed, Ordway had gone to Maris Taylor, editor of Yankton's Dakota *Herald*, to try to convince him to make the *Herald* the administration's mouthpiece. McKenzie didn't know quite what to make of this news. Either Ordway was in the habit of working miracles or else he was a terrible judge of character. Although Taylor's paper dedicated a great deal of space to local and national politics, a reader could look long and hard before running across the name of a politician meeting the cranky editor's approval (with the general exception, in the past, of his crony, Moses K. Armstrong). Going to Taylor had been a mistake, and it told McKenzie something about Ordway, about a man whose ambitions could outdistance his groundwork, whose own sense of power made him incautious. Undeterred (and this McKenzie did admire), Ordway had begun another paper of his own, but this time in the more centrally located south Dakota town of Pierre, which was now the western terminus of the Chicago and Northwestern Railroad.

Yes, it certainly would be a busy session, McKenzie thought, and no, he would not meet Governor Ordway empty-handed.

It was late in the evening, a full week after McKenzie's arrival in Yankton, when the two men met in Governor Ordway's courthouse office. The dishes of the supper the men had shared, sent over from the Central Hotel, remained on the table behind them. Seated in a deep easy chair of leather, McKenzie studied his host who remained standing, his right hand grasping the lapel of his coat as he spoke, posturing, McKenzie thought, like a woman in front of a mirror. The conversation over supper had been to no effect, a shared recitation of the legislative arguments that had taken place elsewhere in the courthouse for the past week. As Ordway performed, McKenzie waited for the governor to empty himself of flowery phrases and begin to speak in the language of greed that McKenzie's sources insisted he spoke.

There were several topics about which McKenzie hoped to get a reading from the new governor, including statehood and the related issue of allegiance to the railroads. It was certainly not in the N.P.'s interests to exchange the freedom it enjoyed under the territorial system for the regulations and restrictions likely to be enforced by a state government. Of course, McKenzie knew, statehood for Dakota must come sooner or later, and when that happened, whether as one state or two or four, he intended to be situated precisely where he would have the most power. And that would not be in Yankton. The old guard here could kick and scream, but they couldn't change the path of a transcontinental railroad. The time had come to see if this governor, Nehemiah Ordway, could be pulled on board McKenzie's train.

Ordway was speaking, admiringly, about the vast resources of Dakota Territory. The words were familiar, a repetition of his opening message this past Tuesday to the legislature, which Maris Taylor in the *Herald* had described as an over-done panegyric similar to what might be expected of an adolescent school-girl's first essay. "The people of Dakota are so well aware of the advantages of their chosen place of residence," Taylor had concluded, "that they need not be told of them by a peregrinating gubernatorial tramp." McKenzie stroked his mustachios to hide his smile, and then, shifting in his chair, prepared to herd the governor's pretty phrases toward a more useful topic of discussion.

"In your opinion, Governor, is there a difference between the resources and opportunities of the territory, north and south?"

"As the fortunate and honored chief executive officer of all of Dakota, my respect, duty, and allegiance are trothed to the citizens of the entire territory, and I make no distinction between the importance of the judge and the farmer, the merchant and the blacksmith," Ordway hesitated, and then added, "north or south."

"Some folks feel that opportunities are growing a bit faster in some parts than others."

Ordway smiled benevolently upon his guest. "You are speaking, Mr. McKenzie, of the northern half of the territory, and your loyalty to the place where you have made your home as well as your good name does you honor. I will not concur—I can not—that the future of one part of the territory is brighter than any other, but I will happily attend to your recitation of north Dakota's fine attributes."

"Well, in some ways, I guess we just got plain lucky, Governor," McKenzie said, looking directly at Ordway now that his host had seated himself as well. "Most of the Indian trouble been down here in south Dakota, you see. Sure, getting them corralled onto the reservations been good for business here in the southeast, but the best of them days are over, and if you ask me, them Indians will just be trouble from now on. Cost the government a pretty penny. Cost a state more if the statehood folks get their way."

"And the Indian to the north, is he not an equal problem?"

"Less so. The Ojibwa on the Canada border got to marrying French fur trappers early on, and anyone can tell you that a half-breed ain't even half the problem of a full-blooded Indian. Then there's the Arikaree, Hidatsa—some call 'em Gros Ventres—and Mandan up in the Fort Berthhold area that'll be friendly enough to anyone that keeps the Sioux away from 'em. As for the Sioux, used to be they mostly just passed through for hunting during the summer. Nowadays they're just not around much at all. Clipping the scalps of a couple hundred of Custer's men back in '76 was their last hurrah. Now they may be in Canada still, what's left of 'em, or they may have all snuck back into Montana, or here in south Dakota, but the point is, they just don't figure much up north."

"You speak of the past, Mr. McKenzie, and not of the future."

"Then let me be just a little more forward, if you will, Governor. I was there the day the Northern Pacific Railroad crossed the Red River into Dakota Territory, and from that day on the future of Dakota was set as firm as them rails. In a couple of years when the line coming in from the west meets our line from the east to make the N.P. a transcontinental railroad for real, well sir, on that day, every city along that route is worth about twice what it was the day before. Even now it's the N.P. that makes north Dakota a part of the rest of the country in a way that these little towns, even Yankton, can't imagine. It's a sight to see, I tell you, watching boxcar after boxcar of Dakota wheat heading east to the mills of Minneapolis."

"Then you would say that the most promising part of north Dakota is the Red River valley? Fargo, perhaps? Cigar?"

McKenzie shook his head 'no' and watched as Ordway delicately snipped the end of his cigar with a gold cutter he carried on his watch chain. He was certain that the governor, like most of his predecessors, was determined to use his office for personal gain. Whether Ordway had the patience to quietly work toward the greater wealth and power realized only by steadfast maneuvering, McKenzie had yet to determine.

"Fargo is important," McKenzie said. "Good for bonanza farmers and merchants, and good for Minnesota, since that's where all the milling gets done. Got maybe five thousand folks living there now, and it's going to keep right on growing, and that's all good. But for return on investment, there are better places for a forward-looking man to... to look forward to."

"And what, Mr. McKenzie, does Bismarck have to offer?"

McKenzie was pleased with the governor's candor at last, for the man had said nothing of substance since their greeting almost two hours earlier.

"For one, it's on the line of the Northern Pacific. Two, an investor picking up town lots and some surrounding acreage for a song today would realize a significant return should it, let's say, take on greater political importance some day."

Ordway smiled. "Greater political importance? Perhaps the home of the capital, for example?"

"Just so, and an investor who had got himself in a position to say exactly where that capital ought to go would be sitting pretty, you see."

"You surprise me, Mr. McKenzie. Your comments suggest that you are not only in favor of statehood, but of splitting the territory in two in the quest for that statehood. Perhaps you may have read in one of the local newspapers that I am in favor of such a move, but I will happily disabuse you of that notion. I speak not as a representative of the federal government, but as a servant of the territory with its best interests at heart. I simply do not believe that the territory's population can support the costs of statehood just yet."

"Me, either, Governor. Me, either. Though it don't ever hurt to be ready ahead of time. In the meantime, maybe the time has come to reconsider the location of the territory's capital. Take a look at that map," McKenzie nodded toward the wall behind Ordway's desk. "You draw a circle with Yankton at the center and you'll hit the better part of Nebraska, Kansas, Iowa, and Minnesota before you get to half of the territory. And how do you get here no matter where you are? Slow. By stage coach or by changing trains a couple of times, and then limping in on that toy train, the Dakota Southern, from Sioux City. What Yankton is now is what Yankton will be in twenty years, if that. The future of the territory is up north, and that's just a cold, hard fact."

"Yet it does not lie with Fargo, you say?"

"Fargo will be the rival of Chicago or St. Paul someday, there ain't no doubt about that. But the center of commerce don't need to be the capital. Better to spread things out. Besides, putting the capital in Fargo would be like making the same mistake as putting it in Yankton."

"Bismarck as the capital of Dakota Territory."

"For now, and for as long as there is such a thing. Let the Yankton folks split away when they can and agitate for statehood all they want. But when the day comes for statehood up north, Bismarck ought to be the capital of the state of Dakota."

"Out of curiosity, Mr. McKenzie, what will the state to the south of your Dakota be called?"

"Whatever folks here like, so long as it ain't Dakota. It's the wheat farms of the Red River valley that made Dakota famous, and that gives us to the north the right to claim the name, you see. Let them name the entire state Yankton for all I care."

Ordway gave a nod and slight smile and then shifted in his chair. "Well, Mr. McKenzie, you are an interesting conversationalist, and I am always pleased to make the acquaintance of a Dakota citizen who thinks so highly of his home. I understand that the idea of capital removal was broached in a previous session, without a great deal of success. I have seen little of my new friends here in Yankton to suggest that their opinion on the matter has altered."

McKenzie could tell that he was about to be dismissed. Sitting forward he prepared to lay down his ace to keep the game alive. "I am not alone in my enthusiasm, Governor."

"I am sure not, Mr. McKenzie. Now if—"

"In fact, I have several loyal friends in the newspaper business. Good men with good newspapers make good friends." To McKenzie's relief he noticed that the governor had settled back in his chair.

"For example?"

"George Walsh of the Grand Forks *Plaindealer.*"

"The president of the Council. We have met."

"Marshall McClure of the Jamestown *Alert*. A. W. Edwards of the Fargo *Argus*," McKenzie said. "Major Edwards, that is. He's in town for the session, so must have left Percy Bingham in charge back in Fargo." McKenzie waited for Ordway to respond.

"I am afraid that I do not know the name."

"No reason to know about young Percy himself," McKenzie explained. Nor was there a distinct reason for McKenzie to have persuaded Edwards to hire Percy Bingham at the *Argus* after the new owner and editor of the Fargo *Times* quite publicly refused to keep Bingham on when the paper changed hands. McKenzie was playing a hunch that Bingham would come in handy some day, and it cost him nothing to store him away for awhile. "His father is John Bingham, one of the bonanza farmers in Cass County," McKenzie said. "Compared to some of the other bonanzas in the valley he's small potatoes, but for one reason or another it's his place that attracts the visitors of importance that pass through. He's an N.P. man—John Bingham, that is."

"Go on."

"Colonel Lounsberry of the Bismarck *Tribune*, of course," McKenzie continued. "George Hopp at the Brookings *County Press* has his hand in about a half dozen other papers as well. Two in Huron. The *County News* in DeSmet. The *County Times* in Estilline. I'm forgetting one or two now."

"And all of these gentlemen of the press are ready to agitate for the removal of the capital to Bismarck, you say?"

"I ain't said that at all, Governor. What I said is that all of these men are friends of mine, and given the opportunity, they'd be friends of yours, too."

"It is kind of you to think about me, Mr. McKenzie, but if I may, I would like to point out that your friends are, for the most part, from the north. They may whistle as loudly as they like in your famous wind up there without affecting in any significant way the business of the legislature here in Yankton."

"Hopps' got a paper in Brookings. N. C. Nash, that runs the *Sioux Valley News* in Canton, might be persuadable. And that's just the beginning."

"Yes, but the beginning of what, precisely?"

"A Press Association."

For the first time in their conversation, a look of some surprise crossed Nehemiah Ordway's face, and McKenzie suspected that he had hit upon something close to the governor's own plan. The look was quickly replaced by a disinterested and delicate yawn.

"I must repeat my point," Ordway said, "and I remind you that my interest is purely of an academic nature. The influence of your associates is limited, for the most part, to the north."

"Newspaper editors can be representatives and councilmen, Governor." McKenzie paused to let his words take effect. "I ain't suggesting a public campaign to stir up the local populations. I'm saying that several of the newspapermen are in a position to seek election themselves, such as my friend, George Walsh, has done. Lots of birds killed by that stone. Each man would be more than a mouthpiece, but a vote as well, you see."

"With a snap of the fingers?"

"It will take more with some than with others. But we have a good start with Walsh."

"'We', Mr. McKenzie? 'We' have nothing here, but a pleasant conversation. Which you may continue, of course."

"I'm just saying that newspapers are an interest we share."

"But you do not own a newspaper yourself, do you, Mr. McKenzie."

"No, I prefer–"

"To own the newspapermen. I see. I am sure you have noticed that the newspaper I own is located at the current terminus of the Chicago and Northwestern. Pierre is as centrally located in the territory as, say, Bismarck."

This went well beyond candor, and for the first time in the conversation McKenzie feared he had underestimated his quarry. It occurred to him that in five minutes he could find himself on the other side of the door, having played his cards with very little to show for the game. Certain that he was dealing with an incautious man, he had lacked caution himself.

"Yes," McKenzie said. "There is certainly a case to be made for Pierre. And for Huron. Maybe Jamestown, too. I ain't a stubborn man, governor. I could see my way clear to supporting most any one of them choices for the right reasons. But first things first, which is to get the ball rolling for capital removal itself, and that gets me back to that Press Association. Maybe you would agree that the final decision for locating the capital itself would best be kept in the hands of a trusted few."

"Certainly, but trusted by whom?"

"By you, Governor."

McKenzie held Ordway's direct look, which slowly gave way to the slightest of smiles and an assenting nod of the head. A knock on the door turned both men in their chairs.

A tall, scrawny boy with alarmingly red hands and a runny nose opened the door just wide enough to peer around. It was the same boy who had delivered the supper earlier, and Ordway simply waved toward the table. Then, standing, and bringing McKenzie likewise to his feet, Ordway said, "I would agree, Sheriff McKenzie, that it often falls to the responsibility of a few to see to the best interests of the many. As governor, I have taken the mantle of protector of the territory upon my shoulders, just as you, as sheriff, have taken upon yourself the protection of the citizens of Bismarck." When the door behind the men closed, Ordway extended his hand. "I am happy to make the acquaintance of a man whose vision of the future so closely," Ordway paused to give his modifier weight, "approximates my own. I look forward to meeting your friends over the next two years, and to a productive legislative session in '83."

CHAPTER XXXIII

In Which We Hear about Scallawags and Scoundrels

Moses K. Armstrong had not left Yankton since his return from Bismarck in '76. His brief foray as a traveling correspondent had not been successful: the bonanza farm piece paid much less than the trip had cost, and the long letter about Indians in Dakota had been edited and cut to a few paragraphs inserted into a much longer essay. Back in Yankton he had run, unsuccessfully, for Clerk of Court and then, Judge of Probate, before accepting that his good name would no longer bring in the votes. Most of the time, these days, he could be found at his desk, collecting, sorting, and occasionally editing clippings of stories that were to become the history of the territory he intended to call *The Early Empire Builders of the Great West*. He had just put his work away for the day when he heard the expected knock upon his door.

"Just in time, Bud," Armstrong said as he opened the door. "Maudie has a fresh pot of coffee ready." He stood back from the door as Maris Taylor shrugged out of his heavy winter coat and turned to hang it on a peg by the door. Taylor had already stamped and scraped on the other side of the door, and now he automatically began the polite wipe-and-slide of winter manners on a series of rag rugs that led to the Armstrong parlor.

"Suppose this snow will ever stop?" Armstrong asked as he followed Taylor into the room.

"Always does, Moses, but never in March. The Bismarck *Tribune* says that the Crow Indians are moving their camps to the highest hills, predicting terrible floods come spring."

"I've been in Dakota for over twenty years now, and have yet to see the Missouri do any real damage." Armstrong gestured toward the horsehair chair next to the coal stove where his friend had come to sit most Thursday nights for the past five years. Together Armstrong and Taylor would chew through the week's news that the rest of Yankton would read in Taylor's Dakota *Herald* on Saturday. "Our northern citizens along the Red will get their feet wet with the thaw, though, should there ever be one. By the way, when Maudie gets here with the coffee, I wouldn't let her pour your cup, if you know what I mean."

Taylor knew exactly what his friend meant. The previous Thursday evening, when he had refused to temper his opinion of the "slab-sided, short-haired, narrow-hipped, square-shouldered, bony-shanked, alleged females" of Nebraska who were agitating for the right of suffrage, Maude had 'accidentally' spilled a bit of coffee onto his lap before leaving the room.

"What is it this week?" Taylor asked, dropping into the chair and stretching his feet toward the stove.

"What A Woman Can Do."

"Oh, for ... Maude, too?"

"Heard from others, have you?"

Taylor shook his head in disbelief. "I spend weeks doing my damnedest to inform the public about the shenanigans of our fine legislature, constituted in the whole of stuffed clothes and jackasses, and all soaked in whiskey, while they bond everything in the territory but the channel of the Missouri. They saddle the territory's citizens with an insurmountable debt for the simple purpose of lining the pockets of the scallawags and crooks who own the legislators, and what is it that I hear on the streets?"

"What a Woman Can Do?" Armstrong repeated with a smile. "Do you find that you have offended your readers equally, male and female?"

"It is the women who come to the point, although every single one seems to have missed it."

"The point? Now, Bud, as an old newspaperman myself, I understand the convenience of a story clipped from another paper to fill in the odd inch, but let's not go so far as to insist upon a point. I will change the subject. Your face is getting rosy and we have not even begun to discuss the Republicans."

"Or how I find myself in the odd position of complimenting our governor."

"That—now what was the phrase that you so generously borrowed from me—that great peregrinating tramp? Ah, here you are, my dear. You see, Bud, you have been forgiven, for you will have dough-nuts with your coffee this evening."

Maude Armstrong had been blessed with sufficient sparkle of eye and fullness of lips to spare her the sexless androgyny of a prairie woman's middle age. Neither the hair pulled so tightly back from a severe middle part that it made her head shiny nor the high-necked black wool dress could disguise the warmth and humor of a woman happy in her home. This particular happy woman meant for her husband's old friend to admit to a lapse of editorial judgment before he enjoyed her food.

"Do you see before you, Maris Taylor, an 'angel of good' or an 'instrument of evil'?" she asked.

"Now, Maude, you know better than that."

"What I would know, were I to rely upon what I read in your newspaper, is that we women are directly responsible for the failures of men."

Moses Armstrong had been enjoying his friend's discomfort, but was sorry to see his coffee cooling. "Do we still have last week's *Herald* about, Maudie? Let's take another look at the offending matter."

"It is by the door," Maude said, "where it is doing some good." She set the tray on the sideboard, out of reach of both men, and left the room, returning quickly with the newspaper, soiled and damp from the boots that had been drying atop it. Holding the paper between finger and thumb, she approached her husband. "You may read."

It took Moses Armstrong a few seconds to find the column, reprinted from the *London Journal*. "'What a Woman Can Do,'" he read. "'As a wife and mother, woman makes the fortune and happiness of her husband and children; and if she did nothing else, surely this would be sufficient destiny'. So far you seem to be on safe ground, Bud."

"Continue, please," Maude said.

"'But who can estimate the evils that woman has the power to do with the cry of late that she has no worthy work? It is this cry that precedes the woman's transformation from angel of good to instrument of evil, the dastardly result being the certain degradation of husbands and the transformation of innocent babes into vile men and women'." Armstrong continued to read the short piece aloud, ending with a look first toward his wife, and then toward his friend.

"What's wrong with that?" Taylor asked, sliding a bit lower in his chair.

"Oh, Bud, for heaven's sake," Maude said. "Of course a woman may find a lifetime's fulfillment tending to a husband and children, but to lay the responsibility for the greed, avarice, incompetence and general dishonesty of the men about whom you weekly rage, at the feet of their wives and mothers... well, you may as well add 'craven' to the list. You need to get married," Maude concluded, and Maris Taylor knew better than to reply. "Good-night," she said, kissing her fingertips and gently touching the thinning spot on the top of her husband's head as she passed behind him.

"Perhaps you should stick to politics, Bud, and leave the proper role of womanhood to the women," Armstrong said. "What, for example, will be the *Herald's* position on capital removal? Will it behoove our territory, as some of the legislators of this past session believed, to spend thousands of dollars to remove the capital from Yankton when we are within a year or two of being granted statehood?"

"There weren't a half-dozen representatives who took the matter of capital removal seriously. That's all a bucket of drivel poured out upon the public by that little louse in the hair of the community, that sty on the eye, that boil under its arm, that bunion on its big toe, that pimple on its—"

"Bud."

"...that goggle-eyed Bowen and his great outhouse necessity, the *Press and Dakotian*. I assume you read Bowen's long-winded editorial in Tuesday's issue of the little fish-wrap up the street?"

Moses Armstrong nodded, but he needn't have, for Taylor was now full steam into his presentation and his weekly rant against his competitor, Wheeler Bowen, the editor of the rival newspaper in Yankton, the *Press and Dakotaian*, and the recipient of the lucrative territorial government printing contracts. Armstrong would come upon these words again (and a few of his own) when he picked up Saturday's *Herald*.

"Yes, of course you read it," Taylor continued. "We all need to read something by the light of the crescent moon. With an air of solemn gravity, that pop-eyed toad informs the public that the north Dakota and Black Hills members came here with a bill already drawn for removal, and it was solely through the efforts of Yankton's very own representative, that drunken shyster Gamble, that removal was prevented."

"Bowen called his friend Gamble 'a drunken shyster'?" Armstrong interrupted.

Taylor waved Armstrong's interruption away. "Not one bit of truth in it all. You notice, of course, that the *P and D* waited until after the legislators had left for their homes before making its lying statement.

Bowen sets the *P and D* up as a special defender of Yankton's interests, whereas it is nothing but a dirty barnacle, which, were the capital removed and its sustaining plunder thereby cut off, would be among the first institutions to pack up and leave."

"Setting aside for the moment the arresting image of a baggage-packing barnacle, Bud, I must point out that your own words—'were the capital removed'—lends credence to the scheme after all. Remember, there was such a proposal put forth in the session two years ago as well."

"And as quickly shouted down. It can come to nothing, Moses, despite your earlier assumption that we in south Dakota are simply a year or two away from statehood."

"The movement is afoot, my friend. I am aware of a number of proposals made to that effect to several of our United States congressmen who might find such a proposal appealing."

"Several Republican congressmen, you mean to say, who believe, accurately, I am afraid, that admitting south Dakota to the Union would bring with it two more Republican senators. Divide the territory into two, north and south, and admit two states, and get four more Republicans in Congress. Throw the Black Hills into the mix as its own state, and get six. But why stop there? Divide it into four parts!"

"That has been suggested, too, I believe."

"And makes as much sense just now as two states. The Democrats in Congress will not let it happen, and that is that. We are not ready for statehood in the south, and the north simply doesn't have the population necessary. The 1880 census–"

"I know the figures, Bud."

"Then you know that the division and statehood movement is a storm in a tea cup."

Armstrong unbuttoned his vest and reached for another dough-nut before answering, although he realized he was taking a chance, for pauses in Bud Taylor's speech were not to be squandered. "I am afraid that I know no such thing."

"Then you support division and statehood?"

"This is not a campaign debate, my friend. I am not telling you what I think *should* happen, but what *will* happen. In as little as two years time, south Dakota will become a state, and its northern boundary will be the 46th parallel, at which point a few farmers to the north will find that their pumpkin patches have achieved statehood before they have. North Dakota will continue on as a territory. That is my prediction."

"You are wrong, Moses. No good can come of increasing expenditures and doubling the number of officials."

"Ah, Bud, despite that famous scowl, you are an innocent at heart. Doubling the number of officials is a temptation not to be withstood by our most ambitious citizens, north and south. Twice the spoils, my friend. Twice the spoils. Watch and see. But I see eye to eye with you on one point."

"All is not lost, then. You have not yet become a madman like so many others."

"What is not to be lost is the capital. Perhaps when statehood does come, a central location will be required. But as long as we are a territory, capital removal is a fantasy entertained by a few northern Dakotans who continue to cast about for a reason to be taken seriously here in Yankton, as they have done since '61."

For a moment both men were silent, savoring this moment of agreement. Armstrong had heard his wife climb the stairs to their bedroom minutes earlier, as, evidently, had Taylor, who pulled a cigar from his jacket pocket, ran it under his nose and inhaled deeply.

"Now as for complimenting the governor, as you mentioned earlier," Armstrong said, "You are referring to his surprising vetoes. But will you go so far as to publicly extol Ordway's virtues?"

"As an honest man—and I refer to myself here, not the governor—I'm afraid I must. With the legislature's utter disregard of anything approaching economy in public expenditures, the governor's vetoes provided the only respite from the humiliation that body of scallawags and scoundrels visited upon the citizens of Dakota."

"For naught, I understand."

"For naught. Ordway's vetoes were couched in sound law and correct principles, and I am man enough to say as much in print. Yet they were overridden with a yell in every instance. The result is a squandering of the people's money almost unimaginable. They've propped up that decaying printing concern of Bowen's with government contracts, they passed measures which will saddle nearly every county in the territory with an immense debt, and they were drunk, to boot, nearly all the session on the whiskey of the men who were prostituting them. We are well rid of them."

"But we still have our governor, whom you now admire."

"He will disappoint soon enough. I take that as my consolation."

CHAPTER XXXIV

Dakota Dirt

Percy Bingham surveyed the half-dozen weather-blasted faces of the farmers gathered at the Pontoppidan Scandinavian Evangelical Lutheran Church to listen to Per Rolfsrud expound upon his newly proposed Norwegian League. Rolfsrud had been, he had explained to Percy several days earlier when he'd stopped by the *Argus* to place an announcement for the upcoming meeting, a "voice in the wilderness" this past legislative session, one of a scant handful of farmers in the company of railroad men, lawyers, and land agents. It had been the "best part" of the Red River valley's immigrant population that had voted him into the legislature, and now was the time to get these citizens better organized. A league of Norwegians, Percy had thought as he jotted down the information, could there be anything more depressing?

They were not a lively lot. Having braved the trip to Fargo in the late-March mix of snow, sleet, and freezing rain, they now sat silently, hats in hands and beards dripping into laps, like an assembly of overgrown schoolchildren waiting for the teacher to appear. The sound of boots on the wooden steps brought their heads around in unison as the door opened, letting in another gust of chilly air and Per Rolfsrud. As Rolfsrud first spoke with the pastor who had stationed himself by the door, and then greeted the seated men with a hearty *"god dag,"* it occurred to Percy that there might not be a single word of the meeting that he would understand. The thought inspired his first smile of the day. Although levity was no longer a habit with Percy, he remained receptive to the ridiculous. When Rolfsrud began his official speech, however, it was in English (with the occasional clarification in Norwegian). Percy was nonetheless engaged in translation as he scribbled his notes. His interest in the proceedings was slight, and he took no more pride in his work for the Fargo *Argus* than he had for the *Times*, but his loyalty to the English language remained steady. It was to his credit, Percy believed, that his sources, be they Norwegian, Dane, German, or Swede, sounded like Percy Bingham in print.

The meeting was mercifully brief, and Percy was soon stepping into a wind that had blown beyond uncomfortable and into menacing. He turned up his overcoat's collar, pulled his muffler up over his nose, tugged his hat low over his brow, and dropped his head to avoid as best as possible the needles of sleet whipped down the street by a north-westerly wind. Taking a quick look up to check for traffic, Percy leaned forward and watched his feet crunch through freezing black slush as he made his way from the Third Street church toward Broadway. An icy chill seeped into his right heel, reminding Percy that he had meant to have his boots mended. There had been a welcome thaw the day before, but then the rain had begun in the middle of the night, slicking the packed snow with running water. Falling temperatures had turned the rain to sleet. The slush in the streets was freezing into ruts and ridges of ice. He was just steps away from the *Argus* building at the back of the lot on Front and Seventh, but by the time he rounded the corner his wet hands were so stiff with the cold that it took him several moments to work the cork out of his flask. Seventh Avenue was empty and Percy took a long pull, fitted the flask back into his jacket pocket, slipped a liquorice candy into his mouth, and opened the door.

Major Edwards had made it clear that he knew precisely why the new owner of the *Times* had not cared to keep Percy on as an employee. He, himself, the Major said, didn't trust teetotalers; nonetheless, if Percy were ever discovered to be drunk on his new job at the *Argus* then he would quickly be let go, no matter who his friends were. Friends? Percy had been tempted to ask, I have friends? But he had not. Increasingly, all he really wanted to know was that his books and his bottle were waiting for him at the end of the day. They were all the company he craved, all the friends he needed. The unrelenting severity of the winter's weather had kept him from seeing his wife and son for weeks at a time. There was at least one moment each evening, generally in that liminal space between the well-being of inebriation and the despair of drunkenness, when he let himself ponder this absence. Sometimes he felt the hopelessness of past choices that had diseased the present and doomed the future. Sometimes he felt anger, blaming Frances or his father for the alienation that had entered into his marriage. Sometimes he felt a surge of purpose and determination, and vowed to begin taking control of his life, his wife, his family, his fortunes the very next day. He would follow this vow with a drink to celebrate his decision, and that drink with another, and then another, and then, in the morning, he would wake in the dispirited funk of self-loathing, able only to stand, to dress, to sip a cup of coffee and force down a hard biscuit before walking to work and to another day that looked very much like the day before.

The story he had to write about the incipient Norwegian League, he had been instructed by Major Edwards earlier in the day, was to be cast in ambiguously positive terms. The *Argus* was a Republican paper, and Norwegians formed a large, consistently Republican, voting block. Where this Norwegian League was potentially a problem, Edwards had explained, was in the chance that it could get mixed up with some of the anti-railroad agitation of farmers in south Dakota. If they get on that path, Edwards explained, the next step would be to support a statehood movement, and that was something the *Argus* was not encouraging. Not just yet, anyway. "Our bread here in Fargo has been buttered by the Northern Pacific, and that's how it will go until all the railroad land is sold along the line," Edwards had said, and then added, almost as an afterthought, "It just might be the St. Paul, Minneapolis and Manitoba that's going to matter then, if Jim Hill comes through with all the branch lines we've been hearing about for the Red River valley. Anyway, the point is, Bingham, statehood would come with a bundle of regulations, and that's the last thing the railroads want. For the time being, that makes it the last thing the *Argus* wants." Thus, regardless of the details of Rolfsrud's proposal, Percy was to write a story complimenting the Norwegians for their industry and their contribution to the settling of the territory, and then use the story to encourage them to be satisfied with the status quo.

Back at his desk, Percy wiped his spectacles clear of condensation and then checked once again to see that the door to Major Edwards' office was closed. Alone in the newsroom, Percy took another swallow from his flask and felt the whiskey's warm slide, an antidote to the shriek of the wind beyond the room's windows that looked out onto an empty street. The story about the proposed Norwegian League took him less than a half hour to pick out on the *Argus'* new Remington. His experience writing brochures to boom the new Northwest for the N.P. had made him an expert at saying very little in glowing terms. Setting his story aside he began to read through the dozen or so regional newspapers that had arrived that week, using a thick pencil to circle the stories Edwards might be interested in copying in the *Argus*: women who shot their husbands (or better yet, murdered their children), bigamists, mob hangings of coloreds in the south, ministers caught with their lovers in the east, and then once a week, a half dozen or so windy editorials collected from newspapers whose political views reinforced those of the Argus.

Percy was circling a paragraph about Thomas Edison and "all the fuss and feathers" over his 301 patents when the background howl of the wind was replaced by the whoosh and suction of a door opening and closing. Percy looked up to see Alexander McKenzie standing before him, picking ice off of his thick lashes and mustachios. Percy had seen McKenzie a handful of times since their first meeting over a half dozen years earlier. Twice McKenzie had gone out of his way to buy Percy a drink, something that Percy was not inclined to refuse, although he found the Scot's conversation less stimulating. Pulling himself to his feet, Percy extended his hand.

"Good afternoon, Mr. McKenzie. I did not know that you were in Fargo. Nasty day to be traveling."

"Mr. Bingham. Got in last night on the '5:50'. Leave again in the morning. Is the Major in?"

Percy nodded toward the closed door at the back of the room, and McKenzie strode past. When the door to Major Edwards' office closed behind McKenzie, Percy retrieved his flask for another pull. He looked up at the clock. He had another story to write, but very little will to do so. It was to be yet another disavowal of the stories of the harsh, and evidently endless, Dakota winter that were increasingly finding their way into eastern newspapers. These stories had at first been met with the usual shrugs by Dakota newspapers. As recently as January the *Argus* had good-naturedly reprinted a humorous item from the Philadelphia *News*:

> For sale—*Fine farm in the new Northwest. Take the train to*
> *Glacier Junction, then the overland bob sled to Frozen City,*

where snow shoes can be borrowed to continue the journey.
The location of the farm house will be recognized by the
chimney smoke curling above the snow drifts. Ring the bell
on the trap door near the chimney.

But then the storms continued on through February and now into March, and the humor was turning to real concern about the effect the unusually harsh winter would have on immigration into the territory. What was needed now, Edwards had instructed Percy, was something to counter the stories, something to reassure the prospective settlers, something to make them want to discount the nay-saying as simple rumor-mongering. "You know how to do it," Edwards had said, adding, "Use that fancy education of yours. Make it something other newspapers will want to pick up and print."

Percy leaned forward and for a moment laid his head upon his arms where they rested on his desk. What more could he say about this god-forsaken land? For years now he had been collecting clichés and expostulating upon the glories of a place he abhorred. There had been a time when he had almost enjoyed the irony of his work, when he had been able to imagine himself a novelist conjuring up the language of a character who was his precise opposite. But now he just felt tired. Lifting his head he found himself staring at McKenzie's muddy footprints that led first to his desk and then to Edwards' door. Percy shook his head in disgust. Several feet of snow amassed so far, and still, somehow and always, it's the dirt that makes its way inside. That is what the settler had to look forward to upon arriving in Dakota in the spring. Dirt and mud. Mud and dirt. And then more dirt.

A slow smile spread across Percy's face. He opened the deep side drawer of his desk and rustled through the loose papers, notes, and newspaper clippings there. Finally, finding what he had been looking for, he set his last assignment for the Northern Pacific Land Department on the desktop before him. Across the top a heavy hand had scribbled, "Ridiculous and extravagant. I will not waste a penny on printing." Although the essay had been returned to him by J. B. Power, the handwriting was unfamiliar. Well, Percy thought, every single thing that he had ever written about Dakota Territory and the Red River valley had been ridiculous and extravagant. That had been the point. Opening another drawer Percy located a pair of scissors, cut off the critique and the opening verses by Byron. Then he picked up his pencil and began to cross out several paragraphs, for the space he had to fill in the *Argus* was significantly less than what had been commissioned by the N.P. Within minutes he reached the closing lines of his story:

Thus, this dirty, disagreeable, unpleasant and sometimes offensive mud becomes to a resident of the Valley a friend, one which not only sticketh to the feet and the clothes closer than a brother, but also to the pocket-book and fills that with eagles, double eagles, bank notes and other legal tenders, and thus makes its friends happy. Why, this fertile mud is a friend of every resident of the Valley. It is beautiful, it is grand, and in their eyes it has more attractions than the whitest of marble.

Percy counted the words, and then set about crossing out a sentence here and there. He was just about finished when the door to Edwards' office opened and Alexander McKenzie stepped out. Percy looked up to see McKenzie studying him.

"It ain't calming down one bit, is it?" McKenzie said as he walked toward the door, and both men were silent for a moment as they listened to the shrill whine of the wind as it worked its way through the slightest cracks in the window frames.

"The light wings of Zephyr."

McKenzie stared at Percy as he pulled his gloves on and settled his hat squarely upon his head. Percy noticed that he had the beginnings of the paunch of a successful man.

"If you say so," McKenzie shrugged. "I'm having supper 'cross the street at the Sherman House in an hour or so. George Kissner still serves the best chop in Fargo for my money. Join me, why don't you."

"Sure," Percy said, "I'll just finish up here."

McKenzie hadn't been gone ten minutes before Edwards stepped out of his office, already buttoned into his heavy coat. "You still here, Bingham?" he said, but did not wait for a reply. "I want you to make the rounds of the liveries tomorrow for a stock count. Horses, mules, oxen for sale. Count them yourself. And don't forget Sears and Stephens. We didn't put them in last week and I still haven't heard the end of it. Lock up on your way out."

Percy nodded and then looked back at the sheet before him, making a few final changes. Relieved to be finished with his afternoon's labor,

Percy worked his feet out of his boots, pulled the one damp sock off and hopped over to put it on a radiator to dry. He hopped back and sat down, crossing his feet on the desk-top as he reached for his flask. He had a good forty-five minutes of quiet drinking before he would cross the street to join McKenzie.

Percy could remember little the next morning, certainly not how the man he had begun calling "Big Alec" had convinced him that he, Percy Bingham, was an increasingly important figure in Fargo, someone whose opinions had come to bear weight. For try as he might to reconstruct the evening before as he lay across his bed in the rumpled clothes of the day before, his head throbbing, and his tongue coated with cotton wadding, he could recall only snatches of images and fragments of dialogue that followed their supper conversation at the Sherman House.

He remembered warming to McKenzie's speech as the early evening dusk grew into full dark, the irregular grammar pleasantly idiosyncratic when rounded and trilled through a warm Scottish cadence. Fully a half dozen men had stopped at their table to shake hands with McKenzie, and then, taking note of his dining partner, with Percy as well. Although McKenzie himself declared that he had no taste for alcohol, he had been liberal in his purchase of drinks for Percy. When the two of them had stepped out onto Front Street after supper, the wind had died down a bit, and the sleet was once again snow. Percy was certain that it was McKenzie who had suggested a game of billiards at the Tivoli Garden across from the Headquarters Hotel, although the big man had proved to be adequate, at best, with a cue, and it had not taken long for Percy to win enough money to allow him to buy a few of his own whiskies as well as a sarsaparilla for McKenzie. They'd been at Jerry Delaney's Delmonico Saloon, too, Percy was certain. The actual trip down to the river Percy could not quite recollect, nor how it was made, but he could remember stepping from the icy cold of the night into the dim, smoky fug of a riverside saloon. There had been a piano. There had been women. Percy groaned as a scrap of memory revealed a woman on his lap as he provided his own verse to a sentimental song.

Percy was pretty sure that McKenzie was no longer in this picture, so how, he wondered, had he gotten back to his rooms? With a sudden gesture, Percy reached for his jacket, bunched into a pillow beneath his head. His wallet was there. And so was his money.

And more. Percy sat up too quickly and was forced to wait with his eyes closed until the wave of nausea passed. Pulling the cash from his wallet he counted it. And then counted it again. It came to just over five hundred dollars, and that was about five hundred dollars more than had been there the day before. Sitting on the edge of the bed Percy dropped his head into his hands and tried harder to pry loose the details of the evening before. It was a little like walking through the deep clayey mire, the springtime 'Dakota Dirt' he'd been describing the day before. Each mental step required an effort to dredge up a phrase or an image from the confusing morass of the previous night. First there was the slow suck of resistance against the attempt, and then, the pop of release. A conversation at the Sherman House over their chops. Complaints about his wife, about his father, about his job. With an audible groan Percy recalled a litany of boasts made over the billiards table: his talents, his education, his promise, all going to waste in Dakota. But there was something more. Something he needed to remember, something he had said. His head now throbbing, an internal base drum keeping time with his pulse, Percy fell back onto the bed, and with the motion seemed to jar the words free. But they weren't his. The words came softly in the cold and dark, and were spoken by the man sitting next to him in the carriage. They spoke of a new start. Of a new home where he could re-claim his family. Of the possibility of a new life in which he could fulfill his promise. All he needed was the right friends. And then the phrases and the images and the moment clarified, unearthed and coherent. He was standing next to the carriage, looking up at McKenzie. Behind him the music of a barroom piano seeped into the cold night air from a near-by riverside saloon. There was a handshake that was more than a good-bye, less than a deal sealed, and then McKenzie's words, heard now as clearly as if McKenzie were bending over his bed. "There's more, Bing-ham. There's always more."

Percy sat up again to recount the money. Folding his pocket-book he let the new weight rest in his palms. He'd handled this much money, and more, in checks or vouchers or cash, always as a courier from the Bingham farm to this bank or that. But each dollar had to be accounted for. This money was unknown. It was a down payment on freedom from his father. By God, he would put it toward a new house in Fargo for his family this very morning. Percy looked out the window at the blue sky, noticing that the wind had blown the storm away during the night. Then it occurred to him that there was something else he was forgetting. There had to have been more. Surely McKenzie had specified the terms of repayment. Percy closed his eyes and tried to remember, but was forced to give up. There was nothing more to remember.

CHAPTER XXXV

Exeunt Power

His career with the Northern Pacific Railroad Company was as good as finished. It irritated him mightily to have it end this way, to have his name dragged through the mud by Frederick Billings. Mismanagement of the Land Department! By God, he had given his all to the N.P. and to the land through which it passed, his time, his energies, and even his health, and was this the thanks he was to receive?

J. B. Power pushed himself back from his desk in disgust at the thought. His stomach had once again begun to churn in anger and he sat for a moment and counted his breaths in the effort to compose himself. He wondered again if there was something he had missed, something he could have done that would have changed the course of events. He reached toward the file drawer that held the letters he had received from Billings, but then stopped himself. He had read and reread them too many times already.

Billings' characteristic tone of irritability had become, throughout the previous fall, downright hostile as he found fault with all that Power did, said, commissioned. They agreed only about Percy Bingham's latest (and last) essay, which was to have been included in an emigration brochure being worked up in the St. Paul office. An impenetrable hodgepodge of nonsense that began with a lengthy quote from Byron's "The Bride of Abydos," and then moved on to a disquisition on the nature of dirt in Dakota, it had indeed been filled with "humbug, bombast, and precious extravagance," as Billings had exclaimed. Power had fired the clerk who had sent the essay on to New York without his approval, and assured Billings that Percy Bingham would no longer be in the occasional employ of the N.P.'s Land Department, but the damage had been done. In retrospect, Power understood that Billings' complaint about the unusable story was just one of many scattered shots across his bow that preceded the bomb-shell he had dropped upon Power's orderly life soon thereafter.

The assault had begun in earnest with a letter from Billings, ordering Power to immediately discharge his manager of the Land Office in Brainerd, C. F. Kindred, and to transfer the Brainerd office to St. Paul. Billings' accusation was, as usual, unsubstantiated: reports "from various quarters" had convinced him that the Brainerd office was chargeable "at least, with favoritism, and perhaps with personal speculation." Soon thereafter it became clear that Billings meant to tar Power with the same charges. Two weeks after Power had been ordered to release Kindred, he was informed that he was to make no more sales at the current prices, an order that brought the business of the Land Department to a standstill. Then came the summons to New York, where he was to meet with a "Special Committee" appointed by Billings and charged with examining Power's "mismanagement" of the Land Department. The meeting provided no resolution, but it did clarify the extent of Billings' suspicions, which had to do with Power's personal right to buy and sell railroad land. Certainly, the charges conveyed a very bad impression, and yet each transaction, Power had insisted, could be explained to anyone disposed to judge fairly.

He had not been charged, however, in order to be judged fairly.

All right, then, Power thought, sitting forward once again to begin the first of several letters. He would fight back. Not for his job, but for his honor. The friends he had made in the Red River valley deserved to hear the truth behind the rumors of the situation, and a good many of those friends happened to be newspapermen. If the N.P. chose to label his personal business a "crime," then the case would prove to be a boomerang to several of the principal officers of the road, including Billings, for the public would hardly draw the line between the rights of principal and subordinate officers in transactions of the kind. Nor, he believed, would the courts. He would hire his own counsel to counter Billings' charges. Then they would see if Billings had the stomach for a public airing of his own "personal" business.

Of course, he would now accept Jim Hill's standing offer and become the new Land Commissioner of the St. Paul, Minneapolis and Manitoba Railroad. Let Billings, flush with forty million dollars in financing newly secured in loans, focus on the western terminus of the Northern Pacific line, and the connection negotiated there with Henry Villard's Oregon Railway and Navigation Company. Unlike Billings, Jim Hill understood the continued promise and importance of the Red River valley, and was determined to build a web of lines connecting towns throughout the region. It was this valley that Power loved. Here he would stay.

In the meantime, however, these changes would require some belt tightening. There would be the costs of his lawyer, and perhaps of a court battle. Sales for the St. Paul, Minneapolis and Manitoba would not be on the same level as what he had known for the N.P., at least not immediately. Power set aside the letter he had addressed to his counsel, and brought a ledger out of his top desk drawer. He supposed he ought to make a list of men delinquent in their mortgage payments to him.

CHAPTER XXXVI

In Which What Goes Up Prefers Not to Come Down

Just how the horse got onto the roof in the first place was easy enough to figure out. It had simply marched up the incline of the snow bank driven against the side of the ice house, a snow bank much like the ones on the north side of practically every house, barn, granary, blacksmith shop, bunkhouse, soddie, claim shanty, and shed in the Red River valley. By mid-December the accumulated snowfall had already exceeded what could be expected during an average winter, with half of the season remaining. In January the newspapers stopped counting the blizzards, simply calling each storm the latest assault of the "Winter of '80-'81." By February Northern Pacific snow plows were having an increasingly difficult time keeping the track between Brainerd and Bismarck clear. Between Fargo and Jamestown the train ran through a tunnel of snow so deep that children, violating their parents' orders, could lie atop the side banks and look straight into the windows of the cars passing by. In March there came the occasional day with temperatures above freezing. Constant wind and daily freezing and thawing made the snow banks beside the train tracks as well as those piled against buildings as solid underfoot as a packed dirt road.

So it was easy to follow the horse's trajectory. He had begun on a patch of level, snow-covered ground and slowly followed the rise of the bank until that bank became roof. From there on he didn't have much farther to go until the gentle pitch of the roof reversed itself, at which point Samson evidently reconsidered his route, making a ninety-degree turn to stand astraddle the low peak of the shed. He probably hadn't been up there very long before the stock hand who had been cleaning out stalls (and who had failed to properly shut Samson's stall door) noticed that an eighteen-hundred-pound horse had gone missing. The stock hand walked to the end of the barn and stood there shading his eyes against the glare of the sun reflected against the solid white landscape around him. What he saw first was Little Carl sitting on an overturned bucket outside the cookhouse, enjoying a rare moment of late-March sun in a rabbit-fur cap and a heavy wool sweater that draped to his knees like a schoolgirl's dress. With a series of upward jabs of the knife he was using to peel potatoes, Little Carl directed the stock hand's gaze to the ice house nearby and to the horse astraddle the roof there.

Little Carl had pulled his bucket and sack of potatoes outside precisely to enjoy the spectacle about to unfold. The handful of hired men who remained on the Bingham place throughout the winter to tend to the stock had taken to relieving their boredom by placing a bounty on the half-dozen or so longish hairs that grew from Little Carl's chin. Waiting until the cook's hands were full as he brought their food to the table, one by one they would attempt to pluck a hair for the reward. It was not an undertaking without peril, for the result was likely to be a crack across the knuckles with a wooden spoon or a bowl of steaming soup in the lap. The game had not increased Little Carl's affection for his fellow man.

A small group of these men soon gathered around the ice house, clucking and calling out the occasional "C'mon, boy" in encouragement. But the horse was now as frozen as the land about him, terrified of taking another step, and rightfully so, for had it continued down the other side it would not have been met by another hardened snow bank, but by a drop of eight feet. Nor did Samson appear to be considering turning around to retrace his path. When the stock man responsible for the horse's escape hurried back to the barn, presumably for a halter, Little Carl turned his attention toward the Bingham house across the yard, and the family group that had appeared on the porch. As he watched, Percy Bingham handed the boy he had been carrying over to Frances, turned and strode down the steps. He was about to climb into the buggy waiting there when he caught sight of the horse on the ice house roof and the men assembled below. Little Carl could not see his expression, nor hear his words, but he could hear Houghton's squeal of delight when he, too, saw Samson. As soon as Percy pulled his buggy away from the house, Frances and Houghton stepped back inside. They returned to the porch just minutes later, bundled into coats and mittens, although neither wore a hat. They crossed the yard toward Little Carl, Houghton, at almost four years old, doing his best to pull his mother into a faster pace. Little Carl stepped back into the cookhouse and returned with a small ladder-back chair and another bucket, which he offered to Frances and the boy. One more trip brought a cup of coffee for Frances, and then the three settled in to watch the show.

"I'm surprised that the roof has held," Frances said.

"So far," Little Carl replied.

Samson, an even-tempered Percheron that could be counted on to compliantly labor in front of a plow for up to twelve hours a day, was not to be led off a roof by a mere human with a halter. The second man to mount the roof lost his footing half way up and slid down the snow bank head first to land at the feet of his fellows, eliciting a shout of laughter from Houghton (and a mumbled comment followed by a guilty look toward Frances Bingham from the tumbled man). Another man scrambled up the bank and onto the roof and for several minutes applied his shoulder to the horse's hindquarters while his partner pulled at Samson's head. Their efforts were vigorous, but the horse remained immobile. A bucket of oats had Samson snaking his neck downward, but his feet remained firmly planted on either side of the roof's apex. For the next fifteen minutes various combinations of men tried to push, pull, and lure the horse off the roof. When one of the men lost his balance again, and brought two others off the roof with him in a jumble, the mumbled language took a decided turn for the worst, which the proximity of a lady did not prevent. For a moment Frances considered taking Houghton back inside the house to watch whatever the resolution would be from an upper window, but she could not bring herself to diminish the pleasure he was taking in the events. With the constant storms they had both been too much inside anyway, and she herself had been dispirited company since Anna's departure almost four months ago.

"What would you do, Carl?" Houghton asked.

Little Carl seemed to weigh the boy's question for a moment, pursing his mouth further and squinting into the distance. "Well, Howie, when all this snow melts, there's sure to be flooding. I reckon if the water gets high enough he could just sort of float off the roof."

Houghton considered the response for a moment, and then broke into a laugh when Little Carl smiled to let him know that he'd been joking. "What would you do, Mama?"

"I think I'd get some boards and nail them horizontally to the roof, like a ladder on its side, so that horse would think he had some footing coming down, and then in between those boards I'd throw down hay, to give him a reason to move. And then I'd leave him alone."

"That's a lot of work to go to," Little Carl said.

"That's a $120-horse, six months wages for any one of those men."

This was evidently what Mr. Johnson, the farm's supervisor, was thinking as he appeared at the front door of his house nearby. "Get that horse off the roof before he falls off and breaks a leg," he yelled to the group as he pulled his coat on, causing the men to enter into an orchestration of shrugs and gestures and explanations of what had been tried thus far. Samson, however, appeared to have been waiting for just such a command. A hesitant step brought a third hoof onto the side of the roof that he had climbed, and then a fourth, and then the horse did indeed lose his balance. With a thud that threatened to cave in the roof, Samson fell back upon his hindquarters whereupon he began a quick and undignified slide on his backside, his front legs working in a blur of tiny backward steps in the attempt to stop. The group of men at the bottom of the slope quickly dispersed, turning in time to see Samson collect himself back onto all fours on level ground, and immediately dip his head into the bucket of oats waiting there.

"That's why Johnson gets the big money," Little Carl said.

"May I, Mama?" Houghton danced to his feet.

"Be careful," Frances said, and with this Houghton was scurrying toward the men now surrounding Samson. "Mr. Johnson," Frances lifted her voice toward the group, and the supervisor turned and nodded when she gestured toward her son's approach. Percy had long ago told Frances to keep their son away from the workers, and had long since, Frances believed, stopped caring. John Bingham had warned the boy not to get in the way of the men, but the year-round crew had become accustomed to having him underfoot.

"Get you more coffee, Miss Frances?" Little Carl asked. When Frances declined, he said, "I can see that Howie gets back to the house if you've had enough of the cold."

"I've had enough of the house, Carl. And it does not seem at all cold with the sun shining and the wind absent for once."

"Almost forty on the thermometer. Just about perfect, like you say, without the wind." Little Carl picked up another potato and began to deftly pare away the peel. After a moment he said, "House must be awful quiet for you these days, what with Miss Anna so long gone."

It was a presumptuous thing to say, and for a moment Frances considered reminding Little Carl of his position. This unwelcome familiarity was her fault, of course, for, as Percy often enough pointed out, she had let herself become too friendly with some of the farm help. She missed her occasional conversations with Jack Shaw, who would not be needed on the farm until the new shipments of machinery began to arrive again early next month. She had no idea how or where he spent his winters. She could not imagine him with the Jews. The other Jews, she supposed she meant, except that she didn't. Nor did she really feel offended by Little Carl's presumption. Watching one of the stock men guide Houghton's hand down Samson's right foreleg, as if teaching him to palpate for an injury, Frances was aware of Little Carl's industry as he worked next to her. To her surprise she discovered that she wanted to tell this odd little man just how lonely her days were, how she woke each morning to an ache in her chest, how she feared that she had undone every bit of good will she had accumulated in one impulsive moment. 'I fear that with her goes my own small store of goodness,' she wanted to confess.

And more. There was more she wanted to say, especially now, given

Percy's news of the night before. To Frances' surprise not only had he remained sober throughout the day, but he had come to bed soon after Frances had retired, casually relating the details of a supper he had recently had with Alexander McKenzie as if years of alienation had not intervened since they had last thus conversed. Stepping out of his closet in his nightshirt, Percy completed his description, explaining that McKenzie so reminded him of some animal, perhaps of a handsome bull, with his wide-set eyes and big head, that he found himself tempted to reach out to stroke the big man's forehead.

"At the risk of a goring, perhaps," Frances had offered.

Percy's rapid change of expressions that followed his laugh occupied seconds, no more, but fleeting as they were, Frances had read the messages there. No doubt he had been reminded, as had she, of the nights they had shared as newlyweds, when they traded opinions more colorful than generous about dinner guests. Percy's face bore a nostalgic regret, then brightened to hope before darkening with intention, like the prairie passing from shade to sun to shade again under swiftly running clouds. Frances' smile melted, and Percy's mien settled back into the scowl he often carried now.

Turning the light down on his side of the bed, Percy said, "By the way, my dear, I have good news to tell you. I purchased a lot on Thirteenth Street and have arranged with a builder to begin work as soon as the weather allows. The house should be ready for you and Houghton to join me by the end of summer, perhaps September or October at the latest."

"I beg your pardon?"

"I said I purchased a lot–"

"I heard you, Percy." Frances sat up to turn the gas up on her lamp. "But how? When? Why did you not first speak with me? Did John–" Frances left this question unfinished.

"Just this past week," Percy answered, speaking now with his eyes closed. "The opportunity availed itself and I took advantage of it. You have known, of course, that this situation could not go on indefinitely, with me in Fargo and you and Houghton here. The ride is too long, and the weather too capricious to make it comfortable, or safe, or," Percy rolled onto his side away from Frances, "natural. And no, father has had no part in this. I have secured my own financing."

"But how?" Frances said again.

"I am employed, dear. I have made friends in Fargo." Percy did not attempt to stifle a yawn. "The details need not concern you."

Frances had waited for Percy to say more, for it was not unlike him to announce resistance, and then offer a grudging compliance, but very quickly his breathing steadied, leaving Frances wide awake and amazed next to her sleeping husband. Frances slid out of the bed and reached for her wrapper that lay across the back of a chair. Silently she passed from the bedroom to the sitting room next door. Standing at the window all she could see was the vague reflection of her own shape and the glow of a lamp behind her. Frances put her hand to her forehead and closed her eyes, as if commanding her mind to calm itself so that she could call forth some forgotten or unconsidered fact with which to refute Percy's decision.

There was nothing. Of course, once Percy provided a house, she and Houghton must make it their home. Why should it matter so? With Anna gone what matter that she would no longer live here on the Bingham farm? What difference would six miles make, or life lived in one house as opposed to another? Abruptly, as if in sudden need of air, Frances tugged the sash upwards. The window had not been opened for months and sounded a sharp crack of release. Frances inhaled the night air. Although the ground remained covered by an increasingly dirty snow, the metallic smell of wet soil seemed to settle upon her tongue. A breeze raised gooseflesh on her arms. There were neither stars nor moon visible, and although several out buildings were close by, even their outlines had disappeared in the dark. Surrounded by endless, black space, Frances felt the approach of the calm she had been looking for. She took another deep breath, and waited for some answer to come forward, an answer to a question she did not know precisely how to ask. And then, for the first time since Percy's assault eighteen months ago, she began to weep. She could not have said, precisely, what she cried for. Impossible dreams. Unspeakable desires. Unquenchable thirsts. Perhaps. Equally likely were more mundane frustrations and fears. She was to be told again where to go and how to live. She was to be confronted with her own impotence. To be closed in once again in a small life, in a small house, surrounded by other lives and houses equally circumspect.

And then, almost to her surprise, she heard her own whisper: "I do not want to leave ... this! This!" Frances said again, opening her arms to the black space before her.

It was a dramatic gesture, a pose that embarrassed Frances almost immediately. She dropped her arms, closed the window, and reached into her pocket for a handkerchief. She was cold, she was tired and miserable, and there was nothing she could do about anything that night. I am a fool, Frances thought to herself then, lifting the picture of Miss Ardwell's Female Institute, Class of '70, that she had moved to a table amongst the nick-nacks arranged there. The lamp's light was too dim to allow Frances to see the picture clearly, but that mattered little. She had held it before her too often over the past decade to need artificial light to bring the figures into view. A fool, a fool, a fool. Ten years, Frances thought. Over ten years, and for what?

There was no one to answer, and now, sitting next to Little Carl, there was no one to tell.

"Yes," she replied. "I do miss Anna."

"Like a knife," Little Carl added, and then directed his own knife toward his chest. "Here."

Frances looked at the little man's profile for a moment, his rabbit fur cap sitting well over his ears. What is it that you can see?, she wondered, finding the silent question strangely reassuring. Standing, she placed her cup of cold coffee upon her chair. "We're about to lose the sun," she said. Without waiting for Little Carl to look up or reply, Frances walked toward the barn to collect Houghton.

CHAPTER XXXVII

In Which A Flood Both Washes Away and Reveals

At some point during the first forty-eight hours of rain the boards laid end-to-end across Front Street (to help pedestrians crossing from the Headquarters Hotel keep their pant legs and hems out of the mud) began to sink. The next day a Fargo citizen reported to the sheriff that lumber deposited a week earlier in front of his Confectionary and Bakery under construction on NP Avenue had been stolen. Sheriff Haggart found it hard to believe that a thief could have loaded several hundred board feet of pine in the steady downpour without getting his wagon stuck and without being seen, but had to agree, standing calf deep in the street's muck, that, indeed, the lumber was nowhere in sight. The lumber would be rediscovered in three weeks, exactly where it had last been seen, just about the time that the boards across Front Street resurfaced. On day four of the rain the Red River began its slow slide over its banks, giving a short-lived industry to a group of boys who met at dark to slip into the chill water to swim the boards that floated free from Chesley and Lovejoy Lumber to dry ground, like giant muskrats come upon a trove of loose marsh grass.

The Red River in flood inspires more dread than terror. With its downriver progress to the north slowed by the remains of Canadian ice, it simply backs up, oozes over shallow banks, and then begins the insidious seep and spread across a level countryside already saturated with snowmelt, as if seeking its former boundaries as a glacial lake. Modestly protected by the earthen levees on either side of the N.P. bridge, the citizens of Fargo proper held their breath.

Things looked less hopeful for the remnants of the old Fargo-in-the-Timber community that lined the Red's banks to the north of the levee. On the fifth day of rain a couple of the shacks and ramshackle buildings there slipped from their foundations to begin the lazy trip up the moving lake. To the south of Fargo the narrow river that once snaked and curled had been replaced by a muddy soup up to eight miles wide at places, putting tens of thousands of acres under water that in another year would have been spotted with teams of men and horses plowing and planting.

The Red did not reach the headquarters of the Bingham farm. Frances, standing upon the balustraded platform atop the house and getting thoroughly drenched as she attempted to keep her umbrella upright while peering through John Bingham's field glasses, believed she could make out in the distance the point where its edges met the overflow of the Sheyenne River. It was from this vantage point that Frances, preferring the rain over yet another hour inside a house that no number of lamps could make bright, witnessed the unexpected exodus of the small Jewish community from the slough land between the rivers. She counted thirty-two figures, some leading horses, some leading cows, some leading children, some children leading others. Even the road had reverted to the gummy black loam of the bordering fields, and the group was making slow progress. Three teams of oxen strained to pull as many wagons, laden with furniture, bedding, pots and pans, crates of chickens, and a few more children. Leading the first team of oxen was Jack Shaw, whom Frances had assumed to be at work across the yard in the machine shed. She went down to meet the procession as it slogged into the yard in the steady rain.

Standing at the end of the raised board sidewalk, Frances listened as Jack Shaw spoke, although very little needed to be said to make the situation clear. Their homes and barns were awash with muddy water, their root cellars had flooded, ruining not only the remaining provisions but the seed potatoes and bushels of wheat set aside for spring planting. And now three of the children had taken sick. Shaw finished his report by pointing to the forlorn bundles huddled atop the wagon. Looking past Shaw and the wagon Frances watched as Little Carl emerged from the cookhouse. The door of the supervisor's house opened, and Mr. Johnson, clad in a yellow oilskin, stepped into the rain. Johnson was a hard worker and a dependable supervisor, but he had stated his opinion regarding the presence on the farm of "that Jew," Jack Shaw, often enough for Frances to prefer that he not become part of the conversation. To Little Carl as he approached, Frances called, "How many men are staying in the bunkhouse now?"

Before he could answer, Jack Shaw said, "Better they should stay in the granary."

"All right. Carl, can you have supper ready for—" Frances began to count, and then asked Jack Shaw, "How many of you are there?"

Despite Little Carl's nod in the affirmative, Jack Shaw said, "Better they should cook their own food, too, Mrs. Bingham." He hesitated before adding, "In their own pots and pans. Only you should spare for us potatoes and onions. Mr. Bingham can take it from out my wages."

"Carl will get you what you need. Mr. Johnson," Frances turned toward the supervisor who had reached her side, "These people will be staying in the granary this evening, and perhaps for a few days beyond. They will need help seeing to their stock. Thank you," she said before the supervisor could reply. "Mr. Bingham will be available to speak to you this evening when he returns from the Number Two Farm if you have any questions."

When Johnson turned away with a scowl, Jack Shaw gave Frances a wan smile and said quietly, "The wolf is not afraid of the dog, but he hates his bark."

"Yes, well, get these people out of the rain, Jack, and then come to the house."

Within the half hour, Jack Shaw and Frances were seated at the kitchen table, each with a cup of coffee. Frances spoke first. "Have the children been seen by a doctor? I can get a message to Dr. Harkness, if you like."

Shaw favored Frances with a short look she did not know how to interpret. "Dr. Harkness does not want to help these children. The same thing with Dr. Jaye in Mapleton. I know what is with them. They are cold and wet and hungry. Only you should call the doctor if they are worse," Shaw added, stirring sugar into his coffee.

"Where will these people go?"

"Some are thinking from Grand Forks. There, at least, there is a rabbi. The young men can think only from California, California, California. There, they say, they will be able to lift up their heads like persons. There is talk of a new settlement in Burleigh County, north of Bismarck, but," Jack Shaw finished the thought with a gesture that had become familiar to Frances, and which, she knew, signified little confidence in the prospect.

"And you?"

"I will stay."

"Here?"

"For now. Yes."

"And the land?" Frances asked. "What are your plans for it?"

The personal nature of Frances' questions did not appear to surprise Jack Shaw who spread his hands as he answered. "It is for me to sell. There is still a small sum to go to the Jewish Agricultural and Industrial Society in St. Paul—a black year on them—that brought these families to this slough land in Dakota. And there are debts in town. I am to send what is left to the families after I have seen to the sale and spent out for the rest. Do you think John Bingham will buy?"

Frances absent-mindedly turned her coffee cup in her hands. When she replied, it was not to answer Shaw's question. "Perhaps you have saved enough money to secure a loan for the land yourself."

Shaw's chuckle contained very little humor. "I am good with machines, not with animals and dirt. In Dakota I will make from myself a person, too, but not as a farmer. And even if I did, I would not choose to farm in a swamp."

"So you think that the land is worth very little. I must say, Mr. Shaw, that your honesty will not serve you well as a salesman. I was under the impression that you people had more savvy when it came to making money."

Shaw opened his mouth as if to reply, then lifted his cup to his lips instead. Setting the cup back on the table, he said, "Wait only, and the land will be valuable. It is with a fine stand of trees, and lumber here is like gold. So, clear the trees, dig a big ditch to drain the water, and then the land is good to farm, and within five, six miles of Fargo, too. But not for me this tree cutting and ditch digging. It will take a buyer of sight... no, that is not right—"

"Vision?"

"That is it. It will take only a buyer who should have vision to see into a day for profit."

"And you believe John Bingham to be such a visionary?" Frances asked with a small smile.

"No, Mrs. Bingham, I believe that is you."

Startled, it took Frances a moment to reply. "I have no personal fortune, Mr. Shaw. Nor, I assure you, is my husband likely to be interested in purchasing your land. I will, however, speak to John Bingham regarding your proposition, if you like."

"I am only thinking out loud on the possibilities. If the Binghams are not interested, I will talk to Per Rolfsrud. Only someone should buy it soon. Rolfsrud, they say, is as rich as a Jew." Jack Shaw looked directly at Frances.

"Yes, well, I do not know about that. I am surprised that you have not put this plan forward to your people. Perhaps the sale of trees would free them of debt and allow them to continue on here."

"You have seen them, Mrs. Bingham. They have had enough."

"It is the rain," Frances said, looking at the window, opaque with running water. "It will defeat many."

"*Gott in himl, no!*" Jack Shaw said with sudden intensity. "It is the dirt. The rain just made the dirt too much to bear. It sticks to shoes in great wet clumps. It makes the animals weak. It is everywhere. My friends, may they find a little happiness soon, have said many times: 'In Russia we were hungry, and here we are hungry. In Russia we were poor, and here we are poor. But in Russia we were not dirty'."

"Perhaps your people would be happier if they returned to Russia, then," Frances said, turning back from the window.

"A Jew does not return to Russia, Mrs. Bingham."

Around 3 p.m. on Friday, April 29th, after six straight days of rain, a patch of blue opened over Fargo, and men in rowboats and make-shift rafts began to take stock of the damage. The general agent of the Northern Pacific in Fargo breathed a nervous sigh of relief as he walked across the railroad bridge. Although the river had sloshed over the le-vees, they had held. The old bridge for cart and foot traffic directly beneath the trestle was no longer visible. Another foot higher and the Red would have been poised to wash out the tracks. Almost as an echo to the agent's sigh came another, but this one from the land itself as a huge chunk of packed soil slid away from a supporting beam where the trestle met the east levee. A flatboat had come loose from its mooring from the Grandin Brothers' elevator and now it bumped and rocked against the piling. The agent turned and hurried back across the bridge to telegraph the agent in Jamestown, where the eastbound N.P. had been ordered to wait for clearance through Fargo. Three hours later the train pulled to a stop in front of the depot at the Headquarters Hotel, let off its few passengers, and then slowly made its way onto the bridge where it stopped again, no longer a vehicle for transportation, but rather, a simple dead weight meant to prevent a bridge washout in case the rain began again.

It did, accompanied by a wind that had been largely absent through-out the deluge thus far. The N.P. agent was not the only man to lie awake that night listening to the increasingly intermittent showers and the slap of water where a week before no water had been. The next morning, on the first day of May, the Fargo residents who had slept woke to a sky of blue broken by quickly passing clouds. The storm had blown over and the bridge had held.

At mid-morning Percy Bingham walked to the gallery and office of F. Jay Haynes, the official photographer of the Northern Pacific who had opened a shop on Front Street in '79. Although the flood had been in every way inconvenient, it allowed Percy to find something to write about other than the daily installments of the Northern Pacific-versus-J. B. Power story that readers could evidently not get enough of, and the related news that the Northern Pacific management had raised the price of its lands from two dollars and fifty cents to five dollars per acre. The increase had brought vigorous protests from citizens along the line who complained that the increase would divert settlement and retard the development of the country. Another "unpleasant feature," as the story Percy copied from the Jamestown *Alert* stated, was the appearance of playing into the hands of speculators:

> *Large tracts of land all through this region have already passed at the former prices into the possession of speculators, among whom are numbered many of those most prominently connected with the Northern Pacific Railroad Company as directors and officers, and people are not wanting who suppose that the fact of their large individual holdings is the reason of the present advance. It is said that the president of the company owns from thirty to fifty thousand acres, and several of the directors nearly or quite as much, all purchased at old prices. On the other hand, the officers of the road claim that they have for some time past disapproved of sales at the old schedule and are even now making an effort to bring the old management of the land department into discredit by refusing to recognize their outstanding contracts. Residents along the line, and especially those whose dealings have brought them into personal contact with Messrs. Power and Kindred, will be slow to believe that their management of the land department has been otherwise than just, liberal and fair, both to the company's interests and to the people.*

In a letter the *Argus* printed a week earlier from an anonymous "Special Correspondent" in New York—Percy was certain the correspondent was, in fact, J. B. Power himself—the bulk of the "N.P. plottings and scandals" were laid directly at the feet of the president, Frederick Billings. There was a ring within the company that was determined to "hog" all the good lands possible, and, in fact, had already gobbled the cream of the Red River valley for themselves. The 'special correspondent' had ended the letter by proclaiming that the sooner Henry Villard took hold of the road in good earnest the better. The latter was a reference to the news that Villard had amassed tens of millions of dollars from investors in order to silently acquire a controlling interest in the stocks of the Northern Pacific Railroad, with the intent to merge the company with his own Oregon Railway and Navigation Company.

The letter from the anonymous 'special correspondent' had spawned a flurry of responses, for it seemed that every other reader of the *Argus* had an opinion on the Northern Pacific, or J. B. Power, or railroad land prices, and frankly, Percy was finding it all just about as dreary as the incessant rain had been. So it was with pleasure that he helped Jay Haynes load his seventy pounds of equipment and glass plates into a rowboat that Sunday morning. Coming upon a half-submerged house by the river, Haynes pointed to the second-story window within reach, saying that it would provide the perfect vantage point for a shot of the bridge and the train upon it. It took some careful maneuvering of the rowboat and a few unsteady moments handing the camera through the window, as well as a bit of explaining to the old-timer discovered sitting in the corner of the room with a shot-gun indelicately aimed, before Haynes was ready to proceed. In the near distance (what Percy was guessing would be the forefront of the photograph) several men leaned against the rail fence on the levee, speaking with a fellow in a rowboat who had tied up to a tree snagged there. The man in the rowboat was trying to coax a bedraggled and terrified cat out of the upper branches.

"That doesn't look too safe," Percy offered, gesturing toward the tableau.

"I imagine it's been a rough ride, all right."

"I meant for the rowboat, tied up to the snag. It could break loose at any moment."

"Long as it holds still for another couple of minutes, I'll be fine," Haynes said as he ducked underneath the black cloth of his camera.

Percy tried to imagine what it was that the photographer was seeing. Haynes' Stereoscopic Railroad Views of the New Northwest had become quite famous over the past few years throughout the United States. Percy had found himself staring at these pictures, fascinated by the images when the reality of the trains themselves and the land through which they passed seemed to him dismal at best. Percy looked over the flooded river below him. He saw muddy water sluggishly moving fallen trees and bits of detritus northward, a few buildings with water up to the rooflines, and a train sitting on a bridge. He opened his notebook to jot down some notes regarding the view before him, wondering absently if he should haul out the expected reference to Noah. For the rest of the morning Percy and Haynes rowed and slogged through the town, Haynes laboriously taking photographs and Percy collecting the occasional flood anecdote. Photography, Percy discovered, consisted mostly of carrying heavy equipment up steps, through windows, and onto roofs, always in search of the highest vantage point.

The special edition of the "Flood of '81" was a great success for the *Argus*, and much to Percy's surprise he was met the morning after it came out with handshakes and stories (and a few questions regarding the location of this Ararat where he and Haynes had tied up their boat). It seemed as if everyone had a tale to tell and a burning need to tell it. Lettie Macintosh's sister, Hattie, had gotten stranded away from home when her buggy got stuck, and what she was doing out in that rain in the first place, Lettie just couldn't say, but probably some mission of mercy, that was just like Hattie, and don't you know that she just unhitched that horse and rode it home bareback and no bridle and her never on horseback before in her life. Big Hank Fink had been seen running along the levee and tossing a lasso over the stovepipe of his converted pig shed that had come free to keep it from floating away. Alf Fredrickson had rescued an entire family from the roof of their soddie just a mile south of Fargo, and him not yet ten years old and out in the rain on a homemade raft. Abraham Jefferson, the one black man to have taken up permanent residence in Fargo, and who had learned a rudimentary Norwegian in order to converse with customers at his First Street Tonsorial Palace, was promising free haircuts for a year to anyone who caught a fish while sitting in his barber's chair. They were stories of courage and triumph and loss and determination and humor, the stories of the individuals who make up a town.

Argus readers couldn't get enough of them.

For a week after the rain stopped and the flood waters began to recede, Percy listened to and chronicled the narratives of the citizens of Fargo. Discovering that his readers actually seemed to prefer the locutions of their fellow townspeople, with their many linguistic irregularities, Percy began to resist the temptation to revise and augment. The individual voices behind the stories, the breathy excitement, the shrugging nonchalance, the suggestive aside, he noted, were themselves part of the tales. One night as he sat on the side of his bed in his rented rooms, tipping the whiskey bottle into his glass, Percy realized with something of a shock, that not only had he had enjoyed a full week of work, but that what he had enjoyed most was feeling part of the stories he told. The people were coming to him. They were stopping him on the sidewalk. He felt as if, and here he stopped himself, embarrassed by what he was about to admit to himself, but then went ahead nonetheless and let the thought come. He felt like he belonged.

Something that Alexander McKenzie had said to him the night of the five hundred dollars came back to him, resurfacing like a lost bucket or tool or board as the flood waters receded and the mud dried: "A person like you, young, handsome enough, educated, you could make things happen. You got the power of print, too. With the right friends and some right thinking, yes, sir, I bet you could be the sort of fellow to make things happen."

Chapter XXXVIII

In Which the Relationship between Dirt and Insanity is Clarified

Here was another reason to miss Anna. Frances glanced across the table at the substantial woman who appeared to be cataloguing the contents of the Bingham dining room while ignoring the oysters upon her plate to much the same degree that she had thus far disregarded Frances' attempts to draw her into conversation. Over the past two years Frances had helped John Bingham entertain the bankers, businessmen, politicians and foreign dignitaries that J. B. Power had sent their way, with stories and images of life on the Dakota prairie, seasoning her observations with humor to turn aside her guests' assumptions of hardship, and drama to dispel fears of drudgery. With each excursion party met and entertained, Frances felt more secure in her status on the Bingham farm, despite Percy's growing independence and the construction, mercifully delayed by the flood, of their new home on Thirteenth Street.

But the distant matron across the table, her large square head pivoting atop a perfectly cylindrical body encased in beaded brocade, resembling a chubby child trapped in a carpet roll, had quickly brought Frances to the limits of her charm, for she could suffer fools for her own benefit, but resented condescension. Perhaps even the quiet grace of Anna, which had so often drawn the reluctant guest into speech, would not have been equal to the formidable resistance of Mrs. Thomas Oakes, who did not need to speak to communicate her opinion regarding the inferiority of the plate, the silver, the gasolier above, the furniture about, and, evidently, the food before, to that which she was accustomed in Boston.

Mr. and Mrs. Oakes, in the company of Alexander McKenzie, had arrived with Percy earlier in the afternoon, allowing John Bingham the opportunity to show his visitors about the headquarters farmyard. Over the years the yard had grown to resemble a small village, complete with barns, machine shed, butcher shop, blacksmith shop, cookhouse, ice house, granary, the supervisor's house and several bunkhouses (the newest of which had a separate room for the small army of housekeepers and cooks needed for the summer months). Then, he had driven them through the countryside. Although the planting had been late, the wheat was a lush, green carpet by late June. Mrs. Oakes had retired immediately to her room to lie down, complaining of a headache brought on by the jerk and bounce of the carriage over the rough road, not to mention the unremitting wind. Upon rising she had required the services of Kirsten as she changed for supper, taking the girl away from Mrs. Ford precisely when the cook could least spare her. Dashing into Frances' room to help fasten her plaits, Kirsten repeated the many disappointments to Mrs. Oakes thus far: the water was too cold, the bed too hard, the window panes rattled incessantly, making it impossible to get a moment's rest or respite from her headache, and the mirrors were too dark. "It is lucky for you that they are dark the mirrors, I wanted to tell the fine Mrs. Oakes," Kirsten summed, with the familiarity that had become increasingly natural since Anna's departure over six months earlier.

Frances had laughed, defined "incessantly" and "respite" for the girl, and then stood to give Kirsten a kiss on the cheek, as was usual now, although this "usual" could not have borne great scrutiny. Such ease between the woman of the house and the immigrant help would have been proof to Percy of the egregious breakdown in distinction of place that Frances' laxness encouraged, and Frances would have been hard put to disagree with her husband's assessment. But the small kisses were too pleasant and had gone unremarked for too long to stop them now, for the very ceasing would lend significance to the thing ceased. As for Kirsten, she had no guide by which to judge the propriety of the friendly buss that excused her from Frances' room, for there was little in the big Bingham house that she had been prepared for in the Knudson claim shack. And she would have been sorry, too, to go without, mostly because that would mean losing the moment when Frances turned those eyes that held both cloud and lightning upon her. It was the look, and not the kiss, that made Kirsten blush as she left the room to take up her duties this evening as the cook's helper.

Alfred and Lydia Harkness had joined the dinner party. They, too, would be spending the night, allowing Lydia to enjoy a leisurely visit with Frances the following day after the other guests left, while her husband saw one of his old patients nearby. Seated at the dining room table, Lydia Harkness had been equally unsuccessful at engaging Mrs. Oakes in conversation. Frances was reminded of an ox that Mr. Johnson had ordered butchered last summer, a fabulous looking animal that refused to pull his share of the load while under yoke.

Frances lifted the bell near her water glass and within seconds Kirsten was there to begin clearing the plates from the first course. The bell (brought out specifically for these occasions), as well as the service, had begun to feel unnatural to Frances. With Percy so often away and John as likely to take his meals with his supervisor at the Number Two Farm or in Fargo as at home, Frances and Houghton frequently ate in the kitchen with Kirsten and Mrs. Ford, and occasionally with Little Carl in the cookhouse. Houghton much preferred the latter, and on those rare occasions when brought to the formal dining table, was certain to pout. Earlier this evening he had happily skipped across the yard to spend the night in the company of the Johnson children.

Frances was about to address Alexander McKenzie, sitting to her left, when she noticed that he was occupied in an appreciative appraisal of the Bingham housekeeper. Frances looked back at Kirsten as she bent to retrieve Mrs. Oakes' untouched oysters, and was reminded that their housekeeper was indeed no longer a girl. She still had that healthy bloom of youth that Frances knew she herself had long ago lost, but the last remnants of baby fat were gone, leaving behind well-defined cheekbones that highlighted the Scandinavian slant of her eyes. Kirsten was wearing a dress that Anna had cast off, let out here, taken in there, and shortened all around. The result was nothing like the elegance of the original, but pleasing nonetheless. To Frances' surprise, and Mrs. Oakes' horror, Kirsten felt the need to excuse the lady for neglecting her oysters as she removed the offensive plate. "I don't blame you," she said in a lowered voice to which everyone around the table attended. "Not like food do they look. More like—"

"Thank you, Kirsten," Frances said. "You may bring in the roast. Lydia, have you heard from Anna lately? My sister-in-law," Frances explained to the guests, "spent the winter in St. Paul with an elderly friend of the family whose poor health has prevented Anna's return."

"I received a letter just yesterday," Lydia Harkness said. "She seems to be enjoying her time in St. Paul a great deal. She had recently attended a very informative lyceum on the dangers of spiritualists and communists."

Frances felt little pleasure in hearing of Anna's happiness so far away. There had been nothing in her letters to Frances that indicated an intention to abandon "poor invalided Sophie" any time soon, although the months of separation had allowed the gradual return of some of their old language of affection. Still, Frances was grateful for the discussion that followed, for even Mrs. Oakes could not feign indifference to other-worldly matters.

Over the roast beef the conversation turned to the weather, the recent winter and the flood that had followed especially worthy of discussion. There was a general recounting of several of the blizzards that had begun early and continued regularly, all couched in the language of pleasant amazement, and ending with the telling, yet again, of the horse-on-the-roof incident. There was no mention of the several deaths throughout the valley, which Frances knew from Percy had far exceeded what had been reported in the local papers, nor of the hundreds of head of stock that had perished. At Major Edwards' request Percy had written mocking letters to the Chicago *Inter-Ocean* and the New York *Her-*

ald, suggesting that their exaggerated reports of the Dakota winter were attempts to keep the citizens of their cities from packing up en masse to move to the new Northwest. There was little Dakota journalists could do, however, about F. Jay Haynes' photographs of the Red River flood. The photograph that showed the Northern Pacific train parked on the bridge to keep it from washing away, a picture that gave the illusion of a train floating directly upon the flood waters, was said to have been particularly popular throughout the east.

When Mrs. Oakes mentioned the photograph, Alexander McKenzie's response was as genial as it was dismissive, "I ran the gang that laid them tracks in '71, and there ain't a rain short of forty days and forty nights could budge that bridge. But even though I take some personal pride in that particular span, I got to say that for pure impressiveness you ain't seen nothing 'till you get a look at what is shaping up in my neck of the woods."

For several minutes the conversation followed McKenzie's lead to the bridge begun across the Missouri River at Bismarck which, when completed, would end years of ferry boat operation in the summer and rails laid on the ice in the winter. Now that the topic had turned to railroads and bridges and topography, Thomas Oakes became an invigorated conversationalist, and Mrs. Oakes, an enthusiastic listener. As Oakes began to school the company around the dining table about the rivers and mountains of the Columbia River valley of Washington and Oregon—his descriptions having everything to do with elevations and tons of freight, and nothing to do with visual grandeur—Frances had the opportunity to wonder what Henry Villard's right-hand man, as Percy had described Thomas Oakes, was doing at the Bingham home just one week after Villard's much-publicized takeover of the Northern Pacific Railroad, and in the company of the sheriff from Bismarck, at that. There had been no letter from J. B. Power introducing the guests and scheduling their visit, of course, for Power was no longer with the Northern Pacific. The only letter to arrive from Power in the past several months had been an official notification of a loan payment that was past due.

There had been very little warning about the visit, beyond the message Percy had sent out to the farm the day before, saying that Alexander McKenzie and Mr. and Mrs. Oakes had arrived in Fargo that day (along with a shipment of oysters packed in ice) and had accepted his invitation to dine at the Bingham home. Considering Percy's oft-expressed contempt for his father's "entertainments" at the behest of the N.P., Frances found the invitation astonishing, almost as astonishing as her husband's new behavior. He had been pleasant throughout the meal. There had been no indication of morose self-involvement, no sarcastic asides to his father, no complaints about Dakota or Dakotans, not even when the discussion of the winter and the flood offered an obvious opportunity. Most surprising had been his subtle flattery and attention to Alexander McKenzie throughout the meal. No, most surprising, Frances thought again, was that he remained relatively sober by eight in the evening.

Frances turned her attention back to Thomas Oakes when John Bingham asked him if the new management of the Northern Pacific intended to continue the lawsuit against J. B. Power.

"The suit has been dropped," Oakes replied.

"Does that mean that Power has been exonerated?" Frances asked.

"It means that the suit has been dropped," Oakes replied abruptly, producing a small mustache comb from his vest pocket to comb away any crumbs. "In my opinion where there is smoke there is likely to be fire, but the suit itself was ill-conceived by the presiding officer of the road at the time, and did the company more harm than good. These problems are best dealt with privately."

Oakes' speech, a combination of personal rancor and professional pomposity, left the table silent for a moment before John Bingham returned the conversation to the Red River valley. "I have been meaning to ask you, Doctor, did your prediction of increased health problems following the wet spring hold true?"

"Respiratory ailments in particular worsen with damp weather, and there has been no shortage of bronchial catarrh, but I am happy to say that I am most often occupied these days delivering babies."

"It would seem," Lydia Harkness added, "by the hours that my husband has been keeping this spring and summer, that the population of Fargo must have doubled since May. And by Dakota law, no children are to be born during daylight."

Dr. Harkness smiled at his wife before saying, "I do have some unpleasant news, however. There is diphtheria among the Mennonites."

"Mennonites? Diphtheria?" For the first time that evening, Mrs. Oakes became curious, although her dismay seemed to position the colony and the disease as equally astonishing. "Are you sure? Are they near?"

"Five, six miles southwest of here as the crow flies," Dr. Harkness answered. "But they keep to themselves, and have effectively quarantined their community by habit. What I do not understand is how it got there in the first place. Percy," Dr. Harkness said, "I would like to keep this out of the *Argus* for the time being. There is no reason to cause a panic."

"Has anyone died?"

"A boy. The father came to see me this afternoon as Lydia and I were about to leave Fargo. He has two more children who are sick. I could not understand him very well, and I believe he was not acting according to the community's wishes by speaking to me. I may not be at all welcome tomorrow, but I will do what I can. At least I will be able to drop off several bottles of quinine."

Diphtheria, death, and finally, Mrs. Ford's rum-soaked bread pudding, had together warmed Mrs. Oakes to speech, and she not only complimented the pudding, but the Bingham's "cozy cottage on the prairie" as well. With that Frances brought the men to their feet by suggesting that the ladies retire to the parlor for their coffee. As Frances stood back to allow Mrs. Oakes and Lydia Harkness to pass through the door, she turned to cast a final smile upon the men waiting to sit again. To her surprise she discovered Alexander McKenzie studying her with much the same appreciation that he had earlier directed toward Kirsten. Frances glanced toward Percy to see what he thought of this open appraisal, but Percy had not waited for the door to close behind the women before turning toward the sideboard for the bottle of port waiting there.

Seated again, Alexander McKenzie reflected upon Mrs. Percy Bingham. Bingham was evidently a bigger fool than he had imagined if he didn't know how to keep that woman by his side. When Percy had whined over his whiskey back in March that "a man needs his freedom," McKenzie had expected to hear the old story of a man tied to a wife he could no longer tolerate. But as the night wore on McKenzie discovered that the wife was the focus of Percy's anxiety, but not the cause itself. Percy Bingham, it seemed, was just a little boy who was still swinging at his daddy while held away at arm's length. Thank God, McKenzie had thought to himself, that he had been born poor and had had the good sense to knock his own father down one day and set out to make his way in the world the next. Poor Percy Bingham couldn't even figure out how to get his own wife out of his father's house. Well, like most men who used those high-sounding words—freedom, honor, respect—what he really wanted was money. And for once, it couldn't be his father's. With enough money, Percy had said, he could provide his wife and son with a proper home, for it would be impossible to expect them to leave the comfort of the bonanza farm for a couple of rented rooms. With enough money, McKenzie had thought at the time, Percy Bingham was likely to drink himself to death just a little bit faster. But he would be useful in the meantime.

McKenzie liked to watch people, and he had seen lots of unhappy marriages. There were the couples who snarled and snapped, the ones whose iciness toward each other could give a fellow frostbite just by standing nearby, the ones who called each other by pet names while cringing to the touch, but he'd never quite seen a pair like Percy and Frances Bingham. They weren't pretending to ignore each other. They just weren't interested. Well, McKenzie was interested. There was something in the woman's eyes. Something unsettled, not so much hungry as restless. Potential there, one way or the other, he thought, returning his attention to the conversation that had moved from the bonanzas of the Red River valley to points west.

"If I were a young man," John Bingham was saying, "with a little money to invest, I believe that I would follow the lead of some of the fellows who have set up cattle operations north of the Mouse River."

"Cattle bonanzas?"

"More or less."

McKenzie recognized the look on John Bingham's face as he continued to speak of the growing opportunities to the west. It was the expression of a man invigorated by the vision of money to be made, even if it wasn't a vision he intended to pursue. It could be a gold mine, or a cattle bonanza, or a recipe for a new snake oil. The elder Bingham spoke and carried himself like a much younger man, and McKenzie wondered for a moment if the son had more reason than he had mentioned to want his wife out of his father's house. It was an interesting thought, which led McKenzie to wonder if perhaps a woman like that might need to take a trip to St. Paul to make purchases for a new house. And the Norwegian girl would be worth a moment or two in the pantry, too. He would have to make his stops at the Bingham bonanza farm more regular.

"You were there yourself, were you not, Sheriff McKenzie?"

The discussion around the table had followed the Missouri south to Yankton and the destruction caused by flooding there, and from thence on to the business of the recent territorial legislature. McKenzie reentered the conversation easily.

"I was. Escorted a citizen of Burleigh County to the insane asylum. Sad case."

"Male or female?" Dr. Harkness asked.

"Male. Why?"

"Professional interest only. No, thank you, Percy," Dr. Harkness waved aside the bottle offered. "I am of the opinion that madness among men is far less prevalent here in the new Northwest than it is in the crowded and unsanitary cities back east. I have come to believe that the higher incidence of insanity in men there can be accounted for by a man's constitutional need for space, whereas a woman is meant to live a life of relative confinement. Now, after almost a full decade in Dakota Territory where it has been my observation that the majority of our insane are women, I have deduced that this is simply the inverse of the cause for madness in men in tenements and slums."

"Are you suggesting, Doctor," Percy asked, although he appeared to be addressing his glass, "that a woman given too much space in which to move, who, shall we say, finds herself unmoored by the lack of proper boundaries and conventions, will go mad?"

"Not unless there is a weakness of mind to begin with, of course, but that is, I am afraid, too often the case. I see it over and over among the new settlers. The men are engaged in back-breaking labor from before sunrise to after sunset, day in and day out, with barely two pennies to rub together, and yet they look out upon the prairie as if reading a letter of promise. Whereas the women seem, well, they often seem confused and lost. Exposed, shall we say? Bluntly put, I sometimes fear for those who thrive as much as for those who do not. The Dakota prairie threatens to spawn a sexless, or rather, a more masculine, womanhood, with each generation more akin to her father than her mother. The very idea of survival of the fittest forces one to ask: fit for what?"

"A dreary prognosis, doctor," Thomas Oakes said. "What does your wife think of your hypothesis?"

"I was speaking of the immigrant population, those who have little recourse to the comforts and diversions available to American women. As for Mrs. Harkness," the doctor smiled, "she is willing to believe that the female population in Dakota is more inclined to madness than the male, but holds to a more mundane theory. Wind."

"Wind?" Percy repeated.

"Or more precisely, dirt driven by the wind. Any woman would be driven mad, my wife claims, to find pillows of dirt accumulating upon the sill of a closed window, or to discover the white shirts coated with grime in the closet the day after washing, or—and this seems to Lydia to be the moment when all women in claim shacks must certainly go insane—to open the icebox to find even the butter blackened."

"Well, it was another kind of dirt that got to my man," McKenzie said, "although he'd always been a little funny. Sort of nervous and jumpy-like. Married to a pretty girl who up and run off with a soldier stationed at Fort Lincoln one day. At first he was just drinking too much. Got to be a regular at the jail. Mostly for his own protection, since he had a bad habit of picking fights with soldiers half again his size when on a toot. But then he up and disappeared for almost a year and we thought that was the last we'd seen of poor Jake Grunstadt. Then last October, he got back off the train in Bismarck, looking like the ghost of himself. Skinny as a rail. Fidgety one day and acting like he was half-ways between sleep and death the next. Broke into the Dunn brothers' drug store one night and Bill Hollembaek's just a week later. I was sitting there waiting for him when he decided to take his next midnight shopping trip."

"He sounds like a candidate for the penitentiary rather than the insane asylum," John Bingham suggested.

"I imagine that depends upon what it was he was stealing," Dr. Harkness said.

"Just so, Doctor. Just so. Each time it was a half-dozen bottles of cough sirups, pectorals, or pain killers. The last time he had a packet of something-or-other of morphia."

"Sulphate of morphia," Dr. Harkness said. "Your thief was after opium. Laudanum, paregoric, McMunn's Elixer, Winslow's Soothing Sirup, Godfrey's Cordial, each is a preparation of opium or its alkaloids, most commonly sulphate of morphia. They can provide powerful remedies, especially when all else fails. But used or prescribed injudiciously, they can lead to physical and moral failure."

"Well, those sirups did something to Grudstadt's mind all right. It was the family that asked to have him sent to the insane asylum. And him not any older than Percy here."

With the eyes of the men at the table suddenly turned upon him, Percy changed the subject. "Insane asylums. Penitentiaries. There were a lot of plums pulled out of the territorial pie during the last Session," Percy Bingham said. "Looks to me like Per Rolfsrud—our Cass County delegate," Percy explained to Oakes in an aside—"came home empty-handed."

"Well, I was just an observer down there," McKenzie said, "but a man can get a pretty good sense of things if he keeps his ears open, and I got the impression from some of the conversations going on around town that the biggest plum ain't surfaced yet."

"The capital?" Percy asked.

"The capital?" John Bingham repeated. "What's this about? I'm afraid I don't have much time for the newspapers these days."

Percy quickly summed up the opinions of editors throughout the territory regarding the issue of capital removal that had been broached and dropped in the last legislative session. As he warmed to his topic he dropped the self-conscious tone with which he had begun. The synopsis was impressive, for Percy had the bookish man's memory for potent phrases and an actor's deliberate delivery. As Percy spoke, Alexander McKenzie caught the eye of Thomas Oakes, and read there, if not approval, at least a willingness to consider supporting Percy Bingham as the delegate from Cass County to the next legislative session, still eighteen months away. Oakes, McKenzie understood, did not care if the capital of the territory was moved to Fargo or Jamestown or Bismarck or any of the barely populated siding towns in between, as long as it was along the N.P. line.

CHAPTER XXXIX

In Which What Recedes and Returns Fatigues

July 11, 1881

Dear Frances,

I am writing with sad news. Dear Sophie passed away very unexpectedly last night. I thank the Lord that she was taken in her sleep. The doctor assures me that she experienced no pain. I know, too, that she felt no fear, for her faith in God was steadfast, and she had spoken with anticipation of the day to come when she would stand before her Savior, face to face. My shock, however, has been great, for it was not three weeks past that we attended church together, and although she had complained recently of being weak and weary, and was often confined to her bed, her spirits and her mind remained as vigorous as ever. I know that you were fond of Sophie, Frances, and I am sorry to have to share this news with you. We have lost a dear, dear friend.

A shout of protest lifted Frances' attention from the letter. Houghton and the youngest Johnson boy had been intently farming a small square of the house yard all morning with a combination of odds and ends that Jack Shaw had fashioned into miniature farm implements, but now the boys struggled over ownership of a wooden horse. Once he saw that his mother was watching, Houghton let out a second howl. Frances had grown up watching the play of her older brothers regularly erupt into fisticuffs and wrestling matches, and although the Johnson boy was several pounds heavier than her son, she saw no reason to intervene. Returning her attention to the letter Frances wondered if perhaps the shock of Sophie Fredley's death had temporarily deranged Anna, for that alone would explain the reference to their elderly friend's mind as "vigorous." The details that followed were about arrangements for the funeral and Anna's plan to contact a distant nephew of Sophie's. A passing complaint about fatigue surprised Frances, for Anna rarely referred to her own discomfort. Questions about Houghton and Percy, and an expression of hope regarding President Garfield's condition, all but finished the letter, leaving Frances to reread the final two sentences over and over, each time hearing Anna's tone and inflection differently: *"I will necessarily return to father's house in due time. I am certain that much has changed in my absence."*

What had changed?, Frances wondered to herself, refolding the letter and placing it in the pocket of her skirt as she stood. She was about to descend the porch steps to settle the dispute that had irritatingly escalated in pitch when Kirsten came around the corner of the house carrying an empty laundry basket. Frances watched as the boys reluctantly handed the horse over, turned their backs upon each other, and then quietly returned to their farming as Kirsten disappeared once again. Reaching for the broad hat and gloves upon the bench beside her, Frances stepped off the shaded porch and walked to the picket fence that surrounded the yard, where she began to pull the weeds that were faring much better than the sweet peas under yet another day of unremitting sunshine. First a flood, and then a drought. Next should come the locusts, Frances thought, her mood far from cheered by Anna's letter.

Frances recalled the day this past December when she had watched John Bingham help Anna into the buggy already laden with her trunks. A rare break from the winter storms had allowed for travel, but there was very little, Frances knew, that could have persuaded Anna to leave the house in such frigid weather. 'Just me,' she had thought then, feeling as if a band of steel were constricting her chest. 'Just the need to get away from me'. For days she had walked about in confusion, at times angry, at times frantic, as if something precious had been lost, to be returned only if she could solve some mystery, find the right words, discover the correct gesture. In the following weeks and months that steel band released and tightened, released and tightened. Almost always it was during moments of quiet that the sensation of absolute loss returned and she would feel her breath squeezed away. But Frances preferred not to have moments of quiet, so she played with Houghton, and worked on the light accounting and correspondence that John Bingham allowed, and when there was nothing else to do as the wind howled and the storms raged, she drew, erased, and redrew plans for an elaborate garden of hedges, shrubs, and flowers to surround the house, plans meant to please Anna (and which with the arrival of spring and summer had not taken shape beyond a few struggling sweet peas).

Increasingly there had been moments in the company of Little Carl, whose odd combination of patience and brusqueness (and pies and cakes) had completely won over Houghton, who was himself content to sit for hours at a time at the cook's table molding shapes out of the flour and water dough that Carl set before him. Once the spring rains gave way to summer sunshine and the ground regained its solidity, Frances was able to resume her rides upon Raleigh and walks into the prairie to gather wildflowers. On occasion she would stop by the machine shed where Jack Shaw could be found oiling and repairing machinery when he wasn't out in the field doing the same. Listening to Shaw reminded Frances of earlier days with Percy — a comparison that she made with generosity toward both men — when his larger experience of the world served to expand her own. Shaw's descriptions of village life in Russia and tenement life in New York fascinated her, although she suspected that there was a good deal he was leaving out for her benefit.

And there were hours in Kirsten's company, many of which were dotted with bursts of unexpected laughter. Frances had promised Lydia Harkness that she would informally continue Kirsten's education during the young woman's spare hours (of which there were few), although what precisely that would mean besides reading novels and stories aloud, Frances could not imagine. Listening to Kirsten read was a distant experience from that of listening to Anna. Frances missed Anna's modulated tones, precise phrasing, and elegant clarity, but there were pleasures to be found in Kirsten's performances, for the young woman felt that it was only polite to laugh at the author's jokes, and to register her own amazement at a surprising turn of events. She shook her head with impatience when the characters behaved badly or with sadness when they suffered. But she could not be made to appreciate irony, and found it difficult to resist interjecting a personal commentary of exasperation regarding characters who found themselves in unhappy situations of their own making.

Attempts at reading poetry were quickly abandoned. Kirsten's delivery was painful to Frances' ear, and Frances' readings were very little appreciated by her student. Reading a poem, Kirsten explained, was like being told that there was a treasure buried beneath beautiful flowers. "So even if you are good to dig, in the end you have here flowers and there flowers and maybe not much of a treasure after all do you find. The poem is not," she finished proudly, "a model of concision." There was an argument to be made there, Frances knew, but no good reason to make it.

Sitting back on her heels to look at her progress with the weeding, Frances let herself chuckle once again at Kirsten's analysis. The crackling of the letter in her pocket reminded Frances of Anna's imminent return, and it occurred to her then that she missed Anna most when she thought about how much she missed Anna. That is when the steel band tightened once again.

Anna returned to the Bingham farm in early August. Frances met her at the front door with a cautious embrace. Anna responded with a light kiss upon her friend's cheek. And thus was enacted the tacit agreement of mutual amnesia, an example of the legacy that Yankee reserve would contribute to the Dakota psyche: a horror of the expression of all things disturbing or uncomfortable. Wordlessly, Anna's flight to St. Paul had been recast as the flight of a good friend to the side of an invalid in need. There had been no unwelcome advance, no equally unwelcome refusal, and thus, no rupture. Things were to go on as they had before, except of course, that things were not as they had been before.

If Frances had been slowly approaching an understanding of the extent to which her life had changed in Anna's absence, it was Anna's return that brought these changes into relief as Frances began to picture her behavior through her sister-in-law's eyes. She hadn't given much thought to how she looked in the wide-brimmed man's hat that she had discovered in Grant & McCauley's and wore now on her daily rides because it protected her from the sun far better than did her bonnet that caught the wind at a canter and choked her with its ribbons. Nor had Frances considered the informality of the long braid trailing down her back until she caught Anna's startled expression when they came face to face on the front porch one morning as she returned from yet another exploration of the Jew slough, which was lovely this time of year, the untilled land quickly returning to wildflowers. It was much the same look that made Frances aware of the hand that she had rested on Little Carl's shoulder as she bent over him to discuss an order for several dozen cases of canned fruit for the crew, expected to reach over two hundred for the upcoming harvest. When Frances mentioned to John Bingham during the evening meal that there was a discrepancy between the figures provided by the head cook of the Number Two Farm and those shown to her by Little Carl, she was aware of a peculiar tilt to Anna's head.

Weeks passed before Anna gave voice to her concern, and then it was prompted less by something unexpected that Frances said or did than by the peculiar behavior of the young Norwegian housekeeper. It had been a congenial evening for the Bingham family. Even Percy, whose mood had improved significantly with Major Edward's suggestion that he consider running for the Cass County seat for the next territorial legislative session, had seemed like his old self, teasing Anna and easily agreeing with Frances that there was no great hurry for her to purchase furniture for the new house in Fargo since it was not expected to be completed until Thanksgiving. When Percy excused himself to work on a short speech he had been asked to give at the dedication of the site for the new high school (just blocks, he had been pleased to note, from Houghton's new home-to-be), and John retired to his office, Frances and Anna settled in for an evening of reading in the upstairs sitting room. Frances was flipping through the most recent *Peterson's* and Anna was nodding over her Bible when Kirsten, finding a rare moment of rest away from her household duties, entered the sitting room with a pot of tea, sat down next to Frances on the sofa, poured a cup for herself as well as for Frances, and brought out a list from the pocket of her housedress.

"I have finished the story by Mrs. Alcott," Kirsten proudly whispered, believing Anna to be asleep. "But there were many words I did not know."

Frances quietly explained the game of croquet and described a burnoose and a pomegranate. 'Frippery', she could tell by Kirsten's expression, was certain to find its way into the young woman's lexicon, as well as 'indolent'. 'Hasheesh' Kirsten had worked out on her own from the events of the story, although she was suspicious regarding the properties described, and wanted to know if these 'beans' of Mrs. Alcott's were regularly chewed by Americans. Assured that they were not, Kirsten moved on to the rest of her list. Who was this beautiful drowned Ophelia? And what was the legend of The Lotus Eaters?

Here, Kirsten had to be satisfied with Frances' rather vague explanation that it was about people somewhere far away who ate something-or-other that made them forget things. Were Anna not once again fully awake and staring at the scene before her with some incredulity, Frances supposed she would have resurrected the little bit she retained in her memory from Percy's nightly readings of long ago, and then filled in the rest of the story with her own imagination. Instead she handed the list back to Kirsten and encouraged her to leave with a hasty "good-night."

"Good-night," Kirsten said quietly in response, darting a quick look at Anna. "I will read the story again, then."

"When Percy was a boy he could recite by heart Tennyson's entire poem," Anna said as soon as Kirsten was out of the room. She closed her Bible and set it on the table next to the tea tray. "But what can the girl have been thinking? Her curiosity is admirable, but to make herself so at home next to you on the sofa, Frances?"

Frances placed an index finger on the magazine before her, as if marking the end of the paragraph to which she would return, allowing herself a moment to arrange her response. Lydia Harkness' suggestion that Frances continue Kirsten's education could be called upon here, for the doctor's wife was considered by Anna to be one of Fargo's saving graces. But Frances suspected that if she were to dodge Anna's real question, which had less to do with Kirsten's presumption of familiarity than with Frances' evident encouragement, without which familiarity would not have been possible, she would be favored with one of Anna's cool glances. The alternative would be for Frances to express her own surprise that Kirsten's immigrant manners had surfaced thus, and offer to speak with her the next day regarding this breach of propriety by a servant. To refer to Kirsten as a servant, however, was not quite accurate, and even 'housekeeper' no longer defined her status properly. And although Frances would not reveal the extent to which she and the young woman had become comfortable, or the pleasure she had come to take in Kirsten's company, to place the blame on Kirsten seemed simply craven. Frances had no choice but to go with Lydia Harkness and hope for the best.

Looking up from her magazine Frances said, "Lydia," and then stopped, for Anna had once again laid her head against the back of her chair and appeared to be suddenly asleep. "Anna?"

When Anna did not respond, Frances frowned and closed her magazine to study her sleeping friend. It was the second time that day that Anna had drifted into sleep in the midst of a conversation. This time it was convenient, but certainly not flattering.

CHAPTER XL

In Which Kirsten Is Taken for a Ride

Ya, sure, they will come to talk to me now, Pastor Fedje and the men of the church council. They will be with their faces very serious because a good Norwegian girl did go to a picnic and not to church. It is because Ingeborg and Per Rolfsrud can not mind their own business so right out of their way they drove just to see who it was under the big cottonwood tree that stands all by itself in the middle of the field. (Mr. Johnson he wanted to cut the tree down so the men did not have to drive around it, but Miss Frances said, "You shall do no such thing. That may well be the only tree standing between the farm and the Pacific Ocean for all we know," and that is how Miss Frances talks, and it makes me laugh because to look to the west from the farm is to see six, maybe even seven, trees before the horizon, and after that is a mountain, Mrs. Harkness says, and where there are mountains there are trees, and then there is California, and then there is the ocean.) So there we are, then, in a field of stubble under the tree and to have a free day is what we are there to celebrate, because now the harvest is over.

Jack Shaw, who almost never takes a day off is here, and Lars Oleson, the plowing foreman, and his wife, Hege, who does not speak American yet, not one word, she will not even try, and Mrs. Ford, who is sweet on Jack Shaw, I think, but she is not a Jew so I do not know if he has even looked at her that way, and as for him being a Jew, I asked Mrs. Ford one day if she minded and she said that what she minded was being a Mrs. without a Mr., and that is concision. And three nice men from the threshing crew that just finished Mr. John Bingham's wheat and with them are three women from the cooking crew that came with the threshers, because even with me to help now and then and the Swedish sisters who come to the farm during the summer (their names are

Christine and Kari, but everyone calls them "the Swedish sisters") and the extra *hushjelp* to do the washing up, Little Carl can not keep up with a crew of almost two hundred men. So maybe husbands and wives the threshers and cooks are, but maybe not, and at least Ingeborg Rolfsrud did not know about the "maybe not," but she did know that she was looking right at Kirsten Knudson who had decided to be indolent and not to go to the Lutheran Free Church that morning.

So I will tell you what they are to say, the men of the church council, but that will not take long because you can just guess. A young woman that does not have a husband and does not live with her mother must listen to her elders. I am to be in church every Sunday and it is time to marry and have a family. All this I have heard before. When Marit Norstad married Halvor Rolfsrud in June, I said to myself, Kirsten Knudson, you are safe now because never will you be Kirsten Rolfsrud. But I was wrong because Ingeborg Rolfsrud is still to be a problem. About me without my poor Mor to help with the good decisions she says she is thinking, but I think that she is still mad about Homer's land and that she knows about my money in a box in the bank, that is even more now because it was a good harvest and one-fourth of a good harvest on a quarter section is a lot for the *hushelp* (but now I will say it in American, the housekeeper, because even Hege Oleson says *huskeeper* now). I know just how much is in that box because Miss Frances gave to me the little notebook from the bank with my very own name on it, and so now I am to give the notebook, the land, the three dollars I make every week now, and me, too, to some nice man in the church to make Per and Ingeborg Rolfsrud happy? You bet I am not.

Well, I can see that I am not yet back to the picnic, where I am sorry to say I just went flat down on my back like a jackrabbit shot by Little Carl for stew when I saw the buggy of Ingeborg and Per Rolfsrud, but not fast enough, and about this there is not much more to say. Except this that maybe I should not say: I do not want a husband who will take my land and tell me what to do. I am strong and good to work. I am good to clean and to cook and to sew and to do the laundry and to take care of little Howie, and it is a lot but it is not too much. I do not want to be like Mor, with my hands in lye or tallow or hot water or bread dough all day long and my back all bent over from making candles and soap and stirring laundry with a big paddle in boiling water and then scrubbing and scrubbing and scrubbing and baking and cooking and cleaning and spinning and feeding the cows and the chickens and stacking hay, and all of this with a new baby every year and never a smile until I am skinny and sick and old. I want to stay in the big Bingham house that I know from corner to corner, and where the soap is from the store and the candles come in a box and they are just for being pretty and not for light, and where to clean is to touch so many beautiful things and to cook is to be side by side with Mrs. Ford or Little Carl. I do not want to leave my little Howie, who is so sweet and funny, and is just one little boy to take care of and not ten. And I do not want to leave Miss Frances, who is not sweet really but she makes me laugh when she laughs even when I do not know why, but not as much as before Miss Anna did come back.

She is different now. Miss Anna is, not Miss Frances, who is different, too. Except on the day of the picnic, and that is why I do not care what Ingeborg Rolfsrud wants me to do. Here I stay. I will tell you why, then.

It was after the Rolfsrud's buggy was not even a dot and the empty buckets for the sandwiches were all in a stack in the wagon and the pies from Little Carl were gone, except for one piece, and two of the threshers had to arm-wrestle to see who was to have it. The other thresher and Lars Oleson they were sound asleep, and Hege Oleson was talking and talking about her home that she misses so much, and not everything did I understand because there are many words in *norsk* that I do not know now, and maybe they are words I never did know. The three women from the cooking crew they listened to a story that the other thresher was telling them (I think it was not a nice story), and then, just like that, Jack Shaw and Mrs. Ford decided right at the same time that they were so full of the picnic that they would walk all the way back to the farm. Well, I could see that Hege Oleson had many more things to say about *Gamle Norge* and about the beautiful *dal* where she grew up, and that made me want to take a walk, too. And for a late August day the weather was like a miracle because it was not too hot and not even muggy and in the sky there was just one big cloud, the kind that is not really a cloud but is like an old sheet you can almost see through with sometimes the holes here and there, and there was even a little breeze to keep the mosquitoes away but not a wind to try to knock you down.

All of this and on a Sunday, too.

So I said "please excuse me" to Hege Oleson, and set out not in the same direction as Mrs. Ford and Jack Shaw but instead I walked east toward the river and toward Sten's house that is mine on Homer's land because I like to just sit at the table there and think about Mor and Sten and Ole and Haldis and Guri and Far, too. And sometimes I pick flowers on the way. When I was a little girl I could not walk in any direction for over five minutes without picking a handful of beautiful wildflowers, but now it is everything for plowing and planting. Almost everything. So here I am walking and walking and I am starting to think that even a miracle in Dakota in August is hot, so I sit down with the little bit of flowers I did find along the way and I am thinking now of Guri and Haldis when they were little and how never did they want to do one thing but pick flowers and make necklaces. And so I made a necklace right then and there, and that is a funny thing for a grown woman to do, but it is not funny because there are also the tears. And then I made a ring of flowers just like the one I used to make for Guri, but there was no Guri to wear it so I just put it on my head, and then up I stand, and that is when I see the horse and rider. Even though I had to wipe my eyes it did not take me long to see that it was Miss Frances, with her big hat pulled down over her forehead and her braid bouncing. At first she did not see me, but for Miss Frances I did not fall back like a dead rabbit, and pretty soon there she was looking down at me with those eyes that do not smile like her lips. And she just sat there and stared down and did not say a thing, and so I bit my lip and stared right back up, and it sent a little sting into each one of my fingertips, like when I have been brushing the carpet in winter and then touch a candlestick. But then I could not look any longer, and I could feel my face very hot, and I looked down at the ground.

"Aren't you a picture," Miss Frances said, and when I did not look up, she said, "Your garland is lovely, Kirstie."

"I beg your pardon?" I said. That is what Mrs. Harkness taught me to say when there was a word I did not know.

"Garland. Your necklace of flowers."

"About Guri and Haldis I was thinking," I said, putting my hand to my necklace that is a garland.

"Your sisters? What do you hear from them?"

There is nothing to hear from Guri. I knew that Miss Frances would understand me if I said '*Guri er død,*' but it is not for Miss Frances to hear about my sad thoughts. So I said, "From Mor I had a letter in May. After the flood. They did not go to the west of the Missouri River after all, but they are still far away, in Griggs County, Mor says, but I do not know where that is. Mor says there the Sheyenne River is, too, but it must be a different Sheyenne River because she says that they are now to the north and the west of here, and the Sheyenne it goes south."

"It is the same river. If you remind me when you get back to the house, I will show you where Griggs County is on Mr. Bingham's map," Miss Frances said.

Well, that made me so happy that I just kept going with the talk, and I said, "Mor is going to marry Osten Sondreaal, but not until she can prove up."

"Because she needs to be a single woman to homestead," Miss Frances said, nodding her head.

I started to shrug my shoulders, but then I remembered what Mrs. Harkness told me one day a long time ago, that the good Lord gave human beings speech to distinguish them from animals, but that it was up to us to 'maintain the distinction,' so I said, "I suppose so. Osten Sondreaal has a quarter section next to hers. They are working hard and no one is real sick."

It sounded like a little laugh from Miss Frances, but when I looked back up, she was not looking at me, but across the river toward the slough. I could not hear what she said, so I said, "Excuse me?" Which is a lot like, "I beg your pardon," but what I meant was not that there was a word I did not know, but that I could not hear her, although it sounded like she said something about "land and love." Maybe it was "or."

"Nothing important, dear," Miss Frances said, and I almost said "Excuse me?" again, because Mrs. Ford calls me 'dear' sometimes, but no one else, and I know that Miss Frances was not saying that I was 'dear' to her, but still, it was not exactly the same as a plain, old, "Nothing important, Kirstie."

And then Miss Frances said, "What are you doing out here all by yourself?"

So I told her about the picnic and pointed back toward the cottonwood tree. It is funny how you think that the land is so flat here that there is no up or down, but when you point to something that is a little bit far away you can see that the land is not so very flat, because only most of the tree could we see, but not any of the people. Miss Frances just nodded, and then said, "Stand!" to her horse that had decided that it had stood still for just about long enough, and I thought that then she was to ride away, but instead she said, "You have been crying." Just like that.

I did not know what to say. Because they had not really been crying tears, like when Guri died, but just sad tears like for something that is gone but is probably better off gone, and that is how I feel about Haldis and Mor and even Far, to tell a truth, but I did not know how to say that kind of truth, and I did not think that Miss Frances would be interested. So this time I was just to be a disappointment to Mrs. Harkness because I went ahead and shrugged.

Miss Frances she did not say anything and did not ride away, so I looked back into her eyes and there she did smile, too, and this time it was all with the eyes and not so much with the mouth, and that is not so very often with Miss Frances, and again it was that tingle in my fingers, and then she said, "Kirsten, when did you last ride a horse?"

Well, the last horse I rode was Homer, who was not a horse, so I said the truth, I said, "Never."

"Never? Would you like to ride Raleigh?"

"No! I mean, I would not know how to ride a horse so fancy like that, Miss Frances."

"He is quite gentle. Not fancy at all. Come, you can ride in front of me."

Well, that made me laugh right out loud. "I am bigger than Howie, Miss Frances. I do not think Raleigh would like it."

"That is the beauty of horses, Kirsten. If you are good to them, they will do what they can to please you. Unlike most people. Come, it is a beautiful day, and you have been crying, and now you are to be made happy."

So just like that Miss Frances jumped down, and that is when I saw that her dress was not really a dress at all, but like half ways between a dress and a pair of trousers (and with no frippery at all). Well, how to get up, I was going to ask, when Miss Frances showed me how to tuck my skirt together and where to hang on and then with a boost and a little push against my *bakende* I was in the saddle and there I sat, and right away it felt good to be above everything, and right away it felt not so good at all because the horse he started to walk sideways. But Miss Frances just said something to Raleigh's ear, and I am pretty sure that if he could talk he would have said, "Excuse me?"

"Now put your weight in the right stirrup for a moment, or we'll both be on the ground," Miss Frances said, and just like that she was up behind me, but not in the saddle, because like I said, I am bigger than Howie, and it was like Miss Frances heard me thinking because she said, "I'll be fine as long as I have the stirrups, and the reins, and one hand on the saddle horn."

"But what do I hold?" I asked, just as Miss Frances gave Raleigh a nudge to get him going.

"Lean against me and let your back-end, as you like to say, sink into the saddle. Now put your arms straight out to your sides. Really. Do as I say. You will find your balance."

Well, I am not to argue with Miss Frances, and that worked pretty well, and I was just getting comfortable, when Miss Frances said. "Keep them out." And then she made a clucking sound and Raleigh started to trot, and I brought my hands right back to the saddle horn on top of Miss Frances' hand, but Miss Frances said into my ear, "Trust me," and then I felt her move her legs into Raleigh's side, and the next thing I knew I was like a bird flying right over the ground, and I could hear Miss Frances chuckling behind me, and then I knew that I was laughing, too. But that did not last very long, because pretty soon Miss Frances stopped Raleigh, and said to me, "That's hard work." And I knew that she meant for her and for Raleigh, too.

So Miss Frances hopped down, and then this happened, and it is maybe the true reason why I do not want to leave the Bingham house, even though you will say that nothing happened. This is the nothing that happened, then.

To get off of a horse is not hard, I think. All of my life I have been looking at people doing it, but for some reason I decided to get off like Miss Frances usually does, and that is to bring her right leg right over the saddle horn and then slide off. I know that this is not right because Little Carl said to her one day that it was dangerous and not to do it any more. How Little Carl dares to talk to Miss Frances that way I do not know, but he is the only one who does. Sometimes Miss Frances listens, but when he said that she just smiled at him and said that it would be dangerous on any other horse. So up I tucked my skirt again and over the saddle I put my leg, and that is when I saw that I had nothing to hang on to, and there I was about to come down in a tumble, but then there was Miss Frances with her hands around my waist, and then the slide was slow and it was like the time that Halvor Rolfsrud picked me up and set me down, except that this was not like that time at all.

And there was Miss Frances looking down at me from so close and I was looking back and I just wanted to look and look into those eyes that are gray like a silver dollar sometimes and not like a stormy sky, and, well, O.K., I know that they are just eyes and that everybody has two, except maybe for Peter Sondreaal, and that what we are born with is what we get, but still I can not look at them enough. And then I thought to myself, Kirsten Knudson, this is exactly how Miss Frances looked at you that night that the important men from England were at supper, and Miss Frances gave you that kiss that was not on the cheek for putting up her hair. So I closed my eyes and waited.

And then I opened my eyes, because Miss Frances did not move, she still had her hands on my waist, but she did not give me the kiss. She just looked at me like I have never been looked at before. And it was like the walking on the grave again, and I did not know what to say so I said, "I beg your pardon?" and my voice was so small that even I did not sound like me to me.

"For what, precisely?" Miss Frances said, and that is how she talks sometimes, it is like she says something that there is no answer for because it is like she is having a conversation all of her very own.

So I said, "I thought maybe you said something that I did not hear," even though that was not true.

I don't know why that made her laugh right out loud. "No, Kirstie, I did not say anything that you could not hear."

"I mean, what is the word for, for –"

I do not know what I was trying to say, and that is when Miss Frances just smiled that lip smile and said, "Trouble." And then she stood back and waited for me to step away from Raleigh so she could tighten the saddle cinch before she got back on, and I thought she would ride away then, but instead she looked all around her, like there was something or someone to see and not just wheat stubble and stacks of straw that the threshers had left here and there, and the tall grass and trees along the river. And then she said, "I think it would be best if you did not mention our ride to anyone, Kirsten."

"No, Miss Frances."

"You may call me Frances, although perhaps you should check with Little Carl to see if that is allowed," Miss Frances, I mean, Frances said.

Now that is when I should have been quiet, but instead I said what I was thinking without thinking which is what Mrs. Harkness used to say that I did, even though that is not with logic if you think about it. Anyway, I said, "Miss Anna will not like that."

Just like that there goes the smile, lips and eyes both, and then she was gone, too, and I was mad at myself for saying one thing too many, and I suppose Miss Frances, that is, Frances, is right. I am just trouble. But there is more that I could say that I do not. I could say that I have seen how Miss Frances, *Frances,* looks at Miss Anna when she thinks that no one is to notice, but I do, and sometimes it is hungry and sometimes it is sad and sometimes it is just without the patience, like when she tries to get Miss Anna to go for a ride in the carriage, or to try to answer a riddle, and Miss Anna acts like she is about to go to sleep instead. I could say to Frances, 'look at the little brown bottle that Miss Anna keeps in the drawer by her bed to help with her pain'. I could say that to give the housekeeper a ride on a horse because she is sad is not the only secret, then.

CHAPTER XLI

In Which a Coffin is a Bed but an Ox is Not a Coffin

As the autumn of '81 passed and the cold of another winter set in, Frances was granted a reprieve from her move to town by the explosive growth of Fargo's population that had builders and carpenters overcommitted, which is to say, by the universal and timeless benign neglect that characterizes the construction business. Percy's house, a relatively simple affair on Thirteenth Street, which was to have been completed by Thanksgiving, and then by the New Year, in February lacked only the delivery and installation of carpets, curtains, and furniture. Frances was grateful for each delay, and yet there were complications, unspoken, inchoate, and quite possibly, mostly of her imagination, that troubled her days. Anna, Frances had come to believe, was either incapable of forgiving her for her impulsiveness of over a year ago, or else had been inordinately damaged by the advance, for no attentions on Frances' part could return the women to the easy and loving friendship of the past. Where once Frances had dreamt of heat and passion, of sinking into the very being of Anna, of moving past clothes and skin until she had claimed spirit and soul, these days she would have been satisfied with a little warmth. What she encountered as she reached out, however, was a ghostly chill, less a reserve than an absence.

And then there was Kirsten, whose warmth and spirit seemed to grow in direct proportion to the waning of Anna's, and who, upon entering a room, was certain to search for Frances, only to become suddenly unable to meet the older woman's eyes. So Kirsten went about her business, blushing all the while and quickly retreating and then discovering soon thereafter another reason to be near Frances, which drew from Anna yet another sigh. Sometimes the complicated algebra of emotions, the looks and the looking away and the sighs and the silence and the growing understanding that she was the responsible figure at the center of these passive dramatics, drove Frances from the house, to Little Carl's cookhouse, to Jack Shaw in the machine shed, to the barn to stand among beasts whose only longing was for hay. And so, despite her indifference to her appointment in Fargo with Ferdinand Luger regarding a final furniture order, Frances was grateful for a reason to be outside, breathing air unencumbered by sentiment or passion or memory or expectation or hope.

She was pulling out of the second barn in the carriage when Little Carl came along side with his hand raised to stop her.

"Where do you think you're going?" he asked.

"I fail to see how that is your concern, Carl, but since you have asked so politely, I am on my way to Fargo to conduct some business at the Luger Furniture Company."

"You don't want to do that."

Frances looked down at Little Carl from her upholstered seat. As a matter of fact, she was very little interested in furnishing the house in Fargo (and every bit of it on credit, at that), but even Little Carl, whose powers of perception Frances had found at times to be disconcerting, would not have presumed to speak to her quite so personally.

"And why is that, pray tell?"

"Weather."

"Carl," Frances said, completing her unspoken thought with a sweep of her arm that took in the better part of the farmyard, and the field beyond where several head of cattle had been turned out to graze upon the remnants of the cornstalks there. It was a gray February day, but in no way threatening. An overnight dusting of snow lay lightly upon the frozen ground, but there had been no significant snowfall since Christmas. Those same farmers who had complained throughout the winter of '80-'81 of too much snow, could this winter be heard to fret over too little moisture being generated.

"Miss Frances, every bit of me hurts today. I can't barely move my neck, and that is as sure a sign as any that a storm's coming."

"I am sorry for your discomfort, but my neck feels fine, and the sooner I get going the sooner I can return. Now, I am certain that you have something better to do than–"

A call across the yard from Jack Shaw to "wait only," interrupted Frances. Silently Frances and Little Carl watched him hurry toward them.

"Are you going to Fargo?" Shaw asked.

"No."

"Yes."

Shaw looked from Little Carl to Frances before he said, "If the answer is 'yes,' Mrs. Bingham, maybe you will make it for me a little easier and take instead the wagon. Johnson got a call by the telephone from the other farm. A shaft is out on the well pump. If you could only pick up the part from Henderson's and then swing by the Number Two on your way back–" A look from Little Carl caused Shaw to hesitate and amend his request. "Better you should bring me back the part. I will bring it there myself."

"Of course," Frances said, turning an arch smile on Little Carl.

"Only wait a minute and I will get the wagon hitched up," Shaw said, turning to go.

"Give us Dan," Little Carl called after Shaw, who stopped and looked up at the sky for a moment before nodding and striding on.

"Us?" Frances asked.

A winter's wagon ride to Fargo behind a work horse is a longer, colder, more tedious affair than the same journey in a carriage, so Frances was grateful for Little Carl's company, despite his prickly mood, and his opinion regarding the manifold dangers of the telephone line that ran between the Number Two Farm and the headquarters. He was convinced that headaches and, quite possibly, insanity would be the result of vibrations passing through the ear to the brain.

When they reached the furniture store on the corner of Broadway and NP Avenue, Little Carl helped Frances out of the wagon and then got back in for the short trip across the street to Henderson's Hardware. He would pick up the pump shaft there and then move on to Goodman and Yerxa's for the other supplies that he had suddenly remembered needing back in the Bingham headquarters farmyard. He was to pick Frances up at the Harkness home in three hours. In the meantime Frances would meet with Ferdinand Luger. Together they would visit the new house to take some final measurements, after which Luger would drop Frances off for her visit with Lydia Harkness.

But Frances had been in the company of the doctor's wife for less than thirty minutes when her friend rose to answer a knock on the door, returning almost immediately to inform Frances that there was a diminutive man bearing a singular resemblance to a rabbit who was insisting that Mrs. Bingham "get her things and get to going right now." And indeed, when Frances went to the door, Little Carl was standing there with his nose twitching in the air, looking as if he were about to thump a boot against the porch floorboards to warn of impending danger. For a moment Frances considered instructing him to wait for her in the wagon while she returned to the parlor to finish her tea, but she knew that the thought of the little man huddled out there in the cold would be too disconcerting. So she accepted her astrakhan coat and hat from Lydia Harkness, and after an apology for such a short visit, followed Little Carl to the wagon. The day had darkened and the wind had a new bite to it, but not one snow flake fell from the sky.

"I am sorry if your aches have increased, Carl," Frances said as he set

Dan on his way. "But I really must insist that in the future you hold to the schedule we have agreed upon. Your caution is misplaced and your insistence impertinent."

"Mrs. Bingham," Little Carl said, the formality of address telling Frances that his mood had not improved while in town, "I hope that's exactly what you're still thinking when we get home. If it is, I'll say my 'sorrys' then. Here." He reached under the seat for the buffalo robe there.

Frances did not speak for the first half hour of the drive home, at first because she did not want Little Carl to think that she took lightly his presumption, and then because she realized that the day was too quickly falling into dark, the air had grown heavy, and Dan had begun to toss his head and snort in concern.

"Get up, Dan," Little Carl said. "Here it comes."

It came dramatically, with huge flakes dumped upon their shoulders, as if a chute had opened from the sodden air above, releasing the moisture it was no longer able to hold. Within minutes Little Carl's rabbit fur cap had collected enough snow to make it appear doubled in size. Frances pulled her hat further down over her ears and the buffalo robe up to her neck. Her eyelashes were thick with snow. The world had become white, the sky and the land distinguished by texture only. Coming into the trees along the Sheyenne, Frances realized by the temporary protection they offered the extent to which the wind had picked up. Even here the road was getting harder to distinguish from the space around it and they were almost upon the bridge before they saw it before them. Still, Frances felt a surge of relief to know that the bulk of the trip was behind them and there remained no more than two miles yet to travel.

A blizzard may be described objectively by references to wind, to snow, and to dropping temperatures. A man or woman caught outdoors gauges its progress and severity in the gut. The snow that had been driving directly into the face of Dan and the wagon seemed to begin to swirl, and what was once north Frances thought could be just as easily west, or maybe south. Frances swallowed back the panic of vertigo, and looked hard toward the ground to her side of the wagon. She thought she could see where the taller tufts of dried grass by the side of the tracks formed a darker shadow. Holding fast to this image Frances felt her dizziness recede.

Twice Frances heard Little Carl call out a hoarse "Gee" to Dan and felt the wagon shift to the right, although neither time had Frances lost the shadow that she had believed were the snow-mounded grasses beside her. She did not know that the wagon had stopped completely until Little Carl yelled something at her, but even though she was sitting close enough to him to feel his body next to hers, she could not catch his words before the wind carried them away.

"What?" she turned and yelled back.

"He's losing the road." Frances felt Little Carl's breath against her chin as he shouted. "I got to get down and lead."

Little Carl did not wait for Frances' reply and in a minute was lost beside the moving dark before her that was Dan. Frances closed her eyes. Her toes and fingers burned, and she tried to wiggle them within her boots and mittens. Bending over her lap to point the top of her hat into the wind, Frances reached up to give her nose a squeeze under her muffler, and was grateful to feel it sting. For several minutes Frances rode like that, eyes shut, almost completely covered by the buffalo robe, aware that there was not one thing that she could do that would change her situation.

And then something felt different. Sickened now with panic, Frances lifted her head from the buffalo robe and squinted into the dark that was alive with swirling razors of ice and snow. It took her a moment to catch her breath against the wind. She could see nothing. No light remained in the day, no shadow below her promised that she still was upon the road, no body beside her said that she was not alone. There was only the assault of the blizzard and the sound of her own voice, tiny against the storm, yelling, "Carl! Carl! Carl!" Then she felt the wagon seat tilt beneath her and Little Carl was yelling into her ear. They had lost the road. He had no idea where they were. He was giving Dan his head and hoping that the horse could sense his way back to the barn. "Just hang on," he yelled. Frances felt Little Carl lift his arms and bring the reins hard down upon Dan's rump. The wagon jerked forward once again. The robe lifted away from her side, and Frances felt Little Carl climb under its protection. Together they rode on, directionless, inside a freezing tent of darkness.

The disorientation in space lent itself to a similar confusion in time, and Frances could not have said whether it was an hour or several hours later when Little Carl stirred next to her. For a moment she was alone again under the robe, and then Little Carl was back, shouting that she needed to get down. Exhilaration and gratitude surged through Frances. It did not matter that she was in pain, her fingers and toes numb, her back aching from leaning close to her knees to stay warmer. Soon she would be in her bed, with Kirsten placing warmed bricks at her feet and Anna gently chafing her hands.

Trying to help Frances down from the wagon, Little Carl stumbled and they both fell to the ground. Despite the deep cushion of snow the fall was jolting and hard, their bodies too cold to absorb the shock. Frances was the first to regain her feet. Turning in a full circle she looked for the lights that surely must be burning in the Bingham house, or in the supervisor's house, or in the bunkhouses. But all was dark. She felt Little Carl grab her around the waist, and move her toward an insubstantial shape before her, and then she was inside a pitch-black space no warmer than the wagon, but sheltered from the force of the wind, if not its howl, exaggerated now by whistling and creaking. She could sense Little Carl moving nearby.

"Carl?" she asked, surprised to find that her mouth refused to properly shape the word.

"Just a second," Carl slurred. "Got matches. Just can't–"

"What?" Frances said when Little Carl did not finish his sentence and then did not speak at all.

"Can't get my fingers to work. Hold on," and then there was a tiny light and Frances could see a pair of small, disembodied hands moving away from her before the room returned to darkness. A small thud told her that something had fallen to the ground. The clink of metal upon metal indicated that Little Carl had found a cabinet. Then again there was a tiny light, and then more, and then there was Little Carl's face behind the candle that he held in his hands.

"Where are we?" Frances asked, an involuntary shudder punctuating her question.

"Hold this," Little Carl said, handing Frances the shaking candle while lighting another from its flame. "Over here. Hold it up."

Turning in a circle in unison with Little Carl, Frances could see that they were in a claim shanty not quite half the size of her sitting room.

Newspaper-lined walls heaved and fluttered. The floor was packed dirt. There were two hand-made chairs of twisted saplings and board odds and ends. A three-legged stool. A table of three separate rough planks resting on two sawhorses. Two wooden crates nailed to shiplap served as a cupboard. On another crate sitting upended beside the stool there was a kerosene lamp with no kerosene. A small cook stove stood at the opposite end of the shanty. The wood box nearby was empty. And in the corner, where Frances expected to find a bed, there was a long, deep, pine box.

"Old Andy Cooligan. I'll be damned."

"Who? What? Carl, where are we?"

Instead of answering her question, Little Carl asked one of his own, speaking slowly to keep his words recognizable. "Don't reckon Dan would fit through the door, do you? Probably be O.K. up against the shanty out of the wind, but we could use his heat. Here, hold this. Careful, don't drop it. Got to get him unhitched at least. See if you can get a fire started."

Everything that happened in the next hour should have taken ten minutes. Unhitched, Dan would not be led away from the small space out of the direct force of the wind that he had found against the shack, and Little Carl had little faith that the clumsy knot he tied would hold the horse to the wagon should he decide to wander off later in the night. Hugging his way against the shanty so that he would not lose his way back to the door, Little Carl returned to find that Frances had not started a fire.

"There's newspaper to get it started," Frances moved her arms toward the walls, "but not a stick of kindling. I tried and tried to break apart those chairs, but–"

"But you didn't have a proper tool," Little Carl said, lifting the pump shaft that he had dragged in behind him.

With the cupboard crates, the wood box, and the three-legged stool broken up and the stove lit, Frances began to feel safer, if not warmer. Little Carl, she noticed, could not stop the shivering that had begun the moment he first entered the cabin. His face was wet, as was the top of his undershirt, whether from melting snow or perspiration Frances did not know.

"You look like you are soaked to the skin, Carl," Frances said. "I think it might be wise to take off your inside clothes and let them dry next to the stove. You can roll yourself up in the buffalo robe in the meantime."

The look of horror that met this suggestion almost kept Frances from repeating it, but the man was visibly shaking and could not stop his teeth from chattering.

"I am serious. I think that given the situation we may relax proprieties for the night."

"Wh-wh-what makes you think we'll be going anywhere t-t-tomorrow?"

The thought that this blizzard would extend beyond the morning had not occurred to Frances, although she had grown used to storms lasting much longer. Once again she took careful stock of their situation. The shanty clearly had not been inhabited for awhile, and there was no food or water there, although there was snow aplenty to melt, and there were several bags of flour and cornmeal under a tarp in the wagon, as well as a tub of syrup, another of molasses, and a crate of tinned fruit. Much more frightening was the limited supply of burnable wood. Then Frances realized that Little Carl had turned her from the topic.

"It won't help anything to have you come down with a fever from sitting in wet clothes."

At this Little Carl stood and shrugged out of his winter coat and laid it by Frances' boots and mittens next to the stove. Then he reached for the tattered blanket that they had found at the bottom of the long homemade box in the corner.

"I don't know what good that does, Carl. You're still shivering. At least take the robe. It's so much warmer. Give me the blanket."

"Blanket's liable to be pretty l-l-lively," Carl answered.

Had Little Carl's refusal had to do with warmth, Frances would have continued to argue. Instead she said, "How do you know that this is Cooligan's claim shanty? Where is he? Where are we?"

Little Carl nodded toward the corner where the large box sat. "Cooligan m-m-mucks out stalls at Hadley's Livery in Fargo during the winter in exchange for a place to sleep. He proved up the claim a couple of y-y-years ago so he don't have to live here between harvesting and planting. I guess he just ain't got 'round to putting up something more permanent. He's the only settler I know said to sleep in a c-c-coffin. Didn't believe the stories myself, but there it is. That puts us—" Little Carl's sentence was interrupted by a violent shivering fit, after which he seemed to forget that he had been speaking.

"Are you all right?"

"Chilled through is all."

"That puts us where?" Frances prompted Carl.

"We must a' got turned around pretty soon after crossing the bridge. We're over a mile north and still east of the farm. No wonder Dan kept trying to get left on me."

"It isn't much," Frances said, looking around at the walls that continued to shudder in the storm, "but we were lucky to find it. Thank you, Carl." It was meant as an apology.

"Thank Dan," Little Carl said. "There's going to be more than one frozen soul thawed out in hell after this storm. It c-c-come on about as fast as any I've seen. Stand up for a minute, Miss Frances, so I can bust up that chair. Then you can help me drag that box over here. Inside that box, next to the stove, and under the buffalo robe, and you'll be fine for the night."

"What will you do?"

"I'm going to bust up those planks and saw horses and then s-s-sit on this here chair and hope they keep the fire going for a good long time."

With the coffin arranged next to the stove, Frances was about to step in, but hesitated.

"You'll f-f-forget where you are once you're asleep." Little Carl paused before adding, "I promise not to put the l-l-lid on."

It was the first smile that Little Carl had bothered with all day, and it allowed Frances to admit why she was hesitating. "I was actually wondering how... Well, it doesn't seem quite possible to... Oh, dear," Frances looked away from Little Carl, "we are indeed thrown into a rather intimate situation here, and, well, perhaps it would be safe for me to just step outside for a moment."

"It would not, so don't even think about it."

"But—"

"Here." Little Carl stood and walked the two feet with his candle to where the crates had hung, returning with a tin coffeepot. "I better go check one more time on Dan. I won't let loose of the wall." Shrugging back into his wet coat, Little Carl stepped to the door and opened it just wide enough to let himself through, but even that was enough to raise the tenor of the wind's howl from a roar to a shriek. When he returned Frances had arranged herself in the coffin with the buffalo robe tucked around her. She was still cold, but no longer frightened. She had been silent for quite some time before suddenly asking, "Why does he sleep in a pine box?"

"Never heard. Maybe 'cause you never know when you're going to d-d-d—" Another convulsive shudder interrupted Little Carl. "Die," he finished.

Frances did not believe that she would fall asleep in a coffin on an earthen floor in front of a cook stove in a homestead shanty with the wind wailing and the walls threatening to come down around her at any moment. When she woke she didn't know if she had slept for hours or simply dozed off for a moment. Sitting up she could just make out Little Carl in silhouette, rocking in the blanket on the keg chair next to the stove. An involuntary shudder that shook his entire frame released a small groan, almost feminine in its pathos. One candle remained lit next to him.

"I am almost too warm here, Carl, with my coat and the buffalo robe as well."

Little Carl started at Frances' voice, and sat up on his chair.

"Which do you want?" Frances spoke again.

"I'm fine."

"No you're not, and you will do me no favors if you get sick on me here. I am counting on you to get us home. Please." Frances stood within the coffin and moved as if to hand the buffalo robe to Little Carl.

"Just hand me the coat, then, and get back under that robe."

Frances slept fitfully after that, her dreams filled with wondering whether she were asleep or awake. Often she believed herself to be watching Little Carl as he softly stroked the soft lamb collar of her coat as he continued to rock. Only when she realized that she expected to open her eyes upon Kirsten and Anna sitting before her was Frances sure that she had been sleeping. It was the sound of Little Carl bringing the pump shaft down upon the coffin lid in the corner that had awakened her.

The morning brought very little light to the windowless shanty, while outside the storm continued, undiminished. Despite Little Carl's warning the night before, Frances realized by her disappointment that she had expected the worst to be over. Little Carl had already emptied the coffee pot, fed Dan from one of the cornmeal sacks, and was fashioning hard cakes of cornbread, flour, and water. Throughout the day, Frances attempted to engage Little Carl in conversation to help the time pass, but the forced intimacy of space was slowly lessening the ease that had developed between them over the years in the cookhouse. To Frances' questions about his past, Little Carl had answered, "There ain't nothin' more to say on that 'count." When Little Carl did talk it was to tell stories of past blizzards he had lived through, complete with details of how those who had not been so fortunate had met their deaths. Several of his tales were about men who were found in snow banks within feet of their houses, having fallen down and given up without knowing that they were so near to safety. Then there was the story of the entire herd of cows that had frozen to death standing up, and had remained standing in the sub-freezing winter weather for two more months until they thawed and dropped one by one in the spring. Most disconcerting to Frances was Little Carl's account of a settler near Fort Thompson who, stranded unprepared in his claim shanty during a five-day blizzard, had slowly begun tearing down the studs of his home to burn, and was discovered after the storm huddled frozen into the northwest corner that was all that remained of his shack. This is when Frances learned that Carl was about to begin breaking boards from the wagon, now that there remained nothing inside Cooligan's shack to burn except the pine coffin. Despite Frances' insistence that she, too, could sleep wrapped in the buffalo robe next to the stove, Little Carl appeared to have taken it as a matter of personal pride that she not.

Not long after a second meal of cornmeal and flour cakes, while Little Carl dozed before the stove wrapped tightly in the blanket that had become pungent with the stove's heat, Frances lifted her head from her arms where she had been sitting in her box, aware that the sound of the storm had changed. She was about to speak, but then decided not to wake Little Carl, who had settled into a series of regular whimpers while asleep, but no longer shivered. A thump and scrape against the side of the shanty brought Frances to her feet and to the door. It opened inward, revealing a waist-high hard bank of snow. The snow had stopped and the wind had subsided dramatically and Frances looked out upon an expanse of frozen waves of white. Another loud thud from the other side of the shanty sent Frances scrambling over the bank in front of the door and around the corner, where Dan was doing his best to get free of the wagon. She had just taken Dan by the head when Little Carl appeared. Although he was smiling, the past twenty-four hours had taken a toll on his strength, and he did not argue when Frances offered to help lift the harness onto Dan.

The smiles quickly faded when it became clear that the horse simply could not gain sufficient purchase in the banks that had swirled around the leeward side of the shanty to pull the wagon free.

"If it were Raleigh, we could ride double," Frances said.

"If it was Raleigh we'd be dead about now," Little Carl answered, and then added, "and Dan don't strike me as being so particular. We can get on from the wagon. Do you want front or back? I ain't particular myself."

It was slow going for the big workhorse through the deep drifts, and it didn't take long before he was covered in sweat despite the freezing temperature. Within minutes of the ride Frances' fingers and toes were once again numb. Behind her she could feel Little Carl shiver. And then they were within sight of the big Bingham house, a towering square set into an island of outbuildings, surrounded by an undulating yet motionless ocean of snow. Slowly they moved closer, Dan now straining harder against the drifts, and only then did Frances allow herself think about how miserable and cold and terrified she was. She thought she could make out tiny sparkles in each of the house windows, and wondered what they could be, shining into the whiteness of the day that was all light with nothing illuminated. A sudden half-start by Dan almost unsettled his riders, and Frances looked down upon a frozen ox lying on its side, half-buried in the snow, a lead rope around its neck.

"What was it doing out here?" Frances asked, and felt Little Carl shrug behind her in answer. Both knew that the real question had to do with what had become of the man or woman at the other end of the lead rope. They were almost past the frozen beast when it spoke.

Frances and Little Carl put their heels against the sides of Dan in surprise, starting the horse again. Then the frozen ox spoke again, in what Frances had come to understand was a Yiddish accent. *"Mein Gott,"* came the voice. "Is it a person?"

"Who's there?" Frances shouted, and then added, "Where?"

The words that came back were muffled. "In here! Give only a look!"

"In where? Oh, my God, Carl. It's Jack. He's inside the ox. Jack, are you all right?"

"Can't move."

Little Carl spoke quietly, into Frances' ear. "I'm half froze. If I get down, I'll never get back up. We need to leave him here and send someone back. Nothing we can do."

Shaw could not have heard Little Carl, and yet he spoke as if to answer.

"No time."

Frances slid off Dan, doing her best not to knock Little Carl off in the process, but needing to reach up to steady him upon the horse's wide back nonetheless. Breaking through snow past her knees, she made her way to the side of the ox. She could see now that its throat had been cut and its belly slit. A frozen mound of snow-capped entrails lay nearby in the space sheltered from the wind by the ox's belly. Bending to the incision that gaped open three to four inches, Frances searched for a face within, but could see nothing but snow and a crusted black ice. She explained that she and Little Carl were on Dan, but that they did not have the wagon to tie the ox to. She would send someone out to rescue him as soon as they reached the farmyard. When Shaw did not answer, Frances called out his name. This time Shaw replied, but his words were difficult to make out and she had to ask him to speak again. He had to explain to her twice how to cross the thick wagon reins over Dan's chest, cross them again over his back, and then attach them to the rope around the ox's neck. "Only chance," he said. Again, what should have taken a few minutes seemed interminable. Frances had no feeling in her fingers and was using her two hands together like a single pincer. She had no confidence that the fat knot she had managed to tie in the reins would hold against the weight of the ox, even if the lead rope did not break.

And then there was nothing to do but to tell Little Carl to hold on, to give Dan another slap on his haunches, and to trudge behind the path flattened by the ox's carcass, for there was no way to get back onto the horse.

They were within fifty yards of the farmyard when Frances saw a handful of men running as fast as they could through the drifts toward them, and she dropped to her knees. She did not know which of the hired men picked her up and carried her to the house. Seeing the candles burning in every window, faint gleams in the early dusk, she wondered for a moment if it were Christmas. Over her bearer's shoulder Frances saw another man carrying Little Carl in precisely the same fashion, although he was struggling to be set back down. He seemed so small in the stock hand's arms that she wanted to call out to the man to be careful. Perhaps she did. A third man was leading Dan and his burden toward the barn while calling out to a fourth to bring a saw from the blacksmith shop. At the door of the Bingham house, Kirsten waited, gesturing and calling to Frances' carrier to hurry, and then saying something to him in Norwegian. The warmth of the house hit Frances at once, releasing her from consciousness. The last thing she saw before she fainted was Anna asleep in the parlor, her head resting against the back of the sofa where she sat.

CHAPTER XLII

In Which Always is Always (Maybe)

At first Miss Anna she says, "We must pray for their safe return," and then she says, "Surely they would have stayed in Fargo when they saw the storm approaching," and then she says, "Yes, that is what they would have done. Frances is with Percy. She is safe," and then she says, "My hip is causing me great pain this evening, Kirsten. I must lie down. Please have Mrs. Ford prepare a tray for me for supper." Mr. John Bingham he says that there is nothing to be done but to wait and hope for the best. If they are on the road, he says, Dan will get them home, and if they are still in Fargo, so much the better. Wait and hope, John Bingham says. Wait and pray, Miss Anna says.

Hope and pray I do, but I am not so good to wait. So first it is a candle I put in every window. Then I bundle up and go outside to see how much the light they show, but already it is dangerous to go far from the house, so in I go back. It is not so very much later that it is Mr. Johnson at the kitchen door with icicles in his beard and he has good and bad news, and the good news is that the two stock hands who had gone to the cornfield to herd the cattle in had made it back in the storm, and it was my lights in the house they followed, too, but the bad news is that Jack Shaw did not come back, and what does Mr. Bingham want him to do. Mr. Bingham he just shakes his head and says it would be madness to go out onto the prairie to look for Jack Shaw now. Wait and hope for the best, he says. Wait and pray for his safe return, Miss Anna says.

Well, I know they are right and it is not good to go out into a blizzard, but I think that it is almost as bad to do nothing inside because maybe it is Frances and Little Carl, and now Jack Shaw all lost in the storm, so now it is Mrs. Ford who is so full with worry, too, but at least she does not say that all we are to do is to hope and pray. Gather all the mirrors, she says, and that is good because for a little while we are busy finding this mirror and that and then putting each one behind a candle in the upstairs windows to make the light there two times so bright. All night we are looking for something more to do even if it is just to keep bricks warm and to make a big kettle of stew because it is any minute maybe that Dan brings Frances and Little Carl home, because that is what I am thinking, and it is about Jack Shaw that Mrs. Ford worries, but we just try to do and do. There is nothing to say, except when I say, "Go to bed now, Mrs. Ford, and I will wake you if there is something to hear," or when Mrs. Ford says, "Go to bed now, Kirsten, and I will wake you if there is news," but we do not go to bed and it is such a long night with the wind that sounds like a scream and the windows that rattle, and even when it is at last the morning there is still the storm and the scream and the rattle and so I change the candles again. Then Howie he wakes up and wants his mother, and so I say right out loud to him the thing that I can not say to anyone else. "I want her to come home right now, too," and then I tell a little lie, I say, "She will be home soon, Howie." I say it to make me feel good, but it is good for him, too, and pretty soon he is happy again because he is a little boy and he believes me.

Nothing at all do we hear from Mr. Johnson because it is too dangerous to go from one house to the other, we can not even see the big barn from the kitchen window, it is that bad, but then after noon the wind lets up just a little and that is when I put on my coat and hat and boots and mittens and climb up the outside steps that are right outside my bedroom that I share with Mrs. Ford and sometimes a spare girl, and it is slippery and windy and dangerous I think, but then I am on the funny look-out that is on top of the roof that is where Frances likes to stand, and I can only stay there for a minute, it is so cold. I am afraid that I will blow right off of the house, and it is hard to breathe and there is nothing that I can see but still the snow blowing. I have to hold on to the railing with both hands and walk backwards to keep from falling down the stairs, but pretty soon it is back up there again I am. And so it is all afternoon up and down, and down and up, and then I can see the barn again and then there it is something that I see, and I am happy because there is something to see, but I am sad because it can not be Frances and Little Carl because what I see is not big like a wagon, but for sure there is something coming toward the house, and I run downstairs and I am shouting, "Someone is coming! Someone is coming!" and I am out of the house and stumbling through the snow to get to the bunkhouse and all the time I am yelling "Help! Help! Someone is coming!" And then I am back in the house, and Mrs. Ford I am sure is thinking that it is Jack Shaw that is back and we are wrapping the bricks in flannel and pouring the hot water into pans and then I run to the door and it is Frances in the arms of big Ole Halvorson, and I think maybe I am to cry but there is too much to do. Mrs. Ford she helps me get Frances into bed, and big Ole Halvorson, who is a good man, he waits outside the bedroom door making a puddle, because he wants to tell Mrs. Ford that it is Jack Shaw inside the frozen ox, and I say, "Go, I will tend to Frances." So go she goes, but first she says that she will wake Miss Anna to help, and I say, "no." Just like that, I say, "no."

Well, it is very clear that it is a doctor that we need but now it is dark and we can not know if the storm is over for good, and John Bingham says that no one is to go out upon the prairie until the next morning, and so it is more with the waiting and the praying, and it is now Mrs. Ford and me and sometimes Miss Anna, except that Mrs. Ford is back and forth to the bunkhouse to tend to Jack Shaw, and Miss Anna says (and here I will tell you that Miss Anna has not been so very nice to me since she is back from St. Paul, but here she does the good thing), so anyway, Miss Anna says that Jack Shaw and Little Carl are to be brought into the house so they can be taken care of better, but Mrs. Ford says that maybe that is not a good idea because Jack Shaw can not help but to cry out because he is in so much of the pain. She says that he is still all curled up like when they cut him out of the ox and that he thinks that he is on fire. I wish that Frances would cry out but she does not move, she does not even open her eyes, she is like she is not there still. But I was talking about bringing in Jack Shaw and Little Carl to the big house, and so Mrs. Ford says, no, it will frighten Houghton to hear a man scream so and she can see to Jack Shaw in the bunkhouse until the doctor comes, and about Little Carl, well that is something else. No, that is something else *entirely*, as Mrs. Harkness used to say. Because here is what it is entirely with Little Carl.

When it was big Ole Halvorson with Frances it was Kevin McCoy who had Little Carl, and I guess he just fought and fought and even did curse until Kevin McCoy put him down in the cookhouse, and then just like that Little Carl he jumped into his bedroom in the cookhouse and threw the bolt on the door and no matter what anyone said he just said, "Leave me alone. I am fine." And every time it was on her way back to the big house from the bunkhouse she was, Mrs. Ford would stop by the cookhouse and call to Little Carl through the door and it was always, "Leave me alone. I am fine." And then finally it was morning and the wind had blown away the storm for sure and the clouds, too, and there was all of a sudden just a blue, blue sky over the prairie that is pure white and this is Dakota for you because you think that for beautiful there can be nothing else like it on the earth, and then you think that probably here and there under the beautiful is someone dead who does not get to wake up after the storm to see the sun and the blue and the white that now does sparkle like a story in the fairy tales that Far did tell once upon a time.

So now it is safe to send a man to Fargo for Dr. Harkness, and he comes right away and Mr. Percy Bingham is with him, and Dr. Harkness puts his stethoscope (that is just the right word because Dr. Harkness wrote it down for me) onto the chest of Frances, and he looks so serious and he tells Miss Anna just what to do, and that means that he tells me just what to do, too, because he is looking at Miss Anna but I know that he is really talking to me. Then he goes to see Jack Shaw, and about

Frances and Jack Shaw he says the same thing, that we would know pretty soon if it was fingers and toes that they are to lose, or maybe more, but besides that he has different things to say because Jack Shaw is awake and in terrible "anguish," but Frances will not wake up. She does toss and turn and moan and sometimes she fights to get out of the bed, and it takes two of us to hold her down, and she calls out but it is not to make sense, because what she says is, "Let me out! I am not dead, I tell you!" But about Little Carl there is not one thing that Dr. Harkness can do because Little Carl says that no doctor is going to come near him with his "bag of tricks," and that he can make his own (this is his word) poultices that are better than anything any doctor can do for his cough. Well, that Little Carl is stubborn is not news to anyone, but since he is getting up and down and he says that he is fine and Frances and Jack Shaw are not, we leave him alone.

At first it is every other day that Dr. Harkness he comes to see Frances, and that is a long trip to make forth and back from Fargo so very often and for Jack Shaw it is lucky he is to live on a bonanza farm because this is to get good care, and it is from Dr. Harkness that we hear the stories from the blizzard. The very worst one, it could make you cry, is about the teacher from the Canfield Station school that went with her two students that had the longest walk home to see that they were safe and the three of them they found not even two rods from the children's home but on the other side, so they must have walked right past the house, and Dr. Harkness said that they were like a statue with the little boy and the little girl huddled so close to the teacher and her with her arms and her cloak around them and the little boy and the little girl with their hands together like they were praying. And that is a pretty picture, but it is still sad and they are still dead.

Mr. Percy Bingham he was here for four days, but he did not know what to do, he would sometimes sit in the room with Frances and he would read from a book, but not out loud, and not very much did he look at her, and about Frances and Mr. Percy Bingham I do not understand, in fact, sometimes I wonder how that little boy got born in the first place, it is so much apart from each other they are even when they are together. You might say that it is not my business and of course you are right, and I do not care so much about what is right anymore because what is right does not make sense and what is wrong does not

seem wrong and if you think that is all mixed up then you are right. So
sometimes Mr. Percy he was with Frances (but not really with Frances)
and sometimes he was with Miss Anna (who is not really with anyone
anymore, if you ask me), and sometimes he was with Howie and that
was a good thing because it is very much that the little boy wants to
be around his father even if it is clear that they do not know what to
do with each other. Once when I was downstairs I saw Mr. Percy go to
the sideboard in the dining room to pick up the bottle of brandy, but
then he set it right back down, and not until it was dark did he put the
brandy into a glass to drink, and that is a good thing, because Mr. Percy
is a little bit like Far, I think, and no, he does not come into the house
with his eyes swollen shut and straw in his hair and with the smell like
he has been sleeping in the mud or in the barn or in his own you-know-
what, but that is the difference between a rich man and a poor man, I
guess. So anyway, after four days it is back to Fargo Mr. Percy Bingham
goes because it is work he says he has to do, and then it is just me and
Miss Anna with Frances.

And that is not so good now.

Because still Frances she does not wake up, but now she is talking,
and sometimes it is about how her neck hurts, and sometimes it is to
call out for Miss Anna, and over and over she says not to bury her, and
once she said, "Lean back," and then she said, "Trust me." And it was
then that I just wanted to go to her and hold her against me and say,
"I do. I do trust you," but I am the housekeeper and what I can do is
empty the chamber pot, and change the sheets, and bring the bowl of
water back and forth for Miss Anna to dip the cloth into to put onto
Frances' forehead because she does sweat and sweat even though she
shakes with cold. And Miss Anna I can tell is now trying to stay awake
more for Frances, and at night she says that it is Mrs. Ford who is to
sit with her, but me Miss Anna sends out of the house to help cook for
the winter crew because Little Carl can not yet, or to see to Howie (that
Miss Anna says I am to call Houghton), who is starting to complain and
to whine. It is just scared he is because Miss Anna finally let him in to
see his mother and so wide his eyes did go then because her face is swollen and there are patches of skin that are now peeling off because of
the frostbite and that, Dr. Harkness says, is a good thing because there
is circulation there and the same is true of her feet and hands. But Jack

Shaw is not so lucky, his fingers and toes are turning black. Dr. Harkness says that the best that can be hoped for there is that it is just fingers and toes and probably an ear that he will lose, but I was talking about Frances and what Howie did see, and what he says is, "What is wrong with Mama's hair?" And he is right because it is like an old rag on the pillow and not like hair does it look at all, at least not like Frances' hair.

So, even though Miss Anna tries to keep me away from Frances, sometimes at night I say to Mrs. Ford, go now to Jack Shaw, and I will sit here, and this Miss Anna does not know because she is in her bed, and so there I am and it is a week after the storm and still Frances does not know where she is, but she shivers and she calls out and she says that she is thirsty, but only a spoonful or two of broth does she take, and then she says, "Anna, don't go. I am sorry. Anna, please don't go." This she says over and over, and then I start to cry, I just cry and cry and I suppose it is because I am so very, very tired.

Then, it is the morning of the eighth day, I come in from feeding the men their breakfast and there is no Miss Anna with Frances, so I get the magazine from the sitting room next door that I think Frances was reading before to Fargo she went and it is open to a story by Mr. Charles Reade that she likes so much and it has the title, "Man's Life Saved by Fowls, and Woman's by a Pig," and I think that Frances would like to hear this more than another chapter from the Bible that is all Miss Anna reads to Frances, and so I start to read right out loud and I can tell that this is to be a good story because it says, "Men's lives have been sometimes taken, sometimes saved, by other animals, in ways that sound incredible until the details are given," and pretty soon I am so interested in the story that I do not even hear Miss Anna come into the room, and I jump right up out of the chair when she says, "What do you think you are doing?"

And I say, "I am reading to Miss Frances, and she is just now quiet so I did not want to stop."

Miss Anna makes herself stand up very straight and I think that maybe she will stamp her cane down she looks so upset and what she says is, "I do not think that is a good idea. Frances has a very particular ear."

So I say, "Yes, ma'am."

I put down the magazine and I am just about to the door when she says, "Has she spoken?"

And I say, "It is the same. Sometimes she talks, but not to make sense."

"She did not... she did not mention my name?" Miss Anna asks.

"She said your name many times, Miss Anna," I say, "and once even she did say my name, and then it was for her mother that she called."

Miss Anna just nodded and said that I could go now, and that I was to show the doctor up when he arrived. And so it is not so very much later that I am in the room with Frances and Miss Anna again with the doctor, and he is surprised and not happy at all to see that Frances is still not awake because the last time he was here it was three days ago and then he said that she was getting better and here she was not better at all, and maybe even worse, he said, because her fever was "elevated" and this he said could not be "sustained." This is what he said exactly, he said, "The fever must break soon or else there is danger of perma-nent damage to the mind. The next twenty-four hours are critical." And because it is Frances Bingham who is sick, who is a friend of the wife of Dr. Harkness, that is, my very own teacher, Mrs. Harkness, and because Frances is the daughter-in-law of a bonanza farmer, Dr. Harkness says that he will stay overnight, but it is also because this is the day that he is to begin cutting off the fingers and toes of Jack Shaw whose mind is fine and is without a fever, but in his fingers and toes there is no blood. But it is about Frances that I am thinking and what I am thinking is 'twenty-four hours, twenty-four hours, twenty-four hours' and I am thinking that no matter what Miss Anna says I am going to be there beside Fran-ces whenever I can be.

Well, I guess Miss Anna was then too scared to chase me away, and so when I am not cooking for the men or trying to keep Howie happy or doing the laundry in the cellar (because there was even more and more of it with a sick person in the house), I am looking in on Frances, and then, finally, I think that I am about to get sick myself I am that tired and Dr. Harkness says that he will sit with Frances during the night and Miss Anna and I are to get some sleep. He says that we will know nothing until she comes out of her "delirium" and that is when we will know if she is to "recover, mind and body." And I think that there will be no sleep for me and what I am thinking about is not about Frances sick but about Frances healthy and about Miss Anna, who is for so long now wanting to sleep all the time, but for the past few days is sometimes like she will jump out of her skin and sometimes asleep in her chair, but that is because of the brown bottle, I think, and so here is another someone who is a little like Far, too. But even that is not what I am thinking about because really I am thinking about why Miss Anna is no longer so nice to me, because before she went to St. Paul to stay with the old lady it was Miss Anna more than Frances who was nice, and that was because of the good things that Mrs. Harkness said about me, that is what I think. And then I think to myself, Kirsten Knudson, you are not being honest. It is not just Miss Anna who is different. You are different, too. You do not want to be nice to Miss Anna so much any more.

So there I am, thinking so hard and knowing that I am not to sleep no matter what Dr. Harkness says that I am to do. And then it is like it is one minute later and I am awake and so I think that I must have fallen asleep, but it is still dark. Mrs. Ford she is sound asleep next to me and she was not there before so I know for sure that I did sleep, but there is something that I need to remember and then I know that I have been dreaming but it is a dream that is not new and it is as much something that I remember as it is a dream. It is Frances helping Miss Anna into a buggy and I am a little girl watching and Miss Anna looks down at Frances and on her face there is such a beautiful smile and then I am in the buggy and I am not a little girl and I am looking down at Frances and there is a look like never have I seen before and there is something in the gray eyes that are silver with black cracks and I think that I will cry because they are looking at me like that and then I see that they are not looking at me at all but at Miss Anna, and right there I know that I am awake because there is such a pain in my chest.

I know what it is. It is to be jealous. It is what is the "green-eyed monster" that is in the books that Frances reads to me, and it is a terrible thing. Well, I just get out of bed and I do those things that I need to do as fast as I can because I think that I must get to Frances' room right now, and my hair is still down but I do not care I must get there right now, and when I get there I look at the doctor and I do not have to say a thing because it is so serious he looks and he shakes his head, and then he stands and whispers that he will return within the hour and I am to stay with Frances until then, so I go to her side, and lift the clean cloth from the fresh water that I did bring, and when I lay it upon her forehead, she opens her eyes, just like that.

Well, it is like the time that I was to help Sten with the roof on Homer's house, and off the ladder I fell and my breath was knocked right out of my body, and no sound could I make, but I could feel the tears about to come, so I look away and when I look back Frances' eyes they are closed again. I do not let go of her hand that is very hot. And just when I am sure that Frances is again asleep, she says, "How long have I been here?" and I say, "Nine days," and then again she is quiet. I think, well, that will be all for now for sure because still she does not open her eyes, but then she asks, "When did you get back?" and I do not know what to say, so I do not say anything, and then she says, "How long have you been here?" Well, maybe it is not right for me to answer because I do not know if it is really me that she is talking to, but I say what I am thinking and that is "always," and this makes Frances smile.

It is not like the smile of Frances that she has when sometimes I say a thing that is not on purpose to be funny but for some reason it makes her laugh right out loud, no, it is more like a sweet smile like she does sometimes give to Howie and to no one else, and then I think, no, it is like the smile that she gave to Miss Anna when she helped her into the buggy on that very first day, and it is like the smile that she gives to me only in my dream, and this is what I am thinking, and I think well now maybe I am going to cry a little, and then Frances says, "Will you stay?"

Now I have the tears for real and I say, "Yes."

And Frances says, "Always?"

And I say "Yes, I will stay always."

And there I am crying like a baby and I do not know why exactly, maybe, and in comes Dr. Harkness and right away he moves to Frances and he puts his hand upon her forehead and then he lifts the hand that I am not holding and he puts his fingers on her wrist and I know that he is feeling for her pulse and he says, "Her fever has broken. See, Kirsten, how the sleep is different now. We won't have long to wait. Go," he says. "Tell Anna and John the news as soon as they are up." And I am almost to the door when the doctor says, "Kirsten," and I turn and he says, "They are lucky to have you."

Well, that is what happened, and from then on it was all better for Frances because it was not even two hours later that Frances woke and here she was weak but thirsty enough to drink a little broth and full of questions about Little Carl and Jack Shaw and ready to tell all about the blizzard and the night and day in the shanty, and she was so surprised to find out that she had been nine days without knowing a thing and what she remembered about the nine days was not right because she said that she was sure that she had been put into a coffin and that someone was trying to bury her alive, and then she explained about Andy Cooligan. And we all knew that she was getting better when she made Dr. Harkness grow very stern because she said that she "did not intend" to stay in bed for another two weeks, and it was when he said that was not all, that she was to rest and not to leave the house for a month after that still, that there was the old look in her eyes, but the doctor was not one bit afraid of the eyes of Frances Bingham, and that is that, he said.

"We'll see," Frances said.

Just one more thing.

It was not until four days after Frances woke up for good in her right mind that she said to me as I was bringing her tray into the room, "Kirstie, it is Dan that saved our lives, but for the life of me I can not get an image out of my mind about holding on to a pig's tail as it pulled me to safety through the snow." Well, that made me laugh, and since Miss Anna had gone downstairs to say good-bye to Lydia Harkness, who had come out with Dr. Harkness to "see the patient" now that she was better, I found the story by Mr. Charles Reade, and again I did read the whole thing out loud. And it made Frances laugh, and that made me laugh, and then Frances looked at me and said, "Were you here all the time, Kirstie?" And I said, without even thinking, because that is what I do, I said, "Always."

CHAPTER XLIII

In Which a Monster is Revealed and a Friend is Lost: I

The February blizzard, a reminder of the deadly caprice of even the mildest Dakota winter, was followed by an exceptionally warm March and an April of long, soaking rains. Frances' recovery had been steady, although her temper had not been similarly improved by the restrictions imposed upon her by Dr. Harkness and reinforced by the wet weather. Only to Kirsten did she confess to a lingering fatigue and weakness. To John Bingham and Anna she was more likely to protest against the tedium of idleness. To Percy, busy with his new public role as Cass County's Republican candidate for the territory's upcoming legislative session, Frances had very little to say, since he was very seldom around. Easter came and went, and while Frances remained on the Bingham farm to recuperate under the care of Anna and Kirsten, Percy took up residence in their new home in Fargo.

At first the silent contest between Anna and Kirsten over the nursing of Frances took the predictable direction of unarticulated animosity, but hostility required a temperament foreign to Kirsten and a dedication that Anna could not sustain. As the days passed it was increasingly Kirsten who took advantage of every spare minute to tend to Frances. There were not, however, very many minutes to spare, as Kirsten was regularly pulled from her duties in the big house to help out in the crew cookhouse. Little Carl's recovery had been more accurately a series of relapses, and his determination to rise each morning as if he had gone to bed healthily the night before further exhausted his increasingly frail body. With the help of Kirsten and Mrs. Ford, Little Carl was able to keep the farm's small winter crew of stock hands fed, but even with the return of the Swedish sisters he was clearly in no condition to keep up with the expanding crew of laborers who had begun to arrive for spring plowing and planting. He knew well, each time he dropped to a chair next to the stove to rest before continuing to knead the dough for yet another loaf of bread, that he was a man about to lose his job. From Kirsten he learned that Frances had asked Mr. Johnson to give him a few more weeks to recover, but the reprieve gave him little hope. No supervisor was going to risk setting a hundred or so hungry farm hands down to a scant table at the end of a twelve-hour day in the field.

Then came the morning that Little Carl simply did not get out of bed, nor would he speak to Kirsten who tapped at the door that separated his room from the cookhouse kitchen. For three days, Kirsten and Mrs. Ford and the Swedish sisters, now assisted by Hege Larson and the blacksmith's new bride, managed to keep the growing crew fed, but it was a situation quickly deteriorating, a kitchen full of cooks with no one in charge to plan the meals or to order supplies. On the fourth day,

Mr. Johnson introduced the women to the new head cook he'd plucked from the Dwight bonanza farm. Little Carl was told to move his things to the bunkhouse with the other men the next day. He would be kept on as his replacement's assistant provided he could keep up with the work. Little Carl did not stir from his bed as the supervisor spoke to him from the door, but he did mutter a hoarse, "That's it, then," in response.

Plenty of folks reach the point of wishing they were dead, but not too many get to die precisely when they choose. The distance between the wishing and the choosing is the life between breaths and it's only the next one that's hard to give up. So maybe Little Carl was just plain lucky or maybe he was just plain determined, but the next morning he was just plain dead. The Swedish sisters, noticing that his door was ajar, discovered him lying on the covers of his bed, fully dressed but in his stocking feet. A clean pair of pants and a recently mended shirt were folded and placed atop a pair of boots at the foot of the bed. His winter coat and his rabbit fur cap hung from a peg by the door. All of his other possessions, odds and ends of clothing, his soft felt hat, a couple of books and a wallet, he had evidently fed into one of the kitchen stoves sometime in the night. His small room was tidy and swept. Beside the bed there was one piece of furniture, an overturned crate upon which sat a kerosene lamp. There had never been a picture or an ornament or a mirror on the walls. A large metal pot showing the imprint of a horse-shoe upon its bottom sat upside down by the bed and upon that was a cigar box held shut by a twist of 17-gauge wire. Wedged under the wire a scrap of paper carried the instructions, written in a tight, prim hand, "To be opened by Mrs. Frances Bingham ONLY."

The sisters did not have far to run with their news before coming face to face with Frances, for she had slipped out of the house well before dawn to feed a few lumps of sugar to Raleigh and to smell the fresh morning air, determined to test her strength with a brief walk before returning for another day of imprisonment. Frances had not spoken with Little Carl since their trauma together in the blizzard, but hearing from Kirsten the night before that the little man had taken to his bed and was to be replaced as head cook, she had decided that morning on a visit.

The dash to the cookhouse was enough to leave Frances gasping for breath. Reaching Little Carl's door she had to wait with her hand clutching the jamb to let a moment of lightheadedness pass. Once in

the bedroom she pulled the rough curtain to the side of the lone window to let the dim light of dawn fall across the bed and the body there.
Frances put her cheek first to Little Carl's lips and then her ear to his
chest, feeling a rough, ribbed undershirt underneath, but no breath. In
a gesture that seemed altogether too presumptuous, Frances reached up
to close the eyes open to the ceiling. She had forgotten about the two
women wedged into the doorway behind her until one of them spoke
in Swedish. Frances looked around in time to see the other sister shrug
in response.

"What to do?" the first sister translated.

"Get the men fed," Frances answered, adding, "Don't say anything
about this just yet." She shut the door behind the retreating women
before turning to the cigar box that bore her name. For a moment she
thought to return to the house, with her news and the box, but then she
looked back at Little Carl. She had never before seen him bare-headed,
not while he cooked, not while he ate, not during their night in Andy
Cooligan's claim shack. Whether it was the felt hat worn during the
warmer months, or the rabbit fur cap put on once the weather turned
cold, pulled low over his forehead and ears, it had enhanced the cantan-
kerous and solitary impression he presented to the world, an impression
that he had undone a dozen times in Frances' presence with the slip of a
thoughtful response. Frances bent to touch Little Carl's fine, sandy hair,
and then drew her hand down to cup for a moment the cold face of the
man who had saved her life. The jaw was pale and slack, and smooth
as a woman's. Frances straightened her back, looked out the window
into the soft light of the morning, picked up the box and sat down on
the overturned kettle.

She had expected to find a note of explanation, or instructions regarding his burial, or perhaps an address and a request that she notify
some distant relative of his death. Instead she found the meager belongings of a stranger, a letter and a bent photograph of a family of nine.
The father and mother sat sternly in straight back chairs. They could
have been aging twins of indeterminate sex with weak chins and close-
set eyes, the hair of each parted in the middle and combed tightly to the
head. The woman held a baby; the man, a toddler. A small girl in home-
spun, who looked to be little older than the toddler, leaned against the
mother's knee. Behind the parents stood four more children, three boys

and a girl, each one staring at the camera with a look of unblinking astonishment. At the bottom of the photograph the names of the children had been inked in. In the back were Amos, John, Claude and Clara. The little girl was Martha. The toddler, Robert, Jr. The baby, Alfred. There was no Carl.

Setting the photograph aside, Frances turned to the letter. Almost transparent with handling, it was addressed to "Dear Clara," and consisted of a litany of complaints and disasters. Claude had broken his leg in a fall from the roof of a neighbor's house where he had hired out to help with shingling. Pa's cough continued. Alfred remained sickly. The wheat had stayed in the milk too long and a poor harvest was expected. Clara was then instructed to be a good girl and to work hard for her Aunt Mary and Uncle John. By no means was she to come home now. Her Uncle John was not a "bad man," and the family needed the money that she sent home each month. The letter ended with what Frances supposed was meant to be a compliment: Aunt Mary had mentioned in her last letter that although Clara's mending was passable at best, her rabbit stew had become a favorite in Uncle John's tavern.

It was like hearing the final tumbler click before the lock springs open. Frances remained absolutely still, staring at the letter, seeing nothing, and seeing everything anew. She looked again at the date at the top of the letter. It had been written over twenty-five years ago. When she realized that she had been holding her breath, Frances looked up to study the face of the odd little man who had been an odder friend. She knew with absolute certainty that by leaving her this box he was asking her to be a friend in return. To be left alone was all he had asked of the world. It was up to her to see that this privacy not be violated now. Frances stood and walked quietly to the door to throw the bolt on the sturdy lock that Little Carl had installed there. She paused by the bed to light the kerosene lamp before pulling the flour sack curtain back across the window. Gently, as if approaching a frightened lover, Frances began undoing the buttons of the flannel shirt. She did not stop to wipe aside her tears, but let them fall upon the strip of sheeting that she slowly worked to unwind. The revelation, Frances realized, was surprising only to the extent to which she felt no real surprise, merely a tenderness that brought a small sob to her throat. Needing to lift the body away from the bed in order to rewind the binding, Frances pulled Little Carl into a sluggish embrace he certainly would have resisted alive. Gently she worked her friend back into the flannel shirt.

Frances straightened her back and wiped the tears from her cheeks, her fatigue for the moment indistinguishable from sorrow. There remained much to do. She would require help, but first she needed to make sure that no one else disturbed Little Carl's body. Putting the Swedish sisters in charge of guarding the door would suffice. Frances stooped to pick up the cigar box and heard a small click as something inside the box shifted. This time upon opening the box Frances discovered the rather obvious false bottom underneath the photograph and the letter. A moment's prying with her fingernail lifted the thin lath free to reveal the bone-handled pocketknife Houghton had so often begged to play with. "Later. When you're bigger," had been Little Carl's consistent response. Under the knife lay a thick yellow envelope with the words "For Kirsten Knudson" upon it. Frances opened the envelope but did not count the money inside. Along with telephones and stethoscopes, Little Carl had not trusted banks.

Frances' first stop upon leaving the cookhouse was the machine shed. Finding it empty, she crossed to the blacksmith shop, and there, as she had hoped, sat Jack Shaw, explaining the assembly of a piece of equipment, unrecognizable to Frances, to the blacksmith. Holding up his right hand, the one with a thumb and the better part of an index finger remaining, Shaw motioned to Frances that he would be right with her. A moment later he stepped outside the blacksmith shop door, catching the brim of his hat between his left thumb and fingerless fist to pull it at a jaunty angle over his missing ear. Just what would become of Jack Shaw, Frances did not know. For the time being he remained on the payroll, earning his keep by doing his best to teach a couple of the more mechanically minded hired men how to service the machines. But it was a temporary situation. A man with a sum total of not-quite-three digits was not going to remain the chief mechanic on a bonanza farm.

Shaw's sadness upon hearing Frances' news was sincere, as was his offer to be of whatever assistance he could.

I would like you to carry Little Carl to the summer parlor at the back of the house in a half hour," Frances said. "Then wait."

Frances entered the house through the back door to find Mrs. Ford and Kirsten sitting at the kitchen table over a breakfast of coffee and bread and butter. The look of concern with which Kirsten greeted Frances made her wonder if the news of Little Carl's death had somehow escaped the cookhouse already, but Kirsten's words clarified her alarm.

"Where have you been, then? Outside? It is still too cool, Frances. Here, sit down," Kirsten said, getting out of her chair.

"I am fine, but I have some sad news."

"You are as white as a ghost," Mrs. Ford said as she stood, too. "Let me get you a cup of coffee."

"Thank you," Frances said, settling into the chair to which Kirsten had led her, for in fact, she could feel a headache approaching. Then, reaching for Kirsten's hand, she looked the girl in the eye and said, "Kirstie, dear, Little Carl *er død*."

Kirsten stared at Frances in disbelief, and then shook her head. "No, no, that can not be." She made a motion as if to turn toward the door, but Frances did not let go of her hand.

"Little Carl is–?" Mrs. Ford asked, although her expression showed that she had understood Frances' message.

"He–" Frances hesitated. "He passed away last night. The Swedish sisters discovered his body this morning."

For a moment the three women were silent. Mrs. Ford turned toward the coffee pot on the stove, dabbing her eyes with her apron. Still holding Kirsten's hand, Frances watched as the young woman who had dropped into the chair next to hers swallowed and did her best to hold back her tears. Frances could not help but think of how altered this moment was from the evening when she had told the girl about her father's death. Since that night their relationship, as unexpected as that with Little Carl, had slowly developed, although there seemed to be no proper term for it. Kirsten remained the housekeeper, of course, but that was the least of what the pretty young woman was to Frances. She was student and attendant and companion, and more, although that 'more' was something other than friend.

Frances brought a handkerchief out of her pocket and lifted it to Kirsten's face. The eyes Kirsten turned toward her reminded Frances of the kiss that she had given to the girl on the night of Percy's attack. It had been the trauma and the Winslow's Soothing Sirup she had told herself upon remembering the moment the next day. But had it? Or had she turned from her humiliation in Percy's grasp to assert her power over another? And the day when she had held Kirsten's body against her own as the young woman slid from the horse. Harmless, Frances had thought. A pleasant diversion. Nothing more. But was it? How many times had she allowed herself to stroke the girl's arm, or to bring her near to her upon the sofa, simply out of her own desire for the warmth and the smell and intimacy of a woman's body, when the young woman had no choice but to do as she was told? Kirsten had lost father and mother and family, and last night, a friend. What was Frances to be to her now? What had she become?

There is no proper term for that element of time that transforms a shared look of concern, of caring, into a gaze that announces so much more. Frances did not look away from the woman who had entered the house as a girl and who had just this moment found the courage to look back, not as housekeeper to employer, not as younger to older, not as immigrant to American, but as woman to woman. Then Mrs. Ford turned back to the table to set a coffee cup in front of Frances, Frances withdrew her hand, and Kirsten, flushed, looked toward the window.

"Who will see to Little Carl's body?"

Mrs. Ford's question brought Frances back to the present.

"I have asked Jack Shaw to bring him to the house, to the summer parlor. Kirsten, I want you to stay there with Little Carl. Jack will re-main as well. I will join you as soon as I can." Frances took a sip of the coffee before her, and then stood, surprised by the wave of faintness that washed over her. "I must speak to Mr. Bingham now," she said after a moment.

Frances had reached the door from the kitchen before she remem-bered the cigar box that she still carried. She turned back, but Kirsten had already stepped outside to wait. No matter, Frances thought, there would be time to present her with Little Carl's generosity later.

What Frances had expected to be a rather difficult, clandestine op-eration turned out to be easy to keep secret. John Bingham was occu-pied with Mr. Johnson in his office, and beyond their shared relief that a replacement for Little Carl was already on the farm neither had much to say. Anna had not yet risen, although she was awake. Upon hearing the news of Little Carl's death, Anna murmured a soft, "hmm." When Frances understood that this was to be the extent of Anna's response, she turned to leave the room. That is when she noticed the bottle sitting next to Anna's bedside.

"Anna," Frances said, "Is this laudanum? I thought that you said it made you nauseated, and so you didn't–"

"A much diluted palliative, rather," Anna interrupted. "When I was in St. Paul with dear Sophie I visited Dr. MacNeil, who insisted upon it as an anodyne for my discomfort, which I am sorry to say is increasingly difficult to bear. I am afraid I may need to spend the morning in bed."

On another day, Frances would have wondered about Anna's decision, for it was the second time this week that she had chosen not to rise before noon. On another day, perhaps, Frances would have paused to question what had happened to the stoic friend who once could be infuriated only by what she felt to be condescension regarding her infirmity. Maybe she would have even given some thought to her own reluctance, now, and in the past months, to question Anna's growing lassitude. But today Frances was simply relieved that Anna would be well out of the way for the rest of the morning. All that remained was to wake Houghton, help him dress, and see that Mrs. Ford kept him occupied in the kitchen. She would explain about Little Carl later. It would not be easy for the boy. At a month shy of five years old, he had spent much of his life thus far in the company of his friend, the funny little cook.

Kirsten was waiting for Frances in the summer parlor. She had wrapped a shawl tightly about her shoulders, for the north room, used mostly during the hot summer months, was closed off during the winter and even in mid-April retained a damp chill. The room was naturally dark, and Kirsten had not pulled aside the curtains. She had, however, moved several chairs to make room for the long side table that she had pulled away from the wall. Stretched out upon the table, Little Carl lay as primly contained in death as in life. Jack Shaw stood nearby, just inside the door, still holding on to the clean set of clothes that Little Carl had placed at the foot of his bed. Once again the women's eyes met and held.

"Well," Frances said after a moment.

"Well, then," Kirsten answered, nodding. "It is narrow, the table, but so then is Little Carl."

"It will do."

"Will we take him to Lugar's this morning? He has no people near-by. One time when I asked –"

"Kirstie," Frances interrupted, "you and I will prepare his body for burial."

"We will?" Kirsten's voice raised in alarm. "But is that right?"

"It is perfectly right. You must trust me. We are to be Carl's family now. Jack, I am going to ask a favor of you, and the better part of that favor will be for you to ask no questions in return. I want you to wait outside the door until I call for you. Do not let anyone through, I don't care who it is."

Shaw did not speak immediately, but when he did there was a hint of feeling to his voice that he did not try to disguise. "Don't worry for nothing, Mrs. Bingham. I will be right here."

Frances watched the door shut before turning back to Kirsten who had been standing silently, waiting and worried. "Have you done this before?" Frances asked.

"I have watched."

"Then you know what is needed. I will wait for you here." As she spoke a second wave of dizziness washed over her and she felt Kirsten by her side helping her to the sofa.

"It is too much," Kirsten said.

"And so too much falls to you," Frances said, her eyes closed and her head resting upon the cushion. "You do not have a great deal of time. I would not have us interrupted. Forgive me, Kirsten, but you will under-stand soon, and if I have to stand or speak again soon, I will be truly ill."

Frances did not know if she slept as Kirsten worked. If she did she dreamt of a dark room in which a woman prepared the body of an-other for burial. She may have dreamt or imagined or heard the young woman gasp. Certainly from where she lay Frances could not have seen the tears nor witnessed the tenderness of the wash cloth passed over breasts, across the belly, between the thighs, and yet Frances knew each action.

Then, as if from within this dream, Frances heard a voice ask, "What is it that we become? Monstrous to others. Unknowable to ourselves. What is it that we become?" Frances tried to place the voice. Was it her mother speaking? Was it Little Carl? And then there was Kirsten kneeling beside her, saying, "No, Frances. You are wrong. Little Carl he was not a monster."

"What, then?" Frances opened her eyes.

"An unhappy person, maybe?"

"An unhappy woman, certainly. But what kind of man?"

For the third time that day Kirsten returned Frances' gaze in silence, letting it hold for the beat that from that moment on only one would deny. "Who Little Carl was to Little Carl we do not know," Kirsten said. "To me he was a friend. And to you, too. But a *uhyre*, a monster? Not for one minute do I believe that to be true. Mysteries there are, sure, but some of them are not so bad, then."

CHAPTER XLIV

In Which a Monster is Revealed and a Friend is Lost: II

What remains when desire passes? If there has been union, consummation, passion, the waning of desire may follow any number of predictable paths to lethargy, or repugnance, or regret. If there has been waiting and dreaming only, then there is only an end to waiting and dreaming. When Frances realized one late spring day that she did not care if Anna rose from her bed, she did not care if Anna spoke her name, she held herself very still, waiting for the sensation that would accompany the realization. She felt nothing. This, then, Frances thought, is what she had been waiting for all these years. She had been waiting for nothing.

What replaces desire? If you are Frances, it is desire for something else.

Morning after morning Frances rose with the intention of handing over the yellow envelope and its one thousand, two hundred and forty-three dollars to Kirsten. Then she did not. Of course, the longer Frances held on to the gift that Little Carl had so clearly intended for Kirsten the less comfortable she became in the young woman's company. Kirsten's confusion at Frances' growing distance, coming upon the heels of their experience together with Little Carl, was palpable, and Frances berated herself for the moments of tenderness that she had allowed. It had been her illness, Frances told herself, that had allowed for such intimacy, but it was not good for her and it was not good for Kirsten, and there it would end.

It was not the amount of cash that tempted Frances to deceive the person most determined to be her friend; it was, rather, what the cash represented. A happy accident. A sign. Fate, perhaps. The unexpected tool that would pry her out of a present that she had painstakingly, if mistakenly, created, and into a future that would better suit her. This was the point where Frances stumbled in her rationale (if the combination of reluctance and craving that were her motivations can be allowed such a name). She wanted to be free, but she did not want to leave. Although the dream of a life with Anna had evaporated, revealing itself to have been no more substantial than the swirl of clouds that decorate the horizon of a summer dawn upon the prairie, more color than matter and certain to burn off quickly, Frances had no desire to shuffle off to Fargo for a life of tedious domesticity as Mrs. Percy Bingham. She had tasted both independence and consequence in John Bingham's office, copying figures into ledgers and managing correspondence. She had thrilled with each season as the thick black soil of Dakota's Red River valley turned golden with wheat, and marveled as bushels were transformed into dollars. The combination of risk and routine that was farming suited her perfectly, and to be involved in anything less, she believed, would be unendurable.

And yet, leave this life she must, for she had run out of reasons to stay. Percy's nomination as the Republican candidate from Cass County essentially secured his election. His position as a public figure had accomplished what neither humiliation nor remonstration could: he had been almost sober in each of his brief visits to the farm since Frances woke from her illness. His sobriety, as well as his burgeoning sense of importance, Frances had discovered, made him difficult to ignore and impossible to manipulate. Then came the charge. There were to be no more excuses, no further procrastination. She was to get her things together for the move to Fargo immediately. There she would complete Percy's transformation into respectable family man of the community. They would go to church together, husband, wife, and son. She would be by his side during speeches and social gatherings. She would join whatever ladies' societies he thought best.

"Your days as my father's hostess and amanuensis, my dear, are officially over," Percy concluded. "If the rumors I hear in town about the debts of certain bonanza farmers in the area are correct, he will soon need a lawyer more than a secretary anyway. But that is his business now. He works his work. I mine. Although I suppose I should more properly paraphrase to say, I work my work. He his." Frances had watched Percy as he spoke, aware that for a moment he had almost forgotten her as he arranged his words to his satisfaction. She was about to ask what he meant about John Bingham's need for a lawyer when Percy spoke again. "You have two days to pack, Frances. You and the boy will come back to Fargo with me on Sunday afternoon. One of the men can bring your things along in the wagon later."

When Frances had knocked on John Bingham's office door later that day to tell him of her imminent departure, she discovered him frowning at a letter that he was reading. His response to her news was not the least bit flattering in that, clearly distracted by his correspondence, he seemed to have almost no response at all. He thanked her for her help in "tidying" the books. He and Anna would certainly miss having her about the house, but she should not worry that her move to Fargo would in any way inconvenience him. And no, no, he did not have anything just then that he needed her to copy out for him. Yes, he would prefer that she close the door behind her.

"I will help you pack, dear," Anna roused herself to offer when Frances discovered her dozing in the parlor.

To Kirsten, Frances said nothing.

Late that evening when everyone else was asleep, Frances paced within her sitting room. The day after next, with Houghton next to her, she would accompany Percy to their new home. Houghton would not understand, not right away, that they were leaving the farm for good. Oh, they would return often, but they would no longer wake to the sound of the blacksmith's hammer, or to the voices of men calling out orders to each other or encouragement to animals. There would be no more rambles across the country upon Raleigh (although John Bingham had, in a moment of generosity, said that Frances was to keep the horse in Fargo). There would be no more... Frances caught herself as she was about to imagine the moments that would not be filled with Kirsten's chatter and laughter and common sense.

Just as on that damp March night, over a year past, when Percy first told her of his purchase of the lot in Fargo and Frances had been suddenly desperate to breathe the evening air, she wanted nothing so much now as to be free of the walls about her. Tightening her wrapper she slipped out of the sitting room, up the steps to the third floor, and out to the balustraded platform atop the house. The dark night held the balmy warmth of the mid-summer day, and Frances kept her hand on the railing to maintain her sense of balance. In the vacuum of the blackness about her Frances sensed, tasted, acknowledged the fear that had lodged in her chest. It was not a life of lonely domesticity that terrified her, but the plan that had been forming in her mind, a plan that she had been half-heartedly denying was taking shape. She was capable of nothing of the sort, she had been telling herself, so where was the harm in identifying complications and plotting out contingencies. It was like a puzzle that she kept in her head. A riddle. A daydream. The plan involved the three people whom she had befriended in her life on the Bingham farm, and who had come, over the years, to trust her: Kirsten and Little Carl and Jack Shaw. If her plan were not a daydream, if it were real, then she would need to cheat the first, betray the memory of the second, and lie to the third. If successful, she would gain the one thing in this territory that was prized above all else, land to call her own, and maybe, maybe, her freedom. If she were successful she would lose everything else.

Not long after the Jews' exodus during the flood of '81, Jack Shaw had sold the bulk of the Jew slough to a couple of speculators from Chicago. The price he'd received had not been good, but it was better than what John Bingham or the other surrounding farmers were willing to consider for land that was, at the time, mostly under water. Shaw had used the money to pay off the debts the community had left behind. Shaw had kept his own quarter section back, believing that the land would rise in value as Fargo grew. A nearby farmer was working the scant tillable eighty acres there under an informal arrangement that benefited the farmer since it was not precisely consistent with the terms of the Homestead Act. Jack Shaw had this final season to go before the land could be proved up. All of this he had explained to Frances earlier in the summer as he bent over a plow to chisel the dried and caked dirt from the spades, a job that now required both of his hands, but not a full complement of fingers.

I know here," he had paused to tap his chest with a thumb in response to Frances' question whether he had decided what to do with his quarter section, "that it is now not so good for me to sell. I must only wait." Then, straightening his back with a groan, he had plucked out a folded sheet of paper from his shirt pocket and slowly worked it open to display a clumsily drawn graph that meant nothing to her. "Give a look on my drawing, Mrs. Bingham. A series of drainage ditches, like this," Shaw had said, "and the land produces as good as any in the valley. But, that kind of money I don't have, and to tell the truth, I am thinking only from what someone else could do. I was never meant to be a farmer, and now–" Shaw finished his sentence with his abbreviated hands before him. "Why do you ask?"

Instead of answering, Frances had asked her own question. "What will you do?"

"Once, I was to make for myself a repair shop, for machines, but that was not to be either. I am thinking now on dry goods, but fancy, for gentlemen, with maybe also someday things for the house, china, napkin rings, things that are nice, yes, but that a real person can afford, too. Then, maybe even vases, toilet sets, smokers' sets, perfumes. And for children, dolls, tea sets, the horses, you know–" Jack Shaw brought his fists to his chest and his elbows out to his sides and rocked from the waist.

"Hobby horses," Frances said with a laugh. "I see that you have given this some thought."

"Nu? For thoughts I have time. But now maybe I am running out of time. Mr. Johnson will not be sorry to see me go, yes?"

That had been the end of that conversation, but it had given Frances a great deal to think about, and it was not many days later that she found Jack Shaw back in the machine shed, this time with an oil can gripped between thumb and stubbed finger.

"How much would you need to get the store started?" Frances had asked as a greeting.

Jack Shaw did not miss a beat before he answered, "I have saved. Enough I will have when enough I can get for my quarter section."

"And how much is enough," Frances insisted.

"Now I can get, maybe, six, seven an acre. I should sell only when I can get ten."

"You will not get ten for that land."

"There is land for sale in this county for twenty-five."

"Bonanza land, broken and worked and next to the railroad. Not slough land, covered with trees and shrubs, and under water until late each spring."

"In twenty years, when Fargo is as big as Chicago, you will be able to throw a stone only to hit a Fargo citizen on the head. Then it will be worth five times that."

"Twenty years is a long time to wait for a store, Jack."

"Oh, I will not have to wait so long. I am only thinking that for someone it is a good investment at ten dollars an acre."

Standing alone on the top of the house, wrapped in the darkness and the close night air of a humid Dakota summer, Frances did her math one more time. One hundred and sixty acres at ten dollars left her over three hundred and fifty dollars short. She closed her eyes and tried to imagine what it would be like to step outside her own home on her own land in the middle of the night. Would it feel different? Would it smell different? Following the railing back to the steps, Frances lifted the hem of her wrapper with her free hand and carefully descended.

Back in her sitting room Frances opened the bottom drawer of a corner cabinet and reached for the cigar box at the back. She turned up the lamp above the cabinet and opened the box to the letter, the picture, and the knife. She lifted the false bottom and took out the yellow envelope. Once again she counted the money. Quietly she crossed the room to the ornate secretary from which Anna had once preferred to write her letters, before she had decided that it was much easier on her hip and back if she carried out her correspondence from bed. Frances returned to the cabinet with two envelopes. She put twelve hundred dollars in one, and the remaining forty-three in the other. The first envelope she slid into the pocket of her wrapper. The second she returned to the cigar box and then returned the box to the back of the cabinet drawer. She noticed that her hands were shaking. Her forehead was damp with sweat. She thought she might be sick, but there was one more thing to do before she returned to her bed. Tearing the yellow envelope that bore Kirsten's name into ever smaller pieces, Frances made her way down the steps in the dark to the kitchen.

It would be, she thought as she stirred the envelope's shreds into the embers of the oven's firebox, an interesting moment the next morning when she made her offer of $7.50 per acre to Shaw for his land. Not all men have the opportunity to put a precise figure on what their lives are worth.

Book Five:
A Reach and a Grasp

Ah, but a man's reach should exceed his grasp,
Or what's a heaven for?

(From "Andrea del Sarto" by Robert Browning)

Chapter XLV

In Which She Has a Farm of Her Own

Jack Shaw, as it turned out, did not consider the terms of friendship and good business to be exclusive. He had been eager to sell to Frances, as pleased to be able to do what she asked as to get his hands on the cash that would allow him to open a dry goods store in Fargo. As a friend he would keep the transaction quiet, agreeing to Frances' request that they not see to the deed transfer at the court house until "sometime later, perhaps in January." As a businessman, however, he was unwilling to lower his selling price by twenty-five percent. So they compromised. He would sell the land to her for fourteen hundred dollars, twelve hundred down and the remainder to be paid within the next five years at seven percent interest. Frances had nothing beyond her moment of humanity in the snow with which to negotiate, and that had left her two hundred dollars short, so she agreed to Jack Shaw's terms, without the slightest idea of where that final two hundred was to come from. She had no savings, she owned little of value besides her clothes and some pieces of jewelry, and she had no one to whom she could turn for assistance.

And yet, she was filled with an almost nauseating excitement at her daring: she was the owner of one hundred and sixty acres. It would be up to her to decide what was to be planted upon the irregular eighty acres that had been broken. It would be up to her to decide whether to keep or to log the forested acres near the river. It would be up to her to ponder the improvement of the remaining sixty-plus acres of slough land, thick with shrubs and often under water. As to who was to plant, who was to log, who was to improve, and how this was all to be seen to without capital, this Frances did her best not to ponder, for then the nausea moved beyond excitement and into simple terror. She had until the spring, she told herself, to make those decisions. She had until spring to reveal her secret.

Until then, she had a new fantasy to make her days in Fargo bearable, a new destination for her rides. It was a beautiful piece of dirt, although certainly not the best for farming. The trees and the river nearby gave the place a settled, civilized look, more like the landscape of her youth than the stark homesteads farther out on the prairie. Occasionally, Frances would leave Raleigh tied to a shrub while she went inside the eight-by-ten claim shanty that Jack Shaw had put up five years earlier. The shanty had been constructed only to meet the requirements of the Homestead Act, and Shaw had never really made a home there. A pipe for the stove still extended through the roof, but rested inside on an overturned barrel, the stove itself long removed. No sod had been stacked around the tar paper exterior, and on a day with any sun it was colder inside than out. It would be fine for chickens, Frances thought, and then tried to imagine herself as someone who raised chickens. She could not. And yet, sitting in the center of this chill room on a raw, gray November day, on a log that she had rolled inside for just this purpose, Frances felt oddly at home. Her brothers had built her a doll house just about this size in their back yard in Virginia. A thousand years ago now, it seemed, and yet she did not doubt that whatever her daydreams then, they had probably been more realistic than any she'd constructed since. And that included this land for which she had violated every last good thing about herself to get. Well, she thought, with a humorless chuckle, perhaps she was better suited for dirt than for people.

She had no money of her own with which to build a real house. She did not know who would farm the eighty acres. Jack Shaw had suggested Peter Erickson, a successful settler whose holdings had grown to a full section just to the north of Frances' tillable eighty acres. Across the Sheyenne from Erickson's land was the quarter section that Kirsten still insisted upon calling "Homer's land." Frances quickly pushed an image of the young woman from her mind, and continued with her calculations. She knew that John Bingham rented some of his land to local farmers on a share crop basis, generally taking one-third of the profits for himself. The tenants kept the remaining two-thirds, although out of that sum came the labor, seed, machinery and stock that the tenant furnished. Frances put her figures together. Eighty acres averaging, say, a conservative twenty bushels per acre at one dollar per bushel. Minus thirty cents per bushel for transportation costs. That was fourteen dollars per acre profit, equaling $1120. One third of that would be just over three hundred and seventy dollars. Now if she paid Jack Shaw fifty dollars plus seven per cent interest on the two hundred that she owed, that would be sixty-four dollars the first year, leaving her with around three hundred dollars.

For a moment Frances felt the terror recede and the excitement return. Three hundred dollars was a lot of money. But then the anxiety
washed back, like a wave that had collected force during its absence.
How much of that would go for land taxes? Wheat could fall below a
dollar. There could be another wet spring, or a drought, or grasshoppers, or hail, or a hundred other tragedies, and the bushels per acre
could fall well below twenty. There could be no crop at all. And even if
all went well, how far would three hundred dollars go? Would it feed
and dress Houghton? And Raleigh? And what about a house? A barn?
A buggy? Oh, there were too many things to think about and no one
to turn to, no one to say, here, Frances, this is how it is done. What she
had were an assortment of incoherent fantasies and realities. She had a
husband who was not to have any part of this land, but who was very
real himself. She had a son from whom she would never part, but could
not support on her own. The only person she could imagine showing
this place to, the only person who might not think that she had gone
completely insane, was the young woman she had betrayed in order to
have the land in the first place.

Unbeckoned but insistent, a memory nagged at Frances. She, solicitous; Kirsten, grateful; an arrangement made after Torger Knudson's
death to give a grieving girl just one-fourth of the income from Homer's
quarter section that John Bingham was to farm. Now, even that bit
of maneuvering, done to ingratiate herself to her father-in-law at the
housekeeper's expense, was added to Frances' guilt. It had not been
forgotten, after all. Just as Kirsten had not been, could not be, forgotten.

But what was done was done. From now on she would simply act,
and if her actions seemed insane, well, so be it. With the land must come
freedom. One was nothing without the other, and pretty much everything else had been lost. Percy was to leave soon for Yankton. While
he was gone she would go with Jack Shaw to the court house to make
the sale of the land official. When Percy returned, she would ask for a
divorce. She was living in the divorce capital of the world, after all. Men
in frock coats and silk top hats and women in the richest colors of silk,
velvet and chenille regularly stepped off the N.P. to register in the Headquarters Hotel for a 90-day stay, the territory's residency requirement
for a divorce. She would add her number to this cosmopolitan crowd.

And if she did not know what she would do the day after the divorce, then she would just have to wait and find out.

I am alone, then. Now. Not so very long ago when I was in the little house with Mor and Far, not much more than seven strides long was my world, too, and at each step there was another body it seemed. Now I walk fro and to in this big house and see no one except Miss Anna Bingham who does not see me. Even Mrs. Ford is to leave after the first of the year, when she is to become Mrs. Jack Shaw. "Kirsten," Mrs. Ford said to me, "I don't care if he is a Jew. Jack Shaw is a good man." So I said to her, "Well, I guess there is no reason to care if he is a Jew if he does not care that you are a Presbyterian," and Mrs. Ford just smiled and said, "I will miss you, Kirsten Knudson."

I will miss her, too. And I will miss Jack Shaw. But not like I miss Little Carl. He (and he will always be a he to me because he will always be Little Carl and I did not know that Clara person), anyway, *he* was a funny one, so quiet and serious when around the crew, but when it was just Howie and me and us making the cookies then it was stories about stage coaches and Indians and soldiers. And never did I believe one word but Howie believed it all, and it is too quiet without a little boy in this big house. I hope he has found some friends his age in Fargo, and I hope, too, that Mr. Percy was telling the truth about the pony that he promised to get Howie come spring, because that boy is just like his mother about the horses.

Frances.

No, about missing Frances I can not talk. Not yet. So more about Little Carl. One day when he was so sick, after the blizzard, and still he would not let anyone near, he called me from the cookhouse kitchen into his room. "I'm going to tell you something, Kirsten, and then you are going to leave without saying one damn thing. Not one word. I mean it." And so I said, "O.K., then," and that made him sort of hiss back at me (he could hardly talk) "Not one thing!" so I just stayed quiet, and that is for me not so easy to do. That is when he said, "If something should happen to me...not one thing now, Kirsten...there will be a surprise for you. Now go on. Get out."

Well, I guess I was pretty surprised all right, and it was not such a nice surprise, but I am proud that Little Carl thought that I was a friend who could keep a secret, and I am even more to be proud of Frances. When to the Bingham house first I came, and even before that when I would take butter to Mrs. Harkness and the doctor, I thought that to be a Yankee was to always know how to do the right thing. But I am older now, and I have seen some things and I know that it is not the same thing to know how to set a fancy table and to do the thing that is right. But Frances did the thing that was right with Little Carl. I will say it again, not because I am someone who has the right to say this but because it makes me feel good. Little Carl went into the grave like himself and not like this stranger Clara and there is not a person in the world to laugh behind the dead back of our friend, and it is all because Frances Bingham is a person who does the right thing.

So there she is again. Frances. Missing all of the others is nothing like going all day long, day after day, without seeing her. It is like the air is not right for good breathing anymore. Maybe I am like Little Carl, maybe there is something wrong with me, too, only the thing that is wrong with me is inside my heart and is not to see on my body. Two nights before Frances and Howie left to live forever in Fargo with Mr. Percy Bingham, I heard the creak of the outside door to the steps up to the platform on top of the house, and I knew it was Frances because there is no one else who goes up there. Howie wants to all of the time... no, Howie *wanted* to all of the time, but he was forbidden. (Now that is a good, strong word to know.) Anyway, I knew that it was Frances and I wanted so much to go there, too, but I knew that she did not go up to the platform in the middle of the night for company. Still, it was very hard just to wait and wait and wait to hear her steps coming back down.

Well, the next morning I go to her bedroom as she is packing, and she does not even look at me when I come into the room, so I say to her, "Take me with you to Fargo," just like that. I say, "You will need a housekeeper there, too."

"I will keep my own house," is what Frances says then.

"You can not cook," I say, and that is just the truth. Oh, she can cook, but not like to do three times a day, every day. I have never seen her make even one loaf of bread.

"We will not starve," she says, and then she says, "Please leave me now, Kirsten." Kirsten. Not Kirstie.

Sometimes I think it is because of me that Frances left. Oh, I know that Mr. Percy finally put his foot down, but it is not much of a foot. Maybe it was because I let my heart show in my face on the day that Little Carl died. Maybe it was because of what was in her face, too. Or maybe I dreamed that. Or made it up. Like Little Carl's stories about stage coaches with ghosts for drivers, or Indians who could turn into birds. There are so many maybes and not a one of them do I understand, but one day Frances was looking at me with those eyes of a storm and the next day she does not look me at all.

There are people who make things happen and there are people that things happen to. The Binghams make things happen, and that is because they are rich Yankees. Things happen to me, and that is because I am a poor Norwegian. So I will tell you what happened to me. Frances happened to me when she kissed me on the night of the men from England, even if she did not even remember it because of the Winslow's Soothing Sirup. And Frances happened to me when she let me sit right next to her and read out loud when Miss Anna went back to St. Paul. And Frances happened to me when she rode behind me on Raleigh with her arm so strong around my waist. Frances happened to me, over and over, day after day, when she lifted one eyebrow when someone said something that she did not believe, and when she laughed with her head way back and her mouth open and not at all like a lady like Miss Anna, and when she went out of the yard at a gallop on Raleigh with her braid bouncing under that big hat, and when she took Howie by the arms to swing him around and around in the yard, and when she told Arne Magnusson to collect his things and be gone by the morning after she saw him beating Dan, and, and … and the truth is she did not need to do one thing but breathe for Frances to happen to me.

And then she went away without one look back, and there was nothing I could do to change that. Because I am the housekeeper. I do not make things happen.

But I can leave. I am a woman now of twenty years and soon to be twenty-one, and that is old enough to be alone for sure. There will be trouble at the church again, but then "so be it," as Mrs. Harkness used to say. Just last Sunday it was Per Rolfsrud to give the sermon because Pastor Fedje is still flat on his back after his buggy tipped in Fargo. So there we were just one Sunday before Christmas and there is the church all in frippery and there is much to say about the baby Jesus to be sure, and instead it is Per Rolfsrud telling us every single thing that is wrong. A lot of what is wrong, Per Rolfsrud says, is the fault of the big bonanza farmers like John Bingham because they take up so much land that could be farmed by real families that would send their children to school and who would go to church and who would all together make up a big community, and instead there are just miles and miles of land that is only for one family and most of the time that family does not even live in Dakota, and when they do, they think they are too good to have anything to do with the rest of us.

I think that Per Rolfsrud is just mad because Mr. Percy took his place to go to Yankton. Still, when he gets to talking I just slide lower and lower into the pew because I know that people are looking at me and wondering how I can work for such a family. Well, maybe I am part of what is wrong, then, not because I am a housekeeper on a bonanza farm but because I am not married and so I have not been good to be fruitful and multiply, but most because I have Homer's land and there are plenty of good Norwegian men who are in need of land. And that is why there will be trouble, because I am going to move out to Homer's land, and live in Sten's house, and there I will be alone, and alone I will stay.

So this is what I have to say to Frances when she and Mr. Percy and Howie come home to the farm for Christmas, and Frances and Howie stay for a week, and all that time (you will think that this is not possible) but all that time Frances does only once look me straight in the eye. I have thought and thought and I do not know for sure what it is that I have done wrong, but it is something bad for sure. So I say to myself, Kirsten, you will talk to her one more time, really talk like before, and maybe then she will tell you what it is that you have done. I have an excuse for the talk, too. I will tell her that come spring I am going to see if the money that is sitting in the First National Bank in Fargo with my name on it, the money from renting Homer's land out to John Bingham plus my three dollars a week that I have been putting away ever since Mor left is enough to make me into a farmer. I will fix up Sten's house, and I will get a couple of cows so I can make butter to sell, and I will get chickens and maybe turkeys because I have kept my eyes open and that is a good way for a woman to make money. And as for the real farming, I will still rent out the land to John Bingham, if he isn't too mad about me going.

So now it is the day that Frances and Howie are to go back to Fargo, and Howie has been sniffling all morning about leaving the farm until he finally lets Miss Anna hold him on her lap like he is still a little boy, and that is when I see Frances slip out of the room, and walk up the steps, and I know that she is heading toward the lookout where no one goes now that Frances is gone, and no one should go in the middle of the winter even on such a day with the sky so clear, because it is just plain dangerous. I know because I have done it. The stairs are covered with snow and ice and the platform is full of snow, too, and John Bingham says that he is going to tear it down before it makes the roof leak.

Well, then, I just follow right behind Frances, and when I get to the top step I think I will see her looking far away just like she used to, because that is how she is. Some people look at their feet, and some people, like me and like most of us, I think, look at whatever is right around us, but it is like Frances is always trying to see if there is something happening out there where the sky and the land come together. Like she is waiting for something. But she is not looking out, no, she has her face in her hands and her shoulders are moving, and all I want to do right there and then is whatever it is that will make her stop crying.

But instead I say, "Hello?"

And Frances she touches under her eyes with the tips of her gloves and says, "Come to haunt me, have you, Kirstie?"

Well, Frances does say some strange things sometimes, and it is like how she looks for something that is not there on the horizon, sometimes she says things like she is talking to someone who is not in the room. But it was Kirstie, not Kirsten, and that was something at least. So I say, "No, just to talk for a minute."

"I really must be going, I am afraid," Frances says, and still she does not look at me.

"Please. Just one minute," I say. And then I tell her how I am to leave in the spring, and all the time that I am talking her head is turned and she is looking so far away.

"That will be a disappointment for Anna and John, especially so soon after losing Mrs. Ford," Frances says, when I stop talking. "Where will you go? Have you arranged for another position?"

"I am going to live on Homer's land. My land," I say, and just like that up goes the eyebrow, and then comes a laugh, but not the one with her head thrown back, and there is nothing happy about the laugh, just some sort of joke that I think is probably not very nice, and then I think, she is laughing at me, and that makes me a little mad, so I go on and I tell her about the butter and the eggs, and I say that I have been making my own money ever since I was a girl and I think I can manage pretty well on my own, and I am just getting to going when Frances puts her hand on my arm and looks at me for the very first time all week. Well, then just like that there is no more breath and no more talking, and I am remembering how the very first time I saw those eyes I thought that there was something wrong with them, and how a hundred times since I did feel the gooseflesh come up on my arms when they looked at me, and sometimes they would sparkle and sometimes they were like smoke, and now here they are, red from the crying and the cold, and they just look small and sad, like anyone else's, and I can see that Frances has lost even more weight and it is not good for her face, and I would give Sten's house and Homer's land and all of the money in the First National Bank of Fargo right there and then if I could put my arms around her, if I could say, "There, there, Frances. There, there."

But I just look back, and Frances says, "Don't rent your land to John this spring. You can do better. Peter Erickson farms the section to the east of you, across the Sheyenne. He's a good farmer and, I understand, a fair man. Insist upon one-third of the profits from the harvest. Now, I really must go."

But she does not go. She just stands there. And then she takes off her gloves and at first I don't know what she is doing, but then I see that she is unpinning the horseshoe pin that is so much on her high collar, and just like that she hands it to me, and then she uses her hand to close my fingers around it, and she says, "I am sorry."

So there I stand like I am a statue I am so surprised, and then down the steps she goes, and I am all by myself at the top of the big Bingham house and that is when I realize that I am shaking, and maybe it is because it is so cold, no matter how blue it is the sky, and I am just standing there and shaking and thinking the thing that I can not say out loud, but then I think, Kirsten, you are alone, you can say what you want, and so I say, right out loud, I say, "Frances, don't leave me."

And then I say, "Sorry for what, then?"

CHAPTER XLVI

In Which Percy Learns to Dance with the Ugly Ones

Percy congratulated himself on his behavior toward his wife. He had waited patiently for her to regain her health. He had tolerated her reluctance to join him in Fargo. He had even exercised incredible restraint when she had informed him, during their first evening together in their new home on Thirteenth Street, that she preferred that they no longer share a bedroom "as husband and wife." The spare room next to Houghton's remained unfurnished, but he (or she, if Percy insisted) could sleep on the sofa in the tiny back room that Percy liked to call his library. By restraint, Percy meant that he had not struck her there and then, as he so desperately would have liked to do. But he had had an election to win at the time, and then a legislative session for which to prepare. He would deal with her later, when he returned from Yankton. She was thirty, old to be having children, but not impossibly old. If it was dangerous, then it was a danger for which she was entirely responsible. Houghton should have brothers and sisters, and a man of his standing should have a family. Frances had had her own way long enough.

In fact, Percy had been in a significantly self-congratulatory frame of mind during the entire fall and early winter of '82. He had acquitted himself particularly well, he believed, during the ad hoc bipartisan convention that met in Fargo, the purpose of which was to elect delegates to go to Washington to petition for the creation of a new territory out of northern Dakota. A similar convention in Sioux Falls had met at the same time, sending its delegates to Washington to petition not only for division from northern Dakota, but for statehood as well. Percy had needed little tutoring from Alexander McKenzie to understand that the Fargo convention required a delicate and noncommittal touch. "The fact that we don't care one bit for division or statehood just now," McKenzie had explained, "don't mean that you ain't got a job to do, Bingham. If you're going to make it in politics you got to dance with the ugly ones as much as the pretty ones, and make 'em all feel like it's your privilege, if you see what I mean." So Percy attended the convention, he added his voice, and he wrote an editorial in the *Argus* that neither supported the movement nor argued against it, but rather lauded some of the local citizenry for their initiative and others for their caution, taking care to offend none of the attendees, not even the prohibitionists. That he could do this while at the same time invoking praise for the "lifeblood of the valley," the Northern Pacific Railroad (and the wise leadership of its new president, Henry Villard), thereby tempering the increasing anti-railroad sentiment with quiet support of the status quo, Percy believed, was proof that McKenzie's investment in him was well deserved. As for the division and statehood conventions, with their delegates and petitions, nothing had come of them, just as McKenzie had predicted.

Enjoying the amnesia peculiar to purchased politicians, Percy Bingham perceived his election, which placed him in the company of three dozen men who were to comprise the Fifteenth General Assembly of Dakota Territory, as confirmation that he was genuinely liked and trusted by the citizens of Fargo, in part for what he said in his speeches and his editorials, but more importantly, for himself, for the man he had become. He did not consider that it would have been the exception had a Republican not been elected from Cass County. The ironies that Percy once would have been quick to identify—as McKenzie's man he was necessarily the unofficial champion for the Northern Pacific, and thus, was to become a voice and a vote for the industry that he had cursed for bringing his family to Dakota—he was now as quick to ignore as he strode down the plank-boarded sidewalks and tipped his hat and shook hands. He had become someone in Fargo, and from this moment forth Fargo's progress would be his own.

Percy looked up from the Dakota *Herald* resting in his lap early one February day, a month into the legislative session of 1883, to watch two of his fellow assemblymen button their greatcoats as they passed through the lobby of Yankton's Central Hotel and onto Fifth Street. George Walsh of Grand Forks nodded a greeting in passing, causing his companion to look his way as well. Percy dipped his chin in response and then returned to the newspaper. He had been told by Alexander McKenzie to look to Walsh for advice while the legislature was in session, but Walsh had thus far had very little to say to the new delegate. Seeing his fellow legislators gathering in groups of two or three made

Percy feel like a boy allowed into a club, but not told the rules. His insecurity embarrassed him. He would have liked to ask the other delegates from north Dakota if their $4.50 a week for lodging and board at the hotel was being paid by Alexander McKenzie, too. Did each and every one of them receive a free pass, not just on the Northern Pacific, but on the assorted trains it still took to get from north to south? Was this business as usual or was it a secret between him and McKenzie?

Percy could not ask without risking another display of greenhorn ignorance. Just thinking about that first day of the session made his cheeks burn. For weeks prior to arriving in Yankton he had practiced his maiden speech to the legislative body, finding just the right combination of Jefferson, Lincoln, Longfellow and Shakespeare that would announce the arrival of a man of gravitas and import. But when the occasion arose, he was less than two minutes into his oration before he heard the gavel of Speaker Williams strike, and the question that followed: "Just what is it that you want, Mr. Bingham?"

He had wanted to make a grand, impressive speech. He wanted to be someone his fellow legislators patted on the back and invited to dinner, someone written about in the newspapers. He wanted to be known, not because he was the son of the bonanza farmer, John Bingham, but because he was Representative Percy Bingham. As for the normal school for Fargo, which the Republican committee in Cass County expected him to secure, Percy certainly had not expected to so brashly introduce such a bill. And so within minutes of first standing, Percy found himself sitting again, largely ignored except for a few chuckles at his expense. For the two weeks following, Percy had watched as other assemblymen were clearer about what it was they wanted. They wanted a piece of the territorial treasury, in the form of prisons, or hospitals for the insane or for the deaf and dumb, or normal schools, or colleges. They wanted to carve counties out of the vast territory, to be named after themselves or important patrons. They did not seem overly concerned with the taxation of the citizens they represented.

Percy was amazed. Not by the logrolling. Not by the rapidity with which the legislators were securing prizes for their home towns (which is to say for themselves and their friends who would benefit from the resulting sale of city lots). And not by the lobbyists for the railroads and banking corporations back east who provided (along with several cases

of whiskey) the exact wording for the legislation their "friends" in the
assembly were to introduce. It was neither the fact nor the extent of
the jobbing that shocked Percy. It was the openness, the lack of dissembling. Percy's transition from lazy cynicism to determined optimism was
too recent to allow for outrage, but he was well aware that his newly
minted self-respect depended entirely on the good opinion of his fellow
citizens of Cass County, and more specifically, of Fargo. How was this
good opinion to be maintained if the legislature of which he was a part
was revealed to consist of scoundrels who so brazenly engaged in the
division of the spoils of the territory?

More distressing for Percy was his slow acceptance that local popularity and personal merit had not brought him to Yankton. He was
McKenzie's man, plain and simple. As were at least a half dozen other
men he could count, including, he suspected, George Walsh, although
Walsh's own power in the Red River valley was very real, so perhaps,
Percy thought, he and McKenzie were simply in alliance. Reacting to an
old sinking feeling in his gut, Percy reached into his inside vest pocket,
forgetting for the moment that he no longer carried his flask with him.
Percy folded the newspaper, placed it next to a heavy glass ashtray em-
bellished with a tarnished eagle perched atop the ashtray's handle, its
beak sooty from the ashes of cigarettes and cigars rolled upon it, and
stood. The charade was over, but perhaps he need not lose all that he
had gained. He would not be loved by all men, high and low, but he
could maintain his position among the powerful few in the community,
if, and only if, he brought a share of the spoils home to Fargo. He could
tell, now, that there was to be no normal school for Fargo. That had
been decided by other men, most likely by Alexander McKenzie, weeks
or months earlier. There remained, however, the largest prize of all, and
he prayed that McKenzie was with him on this one.

Percy's one social engagement in Yankton had been at the home of
Moses K. Armstrong, but there had been little about the evening to
charm either host or guest. Percy understood that the invitation had
been extended in acknowledgement of the hospitality that the Binghams had twice shown Armstrong, first in St. Paul, and then again in '76
when Armstrong was writing his bonanza story. In the years since that
last visit, Percy noted, Armstrong's famed good humor had diminished.

The immediate cause of the older man's bitterness was evidently Governor Ordway's refusal to grant Armstrong "freedom of the House" this session, a privilege that in the past had allowed him to circulate among the legislators, and which he had been granted ever since his return from Washington. The governor had explained to Armstrong that with the size of the legislative body increasing every session, room for "unnecessary visitors" had decreased.

"Unnecessary visitors," Armstrong spat the words out as he settled in to his comfortable chair. "The 'unnecessary visitor' is the governor himself, that carpet-bagging scallawag. By the way, I hear that George Walsh gave notice that he intends to introduce a bill to remove the territorial capital from Yankton. Just where the seat of government is to go, I have not heard, but considering the complaints by your fellow legislators about ventilation, I suspect that Mr. Walsh contemplates some point to the north, where there could be no trouble on that score."

Percy knew that Moses Armstrong was digging for information. He also knew of Armstrong's friendship with the editor of the Dakota *Herald*, and so was careful not to say anything that might end up embarrassing him in the paper, although in truth, Percy had nothing to reveal. "And it was a south Dakota lawmaker, Frank Washabaugh," he replied, "who answered Walsh with the suggestion that it is time to stop talking about territory this or territory that. His proposal, you may have heard, was to just go ahead and organize a state government and then see what the federal government does about it."

The audacity of the proposal brought a smile back to Armstrong's face. "Well, it isn't quite succession, but it would get some attention," he chuckled. "No one takes all of this nonsense seriously. The people of Dakota are not the least interested in either division of the territory or in statehood. Divide the territory and the same population has to support the cost of running two governments. Gain statehood, and taxation is sure to increase. Not," Armstrong added quietly, "that the average Dakota citizen seems to be very much of much concern to legislators these days. No offense, Bingham, but things used to be different."

For the rest of the evening Percy listened to Armstrong reminisce about days and legislatures past. What 'used to be different' as far as Percy could tell was that the legislative body had once been composed of uncivilized ruffians. By the time he rose to collect his hat and coat

and say good-night, he was thinking that if he had to hear another of
Moses Armstrong's stories about the fistfights and shootings of bygone
days in the legislature, he'd be temped to shoot Armstrong himself.

It was the middle of February, with just under three weeks remaining in the session, when the somnolent afternoons of meetings, motions,
cigar smoking, whiskey drinking, and mutual back scratching were suddenly charged by the appearance of Alexander McKenzie, in town once
again "on business for a friend," as he liked to say as he circulated
among the legislators through the "freedom of the House" privilege he
had been granted by Governor Ordway. Several other prominent north
Dakotans, including Percy's *Argus* editor, A. W. Edwards, had also arrived in town and could be seen with their heads together at the Central
Hotel. Percy watched, well aware of his envy as McKenzie shook hands
and spoke quietly, gaining the attention of each and every man he approached. There were several in the assembly who did not trust Mc-
Kenzie, Percy knew, for his allegiance to north Dakota and his loyalty to
the interests of the railroads were never in doubt. And yet, such was the
personal magnetism of the big man (referred to in the *Herald* by an exasperated Maris Taylor as Alexander the Great, "generous to his friends
and friendly toward his enemies") that he could go anywhere, approach
anyone, with the assurance that he would be heard, if not welcomed.

Percy was a little embarrassed by the pleasure he took in having
McKenzie stop one afternoon to lay a huge paw on his shoulder in full
view of his fellow legislators who had largely ignored him. They needed
to meet that evening, McKenzie had murmured. It was a meeting for
which Percy was eager, for he would soon be returning home with,
thus far, little to show for his time in Yankton. Although Percy arrived
at McKenzie's room with one more whiskey in his gut than the two he
had intended to allow himself, he was still nervous. Within five minutes he had been put at ease by McKenzie's casual insults regarding the
legislators who had not supported Percy's appropriation bill for a normal school for Fargo. And then Alexander McKenzie began to quietly
explain to Percy just why they were both in Yankton, why a full third
of the Council members were newspaper editors or owners who had
received patronage from Governor Ordway in some form or other, how
Percy would be able to hold his head high when he returned to Fargo,

and what was expected of him during the remaining two weeks of the Fifteenth General Assembly. The stage had been set for the territorial capital to be removed from Yankton once and for all, and Percy had a part to play.

"To Fargo?" Percy asked. McKenzie's look in response made him regret the blunt hopefulness of his question.

"I got a dozen good reasons why Fargo should be at the top of the list. That's why you and me are having this here discussion, you see. But don't let's put the cart in front of the horse. Now, listen. What I got to tell you has got to stay in this room. Every man who knows what you are about to know knows it on account of I told him so. One word of this reaches someone who ain't a personal friend of mine and I will need to personally express my displeasure, if you see what I mean. You or anyone else goes mentioning Fargo or Bismarck or Jamestown in that Assembly and right there," McKenzie smacked his fist into his palm, an unexpected counterpoint to his quiet voice that caused Percy to jump, "the whole deal is lost. See what I mean?"

Percy swallowed and nodded.

"Now, listen. Most of your fellow assemblymen is feeling fat and happy and ready to go home. Now's the time to get a capital removal bill going."

"Who will—"

"Just listen. You don't got to know more than I got to tell you just now. Less mistakes likely that way. The moment that bill gets introduced we got eleven 'aye' votes in the House. That's ten plus you," McKenzie bared his teeth in a smile. "That's close, but it don't get us a majority, and it don't get the bill to the Council. That's why that bill is going to fail." McKenzie sat back in his chair and nodded his head and this time Percy knew enough to wait silently for the big man to speak again. "That's when George Walsh is going to nominate Huron as the new capital of Dakota Territory."

"Huron!" Percy almost stood. "What's in Huron? Why it can't have a population of two, maybe three thousand. And the newspaper from there—" Percy gestured with a hand, as if he were shooing away an insect.

"It ain't anywhere near that big. But it's in central south Dakota, and the delegates from thereabouts are the wildcards, you see. They

404 Brenda K. Marshall

ain't feeling so pleased right now about how the appropriations panned out. Sioux Falls got the penitentiary and the Deaf Mute School. Vermillion got the University of Dakota. Brookings, the Agricultural College. Yankton, the Hospital for the Insane. But you get out of this here little corner of the territory and what you got are folks in the rest of south Dakota feeling just plum left out. Huron. Aberdeen. Maybe even Pierre. Them delegates from Mitchell and Chamberlain ain't feeling none too flush either. It don't matter which one Walsh nominates, except that Huron looks just right, not too close to the 46th parallel and not too close to Yankton."

"But a bill to remove the capital to Huron won't pass."

"No, it won't. But just having it dangled in front of the Huron delegate will get him good and hungry, and—"

"—will whet the appetites of the others in mid-Territory, and make them just a bit more congenial to the notion of removal in the first place," Percy finished McKenzie's sentence, and then felt the small warmth of pleasure in his chest as McKenzie nodded his head like a teacher with a pupil just catching on. "So then another bill to remove the capital, without naming the new location precisely, is brought to the floor again, and we're one step closer to—"

"No," McKenzie interrupted.

Percy's glow was extinguished. "No?"

"No, that would be going backwards. Don't ever want to do that. What you can expect at that point is a bill to create a commission charged with the responsibility of, say, collecting bids from interested towns, and making the decision."

Percy's short bark of laughter, quickly covered by a cough, registered his surprise. "Take the decision out of the legislators' hands? Is that even legal? Even if it is I can't imagine that it would meet with much enthusiasm. If my arithmetic is correct, and I add your eleven sure votes plus those of the mid-Territory delegates, I get enough to get though the House, but not the Council. And even then, so much would depend on who got elected to that committee."

"Commission, not committee, Representative Bingham. A commission to be composed of nine citizens of the Territory, to be appointed, not elected."

"By?"

"By Governor Ordway. Then it's up to the Council to confirm the appointments, or rather, nominations."

Percy was silent for a moment before wondering aloud, "But even if a third of the Council votes are assured, that still leaves a handful of unknowns who–"

"Who are still waiting for the governor to sign all them bills that those Councilmen have spent almost two months now getting passed. I guess that's likely to make them pretty agreeable."

Chapter XLVII

In Which Percy is Hanged for a Lamb

It is generally conceded that this legislature is the worst with which the Territory was ever afflicted. With a great majority of members of the last body there did not appear to lurk a single honest impulse. They came to Yankton imbued with jobs and schemes for private benefit and their exertions during the session have all tended in that direction. The Territory has been bonded in large amounts and all the people burdened with an onerous interest bearing debt that ambitious towns might be benefited and the price of lots enhanced by the erection of a public building. The vigorous vetoes which were placed against this kind of legislation two years ago by Governor Ordway were this year stayed by reason of a corrupt compact with the executive, probably the most shameful and disgraceful in the history of the country, not excepting the reign of the carpet-bag thieves in the south. The Dakota *Herald,* Yankton

Across the territory and into the bordering states, newspapers cried "Shame!" and condemned the legislators who jobbed, schemed, appropriated, and most shockingly of all, approved the capital removal commission. They denounced the governor who appointed the removal commission and the nine "ringsters" who were given the power not only "to locate the capital, buy and sell, and build, and pay off their friends," but to "draw upon the public treasury under one pretense and another for almost unlimited sums."

Those few newspapers that absented their voices from the general

hue-and-cry were either run by members of Ordway's "press association" or they represented towns rumored to be contenders for the new
capital. As the Elk Point *Coyote* colorfully explained, "Not a single paper in Dakota with the exception of those directly controlled by the
rascals engineering the Steal, or those whose editors hope for a suck at
some of the trickling streams of swag, support the monstrous scheme."
The Fargo *Argus*, whose employee, Percy Bingham, had not only voted
for the capital removal commission, but had reported via telegraph that
the "capital commission bill is clear and straight and fair," remained
strangely silent regarding the last days of the Fifteenth General Assembly.

Leaving the hornets' nest stirred up by the southern Dakota press
behind him, Percy hoped to encounter little more than a suspicious buzz
back home, which would transform into a hum of approval once Fargo
was identified as a top candidate for the territory's new capital. The
Fargo *Post*, a pro-statehood paper that Percy found lying on one of the
benches of the car in which he rode from Brainerd to Fargo, thus came
as an unpleasant surprise. Not only did it express its disgust with the
capital removal commission, calling it "a scheme worthy of Boss Tweed,
in his best days," but it insinuated as well that the Cass County representative, Fargo's own Percy Bingham ("the equivocating voice of the
vacillating *Argus*") had been paid for his support of the scheme. Why
else, the *Post* reasoned, would a legislator support what was necessarily
an insult to every honest sensibility. With Alexander McKenzie placed
at the helm of the commission by Governor Ordway, the *Post* story continued, Bismarck and Bismarck alone was likely to benefit.

This, Percy thought, setting down the paper and looking out the
window at the passing fields of dirt-crusted snow, was going to be a
rougher patch to get through than he had anticipated. Every acre abutting the tracks had now been tamed by the plow, and still the countryside appalled him with its indiscreet openness and unhampered space.
Even the little towns that were forever bringing the train to a halt and
the many farmsteads that now dotted the prairie did little to tidy the
plains. Percy thought back to his first trip to Dakota. He had changed,
too. Then he had not known what he wanted. Now he did. He wanted
not to be a failure. He did not love politics, but he did not want to be
a failed politician. He did not love his home in Dakota, but he did not

want to fail to bring the capital to Fargo. And he supposed, his sigh misting the window, he did not love his wife, but he did not want to fail at marriage either.

Attention to the latter would have to wait, Percy thought, sitting up and squaring his shoulders. He would weather the rough patch. He had to believe that McKenzie would back Fargo for the new capital. In time, all moral indignation over the means would be swallowed in anticipation of the end, and Percy would become the man who helped Fargo step up to its rightful place alongside the capitals of the nation. In two years he would walk from his home on Thirteenth Street to take his seat in the Sixteenth General Assembly.

So despite the cold stares that met him as he stepped off the train outside the Headquarters Hotel, despite the shoulders turned against him as he stepped up to the bar across the street at the Sherman House for "a short one," despite the mumbled excuses that she was running late and could not stop to talk from a clearly embarrassed Lydia Harkness whom he met coming out of her dressmaker's as he strolled toward his home with his portmanteau in hand, despite, even, the odd expression of concern with which his wife received him upon his return, Percy walked into the *Argus* office of A. W. Edwards the following morning with something of a bounce to his step. He had seen Major Edwards in McKenzie's company too often in Yankton not to feel confirmed in his understanding that his boss was McKenzie's confidante. Here, in this office, Percy believed, he would be made privy to the plan that McKenzie had developed to bring the capital to Fargo. Only in retrospect would Percy remember the ducked heads and muffled replies as he pulled the back door shut against the wind and greeted the men setting type for the next day's *Argus*.

"Close the door behind you, Bingham. Have a seat," Edwards said, looking up just long enough to motion toward the chair opposite his desk.

Percy waited, listening to the shifting pitch of the wind outside. It took him a moment to locate a nearby whistle, coming from the window onto Seventh where the casement had warped away from the stud. When he looked away from the window he discovered his employer studying him.

"You just get back?"

"Yesterday. On the Number One."

Edwards nodded his head and frowned. "I like you, Bingham. I admit that I was a bit reluctant to take you on at first, but you've come along, especially once you stepped back from the bottle a bit. No, no—" Edwards' held up his hand as if to stop Percy's denial. "So I'm sorry to have to let you go, but I'm sure that you understand that I have no choice. For the good of the paper, of course."

For a moment Percy did not speak. When he did, his "what?" came out as a whisper. Percy cleared his throat and tried again. "Let me go? I don't understand."

"Calm down. Calm down." Edwards settled back into his chair, and waited for Percy to sit back in his as well. "The public outcry against the capital removal commission... well, I should say, the newspapers' outcry that is feeding public sentiment in the towns—"

"But the *Argus*—"

"The *Argus*," Edwards looked back down to the sheaf of papers before him before continuing, "the Argus shares the distress of the good men of the territory to find that the recently adjourned legislative body was so obviously corrupt, and that its own employee, who it had taken to its bosom and supported in his campaign for the Cass County legislative seat, should be so easily deceived as to participate in an obvious miscarriage of justice. As a sign of its good faith with the public, the *Argus* has parted with its former employee, Representative Percy Bingham." Edwards looked up. "The boys are setting the type for the story as we speak. That said, the *Argus* will choose to move on to other topics of importance, putting the dealings of the Fifteenth General Assembly behind it."

Percy shook his head as if to clear it of a bad dream. Then it occurred to him that this was a game that the two of them were playing, and that the longer it took him to catch on to the intricacies and nuances of the stratagem, the further he would fall in the Major's estimation. With a small smile, Percy took a guess.

"I see," he said slowly. "The *Argus* must maintain its popularity with its public as well as with its, shall we say, influential friends. I understand. This puts me in a delicate position, unenviable even, at least for the time being, but if I am to now work, shall we say, behind the scenes, I am, of course, ready to help in whatever way these, um, influential friends would prefer." Percy stumbled to a halt. When Edwards did not speak, Percy said, "We are all, I am sure, most interested now in seeing to it that Fargo take her proper place on the territorial stage."

"I beg your pardon?"

Percy licked his lips. If this were a test, he could use some prompting. When it was clear that there would be none forthcoming from Edwards, Percy leaned forward in his chair. "It is my understanding from a mutual friend that Fargo is at the top of the list, I believe those were his very words, at the top of the list for the home of the new capital. If there is some way in which I can be more useful to our friend in making this happen than as a newspaperman for the *Argus*, then, although I would, of course, be sorry to leave–"

"Ha! Fargo the next capital!" Edwards interrupted with a laugh. "Not likely. You won't find the citizens of Fargo banding together to come up with the $100,000 necessary for the bid, and as for the required acreage, look around you Bingham. Who would donate the land? Maybe your father would like to have the capital in one of his wheat fields."

Percy's ears had begun to ring, and his heart was pounding. There was the very real and horrifying chance, Percy knew, that he was about to beg. But so impossible were the words he was hearing that he forced himself to remain alert, desperately hoping that he was just seconds away from breaking the code of the conversation. There was still time to be assured that all would be well.

"Fargo." Edwards was shaking his head. "Is that what you thought, Bingham? Well, I'm sorry to hear it. Perhaps that will go some way toward explaining your vote to your acquaintances, but it will not assuage our readers, to be sure. No, Bingham, you appear to have taken part in what is too often being called a swindle to allow you to be further associated with the *Argus*. There is even speculation that some legislators left Yankton with an extra $10,000 in their pockets in return for an 'aye' vote for the commission. I have no intentions of repeating gossip in my paper, of course, but I can not have a man in my employ under such a cloud of suspicion. I am sorry, but I will have to ask you to clean out your desk on your way out." Edwards stood, and extending his hand to Percy added, "No hard feelings. I wish you the best of luck. Good day."

Percy looked at the hand and then stood, holding on to the arms of his chair for support. His voice was shaking. "It is not a good day. Not for me. And unless we can come to an understanding it will not be a good day for you either."

"You're upset, Bingham. I can understand that. Now go home. Something will come up for you."

"You forget, Major, I know too much to be sent home like a schoolboy. I will not be played for a fool like this."

"Only a fool can be played for a fool." Edwards had lost his benevolent expression. "Now go. And let me give you one last piece of advice. Keep your speculations and accusations to yourself. They will only get you into trouble."

"You spent the better part of two weeks in Yankton yourself, Major. You were as often in McKenzie's company as out of it. Alexander McKenzie as much as promised me that a vote for the capital removal commission was a vote for Fargo, and you knew that was coming all along. I know how the game was played. I can name names, Major. I will name names and yours will be at the top of the list. 'Miscarriage of justice,' I'll be damned. I don't know what you got for setting me up for a double-cross, but damn it all…damn it all…I'll…I'll–"

"You'll what? Everyone is speculating on 'how the game was played,' Bingham. It's in all the papers. And there's no lack of names tossed about. Here in Fargo, it just happens to be yours that comes up most often. All you're threatening to do is to confirm your own dereliction of duty as a legislator. I'm going to say it one more time. Go home."

"And in confirming my dereliction I will confirm yours, and that of all of the members of Governor Ordway's press association." Percy drew himself up as tall as he could as he spoke. "I will add my voice as a chastened legislator to the call for Ordway's removal, and when that happens, that will be the end of the *Argus'* public printing patronage, and that, Major Edwards, will be the end of the *Argus.*"

"You have a somewhat inflated sense of the story you think you have to tell, Bingham. You know full well that as the Cass County newspaper with the largest subscription the *Argus* is simply the logical choice for governmental printing contracts and notices. I have nothing to hide here. You, however, have nothing to gain by being difficult, and everything to lose." Major Edwards' hand closed on Percy's arm and turned him toward the door as he spoke into Percy's ear. "Take my advice. The last man you want to upset is our 'mutual friend'. Sing, and you may well find your pleasant cage has disappeared, and your wife and boy flown home to papa."

Percy made one detour between the *Argus* building on Seventh and his home on Thirteenth, to pick up the bottle that would keep him company throughout the day. When he passed Frances in the hallway he did not meet her eyes, nor did he speak, and a moment later Frances heard the library door close. Hours later, when Frances knocked on the door to say that supper would be on the table in a half hour, there was only a muffled, "Eat without me," in response. Sometime later, not long after she had sent Houghton to bed, Frances heard the front door open and shut. Where Percy had gone, or when he had returned home, she did not know. When he walked into the kitchen, unshaven and bedraggled and asking for coffee well after noon the following day, Frances did not have to ask what had occupied him the evening before. Seated again, Frances returned to her study of the patterns that she had removed from an *Erich's* winter catalogue.

"Where's the boy?" Percy asked after he had taken several swallows of coffee. Frances looked over at him and watched as he first scratched his chin, then dropped his head into one hand.

"It is Saturday, Percy. He is with Mrs. Shaw."

"Who?"

"Mrs. Shaw. Mrs. Ford?"

"Mmm," Percy groaned, and then startled both of them with an involuntary shudder that shook his entire body. "Christ, it's cold in here."

"It isn't at all cold. With the wind dying down overnight I had hoped to be able to open the windows for a moment this afternoon, just for a little fresh air."

"Wind, wind, wind," he moaned. "Godforsaken place." The latter had been spoken in a mumble, almost below hearing.

For a moment Frances did not speak. She was trying to decide what she was feeling. Percy had been drinking, after so many months of control, if not abstinence, and her response to his condition was so complicated that she herself did not know whether she welcomed his weakened state or felt a residue of sadness for his defeat. Or whether she truly cared at all. Some part of her, she realized, had expected this. She had read the newspapers. The *Post* was the worst, but the *Republican* (which had recently absorbed the old *Times*) had been almost as hard on Percy, complaining about his inability to secure a normal school for Fargo, and suggesting that he had chosen to line his own pockets instead. She had noticed that the few neighbors with whom she spoke, and a number of shopkeepers as well, had been clearly embarrassed to find themselves in her presence. Her response was a bemused wonder at her own surprise. Thoroughly distanced from her husband, she had forgotten that others must assume that she necessarily shared his shame. Only Houghton's tears after a row with a neighbor boy could effectively remind her that her husband's status was, in the community's eye, his family's. But Houghton was a resilient boy and children had more interesting things to do than to repeat their parents' insults. By the time Percy arrived home from Yankton, the worst of the storm had blown over for Houghton. It had not, evidently, for Percy. The situation was as inconvenient as complicated, Frances thought. For two months she had practiced the words that would inform her husband of her intention to divorce. Now did not seem to be the right time for their talk.

"We need to talk," Percy said into Frances' silence.

Frances released a short laugh in surprise. "Indeed we do. I mean, yes, of course."

Percy lifted his head from his hand, took another swallow of coffee, and looked across the table at his wife. "Are you well?" he asked.

"Am I well? Why do you ask?"

"You seem agitated. And you look rather, I don't know, flushed. Have you lost more weight?"

Frances resented the question. She had been a long time before her mirror earlier in the day, taking stock of her complexion, roughened by too many hours in the cold wind and the sun, of her figure, too thin, no longer youthful, and of her hair, once her glory but now, with no Kirsten to work it into an intricacy of swirls and braids, and no patience of her own, simply twisted and secured at the base of her neck in a severe bun. On her forehead were the shadows of parallel lines she hadn't noticed before. Still, she did not care to have Percy, with his morning beard and his unkempt hair and his whiskey breath, commenting upon her decline.

"Have you taken a look at yourself lately?" she replied.

Percy scowled. His had been a question of concern. He felt like he had put a hand out in friendship and had it bitten in return. "We need to talk," he said again.

"Yes."

"I have been thinking. It is time to make some changes in our lives. Real, substantial changes. I am through with Dakota. This morning I woke with the understanding that this has been a decade of lunacy for me, for us. Nothing that I, that we, rather, have done has made sense. But," Percy added, dropping his voice to his orator's baritone, "'tis not too late to seek a newer world."

"This morning, Percy, you woke suffering from the effects of an intemperate evening. Perhaps if you go to bed tonight without a bottle for a companion you will see things differently tomorrow."

For a moment Percy did not respond. He very deliberately took a sip of his coffee and set the cup on its saucer. He had begun to nod to himself, agreeing with his own silent conversation. Finally he said, "Really, Frances? Will I have another companion in my bed? Will you and I make sense tomorrow morning as husband and wife?" Percy kept his eyes, bloodshot and puffy, on Frances. "Will I wake with my wife loyal, my reputation intact, my honor unquestioned, my employment returned?"

"Your–?"

"Yes, my dear, Major Edwards has informed me that the Fargo *Argus* can no longer risk association with a man whose character has been so publicly besmirched. Perhaps the Major has done me a favor. It was a mistake to have come here in the first place." Percy stood to pour another cup of coffee, releasing a quiet groan in the process. "Every step I have taken here has been a step further from sanity, and every step we have taken has increased the distance between us. It is time to leave. It is the only way."

"Where will you go?" Frances asked, and then watched as Percy froze with his back toward her and the coffee pot still in his hand.

When he turned, his expression had hardened. "Where will I go? Where will we go, you mean. No?"

Frances sidestepped the question. "Is there money for a move? Have you saved enough to live on until you find something new? The house–"

"The house," Percy interrupted, "is not ours. I am in no position,

without employment, to continue making payments. The down-pay-
ment itself was provided to me by Alexander McKenzie, and he has
received good value for his money. There, too, I have been a dupe, purchased on the cheap. It is said upon the streets that I number among
the legislators paid $10,000 for a vote in support of McKenzie's capital
removal commission, but I am indeed sorry to inform you that I was
purchased for a mere fraction of that. I am to be hanged for a sheep,
when it was only a runt of a lamb that I accepted. Ah," Percy settled
back into his chair, "that is quite a look that you are giving me, but it is
wasted. I assure you that my self-loathing is sufficiently chastening. You
may spare me the wifely censure. In short, my dear, there are no savings.
What I have accumulated, it appears, is the dust of false expectations."
Percy dropped his head to mumble, "Great expectations, perhaps, but
my Magwitch does not, as it turns out, love me after all."

"Speak up, Percy. I can not understand you."

"We will default on the mortgage. As for the furniture, the carpets,
the buggy, everything," Percy made a swing with his arm meant to encompass the house, but ended with his flutter of the wrist that signified
contempt for whatever it was he was pushing away from himself, "with
the exception of what you brought with you, of course, not a stick, not
a stitch of it is paid for. All will be lost. That is why I have one more
mouthful of shit to chew–"

"Percy!"

"–before we leave Dakota Territory, never to return, and it will be
worth it to leave this godforsaken land behind. I will go with my hat
in hand, defeated and contrite and ready to bear my father's contempt,
and will ask for just enough to see us relocated in…in…oh, I don't
know, New York, or Boston, or Philadelphia. My father may despise his
son, but for the sake of his grandson and his precious daughter-in-law,
he will give what I ask, and then we shall escape. And then, maybe then,
you and I will be able to remember why we chose to marry in the first
place."

A small, sad smile crossed Frances' face and the two of them sat
in silence for a moment. With a sigh Frances prepared her words with
care. Percy's clarification of his financial affairs not only explained
the reluctance these past two months of the usually garrulous grocer
(and Fargo's new mayor), W. A. Yerxa, to put her purchases on Percy's

account, and of Mr. de Lendrecie's downright refusal at the Chicago House Dry Goods, but it raised the specter of a new threat to her land ownership as well. If word got out that she owned a quarter section of land, could she be dunned for her husband's debts? Worse, could Percy claim the land as equally his? Why did she know so little, when for so long she had believed that she knew so much? She did her best to keep her voice calm.

"Listen to me, Percy. Listen to me, not as your wife...oh, Percy, I will be the first to admit that I have not been the wife you deserved... but as the friend I once was. We were friends. Remember? We were friends." Frances paused to study Percy's expression. She was reminded of a beaten dog backed into a corner.

"What?" His voice had dropped to a whisper.

"I am saying that I think that you are right. This is not the right place for you. It has never been the right place for you, and I am sorry, truly sorry, Percy, for my part in keeping you here. But you are still a young man. Yes, you are," Frances insisted. "And you have talent, but not for life here. You belong–"

"Where I belong is not the question, Frances. The question is where you belong. I will answer that for you. A wife belongs with her husband."

"Are we husband and wife, Percy? Truly? Oh, Percy, let's be honest for once with each other. Our lives have been so separate for so long, and it pleased us both to have it that way. What is it that we share? Not hopes, not dreams. Percy we were friends, and now we are strangers, but I think we were never truly–"

"Married." It was a statement, not a question. "And Houghton, do you and I not share a son, you and I who were never truly married?"

"A beautiful son. A strong and smart boy who is flourishing here, who–"

"Whose parents were never truly married," Percy finished, shaking his head. "You never cease to amaze me, Frances, with your powers of convoluted imagination. Are you suggesting that I leave here without you? Without my son?"

"I am suggesting...no, I am not suggesting," Frances drew herself up, placed both hands flat on the table before her, and took a deep breath. "I am saying that I want a divorce."

The word, finally spoken, waited there between them. For several moments they looked into each other's eyes, Frances waiting, Percy searching for some piece of information that he had not previously understood. His expression slowly changed from amazement to suspicion.

"What are you planning?"

"What do you mean?"

"Where will you go? What do you intend to do? You have no money of your own? You have no family to return to, only–" Percy became perfectly still. When he spoke again, his voice had gone ugly with threat. "Perhaps you will tell me now that the rumors have been true all along."

"What rumors?"

"Oh, never said to my face, of course. Just the ends of jokes I hear, the sly asides, the insinuations."

"Percy, I have no idea what you are talking about."

"You haven't heard? About Percy Bingham's wife? Said to entertain so charmingly at John Bingham's famous dinners?" As Percy spoke he stood again. With each word he seemed to lean closer to Frances across the table. "A great favorite with the men, they say. The same one who found it more convenient to live with her father-in-law than to move six miles to be with her husband? No? You haven't heard? Well, then, my dear, let me tell you what they are saying about you as you ride west out of town every day ... oh, of course, I know about your daily rides, cross-saddle like a field hand. I have even been stupid enough to think that they would do you good, help you to be happier here in Fargo. Well, my dear, the gossip has it that you are entertaining your father-in-law as well. Is that it, my dear, have I been cuckolded by my very own father? Am I not only a failure but a fool as well, and you, a whore?"

"You are a drunk, and a vulgar one at that." Frances, white-faced, stood. "There are no such rumors. This is the fabrication of a sick mind. I will not spend another night in the same house with a man who has spoken to me as you have. There will be a divorce. And as for what I will do then, I do not know, but I and our son–"

"Houghton." Percy suddenly sank back into his chair, his face pale and his skin oily, sick with the venom of his speech and with his own accusations. His head was spinning and his stomach churned. He believed he might vomit. Had he indeed heard such rumors? Or was Frances right? Was this the speculation born of his own anxiety and dread, nourished within the fog of alcohol? He did not look up, but he knew that Frances remained standing at the end of the table. He had given in to the gratification of fury, the drama of his accusation. He had wanted to inflict pain, and he had, but now what? Frances and Houghton were all that remained. Was there perhaps something he could say, should say, that would undo his words? Taking a deep breath, he summoned up his last bit of resolve and lifted his head ... and was surprised to see that Frances' expression had quickly passed from shock at his words to, what? Her eyes reminded him of the dirty bits of ice that crust at the edges of a melting snow bank. What he read there was cold satisfaction, as if she had just been proclaimed the victor in a contest. His own fury returned.

"Our son? Are you so sure?" Percy said, and then watched as Frances strode from the room.

There. He had done it. It had been his choice, his doing.

CHAPTER XLVIII

Percy's Last Poem

From the sofa in his library where he lay, Percy listened to his wife in the room above packing her bags. When he heard the front door close he sat up to retrieve his flask from the jacket hanging on the back of a nearby chair. The feverish exhilaration of his insult had waned. Lacking any real belief in his accusation beyond a generalized jealousy borne of an old father-fury (of which even he had grown weary), Percy was faced with the cold realization that he had exchanged all hope of reconciliation for the stunned look his words had brought to Frances' face. He had done her violence once, although nothing that was not within a husband's rights, but until that moment less than an hour ago in the kitchen he had not been able to muster the potent combination of surprise, insult and contempt that could touch her to the quick.

And then, once again, she had trumped him with action.

Percy remained in the library for hours, occupied entirely with the flask and a rehearsal of the circumstances that had led to this day. He kept the curtains drawn tight, a man in hiding with precisely no one looking for him. In the early afternoon he slipped out of his house to pick up another bottle at the new National Hotel conveniently nearby. At some point, once again back on the sofa, he fell asleep, waking to an approximation of sobriety that he could not tolerate. He left his home the second time in the early twilight.

He will not remember his return.

Shivering awake upon his front porch the next morning with a bloodied forehead and nose, Percy finds that he is wearing neither coat nor boots. His spectacles, he is relieved to discover, are still wrapped about his ears. He does not have a wallet. He feels about for his flask. It is gone. A shudder shakes his frame. He sniffs, looks down, and sees that he has wet himself. He stands, reaches for the railing for support, and stumbles into his empty house.

Percy is about to drop onto the library sofa, when he reels, retraces his steps to the landing, slowly climbs the stairs, and enters his wife's bedroom. He pulls off his clothes and climbs under the covers of the bed. He sinks his head into the pillow, trying with his weight to stop the bed's orbit. He does not think that he sleeps, but wakes nonetheless to a watery mid-March afternoon light that rests against the window pane, too weak to transfer either heat or illumination to the bedroom. He reaches for his vest to check the time, but his watch, too, is missing. He swings his feet to the floor, and the room is suddenly set free from all physical laws. The walls press against his forehead, the floor pushes against his feet. Bile rises in his throat.

Percy desperately needs a bath, but the stove has gone cold and the boiler is out. It takes him almost an hour to heat enough water for the tub. Easing himself in, he tries to reconstruct the missing hours. He remembers the stench from the N.P. stockyards stirred by a steady northwest wind as he walked into town on Front Street along the tracks. Downtown Front Street had been busy for such a raw Saturday night and yet both O. J. de Lendrecie and Ted Franks had stepped out of their stores as Percy passed to remind him of his winter bill, now that he was back in town. Walking the short block from Seventh to Broadway had been like running a gauntlet in slow-motion, as Percy expected the doors of the meat market, the confectionary, the drug store, the tailor, to open as he passed, each disgorging a proprietor or clerk waving a bill of credit. Looking north beyond the intersection of First and Broadway, illuminated by the new 165-foot electric light tower, Percy had seen George Nicols, the clerk at the Headquarters Hotel, whom Percy had known now for almost eight years, walking toward him. Percy could not pretend that their eyes had not met, so he stood his ground, but Nicols bowed his head with a cough, and turned in the other direction.

Wanting nothing so much as to be invisible, Percy had turned down the alley off Sixth Street to cross over to the Red Light. Within minutes he stepped back outside, a bottle cupped inside his jacket pocket. A short jog brought him onto Washington Street. Percy crossed the street and stumbled down the ditch toward Island Park, an island of leafless, mature trees in a sea of slough grass. He found a seat on a gnarled box-elder with a thick branch the size of a small tree that snaked and looped near the ground. How long he sat there, Percy does not know, but he has an image of himself carefully emptying the remains of the whiskey bottle into his flask. He remembers looking up to see that the wind had blown the sky free of clouds, revealing a perfect half-moon. Perhaps he had meant to retrace his steps back home, but when he stumbled down the bank of Island Park he found himself along the river instead.

At that point he must have followed the Red as it wound toward the N.P. trestle. He remembers being cold, his reluctance for the company of his fellow man paling in comparison to his desire for the warmth of a building. There were very few nearby, the old Fargo-in-the-Timber settlement pretty much a thing of the past. But there had been the sound of a piano in the distance, and Percy had followed the river road past the old steamboat landing until he found the music coming from a sign-less shiplap shack. And then? And then, almost nothing. He had been there for awhile, and then he was there no longer.

Percy stands, feels his head reel once again and steadies himself against the tub. He reaches for a towel, wraps it around his waist, and walks, shivering and dripping, to the kettles that are steaming on the stove. It occurs to him that he might be able to eat, but returning to the warmth of the bath is all he cares to do.

Hooking his legs over the sides of the tub, Percy slides under the water. He does not remember much else of the night, but some of the images that float to him belong to a saloon in Moorhead. He thinks he gave a speech, but he remembers no arguments, no fights, no trouble.

And yet, there is the matter of the bruises, the missing watch, wallet, cigarette case, flask, coat, boots. Percy opens his eyes and looks up into the dim light of the room through the bath water. For a moment his headache recedes. There is calm here, silence. If he could go to sleep, like this, under the water, never to take another breath in his life, would it matter? As though to breathe were life, he recites to himself. Could he, perhaps... with a sudden movement that sends water sloshing onto the floor he sits up and gasps.

The blackness at the edges of his peripheral vision recedes as Percy takes several deep breaths. He sighs and reaches for his shaving things that he has set next to the tub. He dries his hands on the towel there, and sits up with the mirror held between his knees. His hands shake, and almost immediately he feels the razor's sting. A short line of blood forms on his neck, and Percy watches in the mirror as it gathers and pinks a patch of shaving soap to precisely the color of the frosting on the cake in the window of Franks' bakery and confectionary that Percy had passed... could it have just been yesterday? Percy rinses the razor in the tub and sets it aside with the mirror. It is as good a day as any to begin a full beard, he thinks. The steam kettle sounds again, and he stands, climbs out of the tub, and pads to the kitchen, naked except for the towel.

A stack of newspapers next to the kitchen stove catches his eye. Stupid with exhaustion, Percy is unable to stop himself from reading the familiar advertisement for Hostetter's Celebrated Stomach Bitters:

> 'Do you feel that any one of your organs—your stomach, liver, bowels or nervous system, falters in its work? Remember that debility is the "Beginning of the End"—that the climax of all weakness is a universal paralysis of the system, and that such paralysis is the immediate precursor of Death'.

"The climax of weakness is paralysis," Percy murmurs aloud. "Paralysis is the precursor of death." He shudders and looks around the room, then crosses into the parlor and takes a sheet of paper from the small desk in the corner, drops a cushion from the sofa onto the wooden chair and sits.

Percy tries to remember the wording of the 'Notice' that had caught his attention in the Dakota *Herald* one Saturday early in February while still in Yankton. At the time he had felt only amazement for the writer's willingness to make public his shame. At the time, Percy thinks, he knew nothing of shame. Percy closes his eyes. Van Something-or-Other. The name escapes him, but the rest of the words are pretty clear. 'Notice is hereby given that my wife, Mrs. Van Something-or-Other, has left my bed and board without' ... what, Percy thinks? Just cause? Provocation? ... 'and I warn the public against trusting her on my account as I will pay no debts of her contracting'. He could write something to the same effect, although what he hopes to accomplish is probably quite different from what the Dutchman had intended. He will simply spread some of the shame around before he gets on the eastbound train early Monday morning. His N.P. pass from McKenzie is still good. He will find someone in St. Paul to lend him enough money to continue on east.

On the paper Percy writes, "My wife, Frances Bingham, has left my bed and board," but here Percy stops. He can not do it. Paralysis may be the precursor of death, but no desire to get even would excuse this level of public humiliation, even in his absence. Percy sweeps the paper aside, returns to the kitchen for the kettle and walks back to the bath.

The tub no longer looks inviting. He is almost dry. He would like to have a drink, just something to settle his stomach and then crawl back into bed but there is no liquor in the house. He is standing there, kettle in hand and unable to make the simplest decision, when he hears the front door open. A surge of hope further unsettles his stomach. He sets the kettle down and listens for his wife's footsteps. What he hears is the heavy tread of boots. He is still standing in the bath room door when the first man appears, erratically whiskered, red-faced, unfamiliar.

"Who–?" Percy says, but is interrupted when the man lifts his gaze from the towel to Percy's face, and yells, "In here! Pert near naked as a robin."

Percy tightens the towel around his waist. "What–?" he says, but then stops as if expecting to be interrupted again. He is not, and the two men simply stare at each other as they listen to the approaching steps.

The man who now enters the room is another stranger, but this one is clean shaven and dressed well, unlike the first man and the third, who arrives with the information that "ain't nobody else, Mr.–"

A slap across the face stops the third man's speech. To Percy's surprise the slapped man reacts with a merry giggle and then begins to nod his head as if responding to good news that only he can hear. His eyes

are unnaturally wide, and this, with the nodding, gives him the look of
a horse trying to bring something unfamiliar in front of him into focus.
When the well-dressed man unexpectedly smiles as well, puts his finger
to his lips, and hisses, "shhh," the horse-eyed man silently imitates the
gesture.

At this, Percy finds his voice and manages to finish his questions.
"Who are you and what are you doing here?"

"Why, I'm Mr. Shhh, Mr. Bingham. Didn't you hear? And I'm here to
see to it that you do just that. You've become a disappointment to some
of your friends, I'm sorry to say."

"Get out of my house," Percy says, drawing himself up with as much
dignity as a man covered only by a towel can muster, his bare toes
within inches of the strangers' heavy boots.

"Not just yet, Mr. Bingham. Our visit has just begun. Have you seen
today's paper?" The man does not wait for a response as he hands over
the Fargo *Republican* that he has been lightly tapping against his thigh.
With a manicured finger he points to an item under "Local News," and
Percy reads:

> *"A spontaneous, if infelicitous, speech is reported to have been
> given by our recently returned representative from the Fifteenth
> General Assembly Saturday night in an establishment across the
> river better known for fisticuffs than oratory. If the gentleman is
> willing to repeat his information when sober, his testimony will be
> much appreciated by the forces pursuing legal redress regarding
> the now infamous Capital Removal Commission. It may do his
> own sullied reputation some good as well."*

"Who are you?" Percy asks again when he can speak.

"I'm a friend of a former friend of yours who asked me to personally express his disappointment in you before I escort you out of town
tomorrow morning on the Number Two. You will not be returning to
Dakota Territory. These two gentlemen have agreed to keep you company until then."

"That will not be necessary," Percy says. "You have anticipated my
plan. I will board the train of my own volition, quite happy to leave Dakota well behind me." Pleased by the steadiness of his own voice, Percy
adds, "And as for our friend—"

The blow to his gut bends Percy in half for a moment before he drops to his knees, then leans forward with one hand on the floor and the other still grasping the towel as he fights to regain his breath. He is aware of the boots now so close to his fingers. And then he feels himself pulled upright by his hair. His face is just inches from the well-dressed man.

"You don't have any friends," the man says. "That's the point." He releases Percy's hair, takes out his handkerchief and wipes his hands, and speaks to the other men. "Remind Mr. Bingham of what he has left to lose should it occur to him to start squawking again." The man looks back at Percy who has begun to sweat. "The boys will see to it that you are at the train station on time tomorrow morning. You see anyone you know, you smile and tip your hat and keep your mouth shut. Get on the first car. I'll be waiting." He turns to leave, but when he passes the horse-eyed ruffian who has been moving restlessly from foot to foot, he hesitates.

"He has to be able to walk. And not the face. You hear?"

The ruffian smiles and nods, and the well-dressed man turns to go. Just as Percy hears the front door close, he is bent over by a second blow to the midsection. In the beating that follows, Percy can think only to keep his hands cupped over his genitals as he staggers between the two men. The blows fall upon his chest and sink into his gut. A punch to a kidney drops him to his knees again, and before he is aware of what is about to happen, he vomits a watery bile onto the shoes of the horse-eyed man. There is a moment in which nothing seems to move, and then, just as the first man says, "Now hold on, Emmett," a kick at Percy's ribs lifts him from the ground and rolls him onto his side against the tub. From that moment on there seems to be speech and a kick in unison, "That's enough, now" is accompanied by a boot to the sternum. "O.K., stop," crushes his ribs. "God damn it, Emmett!" is the last that Percy hears as a boot sends his cupped hands flying to his sides.

He is whimpering as he wakes to the smell of his own excrement. Both men are standing above him, the first still repeating, "God damn it, Emmett. God damn it." It's a poem, Percy thinks. A child's poem. Then Percy realizes that he has lost consciousness for no more than a minute at best, and that the poem is the first man's attempt to stop the beating to which this Emmett is still devoted. "Christ Almighty," the latter says, wrinkling his nose as he bends toward Percy again. "He shit all over himself! Grab his feet, Fred." The weird giggle returns, and Percy is suddenly lifted from the floor and dropped into the tub. The water is tepid but Percy feels a waking into the full comprehension of his pain. He hears himself gasp, "Enough."

"Just about," Emmett says, and giggles again. The man's wide, pale eyes are almost completely devoid of intelligence as he bends over Percy, grabs him by the hair, and pushes his head under the water. When Percy is dragged up out of the water again, gasping, he hears his tormentor whisper cheerfully, "Rub-a-dub-dub." The clutch on Percy's hair tightens. He hears the giggle again. He can not help but struggle against the arm that is trying to push his head under the water. He knows he should not. He knows that these men do not have orders to kill him, and yet, he can not let himself go under again. His arms reach up to push against Emmett's body and his hand touches the metal handle tucked into the creature's waistband. He jerks his hand away from the revolver just as Emmett's hand drops to the handle, catching Percy's.

Percy cries out, "Let go!" He means 'let go of my hand'. He does not mean to be fighting over a gun with this man with the wide-set, empty eyes and the eerie giggle of an idiot. The gun comes free from the man's waistband and still Percy's hand is locked between the gun handle and Emmett's grasp. Then there is a blow to his chest and Percy looks down to see a pink flower, fluid and mutable, rise to the water's surface.

Chapter XLIX

In Which Percy's Past Improves Whereas Frances' Future is Less Certain

The suicide of Percy Bingham, hard upon the heels of his ignominious return from the recent legislative session in Yankton, made the front pages of newspapers across the territory, and accomplished for Percy in death what he had been unlikely to achieve alive: the restoration of his reputation. Were there to be a couple dozen more suicides to follow, Maris Taylor mentioned in private to Moses Armstrong, the legislators of the Fifteenth General Assembly would go down in history as Dakota Territory's most honorable politicians.

"Present company excluded, of course," he had added.

That Percy Bingham, "son of Red River valley bonanza farmer, John Bingham," had killed himself "in remorse for his role in the Capital Removal Commission scandal" and to escape "the resulting and relentless shame that must necessarily dog an honest man forever after" was the assumption of those editors who continued to seethe and sputter over the commission's creation and mandate. Newspapers from the towns hoping to come up with the money and the land necessary to qualify for consideration as the territory's new capital were more likely to see Percy Bingham's death as the tragic result of the continuing trial by press of the legislators of the recent assembly. Only in the Fargo papers did Percy Bingham's personal life figure in the public speculation over the reasons for his actions.

Although Percy may have been hard put to remember the events of his last evening alive, his death brought forth an abundance of reports from individuals who had talked to or seen him during those lost hours. The reports were pretty consistent, the new Chief of Police, George Holes, discovered, differing mostly in the deceased's state of inebriation and dress, or undress, as the case may be. He had spent his money freely until it was gone, tried to buy drinks on credit, written IOUs, sold his coat and watch. He had complained about his father, his wife, and the loss of his position with the *Argus*. He had denounced, in more than one saloon, the corruption, the logrolling and the outright bribery rampant in the legislature in Yankton. The names that he had sprinkled throughout his rambling speeches, which seemed to be equal parts confession and condemnation, were those of the most powerful men in the territory, and the most respected in the north.

No one came forth to identify the men who had evidently beaten and robbed him and left him lying in the brush along the river where he had been discovered by the owner of the First Street Tonsorial Palace in the pre-dawn hours of that Sunday morning. The barber insisted that Percy hadn't looked all that roughed up to him, more like he'd just tripped and fallen or just plain passed out, but his opinion was given little attention. He had recognized Percy as the man whose story in the newspaper following the flood of '81 had advertised his barber shop as a place for cheap haircuts and shaves, bringing in dozens of new Norwegian customers. So he had laid Percy across his mule and carried him to

Thirteenth Street just as the sun was coming up. He'd thrown a blanket over Percy for the trip so no one would have to see the gentleman like that, the barber explained. He wasn't sure that he'd put Percy in front of the right house, since Mr. Bingham didn't seem quite sure himself. It was then that Bingham had offered to pay him, the barber explained, only to discover that his wallet was missing, along with pretty much everything else it looked like.

"And your still by the river?" Holes asked. "Was that O.K.?"

"Yes, sir," the barber replied, before drawing himself up to ask. "What still? I don't –"

"That's fine, Mr. Jefferson. Thank you for your help," the police chief had interrupted.

It was the truncated suicide note, however, that caught the Fargoans' fancy, and was the basis of much whispered talk in the saloons, over billiard tables and breakfast tables, and along the new plank sidewalks steadily creeping into the prairie in all directions. The wording, repeated in the *Post*, the *Argus*, and the *Republican*, was oddly formal for a suicide note, but then this was Percy Bingham, after all. That his wife's abandonment had been the last straw for the man, however, was clear. The story of how he had begun the note, but found it too painful to continue, of how he had then filled the tub for a last bath before taking his life with the pistol found next to him in the water, was retold with such detail that it was easy for all to forget that no one had actually witnessed these last minutes. The women of the community, noting how Frances Bingham had always been haughty and unfriendly, rarely deigning to stop to speak when met upon the street, felt all the more sympathy for a man thoughtful enough to climb into a tub to shoot himself. The *Post's* maudlin phrase, "with a pistol held to his broken heart," caught the fancy of the town romantics, and was repeated for days. By the time the suicide worked its way into Sunday morning sermons—several of which began with a scriptural reading from the fifth chapter of Ephesians and included, at least in passing, a condemnation of Dakota Territory's easy divorce laws, as well as of the spreading agitation for women's suffrage—the resurrection of Percy Bingham's reputation was complete.

The living Binghams were faring less well. Dakota fever was bringing settlers into the territory by the thousands. Trains pulling dozens of freight cars loaded with household goods, stock and grain, and coaches loaded with hopeful families arrived in Dakota daily, making the streets of the booming towns look like a state fair. The attitude of this burgeoning population of small farmers (and of the shopkeepers and businessmen whose trade depended upon them) toward the bonanza farmers had shifted from one of respect and awe to resentment for the preferential treatment given them by the implement dealers and grain elevators, but mostly by the Northern Pacific Railroad. They resented the sidetracks the N.P. had built for a couple of the bonanza farmers, while the small farmer bore the additional cost of transporting his crops to the railroad's elevators, and then of storage there as well. They resented the officers, former and current, of the Northern Pacific who had profited through speculation (such as Frederick Billings) and savvy investment (such as Septimus Slade, who, it was reported, had received twenty-five dollars per acre for land just west of Fargo that he had secured less than a decade earlier for as little as twenty-five cents per acre). This resentment spilled over to include the bonanza farmers, many of whom continued to remain aloof and separate from local community life. As the story of Percy Bingham's suicide grew, so did that of his estrangement from his father, until the entire bonanza farming operation of John Bingham came to share, in the vague and shadowy way of indirect accusation, in the responsibility for his death.

The wife of a suicide may expect a degree of suspicion along with sympathy, but Percy's truncated suicide note denied Frances all of the latter and increased the former. Alfred and Lydia Harkness extended their formal condolences to Frances, suggested that she should rightly be with her husband's family at a time like this, and made it clear that she and Houghton would be unwelcome in the Harkness home, all with the softest of words and the longest of faces. Her reception at the Bingham farm was less cordial. Anna had taken to her bed upon hearing the news of Percy's death, and there she would remain for weeks, insensible and rousing only to take her 'medicine'. She refused to speak to Frances. Her fragile health would not allow her to accompany her father to St. Paul where Percy was to be buried next to his mother in the cemetery of the First Christ Episcopal Church.

Like the citizens of Fargo, John Bingham considered Frances to be, if not directly responsible for Percy's death, then certainly negligent as

a wife, absent when a gently ministering hand upon her husband's suffering brow could have saved him from his own desperate hand. Sitting
alone in his office for hours at a time, he wondered where his family
had gone, and began to form the decision to sell in half-section parcels
what remained of his farm now that Septimus Slade, making good his
threat to sell, had cut square mile holes in the parcel that John Bingham
had come to think of as his own. Taking a notebook from his pocket he
began to figure the profit on the sale of his land at twenty-five dollars
per acre, less the mortgage and interest now in arrears with J. B. Power,
less the settlement he hoped to make with Slade that would keep him
out of court, less the several outstanding debts and loans to be paid off.
There were still too many unknowns to make the figure he stared at
truly meaningful, but it was, nonetheless, a sobering sum. And he was
no longer a young man. Maybe, with some wise investing, it would be
enough to allow him and Anna to return to St. Paul. Anna, he knew,
would like to be back in the city again. Still, John Bingham thought to
himself, it might be worth looking into what was going on in the cattle
business further west in the Little Missouri country of Dakota. Lower
taxes. Fewer laborers required. A beef bonanza. He liked the sound of
that, even though this time he'd have to be a little more careful about
his initial outlay.

Frances was more saddened than surprised to discover that whatever she had been to John Bingham in the past, it all came to nothing
in the face of his son's death. As for her own son, Frances could not tell
the extent to which Houghton truly understood what had happened.
He complained about being taken away from his new friends, but was
also happy to be back on the farm. His father's absence had been more
consistent than his presence, and Frances watched her son closely as
he directed all of his energies toward the farm's activities. Houghton's
anger, she supposed, would surface several years from now, when she
least expected it. In the meantime, he had a home on the Bingham farm,
John Bingham had told Frances on the second morning of her return
following the discovery of Percy's body. She did not. She was welcome
to whatever she had brought to the marriage, and if Percy had provided
for her in the event of his death, good. But since she had evidently decided to leave the Bingham family prior to Percy's death, he saw no
reason for her to change her mind now. Houghton would be provided

for if the boy remained with him and with Anna.

They were in John Bingham's office when he made the offer. His bag was resting against the door frame. In minutes he would be leaving for Fargo where he would see to the transfer of his son's coffin from Luger's to a freight car on the afternoon N.P. heading east to St. Paul. Frances stood just inside the door.

"No," Frances said, and then again, "No. My son stays with me."

"Where?" John continued to write and did not look up as he spoke. In the silence that followed his question, John tore the check free and placed it in an envelope, opened a ledger book nearby, and made a notation. Then, looking up, he asked, "How will you clothe him, feed him, see to his education? Think about it. It would be a shame to make the boy suffer for your own pride and selfishness."

"It is neither —"

"I will not argue with you," John Bingham interrupted. "I have a train to catch and a son to bury. If the boy is here when I return from St. Paul, he is my responsibility from that day forward. If not, I wash my hands of the both of you. Here," John lifted the sealed envelope toward his daughter-in-law. "I am not interested in seeing you starve while you find a way to take care of yourself. And I do not doubt that you will. There will be no more."

When Frances did not reach for the envelope, John Bingham set it down on the edge of the desk, rose, and left the room. Frances slowly dropped into the chair behind her. She heard the front door shut, and watched through the semi-circle of windows as John Bingham strode across the yard, and soon thereafter drove away in the carriage. She was still sitting there over a half hour later when Houghton found her. He was hungry and a little afraid of the strange new cook who was peeling potatoes in the kitchen and had spoken to him in a language he did not understand. Frances nodded to her son, stood, reached for the envelope, and opened it to read the sum on the check before her. It was more than she expected, not as much as she had hoped. It would see her and her son through three, maybe four months, she supposed. Frances looked at Houghton, made silent and still by his mother's expression. Then, as if answering a question, she murmured, "Raleigh is mine." Standing, she put the check in her pocket and said, "I will make a sandwich for you. Tonight we will eat in a restaurant. You will like that, won't you?"

And then, taking her son's hand, Frances left the office of John Bingham without looking back.

Chapter L

In Which Pretty Much Everybody Misses the Train

While newspapermen shook their editorial fists and ambitious businessmen plotted to bring the capital to their towns, the citizens of southeastern Dakota turned to the courts. As a last-minute attempt to thwart the capital removal scheme, a few determined legislators had managed to insert language into the bill that required the nine-man commission to meet in Yankton to organize. Once organized, it had until July 1, 1883, to select "a suitable site for the Seat of Government." If, these politicians explained to the local citizenry of Yankton, a legal injunction could be secured that would restrain the commission from organizing until the constitutionality of the act under which they had been appointed could be tested (for clearly, they reasoned, the power given to the commission violated the Organic Act of Dakota, which stated that the legislature alone had the authority to locate the capital), then the case could be tied up in court until the July 1 deadline passed. As Maris Taylor proclaimed in the *Herald*, "The governor and his henchmen in the Territorial council did their part in declaring that the capital should be removed from Yankton. Still, it may be well enough to remark right here that the capital has not yet gone."

A joke by Moses Armstrong, delivered to Taylor in response to a rumor circulating that the capital removal commission planned to meet in Yankton on March 30th, inspired several Yankton men to gather into nightly patrols to keep a lookout for the "capital ring." The two friends felt justified in their moment of levity, having learned that the injunction papers that would prevent the commission from holding the meeting to organize were in the hands of officers, ready to be served to the commissioners upon their arrival in town. "Advise your readers to place their hen roosts under lock and key and clear their clothes lines before dark in anticipation of the visit, Bud," Armstrong said, adding after a pause, "Come to think of it, it would be just like those scoundrels to sneak into town in the middle of the night to hold their meeting in secret. It might not be enough to keep an eye on the train station and the Eagle House for the stage coach."

March 30th came and went and the nine-man commission had not materialized. Daily the reports of commissioner-sightings reached Yankton from nearby towns. Three commission members had been seen together in Elk Point on April 1st. Four in Vermillion on the 2nd. A telegraph from nearby Sioux City that evening had a half dozen of the commissioners spotted there. Not a one had been seen in Yankton since the day the legislature adjourned. The patrols continued, the lookouts remained vigilant, and Moses Armstrong was invigorated. The early April nights were chilly, but no tender catechism devised by Maude could get him to admit to the stiffness in his knees when he finally came home for breakfast. He was tired, yes, but he had not felt so young in years.

Armstrong began his watch in the early morning hours of April 3rd in the company of several fellow patrollers, a few of whom were evidently of the opinion that if the commissioners were to sneak into Yankton to organize in the middle of the night, their first stop would be at Wagner's Brewery Hall and Billiards Parlor. When Wagner's closed, they would move to the City Hall Saloon where the proprietor kept more informal hours. By that time Armstrong would have visited with the men stationed at the train depot, stopped at the sheriff's office for a chat with the deputy on the night shift, and strolled toward the warehouses that lined the railroad tracks on the southeastern side of town.

It was a dark night, almost a new moon, and coming upon the storage yard of J. L. Foskett's, Armstrong could just make out the line of open and top buggies for sale. Selecting a Corning buggy upholstered with plush whipcord, Armstrong climbed in for a short rest. It was after five when Armstrong woke with a start and scrambled down to make another tour of the warehouses, looking in windows for a tell-tale light. When he reached the edge of the railroad yards, Armstrong stopped and yawned. He felt a little light-headed, and his eyes scratched as if he'd spent a day threshing oats. It was still too early to call the day dawn, but the quality of the dark had shifted perceptibly and Armstrong could see several feet along the tracks. Without warning, a feeling of foolishness washed over him as he pictured himself, a fifty-one-year-old man, hobbling about the quiet nighttime streets of Yankton looking for bogies, while his more distinguished contemporaries (and the bogies themselves) were tucked warmly in their beds.

Moses Armstrong was tired. He had been tired before, but he had never been foolish. With a rueful shake of his head, he was about to turn back toward the center of town when something along the track just beyond the railroad yards caught his attention. Armstrong squinted into the distance. It was probably a varmint of some sort, but for the sake of curiosity and direction, Armstrong walked toward the spot where he had sensed more than seen the thing. He was almost on top of the three-foot stake before a breeze once again fluttered the white flag tied there. Why the current edge of the city limits had been thus marked he didn't know. He'd have to ask Bud Taylor.

Armstrong turned and retraced his steps along the tracks. Reaching the railroad yards he felt, and then heard, the rumble of a train approaching. Pulling his watch free of his vest pocket he made the time out to be just minutes before six o'clock. The first train scheduled for Yankton was the 8:32 Dakota Southern. Armstrong smiled as if he had been handed a gift and set out at a rapid hobble back into town. If it was the commission, thinking that they could sneak into town on a special train at six in the morning, and not be greeted by a committee at the train station, they were in for a surprise.

Within minutes an engine pulling one coach rolled into sight, and then slowed as it reached the white flag. Even though the train was rolling so slowly that it appeared at each moment to be about to come to a halt, it was all Moses Armstrong could do to keep up as he huffed and puffed beside the tracks. Seeing the silhouette of several men waiting on the platform in the gray dawn allowed Armstrong to stop for a moment to catch his breath, wipe his brow, resettle his hat, and continue on at a more dignified pace. He arrived just in time to stand in amazement with his fellows as the train continued its leisurely progress past the station and out of town.

For a moment no one spoke. Then, from the assembled group came the first words, more expletive than question.

"What the–?"

"Private car."

"Well, yes, but what the–?"

"Hunting expedition, maybe?"

"This time of year?"

"Easterners," Armstrong spoke up, and the group turned toward him. "Who else would hunt for sport during nesting season?"

"You here, Moses?"

"I followed the train in from the railroad yards. Going pretty slow for a train, but pretty fast for an old fellow like me."

Amidst the chuckles, Moses Armstrong took a deep breath of morning air, and felt an old confidence return. The excitement of his race alongside the train and the camaraderie on the station platform had renewed his enthusiasm. The schemers would have to show up in town sooner or later and when they did they would be brought up short, and he would be among the party of Yankton's rescuers to see to that. He was still in the game.

Less than ten minutes. That was all the time the meeting had taken. Alexander McKenzie had left nothing to chance. The final two commissioners had ridden into Sioux City after midnight, just in time for the 2 a.m. meeting at Hubbard House. There the nine members of the capital removal commission had begun their rehearsal. The mock meeting was called to order and the commission organized. Selections of officers followed. With the secretary and treasurer determined, Alexander McKenzie nodded to the new territorial attorney general (the former territorial land agent and the current good friend of Nehemiah Ordway), Alex Hughes. Hughes nominated McKenzie to lead the executive committee for the search and the motion was passed. A date and place were set for the next meeting. The meeting was adjourned and the rehearsal complete. And then, with his watch in hand, McKenzie had them do it again. And again.

At 3 a.m. the members of the commission walked from the Hubbard House to the Milwaukee Road depot. Within minutes an engine drawing a single coach pulled up to the platform. The commissioners, now joined by two "confidential friends" who had materialized in the dark to be present as witnesses, boarded the dimly lit train, and it pulled out of town heading west. In Yankton the railroad superintendent in charge of the yards—a man about to leave town for a better paying position with the Northern Pacific Railroad—had the switches set and spiked, allowing the Milwaukee Road special a clear track. Daylight was just breaking when the special pulled alongside the white flag marking the

Yankton city limits. The train slowed and the meeting to organize the
capital removal commission as provided for by the authorizing bill was
called to order. Once again, the members spoke their parts. Just one
word that had not been planned was spoken, and that was when Burleigh Spaulding of Fargo, at thirty the youngest member of the commission, placed his hand upon the curtain behind him as if to look out the
window.

"Don't," McKenzie said.

Minutes later, with the second white flag approaching, the meeting
was adjourned. The commission, having held its first meeting in Yankton, now legally organized and prepared for further business, left the
soon-to-be former capital of Dakota Territory behind.

CHAPTER LI

In Which the Bidding Begins

The capital removal commission moved quickly to collect bids
from the dozen or so Dakota towns that had managed to come
up with the required $100,000 and 160 acres to qualify as the
site of the new capital. The leading citizens of Huron, Aberdeen, Chamberlain, Frankfort, Canton, Redfield and Mitchell in southern Dakota,
assured by their legislators that their towns would go to the top of the
commission's list, boomed their hamlets in anticipation of the prize.
For sheer hyperbole, Pierre's bid could not be bested. Its location on the
Missouri River made the prairie town a point where the "finger board
of nature had manifestly indicated that a great city must rise, as the
city of Thebes rose upon the Nile, of Babylon upon the Euphrates, of
London on the Thames and of Paris on the Seine." The handful of new
citizens of the paper town of Ordway were smugly optimistic (if not the
least inclined to discuss just where their qualifying $100,000 had come
from).

There really were no citizens of Odessa, another paper town, this
one in north Dakota with precisely one structure (and it still on skids).
Owned by a syndicate that included Alexander McKenzie and George
Walsh, the platted town sites of Odessa increased in value rather dra-

matically (and sold quickly) once it became known as the prospective location for the new capital. The nine commission members studied the bids from these and other towns one by one, crisscrossed the territory to listen to speeches, made speeches in return, and moved on. Nowhere were they more lavishly entertained than in Bismarck. As the special N.P. train upon which the commission traveled throughout north Dakota pulled into the town of not quite four thousand they were met by the rousing music of the Eleventh Infantry band newly arrived from Fort Keogh in Montana. Bunting hung from building to building across Main Street. Entertainment included a scenic steamboat trip to point out the natural beauty of the land along the Missouri, and an early morning hunting excursion for prairie chicken and grouse. The Bismarck *Tribune* editor, Colonel Lounsberry, hosted a formal dinner for the out-of-town guests. The visits to Jamestown and Steele along the N.P.'s return trip east later that week paled in comparison.

The vote, to be held on June 2nd in the neutral town of Fargo, could not come soon enough, in Alexander McKenzie's opinion. The commissioners' early unity that had allowed him to orchestrate the now-infamous April morning train ride through Yankton had begun to fray. McKenzie was faced with the tiresome tendency of men to forget the circumstances of their ascent to power as they began to believe in their own rhetoric about the mantle of public trust that rested upon their shoulders. In short, some of the commissioners had begun to think of themselves as honest men. Worse yet, others believed they always had been. Of course, there remained the few commissioners who were frankly as dedicated to locating the capital in a particular town as McKenzie was set on Bismarck. For these men McKenzie was grateful. They would dig their heels in and divide their votes while he maneuvered at least four others toward his choice. All that was required for the decision was a simple majority.

McKenzie had another reason to look forward to his return to Fargo. Never one to put personal pleasure in front of either personal gain or loyalty to the corporations that lined his pockets, he was, nevertheless, a resourceful man with boundless energy who appreciated the company of women. But Alexander McKenzie was not a man to be found in a saloon with a brightly painted woman on his knee or at the opera with another on his arm. His wife in Bismarck would never be forced to suf-

fer over whispered tales of infidelity. When he disappeared with no trace
for days, sometimes weeks, at a time, to St. Paul, to Chicago, to points
unknown, no one knew about the lonely widow waiting in her tidy
house, or the demure spinster grateful for her small apartment away
from an interfering family. But now there was someone neither lonely
nor demure on his mind. He had passed through Fargo on commission
business several times in April and May, and during each stop he made
certain to visit poor Percy Bingham's unfortunate widow.

Frances Bingham was indeed feeling unfortunate.

As Percy had predicted, the house had been lost and the furniture
quickly repossessed. The money that Frances had accepted from John
Bingham was slipping away much more quickly than she had dreamed
possible. When she returned to Fargo with Houghton, Frances had tak-
en a suite for the two of them at the Headquarters Hotel. Within the
week it became clear that her resources would not last long were she
to remain there, so she and Houghton moved across the street to the
Sherman House. A month later they moved again, this time to the more
rustic Fargo House. Houghton was miserable, aimless and bored in the
hotel room and confused by his friends' reports that they were not to
invite him into their homes. Too often, in a burst of guilt and frustration, Frances would take her son by the hand and they would stride out
onto the street to buy a harmonica, a book of riddles, a toy, anything to
displace his look of melancholy. And then, later that night, as her son
slept, Frances would once again count her money, subtract the cost of
stabling Raleigh for another week, take from that another week at the
hotel with meals, and feel the cold chill of panic creep along her spine.

She had no friends. Anna alone, she had once believed, was friend
enough. With the exception of the occasional afternoon with Lydia
Harkness, her socializing had been restricted for her first several years
in Dakota to the visitors who had come to Dakota as guests of the
Northern Pacific and stayed, in passing, at the comfortable Bingham
home. Over time she had come to prefer the company of Little Carl or
Jack Shaw or, more often, Kirsten. Life, in short, had taken place on the
Bingham bonanza farm. Were she still on Percy's arm, or in the company of John and Anna Bingham, door after door in Fargo or St. Paul
would have opened to her, but as a woman alone she had nowhere to
go. Frances tried to imagine what it would mean to support herself and

her son through her own labor, and then gave up the idea as impossible. Was she, Frances Houghton Bingham, to take in dresses to mend? Was she to apprentice herself, at thirty years old, to the milliner who had constructed her finest hats? Was she to descend to the kitchen of the hotel, take off her brocaded jacket and roll up the sleeves of her silk dress, and begin peeling potatoes and chopping onions?

And yet, doing nothing was an equally untenable proposition, except that doing nothing appeared to be the only thing she knew how to do. Oh, she could compute the wages of a threshing crew in her head more quickly than John Bingham could on paper. She knew how to organize the room and board for a hundred hired hands. She understood the proper tone to use in correspondence with an implement dealer concerning an invoice that was incompatible with a figure quoted earlier. But these were the skills of a helpmate, a wife, a daughter-in-law. Or of a bookkeeper, which is to say, of a man. They were useless to her now.

When her anxiety grew too large for a hotel room, Frances would slip a penny into the hand of Reecher Starbird, the boy who lurked about the hotel waiting to run errands for the guests, asking him to bring Raleigh around, and then to keep an eye on Houghton until she returned. She was aware of the stares she drew as she sat atop the elegant bay in her navy blue riding habit, her short-waist jacket with its rolling collar and her matching straw hat far more elegant than the Sunday dress of the ladies looking up from the sidewalks. Her destination never varied. Throughout the spring Frances would ride to her land, sometimes to sit inside the crumbling shanty, sometimes to walk among the trees by the Sheyenne, sometimes to watch Peter Erickson or his sons as they tilled and planted her eighty acres. Over and over again, Frances would imagine the bushels per acre this fall's harvest would bring, guess at the price per bushel she could get, and calculate her share of the income. Would it be enough to see her and Houghton through the next winter? Enough to pay Jack Shaw and the taxes, too? And what was she to do in the meantime? The shop owners who had once fallen all over themselves to please her had made it clear that there would be no credit extended now. Even the Fargo House would soon become too expensive.

Often, before turning Raleigh back toward Fargo, Frances would ride the perimeter of her land, the northwestern reach of which brought her in sight of the bridge over the Sheyenne. From the bridge itself she could see Kirsten's house and the tiny new barn there. It was no different from the other immigrant shanties dotting the prairie, Frances supposed, with its earthen floor and drafty windows, and yet she could not look at it without imagining order. The home was sure to be set up so that not a step was wasted, within or without. The place would be like Kirsten, warm and tidy and pleasant.

Once, as she was studying the shanty in the distance, she saw Kirsten step out of the front door, and shade her eyes as she looked toward the bridge where Frances had halted Raleigh. Panicking, like a thief spotted on the brink of a crime, Frances turned and galloped away. Another time Frances had looked out of her hotel window to see Kirsten passing beneath her on Front Street, talking to the rather forlorn-looking mule with an empty pack saddle on its back, as if cheerful and determined reasoning could quicken its stride. As she watched she heard the door slam before she could command Houghton to stay with her, and a minute later she was looking at a joyful reunion between her son and her former housekeeper. For a moment she was entranced by the picture before her, amazed by the animation of her increasingly quiet boy, imagining Kirsten's hand touching her son's cheek upon her own brow. She had to resist the temptation to step into the street to humble herself simply for the sake of having those limpid blue eyes turned toward her in affection. Then she saw her son lift his arm to wave at her, and she let the curtain fall as she stood away from the window.

Frances had been once again at that window, her pacing halted for the moment by the sunset colors painted upon the panes on the other side of the street, when there was a knock on the door. Houghton dropped his newest issue of *Our Little Ones* and bounced off the bed to open the door. Alexander McKenzie filled the door frame, hat in hand, an expression of solicitous concern upon his face.

"My apologies for barging in like this, Mrs. Bingham," McKenzie said. "I looked for you at Sherman House and they told me that you and the boy come down here. As a friend of your late husband's, I hoped you wouldn't think it," McKenzie hesitated and Frances imagined the big man in front of her silently thumbing a very small dictionary in search of the proper word. After a moment's hesitation, he started again. "I hope you don't mind me checking in to see if I can be of any help." Each time in the past that McKenzie had stopped to ask if he could be "of any help," Frances had assured him that she was doing quite well, thank you, and turned him from her door. Just what this "help" was that McKenzie had in mind, Frances did not know, but her instincts were to refuse the vague offer and retrieve her hand before he stuffed it in his mouth and began to chew his way up her arm with those alarming teeth of his. She had begun to demur once again when he took another half step into the room, causing her to back up, just a bit off-balance.

"Maybe you and the boy will join me for supper tonight."

"I am not in the habit of going out after dark," she answered. "Thank you."

McKenzie nodded. "Sure. The food here is fine. And we can make it early. Let's say an hour?"

The ease with which he had transformed her refusal into an acceptance startled Frances, and yet, she was hungry. And impatient with boredom. And fed up with worry. So she simply nodded, and then shut the door behind McKenzie. What, Frances asked herself, would people think when they saw her having dinner with this man not three months after the death of her husband? The answer was obvious. They would think the worst, which would in no way lower their opinion of her.

The meal was completely without incident or memorable conversation. McKenzie was in town for the vote to choose the new capital that was to take place in a couple of days, but he had little more to say on that subject. He shared his condolences with Frances once again, adding that, despite the unfortunate allegations and exaggerations that had filled the newspapers after the legislature adjourned, Percy's death ended what promised to be a bright political future. Frances simply nodded and studied her water glass, and then smiled at Houghton to encourage him to absorb McKenzie's lies. She did not know if McKenzie knew that she knew he was lying, or if he knew that Percy himself had come to understand precisely the extent to which he had been a very small pawn in the schemes of others. McKenzie had to have known that the circumstances of Percy's death did not reveal a man whose star was in ascension. Frances did not believe for a moment that her husband's death had been the result of his distress at her leaving. She could not make sense of what had happened, but she was certain that Percy had not meant to kill himself. His death, she suspected, was more likely the result of some moment of high drama gone awry.

None of it mattered. It was good for Houghton to hear pleasant things about his father, but she did not encourage the discussion. Mc-Kenzie's table manners may have left a little to be desired, but he was deft at reading unspoken signals, and quickly changed the subject. He talked about the fine weather for planting that Dakotans had enjoyed and about the hoards of settlers pouring into the territory. He complimented Little Carl's bone-handled pocket knife that Frances had given to Houghton for his sixth birthday. Turning his attention from Houghton, McKenzie conveyed his concern for Frances, alone in Fargo, without suggesting a too-intimate knowledge of her circumstances that would necessarily cause embarrassment. When supper was over, he said good night to Frances and Houghton at the bottom of the stairway leading to their room.

Frances was relieved.

She had not expected McKenzie to stop by the very next morning to offer to take her and Houghton for a ride to enjoy the fresh summer day. Houghton's pleas convinced her to accept. An hour later Alexander McKenzie helped Frances down from the carriage, slipped a penny into Houghton's palm for candy, tipped his hat, and drove away. When he stopped by to offer to take them to supper again that evening, Frances was less surprised and less interested in accepting the invitation, but Houghton was clearly thrilled with the big man's attention and so Frances agreed.

The following day Frances spent much of the morning practicing her refusal of the invitation—for a ride, for a stroll by the river, for supper, whatever it was to be—that would soon arrive. By noon she had begun pacing the room, unable to sit still with her magazine or her inexpert mending of a torn pair of Houghton's trousers, for the waiting had emphasized her absolute solitude. It was mid-afternoon when Houghton burst into the room with the joyful news that he and Reecher had been given twenty-five cents by Big Alec, as Reecher said everyone called Mr. McKenzie. Twenty-five cents! And it was just so they could go to the special puppet show that afternoon at McHench Hall, and Reecher said that all the boys would be there, and, well, could he?

Frances gave her permission, instructed Houghton to be back in the room before dark, gave Reecher a good, long look to help him understand that it would be in his best interest to see that Houghton was home on time, and kissed her son good-bye. Then she waited for the knock upon the door.

This time Alexander McKenzie did not hesitate, but stepped inside the room before saying "hello." Frances had no intention of shutting the door behind him, but the sound of voices coming down the hall made her loathe to risk the curious stares of strangers. She closed the door and turned to face her visitor.

"Hope you don't mind my little bit of generosity towards your son, Mrs. Bingham," McKenzie began. "I saw the handbill, and thought, well, where's the harm."

"No harm, Mr. McKenzie, although I must ask that there be no more gifts. I will see to my son's entertainment."

"Sure. Sure. Sorry I couldn't get away earlier. Business, you see, and I got to get back in a minute. Be working late, too, but maybe we can figure something else out for later."

There were so many assumptions embedded in this short speech of McKenzie's that Frances was rendered speechless. Two suppers and a carriage ride and now the man was addressing her with alarming familiarity.

Frances' moment of silence allowed McKenzie to continue. "Here's what I was thinking, anyway. How about I have supper for two sent up to my rooms at the Headquarters later on tonight." McKenzie paused, but there was very little in his soft-spoken delivery to suggest that he was asking a question.

Frances answered nonetheless. "I could not possibly –"

"No need to worry about the boy. He'll be plumb tuckered is my guess. Fast asleep by the time you leave."

"I am not worried about Houghton."

"Good, good. Then let's say nine o'clock?"

"Mr. McKenzie," Frances took a step back. "I must refuse your invitation."

"Please, call me Alec," McKenzie said. "And there ain't no reason to refuse my invitation to supper, even though I just might have an ulterior motive." McKenzie chuckled at Frances' expression. "It was going to be a surprise, but I guess maybe you're a woman that don't like surprises. I wanted you to see the rooms, is all. I keep a suite at the hotel. Have for years now. But, ah...circumstances are about to make it important that I spend less time traveling and more time in Bismarck. So here's my point, you see. You ought to be living in a nicer place than this, and them rooms go empty most of the time."

"Are you suggesting–?" Frances began, and then hesitated, and then regretted her beginning as McKenzie leaned almost imperceptibly toward her, waiting for her to be the one to put into words the unspoken proposition. Recognizing her error, Frances began again, well aware that a flush had risen to her cheeks. "Your offer is perhaps generous, Mr. McKenzie, but ill-considered. It would be quite impossible for me to accept."

"Alec, please. And it ain't impossible at all," McKenzie said, still speaking in a pleasant and off-hand tone. "Supper seems to me altogether possible. No harm in that." As he spoke McKenzie pulled his watch from his vest pocket. "I gotta go," he said to the watch before extending his hand toward Frances. "Nine o'clock, then."

The door closed quietly behind McKenzie and Frances stood amazed in the empty room. A moment later she realized that she had been holding her breath. Her hands were trembling. Why, she wondered, as she held them out in front of her. She was not excited. She was not nervous. She did not intend to join the man in his rooms for supper. What was it that she feared?

The meeting of the capital removal commission began on the second floor of the courthouse in Fargo that early June Saturday morning with a straw vote. Alexander McKenzie's was the sole vote for Bismarck. Steele received the votes of the two other north Dakota commissioners. Odessa did not receive a vote. Jamestown had withdrawn its bid, unable ultimately to come up with the $100,000 necessary to qualify. The same was true for one of the small south Dakota towns. Three others went without a vote, but no town received more than two. The commissioners sat back, unbuttoned their vests, and settled in for a long day. They discussed the individual bids from each of the towns that had received at least one vote, agreeing to remove the others from the discussion. It was almost noon when they took the fourth vote. Bismarck now had two votes.

During the break for the midday meal, McKenzie found time to speak with several of the commissioners individually. He listened intently, nodded his head sympathetically as each man talked, said a few words, and then either clasped the fellow on the shoulder or patted him on the back as he turned away.

They had taken three more votes by the time coffee and sandwiches were brought over for the afternoon lunch. Two hours and two votes later McKenzie suggested that they all could use a half-hour break to stretch their legs. His were seen stretching toward the Headquarters Hotel, where he spent some time in the telegraph office at the depot there. The windows of the courthouse were beginning to darken when Alex Hughes, Governor Ordway's closest ally in Yankton, received a telegram. The discussions and the voting continued. On the twelfth vote Hughes switched his vote from Ordway to Bismarck, leaving the town short one vote. At eight o'clock McKenzie suggested that the commission not adjourn for supper, but recess for fifteen minutes and then continue on with their work. Twenty minutes later, in one of those political coincidences, the commission member who was to become, with Alexander McKenzie and Nehemiah Ordway, a partner in the Capital National Bank of Bismarck, switched his vote to Bismarck, and a majority was achieved. It was the thirteenth vote of the day. The men stood, stretched, shook hands, and stepped into the Dakota night in groups of twos and threes. When they looked around for Alexander McKenzie, he had disappeared.

It had been a perfect day for McKenzie, filled with quiet intrigue and just a little bit of bullying. Governor Ordway would perhaps be surprised to discover someday that he had sent a telegram to Fargo that day, but he would have little reason to complain. There was the new bank partnership waiting for him, as well as the sale of the land just north of Bismarck that he had purchased upon McKenzie's recommendation this past December. With the increasingly heated calls to Washington for the governor's removal, as well as the accusations of bribery and malfeasance threatening to solidify into actual legal complaints, Ordway would be happy to make north Dakota his new home. McKenzie chuckled to himself as he changed out of his suit coat and vest and into his smoking jacket, which, although he did not smoke, he appreciated for its comfort. Nehemiah Ordway was a greedy man, so much so that he did not understand that by getting his fingers into every pie—into the paper town of Ordway, into Pierre, where his son owned a great deal of property, and into Bismarck—he was effectively dividing his own political capital. It had made dislodging the votes of the men Ordway believed he owned much easier. The difficulty of the day lay in the patience required to wait for his fellow commission members to come around to believing that they had made their own decisions. Lord save us from honest men, McKenzie thought as he sat back in his chair and waited for Frances Bingham to join him.

An hour later Alexander McKenzie set down the newspaper he had been struggling over, rubbed his eyes, and stood to dress for the street again. Within minutes he was standing across the street from the Fargo House. McKenzie did not need to count the windows to find Frances Bingham's room. Every window was dark. McKenzie crossed the street and went into the hotel. He ignored the clerk who stood from behind the desk and then disappeared again when he saw who had walked in. McKenzie climbed the stairs, taking no care to soften his tread, listened for a moment outside Frances' door, then tapped lightly. Then tapped again. Then tried the handle of the locked door. He did not doubt that the woman inside was awake.

All right, he thought to himself as he stepped back toward the stairs. All right, then.

The Alexander McKenzie who knocked on Frances Bingham's door again the next morning was not the soft-spoken, courteous man, "generous to his friends and friendly toward his enemies." This was the Alexander McKenzie who preferred removing obstacles to fighting them. This was the man who would one day have a newspaper office ransacked and its printing press thrown into the Missouri River when an editor refused to see things from his point of view, who had coffins delivered to the front porches of men who crossed him, who had sent a trio of thugs to Percy Bingham's house to "teach him a lesson" before they escorted him out of town. (And who saw to it that these men who had failed to follow his orders were never seen in the territory again.)

Houghton answered the door dressed in his Sunday best, his hair wetted and perfectly parted and already beginning to spring into the curls that he had inherited from his father.

"I thought you were Mrs. Ford, I mean, Mrs. Shaw," Houghton exclaimed, happy to see the man who gave him money for puppet shows and candy. "I'm going to church with her this morning, but not to the real church. Mama and I went to her store yesterday because mama wanted to talk to Mr. Shaw again, and Mrs. Ford–" Houghton hesitated and looked back into the room, and then corrected himself, "Mrs. *Shaw* said that she heard that Grandpa John and Aunt Anna were going to move, but–" Again Houghton hesitated, his attention snagged on this information, "but –"

"–but just now you are going to the Presbyterian church with Mrs. Shaw," Frances finished for her son, as she came to stand beside him at the door.

"And Mrs. Ford, *Mrs. Shaw,* says that we will make a fine pair, and then I am to go to her house for dinner and she is going to have chocolate pudding just like I like it, sort of runny, but mama–"

"–will be waiting here for you when you get back. Run on down now and wait for Mrs. Shaw by the front desk. Do you have the money I gave you for the collection plate? Good. And remember not to fidget during the sermon."

When Houghton rounded the corner of the hallway and disappeared, McKenzie, who had not yet spoken, gestured Frances back into the room.

"We may converse here at the door," Frances said.

"But we ain't going to," McKenzie said, brushing past her.

McKenzie crossed to the window. "Go ahead and keep the door open. Open the window if you want. It's another fine morning." He turned from the window for a careful head-to-toe inventory that took in much more than Frances' riding costume. "Going somewhere?"

Frances did not answer. She could feel her hands begin to tremble again.

"That's your bay at Hadley's Livery, ain't it. Good looking horse. Expensive to keep a horse like that."

When Frances still didn't answer, McKenzie pulled the chair next to the small writing desk along the wall toward him and, unbuttoning his coat, sat and crossed his legs.

"Horses are expensive. Little boys are expensive. Fancy clothes," McKenzie paused as he once again swept his gaze over Frances, "are expensive. Room and board are expensive. Even in a place like this, when there ain't no money coming in. It's a hard thing to be a woman alone, I'm sure. And lonely. You lonely, Mrs. Bingham?"

"You will have to excuse me, Mr. McKenzie—"

"Alec."

"I'm afraid I must go now." Frances said, opening the door just a bit wider as she invited McKenzie to leave with a nod of her head.

"But as I understand it, Mrs. Bingham, you got nowhere to go."

The look that Frances shot toward McKenzie in response, startled, angry, one eyebrow lifted, made him smile. "I was sorry you decided not to accept my invitation last night," he said.

"It would not have been proper. Thank you again for your generosity to my son these past few days, but now I must ask you to leave."

"Come now, Mrs. Bingham, Frances, if you don't mind, we are both adults here. I like you, and I'd sure hate to see your situation get worse. It is already…precarious." McKenzie nodded, pleased to have lighted upon the right word. "You ain't got family and friends to turn to, or else you wouldn't be here in the first place. I'm proposing to become your friend. My offer is generous. It'd be a shame for you to turn it down."

"It is your offer that is shameful, Mr. McKenzie."

"It's a hard world," McKenzie nodded in agreement. "Harder for some than others, but partly that's because they just don't see what's easy and waiting right in front of their noses. Take my offer, Frances. The next one might not be quite so nice."

"For the last time, no. I have listened to your insults long enough. Please leave."

McKenzie shook his head as if saddened by the headstrong refusal before him, then stood and stepped toward Frances. He took her hand that had been grasping the doorknob. When Frances attempted to withdraw her hand, he tightened his grasp. "It ain't really up to you to say when's the last time. Now I'm a patient man, but I am a man who generally gets what he wants." Hearing a train whistle, McKenzie released Frances' hand and pulled his watch from his vest. "I got business to do out of town that's going to keep me busy for a bit. Be back on Friday night. That should give you enough time to make up your mind. I'll tell Nicols to move a cot into my suite for the boy." McKenzie backed into the hall and settled his hat upon his head. "You got no money, no family, no friends. Not here, not in St. Paul, not even in old Virginie."

McKenzie's smile widened at Frances' look of surprise. "You don't seem to understand how much trouble you're in. Just a matter of time before you're sleeping with the pigs."

McKenzie's threat should have been the end of the conversation. It would have been wiser of Frances to leave it hanging there, unanswered. Instead, as if she were refusing a second cup of tea, Frances fought back her trembling and answered in her most polite voice, "I must decline your offer once again. Good day." And then she shut the door and turned her key in the lock, leaving a startled Alexander McKenzie standing alone in the hall, furiously absorbing the rare insult delivered to his face.

CHAPTER LII

In Which Frances Learns What's What and Who's Who (and She's Not)

Frances waited by the door, straining to hear McKenzie's footsteps beyond the roaring in her ears. Was he waiting in the hallway for her to come out? Was he just around the corner? Frances moved quietly to the window, but could not detect his broad-shouldered profile below her on Front Street. Another ten minutes passed as Frances paced around her room, frustrated and frightened, wasting precious time. Several church bells began to ring. In a couple of hours Mrs. Shaw would be back with Houghton. Frances pinned on her hat, reached for her jacket and stepped into the hallway. It was empty, as was the lobby below, save for the clerk who gave Frances an inexplicably remorseful look when she handed him her key.

Once on the wagon path that led to her land, Frances was able to slow Raleigh to an amble as she began to work through the decisions she had to make. She had no intention of becoming Alexander McKenzie's mistress. (And here she felt both irritation with Percy for bringing her into the company of such a decidedly distasteful man, as well as a bit of belated sympathy for her husband, who, she could see now, had clearly been no match for the brute.) Nevertheless, the certainty of McKenzie's assumption that she must accept his proposition quite simply because she had nowhere else to go had clarified the desperation of her situation. She had been waiting, she supposed, for a miracle. She had received something quite other.

There were the trees on her property. She would go to the Fargo Lumber Company first, and if J. J. Shotwell was too busy to harvest and mill the trees now, perhaps he would pay her a deposit should she suggest that other lumberyards in town were also interested. If she could get no satisfaction from Shotwell, then she would have to go to one of the other lumberyard owners. If all else failed she would simply have to call upon Jack Shaw again. There was no one else.

Frances did not have time to dismount and walk about her property, but the ride in the fresh air had done her good. She was breathing again, and she had made some plans, and the world seemed a somewhat less desperate place from atop Raleigh than it did within her tiny room in the hotel. The morning had turned warm and Frances shrugged out of her jacket as she headed Raleigh back toward Fargo. The road was edged on either side by a low carpet of bright green wheat. From this point on the wheat's vibrant color would dull as it grew, until suddenly in late summer the fields would become a landscape of solid, heavy-headed gold. Bringing her attention back to the road, Frances could make out a cart approaching from the east. It did not take her long to realize that it was Kirsten, once again engaged in a one-sided conversation as she walked along with her mule. There was nothing to do but ride forward.

The open pleasure on Kirsten's face at their meeting felt like a punishment. Once, early in their marriage, when Percy had still taken pleasure in displaying his knowledge to Frances and she had still taken pleasure in learning, Percy had spent several evenings reading aloud from a volume of essays by Ralph Waldo Emerson. His essay on Compensation had been a favorite, although Frances had suspected at the time that Percy's lectures were more accurately directed toward an unhearing father than toward his wife lying next to him. "You can not do wrong without suffering wrong," he had repeated, rather hopefully. "You may not be brought before the law for every transgression, and every transgression is not necessarily unlawful, but every infraction is punished. By the loss of innocence. By fear. By suspicion of others." Frances remembered having her doubts, but now she understood. Frances looked into the affectionate eyes of the young woman before her and was forced to look away.

"Well, Frances. It is you after all, then." Kirsten hesitated for a moment, but quickly began again. "I was just thinking about you and that is the truth. For thinking I have all the time in the world because it is forth and back I go to Fargo now two times every week with eggs and butter. Forth and back. Back and forth. Because what do you know? When you sit down at a fancy breakfast at the Headquarters Hotel it is the very same egg before you that was under one of my hens not so very long ago. It is prosperous, as Mrs. Harkness would say, that we are now, New Homer, and the chickens, and the cows, and Kirsten Knudson, and that is what I was saying to New Homer here. I said maybe Frances Bingham is to sit down right now and bite into the same egg that is from me, and then I looked up, and what do you know, I said to New Homer, that is Raleigh for sure, and that is Frances Bingham sitting tall in the saddle right before our eyes, and I am thinking that you are a sight for sore eyes, like my brother Ole he used to say."

"Hello, Kirsten. I'm afraid I can not stop to talk. I am late as it is."

The abruptness of Frances' speech drained the smile from Kirsten's face.

"I am sorry," Kirsten began, and then, in a very un-Kirsten-like moment, fell silent as she looked for the right words. "I mean, I really mean to say that I am sorry. About Mr. Percy. It was Mrs. Harkness that told me about... it. So I made a *krumkake* for Howie. He always liked my *krumkake* so much, and I thought that you and Howie would be at the big house, but when I took the cake there the new cook, who is not so nice like Mrs. Ford, she said that you were not there, and I did not know what to do, then, so I took the *krumkake* over to Birgit Solheim, who is now Birgit Dahl, not that that is a name to mean anything to you, but here she is married to Per Dahl now because Mr. Solheim she lost to the diphtheria and she is having still more babies—last year a new baby, this year a new baby, next year it will be a new baby, and I thought, well, there is a woman to use *krumkake* even if in her house there is no one dead right now."

Frances did not realize that a small smile had crept back to her face as Kirsten spoke. She would have liked nothing more at that moment than to hear the long story of Mrs. Solheim Dahl's hard life as presented by Kirsten, which was sure to be filled with equal parts true concern and less-sympathetic observation, and then forgotten completely at some point when the young woman followed a tangential thought along its path to places unknown.

The smile had not been lost on Kirsten, who burst forth with a declaration that seemed to surprise her as much as it did Frances. "*Love Heron*, Frances, it is good to see you again. I miss you." And then, seeing Frances draw herself up again and look away, Kirsten added quickly, "And I miss Mrs. Ford, who is now Mrs. Shaw, and Jack Shaw. And I miss Little Carl, too."

"Yes, well. Old times. I must go now, Kirsten. Good-bye."

"Ya, good-bye, then. Oh, but there is still one more thing!"

Frances reined Raleigh in again and turned in her saddle to look down at Kirsten beside her.

"There is so much for a little boy to do in a big town like Fargo, with all of his new friends, and next year he goes to school. Can you believe—"

"Kirsten."

"Ya, what I mean to say is, if Howie he wants to spend a day or two with me, well, it is a true thing to say that I miss him, too, and it is good care I would take of him, and keep him busy. There are the chickens to feed, and the eggs to gather, and the cows to milk, and he was always such a boy to be out of doors, and not to be cooped up—" Kirsten's eyes went wide for a moment. "I do not mean that he is cooped up now. I just mean—"

"Thank you, Kirsten. I will ask Houghton if he would like to visit."

"And you, Frances," Kirsten lifted a hand to touch Frances' boot, and then as quickly dropped it. "I know that it is not to poor shanties that you are in the habit to visit—"

This time Frances did not interrupt, but the lift of her head as she turned to look away from Kirsten forced the young woman into silence.

Frances had no way of knowing if Kirsten watched her as she moved Raleigh into a trot, and yet, even when she had gone far enough to be out of sight, she could still feel the young woman's gaze upon her, could still see the melancholy look upon Kirsten's face as Frances had turned away. It had been much like the expression Houghton so often wore now as he approached her. Expectant, a little afraid, and yet, behind it all, a plea to let his own affection make her happier.

On Monday morning Frances dressed in her best walking costume, a light green velvet skirt, with a silk bodice and pannier of a darker shade, and a light pereline to match the skirt, and set out for the Fargo Lumber Company. Within minutes of stepping into J. J. Shotwell's office she was politely ushered back out. Shotwell was sorry, but he was not interested in the cottonwood and ash along the Sheyenne River. The pine that came in from the northern Minnesota forests was of a superior quality for building, and there was little market these days for the local river timber, except for burning. "Sorry you had to waste your time. Get a settler to harvest your trees for you," Shotwell said as an afterthought. "You should get four, maybe five dollars a cord. Good day, Mrs. Bingham." Her visit with Jim Chesley of Chesley and Lovejoy Lumber was equally disappointing. More humiliating was the meeting with Bill White. As one of the founding members of the Methodist Episcopal Church in Fargo, White and his wife had greeted Frances and Anna warmly for several years of Sundays. His greeting at his lumber-yard was curt and his statement of disinterest in doing business with her, abrupt. There was no mention of missing her in church these days.

So it was still before noon when Frances passed under the brand new swinging sign of "Shaw's Fancy Goods." The shelves at the back of the store were still empty, and the center remained as open as a dance floor. And yet, Frances thought, there is nothing like fixtures of brass and the smell of new wood and leather to confer a sense of well-being. For a month now the Sunday *Argus* had carried a half-page advertisement for "Shaw's Fancy Goods," and Frances had smiled at the aggressive optimism of the list of "items soon available" in comparison to the emptiness of the store itself. The advertised 'Plain White French China, Decorated French China, Gold Band French China, Plated Ware, Japanese Ware, Bohemian Ware, Vases, Toilet Sets, Smokers' Sets and Fancy Toilet Articles ("too utterly utter"), Celebrated Perfumes, and Children's Tea Sets, Hobby Horses, and Dolls' were very little in evidence.

Jack Shaw looked up and nodded to Frances as she entered the store, and then went back to plucking pens from a display cabinet one by one to place before the only customer in the store, a handsome man in his forties whose dress suggested that he was perhaps one of Fargo's ninety-day visitors, in town to qualify for residency in order to obtain a divorce.

When she was alone in the store with Shaw, Frances said, "I hope I did not chase your customer away, Jack."

"Not a customer, Mrs. Bingham. A bored gentleman. The whole world should stop still to wait on him for nothing. You are looking fine today."

"Too thin," came a voice from behind Shaw as the former Mrs. Ford stepped through the curtain that separated the store from the stairs that led to the couple's living space above. "Too thin by ten pounds, at least."

"I miss your cooking, that much is true," Frances said. "Thank you for taking care of Houghton yesterday. He gave me a complete report, including the information that Presbyterians sit too much. I hope he behaved himself. "

"He is a good child," Mrs. Shaw said, shaking her head, as if this were a sad thing indeed.

"I am sorry to take you away from your work, Jack," Frances said, "but if you could spare a moment to talk with me in private, I would be very much obliged to you."

"I'll mind the store," Mrs. Shaw offered.

A door at the back of the store led to a storage room. Like the store itself, the room was tidy, with several crates stacked against the walls. In the center of the room sat a partially constructed display case, still lacking its glass cover. A piece of red velvet lay over the edge of the case, next to another of gold. Frances touched both pieces. "This is beautiful cloth."

"A watch, a pen, a tea set, a vase. Set it once on top of velvet and it is already worth more. People." Shaw shrugged his shoulders at the oddity of his fellow man.

"Too utterly utter."

Shaw laughed. "This I saw in the St. Paul paper when I was there to buy for the store. So I think, why not?"

"The store is doing well?"

"*Gott in himl*, no. First I must look like I am doing well like an American. This takes time, to build up inventory and customers. In the meantime, my wife makes cakes for the Keeley Brothers. And you, Mrs. Bingham, how are you?"

Frances thought she could hear reluctance in Shaw's question. That she had not returned to the Bingham farm upon her husband's death had certainly been cause for speculation and gossip in Fargo. Her subsequent moves, from the Headquarters Hotel, to the Sherman House, and then to the Fargo House, were similarly no secret on Front Street. Although few Fargoans, watching her ride through town on Raleigh, or step out into the street dressed as she was today, were likely to be put in mind of a woman in financial distress, Jack Shaw knew better.

Frances lifted her head to meet Shaw's look. "I am sorry to say that I am not getting along very well. Like you, I expect to do better, but I find that I have neither cakes to sell, nor a shop to give me hope." Frances dropped her head as she busied herself with the clasp of her shoulder cape. "In addition, I find myself with very few friends to turn to." She lifted the cape from her shoulders and draped it across her arm before looking up again. "I am sorry, Jack. This is not very pleasant for either of us, but I am here to ask for a loan. Just enough to keep us until the harvest check comes in. I know that you have little to spare—"

"I have nothing to spare."

The bluntness of Shaw's words brought a flush to Frances' cheek.

"There is simply nothing to spare, Mrs. Bingham," Shaw repeated, this time with his arms spread wide. "Every penny I have saved, every penny we make goes into the store. There is nothing else. Some day maybe we all forget from our worries about money, but some day is not now. And I will tell you a secret. There is to be a baby. So you see—" Jack Shaw shrugged.

"That is wonderful news, Jack," Frances said, nothing about her expression or tone conveying the least bit of wonder.

"So, yes. Wonderful. The future is wonderful, but now, if you were to say to me, 'Jack Shaw, to you I will sell only the land at half of what I bought it for,' I would have to say to you, I can not buy

"Sell the land? I am not interested in selling the land. Things are not so bad as—"

"Mrs. Bingham, I am not saying you should sell the land. I am saying if you had this to sell, I would not have with what to buy. But, if you will forgive me for saying this, it is what you have to sell, yes?"

Not exactly all, Frances thought, flashing upon McKenzie's angry look as she closed the door on him the morning before. Frances absent-mindedly brought her right hand to the garnet ear-rings that she had carefully chosen from her jewelry case when dressing this morning.

"Not in Fargo."

"I beg your pardon?"

"If you will sell your jewelry," Shaw said, looking away in embarrassment. "Better you should go somewhere else. Sundberg will not know what it is worth, and Lacy will not pay. Better you should go only to St. Paul."

"Oh, Jack, things are not as bad as all that," Frances put a laugh in her voice. "I was simply hoping to make things a bit less tight until fall. We will be fine. I certainly did not mean to give the impression that I was desperate."

"No, no, of course not. Forgive me my stupid talk. I am thinking always of the worst."

That, Frances thought as she returned to the street, was perhaps the first false thing that Jack Shaw had ever said to her.

When Frances returned to the Fargo House, the proprietor, William Egbert, was waiting behind the desk. "Mrs. Bingham. If I may," Egbert said as Frances passed him with a nod.

Frances' exasperation with the events of the morning prompted her to turn with the words, "If you may what, Mr. Egbert?"

Egbert's shaggy eyebrows lifted toward his bald pate in surprise. "If I may speak to you for a moment, ma'am," he explained with the reluctance of a man asked to waste a finite resource.

"Yes, of course."

Egbert looked about him, and then, hearing someone on the landing above, motioned Frances over to the desk. "I am sorry, but I am going to have to ask you and the boy to leave. I am sorry," Egbert whispered, and then brought his eyebrows together in the best scowl he could approximate.

"I beg your pardon."

"I am sorry," the proprietor repeated, "but I am going—"

"I understood the words, Mr. Egbert," Frances interrupted. "But I do not understand your purpose in saying them to me. I am paid through the week, and I intend—"

"Not now," Egbert said. "Not just this minute, Mrs. Bingham. You may stay through Thursday night. That will give you time to find something else. I will reimburse you for Friday, Saturday, and Sunday. But Friday night, I am sorry, the room will be needed for other guests. No, no—" Egbert waved his hands in front of him, as if Frances were about to offer him a second piece of pie. "You and the boy must go. That is that. Reecher will help you with your trunk. I am sorry," he said again.

Stunned, furious, and unable to think of another thing to say to the apologetic and determined Mr. Egbert, Frances turned toward the stairs.

"Oh, and Mrs. Bingham," Egbert called from behind when she reached the first turn, "if Reecher is up there with your boy, send him down, please. He has work to do."

Frances and Houghton did not speak as they ate their noon meal of bread and sausage that Frances had brought back to the hotel. Miniature soldiers of blue and gray remained at attention at their feet, ready for the battle that had been interrupted by Frances' return and Reecher's departure.

"Which soldiers are yours, Houghton?" Frances asked when she noticed her son's worried expression fixed upon her.

"Reecher won't play unless I let him have the blue soldiers. I'm the Rebels," Houghton said. "I'm going to lose."

"Let's go for a walk," Frances said abruptly, standing and reaching for her son's hand. Once out on Front Street, Houghton slipped his hand out of his mother's grasp, and Frances, understanding, simply said, "Stay near."

The Merchants Hotel was almost next door. When Frances inquired at the desk about weekly room and board, the clerk took a quick look around the small lobby, and then answered in a voice much too loud that there were no rooms available.

"But I did not say when precisely I was interested in a room," Frances pointed out.

"Wait, wait here, please," the clerk said, and disappeared into a back room, calling for a Mr. Haas. A moment later a small man appeared, his dinner napkin still tucked under his chin.

"There are no rooms available now, Mrs. Bingham," Haas said, swallowing and looking over her shoulder. "And no time soon. I am sorry, but you will have to look somewhere else."

Frances walked another block east. She hesitated for a moment outside the Skandinavian House. From the open door, she inhaled the odor of too many bodies in a confined space. A bump against her shoulder startled Frances, and she stepped back as a heavily bearded man swept a shapeless hat from his head, and said something apologetic she did not understand. Frances looked around and gestured to Houghton, and they began to walk east again.

Crossing Second Street she came to the Minnesota House. With Houghton's hand in hers she stepped to the desk and said to the woman sitting there, "I am interested in a room, with board, for a week, please."

The woman looked up at Frances, taking in her walking costume and the boy beside her. "And your name, dear?"

"Frances Bingham."

"Wait here, please." The woman set down the pillow-case she was mending, stood with some effort, and lifted the hinged platform that allowed her to step from behind the counter. Crossing the room she opened a door to the saloon there, and called, to Frances' horror, "Mr. Kjos. It's Frances Bingham come."

A moment later a similarly portly man appeared holding a trowel. His wide face and cloud of curly hair were dotted with white paste. When he spoke his accent was as marked as was the man's who had bumped into her minutes ago, but his words were clear. "There is no room, then. No room at all, Mrs. Bingham."

"When will there be a room," Frances asked, keeping her voice steady.

"There is not to be a room, and that is the short and the long of it, then, and it is sorry I am to stand before you to say this. It is sorry I am." Kjos dropped his head, and Frances thought for a moment that perhaps he was waiting for her to console him.

Instead she said, "This is not right."

"No," Kjos said. "That is what I said to—"

"Mr. Kjos!"

The man turned to look at his wife, dropped his head again, and repeated. "It is sorry I am."

Back out on the street Frances took Houghton's hand in hers and turned to look toward the river. She had not expected this from Alexander McKenzie. The thoroughness was as alarming as the pettiness. Simply knowing that either he, or one of his lieutenants, had spoken her name to every hotel proprietor in Fargo made her long for a bath.

Would he have sent his minions into Moorhead as well?

"Mama?"

Frances felt Houghton pulling his hand away, and realized that she had been squeezing it in fury. "Yes, dear," she said. "What is it?"

"Where are we going now?"

His perplexed face lifted to hers reassured Frances that her son was merely confused by the oddity of their walk, and was not giving voice to her own sense of futility. She forced a lightness into her response. "Oh, nowhere, just now. Nowhere at all. Here." Frances opened her hand-bag, and drew a cube of sugar from within. "Why don't you run to the livery and give Raleigh a good brushing, and if he stands for you, give him this when you are done."

Houghton reached for the sugar, and then hesitated, moving from foot to foot as if he were waiting for permission to leave. "Mama," he finally asked, "Is Raleigh lonely?"

"Do you think he is lonely?" Frances asked.

"Maybe. Without his friends from the farm there with him. I mean, I know that there are lots of horses at the stable, but he doesn't know them very well."

"Then he will be especially pleased to see you, I think."

Houghton answered with a solemn nod, and turned to run back toward the center of town.

Frances knew that it was a waste of her time, but she had nothing else to do. So she retraced her steps west along Front Street, passing the Fargo House and walking two more blocks to the St. Paul House. Moments later she crossed back to Broadway. At three dollars per day, the Continental Hotel was well beyond her means, and yet, unable at this point to cease what had become less a search than a flagellation, she crossed the lobby, lit even during the day with electric lights, only to see the proprietor, J. B. Chapin, disappear around a corner. The desk clerk informed her that there were no rooms available. The same was true at the Dakota House. And the European House. And the Tremont House. She did not try the Germania House or the Farmers Home. She did not return to the Skandinavian House.

The next day Frances rode Raleigh to Peter Erickson's farmstead, and came upon Erickson and his sons framing a granary. Explaining that the land that he had believed he was farming for Jack Shaw was actually hers, Frances proposed that he forward to her a sum that both knew to be significantly less than what they could expect her share of a successful wheat harvest to be. Erickson's discomfort was clear. Even if what she said was true, and here Erickson assured her that he had no reason to doubt her word, he did not have that kind of cash available. "We're all waiting for the harvest," he said, holding Raleigh's head as Frances remounted.

On Wednesday, against Jack Shaw's advice, Frances put her ring, a necklace, two pair of ear-rings, and several pins and brooches in her hand-bag and walked to Lacy's Watches and Jewelry. The jeweler stopped her before she could retrieve her possessions. He was not interested in buying things now, he said. On his face was yet another combination of fear and chagrin that she had seen on the faces of the hotel proprietors and clerks on Monday. She did not visit the other jewelers in town.

If Frances slept on Wednesday night she was not aware of it. It was still dark when she slipped out of bed, careful not to wake her son beside her. Pulling her wrapper around her chemise, she sat on the one chair in the room and watched as the gray light brought Houghton's features into greater clarity. A small tapping startled her.

"Yes?" Frances asked quietly at the door.

"Ma'am?" Reecher's voice sounded on the other side.

"Yes?"

"There's Olly Hadley out front to talk to you. He says to come out now, please, if you will, ma'am."

"Tell him I will be five minutes."

Although Frances had dressed as quickly as she could, there was no mistaking Oliver Hadley's impatience as he stood in the street holding Raleigh, saddled and bridled. He greeted Frances with a brief, "Here," as he held the reins toward her.

"What does this mean, Mr. Hadley?"

"It ain't right. It just ain't right," the man answered, tying the horse up when Frances refused to reach for the reins.

"What is not right? Why have you brought my horse to me?"

"There ain't no use arguing, ma'am. I ain't about to have my barn burned down around my ears on accounta this here horse." Hadley was about to walk away, when a thought obviously occurred to him. "It's a fine animal, though. You ever get the notion to sell, we could make us a deal."

In all of the accumulating disgrace of the week, it had not once occurred to Frances to sell Raleigh. "How much?" she asked.

"Well, now," Hadley rubbed his jaw for a moment. "I got to take a closer look-see, but–"

"He has been in your livery for the better part of three months, Mr. Hadley. You have both looked and seen. How much?"

"I could give you a hundred dollars, maybe. That's generous, but like I said, he's a good horse."

"That is larceny, not generosity."

"Well, if you come to change your mind," Oliver Hadley let his shrug finish his sentence. "But don't bring him 'round otherwise. It ain't right, but I got a business to think about."

Frances watched the man's back as he disappeared around the corner onto Third Street. Her attention was caught for the moment by the reddish sky to the east. The sun itself was not yet visible over the buildings. A gust of wind from the opposite direction confirmed the threat of the blood-hued horizon. Frances sniffed the air. A crumpled handbill driven along the empty street by the gusting wind caught Frances' eye and she watched as it blew against the wheel of an empty dray parked next to the tracks. For a moment it seemed to lodge in the spokes, but then it rolled free, and tumbled on, its course changed by each item it hit, a telephone post, a railroad tie, a pile of horse manure. Despite the wind, it was an eerily silent morning. Across the wide street a line of farm machinery warehouses partially obscured the railroad tracks and the blocks of houses and businesses that each year grew northward. Frances looked to the left, away from the river, following the empty tracks to the western limits of town, not far beyond Thirteenth Street.

This was it, then, Frances thought, as she stepped forward to lay the backs of her fingers against Raleigh's soft nose. This was the moment prepared for her by a stranger for whom she was little more than an afterthought, a convenience, by a man whom she rightly should never have known, an illiterate Scot whose fine suits could not disguise the ruffian beneath, and yet who, the papers were saying, had almost single-handedly wrested the territory's capital from where it had stood for twenty-two years. She understood what it was Alexander McKenzie

intended for her to do. Admit defeat. Step back into the Fargo House.
Wake and dress Houghton. Tell the clerk at the front desk on her way
out to have her things carried to the Headquarters Hotel. There she
would be kept in comfort, and if she were especially amenable, perhaps
someday there would be something more permanent offered her, rooms
above a shop in Brainerd or an apartment in St. Paul. She would continue to wear fine clothes. Maybe she would entertain his friends, several
of whom she suspected she had already entertained in John Bingham's
parlor. Had she, after all, struck such a different bargain when she became Percy's wife? As John's hostess? Had McKenzie simply recognized
her for what she truly was?

Her reputation had already been lost with Percy's suicide and the
town's perception that she might as well have pulled the trigger herself.
Did it matter what strangers on the street thought of her? It occurred
to Frances that she had given up caring about such things when she
had realized that Anna was lost to her. The vanishing of her friend, of
her desire (had it been love?), continued to pain Frances, but in a way
that embarrassed her in its measured scale. She had intended to move
heaven and earth to make Anna hers. Instead, when her fantasy receded
before her, like some ghostly essence she could not coax into materializing, Frances was left with the consolation of neither grand suffering
nor life-altering insight. Had it been such a paltry thing, this magnificent
passion of hers, this desire around which she had framed her life? Was
there a deficiency in her, a coldness that Percy had correctly identified?
Would other losses affect her so little, too?

The groan that escaped from Frances in response to her own question took her by surprise, and she put one hand over her mouth while
reaching for the railing in front of her with the other. Must she give
Houghton up to John and Anna after all? Certainly she could not rear
him as a whore's son. There was irony here, obvious, nauseating irony.
The woman whom she believed she could not live without, she was living without quite easily. The son whom she had not wanted felt no less
necessary to her than a limb, a lung.

And there was more to lose. She knew herself to be a selfish person,
believing that this is how one survived in the world: one developed a
sense of one's own worth and then set about sustaining and protect-
ing this story of significance at all costs. Her story had no room for

mortification. If she were to accept McKenzie's proposition, she would lose herself as well. Then again, had that self, nourished on the dreams of independence ever since she had arrived in Dakota, ever been more than an illusion? The rides across the prairie upon Raleigh, the wind loosening her braid, the plains open before her without barrier, with Houghton held tightly to her chest, that, she had called freedom. But it had been speed, and air, and a moment only. And those hours in the company of Jack Shaw as he explained how a gear worked, or with Little Carl as he silently moved about his cookhouse and then paused to hand out a tiny parcel of prairie philosophy as nonchalantly as he handed over a bit of cake, or with Kirsten as she prattled on about some neighborly nonsense, mixing a copious amount of the mundane with the occasional, searing insight that rarely failed to startle Frances into a laugh... or when Kirsten had slipped so easily into an embrace that day of her ride on Raleigh... or when Kirsten...

Frances shook her head. She had been a fool, nothing less, duped by her own pride. The world was not created anew west of the Red River. In Fargo, as in St. Paul, as in New York, she was as powerless as the immigrants pouring into the territory, filled with their own dreams of a new life. We all live according to someone else's rules, Frances thought. And if the rules, the laws, the decisions were to be altered, here in Dakota Territory, they would be altered as they were elsewhere, by men with money and power. Like Alexander McKenzie. Like J. B. Power. Like her father-in-law and the rest of the bonanza farmers who, having mined the early spoils of the valley, would take their profits and move on, leaving the newcomers to their litany of hopes in the new Northwest. Prosperity. Independence. Freedom.

Which was better, Frances wondered: to know the limitations of your life, as she did now, or to continue to believe in the dream of independence, as did so many of the immigrants and settlers living in their shanties of sod or shiplap and tar paper on the prairie, laboring day in and day out for a harvest that would allow them to spend yet another year laboring day in and day out for the next harvest, while they planted their tiny saplings and shrubs in precise lines around their homes to protect their inward-turning dreams? Frances read the newspapers. She knew the figures. Thousands of immigrants and settlers were entering the territory daily. The boom that J. B. Power had spoken about at the

Bingham table had exceeded even his predictions. But she had also seen with her own eyes the defeated exodus of Jews, wet, muddy, miserable, as they left their homesteads in the slough behind. Not far from there, Kirsten's family, a mother, father, two sons and three daughters, had intended to put down roots. What remained there? One young woman and two graves.

Frances turned her head to look at the rising sun, partly obscured by the low bank of clouds pushing across the sky. A wagon passed by, the generally stolid draft horses shifting nervously in their traces in response to the weather's threat. In front of her, Raleigh, made all the more restive by the short span of rein Hadley had left when he'd tied him up, had begun to move from side to side. Frances looked around to see if Reecher was in sight. She was about to go to the desk to send for him, when she stopped herself with an exasperated, humorless laugh. She had no more pennies to spare. Speaking quietly to the horse, Frances led him around the corner and to the back of the hotel, backing him into a small stall of the stable attached there. A wooden pail hung on the gate, and Frances filled this at the hand-pump and left it at Raleigh's feet. He was as likely to knock it over as drink from it, she knew, but at least he now had the choice.

Odd, how there could be choice without freedom. She was thinking of Little Carl, how in some ways, she was most like him, but without his courage. For surely this unknown Clara, too, had come upon the day when she opened her eyes upon a world in which each and every option available to her was no option at all, and because she could not change the world, changed herself. That funny little, irritable, lonely person had risked the leap. Into what? A greater loneliness, perhaps, but no longer on someone else's terms. What she had lost, Frances could only imagine, but what he had gained was himself. Frances had been less honest. She had wanted the gains without the losses.

A whistle from the Moorhead side of the bridge announced the imminent arrival of the westbound N.P. just as Frances stepped back into the hotel. In twenty-four hours that whistle would announce the return of Alexander McKenzie. He would enter the Headquarters Hotel confident that in his suite of rooms Frances Bingham would be waiting to make his Fargo layover a pleasant interval before he returned to business and Bismarck. Because, he would believe, she had no other choice.

Frances crossed the lobby and began to walk up the stairs toward her room. McKenzie had guessed that, turned out of the Fargo House as he had demanded, she would seek another room in Fargo. He had seen to her failure. He had guessed that she would next try to raise money to make an escape possible, and so he had seen to it that every door was closed to her. Frances was stopped by a thought as she reached the landing and turned toward her door. McKenzie had perhaps given her credit for more resourcefulness than she had managed, in which case there were probably several other businessmen and shopkeepers in town who had been warned away from helping her. The final gesture of making clear to her that even her horse would not be safe if she resisted him had shown remarkable intuition, for the effect of seeing Raleigh tied up in the street had been significant. In short, McKenzie had anticipated her every move, action and reaction. The time had come, Frances understood, for her to admit defeat.

Back in her room, Frances discovered Houghton dressed for the day and waiting in the chair for his mother to return. He had never before woken to find her gone, and had been crying. It did not take Frances long to fill two satchels with their clothes. In a shawl she rolled linens, a second pair of boots, her silver-plated hairbrush and mirror, and her hand-bag containing her jewelry. Then she unwrapped the shawl, removed one pillow-case, tied the shawl back up again, and told Houghton to gather up his soldiers. She put them into the pillow-case, along with his harmonica and the pipe that Percy had occasionally pretended to enjoy smoking, and several of Percy's books. The rest of their belongings Frances packed into the large trunk resting against the wall.

"Do you have your knife?" Frances asked.

In reply the boy touched his pocket.

"Then we will go." Handing the heavy pillow-case to Houghton, Frances said, "I need you to carry this for me."

In the lobby, Frances set down the satchels and shawl and straightened her riding jacket before instructing the desk clerk to have the trunk in her room sent out to the Bingham farm. "If a gentleman inquires after me, please inform him that I have temporarily gone to my father-in-law's farm to prepare for a return to St. Paul, where I intend to make my home henceforth."

"Yes, ma'am, is that all?"

"Not entirely. I believe you owe me for four nights."

The clerk nodded and counted the money out onto the counter between them.

"Hand it to my son, please," Frances instructed, and then nodded to a wide-eyed Houghton to accept the money. "Put it in your pocket, son, and then don't reach in again until I ask for it. Now," Frances turned back to the clerk, "if you would be so kind as to wrap up some biscuits from the kitchen please, for our ride."

"Storm's coming," the clerk said.

"All the more reason to hurry," Frances answered, turning toward the back door. "Please bring them to the stable."

It took several minutes to get mounted, even with the clerk's help. Houghton clung to his mother's waist. The satchels were tied together and hung on either side of the saddle over Frances' legs. The pillow-case and shawl were tied together and slipped in between Frances and Houghton. Raleigh, already nervous with the weather, was decidedly unhappy with his burden, and Frances believed they would be lucky to make it out of town without an accident.

"Just hang on, son," she said. "No matter what. Just hang on to me."

McKenzie had been right. She was defeated. She was not what she thought she was. But she would be damned if she would be what he thought she was either. There was still one choice for her to make. She would not humble herself before the one who knew how cheaply dreams were bought and sold, but to the one who continued on, ignorant, deluded, determined and filled with hope.

CHAPTER LIII

Our Hero

Sure as my name is Kirsten Knudson it is like a picture right out of the stories from Far in the times before he started to escape, when the snow it would fall so deep and the wind it was like a scream, and those stories they were better than anything from *Lars Linderots huspostil*, you bet. There were boats covered with *sjold* (I do not know the American word), and *Vikinger* and battles, and every single time pretty soon it was Ole and Sten to fight then with the lids from the pots and Mor's *tvare* until Mor would say, "*Nok!*" and Far would say, "In American, *kjerring*. Enough!" and that would be the end of the *Vikinger*. Such a long, long time ago it seems now. I was still a little girl, and now I am a grown woman on Homer's land all on my own, but never did Far talk a picture so fine like Frances Bingham coming toward me on Raleigh, with the wind blowing the grass against his legs just like the waves against a *Vikinger* boat, and her tall like there is no wind and rain at all, and about the rain I am sorry because just yesterday before dark I did sweep the yard, and it is like Mor always said, keep your house as neat as if it is Jesus himself to visit, and here is a thing Pastor Fedje does not need to know, I think I am just as happy to see Frances Bingham. But about the mud I am sorry.

And there is Howie hanging on behind with the big bags and I do not know what it all means, but not one question do I ask before I reach up and take two of the bags to put over my shoulder and then Howie he just slides from the horse and into my arms without one question about am I going to catch him. Now, I am not a big woman and Howie is not so much a little boy now, so I have to set him right there in the mud beside me, and then I look up and Frances looks down, and the rain is like so many tears just falling and falling on her face, and there are those eyes and now they really are the color of the sky that is with the storm and no more of the sun that this morning was like a fire in the east. And I will tell you that this morning even with the chickens running around like there is a fox close by and New Homer kicking against his stall and the cow too nervous to give all her milk, about the storm to come I can not even worry because there is not one thing like that sun in the whole world. It is like the prairie is a church that is too big for the walls, and what is in my heart is better than any sermon, and there is another thing that Pastor Fedje does not need to know that I think. So there I am looking into the eyes of Frances, and I think that there is more than a storm there, I think that she is angry and I think that she is sad, but mostly I think that she is here. In my very own yard, mud and all. And for just that minute I think that maybe I am to reach up my arms and she will fall to me like that time after the picnic on Raleigh only around the other way it was, but she is just sitting there looking down at me, and if she is to fall to my arms we would be all in a tumble in the mud and that is not what is to hope for.

So there we are, and not one word, until it is Howie who says, "Mama?" and Frances she turns her head like he is asking her a question and the answer is yes, and she says, "May I come in, Kirsten? I must look a fright." That wakes me up, and I think I will say, "You look like a queen," but then I think what Mrs. Harkness would say, and I say, "Please, *do* come in." There is some trouble with Raleigh because he does not want to go into the little barn that Peter Erickson and his two big sons built just this April for me, and I would like to say to Raleigh that it is a brand new barn and not big, maybe it is just a shed, but it is solid, and it cost me almost all of my money from the First National Bank, and so he should not be too good for my barn that is a shed, but it is probably New Homer and the cow that he is turning up his nose at, and then Frances says, "Never mind the rain, Kirsten, leave the door open a couple of inches so he can face daylight, and he will be all right."

Inside I make right away the coffee. It is Thursday and that is the day to make *flatbrød* so the oven it is warm (and I am proud to say that the top of the stove is shiny because I was this morning polishing and polishing with newspaper, because today is Thursday, which I already said), and I hang their wet things to dry around the room. Howie is like a boy to starve, he is eating the corn meal mush that I fry for him and then give with the molasses as fast as I can take the cakes from the pan, but Frances does not eat, and she should, she is that thin. And quiet, too. I talk about the *flatbrød*, and I talk about the storm that I hope does not bring hail because the spring has been good and the wheat looks good, and already the potato plants are coming up in my garden but not much else, and there will not be hail, I think, because it is too early in the summer for hail, and I say that I am thinking about getting a dog to keep the rabbits and the fox away, and that Howie is maybe an inch taller every time I see him, and he is sure to be a tall boy, and then Howie he says that he would like to have a puppy, too, and then he shows me Little Carl's knife, and then he remembers something in his other pocket, and moves his hand to it, and looks at his mother, and she says, "Later, dear." And that is the first thing that she has said since she sat down at my table, and then nothing more. So it is for Howie and me to talk, but still I keep my eye on Frances, and she is looking at my shanty, and it is not the big Bingham house, but there is a real wood floor, and a window, and no matter the wind, if there is dirt inside this house it is not here for long. The thing is to never let it get the upper hand, as Mrs. Harkness would say, but how one hand is more up than the other I do not know.

Well, then, when Howie is done with his breakfast that is really dinner because it is almost noon, I clean his plate and then I begin to roll out the balls of dough on the table, and I roll and roll because for *flatbrød* that is the secret, even if my *flatbrød* is never to be like Mor's, and pretty soon there is Howie fast asleep with one arm up on the back of his chair and his head on that arm and there is not a picture in Mr. Haynes' window in Fargo that is so fine. I say to Frances with my voice very low, "I will put him in my bed," and she says, "He would wake. It is best he sleeps now." Then she says, "Kirsten, I have something to tell you. Will you sit, please?" Well, that is just like Frances, to come into someone else's home and then invite that someone else to sit down, and I do not mind one bit, except that there is not another chair and now is not the time to sit anyway because in the oven there is *flatbrød* baking, and on the stove there is *flatbrød* ready to turn and on the table there is dough to roll out, and this is what I say. And I say I can listen while I work.

"This is best said quickly, and with as little obfuscation as dignity will allow," Frances says.

"I beg your pardon?" I say.

"You are right," Frances says. "That was not a very good beginning." She smiles the not-really-a-smile smile that I think is her way of saying "There is something sad, here," and so I wait for the sad thing.

"The long and the short of it, Kirsten, is that I have lied to you, and what's more, I have stolen from you. I am neither who nor what you think I am, and for that, especially for that, I find, I am sorry."

Well, it is all I can do to keep from laughing right out loud, because I do not have one thing that a Frances Bingham is going to steal from me, and when I say this, Frances says, "Little Carl left you over twelve hundred dollars in a cigar case when he died. I took the money."

I have nothing to say.

Really and for true. There is a space in my head that is just empty. No words. Not American and not *norsk*.

Well, then, to be true, there are some words in my head. Because I am

468 Brenda K. Marshall

thinking, what did Frances say? What does she mean? I look at Frances and she looks at me, and then she looks at Howie sleeping there, and then she looks at the door, and then she looks down at her hands, and then she takes a big breath, and looks right back up at me. And it is a sad thing, after all, because this is not a thing that a queen is to do, and I do not know what to think.

And then I smell that the *flatbrød* on the stove is no longer just with the bubbles but is now burning, and I turn around and flip it over and then I take the *flatbrød* that is in the oven out and put it on the stack of the ones that are already done, and I am sorry about the *flatbrød* that is not so good now but I am glad that there is something for me to do for a minute because all of my thoughts are going around and around. I can not even think about what that much money is, I am just thinking about why Frances Bingham from the big Bingham bonanza farm would do this thing. Finally, I turn around and I say, "Why?"

"I will not insult you with my reasons," Frances says. "They are dust now, and there is no excuse for such an action anyway. I used the money to buy Jack Shaw's quarter section of the Jew slough. I still owe him two hundred dollars. It is your land, Kirsten. It may not have been how you would have chosen to spend the money, but that is something that I can not undo. In a couple of days when it is safe to return to Fargo—"

"Fargo is not safe?" I say, and I wonder what next I am to hear, maybe that New Homer is not a mule and Pastor Fedje is not a Lutheran, but Frances just shakes her head like that is more of the story that I am not to hear.

"In a couple of days I will go to the courthouse," she says, "and I will transfer the deed to you."

And then all of a sudden I am saying, "No. That is not good enough," and I have in my hand still the *spade* for turning the *flatbrød*, and I shake it at Frances and I say, "You will explain all of this to me." Well, that brings her head right up and up goes that one eyebrow and there is that look, and the gray is silver again with those black cracks so clear and I can see that she did not like hearing that from me one bit, so I set the *spade* back down. But this is my house, and that was my money, or to be true, it was Little Carl's money, and then I am just more mad because it is like she has lied to Little Carl, too, and he was always so much with the "Miss Frances this" and the "Miss Frances that," and so

I just look right back, and I say again, "You will explain this to me."

For a minute, maybe even two, she just looks at me and I look right back, and I do not blink, and my heart is so hard beating that it is louder than the wind, but then she says, "So be it," and I pull over Mor's *tine* from the corner and I sit down on it and she starts to talk.

So there she was in the cookhouse with Little Carl's cigar box on her lap, and there I was laying out his body (and that was not the surprise that he meant after all, although for surprises, that was still a pretty good one). And there was Frances making her offer for the slough land to Jack Shaw with Little Carl's money that was my money but not, and then there, finally, I did understand something because there was Frances crying on the top of the big Bingham house, and there was the beautiful brooch that is a horseshoe in my hand (and is now wrapped in a little piece of felt by my bed where I look at it every day, but I do not wear it) and there went Frances without a look at me. And there she was in Fargo, with Mr. Percy, and then alone, and then with Mr. Percy, and then really alone, but about the suicide there was nothing to say, and that, I agree, is not for me to know. Then there was Mr. John Bingham saying that he would take care of Howie but that Frances was to go away forever, and this is a surprise, because it is like rich people are like poor people sometimes with their problems, and I guess I already did know that because I knew about Mr. Percy and the whiskey that was not so very different from Far and his escapes, and about Miss Anna and the brown bottle ... but that is not part of the story that Frances is telling, and I wonder if that is a story I am ever to hear, and I do not know if it is a story that I want to hear because I am supposed to be mad and I am something, but not exactly mad, because when I think about Frances and Miss Anna and the way that they looked at each other on the day that I first saw them in their beautiful dresses, well, there it is again, that little bit of fire that is no good in my chest. So up I stand from the *tine* while Frances is still talking and I act like I am doing something with the stack of *flatbrød* but I am still listening to Frances and now it is about a man that I do not know. She says that he was at the big house for supper, but of fine suits and big suppers there were so many, and maybe he was the one that tried to get me into the pantry one night, but then he would not have been the only one to think that a housekeeper is for ... well, I will not say for what, but he did not have any more luck with me than with Frances. So there, then.

And then Frances is walking up and down the streets of Fargo, "practically destitute" (I will have to find that one in the big dictionary when I take next the butter and eggs to Mrs. Harkness but I do not want to stop Frances now and besides I am pretty sure that I know what she means), and no family to take care of her, and not one hotel will take her and Howie, and she is almost out of money, and not even her jewelry she can sell, and it is like Frances is reading to me a story by Mr. Charles Reade, it is that full of twists and turns, and I am just getting so mad at that Mr. Alexander McWhoever that thinks he can make Frances Bingham into a you-know-what and put a little boy out onto the street, but to be true I am thinking, too, that this is a very indolent way to spend a Thursday afternoon with the smell of fresh *flatbrød* in the house, and the rain on the roof, and I am not churning butter like I should be, and then I think, "Wait a minute, Kirsten Knudson, this is not a story. This is your life." And then Frances is riding up to my yard and she is wet and she is sorry and here is her word, "defeated," and then it is the end of the story.

I do not say a word. Instead I walk to the door and I take the little umbrella that is hanging there, the one that belonged to Miss Anna but Frances gave it to me because it had a broken spoke, and out I go to the outhouse. To think.

I am there a long time, and when I come back Frances is standing at the door, and she takes the umbrella from me and I point toward the back, but she is not gone so long because I guess she is done with the thinking now that her story is over.

Before I sit down again I say, "Would you like me to make more coffee?"

Well, there is that laugh again, not the real one. "Kirsten," Frances says. "I have come to you as a thief, a repentant thief, it is true, but a thief nonetheless. I am not a house guest."

"What are you, then?" This I say without even thinking about what I mean.

"As I said, a thief."

"No, that is not what I mean. I mean, who are you now?"

"Kirsten," Frances says, "if this is a riddle, I understand that they are all the rage, but I do not think that this is the proper time."

I do not even know what I mean, so I do not say it again. But I do say, "Why did you want the land? So much … so much that you would–"

"Steal from my housekeeper."

"Ya, from me?"

"Yes. From you. It seemed like the answer. Land. I thought that to have land was to have a future. Independence. Freedom. I was wrong."

"No," I say. "About this one thing you are not wrong. If you have land you have a chance." Just then Howie sighs, like he is to agree. "That arm is sure to be sore when he wakes up."

"He is six years old. He will be sore for a minute and then he'll be fine."

"He is not a boy for the city."

"No. He misses the farm."

"Frances," I say, and I make my voice sound very serious (but to be true I am just afraid), "I do not want the land. I want the money." And there goes my heart again, bang, bang, bang, and it is so loud that I think maybe she can not hear what it is I say. So I say it again, I say, "I want the money." And then she laughs. Yes, she laughs with her head back and that wakes up Howie, and sure enough he is not even sore. He is with surprise, I see, to wake up in my little home, but then it is such a smile for me that I can not help but lean over and pull him close to me and give him a big kiss on each cheek. "I think the rain has stopped," I say. "It was not to be such a big storm after all. Will you go to the barn to see if Raleigh and New Homer are friends now?" Howie he looks at Frances, and I think, this boy is now timid and that is not a good thing for a boy, and then Frances nods and Howie is just about to run out the door when he stops and puts his hand on his pocket, and Frances says, "Yes, you may give me the money now." Howie he pulls some coins out of his pocket along with some string and a shiny round rock and the foot of something that might have been a rabbit once upon a time, and then everything but the coins he puts back and runs out the door.

"You may have this, of course," Frances points to the coins on the table. "Beyond that, as I had hoped to make clear, I have almost nothing at all left. I suppose you could report me to the police, but I do not see what you would gain by that."

"You do not have to pay me back, exactly. I mean, all at once," I say.

"No? And how am I to pay you back at all?"

This is it, then.

"For Mr. John Bingham and you and Miss Anna I worked for three dollars a week, but Mr. Bingham he said he would give me four dollars a week to stay."

Well, then, Frances she gives me such a look, it is like a miracle that I do not just fall down dead right there, but I do not. I look right back, because I am thinking of a wonderful thing and it may not be very nice, but I mean to be very nice if only I am to have the time. And then, because I am not going to be able to make my look for very much longer, I say, like I am talking to myself, "Now, where did I put my pencil?" And I stand and I open the *tine* to get out some paper that I have saved from a package I brought back from the store, and my hands are shaking, and Frances says, "One thousand two hundred and forty-three dollars at four dollars a week. That comes to three hundred and eleven weeks. Six years. Without interest, that is." And that is just like Frances, without a pencil and all in her head.

"And then the land is yours," I say, "and I have my present from Little Carl."

"And until then? What is it that I am to do? Am I to cook for you, Kirsten? Scrub your floor? Empty your slops?"

"Oh, no, Frances! Never! It is together we will work. Tomorrow I will show you how to milk the cow. Maybe we will get another cow. And turkeys, too, maybe. There are the chickens, and there can be more. There are never enough eggs. Always they ask at the hotel, can you bring us more eggs? Can you bring us more butter? There is hay to cut and a garden to plant and produce to put up. For work there is always more to do. And so many I times I did think, if only I could ask Frances, about money, about the bank, about how to talk to Peter Erickson, and now," but then I stop, because I can hear in my voice so much of joy, and in Frances' face there is not so much.

But this is what I love about Frances. (Ya, well, I do.) She takes another deep breath, and she sits up in her chair, and there is that posture that the Yankees are so good at, it is what Mrs. Harkness was always trying to teach me.

"Where do I start?" she says.

So thin she is, and so very tired now in the eyes, and so I say. "Do you still have your silver hair brush? Yes? Then it is with brushing your hair we start, and then you will lie down and take a good long nap in the bed and then I will make us an early supper and maybe if there is a book in those bags by the door you will read to me and to Howie tonight. We will make up a pallet for Howie's bed here under the table for now, or maybe he will need to sleep in the bed, too, because it is all so very new. And then tomorrow we will get up, and we will start the day all over again."

But it is one more thing I will tell you because it is good to say. I am happy. There is now to be in my home a child and Frances and life when before it was just me, and I am good to work and good to sing and good to talk, but by myself the working and the singing and the talking are all a way to be not all alone. Maybe you will think that it is not right what I want and that Frances Bingham is not one to feed chickens and milk cows and stack hay, but I think that maybe she will be happy here someday, too.

There. I have said it and good it feels, too. It will not be tomorrow, and it will not be the next day, and it will not be on any one day. That is what I think. And until then I will be happy while I wait because I am waiting for what is already here. And that is what it means to be a model of concision.

The End